E. M. Cooper

GRANTA BOOKS

ALL SOULS' RISING

MADISON SMARTT BELL was born near Nashville, Tennessee, and educated at Princeton. He teaches at Goucher College, Baltimore, and Johns Hopkins University, and is the author of seven other novels and two volumes of short stories. He lives in Baltimore with his wife, the poet Elizabeth Spires.

Also by Madison Smartt Bell

Save Me, Joe Louis,

Dr Sleep

Barking Man and other stories

Soldier's Joy

The Year of Silence

Zero db and other stories

Straight Cut

Waiting for the End of the World

The Washington Square Ensemble

MADISON SMARTT BELL

ALL SOULS' RISING

GRANTA BOOKS
LONDON
in association with
PENGUIN BOOKS

GRANTA BOOKS
2/3 Hanover Yard, Noel Road, London N1 8BE

Published in association with the Penguin Group
Penguin Books Ltd, 27 Wrights Lane, London W8 5TZ, England
Viking Penguin, a division of Penguin Books USA Inc.,
375 Hudson Street, New York NY 10014, USA
Penguin Books Australia Ltd, Ringwood, Victoria, Australia
Penguin Books Canada Ltd, 10 Alcorn Avenue,
Toronto, Ontario, Canada M4V 3B2
Penguin Books (NZ) Ltd, 182–190 Wairau Road,
Auckland 10, New Zealand

Penguin Books Ltd, Registered Offices: Harmondsworth, Middlesex, England

First published in the USA by Pantheon Books 1995
First published in Great Britain by Granta Books 1996
This edition published by Granta Books 1996

1 3 5 7 9 10 8 6 4 2

Printed in Great Britain by Clays Ltd, St Ives plc

A CIP catalogue record for this book is available from the British Library

For les Morts et les Mystères,
and for all souls bound in living bodies,
I have burned this offering

Four hundred years . . .
(Four hundred years, four hundred years . . .)
And it's the same . . .
Same philosophy . . .

BOB MARLEY

Acknowledgments

This novel was completed with invaluable assistance from the John Simon Guggenheim Foundation, the George A. and Eliza Gardner Howard Foundation, the Maryland State Arts Council, and the National Endowment for the Arts. My thanks also to George Garrett and Russell Banks for good advice and good examples, and to Isabel Reinharez, Caroline Gifford, Tom McGonigle, Cassandra Dunwell, Thomasin LaMay of the Goucher College Library, Caroline Smith of Special Collections at the Johns Hopkins University Libraries, Jennifer Bryan of the Manuscripts Division of the Maryland Historical Society, Daryl Phillip of the Cane Mill Museum of Dominica, and M. Emmanuel Leroy Ladurie of the *Bibliothèque nationale* in Paris, for their critical research assistance—may fortune smile upon you all.

Contents

Preface

In 1791, the colony of Saint Domingue, established on the western half of the island which Columbus had named Hispaniola and which the native Amerindians (before their wholesale extermination by the Spanish) had called Hayti, was the richest and most productive French possession overseas, known as the Jewel of the Antilles. Plantations in the colony, run by slave labor, produced fortunes in sugar and coffee, which could create for their proprietors, who were frequently absentees, luxurious lives in Paris. From the point of view of French landowners, locally known as *grand blancs,* Saint Domingue was not a place to settle permanently but a place to get rich quick.

The shock of the French Revolution in 1789 traveled along social and racial fault lines already present in the colony. The *grand blanc* landowners, who owned most of the plantations and most of the slaves, were conservative and royalist by disposition and for the most part unfriendly to French Revolutionary radical ideas. By 1791 the idea was already afoot in this group that at worst the colony might splinter off from the home government and reconstitute itself as a royalist refuge or perhaps make itself a protectorate of the British (who maintained slavery in Jamaica and their other Caribbean colonies). The *grand blanc* royalists in the colony identified themselves by wearing a white cockade and were therefore sometimes known as *Pompons Blancs.*

Meanwhile there existed a lower class of white people in the colony, an artisan class mostly concentrated in the two principal cities of the coast: Cap Français (commonly known as Le Cap) in the north and Port-au-Prince in the western department. Members of this group were not necessarily French in origin; they were an obscure and shifting community, including a great many professional criminals, adventurers, and international fugitives. Some originated from an earlier period when the island had been a haven and stronghold of pirates. These *petit blancs,* who embraced French Revolutionary ideas, were at odds with the *grand blanc* landowners, and between 1789 and 1791 the struggle between these two groups for political control of the colony sometimes came to violence. The *petit blanc* revolutionaries distinguished themselves by wearing a red cockade and were known for this reason as *Pompons Rouges.* Their declared loyalty to the French Revolutionary government led them to call themselves Patriots.

Whatever their differences among themselves, white people were in a minority in Saint Domingue. In 1791 there were about thirty-nine thousand white people in the colony, twenty-seven thousand people of mixed blood, and four hundred and fifty-two thousand black slaves. The large mulatto population, descendants of white landowners and black slaves, had come into being because there had never been many white women in the colony, which had always attracted opportunists and entrepreneurs rather than settlers proper. Some mulattoes were enslaved but many were free, and there existed a class of freedmen, or *affranchis,* who were mostly of mixed race, though some full-blooded blacks were also included.

Sixty-four different shades of color were identified (and named) among the mulattoes, and social status depended on the lightness of the shade. Economically, the mulattoes were a powerful group. Many were wealthy and owned land and slaves of their own, and many had been well educated—sometimes in France. But the mulattoes had no political rights whatsoever. Though required to serve three years in the militia, they could not vote or hold office—only white people played any part in the political life of the colony. Apart from a lively business in prostitution, mulattoes had little social contact with whites, were forced to give precedence to whites in all circumstances, and were sometimes victims of spontaneous genocidal pogroms.

There was a special animosity between the mulattoes, who had wealth but no political rights, and the *petit blancs,* who had rights but little money. These tensions were exacerbated after 1789, when the mulattoes began sending delegations to Paris to petition for political equality and voting rights. These delegations found sympathy among the more radical French Revolutionary factions and among abolitionist organizations like *Les Amis des Noirs*. But in the early phases of the French Revolution, the parties in power believed very firmly that the Rights of Man must apply to white men only. Saint Domingue was one of the few sectors of the French economy still functioning after the Revolution; therefore slavery and the racial hierarchy underwritten by the slave system had to be maintained.

As for the tremendous number of black slaves, only a minority were Creole (a term designating anyone of any race who was born in the colony). In part because absentee ownership was so common, abuses and cruelty were much more frequent and severe in Saint Domingue than in the southern United States or in most other slaveholding societies. Through suicide, infanticide, abortion, starvation, neglect, overwork, and murder, the black slaves of Saint Domingue died off at a much faster rate than they could replace themselves by new births. It was necessary for the proprietors to import twenty thousand fresh slaves from Africa *annually* in order to maintain the workforce at a constant level.

Thus a two-thirds majority of the slaves in the colony had been born in Africa. They came from ten or twelve different tribes and spoke as many different languages. They communicated with their masters and with one another in a patois with French vocabulary and African syntax; this language, also called Creole, is still spoken in Haiti today. The slave population synthesized a variety of different African religious traditions into a common religion called vodoun or voodoo, which was universal among the African slaves and very common among the Creole slaves also—including those Creole slaves who were nominally Christian. Vodoun, which includes a pantheon of gods who take literal and physical possession of their worshipers, incorporated components of African ancestor worship with a new mythology evolved on slave ships. Practitioners believed that Africa, or Guinée, existed as an island below the sea and that death was the portal of return to Africa.

Occupied with their quarrels among themselves, the whites of Saint Domingue gave little thought to the possible effects of the French Revolution on the mulattoes and almost none at all to its possible effects on the black slaves. Because of their common economic interests, some queasy and unstable alliances did form between *grand blancs* and mulattoes. The blacks, who were not generally acknowledged to be fully human, were ignored. Meanwhile, Revolutionary conceptions like "the Rights of Man" circulated freely and noisily through the entire colony and were as audible to the black slaves as to anyone.

All Souls' Rising

Prologue

June 15, 1802 Aboard Le *Héros*

The weighing of our anchor with this morning's tide brought me a lightening of my heart. These last few days we've been in port were most uneasy, owing to rumors of renewed disturbances, perhaps a more serious revolt, to be inspired by the deportation of the brigand chief Toussaint, our passenger and prisoner. All factions in the city of Le Cap or what remains of it are once again aroused against one another. As for the harbor itself, it is alive with sharks, which feed most avidly upon the flesh of those who take the losing part in struggles on the shore.

Thus I was greatly comforted to see us well away, to stand on the stern with the breeze freshening in my face, watching the broken soot-stained ruins sink rapidly enough to the horizon. The town of Le Cap has twice been burned to the ground these last ten years, but even at the height of its ostentation it could not, when seen at such a distance, have seemed any more than a most precarious foothold on this savage shore. Rounding the cape, I see that city give way to rocky escarpments plunging vertically into the waves, and above these the incomprehensible blankness of the forests or, where the trees are cut, the peaks standing out as bare and sharp as needles' points. My sojourn here was brief but more than long enough to satisfy me. Here no enterprise has managed to achieve a good result—the hand of civilized man has done no more than make of a wilderness a desert. Perhaps before Columbus landed, it was some sort of savage Eden here. I believe it would have been better for all if he had never come.

As we set sail, there stood near me, among my fellow officers of the ship, some members of the company of the renegade slave Toussaint, though that gentleman himself remained carefully sequestered, under guard in his cabin below. The others of his party had so far the freedom of the ship, and I observed them closely as I might, with some thought of indicting their descriptions, though for what audience I do not know.

The eldest (and by far the blackest) of the women is Suzanne, the wife of Toussaint. She is said to be older than he and showed her years, appearing confused at moments, appearing not to know just where she found herself or how she came there. But for the richness of her dress (which was, however, modest) she might easily have been taken for any ordinary household servant in the colony. The three young mulattresses in her train (a niece, a daughter-in-law, and a companion as I gathered) struck me as rather more *soignées,* wrapped in that thin layer of hastily acquired sophistication with which one often meets in women of their type.

The lightest of the men is Toussaint's eldest son, Placide, though as our Captain Savary has suggested there are some doubts as to his parentage, suspicion that he may be an illegitimate child of Suzanne's prior to the marriage (yet Toussaint acknowledges and indeed is said to favor him). His light color may have occasioned this speculation, though often the Aradas, from which tribe Toussaint is extracted, are similarly light or of a reddish hue.

As for the two younger sons, Isaac and Jean, it is plain at a glance that they are full-blooded Negroes. The former wears a most extravagant uniform, every inch of it bedizened with gold braid and rosettes, complete with an enormous sword, the tip of it dragging the boards of the deck, whose bearer appears to have no notion of its use. The hilted weapon seems only to encumber the natural movement of his hands along his sides. With all its meaningless pomp this uniform shows marked signs of wear, hard wear at that, and Isaac seems to sulk inside it—a bedraggled peacock, caught in a rainstorm.

I have heard, from Captain Savary and others, that this uniform was the personal gift of Bonaparte to Toussaint's second son. Placide was presented with another like it, on the same occasion, but no longer wears it.

The eighth and last of the party looks a miscellany of ill-assembled and badly chosen parts, being overly tall, gangly, poorly proportioned and clumsy in all respects, all thumbs and elbows. His neck is elongated, with a busy Adam's apple the size of a garden spade, and, above, his head appears ridiculously small. He rolls his eyes and stutters when he speaks, and his outsized, long-fingered hands creep about all over his person like great agitated spiders the while. This singular creature is Toussaint's valet, known by the fanciful appellation of Mars Plaisir. For the moment, he cannot practice his intended vocation, since Toussaint is held strictly apart from all this retinue, not permitted to see any of his retainers or even any member of his family. A pointless severity, I should think, yet I would willingly be deprived of the attentions of a Mars Plaisir. In almost any European village I would expect a creature such as he to be set upon and stoned to death.

Now the very thought of Europe makes me puzzle at my enterprise, for these notes are addressed to no one, nor could I find opportunity to send them anywhere at all these next six weeks at sea. Yet I continue, for there have been other curiosities this day. At even (his family and retainers being at table below), Toussaint was fetched on deck to take the air, under guard of two dragoons detached from Captain-General Leclerc's expedition. Those soldiers seemed to tower over him, for he is only a small Negro man and unremarkable at first glance, more noteworthy for the incongruity of his dress than for any distinguishing feature of his person. He wore a loose white shirt or smock, coarsely woven and open at the neck, over tight trousers from a military uniform, and a pair of high cavalry boots. There was a kerchief bound over his head, and I remembered hearing that Toussaint affected such a covering, not only in his *déshabillé* but often even on occasions of state.

I had the watch, but the sea was calm and the sky clear, with the first stars just beginning to emerge, and I approached a little nearer. He did not seem at all aware of my proximity, but stood near the stern rail to stare most intently down at the water (there being no longer any land in view). Not knowing what to say to him, or if I ought to speak at all, I was silent for some minutes before inquiring, what it might be that he was so carefully regarding.

And here the sentinel's attention abruptly returned to his charge, and he undertook to prevent our conversation, but I overrode him, repeating my question and adding to it, whether Toussaint was looking back toward the island of which he had lately been master, and whether he regretted it.

At this, Toussaint turned half toward me and looked at me with half a smile, but without immediately speaking. I suppose he must have gone a lengthy while without much benefit of human discourse. Still, there was a sort of slyness in that smile. His lips were full and heavy, his teeth long and yellow; he lacked an eyetooth on the left side. The jaw long and slung far forward, stretching and lowering the deep oval of his face. His nose was long also and typically flat, but his forehead was high and his eyes, with their yellowing whites, were large and expressive—his best feature. All in all, a most arresting ugliness.

He was smaller than I somehow had expected, standing no higher than my breastbone. His disproportionately long trunk was set on little bandy legs—undoubtedly he would appear to best advantage on horseback. Some grizzled hair appeared at his shirt's neck, and the gray pigtail hanging from under the kerchief was fastened with a bit of frayed red ribbon. I would have put him in the middle fifties. He was narrow-hipped and distinctly thin, though not to the point of frailty—his arms were disproportionately thick and muscular.

He returned my looks, taking my measure also it may be, and then resumed his staring at the water.

"*Guinée,*" he said, but so softly I scarce caught the word at all.

"Africa?" I said, with some surprise.

Of course he was not looking in the right direction, but one would hardly expect him to be a master of geography, outside of the colony. He is himself a Creole and I believe this must have been the first time he had ever been to sea. I found that my gaze was drawn after his; he continued to inspect the surfaces of the ocean for some time before he spoke. The water had taken on a red metallic glimmer from the light of the setting sun.

"*Guinée, on dit, se trouve en bas de l'eau.*" Still Toussaint kept his eyes fixed on the water. *They say that Africa is at the bottom of the ocean.*

"But you are a Christian," I said, for I was again surprised, though it was not the first time I had heard of this belief. One often finds the slavers complaining of it—how their new-bought slaves will fling themselves off the ships in droves, believing that they may pass beneath the ocean to regain their original homes in Africa.

Toussaint glanced up at me with that same sly smile. "Of course I am a Christian," he said, "but I should like to see Africa all the same."

Our colloquy could not continue past that point, for the dragoons quite brusquely led him away. Improbable as it is that anyone aboard should enter into conspiracy with such a one as he, his reputation for cunning is sufficient that his guard evidently has been ordered to permit that he converse with no one.

Unfortunate fellow, I should not suppose him likely ever to see Africa—not, at least, in this lifetime.

It was well past dark when I was relieved of my watch, and in groping along through the darkness below toward my own repose I must pass the cabin where Toussaint was held secure. Going along the passage, I heard a voice coming from behind the door, and (the sentinel having absented himself, perhaps to the jakes) I paused to listen. The occupant was reading in a loud sonorous voice, this passage from the end of Deuteronomy:

> *And Moses went up from the plains of Moab under the mountains of Nebo, to the top of Pisgah, that is over against Jericho. And the Lord showed him all the land of Gilead, unto Dan.*
>
> *And all Naphtali, and the land of Ephraim, and Manasseh and all the land of Judah, unto the utmost sea.*
>
> *And the south, and the plain of the valley of Jericho, the city of palm trees, unto Zoar.*
>
> *And the Lord said unto him, This is the land which I sware unto Abraham, unto Isaac, and unto Jacob, saying, I will give it unto thy seed: I have caused thee to see it with thine eyes, but thou shalt not go thither.*
>
> *So Moses the servant of the Lord died there in the land of Moab, according to the word of the Lord.*
>
> *And he buried him in a valley in the land of Moab, over against Bethpeor, but no man knoweth his sepulchre unto this day.*
>
> *And Moses was a hundred and twenty years old when he died. His eye was not dim, nor his natural force abated.*

And the children of Israel wept for Moses in the plains of Moab thirty days: so the days of weeping and mourning for Moses were ended.

Here Toussaint stopped, and after a little period of silence began again but in a lower and less certain tone, a murmur unintelligible to me—perhaps it was a prayer. This was for all the world like a regular church service, though with the one man playing the roles of both priest and communicant.

I took my way toward my own berth, but sleep continues to elude me, though the hour is late. Therefore I write—to no one. The wind has risen and the seas run higher than they did at sunset, so that the lamp swings like a pendulum on its chain; it blots my page with shadow, and then once more returns its light. Though the ship is densely packed with men and I can hear my fellows snoring, I feel myself much alone this night.

Out of the groaning of the ship's timbers come again the words that Captain Savary repeated to a few of us at table: a sentence he claimed Toussaint had spoken when first taken onto the ship. *En me reversant, on n'a abattu à Saint-Domingue que le tronc de l'arbre de la liberté des noirs; il poussera par les racines, parce qu'elles sont profondes et nombreuses.** Captain Savary quoted this with a sneer and the following remark that these were fine phrases indeed to fall from the thick lips of a gilded nigger. Then there was laughter, in which I joined. Yet now I hear the words again and not in Savary's voice but in some other. What if they are true? If this man did inspire these last ten years of fire and murder—could he call up two hundred more?

Away with such a foolish thought. I shall not sail this way again. As for Toussaint, the gilt is well worn from him now, his time is past for such pretensions. Toussaint must pass into ignominy, and I into anonymity, remaining at the last without a name.

*In overthrowing me, you have done no more than cut the trunk of the tree of black liberty in Saint Domingue—it will spring back from the roots, for they are numerous and deep.

Part I

BOIS CAYMAN

August 1791

Jou a rive pou n kite Babilon
Moman rive pou n viv an twa pawòl
Se pa mistè pou
Yon moun vin Ginen o
Se sa wap di, sa w panse, sa wap fè
Ki pou an amoni

—Boukman Eksperyans

Chapter One

You could not call it an actual crucifixion, Doctor Hébert thought, because it was not actually a cross. Only a pole, or a log rather, with the bark still on it and scars on the bark toward the top, from the chain that had dragged it to this place, undoubtedly. A foot or eighteen inches below the mark of the chain, the woman's hands had been affixed to the wood by means of a large square-cut nail. The left hand was nailed over the right, palms forward. There had been some bleeding from the punctures and the runnels of blood along her inner forearms had hardened and cracked in the dry heat, from which the doctor concluded that she must have been there for several hours at the least. Surprising, then, that she was still alive.

Pulling against the vertex of the nail, her pectoral musculature had lifted her breasts, which were taut, with large aureoles, nipples distended. Although her weight must have pulled her diaphragm tight, the skin around her abdomen hung comparatively slack. At her pudenda appeared a membranous extrusion from which Doctor Hébert averted his eye. Her feet were transfixed one over the other by the same sort of homemade nail as held her hands.

Sitting his horse, Doctor Hébert was at a level with her navel. He raised his head. Her skin was a deep, luminous black; he had become somewhat familiar with the shade since he had been in the country, but was not knowledgeable enough to place her origin from it. Her hair was cut close to the skull, which had the catlike angularity which the doctor, from the sculptural point of view, found rather beautiful. Her large lips were turned out and cracking in the heat, falling a little away from her teeth, and the look of them made the doctor's own considerable thirst seem temporarily irrelevant. When he had first ridden up, her eyes had shown only crescents of white, but now the lids pulled farther back and he knew that she was seeing him.

The cat-shaped head hung over on her shoulder, twisting the cords of her neck up and out. He could see the big artery bumping slowly there. Her eyes moved, narrowing a little, at their sideways angle. She saw him, but was indifferent to what she saw. The doctor's tongue passed across his upper lip, once, twice, stiff as a file. He turned in the saddle and looked back into the long *allée* down which he had come. This avenue ran east to west for almost a mile, bordered by citrus trees whose branches had laced to the density of a thick hedge. From the far end of the *allée*, the pole had first appeared to him centered like the bead in a gun sight. Now the red round of the sun was dropping quickly into the notch where he had first entered, and the glare of it forced him to squint his eyes. He had gone astray some time that morning and had ridden through the afternoon over ill-made roads, if they were roads at all, without meeting anyone. When at last he came to the edge of the cane fields, he had called out to the cultivators there, but had not been able to understand what they said in reply.

Night came quickly in these parts. It might be dark before he could retrace his way to the other end of the *allée*. Doctor Hébert pressed a heel into his horse's flank and rode around the pole. The citrus trees, more sparsely set, fanned out around the edges of the compound as though they had meant to encircle it but failed. What vegetation there was looked completely untrained and much of the yard was full of dust. From one of the scattered outbuildings, a deep-voiced dog was barking. The doctor rode within a few yards of the long low building which was the *grand'case*, dismounted and walked the remaining distance to the pair of wooden steps to the gallery, where a white woman in *déshabille* was sitting in a wooden chair with her head sunk down on her chest.

"Your pardon," Doctor Hébert said, mounting the first step.

The woman raised her head and rearranged her hands in her lap. In one hand she held a glass half full of a cool-appearing liquid with a greenish tint. "Oh," she said. "You have come."

The doctor stepped onto the planks of the gallery, removed his hat and inclined his head. "I have a terrible thirst," he said. "I beg you."

"Bien sûr," she said, and clapped her hands sharply together. The doctor waited. His horse, waiting in the yard with the reins on its neck, lowered its head and snorted at the dust and raised it. There were steps from within and the doctor turned. A mulatto woman in a madras turban came scurrying out of the central door, carrying another glass which she presented to the doctor with a sort of crouch. He took a long rash gulp which made him gasp, and held the glass a little away from him to look at it. The concoction was raw cane rum with lime juice and a cloying amount of sugar. He finished the drink in several more cautious sips, while the white woman spoke to the mulattress in Creole.

"It is arranged," she finally said, turning back to the doctor, who now noticed that her eyes seemed a little bloodshot. "My husband . . ." Her head swung away as her voice trailed off. She looked out across the compound toward the pole.

"Je vous remercie," Doctor Hébert said. There seemed no place to leave the glass; he stooped and set it on the floor. The horse shook its head as he approached. He took the reins and led it around the back of the *grand'case* and wandered among the outbuildings until he discovered the stable. At the rear of the roofed hall was a water trough made from an enormous dugout log. The horse drank and snuffled and blew onto the water and drank deeply again. The doctor watched its big throat working, then knelt and put two fingers into the trough. The water was cool and clear and he thought that it must often be replenished or changed. He cupped his hands and drank and ran his wet palms back over his hair. With a forefinger he detached a long soggy splinter from the side of the trough and watched it drift logily to the bottom.

A groom of some sort had appeared at his back, but Doctor Hébert waved him away and led the horse to a stall himself, where he unsaddled it and gave it a bit of cane sugar from a cake he carried in the pocket of his duster. Slinging his saddlebags over his shoulder, he left the stable and walked back toward the *grand'case*.

The barking had taken up again and the doctor approached the shed it seemed to come from. When he put his eye to the crack in the door a big brindled mastiff smashed against it, backed off and lunged again, striking head-on into the wood with all its weight and force. The doctor withdrew abruptly and continued his path to the house.

A dark-haired man of middle height stood on the gallery. He wore a white shirt and breeches bloused into riding boots, and he held a gold-pommeled cane in both hands across his thighs.

"*Bienvenu,*" he said, "to Habitation Arnaud. I myself am Michel Arnaud. You will dine here. You will pass the night."

"*Heureux,*" the doctor said, and bowed. "I am Antoine Hébert."

"Please to enter," Arnaud said, indicating the open door with his cane. As the doctor passed through, another domestic relieved him of his saddlebags and carried them away through another doorway at the rear of the large central room. It was dim within, the oilpaper over the windows admitting little of the fading light.

"In perhaps one hour we will go to table," Arnaud said. Standing at the outer doorway, he swatted his thigh with the cane. "You will wish to rest, perhaps."

"Yes," said Doctor Hébert. "Your people, they will feed my horse?"

"Immediately," Arnaud said, slapping himself once more with the cane as he turned farther out onto the gallery.

In the small room at the rear the slave had hung the doctor's saddlebags on a peg on the wall and stood waiting beside it, bobbing his head. He was barefoot and wore short pants and a loose shirt of the same coarse cloth and, incongruously, a black coat that looked as if it might have been cast off by the master.

"*De l'eau?*" Doctor Hébert said, without absolute expectation of being understood. The slave bowed out. Doctor Hébert hung his duster on the wall beside the saddlebags and sat down in a chair to remove his boots. His temples pounded when he straightened up, the rum undoubtedly contributing to this effect. In the room were one other wooden chair and a *paillasse* and one small oilpapered window. With a little clink, the slave set down a crockery pitcher and cup on the floor, then backed out quietly, closing the door. Doctor Hébert poured a cup of water and drank it and lay down on his back. The papered window was no more than a pale patch dissolving slowly on the wall. After a time he became aware of the shifting of bare feet in the outer room. At the jingle of a little bell he got up and replaced his boots.

Four candles in heavy candlesticks were burning on the long table in the main room, and the table was laid with covers of silver and heavy imported *faience*. Arnaud, standing at the head of the table, indicated to the doctor a place at his right. A slave drew back the chair and then adjusted it once the doctor had seated himself. The slave in the black coat, who seemed to fill some sort of butler's role, settled Arnaud in the same way, stepped back and waited. Above the table, a circular fan of boards began to move when a boy in a corner pulled a rope. At the end of the table opposite Arnaud, a fourth slave stood in attendance, although no place had been laid there.

"My wife is unable to join us at this moment," Arnaud said.

"She is unwell, perhaps," the doctor said, wondering if his glance had betrayed some false expectancy.

Arnaud stared at him. *"Pour un coup de tafia elle ferait n'importe quoi,"* he said. *For a shot of rum, she will do anything. "Alors, mangeons."* At that, the slaves moved forward to lift the covers and present the several platters one by one. This burst of activity allowed the doctor to cover his moment of confusion. He had been on the point of offering his professional services, which evidently would not have done at all.

There was a platter of highly seasoned pork slices, a sort of ragout of sweet potatoes, nothing green. A bowl of pickles, one of jam, and a loaf of rather leaden bread. The wine was more than tolerable and Arnaud poured it liberally, or rather caused it to be poured, by making minute gestures with a finger. As on other such occasions the doctor was slightly unnerved by the silent presence of the slave behind his chair; whenever he thought of reaching for anything on the table the slave would move to anticipate him.

Arnaud ate with dispatch, if not relish, and did not seem disposed to offer further conversation. In the candlelight his face had an olive tone. He had a weak chin, plump cheeks and a small plummy mouth like a woman's. In spite of the fan's agitation a sheen of sweat had appeared on his forehead. The doctor himself felt a little flushed, perhaps by the high seasoning of the food. He hoped most sincerely that he was not taking fever.

When the edge of his appetite was blunted, he allowed his eyes to slide around the larger area of the room, though there was little for them to dwell on. Only the other doorways interrupted the walls; there were no pictures and no other ornament except for a large gilt-framed mirror. Toward the door to the gallery some more empty chairs were grouped around a low table made of local wood.

"We are very plain here," Arnaud said.

"Perhaps your stay is temporary," said Doctor Hébert. "You will make a great fortune and return to France."

"It seems unlikely that France will be any longer in existence when and if I ever amass a great fortune," Arnaud said. "News reaches us so slowly, it is more than possible that they have already burned and murdered their way from one end of the country to the other at this moment, only we have yet to hear of it."

"I do not believe that matters are quite so desperate," the doctor said. "Although certainly they may set one's head awhirl."

"You may expect heads to be whirling down the public roads before this time is done," Arnaud said.

"Of course," the doctor said, "one hopes for a degree of moderation."

"I do not see that any middle course is viable," Arnaud said. "Not if the madmen in the National Assembly fall any further under the sway of *Les Amis des Noirs*. They understand nothing of the real conditions here. All this jabbering of liberty may be very well in France but among us it is nothing but incendiary. We will be brought to anarchy. Civil war. And worse."

He snapped his fingers and the three slaves moved to clear the table of the platters. When they had gone out toward the kitchen shed, the room fell quiet, except for the creaking of the fan. Doctor Hébert watched the black boy who crouched in the corner, pulling at the rope. His face was turned away toward the wall and a large ear stuck out at right angles to his head.

"Restraint on the part of all factions is undoubtedly to be desired," Doctor Hébert said. He had accustomed himself to uttering such platitudes since he had first arrived in the colony. All political subjects were dangerously volatile, and he found it difficult to make a quick and accurate estimate of where anyone stood on them. He would have hesitated to express a sincere conviction even if he had had the opportunity of forming one.

"I should like to see the *Pompons Rouges* restrained with a weight of chains," Arnaud said. "That rabble at Port-au-Prince will ruin themselves as well as us if nothing is done to contain them. Though they do not know it. It is an appalling blindness. We got off easily from that affair of last October but I would not expect such a matter to go so fortunately a second time."

The slaves were now returning from the yard, carrying a silver coffee service and a platter of mango and lemon slices and another of small dry cakes. Doctor Hébert accepted some pieces of fruit, tasted the mango, and sipped at his coffee.

"One might say that it went quite unfortunately for Ogé," he said.

"I am little concerned with Ogé's fortunes," Arnaud said. "He had done better to remain in France."

"Where many think it a hard punishment to be broken on a wheel of knives," the doctor said. "For a mulatto or for any man."

"Let it dissuade them from following his example, in that case," said Arnaud. "Ogé would have raised the cultivators. It is unthinkable."

"You speak freely," Doctor Hébert said, with an involuntary glance at the slave who stood behind Arnaud's chair, his face composed to a perfect blank.

"Free?" Arnaud said. "Sir, I have begun to develop a distaste for the sound of that word."

Above them, the fan creaked on its axis, wood fretting against wood. A film of sweat on the doctor's forehead was turning slightly chill. He moved his hand toward his wineglass and the slave behind him leaped forward to refill it.

"You are lately come from France yourself?" Arnaud inquired.

"I have been here for about five weeks," the doctor said.

"And where were you bound when you came here?"

"From Ennery to Le Cap," Doctor Hébert said. "From Habitation Thibodet, near Ennery. The husband of my sister was the proprietor there."

"I do not know him."

"I believe you are fortunate," the doctor said. "He appears to have been seven parts scoundrel. The marriage was inadvisable—by the result at least. My sister had departed before I arrived and as yet I have been unable to trace her."

He stopped speaking and cleared his throat, realizing that in his haste to avoid politics he had steered too deeply into personal confidences. He did not much care for the fruity smile on Arnaud's little mouth.

"And what of his other three parts, this Thibodet?"

"Oh, I would not deny him a degree of roguish charm, when he wished to exercise it. But he was three parts solid gold. I do not mean to be metaphorical. He was an extremely wealthy scoundrel."

"You employ the past tense."

"He died," Doctor Hébert said. "Quite suddenly, soon after my arrival at his house." He had not killed his brother-in-law, but there was that about Arnaud that made him wish it to appear as if he might have done so.

"It is an unhealthy country," Arnaud said. "Many die here."

"Yes," Doctor Hébert said. "I should mention that I am myself a physician. And I would repay your hospitality—"

"We have no illness here," Arnaud said. "Though you are kind." He pushed his chair back, and the slaves again commenced to clear the table, as though his movement was a signal.

"And yourself?" Doctor Hébert said. "In what part of France did you originate?"

"I was born here," Arnaud said shortly, and stood up. "Excuse me."

He picked up a candlestick and moved to a door behind his seat, which was shut with a padlock, and opened it with a key he took from his breeches pocket. From behind, his plumpness made him almost pear-shaped, and there was a hint of effeminacy in his step. The slave in the coat followed him into the room, where there must have been a draft, for the candle guttered. It was a storeroom, the doctor saw, with shelves of flour and other imported foods, many ranks of bottles, and more shelves of tools. Arnaud emerged with an ax in his hand. The slave came after him, carrying two mattocks.

"I have a little task outside," Arnaud said. "I will return momentarily."

"I believe I will accompany you," the doctor said.

Arnaud arched an eyebrow, but said nothing. The doctor followed him through the outer door. The slave who had waited on him at table now stood on the gallery with a lighted torch. At a word from Arnaud he led the way down the steps into the compound; Arnaud and the slave with the mattocks went after him.

Doctor Hébert lagged a little way behind the procession. It was markedly cooler outside by this time. Though there was no moon, the sky was clear and so long as he kept away from the torchlight the stars were extraordinarily bright.

At the foot of the pole, Arnaud stopped and took the torch from the slave and raised it. From a few feet back, Doctor Hébert saw the woman's body illuminated as high as her rib cage. There was no evidence of breathing.

"Well, it is finished," Arnaud said. He spoke to the slaves in Creole: *"Ou kómâsé travay la."* With a reluctant sluggishness the two blacks took up the mattocks and began digging at the base of the pole, which the doctor now saw was supported by a packing of rocks and earth. Arnaud watched the mattocks swinging. He set the ax head on the ground and leaned his weight on the handle. When the slaves had cleared the base of the pole, he smacked it with a one-handed swipe of the ax's blunt end. The two slaves sprang away as the pole fell backward. The woman's head bounced slackly against the wood, with a dense, compact sound. The pole rolled over a quarter turn and was stopped from rolling farther by her body.

Arnaud passed the torch back to the slave who had been holding it before and stood looking down at the corpse. He held the ax in both hands across his thighs in the same way he had earlier held his cane, the handle indenting his flesh slightly. The doctor stepped a little nearer to him.

"And what will become of the infant now?"

Arnaud snapped his head around. "How did you come to know about that?"

"My profession," the doctor said drily, and pointed. "She had not even time to pass the afterbirth."

"Time?" Arnaud said. "She killed her child the moment it was born. She stole a nail and drove it through its head. *That* nail." He raised the ax high and struck down at the impaled hands, severing them both crisply at the wrists. The doctor was impressed by the force of the stroke.

"It was a child of the *pariade,*" Arnaud said. "Some sailor's bastard, a half-breed like your Ogé." He swung the ax again, and again. It took him four or five blows to cut through the ankles and he was breathing hard when he had done it.

"There," he said. "Let them raise that."

Doctor Hébert glanced at the two slaves, who stood as woodenly as they had behind the dinner table. "Do you really believe that they can raise the dead?"

"It is not a matter of what I believe." Head down, the ax angled out from Arnaud's hand, describing a pendulous arc over the dead woman's head. "I paid twelve hundred pounds for that, and not eight months ago. Breeding stock, if you like. It is ruinous. If not abortion, it is suicide. They are animals."

"One does not ordinarily torture animals," the doctor said. "I have never known an animal to be a suicide."

"You are a sentimentalist, perhaps," Arnaud said. "You believe they are like little children."

"I believe they are like men and women," Doctor Hébert said.

"Indeed," said Arnaud. "Then you must be a Jacobin."

"I consider myself to be a scientist," the doctor said.

Arnaud stared at him, then sighed. "You have lost your way," he said. "If you were going to Le Cap you have strayed considerably. There is a passable road from here to Marmelade and there you may rejoin the *grand chemin*."

"Thank you," the doctor said, looking back toward the *grand'case* and the small yellow squares of its candlelit windows. Behind the house the dog had recommenced to bark. "Well, I see that it is late. I had better retire."

"I am in a position to offer you a glass of brandy," Arnaud said.

"I think I had best decline," the doctor said. "I have had a long ride today and look forward to another tomorrow." He bowed and walked out of the circle of torchlight.

There was a glow from the crack beneath his bedroom door when he approached it, but he thought nothing of this; a slave had probably brought a candle while he had been in the yard. Head lowered, he sat down on a chair and dragged off his left boot, not looking up until something suddenly blocked the light. A woman stood between him and the candle, which glittered through the loose weave of her clothing and outlined every detail of her body in black. The doctor had not yet got used to the degree of undress Creole women affected. He stood up abruptly and stumbled forward on his unshod foot. The woman hooked her hands into the waistband of his breeches and sat down backward on the *paillasse*, drawing him down after her.

The doctor was obliged to brace his hands on her shoulders to keep his balance. The bare skin was a bluish white and hot to his touch. He had suspected some misguided extension of Arnaud's hospitality, sending a mulattress to his bed, but it was the same woman he had seen on the gallery when he arrived, Madame Arnaud, presumably. She had let her hair down; it hung in thin pale crinkles into the loosened throat of her negligee. Her face still had a prettiness about it, but was puffed out of shape, and the spots of high color at her cheekbones looked unnatural, though they were not paint. Her eyes were gray-green and the left pupil had shrunk smaller than the right because it was nearer to the candle. The eyes were aimed at Doctor Hébert but he would not have ventured to suppose what they saw in his place.

Removing her hands from his waistband felt like plucking the claws of a dead bird from a branch. He took a step backward, unsteady between his bare foot and his booted one.

"I am sorry to see that you are unwell," he said. "I do not think it very serious, however. An agitation of the nerves. You must rest for three hours in the heat of the day and of course take care to avoid the sun. Have your cook prepare a strong *consommé* each evening. Lemons and oranges are plentiful here; I would suggest that you partake of them often. It would be best to abstain from spiritous liquors for a time. Some wine, perhaps, to strengthen your blood. But for the moment, sleep will be your great restorer."

Madame Arnaud had gathered her hair and was holding it with one hand at the nape of her neck. A thin blue vein wriggled beneath the clear skin of her temple. Doctor Hébert recalled what her husband had said, *For a shot of rum, she would do anything*. However, it was common usage to keep the storeroom locked wherever there were so many house slaves. Also common usage for the mistress of the house to keep a key.

Madame Arnaud put her head to one side and smiled at him with a queer jerk, the style of coquetry one might expect from a marionette on strings. The smile erased itself as quickly as it had appeared, and she rose and moved past him in short tripping steps and left the room. As she opened the door to depart, the doctor thought he might have seen Arnaud standing on the gallery, fidgeting with his cane. He shut the door after her and leaned on it with his palm. His head felt light and his stomach was uneasy, and when he pulled his hands away, he saw they had acquired a tremor. He undressed rapidly, hanging his garments one over another on the last peg on the wall. Kneeling beside the *paillasse* he crossed himself and said Our Father once hurriedly. At the rear of his mind the phrase repeated, *O let it not be fever*.

After the brief prayer he swung his legs up onto the bed and covered himself and lay there, concentrating on composure. The fevers here could cut a man down almost as quickly as the guillotine. The doctor breathed with care, deeply and deliberately, in and out. In a high corner of the room, shadows wavered over a spiderweb. When he reached to pinch out the candle, his hand had grown perfectly steady once more. But a little light still reached the room, over the partition walls, which stopped a few inches short of the ceiling. In the next room he could hear the sound of someone breathing. He lay in the half dark, rubbing the burned tallow from the candle between his thumb and forefinger, thinking uselessly of one thing and another. Thibodet had seemed in perfect health the day he had arrived. Afterward, his affairs appeared a wretched tangle, despite the evidence of great wealth somewhere, or perhaps it was only because the doctor understood so little of plantation management. He did not much trust the *gérant*, who appeared to have partnered his brother-in-law in most of his debaucheries. Perhaps he too would die before long. In a week Thibodet had lost half his body weight and his skin had shrunk and yellowed on his skull and a black effluvia poured from his every orifice, soiling the bed faster than the slave could clean it. He lashed his head from side to side and cried that he had no notion where Elise might have gone, though he hoped she was at the devil. She had had as many lovers as he, he declared, and had probably eloped with one or another, to Jamaica or Martinique. She might have sailed in an American naval vessel, she might have run away to join the maroons. Thibodet bolted up and turned to vomit into a pan. The movement tumbled him out of the bed and the doctor felt himself spinning too, delirious, as he saw her coming painfully toward him on the stumps of her ankles, arms outstretched. Madame Arnaud, or no, it was Elise herself, younger than she ought to have been, her face at sixteen, seventeen. Her gown was hanging off one shoulder. Blood spurted mightily from her severed wrists, and as she reached out to embrace her brother she opened her mouth and howled like a wolf. The doctor was on the floor beside the *paillasse*, bunched on his knees and knuckles, gasping and trembling. He shook himself and sat back on his heels. Now it was completely dark in the room, and a cool sweat bathed him. In the shed outside, the howling declined and broke off into that same deep-throated barking as before.

No, it was not fever, the doctor thought with a slight inward smile. Merely an agitation of the nerves. He got up and found his trousers on the peg and put them on. Barefoot and bare-chested, he went out to the gallery. A breeze was shivering the cane mats that closed either end of the long porch. In the exhilaration of his escape from the nightmare, the doctor felt preternaturally sensitive; he could have counted the hairs on his chest when the breeze lifted them, or numbered the splinters on the post when he placed his palm against it. He was not leaning for support, but only caressing the wood.

Behind the house the dog stopped barking and he heard the scratching of its claws against the dirt as it began to run and then the muted smash of its body against the heavy door. There was something else. He went down the two steps from the gallery and started across the compound, toward the ragged line of trees that scattered away from the denser hedging of the entrance *allée*. His feet were tender; he could feel the powdered dust caking up between his toes, and whenever he stepped on a pebble, he winced a little. By the time he had reached the trees his eyes had adjusted to the starlight. Beyond them the land dipped gently down and rose farther on and he could see one field after another checkered by the tight shrubbery of citrus trees that divided them, and he saw the starlight shining on the narrow channels that brought the water in. Where the cultivation ended the land rose sharply up and up and was a mountain, and he could not have measured the height of it if not for the stippled patterns of stars that began to appear at its limit. That was where the drumming came from, one pattern so low he could not really hear it, only feel a dim vibration of the small bones in his ears, and another drum sounding higher, beaten intermittently, like a voice calling to someone and waiting for answer and calling again. Surely it would have awakened any dreamer. The doctor's hands were curled over the prickly twigs of the two trees he had stopped between. His heart and lungs were working powerfully and there was a potent sense of health and vigor that seemed to rise through the soles of his bare feet and work through every vital part of him. He stood still there for quite a time and then began to circle around the edges of the compound.

The pole still lay where it had been, but every part of the body had been removed and the nails also had been pulled out. Doctor Hébert stepped over it and walked back toward the *grand'case*. Arnaud was sitting on the gallery, dandling his cane, balancing it and letting it drop from the vertical and catching the ornate pommel just before it tilted out of his reach. The reddened point of his cheroot glowed and faded and swept down to his knee. The doctor wondered, as he came up, if he might have failed to notice his host there when he first left the house.

"You are wandering," Arnaud said. He rested the cane against his outstretched leg.

The doctor walked up the steps and stood beside him. "Something woke me," he said. "A silence. The dog stopped barking."

"That's how it is," Arnaud said. He held a bottle up to the doctor, who swallowed from it, tasting a grapy thickness of sticks and stems and then the brilliant heat of *eau-de-vie*.

"The dog," the doctor said. "That is an animal you have there. Do you always keep him penned?"

"It's necessary," Arnaud said. "I trained him for the *maréchaussée*. He only understands killing, this dog. There is a band of maroons in the area, very troublesome."

"There?" Doctor Hébert said, swinging his shoulders toward where the pitch-black of the mountain interrupted the spangled blue-black of the sky. The movement of the deeper drum still trembled at the limit of his hearing. He noticed the shape of the mountain's dark to be vaguely reminiscent of a hog's head.

Arnaud pulled at his cheroot and flipped it over the edge of the board floor. It rolled a little way, sprinkling sparks, then stopped, the coal paling against the ground. Arnaud took the bottle from the doctor's hands and poured from it into the glass he held. "That may be," he said. "There will be slaves from this plantation, certainly. And from others which are near."

"Why do you not forbid such gatherings?" said the doctor.

"Oh, of course they are forbidden," Arnaud said, proffering the bottle. Doctor Hébert took it and held it out from the overhang of the roof so that it caught a glitter of the starlight. It was a slender, tapered vessel, the body just double the width of the elongated neck.

"They will be dancing," Arnaud said. "There are dances for the dead. One knows, even when one does not hear."

"Truly," Doctor Hébert said.

Arnaud swallowed noisily from his glass. "To them everything is forbidden," he said, "and to us everything is permitted. As you are a scientist, I leave it to you to determine the precise difference of our conditions."

"You surprise me," the doctor said, and took a last drink from the bottleneck. "Well, that will not be the work of a moment. I thank you again for everything." He set the bottle on the floor by Arnaud's chair and withdrew into the house.

The remainder of the night he slept without stirring, and woke automatically just at first light. He dressed quickly and quietly, lifted his saddlebags and passed through the main room, which seemed dim and dingy at this hour. There was no sign that anyone else had awakened within. Outdoors the compound was also deserted, except for a pair of chickens picking gravel around the back, but the dog began barking when he passed its shed. The doctor's temples tightened at the sound.

In the stall the horse was nosing at the last scatter of a flake of hay. Doctor Hébert saddled and bridled it and gave it water at the trough. He had no appetite himself, and was eager to be gone. When the horse had drunk, he broke off another corner of sugar to give it. The horse took the sugar and then went on nuzzling and lipping the butt of his palm. The doctor curved his hand up to stroke the soft dark skin around its nostrils and spoke to the horse in gentle nonsense syllables. Thibodet had named it Espoir, which struck the doctor as somewhat ridiculous, considering that it was a gelding.

The dog broke off its barking sharply as Doctor Hébert led the horse outside and swung up into the saddle. He had scarcely had time to take note of the silence when he saw the chickens scatter and loft themselves into clumsy flight and the dog coming grimly between them, straight for him at a dead run. He yanked the horse in the direction of its leap and the dog struck the horse on its shoulder, sprawled back on the ground, and was up again instantly. The horse reared and let out a panicked whinny, wheeled and bunched itself to kick. The doctor leaned down into the horse's mane and groped in the bottom of his right-hand saddlebag, blindly turning over his instruments and the sacks of medicines there. Again the dog was trying to close and, turning the horse more tightly with his left hand, the doctor kicked out at it clumsily with his boot still in the stirrup. The dog's teeth clicked against the stirrup iron and it fell back and recouped itself. Doctor Hébert straightened up in the saddle, bringing the heavy double-barreled pistol out of the saddlebag and bracing it over his left arm, which held the reins. When the dog launched itself he shot it once in its open mouth, and the bullet, exiting from the base of the skull, flipped it over backward. The dog lay thrashing on the packed ground and the doctor sighted at a place behind its ear and fired the second barrel. The dog convulsed and stretched its legs, and the doctor felt confident that it was dead.

It seemed brighter and warmer than it had been, and from all sides there was a jabbering in Creole. Several of the house slaves had come out of the different outbuildings and were edging in cautiously on the carcass of the dog, whose big splayed paws were still twitching in the dust. The horse was moving in nervous jerks, and Doctor Hébert stroked its neck with the two free fingers of his left hand to calm it. His right hand still held the pistol pointing straight up. His ears were ringing from the shots and he felt giddy, as though the gunpowder smell had made him drunk. Arnaud had come out the back door of the *grand'case* and stood with his feet apart, looking from the doctor to the dog's body and back.

"Accept my apologies," Doctor Hébert said. "I had to give myself permission. You understand the predicament, I am sure."

Arnaud said nothing in reply, but merely went on looking. He was standing just as the doctor had first seen him when he had arrived the afternoon before, holding his cane in two hands and pressing it into the meat of his thighs. The doctor contemplated the curious thought that possibly everything which had occurred between the one stance and the other was an illusion and no time had really passed at all. He saluted Arnaud with the sulfurous barrel of the pistol, and kicked the horse and cantered around the corner of the house toward the mouth of the green *allée*.

Chapter Two

THE WHITEMEN BELIEVE that everything is a story. In their world that may be so. I will never live there. What men may do is flat like a road and goes along the skin of the world but because it does not begin in one place or end in another it is not a road at all. At the crossroads is where we must always meet but the other road does not lie on the earth. It comes out of the sky down the *poteau mitan* and through the earth *en bas de l'eau*, where Guinée is the sunken island beneath the waters, where the *loa* wait to meet us. That is the cross and what it means and it is everywhere. The white men say they nailed a man onto it, the man which their god chose.

Their story is not the same as ours. This is a story told by god, but a different god chose me.

In the summer before Boukman danced the death of all the whitemen at the edge of Bois Cayman, we were near the top of Morne Cochon, at the place we call the Pig's Ear. There was a long narrow way between the rocks and then a wider lower spot and on the slope behind a shallow cave with a spring below it. A good place. At the bottom below the rocks we made a hut where a man would wait and watch for the *maréchaussée*, but we knew the *maréchaussée* would never come so high. The going was too steep for horses. A man who sat on the rock above the cave could see a long way over the northern plain to the curving of the ocean where the boats of the whitemen would come and go.

We were few and there were more men than women with us. I did not have any wife of my own, but I had been with Merbillay for three days in a place behind the Pig's Neck, and I believed that she was big because of me, although Achille did not think so. Achille said that the child would be his and that it would be a son. He said that his *maît'tête* Ghede had told him so when Ghede was in his head, and no one would say differently because Achille was the *hûngan*. Achille was small and ugly and shriveled. When he was born his back was not straight and it never did straighten, and at the *habitation* which he had come from the whitemen used to laugh when they said his name. But he told us that he had poisoned the *gérant* and seen him dead on the floor of the *grand'case* before he ran away, taking the rifle. He had the rifle, that was true. It was our only gun.

Merbillay stayed with Achille again after we had come back from behind the Pig's Neck, and I did not mind whatever she did, although I sometimes would remember how fat and tight her skin had felt, those three days and nights around the peak of the mountain. We had gone out gathering, I much farther than anyone else, to find new trees that no one had shaken or climbed. I went so far I thought no one could be near me, and so when I saw her coming through the lianas that hung from the lowest branch I knew that she must have been following me all that way. When I asked she showed me the white of her eyes and said that she had only come looking for something to fill her and I asked her what it was she hungered for. When I asked, she showed me the soft brown of her eye, so we both knew. Sometimes I could see again how she looked then, later when she was sitting with Achille and I sat on the rock above the cave and looked out over the ocean, or if at night I should suddenly wake and feel my *ti-bon-ange* traveling from my head.

There is my *ti-bon-ange* and my *gros-bon-ange* and my *gros-bon-ange* belongs to the life of all, but my *ti-bon-ange* is I, Riau. Waking at night, I would think that I wanted to take Merbillay and go around to the far side of the mountain with her to stay there, or to take her and go south perhaps. Or I heard my voice tell how I might whisper to the others and turn them from Achille, or pick poisonous herbs for him, or give him graveyard dirt to eat. Then my *ti-bon-ange* would whisper that after all Achille was a strong *hûngan*, who served the *loa* very well, and he was honored of the *loa*, even if Ghede had lied to him about the child. Also that we had all followed him from one good place to another, and that no harm had come to anyone in following him.

Merbillay changed in her *grossesse,* and from where I was watching I saw her temper sour. In the spring when we fed the *loa,* it was always the beautiful and loving Maîtresse Erzulie who came down into her head, who smiled with joy at the gifts we made her, a madras cloth or a polished stone or a bit of glass to see herself. But in that summer when we danced, it was Erzulie-gé-rouge that took her body, so red-eyed with weeping it appeared that her eyes themselves had been torn out from their holes. Erzulie-gé-rouge sat on the ground and clawed and beat on the dirt with her hands and screamed and cried and no offering could comfort her for her terrible losses. Also we had little to offer her by then.

Every day it was hot and dry and the winds on the mountain would make the skin rasp. Above us the peak of the mountain had turned red and bare. This Morne Cochon was not a true high mountain where a cloud always sits, only a small hill above the plain. The spring began to falter, running a little less each day. The wild pigs had gone lower on the slope, and the dry meat was coming to an end. Our only fresh meat was small birds caught with glue on the branches. Also there began to be a smell because Ti-Marie, who was old and lame, would not go farther than the edge of camp, and because it would never rain.

Merbillay was swollen at the belly but her face and her arms grew thin. There were new lines on her face which all pointed down and at night I knew she whispered to Achille that she wanted to go down to the plain, and for us all to go. My *gros-bon-ange* did not want to go raiding on the plain, and my *ti-bon-ange* was silent. I knew that Merbillay wanted to go to a *habitation* where other young women would be, she wanted to make a tall cone of cloths around her hair, and eat meal cakes and drink rum and dance at a big *calenda.* About being caught and sent into the cane field with a heavy chain on her feet, she was not thinking of that.

Then I went down to the hut below the rocks and sent Paul Lefu back up. There I stayed for most of two days. It was quiet and I had stopped talking in my head and my *ti-bon-ange* was silent. The runoff springs had stopped completely, but I had brought a little water with me in a skin, and I did not move much so I did not often need to drink, and I was not hungry. On the second day I saw a pig who had himself become thin, and I went after him for a way, but I could not catch him. Then there was a sound which was not the pig. I hid myself and saw Jean-Pic coming from behind a ceiba tree.

"Riau," he said.

"Well, you have come back," I said.

Jean-Pic was coming back all alone, and the sack on his back was wrinkled and limp. If he had got any food he had eaten it on his journey, and he had not any rum or gunpowder either. I went with him back to the main camp. The spring had become only a wet spot on the ground. I got water by pressing the back of my hand in the wet leaves and waiting for my palm to fill. The smell was worse. Merbillay was sitting on the rock above the cave, looking toward the ocean and saying that she wanted to eat a fish. Then she said only the one word again and again, *pwasô, pwasô*. Jean-Pic had not brought anything back in his sack except for a little cornmeal.

When the sun began to go down to meet the ocean I stood up and crossed over to Achille and asked him to make a *vévé* for Ogûn. He looked at me a little time before he nodded. His face was thin and sharp and he had a long nose like a whiteman's, but there was no white blood in him. He nodded and picked up a spear and put it into the ground for a *poteau mitan*. He picked up the bag of meal. There was too little to waste and not enough to save. Achille mixed meal with some ash he took from the edge of the fire and crouched to make the *vévé* at the left of the *poteau mitan*. The mixed meal spilled in fine lines from the bottom edge of his hand and he moved over the ground like a spider, making the diamonds with the stars inside and lacing them together, never stopping till he made the last twirl at the corner of the square.

The *vévé* of Ogûn was there. Achille knocked on the ground beside the *poteau mitan* and stood and raised the *asson*. The strings of stones clashed on the side of the gourd. Achille turned and shuffled and began to sing.

Ogûn travay o li pa mâjé
Ogûn travay-o
Ogûn pa mâjé
Yé o swa Ogûn dòmi sâ supé . . .

The *asson* said aclash-aclash and behind me I heard César-Ami beating the little drum, but there was a stone sitting on my teeth and my mouth would not open. Jean-Pic had begun to sing and

Merbillay stopped saying *pwasô* and slipped down from the rock and began to sing the song for Ogûn.

Ogûn works, he doesn't eat
Ogûn works-o
Ogûn hasn't eaten
Last night Ogûn went to bed with no supper . . .

Clash-aclash the *asson* said. Ogûn was talking to the drum but my feet were buried in the ground, I couldn't lift them. My eyes were looking at the sun where it cut down through the clouds toward the water. It was round and red and its edges were sharpened like a knife. Jean-Pic stood up to dance. Merbillay's hips went back to front and side to side. Then my knees loosened and my feet came free and I was moving with the two of them and with Achille. The *asson* said clash-aclash and the drum changed. My eyes were still on the red of the sun. I saw Achille jerk his head and he began to sing the song for Ghede.

Mwê li brav-o
Rélé brav-o, gasô téméré
Bat' bânân li téméré
Mòso pul li téméré
Gnu ku kléré li téméré
Mòso patat li téméré
M'apé rélé brav Gédé—

Then we were all dancing because we were hungry and others too were singing the song of Ghede.

I say brave-o
Call him brave-o, a bold fellow
His banana end is bold
His piece of chicken is bold
His bowl of rum is bold
His piece of sweet potato is bold
I am calling brave Ghede!

Achille's mouth had fallen loose. His head was rolling unstrung on his neck. The *asson* swung low at his knees like an end of rope. Jean-Pic took the *asson* from his fingers and propped him up a little from behind. Achille had stopped singing but the others went on.

M'apé rélé brav Gédé—
V'ni sové z-âfâ la-o
M'apé rélé brav Gédé—

The drum changed. Ghede pushed himself up and away from Jean-Pic's arm and walked away from him without looking back. Jean-Pic raised the *asson* high and shook it, clash-aclash. Ghede walked in a wide circle to the left around the *poteau mitan*. His knees came up almost to his chest as he marched, but his hands did not move at all. His arms were sticking at his ribs like the arms of a wooden man. Ghede's neck was long and very stiff but he could not make Achille's back come straight.

I am calling brave Ghede
Come and save the children here
I am calling Brave Ghede—

The voice was coming out of Merbillay, though her mouth was no longer seeming to move and her eyes had closed in on her dancing. The rapping of the drum slowed and began, slowed and began a new speed. Ghede stopped before Jean-Pic and began to accuse him: *You have brought no bread for Ghede. You have brought no meat for Ghede. You have not brought any rum for Ghede. Ghede's hunger is very strong. Why will you not feed Ghede?*

I was dancing in a wave, rising and falling. I did not need to move my body anymore because the wave moved it all of itself in time to the changes of the drum. The wave came up over my head and then went down and then again. I could still hear Ogûn's song although no one was singing it out loud any longer.

Ogûn travay-o
Ogûn pa mâjé
Yé o swa Feraille dòmi sâ supé . . .

Ghede stood before me, watching. His lips were thin and his eyes were glassy and wide so there was a white line all around the balls of them. Ghede put his head on one side and then on the other. I could not hear what he was saying because I was shrinking far away. Riau was shrinking, shrinking far away. He felt the pushing in his head as Ogûn pushed out his *ti-bon-ange* to make space in the head to put himself. The drum changed and the wave closed over Riau's head and Riau was gone and there was Ogûn.

Ogûn Feraille! Ogûn turned his back on Ghede. Ogûn took up a cane knife and swung it in circles around his head as he walked around the *poteau mitan*. He put the cane knife down into the middle of the fire and left it there to burn with heat. The sun had struck into the edge of the sea and was sinking in a blood-stained mist. The edge of the cane knife was glowing red hot when Ogûn took it from the fire and kissed it with his lips. Ogûn touched the knife with his tongue. The hot iron had no power to burn him. Ogûn Feraille! He took the shining cane knife and stabbed it into the wet dirt of the dying spring. The hot blade sizzled and went dark and Ogûn cried out in a loud voice that he was hungry too and that his hunger was greater than the hunger of Ghede.

ON THE NEXT DAY Riau was tired. The muscles in his arms and legs felt stretched and rubbery, as if he had been swimming a very long way against a very strong current. Merbillay put a piece of mango on a leaf down beside him and went away without saying anything. Riau ate a little of the mango, chewing the pulp a long time. It seemed hard for him to swallow it.

Riau saw his cane knife sticking out of the dead spring and went and picked it up. For a long time he sat with it on his knees. The heat had made a rippling pattern on the surface of the metal and there was a white ashy dusting where the blade joined the hilt. When someone called to him, Riau got up and put the cane knife into his waistband and began helping the rest of us get ready to leave. We had decided to go away from the mountain all together, and Riau was coming too although for the moment it seemed to make little difference to him whether we had decided to go or remain.

We cooked the meal into flat cakes and ate the fruit that we could gather. For two days there was no spring or stream and we got water by cutting vines and draining them. We did not go so very fast because Ti-Jeanne was always lagging. There were two children who could go as fast as anyone, and one boy named Epi who was too small, and so we took turns carrying him. When I had him on my shoulders he held on to one of my ears and said *Riau, Riau,* whispering it over. By then I had returned all the way from Ogûn and I was once more I. On the sixth day we found the small stream called Petit Ruban that runs out of the ravine onto the plain and turns at the edge of the cane fields at Habitation Arnaud.

Then we all hid ourselves behind the rocks because a whiteman on a horse was crossing the stream. He was on the way to Habitation Arnaud but he did not know it. It was plain from the way he looked about himself that he did not know where he was at all. The horse was tired and walked with its head low. Jean-Pic wanted to follow and pull the whiteman down from the horse, but Achille said that it was not wise. There was no powder for his gun and he did not know whether the whiteman had a gun in his saddlebags. Jean-Pic said that he could take the whiteman so quickly and quietly that whatever might be in his saddlebags would be of no use to him but only to us. Achille said that if he failed he would bring out the *maréchaussée*, or perhaps even if he succeeded, for someone might be expecting the whiteman to arrive somewhere. If we were hunted through the low country not all of us would get away.

The whiteman went riding away down the road and instead of following we turned with the stream and went along the edge of the outermost cane piece, which was bordered by a thicket of orange trees. The stream was low but it was still running and the oranges were ripening there. We all picked and ate a few. Achille made Merbillay go back to pick up some peelings she had dropped. The hedge kept us from sight of the field but when we had gone a little way farther we could hear the voice of the *commandeur* crying out harshly.

We sat down quietly then and waited until the *commandeur* had gone by on the other side of the hedge and away into another part of the cane piece. We could still hear the sound of the cane knives cutting not very far away. There was a low gap in the hedge that a dog might have been using, and Jean-Pic and I crawled through. I did not like to be in a cane field again. The cane was very dry, too dry, and the long leaves were brittle when I touched them.

Jean-Pic put his hand on my arm to make me be still and he parted the cane leaves to look through. On the other side a man was bent over working. There were old scars on his back from the *commandeur*'s whip and a fresh stripe which might have been from that same day. His head was in a tin cage with four foot-long spikes sticking out on the four sides of it, closed on the back of his neck with a rivet. He put down his knife and went down the row to where a woman was working with a calabash of water beside her. When he lifted the calabash we saw that he could not drink because there was a mesh gate over his mouth, locked by a key. He wet a rag and worked an end of it through the mesh and stretched out his lips and tongue to suck on it. Then he put down the gourd and came back to the place where he had been working.

"*Ho, gâso brav,*" Jean-Pic said, speaking in a whisper that carried like a breeze. The slave jerked his head to the side and the spike in the front of the cage rattled among the leaves. His eyes found Jean-Pic on the other side of the row of cane.

"Be still," Jean-Pic said. "What happened to you, did you run?"

"No," the slave said. "I ate. They caught me chewing cane in the field."

"Ah," Jean-Pic said. "I don't hear anyone singing in this cane piece."

"You won't hear anyone singing today," the slave said. "The *commandeur* may wear out his whip hand but no one is going to sing today."

"Why?" said Jean-Pic.

"He is killing a woman today."

"Arnaud?"

"Himself," the slave said.

"And what is it he is killing her for?"

"She is an Ibo," the slave said. "Bought eight months ago, out of Le Cap. Last night she delivered herself of a son."

"Does he kill for that here?" Jean-Pic said.

"The child is dead already." The slave licked his lips and the underside of his tongue brushed over the metal mesh. "The woman is probably not dead yet."

"Ah, so that's how it is," Jean-Pic said. He asked another question and the slave began to tell him how they planned to meet at night and dance the *petro* dances. But I was not much listening any longer. Though I understood now how it must have been with the woman and the baby, I was not thinking of that either, but I was remembering those many years when I myself had been dead to life.

. . .

THAT NIGHT there was a big calenda with food and plenty of clairin. I danced, but Ogûn did not come to me. In the dark outside the circle of the fires I lay with Merbillay, then slept. At dawn I woke when Merbillay slept on, and nearby Achille lay on his back with his arms thrown out and snored. Ghede had carried him all the way into the dark. I got up and walked down toward the grand'case all alone, to the edge of the stable yard where the cabins of the house slaves were. It was in my head that there might be things to take from here, salt or sugar or even gunpowder, but also I was a little afraid to go among these cabins because the house slaves would know me for a stranger. Also I could hear a dog somewhere close by, barking in a loud deep voice.

While I was thinking there at the yard's edge the horseman we had seen on the road the day before came out of the barn leading his horse. As he was mounting I heard the dog stop barking and then the dog was charging and leaping at the horseman, not barking anymore because this dog was trained to kill in silence. I never saw the horseman shoot, only the pistol pointed at the sky with the sharp powder smell smoking out of it, and the dog lying in the dust of the yard. I did not believe this whiteman had killed the dog of his own power, such a shot from the back of a bucking horse—it was the work of a *loup-garou*. The dog's big paws were kicking the dirt and his jaws were snapping and he still wanted to get up and kill the horseman. It was the only thing he wanted. The house slaves had come out and stood near the dog, though not too near. The horseman had gone. Then I went away myself and ran into the cane field.

The hooves of the horse were still beating down the *allée*. I could not catch him up no matter how I ran, but I knew where the road turned alongside the cane field, and I thought that I might meet the horseman there, if he chose to ride back the way he had come. I went running through the cane field with the broad leaves stroking along my back, crossways toward the orange hedge at the far corner. Then I ran into an irrigation ditch and fell and bruised my arm against a stone. When I got up again my arm was numb because my elbow had struck, and I saw that the horseman had turned and was still going at a canter, so that I would never reach him.

But they were coming into the bottom of the cane piece now, and

I heard the voice of the *commandeur* calling *"Chantez! Chantez!"* Silence, and the whip's braid uncurled through it and snapped, and snapped again at the end of a long uncoiling. I heard one voice take up a weary song and then another, I could not make out the words. I got up out of the irrigation ditch and shook myself and began to hurry out of the cane piece.

When I came near the orange hedge I could hear harness jingling and the creak of the wheels of a coach. I hid myself behind the trees and bent down a branch. The horseman had stopped to ask his way and I could see him, sitting his horse, who was still nervous, shifting and turning, like his hooves were on coals. The rider sat well, but he didn't try to stop the horse from shying. He was a small man, with small neat hands, pale on the reins. He had taken off his hat and I could see that he was balding, the top of his head round as an egg, but speckled and peeling from sunburn. His beard was rust brown and clipped to a short point. I didn't know why I had wanted to see him again, to see him nearer and remember him. There was nothing strange to see him near. What power he had came from his pistol, I thought then, but inside my head I saw the flash and saw the dog drop, still. I didn't know. He had put the pistol away out of sight.

When the coachman spoke I was so amazed to hear that voice that I almost gasped out loud. Though after all it was not so far from Haut du Cap. I moved a step or two along the hedgerow to a wider gap and saw him then, sitting on the box. His coachman's dress: the worn green coat with the brass buttons, and ribbons at his knees. His feet were bare. Both his hands were on the reins and the whip was in the stand. Toussaint had never whipped a horse or needed to.

From inside the coach Bayon de Libertat said something in a thin silvery voice. The horseman bowed from the saddle and replaced his hat and rode by. Toussaint gave the reins a shake and the coach began to creak and jingle along the road. There was white dust, I saw, on the shoulders of his coat.

The slaves had fanned out into the field and I could hear them weakly singing, some not far from me. These were not the songs of the night before, during the *petro* dances. The slaves were weary, and unwilling. It was a misery to hear them. I crawled through the orange hedge into the road and began to run again, around the three corners of the cane piece and back toward the stable yard. The sun had come up out of the mountains and I felt naked in the bare new light. The coach was standing in the stable yard as I had hoped, and he had already unhitched the horses. Of course there was nowhere to go on this road except for Habitation Arnaud.

Someone had carried the dead dog away, and there was a ragged stain where his blood was darkening on the dirt. People were going back and forth on different errands between the cabins and the *grand'case*, and I waited for them to stop, but the yard was never empty. At last I stepped out into the yard and began walking toward the barn. A chicken ran squawking from under my feet, and I was afraid then. A woman in a long checked dress looked at me curiously but she said nothing. Then I came under the high lintel of the barn door and into the shadows of the hall.

Toussaint was standing by the water trough at the back, brushing one of the matched pair of grays. One of Arnaud's grooms was going away from him—Toussaint would have sent him away. I waited until the groom had gone and went a little nearer.

"*Parrain*," I said. When I was a small boy, I called him so, and now it came again out from my mouth.

Toussaint looked over the horse's back and nodded. "Riau," he said. "You're thin."

"It's dry," I said. "Besides, you're thin yourself."

"It's how I'm made," Toussaint said. A thick band of leather bound the brush to his palm. He stroked it over the gray's back and shoulders, sweeping away the dust of the road.

"*Fatras-Baton*," I said. I used the old nickname of Thrashing-Stick because I thought he didn't like it. It made me angry that he wasn't surprised to see me there, to think that he had somehow known my presence earlier, on the road. It was not possible. Toussaint smiled his secret inward smile.

"I remember when you were fat," he said. "Wasn't that two years ago?" He came around the near side of the horse and took my upper arm and squeezed it. "Oh, but you are still strong," he said.

"What did you come here for?" I said.

"To drive the master." Toussaint turned from me, and brushed along the horse's flank.

"Why would he come?" I said. "He's a different man from the master here."

"They have affairs," Toussaint said. "The times are strange. You don't know—" He stopped speaking and turned the horse, crowding me over against the wall. A pair of Arnaud's grooms were walking through, talking to each other.

"You don't know, hiding in the mountains," Toussaint said, when they had passed.

"Have I missed so much?" I said.

Toussaint shrugged, and put the brush in his coat pocket.

"It's all right for you," I said. "You have the coach and the horses and the ear of the master. You understand what there is in books."

The horse nipped at the green cloth of his forearm and Toussaint slapped him lightly on the nose. "Stop it," he said.

"I don't understand why you are here," I said. "Bayon de Libertat is a kind master, as it goes, and Arnaud is a cruel master." I was wondering if Toussaint knew about the woman and the baby, and what he would have thought. But after all it was not so far from Haut du Cap, and I had heard the stories about Arnaud at Bréda when I was still a slave there.

Toussaint took a curry comb from his coat pocket and began to work out the tangles from the mane of the gray. The horse tossed his head against the pulling.

"Yes," Toussaint said. "And if he catches you, Riau, he will bury you to the neck in the ground and wait till the ants have eaten your eyes."

"Truth," I said.

"Where will you go?" Toussaint said.

"Why?" I asked him. "Have you begun to ride with the *maréchaussée?*"

Toussaint stopped his combing and turned toward me, one hand still knotted in the horse's mane. He looked at me till my knees grew weak. His eyes looked yellow, in the dim.

"I think we are going south," I said. "I don't know where we'll go."

"Go where God sends you, Riau," he said. It was the pompous voice he used when he was reading Bible verses.

"Where else could I go," I said. We did not mean the same thing, and he knew it. So I turned and went out of the barn, and heard my heart stop.

Arnaud, the master, was standing in the stable yard, switching his cane at the dark place in the dirt where the dog had lain. He looked at me, but he didn't see me. He saw something, but not Riau; he saw something like a chicken or a horse or an ox. When I could breathe again I walked past him, under his eyes, until I had put a cabin between us. Then I began to run and I didn't stop running until I had come all the way up the first slope among the wild trees, to the clearing where Arnaud's slaves had their provision grounds.

Merbillay and Jean-Pic were digging up sweet potatoes with pointed sticks; already they had a heap between them. The two small boys were gathering greens and stowing them away in a sack. Achille stood at the edge of the clearing, propped on his gun barrel, its stock braced against the ground.

"Did you get any powder?" I said.

"It's all locked away in the *grand'case,*" Achille said. "No, I couldn't get any."

"There was powder last night for the *petro* dances," I said.

Achille stared at me. His eyes were unclear, they didn't meet, he looked like his head was hurting him. "And you know what they did with it," he said.

"They burned it for the *petro loa,*" I said. "Yes, I know. When does Arnaud let the people go to the provision grounds?"

"Two hours at midday," Achille said. "We have already stayed too long."

"Truth," I said.

"I would be gone before now," Achille said, and pointed. "Jean-Pic wanted to wait for you until the sun was there."

We shared out loads of sweet potatoes and filed out of the clearing. We went along the lower slope, following the curve of the *morne,* moving as quickly as we could on the uneven ground away from Habitation Arnaud. By the noon hour we were far enough away that we could not hear the wailing and shouting of Arnaud's slaves when they discovered all we had stolen from them. There was nothing to hear except birdcalls in the brush until the evening had turned purple, and Jean-Pic caught at my arm.

"Listen," he said.

I stopped, but there was nothing to hear, only insects singing in the twilight.

"No, listen," said Jean-Pic.

I could hear the others going away from us along the slope, passing out of earshot. Then a long long way away, down on the plain, there was something barking.

"That is a mile from here, or more," I said. "That is only some *habitation* with perhaps a visitor."

"You say so," Jean-Pic said. "But listen . . ."

I thought I heard voices then, calling the dogs together, but it was so far, so faint, I wasn't sure. Jean-Pic plucked at my wrist and led me. Not far from us was a dry gully and above one side of it a pointed shelf of rock stuck out, from where we could look down the gully to the plain. I didn't see anything when I looked, but it seemed I could hear more plainly.

"Well, they have not shot all their dogs," I said. Then down on the plain I saw a spark, another spark, a chain of orange lights, and I knew that they were lighting torches.

"They have not," Jean-Pic said, between his teeth.

"Still, they're far," I said.

"And they'll come fast," said Jean-Pic. "We have to go higher on the mountain where horses can't follow."

So we climbed down from the rock then, and began to trot into the bush to overtake the others and warn them. The sound we made was enough to cover the barking of the dogs, if they were still barking, so far away behind us. Under the trees it was already very dark, so that running at arm's length from Jean-Pic I could hardly see him. I didn't know how the others had gone so far ahead of us. We must have waited longer than we knew, looking over our back trail. Then there was a sound, a crashing sound very near, and I went up a tree so fast it seemed that it had sucked me onto its highest branch.

In a tree nearby I could hear Jean-Pic breathing, it made me angry how loud he breathed. When I looked for a long time I could just see him plastered against the gray-green gleaming of the bark, with his sides blowing in and out like the skin of a frog. The noise had stopped. Then I heard it again—it was in one place—a thrashing sound, and someone groaned. It wasn't far away at all.

Slowly I slipped down from the tree. The insides of my legs and arms were sore from the sudden climb.

"Where are you going?" Jean-Pic said.

"It's not them," I told him.

Jean-Pic hissed at me, no word, just anger—fear.

"It isn't them," I said, and I went back the way we'd come. I could hear the thrashing stop and start again, and stop, to the left down the slope from the path we had broken for ourselves. The sound of the *maréchaussée* was still far below, but I thought I knew what they were after now. Not us. Or not only us. I smelled him before I saw him, the sweat from running and the sweat from fear. He had fouled himself too. My toe found a little wet at the bottom of a drying stream and I stopped and saw him there on the other bank where I had expected, bent double with the spikes of his tin headstall tangled in the vines. He was trying to be still now, because he felt that I was near, but I could still hear the sob and the catch of his breath.

It surprised me he had managed to come so far. I remembered him, the night before—they had unlocked the gate over his mouth when he left the field, so he was eating meal cakes, and drinking *clairin*, and he had danced for a long time, tossing his long-pronged head whenever the powder flashed with the drumrolls. I moved a little closer now, and he jerked away like a horse shying. His back and legs were scratched and bleeding from running in the bush.

"Be still," I said. He jerked and pulled a little away. The whites of his eyes rolled in the headstall. I saw they had locked the gate again. He must have been running a long time without water.

"Kill him," Jean-Pic said. He had come up behind me on cat feet.

"I don't know," I said. The slave made a strangling moan with many syllables but no words and began to thrash his head from side to side. The vines tightened on the spikes of the headstall. At the back of his neck where the rivet closed the tin there was a thin line of blood.

"It's a trick," said Jean-Pic. "He came to see which way we would go."

"Maybe not," I said. The slave stopped moving and lay there gasping his crying gasp.

"He brought them after us," Jean-Pic said.

"Yes," I said.

"Kill him or leave him," Jean-Pic said. "You know what's right."

I took my cane knife out and looked at the edge of it. Above, the sky had silted over, a damp black. There was a single star.

"Go on," I said to Jean-Pic, and again I said, "Go."

Then Jean-Pic went padding off into the trees, and soon I heard him start to jog. The cane knife came up and up and pointed at the one high star. I thought, is it my *z'étoile*, or his? When we die the *ti-bon-ange* must leave the body, but that is only the beginning of the journey, and the *z'étoile* is master of where the *ti-bon-ange* will go and of what things it will do. I felt the handle turn in my hand and when the knife struck it was with the blunt edge, clanging on the rivet. The slave's head bounced and sprang back from the snarl of vines, but the rivet held and I saw the knife rise and chop down once again and then the rivet broke. So I bent over and pulled the tin of the headstall apart. His head came free and he slid down the bank and lay in the creek bed with his face in the wet. He breathed and then his tongue pushed out and began to lick at the damp leaves.

The cane knife swung down at my side. The cage of tin was twisted up among the vines, broken edges shining in the starlight. Two or three smaller stars had come out next to the one big one and away down the mountain I heard the dogs' voices toll as they found sign.

"Come on," I said. "It's time to go."

He spoke without lifting his head from the mud. "I can't any-more."

So I kicked him in the ribs a time or two until he rolled up on his knees. "Get up and run," I said. "You don't yet know what you can do."

Chapter Three

CREAKILY BAYON DE LIBERTAT GOT DOWN from the coach and paused to look up at Arnaud, who stood on the gallery of the *grand'case*, caressing the pommel of the cane he held across his legs. A harness bell clacked as one of the grays tossed its head to shake off a fly. Toussaint closed the carriage door behind his master and moved to the horse's head and stroked the line of its jaw to quiet it.

"I hadn't looked for you so early," Arnaud said. "The Sieur Maltrot has not yet come."

Bayon de Libertat sneezed, drew out a cambric handkerchief from his coat pocket and blew his nose. Toussaint had turned to face him, stooped in a sort of frozen bow, eyes raised and querying. Bayon de Libertat nodded as he folded the handkerchief away, and Toussaint led the coach and horses around the rear of the *grand'case* toward the stable.

"You're well, I take it?" Bayon de Libertat said, a trifle testily. *"Et madame?"*

"—is still abed." Arnaud smiled suddenly and skipped down the plank steps, reaching for the other's hand. "Welcome, then. You'll inspect the fields with me? Come, I'll order a horse for you."

Bayon de Libertat, who would have preferred coffee or a glass of water, and a chance to limber his rickety legs and back, began to open his mouth, but the voice which emerged from behind Arnaud's fixed smile kept rushing over him.

"Come," Arnaud repeated. "You're only stiff from jouncing over these bad roads. An hour in the saddle will do you good."

But when they once were mounted, Arnaud again was silent and morose. Bayon de Libertat asked such polite questions as occurred to him, his voice brittle with annoyance. His stomach was uneasy, his knees sore, his left hand cramped arthritically on the reins. Age told on him, though he would not think of himself as old, but blamed his discomfort on his host's discourtesy. He was too irked to show his fatigue now. It was already very hot.

"You've had another guest," he forced himself to say.

"Eh?" Arnaud said, raising his head from a muttered conversation with his *commandeur*. "*Pardon?*"

"A visitor? I met him on the road as I came in. He stopped the coach to ask his way . . ."

"Oh, that fellow." Arnaud gouged a heel into his horse's flank and they trotted toward the next cane piece. "Some freethinker, I suppose, just out from France. He called himself a doctor."

"No close connection then?" Bayon de Libertat said, and added mockingly, "A relative, perhaps?"

Arnaud glanced over his shoulder. "He was lost." Again he faced toward the cane piece ahead, where the rise and fall of knives set up a painful intermittent flashing in the sun.

"You're cutting early," said Bayon de Libertat.

Arnaud grunted. "It's twelve-month cane . . . fourteen, maybe." He pulled up his horse and got down and went through a gap in the hedge to the first cane row. The horse lowered its head into a swirl of dangling reins, which Bayon de Libertat eyed disapprovingly. Arnaud said something curt to the slave nearest him, who chopped a six-inch section from a stalk of cane already felled and presented it to the master with his face turned away. Then he moved on down the row, raising his knife and swinging it down to cut each stalk as near the ground as possible.

Arnaud walked back toward the horses, peeling the section of cane with his penknife. He split off a wedge and offered it to Bayon de Libertat, who chewed it reflectively, looking wise and saying nothing. He thought this cane would only do for rum or very low grade sugar—then again, Arnaud did have his own distillery, he knew that.

"It's been too dry, as everyone knows," Arnaud said. He gathered the reins and swung back in the saddle; the horse stirred restively as his weight returned. Arnaud spoke defensively, as if he'd read the other's mind. "Why, I've hardly been able to replant this year." He waved his arm to the adjoining cane pieces. "Half this land is only in ratoons."

"*Faut arroser,*" said Bayon de Libertat, shifting the bit of cane to the left side of his jaw where his good teeth matched each other.

"Of course," Arnaud snapped. "But with what? When there's no water in the stream itself, or next to none . . ."

Bayon de Libertat withdrew the splintered cane from his mouth and flicked it into the dirt beside the citron hedge. He kept his silence, looking away. Arnaud swung his horse's head back toward the central buildings.

THEY FOUND THE SIEUR MALTROT sitting on the gallery with his legs stuck out before him and a damp cloth laid over his eyes. Bayon de Libertat took note of the white cockade on the bicorne hat he'd laid aside. The taste of sugar had brightened him slightly, never mind the quality. Arnaud clapped his hands and when his mulattress house servant appeared he ordered coffee. The Sieur Maltrot pulled the compress from his forehead and sat up to track the taut lifting of her hindquarters under the shift as she withdrew. He shot Arnaud a knowing glance, but the host's expression gave him no encouragement. The pleasantries which followed were accordingly rather stiff.

Shortly the yellow woman came back with a coffee service and a dish of sliced papaya, overripe and almost deliquescent, interrupting the Sieur Maltrot's string of observations on the weather. As she handed round the cups, his eyes stroked her from head to toe, lingering on the high arches of her feet and her long toes spreading on the plank floor. Bayon de Libertat also looked down. He rubbed the knuckles of the arthritic hand that lay in his lap like a broken-winged bird, and pulled on the fingers to ease their stiffness.

"*Bien,*" Arnaud said, as the woman left. "What news, gentlemen?" His eyes were on the Sieur Maltrot.

"Mostly bad," Maltrot said cheerfully, stirring spoon after spoon of sugar into his cup. "Mostly bad. Why, Paris is a madhouse, as you've surely heard. They've made Ogé a hero in the theater, among other things, but let a colonial planter show himself in the streets and likely as not he'll be stoned or hung."

Arnaud drew in his plummy lips and tightened them to a white line. Unhurriedly, the Sieur Maltrot tilted some of the viscous coffee syrup into his mouth.

"In the west, the news is a touch more interesting," he said. "A touch more hopeful, I'll declare. Despite the late catastrophes at Port-au-Prince . . ."

Bayon de Libertat shifted in his chair; one corner of his mouth drew down like a cramp. "I can scarce credit how the Chevalier Mauduit was used there . . ."

"You may believe it," said the Sieur Maltrot. His tongue flicked in and out with snakelike speed. "I have it from a witness in the town. They tore him limb from limb like Furies in the street and Madame Martin, a *white woman,* if you please, cut off his balls herself with a knife and carried them to her house for a trophy."

In the ensuing speechlessness, an insect thrummed loudly under the porch boards. From the cane fields came a dispirited chorus of song measured out by whip cracks. Maltrot sipped from his syrupy cup.

"I hear but I cannot believe," said Bayon de Libertat eventually. "What sort of creature must she be?"

"A harpy," said the Sieur Maltrot. "Think no more of her—she is a mere beast. What *is* encouraging is that the colored men are negotiating with Hanus de Jumecourt at Croix les Bouquets."

"I'm charmed," said Arnaud, acidly. "To what end?"

"They're royalists, essentially," said Maltrot. "We have that much in common. They share our interests—to a point. And the point is to turn the *Pompons Rouges* back out of Port-au-Prince."

"But at what price?" Arnaud reached for his cane where it balanced against the railing and laid it sideways across his lap.

"Naturally," said the Sieur Maltrot, "enforcement of the May fifteenth decree."

"But that's disgusting," Arnaud shouted, leaning forward across the cane. "I won't have the law dictated to me by sons of our slaves. No decent white man will."

The Sieur Maltrot snapped erect in his chair, gathering his feet below. "Calm yourself," he said, and stared Arnaud down till he seemed to have subsided. Bayon de Libertat was startled at how quickly his foppish mannerisms had fallen from him. "You must understand," he continued, "it's not the decent white men you have to consider, but the indecent ones. Praloto and his renegade troops, the Port-au-Prince *canaille*. Recall that since Mauduit's unlucky end, that town is lost to us entirely. At least the mulattoes are willing to wear the white cockade, and why? Because, whatever else, they're men of *property*."

"Mauduit would not permit them to wear the *pompon blanc*," said Arnaud. "'Let them wear yellow,' he said, 'as they are yellow men,' and he was right."

"The course of events has discovered defects in the judgment of our late friend Mauduit," the Sieur Maltrot said. "Do you not think so? These mistakes we would be well advised to amend."

Arnaud crossed and uncrossed his legs. "The May fifteenth decree," he pronounced, "is a work of anarchy, abominable. And unenforceable as well, may God be thanked."

"Of course," said the Sieur Maltrot. "You and Governor Blanchelande are of one mind, to be sure. So far. But what will Blanchelande say if the *Pompons Rouges* chase him out of Le Cap too? You won't even be able to reach a harbor if that happens. Where will you sell your sugar then?" Maltrot picked up his cup again and began to eat his own coffee-stained sugar with a tiny spoon.

"That's most unlikely," Arnaud said. "There's been no trouble in Le Cap, not of that kind. There'll be none till the Colonial Assembly meets."

"Yes, and then there'll be trouble enough for all," said the Sieur Maltrot. "I prophesy. Are you not weary of these idiotic legislators yet?"

"Exhausted," Arnaud said, rocking back in his chair, "*absolument*." He rolled the cane on his upper thighs, like a baker rolling out yeasty dough.

"The Colonial Assembly will accomplish nothing," Maltrot said. "More wrangling about the May fifteenth decree, and they may stir up the mob to some foolishness into the bargain. Meanwhile Port-au-Prince is just as bad as Paris. Worse, it's a state of open war. And it could easily happen at Le Cap, you know it could—the Colonial Assembly will furnish a handsome occasion."

"The May fifteenth decree is completely intolerable," Arnaud said.

"So you say." Maltrot touched the rim of the fruit plate, rotated it with a whisper over the woven cane table the mulattress had brought out to support it. "I would suggest you choose your evils carefully. After all, the decree applies only to four hundred people, even Blanchelande admits that much. Four hundred colored men whose *parents* were born in freedom *and* can prove it, and out of how many thousands? Let them have their political rights, they couldn't throw a shadow on our governance. The decree is a token and that is all."

"It is a token," Arnaud said. "But that's not all."

"He's right," Bayon de Libertat said, and cleared his throat. "Thus far. It's a matter of principle."

The two men looked at him, turning their heads in unison. Bayon de Libertat's breath went heavily in the soggy heat; sweat ran from his temples and down the leathery creases in his neck. He reached for his handkerchief and dabbed his forehead and his sweat-stringy hair. Arnaud clapped his hands and called into the house. A sixteen-year-old Negress, stomach rounded by an early pregnancy, came out and began to haul on the rope that turned the fan over the gallery.

"Liberté," Arnaud said grindingly. *"Egalité. Fraternité.* You'd have me claim brotherhood with the yellow niggers, would you?"

"Oh no," said the Sieur Maltrot. He lifted a slice of papaya an inch or so above the plate and held it while the juice dripped down, letting his wandering eye graze over the black girl's rising belly. "Oh no, nothing so near as that."

"You'll give them notions," Arnaud said. *"Ideas."* He bit down on the word with the same contempt. "Let one yellow cur have the rights of a white man and they'll all be howling for the same. I know you haven't forgotten Ogé since you talked of him yourself."

"By no means." The Sieur Maltrot snapped the fruit into his jaws and swallowed. He stretched his legs out comfortably again. "Ogé has done us all a great service," he said. "I know you don't believe it but he did. And remember, he was a Creole in name only, really just another troublemaker from Paris, no different from that white trash that plagues us on the coast. He came here and called for mulatto rights and armed his band and even tried to raise the blacks, and what came next? We *crushed him."* Maltrot licked fruit juice from his fingers, smacked his palm down on his knee. "Easily as that. Ogé proved that it *cannot be done."*

"However interesting that may be," Arnaud said, "you've a long way to go to convince me to claim kin with him, or any of the yellow rats."

"Don't think of it as a love match," said Maltrot. "It's a marriage of convenience. Temporary. So long as our interests coincide, however long it takes to dispose of that mob of *petit blancs* at Port-au-Prince. Afterward," he waved his sticky fingers airily, "everything will return to the way it was before."

"As easily as that?" said Arnaud.

"Why not?" said Maltrot. "You've commanded mulattoes in the *maréchaussée*. They do their job excellently, do they not? And afterward they lay down their arms and go home peaceably? They haven't terrorized the countryside."

"The point is well taken," said Arnaud, "but—"

"In any case," Maltrot said, "it's not our territory, nor yet our affair. Let Hanus de Jumecourt make his own arrangements. There's a very small part that you might play, but afterward we'll come to that—it's not what brought me here."

The Sieur Maltrot sat straight again and withdrew a tiny silver snuffbox, embossed with a fleur-de-lis, from his vest pocket. He sniffed a pinch, sneezed hugely into a lace-trimmed handkerchief, and put away his apparatus.

"Never mind *les gens de couleur*," he said. "The mulattoes are not the problem. It's the *Pompons Rouges* . . . the *petit blancs* in general."

"But the *petit blancs* hate the mulattoes more than anyone," Arnaud said.

"Of course they do," Maltrot said. "Well that they should. Those parties will have their chance to undo each other, *cela s'arrange*. But at the moment they seem to hate us just as much, the *petit blancs*. And that must stop. Our towns have become a breeding ground for Jacobinism and freethinking. Ideas are like diseases, Arnaud, you understand that perfectly."

"You confuse me," said Bayon de Libertat.

"My apologies," said the Sieur Maltrot. "It's entirely simple. At the finish of it, everyone must cleave to his own skin. Must and will. It's natural law. The *petit blancs* have forgotten this, however. They need a demonstration."

"Of what character?" said Arnaud.

"Imagine," said the Sieur Maltrot, "an insurrection on the northern plain."

"The worst catastrophe anyone ever dreamed of."

"Exactly," said the Sieur Maltrot. "Exactly. Everyone would have to pull together then. No more squabbling with the *Pompons Rouges* when they understand their skins are only safe with us. No more troop mutinies, the soldiers fall back into line, and even the mulattoes would line up behind us where they belong, because after all they own slaves too."

Arnaud passed a hand over his eyes; the cane rolled off his knees and clattered on the floor. He bent to pick it up, and straightened with a shaky laugh. "It's bold," he said. "I'll give you that."

"You mean—" said Bayon de Libertat. "You can't mean that."

"Oh, but I do," said the Sieur Maltrot. "It wouldn't be a dangerous insurrection but, between ourselves, a nice imposture. The secret is good *commandeurs*, the strong and loyal ones—I think that you know such a one." He nodded at Bayon de Libertat. "Let them lead the *ateliers* into the mountains for a few weeks, no more. Possibly burn a couple of cane fields." Maltrot smiled in the direction of the rows of ratoons that lay beyond Arnaud's compound. "The ones that aren't producing well, those only. And there you have it in your hand. Let the *Pompons Rouges* have a glimpse of the *black* face of freedom and you'll see the end of politics."

"That's throwing a coal in the powder keg," said Bayon de Libertat.

"We'll damp it out," said Maltrot. "Remember Ogé. And nothing venture, nothing gain. The situation is precarious and our party is small. If we do not use our power while we have it, we may indeed lose everything."

"And Blanchelande?" said Arnaud.

"Well, he could hardly show his hand in this," Maltrot said. "But tacitly?" He waved his hand. "It will go forward, you must know. Someone's already visited most of the *habitations* here about. The only question is whether or not you're for us."

Arnaud swung his head and gazed over the gallery railing, clicking his tongue softly. Above them, the fan creaked on its wooden axle, flogging slow, sodden air. The little Negress pumped the rope mechanically, her face turned toward the house wall.

"Bien," said Arnaud. *"Pourquoi pas."*

Maltrot turned his eyes toward Bayon de Libertat.

"I'm for king and country," said the older man.

"For the king, to be sure," Maltrot said in a near whisper. "But at the end, what country will it be?"

Again it was silent but for the fan, which had found an excruciating friction point, squealing painfully with every revolution now. Arnaud had dropped his head and cocked it to one side, as though listening. A gigantic leopard-spotted mosquito hovered over Maltrot's knee; he waited till it had just lit, then pinched it dead and cleaned his fingers with a snap. Arnaud got up rather suddenly, letting his cane fall, and stood with his fingertips on the railing, staring out and biting his lips.

Indeed there seemed to be a distant tumult from the fields and coming nearer. Then someone came running into the compound, staggering and shouting in a hoarse voice; evidently it was Arnaud's *commandeur*. He wore shoes as a mark of his rank, but the buckles were broken and they hindered him as he tried to run. Arnaud snatched up his cane and went to meet him. Bayon de Libertat watched him jerk back angrily from what the slave had said, then lash him across the face with the cane's point. The *commandeur* spun away and dropped on all fours, tucking his head in. Arnaud made to strike him across the shoulders, but stopped himself and came back onto the gallery, beating the cane's pommel against his palm.

"Damn that little Jacobin rogue of a doctor to the last circle of hell," Arnaud hissed, "for shooting my best dog this morning . . ."

"What?" said Bayon de Libertat.

"Oh, I apologize," said Arnaud, coming to. He turned about, flicking his cane against his boot tops. "A maroon raid on the provision grounds. And there's a runaway. *Un petit marron.*"

"Of course they usually come back," Maltrot said.

"Oh, he won't go far," Arnaud said. "He's already wearing a headstall. But all the same I'd better go after him. It's the look of the thing, you know."

He dashed down the steps, then paused to look back. "Excuse me please, I trust you will—my house is yours." He strode around the corner of the house.

The Sieur Maltrot cocked an eyebrow, then rose and went into the *grand'case* with no remark. In the yard, the *commandeur* scrambled to his feet. His cheek was bleeding where the cane had struck it, but he trudged off toward the fields without even raising a hand to examine the wound. Bayon de Libertat pushed out of his seat and also went indoors.

The interior seemed dim and muzzy—despite checks of searing light which came through the woven shades and broke and scattered on the floor. Bayon de Libertat saw Madame Arnaud lift herself in a cloud of white muslin from a chair at the end of the room.

"*Messieurs,*" she said, and trying a curtsy, she almost lost her balance and fell. She caught herself on the wall, gave a birdlike nod of her head, and turned to withdraw. Bayon de Libertat's eyes had adjusted enough to see that her hair had come undone behind.

"His house is ours," said the Sieur Maltrot when she had gone. "*Quel bonheur!* My stars, I believe that woman was drunk."

"Ill, possibly," said Bayon de Libertat.

The Sieur Maltrot sniffed. "Where did he find her? I'd almost take her for one of the Paris prostitutes they sent out here when the first colonists asked for women."

"Really," said Bayon de Libertat. "After all, we are her guests."

Like Arnaud, the Sieur Maltrot carried a foppish little cane. Now he began to stroll about the room, indicating articles of the sparse furniture to himself with the cane's point.

"Besides," said Bayon de Libertat. "She'd be a hundred years old at the least if she were one of those."

The Sieur Maltrot, who'd stopped before the mirror, chuckled softly along with his reflection.

"She was a girl of good family in France," said Bayon de Libertat.

"Ah," said the Sieur Maltrot to his image. "So many of them fare poorly here. A pity, I think it." He turned from the mirror and paced along the wall, dandling the cane lightly from two fingers. In a corner a fat toad hulked, large as a brick, his sides inflating and deflating softly, otherwise completely still.

"What a fellow, our Arnaud," said the Sieur Maltrot. "Vain, self-indulgent, not a little stupid probably, concupiscent, impulsive, cruel, reckless, selfish and irresponsible—a typical Creole, in short."

"He's quite a good horseman," Bayon de Libertat said temperingly.

"No doubt," said Maltrot. "He could ride a good horse to death in no more than two hours, I'll wager."

"The brutality does trouble me," said Bayon de Libertat. "There's things go on here that could stop your heart, you couldn't bear to name them."

"Yes, and it's impractical too," Maltrot said. "It's not as if there were profit in it—too many die, or run away, they kill themselves and kill their children." Clasping the cane under one arm, he dipped more snuff, then blew his nose. "All the same, terror can be a useful instrument," he said. "So long as it's used judiciously."

"And this charade of an insurrection?" said Bayon de Libertat. "It's judicious, you're convinced."

"All in choosing the right leaders," Maltrot said. "Give us a few good *commandeurs* and we'll only be sending our crews to a different task. Toussaint serves as your coachman, does he not?"

"You know him, then?"

"Why he's famous, you must know. Well traveled as he is, with his *liberté de savane*—I'll warrant he's happier than a freeman. You trust him absolutely, don't you?"

"With my life," said Bayon de Libertat. "And with my family."

"Have someone call him, won't you? I'd like to see this prodigy with my own eyes."

Bayon de Libertat stepped to the doorway and called an order—the little Negress jumped from her seat by the fan's pulley and ran around to the rear of the house. For a moment he remained in the doorway. A small brown hen and a rooster with a red plumed tail were scratching in the dirt, near the scuffed area where the *commandeur* had been knocked down.

"What business do you have for Arnaud in the west?" he said, drawing his head back inside.

"De Jumecourt will be needing guns." The Sieur Maltrot observed the toad and prodded it with the tip of his cane. "He can hardly get them through Port-au-Prince as things stand now—they'll have to come from the Spanish side."

"That's a dangerous undertaking."

"One which requires an expendable person." The Sieur Maltrot poked the toad again; it made a lumbering, bearlike step forward. "Do you not agree? Look at this monster, big as a cat. Too fat even to hop . . ."

He glanced at Bayon de Libertat, who said nothing. From the rear of the house came the sound of a door closing. In a flash the Sieur Maltrot whipped the wood from his sword stick and skewered the toad on the rapier blade. Held high and framed in the light of the doorway, the toad wriggled its legs and moved its mouth in a gasping silence, the thin blade flexing slightly under its weight. The Sieur Maltrot flipped it out the door and over the gallery rail into the dirt.

"What a country," he said, and slapped the sword back into the cane. "Oh. There you are."

Toussaint had come silently into the back of the room and stopped. He had removed his coachman's hat—a kerchief bound at the nape of his neck covered most of his grizzled hair. His head was lowered and he smiled politely, watching the Sieur Maltrot with his eyes only, keeping his face turned toward the floor.

"There you are," the Sieur Maltrot repeated as he walked near. "A credit to our system, to your master and the Comte de Noé . . . Well, then, what do you say?"

"Doucement allée loin," Toussaint said. *The docile way goes furthest.* His smile finished with his words.

"Both eloquent and suitable," said the Sieur Maltrot. "Yes, and the meek shall inherit the earth one day. We've all been waiting for that, haven't we?" He clapped Toussaint on the shoulder and made a half turn to include Bayon de Libertat in his remarks to the slave. "You're a good nigger, I know you are. If they were all like you, we'd never have a difficulty."

Chapter Four

VIA THE INSTITUTION OF SLAVERY, Doctor Hébert observed, the farrier Crozac was able to make use of ten men to do the work of two. The moment he rode into the yard, two blacks raced each other to his horse's head; a third stooped and laced his fingers to make a second stirrup to aid him in his dismount. The doctor bypassed this assistance, however, and slid directly to the ground. His legs were watery after the long ride. Just within sight of Le Cap the bay gelding Espoir had thrown a shoe, and coming into the city the horse had gone slightly lame, so that the doctor thought to bring him here directly, before finding an inn or pursuing his business. He'd been advised by the late Thibodet that Crozac kept a clean stable and a blacksmith's shop as well.

Rocking forward on his shaky legs to loosen Espoir's girth, the doctor was anticipated by another black, to whom Crozac shouted orders and abuse from a stool beside the forge. This slave himself moved with a quieter authority, directing the other blacks with nods or signals of his hand, under the stream of Crozac's ranting. He was thin and stringy as an old chicken, but the doctor admired how the horse quieted under his certain touch.

As another slave carried the saddle away toward the stable, Crozac pushed himself up from the stool and began his approach. He was big-bellied, bow-legged, and virtually neckless. His dress was absurdly elegant for his trade, though none too clean. The doctor took passing note of the red cockade pinned to the crown of his broad-brimmed round hat. His eyes were small and sunken behind wedges of flesh that looked like white fatty slabs of bacon. The doctor grew somewhat uneasy under their chill inspection.

"If I may serve you . . . ," Crozac said, but still with a certain *hauteur*. Two slaves stood in waiting just behind him, one carrying the stool and the other his box of tools.

"Only one shoe lost," the doctor said, and touched the horse on the withers. "He seemed a little tender on that foot too."

Crozac grunted, and indicated a spot for the stool to be set down, then called for the slave to make a slight adjustment. When he was satisfied, he lowered his broad buttocks to the seat and spread his vast stomach over his thighs like an apron. It was another slave who lifted the horse's foot and held it pinched between his knees, presented to the farrier's inspection. Another moved nearer with the toolbox and presented instruments as they were needed. Crozac cursed him occasionally, more from habit it seemed than for any apparent error. The farrier was ham-handed with the hoof-pick, the doctor saw, working around the tender frog. Espoir trembled and stepped with restless hooves, but the slave who held his head calmed him with slow strokes.

Crozac spat on the ground and accepted a new shoe from another of his minions, then fit it on the smooth line of the fresh-cut hoof. His hammer made a shallow tacking sound, driving the narrow nails through. With pliers he snapped off the nail points and beat them back into the horn. Briskly he rasped the hoof-edge even with the shoe, then handed the file back to the slave and stood up.

The slave who all this while had held himself in a half crouch to support the foot at the right position now let it down and straightened. Espoir readjusted his weight to four legs, snorted and lifted his head against the halter rope.

"You'll take him now?" Crozac said to the doctor. In spite of all the assistance proffered him, the farrier was in a mighty sweat. A runnel flowed from his ear and dampened the grimy frill of his neckcloth. Looking at him, the doctor felt himself more oppressed by the heat as well. He loosened the drawstring of his purse and gave Crozac one coin, then another.

"I want to stable him," he said. "Let him be fed and let him rest. I'll go on foot at least until evening."

"As you say," Crozac said, pushing the coins across his plump palm so that they clicked together. "You'll stay how long?"

"I can't be certain," the doctor said. "I'll stop here again before evening."

Crozac answered him with only a nod, pocketing the coins as he waddled back toward the forge, his slaves carrying his equipment after him. The black at the horse's head clucked softly, turned and led him toward a stall. Watching Espoir's hooves, the doctor thought that the limp had lessened. The metal of the new shoe blinked in the sunlight. Under the tattered cuffs of his breeches, the slave's high-arched feet set down silently one after the other, crossing the packed earth of the yard.

Doctor Hébert crossed the Place d'Armes and walked on the unpaved street toward the quay. At the height of the afternoon heat there were few people abroad, and those he did pass seemed bent on their business, whatever it was. The gaggles of brightly dressed mulatto women he had admired when he first passed through the city must be seeking shade indoors until evening. The buildings which lined his way were mostly of stone and none high enough to cast a shadow. The street was dotted here and there with animal ordure and cracked in rigid geometric patterns from the drought and heat. The doctor's boots kicked up little whispers of dust as he went along. The heat pressed down on him like a damp thumb; he took off his stained duster and carried it over his arm.

When at length he emerged on the Quai Saint Louis, the breeze off the harbor did something to relieve the sodden heat. The quay was busy, ships unloading or taking on cargo at most of the available moorings. The doctor turned north and walked along the paved seawall, passing through a short promenade of stunted trees, whose branches twisted in the salty air. Another ship was taking on water at the Fontaine d'Estaing, and he paused there to watch the procedure, stroking his sweat-matted beard. After a time he put aside his dignity and cupped his hands into the fountain and bathed his face and head. He went on his way with his damp beard stringing and the tonsure band of hair that remained to him plastered wetly to his sunburned skull.

The house of Monsieur Bourgois, who had been Thibodet's broker, was only a couple of blocks away on the Rue Neuve, but by the time the doctor had reached it, he was sweating again, through the glaze of cool fountain water which had scarcely dried on his skin. This building had a second story, so that Monsieur Bourgois's private office caught the harbor breeze. The *négociant* himself was an older man than Doctor Hébert would have expected (though why he should have expected anything was a mystery too) with watery eyes and a red nose that spread and softened along his cheekbones like waterlogged cork. He replied to the news of Thibodet's death with strictly formal condolences, and after the slightest pause began to quiz the doctor about crops and deliveries. Doctor Hébert found himself promising to provide particular quantities of brown sugar, particular quantities of white, by certain dates which Thibodet apparently had arranged much earlier.

In this respect, at least, the broker seemed to have his wits about him. The doctor, meanwhile, had only the faintest idea of what he was discussing and agreeing to. These matters would have to be taken up with Thibodet's *gérant,* or his replacement, if he must be replaced . . .

"Et Madame Thibodet?" the broker said, resuming his tone of formal politesse. *"Et la petite?"*

"La petite?" the doctor repeated stupidly.

"The daughter," Monsieur Bourgois said. "There is a daughter, is there not?" A strange avuncular smile. "Would she be six months old, or is it four?"

"You astonish me." The doctor got up and walked to the open casements. Over the low roofs of the intervening buildings he watched a ship under half sail angle in to the quay. Given the length of the crossing to France it was quite possible this news might have failed to arrive before his own departure. Why Thibodet might have kept silent about the birth was harder to comprehend.

"Madame Thibodet—" Doctor Hébert turned from the window, took a step in the direction of Monsieur Bourgois's desk. "Elise, my sister—" He stopped again, passing his palm across his forehead and pausing to inspect the dampness gathered there. As he had anticipated, it was difficult to begin. He cleared his throat. "I have not seen her, not since I came to the colony. I do not know where she is at all. Nor did her husband before he died."

"I see . . ." Monsieur Bourgois's expression seemed to blur as he turned his head to the left, directing his dim gaze over the doctor's shoulder to the open windows behind him. Hair lifted coolly on the back of the doctor's neck, maybe from the humid breeze.

"I had intended to ask you," he said, "if she had come here. To draw money perhaps. She might have done that."

"Ah." Monsieur Bourgois braced his hands on the arms of his chair and pushed himself to his feet. Gingerly he walked to a mahogany cupboard—lamed by gout, the doctor surmised. He opened the cabinet with a small key from his watch chain and took out a bottle of brandy.

"Will you join me?"

"No, thank you," the doctor said.

Monsieur Bourgois inclined his head and poured from the bottle into a straight tumbler, two fingers' worth. From a carafe on the desk corner he added a lesser measure of water and drank off the mixture in a single draught.

"*S'il vous plaît,*" he said to the doctor, stroking the bottle he'd set down beside the carafe and glass. "If you should reconsider—allow me a moment." Monsieur Bourgois limped goutily to the door and crossed the landing into the clerk's chamber, leaving both doors ajar.

Shifting through the casements, the harbor breeze disturbed some papers on the desk. The doctor walked over and shifted a polished stone to secure them. He picked up the brandy bottle and sniffed the cork: good, well-aged spirit and assuredly from the metropole. Beside the brown-stained drinking glass sat a hard-shelled iridescent beetle, big as a baby's fist. Just as the doctor noticed it, the beetle clicked out transparent wings from under the halves of its carapace and flew with a whirring sound toward the door. The doctor replaced the bottle on the desk as Monsieur Bourgois came back into the room.

"It's as I thought," the *négociant* said. "As I remembered. She drew on us two months ago, and for a considerable sum." He handed a folded slip of paper across the desk. When the doctor opened it, his lips formed a round and he exhaled with a sound like wind across a bottleneck.

"Indeed," he said. "More than considerable."

"We love luxury here, some of us do . . ." Monsieur Bourgois fanned his fleshy hands. "One cannot say. For such a price one might obtain . . . a lady's maid, perhaps, already trained. They're dear. Perhaps she had some other notion."

"She may have planned a journey . . ."

"It's possible," Monsieur Bourgois said. "Of course it would not become me to ask intrusive questions of Madame Thibodet. A Madame Cigny, however, I know to have been her intimate friend; she stayed at the Cigny house whenever she was in the city." He wrote the address on the slip of paper below the figure and the doctor thanked him for it.

"Our house has agents in Port-au-Prince and Les Cayes," Monsieur Bourgois said. "Also at Guadeloupe, and Martinique. I could make inquiry, on your behalf."

"Discreetly," said the doctor.

"*Entendu.*"

The same flying beetle or another like it flew in the window, whirring and bumbling toward the desk. Monsieur Bourgois swatted at it with the back of his hand and almost as if by accident knocked it stunned into a corner. The doctor picked it up and carried it to the casements to look at it in better light, but before he could make a close examination the insect recovered itself and flew. He turned again to the desk.

"You're absolutely sure there was a child," he said.

"Without a doubt," said Monsieur Bourgois. "Why, I've met her myself, *chez Madame Cigny*. A little dumpling. Her name is Sophie, I believe."

The doctor stared at his empty palm, the creases crossing it. He could still feel the pricking of insect legs on the skin. "I've reconsidered," he said. "May I take some brandy?"

"Of course." Monsieur Bourgois nodded to the bottle. The doctor poured himself a short measure and sipped it undiluted.

"She's got black hair, your niece," Monsieur Bourgois said. "Brown eyes, but they had a light. I saw her on her mother's knee and she looked me through and through . . . I'm fond of children. And yourself?"

"It's human nature," the doctor said, and set down his glass. "I'm grateful for your patience and discretion." He made his farewell and went down to the street.

Calling upon Madame Cigny he found no one at home, and saw no use to leave a note since so far he had not found lodging. A little footsore now, to complement his saddlesoreness, the doctor walked back toward the Place d'Armes and engaged a room at an inn near

Crozac's establishment. This business done, he crossed the way and entered the stable to see to his horse.

Espoir had been brushed to a sleek shine, tangles combed out of his mane and tail. There was hay in the manger and a trace of grain in the feedbox. The doctor was pleased. He lingered, savoring the quiet and the warm horse smell. Outside the light was failing quickly and it was quite dark within the stall. He stroked his horse and fed it sugar; odd how easily he thought of it as his, when properly it belonged to—not Thibodet, who could own nothing any longer. To Thibodet's widow, or failing that, his child. It bore in on the doctor that for the time being he was responsible and alone. There would be much to do and to learn, and in his fatigue of the moment he was unsure he would be equal to it all.

AT THE INN he ate a dish of chicken served in the common dining room, and drank half a bottle of sour red wine, all that was available there. He was alone at his table and the only one dining, though several parties of men had come to drink and gamble, both white and colored, though they did not mix. Yet at a table among white men playing cards was one the doctor could not place. His skin was pale, but covered with a skein of freckles spiraling like a weird brown galaxy. But for color his nose and cheekbones were those of a Negro, and still his eyes were green. A *sacatra*? Or a *griffe*? The doctor had not learned all the dozens of classifications for mixed blood and in fact he doubted if anyone fully understood the system well enough to apply it on no more evidence than sight.

The chicken tasted good to him, though its peppery seasoning was unfamiliar. There were sweet potatoes too, and fried plantain. He ate slowly, though he was very hungry, and quietly looked about the room. To his left, the strangely speckled mulatto, if mulatto he were, tossed down his cards with a whispered curse.

The doctor's legs had stiffened while he sat at the table, and his saddlesore thighs chafed in their tight breeches as he strolled toward the theater. There was little to distinguish the building from any other from without and he might have missed it altogether if Captain Maillart had not been waiting for him outside as they had agreed by letter. Their embrace was warmer than the doctor might have looked for; they'd known each other from childhood, both being Lyonnaisse, but had never been close friends.

Maillart held him at arm's length. "The sun's told on you," he cried, examining the doctor's peeling scalp. "But you look well. Where do you stay?"

Doctor Hébert mentioned Crozac and the inn. Maillart jerked his jaw with a cross emphasis. "I'd have found you a better farrier in the regiment," he said. "But it's a whole thieves' alley thereabouts, no wonder. You'd be better off with a berth on a ship, or a billet with me at Les Casernes. But never mind, we'll find something for you."

Arm in arm, they entered the theater. The walls were washed to a pale shade and pleasantly lit with candles in sconces. The theater seemed about half full; Maillart let him know it would hold fifteen hundred spectators. He pointed out Governor Blanchelande in his box, and the other box reserved for the *intendant*, the latter empty this evening. Maillart himself had taken seats in the amphitheater along with several other young officers of the Regiment Le Cap. The doctor passed through several rapid introductions, not quite catching the names. He was pressed for news of Paris, but he'd been long enough at Ennery that most of the officers were more current than he.

As soon as the colored women began to enter their boxes, the political talk died off. Of course the mulattresses didn't come directly in with the officers; their boxes were in the rank above, and reached by a separate stairway. But once they were in place, they were no more than a hand's reach away. A rotund young captain whose name the doctor thought was Baudin tore the white cockade from his hat and tossed it upward as a favor, addressing the woman who reached across her rail to catch it by her first name, Fleur.

Fleur, Jasmine, Chloe and Nanon were the four women in the box immediately overhead—so the doctor could gather from the banter that passed between him and the members of his party. The women knew the officers by their first names as well. All four were slim and lovely, close to white whatever mix of blood they carried, and dressed and coiffed to rival ladies of the court. To the officers' banter they responded not with the minced coquetry of French *demimondaines*, but with a slow and balanced languor, a rich dark energy like waves moving through molasses.

All this while the officers chattered to them loudly, an excruciatingly circumstantial discourse couched in language that would have embarrassed a barnyard animal. A raw blush struck the doctor at the roots of his hair and stained him halfway down to his navel, so it felt; he was relieved to think that in this light it probably would not show. He turned to the stage, where the blue curtain was slowly lifting from behind two gargantuan busts of satyrs.

So the play began, a comedy. To the doctor it seemed poorly written, worse performed, the actors often faltering, requiring prompts, and yet he did his best to bend his mind upon the stage. The officers' raillery with the girls continued apace, though *sotto voce* now. The room seemed close, even underfilled as it was, and the doctor was in an uncomfortable sweat. Mosquitoes plagued him too; a cloud of them hung over the whole amphitheater. Maillart and the others seemed insensible of the bites, though now and again one of them would automatically slap himself.

Finally the play lurched to its intermission and the curtain lowered for the *entr'acte*. The doctor got up and followed Maillart into the bustling corridors. A cluster formed around the governor, men of affairs taking this opportunity to catch Blanchelande's ear in an idle moment. Captain Maillart cut efficiently through the crowd, the doctor washing along in his wake.

"What do you think of our players?" Maillart said over his shoulder.

"Abominable," the doctor said, with no pause for reflection.

Maillart chuckled. "Ah well. There was an actor here who told the committee, 'You'd be in poor shape to pay me if I *did* know my parts.'"

The doctor smiled, turned his head in owlish circles, looking at the people. There were many of the merchants and the planters there, some with their wives or daughters, white women in fair numbers too and in their full regalia. He was thinking that Monsieur or Madame Cigny might well be in the company, if he could find someone who knew them and would make the introduction, but Captain Maillart seemed to have another course in mind. Quickly, he drew the doctor out of the building.

Outside it was certainly cooler, the night air almost chill. They overtook the other officers of their party in the *promenade du gouvernement*. A tall young rake with great mustachios, whose name the doctor had not caught, had drawn the woman called Chloe into a niche and was kissing her and pinching her haunches with great freedom, while she giggled and feigned to push his hands away. All along the promenade were other couples similarly engaged, but the doctor and Maillart came face to face with Nanon and Jasmine, who were for the moment unattached.

"Oh Nanon," Captain Maillart pronounced in an artificially lisping tone, *"Je te présente mon grand ami, Antoine."*

The woman smiled, revealing a top row of small, white, perfect teeth. Her lips were heavy, blade-shaped and blood-red. The doctor bowed slightly from the waist, keeping his eyes on hers, which were large and almond-shaped and looked black to him in the indistinct light, which turned her skin the color of old ivory. Her dress was tightly fitted and clung to her thighs, with the bodice cut low, almost to the nipple, a star of multicolored orchids resting on her mostly naked bosom. She offered her hand to the doctor; it floated toward him along a graceful liquid arc. Her palm was cool and dry when it met his, long yellowy fingers creeping round his wrist, a nail turned in to catch his pulse between the tendons.

"Oh, isn't she lovely," Maillart breathed into his ear, but audibly enough to carry. "She's made for love—and yours for the asking."

The doctor's heart slammed rubbery against his ribs. The chafed swaths along his inner thighs began to blaze. To hold a woman's hand and look her in the eye and hear a proposition such as this—he did not know what his feeling was, but it was strong enough, for an instant, to paralyze him. Nanon breathed; the orchids rose on her breast, and from the skin beneath them lifted a cloud of drunken scent which sealed him in its sphere. She stroked her top lip with the tip of her tongue, a cat's gesture; her whole head had the catlike beauty he knew he must have seen somewhere before.

"I beg your pardon," Doctor Hébert said in his most formal manner. *"Je vous en prie*—I'll hope that we may meet again, but on some other footing."

He pressed her hand between his two, once firmly, and released it. With her fingertips she caught her skirt and gave him a half curtsy, an opaque movement, uninterpretable. She was gone; both women had retreated.

Captain Maillart seemed a little glum, going back into the theater. They took their seats in silence. The hall looked empty, quieter than before; about half their party had not returned when the curtain rose on the second act. The doctor crushed a mosquito on the back of his neck and brushed away the broken bits of it. Grimly, he concentrated on the sluggish movement of the play. Maillart sighed and draped a hand across the doctor's shoulder and began to rearrange and fondle his lapel.

"You mustn't be shocked," he said in a tender voice. "It's what they're good for. After all, they're not white women."

The doctor looked around the seats. Only Jasmine and Fleur had returned to the box above them. But Captain Baudin had corkscrewed around in his chair and was blowing kisses and talking moonily enough for a dozen.

"Ah, tes fesses, Jasmine," he rhapsodized. *"Tes jolies fesses, comme j'aimerais les baiser encore une seule fois."*

"Never mind," Maillart went on meanwhile, still whispering to the doctor. "You've only got to learn our ways."

"Perhaps you're right," the doctor said, and snorted out a sort of laugh. "After all, it seems there's a better comedy in the back rows than there is on the stage."

Chapter Five

Before dawn the baby woke and cried a little, snuffling against his mother's side. Suzanne hushed him, turning to give him the breast, turning toward her husband as well, since the baby slept between them. The man lay so still that she did not disturb him with a word, though she didn't believe he was sleeping. Two roosters were crowing, far apart, one in the barnyard and one in the hills, and Toussaint, who had wakened with the baby's first cry, rested quietly on his back and listened to them. The young cock had trounced the old rooster the week before, flattened him in the dust and kicked him bloody with his spurs and driven him off into the jungle. Each time Toussaint heard the loopy lifting of his voice above the other jungle noise he was surprised to know he'd made it through another night.

He groped with his left hand in the dark and stroked the narrow back of his youngest son, Saint-Jean, and rubbed the tight thin curls on top of his head. The baby pulled loose from the nipple and grazed his father's arm with a small slack-fingered hand, humming a low note, just beginning to whimper. Suzanne murmured to him and guided him back to the breast. Toussaint folded his hands across his navel, let himself drift. When he next came to, Saint-Jean had fallen back to sleep and Suzanne had risen and gone for water. The baby wormed his way toward him on the pallet, searching in his sleep, and nuzzled along his ribs. Toussaint smiled at him in the dark, and disengaged himself carefully so Saint-Jean would not wake.

He got up and crossed the room barefoot to wake his two older sons, Isaac and Placide, who were six and seven. The boys sat up at his first touch, quickly and silently, as he had taught them. Toussaint hustled them out the door, into the first gray twinge of light. Over at the main compound, the bell tolled to rouse the field slaves for the morning. Suzanne had returned with the water and she poured a generous measure on each of the boys, from a big clay urn. Isaac jumped giggling from one leg to the other as the water struck him, but Placide stood stiffly under the stream, legs apart, and only shook himself once, like a dog, before he scrubbed. The light was coming up suddenly, silvering the droplets as they flew. Toussaint washed himself, slowly and with greater care, after the others had gone back into the cabin.

The light swelled. Already he could begin to feel the heat. Inside the cabin it was bright enough to read by the time he reentered. He put on his shirt and reached his Psalter down from the board above the door where it was kept with a few other books and sat down and opened it on the ribbon. When he signaled to the boys they came and stood at his either hand, not eagerly but with their smooth habitual obedience.

"Save me, O God," he read from the Sixty-ninth Psalm, "for the waters are come in, even unto my soul.

> *I stick fast in the deep mire, where no ground is, I am come into deep waters, so that the floods run over me.*
>
> *I am weary of crying; my throat is dry; my sight faileth me for waiting so long upon my God.*
>
> *They that hate me without a cause are more than the hairs of my head; they that are mine enemies, and would destroy me guiltless, are mighty . . .*

He read in a low voice, little better than a monotone, though he pronounced each word most clearly and went very slow, marking the page with the cracked yellow nail of his forefinger, so that Isaac and Placide could follow. Placide could, indeed, already read many of the words, and his eye went darting ahead on the page. Toussaint continued:

> *I am become a stranger to my brethren, even an alien unto my mother's children.*
>
> *For the zeal of thine house hath even eaten me; and the rebukes of them that rebuked thee are fallen upon me.*

I wept, and chastened myself with fasting, and that was turned to my reproof.

I put on sackcloth also, and they jested upon me . . .

Suzanne, too, sat in an attitude of reverence, but keeping her hands busy. She cut fruit for the family to eat when prayer was done, and sliced cold yam and put it salted into a bag for them to carry for their midday meal.

But, Lord, I make my prayer unto thee in an acceptable time.

Hear me, O God, in the multitude of thy mercy, even in the truth of thy salvation.

Take me out of the mire, that I sink not; O let me be delivered from them that hate me, and out of the deep waters.

Let not the waterflood drown me, neither let the deep swallow me up; and let not the pit shut her mouth upon me . . .

The light was coming in at the cabin door, and with it a little blue-striped lizard, which froze just across the threshold, hanging in a brilliant beam. Toussaint felt Isaac shift his head to look at it. He continued to read, watching the child from the corner of his eye, thinking that these two might already be acquainted, for the lizard had given up one tail. A skinny new one was just beginning to sprout from the fat socket of the old. He caught the back of Isaac's head in the pinch of his thumb and forefinger and so turned his attention to the Psalter again.

Draw nigh unto my soul, and save it; O deliver me, because of mine enemies.

Thou hast known my reproach, my shame, and my dishonour: mine adversaries are all in thy sight.

Reproach hath broken my heart; I am full of heaviness: I looked for some to have pity on me, but there was no man, neither found I any to comfort me . . .

Before he'd finished reading, the boys' eyes were sliding toward the food, but he went on to the end of the psalm at the same slow rate and guided them through the Our Father before he let them eat. There were some cakes of cassava meal as well as mango and banana, but Toussaint took only a few slices of fruit and ate them quickly. Saint-Jean still slept, turned on his back. Toussaint knelt and laid his palm above the baby's naked stomach, not quite touching, but near enough to feel the warmth. He moved his hand so that the infant's breath stirred across his fingers, the broken one, stiff from its old injury, seeming to lift and flex with it. Sitting on the pallet's edge he drew on his boots, then rose and took his green livery coat down from its peg. He stood fingering the faded bloodstains on the shoulders for a moment before he put it on. Suzanne was watching him from the corner, her lips drawn in.

He shrugged into the coat and snapped his fingers. Isaac and Placide ran out shouting into the new light. Toussaint moved to the corner, reached into the dim to take his wife's hand. She bent her neck, for she was taller than he, and he touched his forehead to hers. Without saying anything, he went out after the boys, following them through the screen of trees between them and the row of other slave cabins, all stoutly built of plank, like the one they lived in, but thatched in the old way, with broad palm leaves. The young yellow rooster, new cock of the walk, strutted up and down before the empty doorways. The slaves in the main crew were already on their way to the fields, and Toussaint could hear their songs receding as he and his sons went toward the barn.

He walked with long assuring strides, though he was bandylegged, and fast enough that a lace of sweat broke out across his high forehead. The heat was thick, like a damp blanket. He waved the boys into the barn and walked down to the stone water trough, which two slaves were just refilling. There was a tree beside the trough and Toussaint hesitated in its shade, feeling the sweat beads popping along the tight inner seams of his coat. The other slaves withdrew with their emptied vessels and Toussaint looked down at his own shadow trembling on the ruffled water, watched a green-winged dragonfly come hovering across the indistinct reflection. It was here, long ago when he was young, that he'd struck Béager, who'd been *gérant* in the days before Bayon de Libertat. For some reason his mind had run back almost daily to that time, ever since Bayon de Libertat had brought him to the Sieur Maltrot and their scheme had been partially unfolded.

Again he felt the rude shock to his knuckles, the twisting pain in his elbow since his blow was awkwardly struck. He saw Béager's head snap to the side and then return, and felt again the strange airy certainty that now, no matter what followed, he would surely die. The dragonfly lifted from the stilling surface of the trough and

Toussaint said a silent prayer of thanks to Jesus, that god who softened the hearts of white people. Sometimes softened them. At the same time a verse from his Psalter, not the one he'd read this morning but the one he would be reading three days hence, came unbidden into his mind.

Forsake me not, O God, in mine old age, when I am gray-headed, until I have showed thy strength unto this generation, and thy power to all them that are yet for to come. But this thought made him uneasy; it did not belong in any prayer to Jesus, but was addressed to the angry, powerful God who was his father. It was wrong to invoke the two together, Toussaint felt, and it unsettled him to have done so inadvertently. But a shout from Isaac took his mind away.

Isaac was locked in a tug of war with the black gelding weirdly named Tire-bouchon. The horse had set his feet and Isaac had turned to face him, his teeth gritted, swinging the whole inconsequential weight of his body on the lead, while Tire-bouchon fought the halter with strong rips of his neck that fairly lifted the boy off his feet. Placide was watching from a couple of yards off, holding a brush and a curry comb in either hand.

"You know better," Toussaint called to Isaac, taking a few steps toward them, but not coming too near. "Don't face him so, you make him afraid . . ."

Immediately Isaac relaxed and turned to face forward, eyes just slightly interrogative. The horse stopped lunging but still wouldn't follow.

"Yes," Toussaint said. "Take the halter, under the chin. Like that. Don't jerk him, but pull steady. Now, that will go better."

Tire-bouchon snorted once, then gave in and followed the child, who led him to a mounting block beside the barn wall. Placide climbed the block and began to comb out the horse's mane, while Isaac held the halter, his face blank and neutral now, though he was breathing a little hard. Toussaint watched them from the door. Placide was by far the lighter-colored, and it was true he had been born before Toussaint and Suzanne married—still Toussaint knew that many Aradas had that reddish tint. His own father, Giau-Ginou, had had it . . . So too did Jean-Baptiste, whom Toussaint called his *parrain*. Placide had large and luminous eyes which Toussaint thought resembled his own and he had long thought Placide to be the more intelligent.

He went into the barn and saddled the stallion Bellisarius, a mottled gray, his coat veined like blue cheese. Both boys brightened when they saw him lead the big saddlehorse into the yard. He would not let them use the block to mount. But once Toussaint himself was in the saddle, Placide was able to scramble up behind, clutching at his father's knees. Bellisarius yawed around as the weight shifted, picking his feet up high, till Toussaint stilled him. Isaac couldn't manage without help and after a false try or two Toussaint bent and caught his arms and swung him up in front, just before the saddle. Triple-mounted, they rode out of the yard.

On the road that ran between the cane fields, Toussaint pressed his heels lightly into the stallion's blue-cheese flanks and brought him easily to a canter. Placide's hands tightened on his hips as the horse picked up speed, hooves clattering on the heat-hardened track. Isaac rocked back against his father's chest, and tried to hold on to the saddle, but Toussaint unpeeled his fingers one by one and rearranged them on the reins by his own hands, to show him how. It was not long before they had passed the cane fields and crossed the last irrigation ditch that brought water in from Rivière du Haut du Cap.

A half mile farther he pulled the horse up and left the road, guiding Belisarius at a walk over broken ground. Behind him, Placide relaxed his grip as the horse slowed, and let himself sway free of his father's back, holding himself stable with his knees clamped to the dent of horseflesh just behind the saddle.

"Can I ride him?" Placide said. "Alone, can I ride him alone?"

Toussaint smiled privately, over Isaac's head, but said nothing for the moment. They had come among the trees, where it was a little cooler under the shade, along the paths which the cattle had worn with their foraging. At any rate the cows had cleared the way enough for them to go through mounted. Placide leaned forward again; Toussaint felt him lay his cheek against his back.

"What do you remember," Toussaint said, "from the psalm this morning?"

Neither boy answered. Toussaint gave Isaac a prod with his thumb; Isaac squeaked but said no word.

"Do you remember the first psalm from this morning?" There was no sound but the whisper of the horse's hocks through the underbrush.

"'They gave me gall to eat, and when I was thirsty they gave me vinegar to drink.'" Placide said suddenly. "What's gall?"

Toussaint didn't answer. His bones moved to the rhythm of the stallion's gait and to the beat of the verses that ran on in his head. *Let their table be made a snare to take themselves withal; and let the things that should have been for their wealth be unto them an occasion of falling. Let their eyes be blinded, that they see not; and ever bow thou down their backs. Pour out thine indignation upon them, and let thy wrathful displeasure take hold of them. Let their habitation be void, and no man to live in their tents.* His lips began to move as he followed the beat of the words with a whisper.

"What is it?" Placide repeated.

"It's bitter," Toussaint said. *Let them fall from one wickedness to another, and not come into thy righteousness. Let them be wiped out of the book of the living, and not be written among the righteous . . .* "It's the bitter fruit." Isaac twisted in the saddle, looked up round-eyed at the underside of his father's jaw.

The ground grew steeper, as they went on, Toussaint rehearsing the psalm from the beginning, over and over, till both boys could repeat the first five verses. They rode up over a spur of Morne du Cap, and down into the ravine on the far side. Here Toussaint saw fresh cow patties, new marks of gnawing on the bark of the trees either side of the path. The fresh sign continued to where the ravine opened out into what had been a small grassy field, overgrazed now and gone to dust in the drought. Beyond the small expanse of this *petit savanne*, cloud-covered mountains rose in the interior.

At the field's edge he noticed a spear belonging to the herdsman, Ti-Paul, lying beside a tree and when his eye traveled up the trunk he found the young slave himself in a high fork.

"*Ki sa ou gêgnê?*" Toussaint said. "What's got after you?"

"*Casques*," Ti-Paul said, with a queasy smile. His lanky legs were twined around the tree's bole like a vine.

"*Môntré mwê yo*," Toussaint said. "Show me."

Ti-Paul's smile flickered, then went completely out. He slid down the tree, and at Toussaint's gesture he stooped and recovered his spear. He had grown much in his sixteenth year, so that the diminutive no longer suited him; now he stood high as the stallion's shoulder. Still mounted between his sons, Toussaint walked Bellisarius after Ti-Paul, who waved his spear at the lean-to *ajoupa* which the wild dogs had wrecked. The broad leaves that had roofed it were broken and scattered on the ground among the windfall stakes. Ti-Paul dug his spear point into the ground among the dog tracks faintly circling in the dust and Toussaint peered down from the saddle at the prints. There were three different sets he could distinguish, and one whose large tracks wound away from the others seemed to be missing a foot.

"Did they kill?" he asked Ti-Paul.

"They got my food," Ti-Paul said. His Adam's apple shuddered in his skinny neck. "I had it hanging from the top, so that's how they came to knock down my *ajoupa*."

"Ah," Toussaint said. "What food had you?"

"What I'm given," Ti-Paul said, puzzled. "Yams and maize cakes, a little molasses."

"They came a long way to eat cornbread, these *casques*," Toussaint said. "They've not been seen here for ten years or more . . . Where are the cows?"

Ti-Paul cut off the reply he would have made, raised his spear and pointed, superfluously, for Toussaint had already made out the puff of dust, halfway across the small savannah to the next spur of the mountain rising like a bare worn bone.

"Wait here," Toussaint said shortly. He headed Belisarius around and made toward the cattle. The movement was sudden enough that Placide, who'd leaned over to look at the dog tracks, was almost unseated. He caught himself on a fistful of Toussaint's green coat, and let go as soon as he'd regained his balance.

"He's afraid, Ti-Paul," Placide said. "Is he afraid of the dogs?"

Toussaint shrugged. "It's lonely, out with the cattle. It would be better to have two men, in case of trouble, but the master doesn't like to lose *main-d'oeuvre* from the fields at this time."

"Were you lonely?" Isaac said.

Toussaint rode on silently a little way, watching the backs of the cows define themselves more clearly, reflecting on the time he'd spent as cowherd in his teens, before Béager brought him back to work with the horses. "No," he finally said. "It didn't bother me."

As they came trotting up the cattle spooked, perhaps at the sight of three riders on one horse. Toussaint dismounted and lifted Isaac down. The cattle regrouped themselves, eyeing the people. They were long-horned, shaggy and scrawny in the flanks; some had bloody foaming mouths from trying to eat the spiny nopal when there was nothing else to eat. He counted. All the full-grown cows were there but he didn't have any previous count of calves to go by.

Of a sudden the cattle began to shift and low, their eyes rolling. They circled tightly in on themselves, dust rising from their hooves as if drawn by a small tornado. The little scrub bull hooked his horn toward the ground and veered away, and out of the gap he left in the dust swirl came loping the wild dogs which were called *casques*. There were four of them and the leader was making good time on his three legs—all four of them stretching out a little faster as they made straight for the children on the ground. Toussaint, who was unarmed except for a two-inch penknife, sprang into the saddle quick as a cat, not even touching a stirrup. Placide was up behind him on the instant, but Isaac couldn't make it, and Toussaint turned the horse tightly on his hindquarters to shield him from the dogs. The second of the pack made a lunge for the horse's head, and Bellisarius reared and struck at it with his front hooves. Toussaint could hear Isaac screaming—he brought the horse down with an effort and snatched the child one-handed from where he clung to the stirrup iron, heaved and loosed his grip and caught him again by the seat of the pants and slung him across the horse's neck like a sack of meal.

The dogs fell back. Again Bellisarius clenched hindquarters as if he would rear, and Toussaint loosened the reins and stroked him and talked to him until he was able to stand foursquare, though still snorting and trembling some. He lifted Isaac then, and set him astride before the saddle. Placide's arms were locked around his waist, and he could feel the smaller boy's heart thumping against the flat of his hand, but there were no tears and he was pleased by that. He took a long full breath and sighed it out. The *casques* had disposed themselves around the horse like points on the compass. Only the three-legged leader was still bristling and snarling. He was prick-eared and vulpine, the fur of his humped back gone to silver, and his teeth were worn and brown with rot. He stopped snarling and looked at the horse and riders with an expression of intelligent consideration. One of the other dogs sat down abruptly and began to pant, tongue lolling, lips pulled back in what appeared to be an amiable smile.

"So after all they exist, his *casques,*" Toussaint said. "Are you afraid of them? Like Ti-Paul?"

The boys kept silent; Placide tightened his grip. Toussaint touched up the horse and rode toward the cattle, who'd bunched again a couple of hundred yards away. The *casques* did not follow, but filed off back toward the mountain slopes, the old three-legged one still leading the line.

"But you saw the tracks on the ground before," Placide said, twisting around to watch the dogs retreat. "I saw them myself, *m'pè.*"

"I saw them, yes," Toussaint said. "But who knows for certain if it's real or not, what he sees?"

At the edge of the savannah Ti-Paul stood in a frozen pose. He wore only a loincloth and with the long spear held butt-down on the ground, the blade sticking a foot or more above his head, he looked like a warrior of Guinée, though of course he was a Creole. There were more infants born at Bréda than at many plantations, and more of them survived. Still, when Toussaint looked at Ti-Paul, somewhere down at the base of his brain he felt the tidal memory of Africa, that country which he'd never seen. He pulled Bellisarius to a halt in front of Ti-Paul and laid the reins loose on the stallion's mane.

"So," he said. "All the cows are there that should be. It's been a long time since I came here, so I don't know about the calves. But when I next come, then I'll know."

Ti-Paul looked away, thrusting out his lower lip.

"Have you seen maroons?" Toussaint said.

"No." Ti-Paul's tone was sulky, and he didn't look up.

"Ah," said Toussaint. "I saw some, and not a day's ride from here. Riau's band—do you remember Riau? Well, you were just a baby when he ran away from Bréda."

Ti-Paul jerked his head up. "They were *casques,*" he said. "Five or six of them, one with three legs. One red dog with a torn ear too. Didn't you see their tracks everywhere?" He swept his free hand over the tracks.

"It's as you say," Toussaint said. "I saw them on the plain. The maroons also keep dogs, you know. When the weather's hard like this, even a maroon's dog might go wild."

Ti-Paul's head dropped again, in confusion now, Toussaint thought, rather than guilt.

"You mustn't feed them if they come," Toussaint said. "Keep them away from the cattle. Send them away, all of them. If the dogs come back, use your spear. And keep your fire up. The *casques* won't rush a burning stick."

"Yes," Ti-Paul told the dust.

Toussaint reached into the square side pocket of his coat and took out the bag of food. The boys' heads tracked in unison as he lowered it to Ti-Paul, and Isaac sighed, just audibly.

"Hunger is a bad master," Toussaint said, "often it is. Tomorrow or the next day more men will come to drive the cows back down to Bréda. And all the calves will be here, will they not?"

"Yes," Ti-Paul said, closing his hand around the neck of the bag. "Yes, all of them."

They rode back to the main plantation more slowly than they had come out, for the heat was climbing to its peak. In the jungle Toussaint stopped once to cut some leaves from a bitter-bush and stow them in the bag he carried for gathering such herbs as he might chance upon. Even when they reached the road he didn't gallop, for fear of overheating the stallion. Placide hadn't asked again if he could ride him unassisted. Toussaint could hear both boys' stomachs growling but neither of them complained. The field hands had already come in for their midday break, had eaten already and were resting.

Toussaint let the children off at the cabin, so that they could get a meal, and rode back toward the stables. A few slaves were sitting out of doors, their backs against the mud walls of the cabins, motionless as ironwood carvings; in this heat even the small children were still. The young cock had mounted a speckled hen in the middle of the way, and he rocked atop her with a feathery motion. At the water trough Toussaint dismounted and while the stallion drank he soaked his headcloth in the tepid water and retied it over his brows. He led Bellisarius into a stall and unsaddled him. Just as he finished a junior groom came to tell him he was wanted at the *grand'case*.

A fresh sweat broke out through his headcloth as he climbed the little rise toward the house. The heat shimmer sent ripples over the brick facade at the head of the knoll, so that the whole house seemed almost a mirage. He walked up through the garden of tea roses, faded and withering under the sun, climbed the gallery steps and went around to the front of the house. Between the pillars of the gallery he could look down across the wide expanse of cane fields, quiet and empty for the moment, since at Bréda the Code Noir was observed and the slaves were given their full two hours respite from the midday heat.

Bayon de Libertat turned his head as Toussaint creaked across the whitewashed boards. Beside him sat the Sieur Maltrot, and on the rail, one boot cocked up, was perched the freckled mulatto everyone called Choufleur, believed to be Maltrot's son, or else his brother's, out of a *griffonne* in Le Cap. Toussaint glanced at the others under a lowered eyelid and presented himself to Bayon de Libertat, heels together, hands at his sides.

"And what of the cattle?" Bayon de Libertat smiled and stroked his arthritic hand.

"*Casques* have come down from the mountains," Toussaint said.

"*Casques?*" Bayon de Libertat passed his good hand over his forehead, then returned it to his lap to cover the other. "I thought they had all been destroyed years ago. We must send someone with a gun."

"Yes," Toussaint said. "It would be better to bring the cattle in as well."

"There's no grain to spare," said Bayon de Libertat. "There's no grazing here."

"The pasture's worn out where they are," Toussaint said. "They'll kill themselves eating nopal up there."

"What would you do, then? How would you have it done?"

"I would kill a good few and dry the meat at once," Toussaint said. "Corral the breeding stock and feed them as we can and wait until the drought has ended."

Bayon de Libertat nodded.

"Good husbandry," said the Sieur Maltrot. He took out his snuffbox and thumbed open the lid. "I'm told by your master that you have been equally provident in the other arrangements you have made."

"Master," Toussaint pivoted on his heels and faced him with a little bow. "Everything is in good order."

"Ma foi," said the Sieur Maltrot. "I believe you are the most remarkable nigger I have ever met." He sneezed mightily into his handkerchief and snapped his snuffbox shut. "And the conditions, they are satisfactory?"

"Three days *congé* each week for all and freedom for the leaders," Toussaint said. Behind him, Choufleur plucked a sprig of jasmine from the vine that twined around the nearest post to him, and twirled it in his fingers. Toussaint, distracted by the movement, shifted his feet slightly so he could see Choufleur from the corner of his eye.

"Three days a week is not a negligible price," Maltrot said, musingly. He spun his sword stick in his hands, fidgeting with the catch that released the blade. "For all of the slaves on the northern plain."

"They work more efficiently when they are well fed and well rested," said Bayon de Libertat. "Well treated generally. As you yourself have remarked."

"Of course," said the Sieur Maltrot. "Still, even here you don't allow *three days* . . ."

"Much of this time would be spent tending the provision grounds," said Bayon de Libertat. "There would be a saving there . . ."

"And much of this time would be spent dancing the *calenda,*" Maltrot said. "No doubt." He eyed Toussaint. "What of these leaders who will be made free?"

"Jean-François Papillon. Boukman Dutty," Toussaint said. The Sieur Maltrot nodded at both names. On the porch rail, Choufleur stripped leaves from his jasmine sprig. He squeezed a drop of juice onto the inside of his wrist from the torn stem. The fresh sweet smell of it spiraled toward the others.

"Georges Biassou. Jeannot Bullet." Toussaint stopped.

"Not quite a handful, even," said Maltrot. *"C'est bien, ça.* They are sufficient?"

"They're all strong men in their own *ateliers,*" Toussaint said, "and well known among many of the others."

"Bon," said the Sieur Maltrot, "but who's this Dutty? I dislike the sound of an English name."

"He was sold here from Jamaica," Toussaint said, passing over the point that Boukman had also fought with French regiments in the American Revolutionary War.

"Ah," said Maltrot. "I hope he is not a sorcerer, or some *mauvais sujet*. You know that little scheme of the English."

"No, master," said Toussaint, who also knew that the French tried to fob off whatever *hûngans* they could identify on the English. "He is not."

Maltrot raised his eyebrows and looked up at him sharply. "I trust you don't dabble in witchcraft yourself," he said.

"I follow Jesus," said Toussaint.

"Yes," Maltrot said. "Commendable. Your master," he nodded at Bayon de Libertat, "has told me that you know how to read."

"I read my Bible and my Psalter," Toussaint said.

"Naturally," said the Sieur Maltrot. "You were coming from church, were you not, when one of our good gentlemen of Haut du Cap gave you a beating upon seeing you with a book?"

Toussaint's hand involuntarily lifted to the bloodstains on the shoulder of his coat. He had not expected the Sieur Maltrot to have heard of this episode.

"Many times I have offered to give him another coat," said Bayon de Libertat. "He will not have it, but insists on wearing this one year after year."

"Oh, an eccentricity," said Maltrot. "What do you mean by it, Toussaint?"

"A token," Toussaint said smoothly. "A reminder of a lesson in humility I have learned."

"Mais comme il est raisonné!" the Sieur Maltrot said delightedly. *How well-reasoned he is!* "Choufleur, you must give him the money at once."

Choufleur reached into his elaborately embroidered waistcoat and drew out a leather purse closed with a drawstring. Toussaint accepted it into his palm, his nod dropping his eyes out of the other's line of sight, though he was still looking sidelong. Choufleur wore his piebald skin like a mask, and his expression was hard to read beneath it, as if he really had two faces. All around the four men on the gallery the air was extraordinarily motionless; it felt like being submerged in warm, still water. The coins shifted in the sack with a muted ring of gold.

"A discretionary fund," said Maltrot, smiling. "Something in case of any sudden necessity, and to keep your leaders happy, and by all means something for yourself. There will be more as needed."

Toussaint flexed his fingers around the purse and made another hint of a bow.

"So many are convinced our slaves must be kept in ignorance," said the Sieur Maltrot. "I myself have not fully formed an opinion. Tell me something you have read."

Toussaint hooded his eyes, turning back verse upon verse of the psalms in his mind. Indeed there must be something in the Bible to suit any occasion or answer any inquiry. There was a line from that same psalm they would study at the cabin in three days' time.

"My lips will be glad when they sing unto thee," he said. "And so will my soul, whom thou hast delivered."

"*Et comme il est sournois,*" the Sieur Maltrot said. *And how sly he is, also.* "I'm sure you'll manage the whole affair most wonderfully."

Chapter Six

ARNAUD HAD BROUGHT HER the girl as a gift, he said, a lady's maid, a touch of luxury to color her days on the plantation more pleasantly, to heal her longing for France. She had smiled at the present, however brittly, and given the girl some name which suited this imaginary character and which she could not even remember now—Arnaud had taken to calling her Mouche, and this was the name that had stuck. Now Claudine sat before her mirror, biting her lips as she examined her bloodshot eyes, and struggled to stop herself from trembling visibly, for she had awoken shaky and nauseous. She watched Mouche, deeper in the looking-glass reflection, fumbling uselessly with the dress that she, Claudine Arnaud, meant to wear that day.

Interesting excuse for a lady's maid, certainly, a *bossale* fresh off the boat and fresh from Africa; Claudine was to be assisted in putting on her clothes by a girl who came dressed in nothing but a gloss of palm oil and perhaps a string of cowries around her hips. To this objection her husband had replied that since the girl was unschooled, Claudine would have the opportunity to train her altogether to her own liking. That had been six or seven months ago, and in the intervening time Claudine had been able to teach Mouche to cover her own nakedness, at least some of the time, but not much more. On several occasions she had suggested that the girl was not biddable and might be better sent to the cane fields since she was young and strong. But still she hung about the house. By this time she had learned enough Creole to fetch things on demand and carry simple messages; she helped a little in the kitchen, or pulled the ropes that turned the fans.

Claudine studied her in the mirror, as the black girl fidgeted with the ribbons on the dress laid out across the just-made bed. Mouche's underlip shoved out like a cushion, her mask of uncomprehension, and in the misty recesses of the mirror Claudine could see the whites of the girl's eyes. Her stomach heaved, and she put her fingers across her lips and held her breath. The heat swelled into the room like fog; the white cotton shift she'd tried to sleep in was creeping with sweat where her thighs touched the chair. When the spasm passed she twisted around and snapped at the girl.

"Leave it," she said. Mouche started, flinched at the sound of Claudine's voice. She jerked her hand away from the ribbons as if she had touched a live coal.

"Leave it," Claudine said. As she stood up, another wave of nausea hit her and she had to bend over, holding the back of the chair. She saw herself in this posture in the mirror, her hair hanging down in strings; she looked old, sick—she looked how she felt.

"Leave it," she said. "I don't feel well, just go." She straightened up and made her way as far as the bedpost while Mouche scuttled toward the door. A bolt of pain shot through her head from one temple to the other, like a nail. "Only bring some water," she said, as Mouche backed away. "*Et ma petite chose.*"

As Mouche scraped out, the jerks of her legs pulled her calico tight over her pregnancy. She had come in the same lot as that infanticide of whom Arnaud had lately made an example, but hers was no child of shipboard rape. She was more newly swollen . . . Claudine sat on the bed's edge, swung her legs up. She lay. The pain kept a distance from her so long as she did not move her head; her stomach boiled, then subsided. She sighted down the length of her legs at her toes. It was quiet in the house except for the whisper of the slaves' bare feet on the wooden floors and the sound of insects working, working. They would gnaw until they had carried the whole *grand'case* back to the jungle in their jaws.

Mouche carried in a tray, a carafe and two glasses; she set it down on the stool beside the bed. Claudine waved her imperiously away, and blushed with relief as soon as the girl was out of the room. *Ma petite chose*—if Arnaud had seen them bringing it to her he might well have prevented it. She raised herself on an elbow, pain ringing through her head like a shot, and drank the glass of rum in rapid birdlike sips, then poured water into the glass, thinking that perhaps her husband wouldn't know . . . Her intestines clenched, snaked against themselves, abruptly as a bullwhip cracking back on its own length. She dropped back onto the bed in the spasm, her knees drawn up. After a time her belly relaxed and faintly she began to feel the glow.

The headache was not gone but she felt now that it had been wrapped in a cloud of unmilled cotton. She heard the sound of Arnaud's boot heels mutedly crossing the gallery. She lay half in a trance, watching a long-legged spider stitching a web to close the gap between the partition wall and the ceiling above the bed's head. Arnaud was turning about in the main room; she heard him stop at the bedroom door.

She shut her eyes as the door squealed open; in the dense humidity the wood had swelled into the floor. Without sight she could yet sense Arnaud's eyes dispassionately stroking her from toe to head, then shifting to the carafe and the pair of glasses. Perhaps he would lift the glass she had used and smell the dregs. Instead, he left the room, dragging the door shut behind him.

A giggle—it was Mouche's voice. Some muttering from her husband, then a higher squeal from Mouche, as if she had been pinched. Mouche was protesting, in her rudimentary Creole, and Arnaud reassuring her—*Don't worry, she's asleep like a dead thing*. Another titter and a sound like fabric ripping. Claudine could hear them as plainly as if they were in the room with her, though in fact they must have been two rooms away, in the cubicle used for the doctor or for whatever other infrequent guest might happen by.

Mouche giggled and tittered through the whole affair, bouncing, as Claudine could too well picture it, like a black rubber ball. Arnaud was silent, grim at the work. Of course, she was unsurprised. Often a Creole husband would defile the marriage bed itself, although of late Claudine had seldom strayed far enough from their bed for this particular insult to be probable. But certainly she had always known why the girl remained in the *grand'case* despite her near-perfect uselessness, why she had been purchased to begin with probably, and who had put the child in her belly. But to do it here and now—such carelessness could only be born of an unutterable contempt. She, Claudine, had conceived no child. Arnaud, however, had been sure to prove that this was in no way *his* fault; her husband's face grinned back at her from every yellow brat in the yard.

A giggle and a grunt—perhaps they had only been resting, perhaps they were beginning again. Claudine bared her parched eyeballs, stared at the ceiling. *Ouais, mon homme,* she thought, *t'as ta petite chose toi aussi.* As she framed the words she almost laughed, but bile backed up in her throat instead. From the other room came a snicker, then a deep sigh, close to a moan. The sighing went on, at an even rhythm, like a saw grinding back and forth on the crying emptiness of a barrel. When finally it ceased, the noise of the insects rushed up to fill the gap like a string section in an orchestra.

Claudine dozed a little, along with the fatigued lovers, possibly. The sound of the insects still hummed at her ears, but at the same time she thought that she was dreaming, a dream of lying beside Arnaud in the next room, or in that other bed in Nantes, the great carved wooden monstrosity where he had murdered her virginity, left her stabbed and bleeding in her tenderest recess while he amused himself with the better-experienced whores of the town. But when she woke she found him standing in the doorway, looking down on her with the whetted expression he wore when some slave had particularly offended him.

It was considerably later. She knew because the color of the light had changed, a bar of sunshine had advanced in its position on the wall. Arnaud crossed his feet, propped a shoulder on the door frame.

"Will you be dressing yourself today?" he inquired. "Will you be rising at all?"

"J'ai mal à la tête," Claudine murmured. She stretched out a hand and felt the dress that was crumpled partly under her.

"Indeed," said Arnaud. *"Encore une fois . . . ou gueule de bois, je dirais."*

Claudine passed over the allusion to hangover. "I can't seem to find my maid," she said, more acidly. She hiccuped, tasted vomit on the back of her teeth and swallowed it back. "Perhaps she's otherwise engaged?"

Arnaud's fruity lips pulled back against his teeth, his thinnest smile. "I'll call her for you," he said. "On my way out."

Claudine swung her legs to the floor. She gathered her hair behind and twisted it, tightening the skin across her face.

"I shall be gone for quite some time," Arnaud said. "That little errand for the Sieur Maltrot, *tu comprends*. The journey must be overland, it will take several weeks. I'll take Orion with me but no others. No doubt you'll manage well enough. I've left instructions with Isidor."

"No doubt," Claudine said. She reached her hand as far as the bedpost; the movement seemed steady enough. "I wish you a safe journey," she said stiffly, peering up at him from her bloodshot eyes.

"Eh bien, mon bijou," Arnaud said. *"À la rencontre."* He smacked his palm against the tight fabric of his riding breeches, and spun out of the door frame and away.

Claudine stood up, she drank a glass of water, cleansing her throat. She did not feel so ill as she had earlier, though her head still dully hurt. She called out for Mouche and while she waited she rinsed the rheum from her eyes with a splash of water from the carafe, and changed into a fresh chemise.

The dress was still wearable despite having been slept on. She shook it out and had got partway into it by the time Mouche arrived to help her, with her multiple thumbs, to achieve the complex fastenings. Claudine sat at the mirror then, allowing Mouche to brush out her hair, though the girl was so afraid of pulling that her strokes were uselessly weak. Claudine could smell it on her skin, the sickening melony musk. Her hardened belly pressed into the chair back.

"Oh, give it up," Claudine snapped, and grabbed the gilt-backed brush from Mouche's hand. "I'll take coffee on the gallery. In ten minutes."

When Mouche had gone, Claudine arranged her own hair as best she could, not troubling much about the back. Done, she got up and wandered about the room. The idea of Arnaud's lengthy absence rather cheered her. She opened a drawer at random and poked through a jumble of his things: tarnished brass buttons cut from a worn-out coat, a locket with some unknown infant's portrait, a barber's razor. She picked the razor up and touched the flat of it to the inside of her wrist. For some reason she'd expected cold, but of course the metal was as warm and sticky as the suffocating air inside the room.

Her dress had a puffed sleeve that just covered her shoulder, leaving the whole white length of her arm bare. Standing before the mirror, she touched the blunt corner of the razor to the skin just below the ribbon's gather, and drew it swiftly all the way down to her wrist. The stroke made a faintly pink crease on her blue-marbled skin, which quickly faded to its normal pallor. She turned the razor over and set the sharp edge against the same soft spot below the sleeve, only to see how the least touch of it would feel, but she must have twitched, for without meaning to she nicked herself. She gasped, a sharp intake of breath. An infinitesimal star of blood bloomed on her inner arm, no bigger than an asterisk.

The merest scratch. She wet her finger and dabbed the place clean. For a moment she studied her arm, the network of veins below the skin that gave it its milky bluish cast. The arm seemed more fully hers than it had before. It thrilled her. The razor had a little leather case; she sheathed it and tucked it into her bosom, out of sight. In the main room, Isidor was shuffling round the furniture with a feather duster, wearing as always that cast-off coat from which the buttons had been cut, his version of a butler's uniform. He came to attention the instant he saw her, but she passed through without noticing him, and went onto the gallery.

Presently Mouche appeared with coffee on a tray. Claudine heard Isidor whispering to her as she passed through the inner room. Perhaps he would have taken the tray, but Mouche seemed bent on performing the service herself. Claudine took her cup, stirred in her sugar. At the first sip her brows broke out in perspiration. She turned to order Mouche to work the fan, but the girl was standing too near at her elbow, or else it was through her natural inborn clumsiness that she overset the tray.

The china pot burst in a thousand shards, sending out a circular wave of coffee. In slow trickling stains, it browned a crescent of spilled sugar. Dangling the tray from one thick-fingered hand, Mouche gaped at the wreckage, at the numerous black ants that had flipped up through the floorboards and were training on the sugar spill. Claudine turned blue with fury. Her chest pulsed, the razor shifted uncomfortably between her breasts. She leaped up and seized Mouche by the ear and wrenched it, and so dragged the girl off the gallery and around the back of the house toward the barns, screaming all the while for Isidor to come quickly and to bring some cord.

Claudine held the black girl's head twisted low, at her own waist, while she dragged her stumbling through the dust of the compound. Of course Mouche was much stronger than she, but they had played this scene together often enough before that the black girl knew her only choice was submission. At a rear window of the house popped up the sallow face of Marotte, the mulattress housekeeper. Claudine yelled again for Isidor to hurry with the cord as she hustled Mouche into the shed where Arnaud had kept his mastiff penned.

Isidor crept into the stall with a bundle of coarse twine. His flat face was prickling with an anxious sweat; Claudine could smell it. At her breathy instruction he tied Mouche's wrists together and secured them to an iron eyelet on the wall above her head. "Tighter," Claudine insisted. "Tighten it—" Isidor's face pinched shut, but he pulled on the knots until Mouche's hands began to swell.

"Leave us," Claudine ordered. "*Maintenant.*" Isidor retreated and Claudine stood for a moment, catching her breath. Mouche was slumped against the wall, her cheek laid against the rough half-logs. There was a rip at the neck of her calico smock, perhaps from Arnaud's greedy hand that morning. Claudine went to the tack room and came back with a riding crop, tan leather braided around whalebone. For a moment she hesitated, contemplative, as though she anticipated a touch of love. Her left hand closed on the tear at the girl's neck, and she jerked it down, baring Mouche to the swell of her buttocks. Her back was dotted with marks of old beatings, maggoty white blotches on the dark skin, some encrusted with drying scab.

With a little strangled shriek Claudine lashed the riding crop across the patchy skin, and again on the backstroke she hit, and again. The inch-wide loop at the crop's end raised an oval welt if she struck well, and still she felt it was insufficient, every time. Though Mouche gasped and pressed herself more nearly to the wall, the blows were not strong enough to *force* her; she was only shrinking from the sting, and Claudine wished she had the strength to manage a bullwhip, she wished she could flay the bitch to the bone. Anything to change the timbre of her insincere cries so they no longer would remind her of the self-same moaning Mouche had given up when she was covered by Arnaud. The crop could barely scratch the surface of Claudine's deepest indignation and as Mouche arched her back and twisted her neck, uttering those unconvincing doglike yelps, their eyes met, and Claudine recalled in spite of her loathing how her parents had sold her to Arnaud for the money they believed he possessed, believing stupidly that all Creole planters were richer than Croesus, how whoever had sold Mouche from her home would have made a better bargain, receiving a few sticks of tobacco or an iron ax head in exchange for her life, something real to the touch and to use. Oh, the intolerable thought—the strokes of the crop must wear it away, but they would not, and still their eyes were locked. That crackling connection brought them to a communion larger than themselves; all over the island masters and slaves were expressing their relation in similar ways, and it was nothing to lop an ear or gouge an eye, even to cut off a hand, thrust a burning stake up a rectum, roast a slave in an oven alive, or roll one down a hill in a barrel studded with nails. All these were as sacraments, body and blood.

Panting and biting her lips in frustration, Claudine bent the whalebone double; when she released it, it hummed across the room like a dragonfly, rebounding from the wall. She made a catlike swipe with her bare left hand, scoring the flesh with her nail points, and Mouche gave a shout of surprise at this, but still it was not all she wanted. Besides, she had torn her nail; it dangled from the finger where she wore her marriage ring. She bit it off, with a tingling taste of her own blood, while Mouche's melting brown eye still watched her through a slit. Exhausted from the encounter, Mouche breathed on that same sighing pattern. Claudine thought that while her power over the girl was absolute, Mouche did not fully recognize this truth. Yet she would make her know it.

She picked up the crop and stalked back to the house, snapping the leather loop into her palm. The torn cuticle was stinging her . . . "Isidor," she cried. "Open the storeroom."

Isidor came shuffling, reluctant, shaking his bowed head, with Marotte hovering around him, wringing her long yellow hands. "Eh madame," Isidor muttered, "Eh madame, the master told me—"

"Open it!" Claudine said. "You will take your orders from me."

"Madame, he hasn't the key," Marotte said.

"Liar!" Claudine slapped her with all her force, enough to smash the mulattress's face sideways. The shock of palm on cheek was sweet to her. Marotte had once been her husband's fancy, before Mouche, before that other "lady's maid" who finally had run away to the mountains, abandoning (of course) her string of half-breed children. Claudine inhaled, swelling her bosom against the sheathed razor. "The master is gone," she said. "I *will* be obeyed. Do you hear me? Fetch a pry bar."

She turned her back. In the big gilt-framed mirror that was the main room's most significant ornament, she saw Isidor and Marotte, who still cupped her hand over her face, exchange a shivering look. Marotte went out to the gallery then, and Isidor left by the back door. She waited, confident now, for his return, and kept her back turned to him when he came. There was a clatter of metal on metal; Isidor grunted, and then came the tearing as the wood gave way around the lock.

Inside, the storeroom was dark and sweltering; it was the stomach of the house. It held all she had to hope for. A white woman could not run to the mountains, though Claudine did have her mad fantasies; she would have gone away with that ridiculous little doctor, even. Along with special tools, the room held a military musket and a fowling piece, powder and lead, a meager store of wine and the bottles of *eau-de-vie* which Arnaud tried to keep from her. She took one from the shelf and broached it. The liquid seemed quite tasteless in her mouth, though farther down she felt the burn. She stroked her fingers over the curving slats of a powder keg and sniffed the acrid tang of it. For some of her husband's friends it was a sporting pastime to pack the anus of a wayward slave with gunpowder and blow it by a fuse, *faire sauter un nègre,* they called it, to make him jump.

Lolling against the rear shelves, she nursed from the long slim neck of the bottle. The white brandy was a spiritual essence, so infinitely superior to the crudely distilled rum she could usually obtain. The bottleneck seemed to curve into her hand, glimmering like starlight in the shadows; each time the rim met her lips it was like exchanging kisses with a swan. Each swallow was an inspiration; she could feel her feet levitating from the floor. Transported, she set the bottle uncorked on a shelf and wandered out into the midday blaze and heat, empty-handed, for she had dropped the crop somewhere, and had even forgotten about it.

Very likely she would not have returned to the shed then, if she had not heard Mouche singing. The voice was deeper, stronger, than the girl's speaking tone, and the words came from the savage language of her birth, if there were words. Claudine could make out no divisions; it was a singular liquid sound, like a long wave rippling all the way back to Guinée. She hesitated on the threshold of the shed. Mouche had shimmied all the way out of her dress and was naked. Her swollen fingers bunched, like overripe fruit born of her bound hands. She sang to herself with her eyes closed, the crinkly puff of her matted hair rucked up against the wall. The voice came out of her essential African self, and Claudine recognized that after all she was still untouched in her identity; it was infuriating. Rage shimmered across her brain from pole to pole. After everything, still the girl did not know, but she would make her know.

Dizzily she stepped through the doorway into the shed, blinking with the change of light. The stitched edge of the razor's sheath pinched a fold of her skin; she reached into her bodice and drew the blade out bare. Mouche sang on, unaware of her, until Claudine took her shoulder with a certain gentleness and turned her so her back was to the wall. Her eyes rolled open an instant before the voice ceased, as Claudine let the razor decline through a slow curve and come to rest against the point just below the sternum where the taut rise of the belly began.

Mouche's throat worked, silently now, and Claudine saw her eyes widening and saw that she *had* understood, at last. She herself had no further intention, but to make her point, but when Mouche saw there was no limit, that truly nothing could stop her now, Claudine could no longer stop herself. Or possibly it was her hand or the blade itself on its own agency that was not stopped, because she had not, herself, intended anything more. Only Mouche's body opened down the plumb line to her center and beyond, like a banana peel splitting down its seam. The blade furrowed through a whitish layer of fat; there was no blood, oddly, until the viscera slithered and slapped down tangling over Claudine's feet, and then she bled. An awful scream was uttered from somewhere, Claudine couldn't tell where, for Mouche was singing again now, and that was what Claudine could not bear. Maddened, she swung wildly at the neck, spinning herself half around, and as she came back, blood from a severed artery showered her, drenching the front of her dress. She stepped back and looked down, inexorably, at the snarl of vitals on the dirt floor. Something else was among them, pulsing inside its membranous sac; it was not exactly independent life, but it still lived a little, as her organs were still slightly living, though Mouche was surely dead. It was the thing, Claudine was confident, that she had wanted to uncover, and she had a desire to open it further, to see and know more, and more, but she did not gratify this wish.

Outside in the yard she stopped, a few feet from the door, to look down at the blood that covered her. She dabbled two fingers in it, noting that Mouche's blood was just the color of her own, precisely. She made a print, an oval dot, over the place where she'd nicked herself that morning, then stroked a double line down her cheek with her two fingers. The movement dragged down one side of her mouth and when she took her hand away her face stayed fixed in that position, catatonically, as it might in a victim of apoplexy. Isidor stood in the middle of the yard, staring at her, with Marotte several yards behind him. The two gave forth no expression, but stood unmoving like obelisks in a desert. She began to walk, passing Isidor, advancing toward Marotte. When their eyes met, Marotte dropped to her knees like someone had clubbed her, and let out a terrible groan. Claudine passed her blindly by and went into the house.

In her delirium the thing came to her and told her that the work of destruction she'd begun would be unending. It had not yet developed to a human shape; it was something different, primal, beaked and gilled, damp and clammy, and always slicked with putrid blood. Sometimes it showed her different visages: a monkey's face, or an elephant's trunk, the face of her husband to be sure, or more infrequently her own. She knew it for hallucination, born of delirium tremens, and she knew that drink would stop its coming, but she did not drink. For days at a time she lay in her own ordure on the bed, or wandered through the empty house—Isidor and Marotte had run away, and no one else came near. Like a ghost she walked within the walls, alone or in the company of the thing, which held her finger in a wet, webbed claw, or slithered ahead of her on flippers. If the thing was absent she saw other phantasms, sulfurous fires that swept the cane fields hedge to hedge without consuming them, berserk slaves who danced in clouds of lurid flame, uncaring—she saw Mouche roaming the compound as a headless zombi, her stumped neck a fountain of blood, singing that same song from the wiry flutes of her severed trachea.

But always the thing returned, and when she least expected it—she never learned to expect it, but she might wake to find it settled on her navel, wiggling in a puddle of afterbirth and staring down at her with a dolphin's black eye or, during her solitary ramblings through the house, it might come on her suddenly from out of the other rooms. It had a metamorphic power and it showed her all its changes from a dot of plasm to a fish into a being like herself, but it let her know that her own being was as futile as some ancient extinct beast. She implored the thing to give her peace, and when that failed she threatened it, and finally made it promises—she said that she would take it into her own body and carry it to its term, but it made no answer to any of her proposals.

Then it went away. She lay there, dreading its return. Her body had died, it seemed. If she raised an arm above her head it would remain there tirelessly; if she bit into her finger or her wrist she could feel nothing, though she saw the tooth prints' bruise. Still the thing did not come back, and one afternoon she woke to a shadow of sensation. She felt a finality in its absence, though she dared not trust it. For the first time in many days she could feel her body, face her reflection, smell herself—a nasty smell. She felt hollow, burned to a husk, like a bit of *bagasse* blown off the cane fields. Curiously she regarded herself in the gilt-framed looking glass, her dress hanging in brown-stained rags from her shriveled body. In a week she had aged ten years. Behind her the broken door of the storeroom lolled like a tongue from the head of a corpse.

All the children had disappeared from the yard, the chickens were gone too, and it was deathly still except for a fringe of dust that a small breeze carried low across the parched and cracking earth. A red-headed, wrinkle-necked vulture stood on the ground near the door of the shed. Claudine expected it to evaporate when she approached, but it only shrugged its shoulders at her and clawed a few steps away, and finally when she came too near, it lifted itself on its ragged wings and flew to the shed's roof tree, where three others roosted. She stooped and flung a clod at them with a hoarse cry, but only one was moved to flight, lifting higher and higher on a spiral till it was only a small cross circling in the sky. She waited for it to disappear utterly and so prove itself delusional, but it remained there, slowly turning. She knew that she ought to go into the shed and face whatever was there, but she did not go.

Inside the barn, she washed herself at the horse trough. There were horses still in the stalls; they hung their heads out and whickered at her, but they didn't seem panicky or restive so she knew that someone must be tending them. The water was reasonably fresh as well. She peeled off the sodden rags of her dress and abandoned them. Her body came clean, staining the water. She thrust her head under and scrubbed her scalp. When she sat up, wringing out her hair, she thought she saw a flicker of human movement, felt an eye upon her, though she hardly cared. She pushed her head under the water again and tried to breathe in, but her body repelled itself and she sat back, spluttering. This time she saw the boy jerk his head back into a vacant stall and she darted after him and trapped him there. A little mulatto, about twelve or thirteen, she didn't know his name but she thought she'd seen him working as a groom. His teeth were chattering and he wouldn't look at her.

"Yes, I am a madwoman," she hissed at him, and pinched his cheeks and drew him close. "I'm a witch, or worse. You must do anything I say, anything, do you hear?"

The boy's eyes squinched shut, he trembled to his toes.

"Harness the horses," she snapped, releasing the folds of cheek and pushing him away. "Bring the coach to the front of the *grand'-case.*"

She watched him scurry off, not knowing if he would obey or not, if he had even understood her through his terror. Naked and dripping she went to the house, where she found some dried beef and chewed it ferociously, floods of flecked saliva running from the corners of her mouth, as if she were starving—she *was* starving, of course. She dressed herself as she might for church and packed a small portmanteau. The coach was waiting when she stepped onto the gallery, the boy astride the left horse of the pair. She climbed in and ordered him to drive to Flaville plantation, and when he hesitated, told him that she knew the way.

Chapter Seven

Isabelle Cigny was beyond delicate, she was bone-thin, as frail as a consumptive, though she lacked the consumptive's inwardly gnawed appearance, and her bright animation did not seem feverish to Doctor Hébert's eye. If she stood in the center of her drawing room, twirled to spin out her skirts from the waist in a spiral of silk taffeta, she looked lissome, willowy, though in truth she had no height. It seemed that one could lift her with one hand, and no doubt there were those who would have liked to try it, for Isabelle was a pretty thing, with a weight of dark hair that looked too heavy for her slender neck, and skin whose icy pallor colored quickly whenever she was stirred.

She appeared very young, and certainly she must be younger than her husband. The doctor had waited upon Madame Cigny four times running and failed to find her at home, and at last had called upon Monsieur Cigny at his place of business. Cigny was a burly man in his fifties, beginning to run to fat, who wore a bushy untrimmed beard like an apron over his chest. He received the doctor courteously enough, but the mention of Thibodet brought only a black look, and he could report nothing of Elise beyond acknowledging the acquaintance. Doctor Hébert drew the impression that Monsieur Cigny and his wife moved in fairly separate social circles. At any rate, he had been able to learn at what hours he would most probably find the lady of the house at home.

Two gentlemen were already seated in her parlor when the doctor was admitted. He paid his compliments, which she accepted rather casually, and took a seat at the edge of the room, near a window. A youth dressed in the uniform of the Regiment Le Cap sat near Madame Cigny, on an ottoman, fixing upon her a doglike concentrated look. He seemed inordinately fascinated by her white-stockinged foot, from which she dangled a satin shoe with a blue bow. Each time it looked about to drop, he started forward to retrieve it, but always at the last moment she twitched it back against her sole, so that he sat back crestfallen, under her teasing sidelong glance. Meanwhile she gave more of her attention to the second young man, who sat beside her on the sofa, dressed in the costume of a Paris dandy, cream-colored *gilet* and striped silk *redingote*. She was reading, or pretending to read, a book whose latter pages were uncut, and whenever she turned over a packet of unopened leaves she presented it to this gentleman, who with a wriggle and a simper used a paper knife to slit it.

The doctor sat somewhat uncomfortably, both feet flat on the floor, on a chair which was rather too small for him. All the furniture in the room looked as if it had come from France, probably packed in hogsheads of straw, given its fragility. A servant in ornate livery came in and served him coffee. Desultorily he sipped, his glance wandering around the room. The cup he'd been given was eggshell-thin, banded with gold around the rim. He thought that Madame Cigny had forgotten he was there, but presently she tossed aside her book and crossed the room to where he sat. So small she was that he was almost eye to eye with her when she stopped before him. Her eyes were large and luminous, quite dark, and certainly she was very pretty when she smiled.

"Give me your news of Elise," she said brightly.

The doctor cast about for somewhere to lay down his cup and saucer, but there was no table near. "My news," he said. "Well, I had rather hoped to hear something from you."

"Oh, she is naughty," said Isabelle Cigny, and tapped him teasingly on the wrist. "She does not write to her brother."

The cup and saucer rattled in the doctor's hand. Madame Cigny signaled the slave to come and remove the utensils.

"I—" The doctor swallowed, looking over at the young officer and the dandy, who were eyeing each other across the abandoned book as if they might dispute its possession. The topic was awkward enough without an audience. Isabelle Cigny turned, gaily fanning out her skirt. One of her hands rested on her waist; one of his own might have encircled it.

"Henri, Pascal, do leave us, please," she said.

The dandy hopped to his feet, with an expression that suggested protest, but Madame Cigny raised her voice slightly before he could speak.

"Oh, don't be tiresome," she said, a shade of acerbity in her twitter. "It is not discreet."

The two gentlemen made their departure then, and as they passed through the door, the servant returned to serve fresh coffee, then withdrew to stand against the wall, his arms folded across his frogged coat. Madame Cigny took a seat beside the doctor and helped him to some sugar.

"I do not take them seriously, you understand," she said, nodding toward the door. "Only it can be tedious here sometimes. The days are long, and hot of course, as you will surely have noticed."

"It is a beautiful country," said the doctor, touching a film of sweat from his upper lip with his handkerchief.

"I was educated in France," said Madame Cigny. "After my marriage, we might have remained there for all of me—you know my husband is not a Creole—but he thought it better to come here so as to look after my interests." She smiled. "And his own, naturally."

The doctor was a little startled by this candor, but perhaps she had noticed his unease, and meant to make him an invitation to confidence. He might as well assume so, it occurred to him.

"I will be frank, *madame*." With some concentration he avoided looking at the slave who posed against the wall, having learned that the Creole sense of discretion did not extend to blacks. "I have no news of my sister whatever, I have not even seen her since I came out from France, I have only lately learned that she has borne a child—if it is true."

"Oh, the dear little Sophie, yes, she is quite genuine," Madame Cigny said. "I believe they quarreled over that, Elise and that regrettable husband of hers."

"*Pardon?*" said the doctor. "Did Thibodet wish so badly for a son?"

"Oh, it was not that at all!" Madame Cigny flicked him again on the wrist, got up and strolled away from him, along the row of windows. "No, it was . . . *il lui semblait qu'elle avait une touche de la brosse, la petite—comme on dirait ici.* Since she was so dark when she was born, and both the parents fair."

The doctor watched her back. She turned abruptly and a stream of sunlight flooded her eyes; he saw that they were not black as he had thought, but the deepest blue. She beckoned to the servant, who came over and partially lowered the blinds.

"Of course there was nothing in that," Madame Cigny said. "Only that Thibodet was an idiot—they had other differences, before. I'm sure the child takes after some grandparent. Besides, her hair is good." She seated herself and once more tapped him on the wrist. "Of course one hears the most extraordinary stories. In Paris I knew the wife of a Polish officer who gave birth to a perfect little Negro—she put it down to being startled by a black coachman while she was *enceinte.*" She sparkled at him, then turned to peer through the slats of the blind. "That explanation wouldn't wear well here," she said. "It would become rather *too* universal, do you not agree? And *all* our children would be black. But stay, you must meet mine."

She sent the servant out, and presently in came a black nurse, carrying an infant in her arms and leading a little boy along by the hand.

Madame Cigny rushed to take the baby. "Héloïse," she said, holding her so that the doctor might see, *"et mon petit Robert."* She cradled the baby into her bodice and laid her hand on the boy's head. The infant Héloïse waved her small pink hands in her mother's face, and Madame Cigny began to croon to her. The doctor stood.

"Why, how handsome they are." He stooped and offered his hand to Robert, who clutched a pleat of his mother's skirt and drew it in front of himself. The doctor peeked at the face of Héloïse and realized she must be scarcely three months old.

"They're close in age, your niece and Héloïse," Madame Cigny said, as if she had read his thought. No doubt that she was stronger than she seemed, the doctor mused, and maybe deeper too; she looked as if childbirth would kill her. She gave the infant a series of quick pecking kisses and passed her back to the nurse. Immediately Héloïse began to cry, but the nurse took her to a seat in a corner and hushed her with the breast.

Madame Cigny detached Robert's hand from her skirt and curled herself on the sofa, shifting the book to the table. The doctor lowered himself into a chair adjacent, and she turned to him with a serious look.

"Your sister was a model of fidelity," she said. "Unlike some, and not that her husband much deserved it."

"I dare say he did not."

"I wonder if you know what a Creole husband can be," Madame Cigny said thoughtfully. Robert picked up a china figurine from a table and snapped the head off it. Madame Cigny clucked her tongue at him, but made no further remonstrance. The nurse, who had soothed the baby into a doze, took him by the hand and led him out.

"I hardly know what to tell you," Madame Cigny said.

"I thought perhaps she had been here," the doctor said. "That she might have spoken to you."

"Yes, she has been here, but she didn't speak—I mean, nothing of moment." Madame Cigny touched a finger to her lips. "That would have been a couple of months ago. Yes, and I wondered that she would be traveling with the baby so small . . ." She colored, charmingly. "Of course Héloïse was very new—I fear I was distracted."

"*C'est tout á fait naturel,*" the doctor said.

"We have been great friends, your sister and I," said Madame Cigny. "But she might have chosen to tell me nothing, if she *did* have intentions. Then I would have nothing to tell Thibodet if he came inquiring. But I believed she was returning to him when she left here."

"Anything that you could tell me would be useful," the doctor said. "I know so little of her pastimes, her acquaintance."

"She does have one particular friend, or did," said Madame Cigny. "Xavier . . . oh, I don't know him well myself. Xavier Tocquet, yes, I believe. I'm told he has a little coffee plantation somewhere, and he imports cattle from the Spanish side. It may be that he owns property in Santo Domingo."

"Indeed," said the doctor.

"*Après tout,* she is a widow now," said Madame Cigny. "If she knew that her husband were dead she might well return. Of course you must take care to insert a notice in the Spanish papers, and in the Windward Isles too. I'm certain that it all can be retrieved with little damage. A reputation is less easily destroyed here than in Europe."

The doctor inhaled, then sighed out rather forcefully. "You reassure me," he said. "I will certainly follow your suggestions." He uttered a few pleasantries about the Cigny children, and stood up.

"You'll give Elise my love when you see her," Madame Cigny said, rising in her turn. "Let her know that she is welcome here, as always." The doctor bowed over her hand and went out.

OUTDOORS HE WAS DISORIENTED by the light and heat, and in any case he had no plan. He had forgotten to ask for Tocquet's address, and he didn't like to go back for it so soon. Perhaps Bourgois would know the man. He recalled having heard somewhere that the Creole model of fidelity was to limit oneself to a single extramarital lover at a time. Mulling this over, he found himself carried along in a thickening stream of people, blacks and mulattoes mostly, washing along toward the Place de Clugny and into the midst of *le marché des nègres*.

He had not imagined such a crowd, the largest assembly of any people, black or white, he'd yet seen in the colony. There must literally have been thousands of them packed into the square, mostly dressed for festival, and all chattering frantically in Creole. The doctor was learning to make out some words of the *patois*, but here the voices merged in a single roar. Still, if he let his attention lapse, the choir was close to musical, and certainly it prevented him from concentrating on his worries. He let the shiftings of the crowd carry him around at random. Soon he was shuffled up against the butchers' booths. The meat was wrapped in netting to keep off flies, but nevertheless the smell was strong, and the doctor fought his way a little farther, along the west side of the square, among the vendors of live poultry. Here a speckled cock and a red one were managing to fight, despite the string that tied their legs together. Some women had formed a half circle around them and were pointing and shouting encouragement; it seemed to the doctor that they might be betting on the result.

At other stands were fruit and vegetables of every description, some transplanted here from Europe and others the doctor had never seen before and could not have identified. Those who sold goat meat were quartered among the vegetable stalls, separate from the other butchers so that they could not fraudulently substitute their meat for mutton; the skinned goats still wore their hairy tails, as a further indicator. The doctor watched exchanges. Many were barter, the city blacks exchanging their goods for produce brought in by the Negroes of the plain. He stopped before a fish stand, admiring the bloated spiny puffer fish that hung from strings. Farther on he paused to finger a shelf of carved gourds, elaborately worked and colored with fire-blackening and vegetable dye. Most were intended as containers of one kind or another, but some smaller ones had been left whole with their dry seeds inside, as rattles. The doctor thought of buying one, but considered that he had no use for it.

The crowd swelled up against his back, and he moved on, to another booth where two men were selling songbirds in small basketwork cages. One of them, busy in a rapid negotation with a tall mulatto woman who balanced a basket of fruit on her head, quite resembled one of Crozac's grooms. The woman he was dickering with was more than striking, though simply dressed in a single wrap of flower-printed cotton that dropped sheer from its binding to her calves, leaving her handsome shoulders bare. She wore a necklace of gold links and a dozen or so thin gold bracelets on one arm, jingling them as she gestured and swung her hips. The doctor could not understand how the basket failed to fall from her head, when she was almost dancing as she spoke. He was staring. She caught his eye and kissed her heavy lips to him, and he realized that he knew her too, one of the women from the theater; she was Nanon.

He took a step back and trod on a bare foot. There was a yelp, but when he turned he couldn't make out whom he had affronted. One hand on the rough plank that served as a counter, he made his way around the corner of the booth, while the other vendor handed out birdcages over his head and caught coins in return. When he reached Nanon she laid one narrow hand on his shoulder lightly, leaned toward him and pointed into the dim recess of the booth.

"See the funny monkey," she said. The doctor squinted. Back there in a larger cage was a little spider monkey with a long tail and puffs of white hair at its cheeks. It chittered and wiggled its black fingers.

"Allow me to make you a present of it," the doctor said, and reached into his pocket. The vendor flashed a grin and named a price, which the doctor paid without question. Nanon began giggling at him as he lifted the cage by its wicker loop.

"Oh, you are too rich," she said, laughing as if the thought amused her hugely. "You don't bargain."

Before the doctor could answer she took his hand unconsciously and gave it a friendly squeeze across the knuckles and led him away from the stall. In the press of people he was forced back behind her, but she kept him in tow, her crooked forefinger linked with his. Meanwhile the monkey's tiny hands thrust through the lattice and plucked at the fine hairs on his wrist. He kept his eye on Nanon's head and the miraculously balanced basket. Her hair was done in a chignon, curving down clublike on the back of her neck, and caught in a fine web of gold thread. She was cutting diagonally across the square, toward the monumental fountain in the center, which displayed an image of the sun atop an Ionic column. When they reached it the doctor pulled her up and stopped to read the inscription.

"They executed Ogé here," Nanon said. "*Chavannes aussi . . .*"

The doctor jerked his head up, but her expression was unreadable. She took his hand again and pulled him forward through the crowd, and he followed with no demurral, though his head was humming. He knew little of Ogé except that he had raised an ill-organized and unsuccessful rebellion last October, intended to force compliance with one of the inscrutable decrees from the metropole which seemed to guarantee some political rights for some of the mulattoes. Events had proved him a fool, and his attempt had accomplished nothing or worse, but many said he had died bravely, under terrible torture, and here on this spot. The doctor watched Nanon's chignon bobbing; she had not once looked back. By caste and color she would be Ogé's partisan, but reprisals against mulattoes had been so vicious after the rebellion failed, here in Le Cap and everywhere, that who knew what she might be thinking? He knew just as well that his skin could not reveal to her his sentiments. So far as she could tell he might be a royalist, or one of the faction seeking independence or even an English protectorate for the colony, or the sort of scurvy revolutionist that had surfaced in the coastal cities in reponse to all the movements back in Paris. Or something altogether else; he supposed this last case was the truest. He did not think of letting go her hand.

Nanon lived in two rooms below the Place d'Armes; in fact it was not far at all from the inn where he was staying, and Crozac's stable yard. Much of her furniture was painted wickerwork, and there were a few pieces in mahogany, including a small cabinet which displayed some china bibelots from Europe, a wooden matrioshka doll, and several curious carvings that looked to be of local origin. The doctor set the monkey's cage down on a low table and followed his hostess's beckoning hand into the second room, where the first thing that caught his eye was rack on rack of extravagant clothing, filling half the space; the dresses ranged from European fashion to the sort of improvised garment she was wearing today. She laughed to see him so startled, and gathered a great mass of the clothes into herself, hugging them close and smiling with her cheek pressed against a carnation of multicolored fabric. The doctor blinked. There were two beds in the room, one ordinary, covered with a cinnamon Persian rug. The other was a low daybed, with head and footboards carved like a sleigh, but double width. The doctor nodded as if to affirm something, he knew not what, and withdrew into her *salon*. Nanon let the dresses fall back on their hangers. One slipped to the floor, but she ignored it, following him.

The light was lowering, glaring in the window that overlooked the street, and reflecting back from the large mirror that hung on the opposite wall. Triangulated by the beams, the monkey scrambled in its cage, which allowed it little room to maneuver. Nanon walked around the doctor and stooped to look at it. She closed one eye, then the other, back and forth. The monkey stopped what it was doing and stared at her.

She smiled up at the doctor. "Oh, take him out," she said. "I want to hold him."

His misgivings were insufficient to stop him from opening the door of the cage. A brown blur, the monkey raced up his arm and clawed its way to the top of his head. The doctor ducked and whirled around, but the monkey seized hold of his ears and held on desperately. Nanon was laughing herself breathless, her head thrown back, while the doctor slapped at his head as if it had caught fire. The monkey gathered itself and sprang to the top of the rolled blind above the window, where it clung with all four paws, its head twisted around like an owl's to scream its indignation down at them.

Nanon doubled over, her laughter tailing off into gasps, then straightened up and caught her breath. The doctor reached for the monkey's dangling tail, but it twitched up out of reach immediately, and he stood with his arms akimbo, frowning. Nanon undid the net from her chignon and shook her hair down to her collarbone.

"Let down the blind," she suggested.

The doctor found the strings and worked them to unwind the roller, but the monkey walked the spool like an acrobat on a floating log, and was still holding its position when the blind dropped to the sill. The doctor cast about for a cane or stick or something to dislodge it, but he couldn't see well in the suddenly darkened room. His ears were red where the monkey had mauled them.

"Let him be." Nanon's voice sucked down to its center like a whirlpool. "Let him stay there . . . for a little."

The doctor turned in time to see her touch herself cunningly just above the breastbone. The cotton wrap came undone spontaneously and whispered to the floor. The necklace winked at him, her bare skin changed its surface like a leopard's coat as she moved forward under the white-hot dots and bars of light that leaked through the weave of the blind. Her bracelets softly belled together as she reached out, and wherever she touched him a piece of his clothing fell away as though cut with a hot knife.

Now he understood the function of the daybed. He lay on his back, her hair curtaining him from the navel down. Its fringe moved on his belly in a slow caress. It was happening very slowly, and still at a speed he could not stop, but she stopped sharply, with a low hoarse cry, and swung her long ivory leg up and over him. He saw her eyes. Her lips, which looked so large and cushiony, were lively, muscular on his. Her skin was hot, and acidly tart. He seemed to feel none of her weight, but only a slow stroking movement, her nipples circling on his chest; maybe she was supporting herself on knees and elbows, or maybe she was levitating. Cell by cell he was being strained into her. He caught at her hips, the knob of bone at the small of her back, and bridged himself up and nearer.

Their mouths pulled apart with an audible rip. He saw her eyes barred by her lashes, and heard her breathing over him, "*Tournes-toi, vite, comme ça.*" With a lithe and powerful movement, she reversed herself and slid under him, agile as a stoat. Instantly they were engaged again, if they had ever come apart. He put his hand on the back of her neck and she flattened herself willingly against the sheet, clinging to the scrolled headboard with both her hands. Her mouth uttered some phrases of Creole, then no words, while from the waist down she moved in ways his study of anatomy would not have led him to think possible. He watched her cheek flushing, her mouth bloom to a burning red as it spread against the fabric. A wave surged up and carried him high but instead of crashing down when it broke he went sailing away into space.

Lying half across her back, he felt her heart pulsing toward his through his chest wall. He rested a little, then slipped to the inside of the bed, drew her over on her side and touched her face between his two hands. She looked at him, and curled her fingers around his wrists. Motes of gold swam in the brown swirl of her eyes. The cool rings of her bracelets pressed against his inner arm. He'd lost all sense of his identity; the last vestige of the personality he'd brought into the room eddied somewhere high above like a flake of ash from some great conflagration. Perhaps it had an eye, and watched the scene. He'd slipped his boundaries; there were capabilities in him he'd never known. This was vertigo. He might have slept a little. When he came to himself the light was slightly fading and Nanon was up and wrapped in her sarong, slipping out the door and signaling him with a palm-down gesture to remain.

He lay on his back, sweat drying on the small hairs of his stomach, and watched the dust flecks spinning in the planes of light that penetrated the window lattice. But he felt too alert to doze again, and besides, the mosquitoes were beginning to come whining in. After a while he got up and put on his trousers and shirt. Barefoot, he padded into the other room. The monkey had got the curio cabinet open and was picking out each piece for a close scrutiny and then dropping it to the floor; miraculously none had yet broken. With a quick occult movement, the doctor caught it by the furry nape of its neck. The monkey shrieked and screwed its head around, but it couldn't reach to bite him. As he put it back in the cage he caught sight of himself in the mirror and smiled.

Returning to the bedroom, he put his eye to a gap in the lattice over the window and looked into the inner courtyard of the block. Under the eave of the house was a clay oven and some iron cooking pots stacked beside a fire, which had burned down to coals under a layer of white ash. Nanon hunkered on her heels by the fire, chattering with two black women in starched white headcloths, and stirring a pot with a long-handled spoon. Under her left arm sat a black hen with a red wattle, its eye glassily lidded, as if in a trance. The doctor watched her with admiration and a trace of envy too. He felt hollow, drilled out inside, a nameless vacancy that matched his dizziness. She could squat by the fire with the blacks or come into these pleasant rooms with him; she was more free.

This thought was yet half formed when he was distracted by the sight of a man in dandy dress approaching the cook fire from across the court. Nanon laid down the pot and stood up smoothly from her heels to greet him. The hen cackled and struggled under her arm; she adjusted it and soothed it with little strokes along the length of its wings. Her back was to the doctor, and over her shoulder he could see the man's face; it was that same strange speckled mulatto he'd noticed before at his inn. He seemed angry, or somehow distressed. His hands moved before him in cramped imperious cuts, but his voice was too low for the doctor to make out, and beneath the suspension of his freckles his expression was very hard to read.

Nanon's voice rose to a sharp note. She stepped aside, closing her hand over the hen's head entirely, and whirled it around so that its own weight broke its neck. The black wings jerked convulsively as she tore the head right off with another twist, and directed the bright jet of blood into the courtyard. The man jumped back, while the black women cackled at him from around the fire. The doctor watched him stalk away, brushing irritably at spatters, real or imagined, on his fine clothes.

In the other room Doctor Hébert picked up the trinkets and rearranged them in the cabinet. The monkey chittered at him constantly; he supposed it wanted food. He went back to the daybed and stretched himself out, only long enough to clear his head, he thought, but he did sleep, and heavily. When he awakened it was dark and Nanon was calling him to the table.

She gave him oyster stew and roasted chicken stuffed with nuts and pineapple. There was a dish of spinach and two kinds of melon; she had a very creditable wine. The doctor ate with fervor. Some part of that emptiness he'd felt was hunger, so it seemed. He was coming back more and more to himself as he ate, but it was not altogether a pleasant sensation. Nanon had eaten rather more lightly. She was slipping bits of chicken through the slats of the monkey's cage.

"See how he eats," she said. "He's like a little man."

Solemnly the monkey shredded chicken and fingered it into its small mouth. The doctor smiled awkwardly, beginning to feel himself uncomfortably apelike. He did not quite know how to manage the thing he thought must be expected of him.

"I—" he began, and flapped his aimless hands around the table. "All this, *everything*, I should— I'd like to . . ."

Nanon gave him a cool look. "We will be friends," she said. "You've done a thing for me already, the night we met, and I remember it, *comme tu vois*." Their eyes connected; again the doctor felt the vertiginous depth of the self he didn't know. She smiled. "Of course, you may bring me presents if you like."

The doctor scratched the back of his neck, unconsciously, where a mosquito must have bitten him. He was unsure if he was dealing with professional euphemism or something altogether apart from that. So far as his person was concerned he was without much illusion; he knew that he was prematurely bald, and pear-shaped (though stronger than he looked), that he had spent the greater part of his youth blinded to the world by his studies, that he had no conversation, that he was uninteresting to any woman he had ever met. Heretofore he had expressed his carnal nature only through transactions much more plainly professional than this.

"To be sure, I approve of friendship," he finally said. He toyed with a melon rind, and went on without knowing that he would. "Who was that man I saw you with outside?"

For just an instant, the barest glimpse, she looked as if she'd been stabbed with ice. Then she was laughing merrily as ever. "Oh, you are jealous," she said. "*Bon ça*." She rose and came around the table toward him. "I think you must have eaten and rested enough, then," she said. "Let's see how well you are restored."

Chapter Eight

All the way down into Bois Cayman, I was thinking of Macandal. We were going there, to LeNormand plantation, where he once lived, or where his death began. The whitemen might say he died for love—whitemen believe that things happen for reasons, or if they don't believe it always, they always wish that it were so. All that happened before I was born, when my *gros-bon-ange* was still with *les Mystères*, and my *ti-bon-ange*, eh, where was that? But I knew about it, everyone knew, and as we were coming down from the mountain I knew the others would be thinking of it too.

In Guinée, Macandal was a Mandingue but at Habitation LeNormand he was a slave who fed the sugar mill. He stood at the end of the line and pushed the trimmed cane through the place where the raised edges of the grinding wheels meshed together like teeth in a mouth as they pulled inward. The mules that powered the mill walked around and around at the ends of their long poles, led by yawning children, half asleep, because at LeNormand they ran the mill at night. It's not such hard work feeding cane into the mill, not dangerous, so long as you stay awake, but a slave who has been in the fields all day and then goes to the mill at night may grow tired and drowse and give the mill a finger or a hand. That's why they always sing in the mills at night, to keep themselves awake, and I wonder what they were singing then, before Macandal's scream cut through the song and someone stopped the mules, too late, when the mill had already taken his arm to the shoulder.

Or maybe there was no scream, maybe he never cried out at all, even when the mill ground to a stop and someone took a cane knife and cut his arm off at the shoulder to get him loose from it. And they were singing to him all the time, whatever song it was, they never stopped, and he was singing too, and kept on singing when they cut him away and his arm came out the other end of the mill with the flesh in ribbons and the bone crushed into the frayed and flattened *bagasse*. His blood ran down into the syrup, and somewhere in France a whiteman stirred it into his coffee, Macandal's blood poisoned him, and he died. Yes, it must have been like that. When we were coming down the mountain into Bois Cayman, I saw how he would have taken the knife himself and cut through his own arm, or gnawed it through with his Mandingue teeth like an animal will do with a leg in a trap, because once the arm was severed, he was cut through. No one sends a one-armed slave into the mill or the fields again.

Another man would have died from the wound, and seen his *corps-cadavre* put into the ground, but if Macandal died he was born again. They made him a herdsman. I know how it was for him, that part of it, because Toussaint once let me go myself, to watch the cattle. So he was alone, out there for weeks at a time, running out of food most likely, having little water, but able to think and learn, how to live from the land, what vines to cut for water. To protect himself from the wild dogs and protect the cows, and from the maroons too. There were always maroon bands passing through the foothills, here in Bois Cayman where stray cattle might wander. It might not be the first time, not the second, but one time he would follow them. But he was Macandal, he would not follow, he would lead.

Bois Cayman is an old forest and we were in it a long time. It was a living place and we cut nothing to get through it. The paths were few and they went nowhere or just ended. Sometimes we could hear other bands moving in the jungle near us, large or small. Some seemed to know their way and passed us quickly, and there were others that we passed ourselves. Macandal would have known them all, he went from one band to another. He was everywhere on this side of the mountains, and many places on the other. He learned all that was in the forest, and learned the secrets of Guinée that the old maroons had saved for him, and he learned secrets which the *caciques* knew before the whitemen killed them all.

He learned herbs, and medicines, and poisons, especially those.

He gave poison to the maroons and gave it to herdsmen too, and field slaves, and house slaves finally, best of all. They killed animals in the fields with it, and of course they killed each other, and themselves sometimes. Macandal knew what we all do. Any death can hurt a whiteman somewhere. If it is only a slave or a cow, he is less rich. You make a man like Arnaud grow a little smaller if you kill only his dog. But soon the whitemen began to die in their own houses too. The slaves learned to find new poisons in the house, arsenic and lead. Then there were trials and torture and burnings but the poisoning did not stop. Macandal filled the city of Le Cap with it. Thousands of slaves were saving poison, waiting for that single day when they planned to use it once to destroy all the whitemen. Then the whitemen would be finished in this country and the city would belong to the maroons.

But there was love, if it was that. Macandal went to a *calenda* and they say he went to see a woman, that he would not have gone only to dance. Some say he had taken the woman off into the forest before and that it was a lover of hers, still on Dufresne plantation where the *calenda* was held, who saw him and told the *gérant* that he was there. They all say he was betrayed. The whitemen couldn't catch Macandal by themselves. But the *gérant* did come to know of it, somehow, and because no one had ever taken Macandal by force he used cunning. He had barrels of rum sent to the *calenda,* and then, when the dancers were all drunk and asleep, he tied up Macandal and took him that way.

So then he died again. Not easily or all at once. He broke the ropes and got away before they left Dufresne, but dogs ran him down before he could go far. They took him to a prison at Le Cap and that is where they burned him. Inside the fire he broke the chains that held him to the stake, but he did not walk out of the fire still in his body. The fire took his *corps-cadavre,* but he turned his *ti-bon-ange* into a mosquito and it flew away. The mosquito is still here somewhere. Many saw it. Achille says that he was there and saw it all, though he may be lying. But he says that he saw everything and that he shouted out when the others did, *Macandal is free.*

That must have been a fine *calenda* there at Dufresne, where Macandal was taken, or he would not have come, but I don't think even it could have been so big as the one we danced at Bois Cayman. At once I could see that the people must have come from plantations all over the northern plain and there were as many as at the market in Le Cap. Thousands—and that is only the number of the living.

A long way off still, we could hear the drumming. It was *rada* drumming we heard first, though both *rada* and *petro* drums were there. It was thick dark by the time we came near but we could feel more and more people moving around us in the jungle, and when we began to come into the clearing it seemed that there were even more people than trees. There were more and more people coming out of the jungle all the time so it looked like the trees were giving birth to men.

Boukman and his people had made a big *hûnfor* in the clearing. No altar sheds, but at the center of the peristyle they had topped a straight tree and left the peeled trunk standing for a *poteau mitan*. Damballah and Aida Wedo were wrapped in a painted spiral around it to the ground. There were forty young *hounsi*s all dressed in white, and a *mambo* whose name I never learned, though she was as big as two houses. I looked around and saw at the edge of the clearing the mapou tree which was Damballah's house. I knew Damballah must live there because a bowl of milk and egg had been put there for him to eat, nailed up in a crate so no one but Damballah could slither between the slats to eat his food.

Damballah had not raised his head or come out of where he lived in the tree, but in the peristyle the *hounsis* sang a song for him while they clapped their hands and rolled their hips with the drumming.

We come from Guinée
We have no father
We have no mother
Marassa Eyo!

Papa Damballah, show us
Show us Dahomey again . . .

I listened to the song of Damballah, standing there beside Jean-Pic and also with the new man, who had run away from Arnaud's plantation. Aiguy, we called him. It was what he called himself, though we didn't know if this had been his name when he was a slave in Arnaud's cane field. Some men who we knew from the town of Le Cap came to us then, and I told them the name of Aiguy.

When I looked at Aiguy then I still saw him as he had looked before, wearing the headstall and thrashing his head around like a wild cow crazed for water. The stall was gone now, and the only sign of it was a thick weal healing pink across the back of his neck, and some other hook-shaped slashes where the tin collar had cut him each time he hung the prongs up, running through the jungle. Aiguy began telling the men from Le Cap what had happened and what Riau had done. How he had lain with the headstall caught in lianas, waiting for the dogs, and how he heard us coming, Riau and Jean-Pic, and heard Jean-Pic tell Riau that he should kill him.

Aiguy believed that Riau would do what Jean-Pic had said, or else he would be left there for the dogs. He knew that there was no love between maroons and slaves, and that the maroons did not trust the slaves who ran away to them, thinking that they might be spies who would deliver them all to the whitemen again. But still, the maroons must have been slaves themselves sometime, except the ones who were born in the mountains. Anyway there was nowhere else for Aiguy to run, and he had seen that if he stayed on Arnaud's plantation he would surely die. Then he would rather die in the jungle, and he thought that he would rather be killed by Riau's cane knife than wait for the dogs to find him there. So when he heard the knife blade go humming up and then start whistling a little as it dropped he expected to return his *gros-bon-ange* to *les Mystères* . . .

When this story was done I asked of the men of Le Cap how many had come here to Bois Cayman from that place, and he told me there were very many. In the city too the word had passed from *hûngan* to *hûngan*, *hûnfor* to *hûnfor*, the same as in the mountains and all over the plain. There were maroon bands from everywhere in the island too, even a band from Bahoruco, over beyond the torches on the far side of the peristyle.

I stood on my toes and craned my neck to look for the Bahoruco maroons, who I had heard much about but never seen. People said that they had a big fortress in ancient caves the *caciques* had used, and where the gods of the *caciques* still lived. Somewhere they must have found a great power, the people said, because they had fought a war with the whitemen and won it, and made the whitemen give them their own country and write a paper that said that it was theirs. So I was looking hard to see these strong maroons, but before I could see them there was a stir in the crowd and someone came through handing out papers.

No one could read but still everyone was reaching for the papers and some were fighting over them. Except Riau, I, Riau didn't want a paper, not this night. But Aiguy got one and clutched it in his hand. It was a single sheet, but made to look like a page of a *journal*. No one knew till a long time later that these papers were false and that Toussaint had got them to be printed. Aiguy ran his eyes up and down it, sticking his lips out like a kiss. He was holding it sideways so the words dropped down in columns instead of running in rows like they should. He gave the paper to Riau then and all by itself my hand turned it right way up. The letters were rattling like chains linked together on the paper. They wanted to start speaking to Riau, but I threw the paper down. Jean-Pic picked it up and glared at me, because he knew.

Just the same the words began to talk. On the edge of the peristyle, a big Ibo field hand lifted a smaller mulatto onto his shoulders. The mulatto wore rich man's clothes and had a funny freckled face. Jean-Pic shifted beside me.

"I don't like to see him here," he said. "He has a white father."

Of course it was plain that he had a white father, like any *homme de couleur*, but what Jean-Pic meant was that he had a father who protected him and gave him property, and that probably he owned slaves. I was near enough to see his face well. Except for his pale skin and his funny spots he had the face of a man of Guinée, but the expression of a whiteman—cruelty, and the habit of power his whole life. But he opened his mouth and the paper spoke through him.

The paper said that the King In France had made a new law for the slaves here, we. The new law was that there would be no more whippings now. *Abolition du fouet*—there was shouting when the paper put these words in that mulatto's mouth. And the law said that the *colons* must give us three days free each week, Sunday and two others these three days *congé*, to rest or work for ourselves in our provision grounds. And for this the shouting was even louder than for what the paper had to say about the whip.

The whitemen would say that we were foolish to believe these things the paper said. Sometimes it happens to one of us too, the good blood of Guinée drains out, a man becomes old and pale to transparency and he can't know what to believe anymore at all. But it was easy to believe what the paper said then. The King In France had made laws for us before this time. There was the Code Noir, which said that our masters must feed us, and limited our work, and outlawed the worst punishments, but many of the *colons* did not obey this law. Lately there were new laws about the colored people, but the *colons* would not obey these either.

Also, some of the people then at Bois Cayman had been kings in their own country. It was not hard for them to believe that these whitemen would go against the right of a king. Some said that the whitemen had made the king a prisoner in France and that they sent him to work in French fields every day with his family. Some said that the King In France was a black man and came out of Dahomey like ourselves.

Boukman stood up. He did not need to sit on anyone's shoulders to be seen, he was head and shoulders above the rest, standing on the ground. He wore white trousers and a red sash with a sword in it. His head was big enough for two men and the lower part of his face hung over his bare chest like an open door. Before he spoke we all could feel his *esprit*. It was not one *loa* riding him that night, but all *les Morts et les Mystères*.

Boukman told then that the King In France would send his army over the sea to make the *colons* obey his law. But that we, the people of Guinée, must not wait for the king's army to cross the ocean. We would rise and claim the new law for ourselves.

Then Boukman looked at the *petro* drummers and they began to beat. The *la-place* began going backward around the *poteau mitan*, as if he would undo time and bring us home to Guinée where we came from. It was Jeannot who was dancing *la-place* that night, and as he moved backward the *hounsis* began to sing to Legba, as we must always do at the beginnings of things.

Papa Legba
Open the way for me
When I have passed
I will thank the loa
Papa Legba
Open the gate . . .

Then Legba came to ride Jeannot. I watched carefully because it is rare. Jeannot toppled back and the *hounsis* caught him and when he could stand again he was Legba, Legba grown old, crippled, walking on broken legs and his arms twisted in deformity, his whole self crushed down under the weight of the big *macoutte* he had to carry as far as the end of the world. The *hounsis* sang.

Attibon Legba, limping along
It's a long time since we have seen you
I will carry Legba's macoutte
Put his straw sack on my back . . .

Legba was coming toward where we were standing now, and in his face I saw Grand Bois D'Ilet, master of the Island Below Sea, where the *loa* live among *les Morts et les Mystères*. He was coming down, down into the mirror himself, already Legba could see his shadow rising there. A step ahead of me, Achille stiffened and dropped his gun as he was taken, but it was not Ghede this time. His ruined body straightened and became young and strong again for the *loa*, the muscle throbbed across his back as he lifted his arms in the shape of a cross, ridden by Maît'Carrefour.

Legba, Grand Bois, Legba—inside Jeannot's body Legba saluted Carrefour with his sly smile. These *loa* know each other well, because they both sit on the gate. Legba opens the way for the day *loa*, but the *loa* of night, who must sometimes work evil, all pass through the hand of Maît'Carrefour. So they cannot always agree, but tonight they smiled on each other like brothers, and danced with each other, hand in hand. I didn't see Ghede, not yet, but I knew he was there, below the bright surface of the mirror that turns your image back, his hand now holding Carrefour's other hand. The *hounsis* sang.

O Creole, sondé miroir, O Legba . . .

By my side Aiguy trembled as Baron Samedi mounted him. He stepped forward to join Legba and Carrefour, dancing around the edge of the peristyle. The high whine of *petro* drumming shrilled inside Riau's head. *Yo di,* the mirror breaks through rock. The ocean is mirror, mirror is ocean, by day we see ourselves in it, but when it turns transparent then we see through into the Island Below Sea which is the world of death, where *les Morts et les Mystères* reach up into our world, climbing Grand Bois's tree from the dark side of the mirror. They were shooting up the *poteau mitan* now, as fast as the *vévés* written in gunpowder could burn. Now I saw Ghede dancing everywhere in the peristyle, one, two, many Ghedes. The drum scratched at the inside of Riau's head, Ogûn wanting his body to dance, wanted his *ti-bon-ange* to make way for Ogûn. But I wanted my own head for thinking with, and so I stepped away, moving somewhere I could not hear the drums so well.

But the forest itself was crowded with *esprit.* I walked in the shadows just outside the tree line, feeling it. I was farther away but still I was circling the *poteau mitan.* There were so many to be drawn up from the Island Below Sea. I knew that our living people outnumbered the whitemen ten to one. The whitemen knew it too and were afraid—this was the fear that drove the whip. But what the whitemen never knew was that every one of us they killed was with us still. And by this time they had killed so many, a hundred to our one. A dead white person disappears but our dead never leave us, they are here among *les Invisibles.* They were coming now, all *les Invisibles,* through the mirror from below the waters, and every tree in Bois Cayman became a *poteau mitan* for their arrival.

Walking around the edge of the clearing I came to Damballah's tree and there I stopped and squatted down. Damballah came out of the hole in his tree. No one was watching him, only me. He crawled between the bars of the crate and put his head in the bowl to eat his food. His split tongue flicked in and out of the egg and milk, trying it before he drank. His scales were dark and glossy on his back and his small round eye shone when it looked at me. I raised my head then and I saw Toussaint, squatting down on the other side of the crate. I don't know when he had come there. Jean-François and Biassou were sitting a few yards in back of him, talking together in low voices. I couldn't hear what they said.

Later, a long time afterward, people said different things about what Toussaint was doing that night. Some say he led the ceremony himself and cut the black sow's throat with his own hand. Some say he never went to Bois Cayman at all. I know that he was there. Who knows what is true? Maybe he was there, or not there, but I know that I saw him, if few others did. All the time they were feeding the *loa* he and I sat talking quietly beneath Damballah's tree.

"*Parrain,*" I said. I was the first to speak.

Toussaint nodded. I could see his face plain in the torchlight from the peristyle. His mouth was pursed slightly like he was whistling and his eyes looked cheerful, torchlight flashing in them. Like always he wore the bandanna tied around his head and he wore the green coat with the old bloodstains. He looked like he had been squatting there for a year, but I was surprised to see him there at all, because I thought that he served jesus, who had made him swear against serving the *loa*.

"*Ehé, Riau, sa ki pasé?*" he said. "What are you thinking?"

"I was thinking about Macandal," I said. When I said this, I knew where my thought had gone. Macandal was with us now, he had come up the *poteau mitan* at the head of *les Invisibles*. And with Macandal leading, the whitemen must all die. They were singing it now within the peristyle.

Eh, eh, Bomba
Canga, bafio té!
Canga, moune de lé!
Canga, do ki la
Canga, li!

The *mambo* stood up, all stained with blood from the sacrifice. Boukman was mixing blood with gunpowder and *clairin* to feed the *loa,* and most of the people were pressing forward to get some, whether the *loa* had mounted them or not. Jeannot raised his cup above his head and screamed into the sky before he drank, but I, Riau, I did not taste the blood that night.

Toussaint was looking at me as he would do when I was small, when I had understood something and he was trying not to show his pleasure. Then he turned his head to watch what was happening in the peristyle. In the torchlight I could just see the tips of his teeth. A big mosquito landed on his broad flat cheek and fastened itself to feed.

"You know what happened to Macandal," he said. "The whitemen burned him to death in a fire. And it was one of our own people who gave him up to the whites."

"Do you think Macandal is like Jesus?" I said. "You are wrong."

Now Toussaint smiled a little, openly. He felt the mosquito, finally, and flicked his finger at it. He didn't kill it though. Maybe he didn't mean to kill it. The mosquito lifted, whining high above his head, and vanished in the dark.

"I know what happened to Macandal," I said. "Macandal turned himself into a mosquito, *yo di*. Who knows? Maybe this is the mosquito who has bitten you."

July 1802

From the deck of Le *Héros,* Placide surveyed the harbor of Brest. The dawn was windy and warm, a pleasant July day in store. Later it might grow hot, but nothing to match the stifling heat of a tropical summer. In spite of himself, Placide was refreshed by French weather, French summers at least. He'd grown accustomed to them during the years he'd spent here as a student, or as he now more bitterly conceived it, as a hostage. Though the winters were hard, indeed, and made him wish for Saint Domingue. They had embarked in winter, scarcely six months before, and from this port. Even then Placide had not believed the blandishments of the First Consul, yet his heart had been sweetened by the thought of home.

He watched a sailor now, or maybe he was some sort of longshoreman, unfastening the mooring of a longboat from a stanchion on the quay. He was whiskered and wore a striped shirt and on his head an old liberty cap, conical with the odd forward roll of its peak. Or once it had been that. They had made the old King Louis wear such a cap before they killed him, and wearing it, he drank a toast to *liberté, egalité, fraternité.* Placide had seen an engraving in a newspaper, the *bonnet rouge* shoved down over the king's powdered wig. The king looked bilious, sickly, holding his wine cup at an insecure angle as if he would spill it. From his lips scrolled the phrase *Vive La Nation,* upside down and curling sideways, like a thread of smoke.

The sailor let the stern rope slither down into the boat, which rocked and drifted out from the posts of the dock. The cap he wore was ancient, grubby, faded to a scabrous brown, though once it had surely been red as a poppy. The tricolor cockade had been cut away and someone had flattened the peak and tacked it down backward with a few stitches, further to disguise its original shape. The sailor left the bowline doubled around the stanchion while he scrambled down, then pulled it free and coiled it neatly under a bench seat before he sat down and engaged the oars. A spiral of silver twirled out from the starboard blade as he brought the bow of the boat around toward the harbor. Placide watched as he settled to a longer, even stroke; the boat was too heavy for him to move it very quickly. Somehow he doubted that revolution had much bettered this sailor's lot.

The harbor was full of warships; the sailor was rowing in the direction of one of these. Pennants snapped briskly from their rigging in the freshening morning breeze. All around the talk was of war renewed with England. Perhaps with all Europe, once again. No one would tell them anything directly, but the rumors were in the air. It had been the same when the fleet sailed out from Brest with the army of Captain-General Leclerc: official silence through which the rumors breathed of Napoleon's real intent.

The ship's officer Chabron drifted up to his elbow, and when Placide did not immediately recognize his presence, Chabron plucked at the sleeve of his plain brown coat. Placide hesitated, looking over the water. The sun had just cleared the roofs of the town and that sailor's longboat was burned away in the reflective blaze.

"*Venez, monsieur,*" Chabron said. "He's ready for you."

Placide nodded and followed Chabron below decks. All during the voyage they had kept Toussaint sequestered from his family and even from his body servant, Mars Plaisir, but in the fortnight they'd been docked at Brest, Placide had been permitted to serve as his secretary. Chabron unlocked the cabin door and stood aside, his face averted, for Placide to enter. Placide could hear the key grinding in the lock behind him, once the door had closed; he heard no footsteps moving away.

The cabin was close, almost airless, with a ripening odor whose source was hard to fix. During the voyage Toussaint had been allowed a weekly bath but he still had no clothing but what he'd been arrested in. Placide could hear rats scrambling between the cabin wall and the ship's hull. Toussaint sat calmly at the table, eyes shaded by one hand. A whale-oil lamp was the illumination. Because there was no daylight, this always seemed a timeless place.

The quill and ink pot sat on the table, by a stack of vellum which the Bible weighted down. Placide knew that Toussaint would have made no notes, that he would have spent some part of the night and the earliest hours of the morning composing in his mind the things he meant to say. He sat down. Toussaint, reaching to move the Bible from the sheets of paper, brushed his hand as if by chance.

"*Bôjou, Placide.*"

"*Bôjou, m'pé.*"

They sat side by side, for Toussaint liked to read over his work as he progressed. But he would not begin at once.

"*Ta mére?*" Toussaint asked him. "*Tes fréres?*" The same questions each morning of the fortnight. "*Tout va bien?*"

"*Oui, ça va,*" Placide said, and when Toussaint inquired of his niece and daughter-in-law, Louise and Victoire, Placide replied that their health was also good. With his thumb he turned up the cap of the inkwell on its hinge, and then sat back.

"There's talk of war with England," he said, and then added quickly in Creole, "I wish it had come sooner."

"That would be a treasonable thought," Toussaint said stiffly, and in good French. "You know that I have always been loyal to France."

What Placide knew was that Chabron or someone else must certainly be listening at the door, but again he thought he knew that dissimulation was pointless now; appearances no longer mattered. Irritably he fidgeted with the inkwell, flipping the cover open and shut.

"If there had been war with England," Toussaint said precisely, "the Captain-General's fleet would not have sailed, perhaps, and then I would have missed the sight of you, my child."

Placide jerked his head toward the porthole, but it had been nailed shut. So fearful they were of Toussaint's escape, they'd kept it boarded over even in the middle of the ocean.

"Come," Toussaint said. "It's time that we begin."

Placide drew a sheet of paper toward him from the stack, picked up the pen and dipped it. Toussaint composed himself, drawing his hands back from the table and folding them in his lap.

"Citoyen Premier Consul," he began. Placide wrote down the phrase, waited a moment, then wrote the date above it. *22 juin 1802*. Toussaint tilted his head to look at his writing and gave an affirmative nod. He cleared his throat and spoke again, repeating the salutation.

*"Citoyen Premier Consul, je ne vous dissimulerai pas mes fautes, j'en ai fait quelques unes. Quel homme en est exempt? Je suis prête à les avouer. Après la parole d'honneur du capitaine generale qui represente le gouvernement, après une proclamation promulgué à la face de la colonie, dans laquelle il promettait de jeter le voile de l'oubli sur les évènements qui ont eu lieu à Sainte Domingue, comme vous avez fait le 18 brumaire, je me suis retirê au sein de ma famille . . ."**

At other times Toussaint might grope, fumble for a word, torture his amanuensis for alternative expressions. Sometimes he would have several secretaries compose versions of the same letter before settling on a final result. But Placide thought that he must have worked out this phrasing completely and probably memorized it the night before.

"À peine un mois s'est ecoulé que des malveillants, à force d'intrigues, ont su me perdre dans l'ésprit du general en chef en lui inspirant de la méfiance contre moi. J'ai reçu une lettre de lui qui m'ordonnait de me concerte avec le general Brunet: j'ai obei . . ."†

He spoke in a high clear voice, as if he were giving a speech, and loud enough to carry well beyond the door. His only pauses were oratorical, for effect, but they did give Placide time to write. He felt as it were two invisible threads competing to control his quill. One ran to the hand of the Abbé Coisnon, the preceptor who'd had charge of Isaac and Placide here in France, who'd taught Placide the fair hand and the proper spelling he now used, which Toussaint's sidelong glance approved.

* Citizen First Consul: I will not conceal my errors from you; I have committed some. What man has not? I am prepared to admit them. After the word of honor of the captain-general, who represents the government, after a proclamation made all over the colony, in which he promised to cast the veil of oblivion over the events which had taken place in Saint Domingue, I retired into the bosom of my family . . .

† Hardly a month had gone by before some ill-wishers, involved in intrigues, discovered how to destroy me in the eyes of the general in chief by inspiring his mistrust against me. I received a letter from him which ordered me to meet with General Brunet: I obeyed . . .

*"Je me rendis, accompagné de deux personnes, aux Gonaives ou l'on m'arrêta. L'on me conduisit à bord de la frégate La Creole, j'ignore pour quel motif, sans autres vêtements que ceux que j'avais sur moi. Le lendemain ma maison fut en proie au pillage; mon épouse et mes enfants arrêtés: ils n'ont rien, pas même de quoi se vêtir . . ."**

The other filament, meanwhile, was strung more tautly over the years, stretched to transparency before it reached the plank cabin at Bréda where Toussaint had first taught him how to make the letters. Placide half wanted now to see his father's own crabbed hand and broken orthography scrambling over the page beneath his pen; it would seem somehow more just. But he continued to write in the clean correct fashion which the Abbé Coisnon had drilled into him.

"A new paragraph," Toussaint said. *"Citoyen Premier Consul, une mère de famille, à cinquante-trois ans, peut mériter indulgence . . ."*

The pen had dulled. Placide shifted in his seat and automatically felt his pockets but there was nothing there. He clicked his tongue irritably and got up, quill in hand, and crossed the cabin to rap sharply on the inside of the door. The pause that followed was forced; Placide knew that Chabron must be standing just outside the door, counting off one, two minutes, to make it appear that he was coming from a distance. When he opened the door at last, Placide passed the quill to him wordlessly. Chabron would not meet his eyes. He knew the officer found this procedure shameful, gave him credit for that much. They would not let Toussaint come near a penknife, though it could not be that they feared his suicide, which would have gladdened them indeed, but that with so slight a weapon he might seize control of the ship.

Chabron sharpened the quill with his own knife, eyes fixed to the work as though it required his utmost concentration, and passed it back to Placide when he was done. Toussaint was waiting, the words began to flow from him as soon as Placide had resumed his seat.

"Citoyen Premier Consul, une mère de famille, a 53 ans, peut mériter l'indulgence et la bienveillance d'une nation genereuse et liberale; elle n'a

* I presented myself, accompanied by two people, at Gonaives, where they arrested me. They took me on board the frigate *La Creole*, for what reason I know not, with no other clothes than what I had on. The next day my house was prey to a looting, my wife and my children arrested: they had nothing, not even anything to wear . . .

*aucun compte à rendre, moi seul dois être responsable de mon conduite aupres de mon gouvernement. J'ai une trop haute idée de la grandeur et de la justice du premier magistrat du peuple français, pour douter un moment de son impartialité. J'aime à croire que la balance, dans sa main, ne penchera pas plus d'un coté que de l'autre. Je réclame sa genererosite."**

Toussaint reached to take the sheet from under Placide's hand and held it near the lamp, reading it over while the last line dried. He took the pen and signed it. Placide blotted the signature, blew on it and watched the ink darken. There was no sealing wax so he simply folded the sheet in three and passed it out the door.

Two days later the news came that Toussaint was to be stripped of all his property, by the order of the First Consul. Henceforth he would truly own nothing but the clothes he had on. Placide was with him when the notification was delivered. Seldom had he seen his father really shaken, perhaps never. The spectacle frightened him, and Toussaint's voice was not entirely steady.

"But I had no answer to my letter . . ." he began uncertainly.

"You have your answer there," Placide snapped. His own fear made him cruel.

Then Toussaint disappeared behind his face. Placide had seen it often, during the campaign against Leclerc, most especially in those months Toussaint had spent at Ennery, "retired into the bosom of his family." He thought he remembered it from his early childhood also, but was not so sure. That spark which was himself would sink away behind his features—you must know him well to know that it had not been extinguished altogether. In front of him he'd leave his face as hieratic and inscrutable as a carved wooden mask that some old African dancer might have worn. That was the aspect which made men smile and call him *old Toussaint*, and shake their heads in admiration of his cunning. What they meant was that Toussaint was old as Legba.

Placide dropped onto his knees and kissed his father's hand. He closed his eyes and laid his cheek against the fraying shiny seam of

* Citizen First Consul, the mother of a family, at 53 years of age, could merit the indulgence and goodwill of a generous and liberal government; she has no account to make, I alone must be responsible for my conduct before my government. I have too high an opinion of the grandeur and justice of the first magistrate of the French people to suspect his impartiality for one instant. I like to believe that the scale, in his hand, will not tilt more to one side than the other. I claim his generosity.

the old uniform trousers. After a little while Toussaint's free hand lowered gently onto his head as if to give a blessing.

It was left to Placide to break the news to his brothers and the women. Of all the group only Justine, the *femme de confiance*, wept openly, while Mars Plaisir groaned and wrung his elongated hands. It frightened them more deeply, Placide thought, to see their protector's strength undone. Suzanne took the hands of Victoire and Louise and bowed her head to say the Lord's Prayer, half in a whisper. Placide did not pray with her; he kept his head up, but the words still calmed him somewhat, each an old touchstone. After the Amen, his mother raised her eyes.

"I never cared for the good things we had," she said. "But what will become of us now?"

"I fear we may be separated," Placide said.

He was thinking that he himself would likely be distinguished from his brother Isaac, since he had chosen to join the rebels while Isaac had remained with the French. In the back of his mind was an idea that did not quite qualify as hope, that after all he might stay with his father, for that reason, still. But that afternoon Toussaint was taken off the ship to a cell in the château of Brest, while Placide remained in his quarters on board.

ON THE OTHER SIDE OF THE WORLD Captain-General Leclerc took up his pen to report on his mission from his brother-in-law Napoleon: to subdue the blacks of Saint Domingue and to restore slavery there. Again, and again, he wrote to the Minister of Marine Decrès: *"Vous ne sauriez tenir Toussaint à une trop grande distance de la mer et le mettre dans une position très sure. Cet homme avait fanatisé le pays à un tel point que sa presence le mettrait encore en combustion . . ."** A similar letter, more measured in tone but of the same general drift, had been delivered by Le *Héros* itself. All the way over the ocean it had smoldered in the captain's cabin like a bomb on a slow fuse, burning word by word to its conclusion:

"Il faut, Citoyen Ministre, que le Gouvernement le fasse mettre dans une place forte située dans le milieu de la France, afin que jamais il ne puisse

* There is no distance too great for you to hold Toussaint from the sea, no place too secure for you to put him. That man has fanatisized this country to such a point that his presence could blow it up again . . .

*avoir aucun moyen de s'echapper et de revenir à Saint Domingue ou il a toute l'influence d'un chef de secte. Si, dans trois ans, cet homme reparaissait a Sainte Domingue peut-être detruirait-il tout ce que la France y aurait fait . . ."**

Still Leclerc could not leave his theme. He wrote constantly, constantly begged for more men, more money to pay them, again more men. He was transfixed by his belief that if Toussaint were able to so much as wet his boot toe in the water of any French port, he would be magically translated back to Saint Domingue to spread fire and ruin and destruction. Leclerc's wife of course was unfaithful to him, so were his troops disloyal—most of the surviving men had belonged to Toussaint's black regiments. He was sick and feverish, mere months away from his own death. In a shaky hand he wrote Decrès: *"Ce n'est pas tout d'avoir enlevé Toussaint; il y a ici 2000 chefs à faire enlever . . ."*† Each night in his febrile sleep he dreamed that Toussaint had never really left the island.

NEXT DAY IN BREST THE WEATHER TURNED, the sky shelved over gray as slate, and spat cold rain. An unfamiliar army captain presented himself in Placide's cabin, not troubling to give his name.

"You are ordered to remove and surrender the uniform of the French army," he announced. "Being divested of your rank you are no longer entitled to wear it."

Placide pointed out that in fact he was already in civilian attire. The captain nodded, quite as if he had expected this reply.

"You don't wear the French uniform because you know you have disgraced it," he suggested. "Because you are a traitor to France."

"I am as much a traitor to France as my father was," Placide said. "No more and no less."

"Then you must be a very great one," the captain said. "But the slave Toussaint cannot be your father." He jerked his jaw at Placide's reddish Arada skin. "Anyone can see that you are a mu-

* It is necessary, Citizen Minister, that the government should have him put in a strong place in the middle of France, so that he can never have any way to escape and come back to Saint Domingue, where he has all the influence of the chief of a sect. If in three years this man reappeared in Saint Domingue he might destroy everything which France has accomplished there . . .

† It's not everything to have removed Toussaint; there are 2000 chiefs here to have taken away . . .

latto half-breed, neither white nor black. Some white man got you on the nigger whore, your mother."

The captain's tone was rote, however. The insults were not heartfelt, but formal and obligatory; Placide understood that he must say these things in order to divorce himself as much as possible from his own actions. For himself it was a formal occasion too. No matter what age he might survive to, his life was ending here and now.

"In heaven my father is God," Placide said. "And everything you do, God sees. On earth, my father is Toussaint-Louverture."

On deck, two dragoons were waiting. They fell in step on either side of Placide as he drew abreast of them, but he walked between them in such a fashion as to abolish their existence. The cold drizzle wet his hair, ran in his eyes, but he was unaware of it, recalling how Toussaint had looked, coming into Le Cap to make his submission to Leclerc, how people had said his entrance into the city was more like a triumphal procession. He crossed the deck toward the gangway, walking as if he owned the ship, as if the world were his, walking the way Toussaint had taught him, like a free man.

Part II

LEUR CAFÉ AU CARAMEL

August–November 1791

We got thunder
(thunder . . .)
Lightning
(lightning)
Brimstone
And fire
(fire, fire, fire . . .)
. . . wipe them out of Creation . . .

—Bob Marley

Chapter Nine

HER LOVER HAD GIVEN HER A NEW MIRROR, a smaller one, half-length with a prettily painted frame. Nanon hung it on the wall directly opposite the long pier glass she already had. She had illuminated many candles in the room and along the axis of the paired mirrors their flames repeated down an endless corridor of illusion till they blurred to one.

She had bathed as slowly as she liked and dressed herself in comfortable luxury, dotted certain areas of her skin with perfumed oils. She was robed *à la chinois,* her hair let down across her back. She was waiting for Antoine Hébert, with a restlessness no more acute than pleasure. At moments she walked up and down the room, her hem and the points of her Chinese sleeves stroking the floor with her movement. In the matched glasses, her image multiplied. A bowl of fruit sat on the table; she cut a piece and touched it with the point of her tongue.

Beside the fruit bowl there were chessmen; the doctor had been trying, with poor success, to teach her how to play the game. From its wicker cage the little monkey surveyed her lost position. Nanon took it out and gave it fruit. The monkey sprang to the table and overset most of the chess pieces, while she pressed her fingers to her wide red underlip and tittered. The little beast was tamer now, and came easily enough to her coaxing, to the offer of a bit of banana she held out. It clutched her finger with its hind paws and balanced as a bird would on a perch. She stroked the tufts of whisker on its face and put it in the cage again, then rearranged the chessmen in the manner which best pleased her eye.

She sat in the deepest chair with her arms folded and her eyes three-quarters shut. As a sort of exercise she drowned her mind, letting it sink into her senses as if into a swamp. Beneath her palms, behind her navel, a warm bright light unfolded, stretching its sparkling tendrils to the limits of her body and beyond. She knew this electric energy could draw the man to her from across the town or even from across the sea. When the knock came she rose to answer with her eyes still mostly shut, a magnetism sweeping her to the door with her silks trailing a liquid murmur behind.

"I see you are disappointed," Choufleur said, after a noticeable pause. She blinked, slowly as if her lashes were hung with lead. When Choufleur raised his foot across the threshold she took a lengthy backward step.

"*Pas du tout*," she said, and turned her back. Choufleur entered the room. He shrugged back his shoulders, switching his coattails behind him, and put his thumbs in the waistband of his trousers, near his hips. It was the planter's pose, surveying the terrain, *au grand seigneur*. She saw his image in one mirror but it was not repeated in the other, so that it seemed to her that he must be a ghost, or *zombi*, though she knew the illusion was only because of the angles at which they were standing.

For a moment more they hung balanced and entranced, then Choufleur walked to the chessboard, picked up a knight and scrutinized it, staring into the red chips of glass that were its eyes. Replacing it, he saw the nonsensical arrangement of the other pieces and chuckled to himself. His eyes rose toward her with a canny, yellow look.

"A new pastime," he said. "*Ton petit ami*?"

"*Oui . . .*" she said, letting the word trail away as she made an enervated turn in his direction. The brown cloud of freckles twisted starrily on his face; beneath, his pallor told his tension. She had known him many years, since they were children, but after his time in Paris, he had changed.

His hand entered the fruit bowl, tested a papaya for ripeness. A knife lay on a plate beside it, and he picked this up and cut a slice and took a bite. He cut a lemon and squeezed a drop of juice onto another slice of papaya and offered it to Nanon. She shook her head.

"He amuses you then, the little doctor?" he said. "With his chess and his ideas . . . and in other ways, doubtless."

"Yes . . ." she said again, trailing the word. "*Comme ci, comme ça . . .*"

Choufleur flicked his fingernail against the slat of the monkey's cage. Within, the monkey hissed and showed its teeth.

"*Je vois bien,*" he said, "whoever you are expecting is not the guest who has arrived."

She didn't answer him. He dangled the pause for a moment before he went on.

"No matter. It's another of your special friends who interests me more. That gentleman of distinction, the Sieur Maltrot."

"It's been some time," she said, then with less languor called, "I don't like him anymore. If I ever liked him . . ."

"Of course that makes no difference." His lip curled in a smile quite like that of the Sieur Maltrot. "So long as he likes you." His smile vanished. "He'll come," he said. "I know him." He took a clear glass vial from his waistcoat pocket.

"If you dislike him you may find relief here." The vial was shaped like an alchemical retort, but with the bulb and neck both flattened so as to better fit a pocket. He unstopped it and shook a little of the liquid onto another papaya slice.

"What is it," she asked him.

"Tincture of arsenic." Choufleur made as if to give the poisoned slice to the monkey, whose hairy arm reached out of the cage to snatch . . . Nanon stepped near him and slapped his wrist; the bit of fruit flipped onto the floor. Choufleur clutched his wrist and made a little *moue* as if he had been really injured.

"I didn't know the animal was so dear to you."

"Why?" she said. "Why arsenic?"

Choufleur dropped his arm and smiled sidewise at the floor. "A white man's poison for a white man, it seems suitable, does it not? Besides it's hard to know if the *hûngans* give you what you really want."

"I won't do it," Nanon said.

"It can be given slowly," Choufleur said. "The Italian way. A man takes months or years to die; it looks like illness." He shook his head. "But here they always suspect poison when anyone is sick. You must give it to him all at once. There's not much time."

"I won't," Nanon said.

"Do you really believe that you *know* what you'll do?" He stepped to her, put the vial in her hands and folded her limp fingers around it. When he released her, she still held the vial. He slipped his fingers under her hair to the hollow at her skull's base and pressed the points in, not hard enough for pain but enough so that she felt his strength. By old habit she let her bones dissolve, her head roll back into his hand's support. In her mind's eye she saw him scrambling barefoot over the rocks near Vallière where they'd been children, quick and nimble as a long-legged spider, tenacious and ruthless as the maroons he pursued in the *maréchaussée*. She noticed that he had been chewing cinnamon stick to sweeten his breath.

He put his other hand at the small of her back, flattening his palm down over her buttocks' first rise under the Chinese silk, and drawing her not quite near enough to touch. She unbalanced, giving her weight up to him as a swimmer gives it up to water. From behind the screen of freckles his green eyes regarded her like animal eyes peering out of a thicket.

"One day there'll be no one left but you and I," he said. "And that soon." He let her go so suddenly she staggered. Without another word, he walked out the door.

She put her hand over her breast and held it there until her breathing slowed. At the length of her other arm the poison vial still dangled. She went into the bedroom, thought for a moment and hid it in a secret pocket of a dress she'd ceased to wear. All the fruit that he had touched she threw out into the yard behind the houses, except the poisoned slice, which she feared someone might scavenge. Not knowing a better way to dispose of it, she used the side of her foot to push it under the fringe of a drape that covered a small table.

In the mirrors the candle flames trembled, then pricked up like hot little tongues. It troubled her that the doctor was so late, but certainly it was better that he and Choufleur should not intersect. With a small effort she was able to reenter the mood that she'd been in before.

AT THE CLOSE OF MONSIEUR PANON'S PRESENTATION, *le Cercle des Philadelphes* rose from the seats and realigned itself in new geometries. Bottles of brandy were handed round, poured into crystal balloons as light as soap bubbles. Doctor Hébert tasted his spirit, then passed the snifter under the nose of Captain Maillart, who had the ability to sleep while sitting upright with eyes convincingly half open. The captain shook himself, looked cautiously around, and sighed with relief when he saw the lecture had concluded. With a slightly suppressed moan he rose and moved in the direction of the nearest unattended bottle.

The doctor orbited the circle of his acquaintance. He greeted Monsieur Arthaud, *médecin du roi.* All the legitimate doctors of the town were members of the recently chartered *Societé Royale des Sciences et Arts,* and some of the surgeons too, though of course not every sawbones or apothecary. Doctor Hébert paid his respects to the captain's cousin, de Maillart, to whom he owed his own inclusion in the group. There were present a couple of traveling priests who were housed in *la maison de la préfecture* next door, and he exchanged a word or two with them. As the clerics disengaged themselves he was confronted with the smiling, sweating countenance of Monsieur Panon. He hesitated, bowed, and turned away without a word.

By the reflection of a pane on one of the specimen cabinets lining the walls, he saw that Panon seemed to take no offense, but immediately engaged the itinerant priests in conversation. Within the cabinet were arranged on shelves several stuffed birds and lizards, also the mummified head of an Indian, one of the Arawaks who had once populated the island, before the Spanish completely extinguished their race. It was the project of several members of the Royal Society to extend the classifications of Linnaeus to the flora and fauna of this place.

The doctor had been struck by the ambition of the society, its accomplishments too; at a glance it hardly seemed to be burdened with any colonial backwardness. The experimental laboratory was quite up to date and the group had instituted a botanical garden. With interest and pleasure the doctor had studied Monsieur Arthaud's *déscription médico-topographique du Cap.* He had heard a discourse on *les Épizooties de la Colonie,* and another only slightly more fanciful called "The Crocodile and Natural Law." Monsieur Panon had headed tonight's lecture with a similar splicing of the abstract and the particular: *"Le Nègre et la Bienfaisance."*

You could not doubt the man's sincerity; he even seemed to be full of goodwill. In the glass pane, the doctor watched him expatiate to the two priests, who might very well concur with him that the blacks had been specially supplied by God's Providence to serve as laborers in these colonies. The Negro was neither ape nor man, but Panon would classify him, according to the Linnaean system, somewhere between these two. Much the same as a mule, the Negro was providentially designed for the bearing of burdens. Within the best of all possible worlds, *la bienfaisance* had arranged the constitution of the Negro so that he (like the mule again) could best be retained in the path of virtue by beating and whipping. Not to mention, the doctor added privately, by crucifixion, roasting in ovens, crushing in cane mills and the like; these also must be requisite for the Negro's fulfillment of the highest potential of his nature.

He had not made any such statement aloud, however. Every proposition of Monsieur Panon had been received by the group with perfect equanimity; no member of *le Cercle des Philadelphes* had challenged him in any serious way. Well, the doctor thought, from the vantage of current philosophy perhaps the Society was somewhat behind the times. In Europe the whole notion of *bienfaisance* had seemed drastically outmoded since the Seven Years War.

He drank some brandy and rolled the remainder around the bell-shaped glass. Perhaps the fumes would smoke his most uncomfortable ideas from his mind. He toasted the desiccated Indian's head behind the cabinet's pane. The eyelids were sewn shut with a black cord but the lips shrank away from the ragged row of teeth in a strange knowing smile . . . He heard the captain's boot heels muted on the rug behind him.

"I believe the time has come," Captain Maillart said.

"*Sans doute.*" The doctor flipped open the case of his watch, then repocketed it. He was as eager as his companion to be gone; if politeness had allowed it he would have abandoned the captain among *les Philadelphes* so he could hasten alone to Nanon. The next morning he intended to make the trip to Ennery, begin trying to attend to Thibodet's plantation. His inquiries about Xavier Tocquet had all been virtually fruitless; the doctor had come to think that most who knew him were a little afraid of the man. As for Elise, it was almost as if she had never existed in this place.

The two emerged into the Rue Vaudreuil, from under the Society's coat of arms, a beehive with the motto *Sub Sole Labor*. They walked for a while without speaking, before the captain began to rub his hands together.

"Well now," he said. "There's still life left in the evening."

Inwardly the doctor quailed to see his friend reviving. He particularly wanted to escape the captain before going to Nanon's rooms for this last night. But for every meeting of the Society he was persuaded to attend, Maillart wished to convey the doctor to some session of drinking, gambling and whoring among other officers or young blades of the town. The doctor had no head for cards and his taste for women was for the time being more than adequately gratified. On the other hand, his attraction to the pleasure of drunkenness was so great that he had become chary of indulging it too often. Still, he knew that if Captain Maillart guessed where he was going, he would be difficult to detach.

Their boots thumped a rhythm on the hard-packed earth of the street. It occurred to the doctor that he might *bore* Captain Maillart into surrendering his project for the night.

"Have you considered," he began, "that all provisions of *la bienfaisance* must be reciprocal?"

Captain Maillart groaned.

"So that," the doctor continued, "if the Negro must needs be beaten, the master must have his equivalent need to beat someone. In a world of ideal arrangements, does it not seem a curious requirement?"

"I had *thought,*" the captain said, "that love itself might cure your obsession with philosophy."

Forgetting that he had only intended to mount a diversion, the doctor stopped short and caught the captain's sleeve. "Listen," he said. "If you think of love, then think of this." He was a head shorter than Maillart, who had to look down to meet his eyes. In his head rang a phrase of Monsieur Panon's: *Je n'assimile le nègre ni au singe, ni à l'homme Européen . . .*

"If a man should copulate with a sheep or a duck," the doctor said, "their union will be barren. So for all creatures—there is only fertility within their kind."

"Yes, of course," Maillart said, his eyes glazing over.

"Then if a white man and a black woman come together," the doctor said, "what will you call their offspring? Is it something else or is it human?"

Restlessly the captain cleared his throat. "You didn't ask that at the meeting?"

"If I had asked it," the doctor said, dropping his eyes, "I believe the commotion would have awakened even you, my friend."

Maillart nodded. "I see I mustn't keep you," he said. "It's late and tomorrow you will have a long ride. Will I walk you to your lodgings?"

"No," the doctor said. "I won't take you so far out of your way."

The captain took his hand. "Have a care, Antoine," he said. "The road is uncertain, but no more than these streets. You can't be frank with everyone you speak to."

"I understand you," the doctor said. He pressed the captain's hand and let him go. But at the end of the block Maillart turned again and shouted cheerfully, "*À la rencontre, Antoine!*" At that, the doctor smiled as he went on his way.

In Nanon's rooms the candles had burned low, grown fringes of lacy wax on their leeward sides. She rose a little sleepily to let him in. "They kept you long," she said, in tones of sympathy for his inconvenience. She gave him wine and as he sipped she stood behind his chair, kneading his neck and shoulders with her slim strong fingers. Leaning back, he rested his head against her, feeling the warmth of her skin on his bald spot, through the silk. The robe opened to him and he put his hand inside, then followed with his lips and tongue.

Often she would lead him as an expert dancer leads without appearing to, creating subtle vacancies which suggest a step. So she'd encouraged tastes in him which now seemed to be his own, although before he'd never been aware of them. Tonight the hunger seemed more hers. She sucked his tongue half out of his head, wrapped herself around him like an anaconda. His conscience, consciousness, swirled out of him into the vortex. He passed out. Deep in the night she roused him again with a wild voracity. In the velvet dark he could not see her at all and she was silent as a succubus. The choral voice of the insects gave the music to their movement. Again he dropped out of his mind into a trancelike sleep.

Near dawn they woke as if by mutual inspiration and coupled a third time.

Afterward she slept or seemed to, but the doctor could not, though he was drained and hollow as a gnawed-out melon rind. Hands behind his head on the pillow, he watched the rapid spread of light through the latticed windows onto the walls. In its cage the monkey turned and grumbled. He got up, staggering with a sudden dizziness, and fed it fruit from the bowl. Having washed himself carefully he took the pitcher to replenish it from the courtyard well, a parting courtesy. He would not wake her before he left. She lay on her back with the rug tight against the bottom of her chin, so perfectly still that an impulse led him to pass a finger under her nostrils to ensure that she still breathed. In this gentle sleep she looked childlike and unknowing. A whisper of an exhalation crossed his knuckle and he withdrew his hand. Already he could feel the suction that attached him to her tearing, as if he were already mounted and riding from the town. After all, it would be a relief in many ways to be free to inhabit himself completely once again.

NANON SLEPT TILL AFTERNOON, then rose and bathed and dressed herself most opulently, although she did not intend to go out. A pastime, she had no other plans. A miniature Swiss clock ticked from her curio cabinet across the still room from her seat. Out from under the draped table, a scaly tail protruded, rigidly. Investigating, she discovered a large brown wharf rat, which must have eaten all of the poisoned fruit, as it was nowhere to be seen.

She threw the carcass out the back door, then walked to the well to wash her fingers. The sun was glowering down on the top of her head, and the air was still and humid. She walked gingerly back toward the house, saddle sore (as it were) from riding the doctor so hard all through the night. When she reentered she found the Sieur Maltrot standing on the carpet in the middle of her front room.

"I thought perhaps you were out," he said, twirling his sword stick between his thumbs. "Though the door was open, as you see."

Nanon curtsied, well across the room from him, trying to recall if he would still have a key to her front door, thinking it likely that he did. "Will you take coffee, sir?" she said as she rose from her obeisance.

"Oh, no need for such formality," said the Sieur Maltrot, arching his brows with a contrived air of surprise. "Even if it has been, well . . . a longish separation." As he spoke he crossed the room and made to embrace her.

"Monsieur, je vous en prie—" Nanon squeaked and twisted away, banging the point of her elbow into his ribs as she did so. Maltrot lost control of his stick and stooped to catch it with a jerk before it hit the floor. She scurried into the bedroom, dug among the flounces of her clothing on the racks. The contour of the arsenic vial felt hot and moist in her palm. She pushed it deep into the bodice of the dress she wore. From without, his voice called to her.

"Well, then, coffee—just as you like. Perhaps a taste of brandy too, *un soupçon . . ."*

When she brought in the coffee service he was lounging in the chair the doctor had preferred. "You've got new things," he noted, glancing at the monkey's cage, the newer mirror. "New friends as well, I may infer?"

Nanon seated herself in a chair on the opposite end of the room, turned her head aside and looked at him through her lashes. She knew he would have taken care to inform himself of her recent company before he ever came here. Slowly he stirred sugar into his coffee, to such a syrupy thickness that the spoon would almost stand, then topped it off with brandy from the bottle. He sipped, and set the cup aside while he indulged himself with snuff.

"Chess," he said, sneezing and reaching with a languid finger to push over one of the men on the board. "I don't think I approve. It brings out the intellectual faculty too strongly for a woman . . . not to say a woman of your type."

She glanced at the floor where the rat's tail had appeared. Without knowing when it had eaten the fruit she could not guess the speed of the poison's action, but it seemed that the rat had died on the very spot where it had eaten, with no time to get away. Maltrot was upon her so quickly she could scarcely rise. This time he was prepared for her twist from him, and caught her under the arms so that she couldn't reach him, drawing himself tight against her backside. She dropped her head and he pressed his mouth on the exposed curve of her neck, then bit her painfully.

"Laisse-moi tranquille," she said in a smothered shout. *"Je suis enceinte."*

"Oh indeed?" Keeping his grip with one hand, Maltrot gathered her brocade skirt with the other and raised it high, to the bottoms of her breasts. He rotated her toward the mirror, so as to examine her reflected belly, whose curve to the puff of hair at its base seemed no greater than before.

"It doesn't show," he said. "But what fortunate man can claim the honor? Or do you know?" His regard was dispassionate, as if he were considering her for purchase. He dropped her skirt and let her go.

She moved off from him, adjusting herself. "You've torn my dress," she sulked.

"Have I now?" The Sieur Maltrot raged into her bedroom, his sword stick suddenly bare in his hand. She followed only as far as the doorway, saw him slashing at her clothesrack with the point of the blade. "I paid for that one," he hissed. "That one too." He gored some gathers of blue fabric; the dress slipped to the floor.

She withdrew to the front room, knowing that if she showed no concern he would stop before he did much damage. In fact, it was only a moment before he rejoined her, taking her arm and twisting it experimentally, watching her face attentively as he did it. Her pain was something she could now deny him. The burn and blade scars scattered where they would not show had taught her that. She went numb, her skin chilled even to herself. "Do what you want," she muttered, thinking of him stiff between her legs, dead uneven rat teeth pressed into the sheet from his petrified half-open jaw. Maltrot raised her arm and let it drop; the limb fell slack and rubbery against her side.

"You have become too subtle," he said. "You've learned to frustrate better than you please." He walked away from her and she sat down in the nearest chair.

"No, I don't want you," he said, and grinned. "But perhaps your child will be a daughter . . . *that* might interest me, in time."

Nanon didn't bother to turn her face from him. If he was left with only words to injure her, he would soon go. But not immediately. He hovered by the monkey's cage, then reached to open it. She didn't see exactly how it happened, but in a flash the monkey climbed his arm and as he pulled back it sank its teeth into his thumb. Maltrot cried out, a shrillness of real fear, but the monkey had wrapped its tail so cunningly around his forearm that no amount of flailing would shake it loose. He brought his hands together and there was a muted snapping sound. The monkey dropped to the floor, neck broken.

Maltrot gasped. Blood was bubbling up from his thumb. When she made no move to help him, he wrapped the wound in his snuff-stained handkerchief and cradled it against his waistcoat. He had paled and was visibly trembling; it was fortunate, she realized, that he did not find his own pain especially erotic.

"My apologies," he eventually said. "I'll buy another, if you desire it—dirty creature." He kicked at the monkey's corpse with the toe of his gold-buckled shoe. Nanon said nothing. Maltrot folded his fingers over the hurt thumb and bloody handkerchief, picked up the sword stick with his unhurt hand, and flung out, leaving the door ajar.

Through the crack, she watched him down the street. Had he been found dead in her rooms here, she would more than likely have been burned alive in the Place de Clugny, which thought had deterred her from poisoning his cup. As for the monkey, she did not much regret it. It was half-wild still, and troublesome; another man would not like it. She did not really expect that she would ever see the doctor again.

Chapter Ten

"DOMINE, NON SUM DIGNUS," Père Bonne-chance intoned, kneeling before the altar of his church—no more, actually, than a bench of board which supported two planks nailed together for a cross. The cross was wrongly proportioned, closer to equilateral than it ought to have been, like a Maltese cross. Père Bonne-chance was an extraordinarily poor carpenter, though there was no reason to include this defect in his act of contrition, he did not think . . .

"Seigneur, je n'suis pas digne," he muttered, and then in a somewhat clearer voice, "I am addicted to rum, and concupiscence. Cigars too. I am slothful as a hog." He thought for a moment. "And not much cleaner. I am nothing but a little fat man after all. Gluttonous and malodorous to boot, O Lord, I am not worthy . . . My will is weak. Each day I break my vows to the Church, O Lord, and daily I affirm my faith in You."

He fingered the rosary which depended from his belt, and which he used less to remember prayers than to enumerate his failings. "Lord, have mercy upon us. Christ, have mercy upon us."

He stood up and turned to face the congregation, although as usual the tiny church was empty. The walls, made of split palmiste, were bare too, except for a random ornamentation of dirt-dauber nests molded from the pale natural clay. Through the palmiste walls came long irregular slices of the outdoor sunlight. Above, mice scrambled in the palm thatch, and a frond detached, sailing winglike to the bare earth floor. But for its single Christian symbol, this room was no different from the *ajoupa* where Père Bonne-chance lived, beside it.

It was the norm for him to have no other celebrants at his service. Sometimes the outlying planters would send a string of *bossales* for baptism, those who did not care to let them go as far as Abbé Osmond's church in the town of Ouanaminthe. The white families on the three plantations nearest by might sometimes appear at Sunday's Mass, though not on major feast days, when they like others would go to the town. He did not know what moved them to make their rare appearances, some private spiritual quavering he could not guess, and which they did not confess to him. They all despised him because he was not chaste, and he accepted their contempt without resentment, as his due. For the most part he ministered only to the slaves of their plantations, whose motives were considerably more clear to him; he knew that they sought repeated baptisms in much the same spirit that they replaced the *macandals* and *ouangas* strung around their necks, but he saw no great harm in indulging them.

He stepped over the fallen scrap of thatch and bent his head to pass through the door, flinching a little as the gay, bright sunlight struck into his face. When he had awakened this morning he had thought as he sometimes did that perhaps he would not drink *at all*, this day. The stress of this conception was such that he already craved a drink, though usually he did not take one before noon, and often not until evening. With the desire upon him, he broke into a sweat. But then his youngest child came running up, all naked, his tawny skin shining and sweet. He smiled and raised his hands and Père Bonne-chance picked him up and kissed his face. Set down, the child scampered happily away and the priest stood admiring how miraculously well his limbs were hung together and how easily he used them, without thought.

His own sweat had an unpleasant scent of anxiety and alcohol, as he had mentioned in his prayer. The priest loosened his ceinture, thinking that he had as well go for a swim, to cleanse his body at the very least, and perhaps distract his mind. The River Massacre ran just behind the church and his *ajoupa*.

At the point where he undressed, a few trees stood, enough to give him a measure of privacy, though most of the riverbank here at the French side of the elbow was cleared. He left his Dominican habit hanging on a low limb to air and waded out into the water, knee-deep. The water was quite cold, running clear from its mountain source. If he looked down he could see his hairy toes curling to grip the gravelly silt of the bottom, a little magnified and distorted by the water. The cold spread up his spine and pained him in his back teeth. He patted the surface of the water with the flats of his meaty hair-backed hands and looked up and down the river carefully for caymans, which were not unknown here, though the temperature this far up the Massacre did not really agree with them.

He walked waist-deep into the water and suddenly flung himself forward upon it, sending up a glistening wave as he submerged for an instant. Then he bobbed back up. He swam in a splayed crawling stroke at an angle against the current of the river. When he first struck the water the cold had made his vitals shrink but with the exercise he soon became fairly comfortable. He was very buoyant because of his fat although the shape of his stomach made it awkward for him to swim belly-down. To compensate, he had developed a powerful backstroke and now he resorted to this, swimming diagonally toward the middle of the river.

The sky above was a faultless blue, curving unlimited down into the cleared western bank. On the far side, the Spanish shore, it cut off at the treetops along the sharply rising mountain range. Along these peaks the sky was flocked with cloud. The verdure on those wrinkled slopes was unbroken, bearing no visible trace of any human passage. At the farthest distance the jungle green smoked into a slate-blue haze.

Père Bonne-chance stopped swimming and floated idly on his back. His legs dragged sideways in the current, and, peering around the mounded contour of his stomach, he could see his own compound, such as it was. The voices of his children came toward him thinly as they chased each other over the hard-packed earth between the small thatched squares of the church and the *ajoupa*. The boys wore only tattered trousers, ragged to the knee, the girls hemless cotton shifts, much the same garb as the slaves on the neighboring plantations, though they were free. At the corner of the *ajoupa* was tethered a dun cow and the woman—he could not call her wife—was balanced on a one-legged stool to milk. Fontelle. Her head was bound in a tall turban of multicolored scarves, funicular, like a beehive. The priest watched as she finished the task. Balancing the milk pail on her head, she unleashed the cow and sent her away to graze with a slap on her skinny hindquarters. Fontelle had aged, bearing the numerous children of Père Bonne-chance, but she still had her height and grace of movement. Her nose was exceedingly long and had two peculiar swerves along the length of it; she was snaggle-toothed, with a weak chin. He knew most men would find her ugly—let them think so.

He rolled onto his side to inspect the river surface. A way upstream from him something lifted briefly; he couldn't make it out entirely in the water's reflected glare, but it seemed about the size of a cayman's eyes and snout. He swam a little nearer his home shore, watching. Whatever it was dipped up and down in a lifelike manner, but perhaps the movement was a little too regular. When it floated nearer he saw it was only a crook of a floating branch which had deceived him.

He rolled onto his back again and relaxed into the water. With his ears submerged the shouts and whistles of the children were cut off. He might even have dozed. But suddenly a flight of doves splintered in all directions across his tranquil sky, as if something had startled them. He swung himself to the vertical and trod water, turning his bullet head to and fro. A white man on horseback was riding up toward the compound from the direction of Ouanaminthe, abreast of a slave who rode a mule. A *nègre chasseur*, the priest thought he must be, since he carried a long-barreled fowling piece crossways over his saddle.

In the still air he could hear their voices plainly, though the riders were still several hundred yards off. The white man pointed to a tree. *"Orion,"* he cried, *"Là, voila."* The priest watched the black take his aim. The several species of *ramier* in this area were so seldom hunted they were virtually tame. At the shot, two fell, and the rest of the covey rose in nervous flight and circled the tree and lit again. A pair of white goats which had been grazing near the trail picked up their heads and moved farther off.

Orion, the *nègre chasseur*, hopped down from the mule and ran to collect the fallen birds. One was not completely killed and he wrung its neck and scurried back to remount. The children, meanwhile, had bunched up like a flock of sheep. They hid behind the church in a cluster, giggling and whispering and peering around the fraying palmiste corner of the building. The men passed them, riding up to the *ajoupa*. Fontelle came out and answered some question the white man put too low for the priest to overhear. Her turban switched back and forth like a rudder as she gestured with her head.

The two men rode toward the grove of trees where Père Bonne-chance had left his garments. He saw that infallibly they must reach it before he could, though their pace was leisurely. Still, he flopped forward and swam as briskly as he might—in his labored crawl, feeling that his backstroke would be unseemly before such an audience. When it was shallow enough for him to touch his foot, he stood up and began to wade out. The strangers had pulled their mounts up near the bank and were waiting.

Naked, Père Bonne-chance came out of the river, water streaming from the hair that covered him. He was pelted front and back like an ape or a small black bear. He smiled at the visitors. The black looked away, out of discretion. From the pommel of his saddle hung a string of birds, and a thin trickle of blood stained the mule's forequarter.

"You are prolific," Arnaud said, gazing frankly at the crook in Père Bonne-chance's organ of generation, "for a priest."

"Oh sir," said Père Bonne-chance, smiling still more brightly at his guest. "You must have come a long way to pay me such a compliment."

Arnaud's plump lips formed a sort of heart-shaped smile. Slowly he turned his head to examine the priest's old Dominican robe where it swung idly from its branch. Père Bonne-chance's skin prickled, hairs lifting on their follicles. Arnaud looked knowing, as if he could somehow discern, seeing the priest shucked bare of his costume, that it was only a disguise for Père Bonne-chance, who had stayed in the colony unlawfully after the expulsion of the Jesuit order. Though in fairness one could hardly say that he was truly a Jesuit any longer, yet certainly he had never been a Dominican either. For an instant he was frozen. But there was no real penetration in Arnaud's look, it was only the Creole aristocrat's reflexive sneer. Besides he was not much the sort of gentleman to interest himself in sectarian differences among monks and priests.

"Not only for that," Arnaud said, "dear Father. Not only for that. I'm told there is a passable ford somewhere in this vicinity?"

"At Ouanaminthe, do you mean?" Père Bonne-chance said, full of false malicious innocence, for he had seen very well that Arnaud had come from the direction of the town.

"Non, quand même," Arnaud snapped. "Is there not another farther up the river?"

"Justement," said Père Bonne-chance, unkindly smiling still. "Past that bend there," he stretched his arm, "and then it's not more than a mile, perhaps three-quarters. On the Spanish shore," he said, "you'll see a bare cleft rock, and on our bank a tree stump, *acajou*. You must head your horses strictly on a line between these marks, because the way is narrow and the current is strong."

Arnaud nodded and laid a finger against the broad brim of his hat as a mocking salute. He scanned Père Bonne-chance ironically from head to foot once more and without thanks or any other word spurred his horse and trotted away up the riverbank. Orion pulled the mule around to follow.

Père Bonne-chance assumed once more his musty habit. The exhilaration of his swim had rather faded from him. Watching the horse's tail switching at flies as Arnaud receded, he half-attentively apologized to God for needling the man about the ford. This had been deliberately unpleasant of him, since he knew Arnaud must be engaged in smuggling. If he had been interested in any sort of legitimate commerce he would much more conveniently have crossed the river at Ouanaminthe to the Spanish town of Dajabón—like any other trader.

He returned to the *ajoupa,* where Fontelle had prepared for him hot cassava and a bowl of milk fresh foaming from the cow. After he had eaten he lit a thin cigar and went out into the yard to gather such of his children who could be found and give them a lesson in the writing of French. They sat upon the earth to scratch in the dust with sticks for styluses. The priest had no books suitable for this instruction, only some volumes in Latin and a few French novels whose content was wholly inappropriate, he recognized, even for such children as his. Indeed, now that his older daughters were semiliterate he kept the French books hidden. There were some old newspapers from Le Cap and from France which he had carefully saved to read and reread during these sessions, but by now their news was very cold.

The cigar at least was excellent, having come from the Spanish side. As Père Bonne-chance savored the smoke it came to him that Arnaud must be going after guns. There was no other commodity that would require his surreptitious route, not even slaves. Regardless of whatever proclamations might obtain, anything and everything else was freely traded between Ouanaminthe and Dajabón.

The idea brought him only a heaviness, however. When the children had wandered away from the lesson he stubbed his cigar out on the ground and went into the *ajoupa* to seek his pallet there. With a dim sense of satisfaction he realized that by diversion he'd managed to elude his wish to drink.

It was late by the time he awoke, as he could see by the deepening color of the light dropping through the *ajoupa*'s open doorway. He dipped water from the pail by the door and took a sip and splashed the rest of the gourd against his face to rouse himself. With the trickles drying on his throat he stood in the door and watched the light's shade muting on the surface of the river. As they would each evening, the doves were calling loudly all around, as if the morning's slaughter made no difference to them. Again the sound of hooves was somewhere on the trail.

He poured himself a thimbleful of rum and drank it and went out. It might have been Arnaud and his huntsman returning, and though their encounter had not been so pleasant for the priest to wish much to repeat it, he was curious. But strolling around the corner of the church he saw that it was a group of new riders coming up from Ouanaminthe. They were mulattoes all five of them, all with excellent horses and well dressed. Of the wealthy, educated classes. Père Bonne-chance did not know them; he did not think they were of this quarter, probably. One or two of them looked familiar, though, and he thought that he might have seen them previously. It was possible, even likely, that this was so, for many if not most of Ogé's party had remained at large after the leaders were taken.

The warmth of the rum spread leaflike veins all through his chest, tendrils curving down into his stomach. He licked his lips and walked a little nearer the trail, wondering if he would hail the riders, or they him. The leader had a strangely freckled face that Père Bonne-chance felt certain he would have recalled if ever he had seen it before. His aspect was forbidding, and his eyes passed over the priest coldly and without a pause.

The same two goats were cropping grass beside the trail again, and Père Bonne-chance changed his course, as if all along he'd only been going to round them up. As if the passage of these riders were so wholly unremarkable that he had not even noticed them. They passed on.

He had not been much frightened by Ogé's rebellion; really it had gone over too quickly for him to take alarm. In these parts the whole affair had been very smoothly managed, with only one white man killed and that by accident. As well, the mulattoes might have taken him to be in sympathy with their faction, since he lived openly with Fontelle. She was a *quarteronnée* and their children therefore were all officially *sang-mêlés*: that is, one sixty-fourth-part Negro. Père Bonne-chance had been sensible of the idea that Ogé was fighting for their rights.

But the unlucky little army had paid him no mind, as if he'd been a *bête de cornes* himself, grazing blindly by the trail. It was thus that he'd come to know that a few days before his capture Ogé had cached most of his arms somewhere up the river, where Arnaud and the other party had gone. The two journeys might well be connected; on the other hand perhaps they were not. Thinking these things, Père Bonne-chance continued to pursue the goats, which went their own way, ignoring him.

Chapter Eleven

THE EVENING OF AUGUST 22 found Claudine Arnaud sitting upon the gallery of the *grand'case* at Habitation Flaville. Wine had been offered her; she had refused it. An embroidery hoop lay on her skirted knees, and once in a long while she might make a few desultory stitches, but her real purpose was to hold one hand concealed beneath the pale square of linen. If any hallucination appeared to plague her she would surreptitiously prick her thumb with the needle's point and the sharpness of the pain would most often banish the specter, whatever it was.

She was alone on the gallery but for the girl Marguerite, who sat idly, her plump milky hands folded in her lap. This was some distaff cousin of Flaville's *gérant*, an orphan or something of the sort, who'd been sent out here from France to catch herself a husband. Claudine's near-professional appraisal was that the girl made quite delicious bait. She was well formed, a flaxen blonde, with large liquid blue eyes that seemed to show intelligence, though in truth there was next to none. In its place were a few decorative accomplishments—watercolors, playing the spinet—and a deep bovine tranquillity. She sat now, a slave fanning her, her lovely blue gaze bent on nothing at all, as pleasantly vacant as a cow chewing its cud. Some man would surely value this quality, Claudine suspected, if not to preserve and protect it, then to lay it to waste. Since she had come here she had shared a bedroom with pretty Marguerite and she believed the girl was so perfectly blank she did not even dream.

Within there was a dampened clatter of plates and utensils being laid for the evening meal. Out of the speedily gathering dark at the end of the lane which led through the cane fields in the direction of Le Cap, Claudine thought she saw a horseman coming. She moved the needle nearer her thumb beneath the hoop, but this rider lacked the pearly shimmer of most of her other phantasms . . . only the tails of his duster fluttered deliriously over the hindquarters of the horse. She glanced at Marguerite but of course there was little to infer from the lack of reaction there.

As the horseman came nearer, at a brisk trot, she thought she could see a white blaze on the horse's forehead. A moment later, she recognized the doctor. Now that was a peculiar cruelty, and a new one, a phantom appearing to remind her that there had been *a time before*—when she had seen him coming just this way, expanding from a dot at the farthest remove down the string-straight line of Arnaud's *allée*. To imagine that on that day itself she'd thought her situation was unbearable, that thought seemed laughable now. This zombi had been sent to tantalize her with the thought of going back in time to reach that day of innocence again. She sank the needle deep into her thumb and twisted it, biting her lips the while. When she opened her eyes again the doctor was still there and had in fact dismounted from his horse.

"Your pardon, ladies," he began. "Can you tell me, how far have I to go to reach Ennery?"

Claudine began to speak and caught herself. She cut her eyes toward the girl, in search of any clue at all. Marguerite overlooked the apparition blandly and spoke in her most musical tone.

"I don't know how to answer your question, *monsieur*, but I'm sure you are most welcome here."

Claudine breathed out. She rose to her feet, blotting her wounded thumb on the underside of the embroidery before she laid the hoop down. She saw from Doctor Hébert's look that he had not recognized her. Assuming an ironic smile, she made him a curtsy, thinking that if she had attempted any such gesture at their first meeting she would most likely have fallen down. But she was well beyond embarrassment and now that Marguerite had answered for the doctor's presence on the physical plane, she found that the unlikeliness of the event almost amused her.

"You are well out of your road once again," she said, rising and putting out her hand with a mock-regal gesture as he came up the few steps to the gallery. "This is not Ennery but Acul."

"Madame Arnaud," the doctor said. "My happiness to see you." He bowed over her hand. "But how . . ."

"Oh, I am a guest here myself, you understand." Claudine emitted a sort of social laugh, but this joviality was too much and nearly strangled her. She cleared her throat. "This is Habitation Flaville, but as the family is from home, Monsieur and Madame Lambert are my hosts and will be yours."

The doctor released her hand. "Oh, but I should not intrude."

"Nonsense, you will stay, of course." Claudine smiled, not quite cuttingly. "After all, the road you can't find by daylight is unlikely to appear to you after dark." She turned, rustling in her crinolines. "Marguerite, had you not better go and tell Madame Lambert that there will be one more to dine?"

The blonde girl rose from her seat and turned her face aside as if in modesty, most wonderfully displaying her soft profile and long alabaster neck. She held the pose for a moment, then moved with her sleepy rippling grace into the house. Claudine watched the doctor narrowly, but if he'd been impressed he did not show it.

INSIDE THE HOUSE, the doctor delivered himself of a group of apologies, demurrals, and finally thanks to Madame Lambert. She was a short woman, tiny almost, but she seemed strong and full of practical energy. Her three daughters all bustled about, ordering adjustments to the dinner table and sending house slaves to make up another room. The doctor's saddlebags were sent for, clothes hung up and brushed. Someone pressed a drink into his hand. In the midst of all this Monsieur Lambert returned from overseeing the cane fields, with him a youth named Émile Duvel, who was an expected and invited guest for dinner and the night. Introductions were made. The doctor tottered on his rubbery legs. Long hours riding after his idle stay in Le Cap had left him saddle sore again, and he was chagrined at having lost his way so thoroughly. Madame Lambert plucked at his elbow and conveyed him to the rear of the house on the pretext of showing him his room.

Within the chamber she slapped the door shut with her round forearm (she was rather a stout woman though small) and wheeled on him with a bristling vigor that was almost alarming. He took a step back.

"As you are a physician," she said, "you must tell me what you think of Claudine." She spoke in a loud forced whisper. Short as he was himself, she scarcely reached his breastbone. Her round black eyes crackled at him, their pupils large.

"Tell me, what is your concern?" The doctor made a series of evasive motions with his hands.

"Oh, I cannot say exactly. She has changed. She scarcely will eat a mouthful at any time of day, and takes no wine or spirits either, when she used to be so, so . . ."

"Enthusiastic?" the doctor finished, thinking he saw in her expression some knowledge of Madame Arnaud's dipsomania. Madame Lambert looked at him closely and he was careful not to smile.

"Might it be some wasting fever?" she said. "Often she seems to stare at nothing, sometimes I seem to hear her speak to no one. In her room she speaks when no one is there."

"I see," the doctor said. As it struck him, these were symptoms of insanity rather than illness. "Of course, if the lady does not choose to consult me . . . but I will be as observant as I am able."

Madame Lambert seemed a little deflated. "I should be grateful for any opinion . . . I fear for her, indeed. She was once a dear friend to me, and yet she always seemed ill-suited for this country." She nodded to him and went out. The doctor followed her back to the others.

At table he endured some raillery about his poor sense of direction. Claudine Arnaud began the joke, but did not join in the laughter it produced. The girls were giggly, all but Marguerite, whose bland state of calm seemed quite unshakable. Émile Duvel, who clerked on the nearby Noé plantation, cut through the hilarity, raising a finger as he looked at the doctor.

"Still it is no laughing matter to ride over this country alone, whether one knows his way or not. So much unrest among the cultivators." The table quieted, but for Duvel's voice. "And if there really were to be—"

"*Assez.*" Monsieur Lambert spoke from the table's head. "Why look for trouble? I'm sure it's all been settled now, besides."

"*Monsieur*, you are too good." Duvel turned to the doctor again. "Do you know what this man did?"

"Émile . . ." said Monsieur Lambert. But Duvel continued. The girls on either side of him were smiling, anticipating this version of a tale they'd heard before.

"Last week a fire was set to some buildings at Chabaud's. They caught the man who did it—he proved to be a *commandeur*, but from another plantation. And when examined he confessed there was a plot among many *commandeurs* to raise a general insurrection of slaves in these quarters." Duvel looked to the head of the table. "And why should he confess it if it were not true?"

"Naturally, to shift attention from himself," Lambert said. "And under such 'examinations' as they are wont to give, a man might contrive any fantasy."

"Perhaps," said Duvel, "and yet, a *commandeur? Après tout*, he was not some *bossale* or maroon as you know. And if there was no plot what would bring him from Desgrieux plantation to work such mischief on Chabaud?"

"If in truth he did so," Lambert said mildly. "It may be that since he had come from elsewhere he was the likeliest to be falsely accused."

"You are ingenious in your defense of them," Duvel said. "Be that as it may, the authorities of Limbé determined from this fellow that there was indeed a plot and that several of the leaders were here, *chez Flaville*. Can you imagine what would take place if such an intelligence came to some other *gérant*?"

Sidelong, the doctor had been looking at Madame Arnaud, as his hostess had requested. It was true that she only picked at her food, and interesting that she took neither wine nor liquor. She seemed inattentive to the anecdote, but the doctor would not necessarily have said she was in worse health than when he had first met her. One corner of her mouth was drawn down, though; perhaps she'd been victim to apoplexy?

"Can you imagine?" Duvel was repeating. The doctor roused himself.

"Indeed, I think I can," he said. His eyes were on Madame Arnaud's hands lying idle by the sides of her plate, but what he seemed to see was a pair of black hands crossed and transfixed with a nail through their pale palms.

"Quite," Duvel said. "But this gentleman gathered all his slaves together and when he told them of the accusation he said that he could not believe it. Your words, sir—" Duvel raised his voice to overwhelm Lambert's nascent protest. "Your very words: 'If I have given you any reason to seek my life, you may take it now with no resistance and without the trouble of a general riot.' And to be sure they all wept and protested their fidelity."

"I took no risk," Lambert said.

The doctor looked at him. His close-cut curly hair was grizzled and his face was creased with friendly wrinkles, like an old hound's.

"Kindness is repaid with kindness," he went on; "abuse with abuse."

"Well, we must all hope that you are right," Duvel said. The doctor noticed that his tone had changed, and he now looked at Lambert with almost a doglike devotion.

"If all the owners and *gérants* shared your goodness," Duvel said, "it's true we'd have much less to fear."

"I believe we have dispatched this subject," Lambert said, and nodded to the doctor. "Do tell us something of yourself."

In his effort to comply, Doctor Hébert let it slip that he was unmarried. This news created a partially suppressed sensation, for it seemed that Duvel was the only frequent courtier at this house, though not for any want in its attractions. The Lambert daughters were pretty and charming all three: Héloïse, Madeleine, Emilie. They were small and dark-haired like their mother, with ice pale skin carefully maintained. Their being close in age, the doctor had trouble distinguishing which was the elder, which the younger; besides they often seemed to speak and react almost in unison.

When they had dined and the slaves had cleared away the table, Marguerite made a display of her skill at the spinet. Émile Duvel stood by the instrument, joining his tenor to her high piping voice, until the three sisters became restless and organized an attempt at dancing. Claudine sat at the room's farthest edge, near a window covered with mosquito net, one hand covering the other with the embroidery hoop caught between, studying the situation as it evolved.

The shift to dancing was a little coup for the Lambert girls. Claudine was aware of a rift developing between them and Marguerite these days. They were bright and quick where she was slow and languorous, so perhaps it was natural they should not well like her, all but Emilie, who had formed an attachment. But even she would not break with her sisters in the matter of Émile Duvel, who was their property as they saw it (though before Marguerite had come they had not liked him so much either). So they would dance, leaving Marguerite to the provision of accompaniment, fastened to her bench.

The doctor was game to play his part, though shaky from the saddle as Claudine could well see, and she surmised he was no virtuoso of a dancer at the best of times. He propelled Héloïse around the floor in a bearlike fashion, and though she tried to engage him in conversation he was too much occupied by his effort not to step on her feet or knock over the smaller articles of furniture. Duvel was far nimbler, but perhaps less obliging. The two men kept dutifully sharing the three sisters round, but Duvel's eyes kept running to Marguerite, over the neat dark head of his partner.

There was a crackling sound that seemed to come from beyond the window, plainly audible to Claudine over the spinet's tinkling, yet knowing it must be an echo from within her skull, she tried to ignore it. At last she could not help herself from glancing out to see the phantasmal tongues of flame licking through the cane fields. Her lips worked drily. Often the appearance of her demon was foretold by such displays, and this time there even seemed a taste of smoke in the air. She stabbed her needle deep into her thumb, gasped, and resolutely turned back toward the frail bright bubble of the room, where the parents overlooked the dancing with fond glances, or maybe only with fatigue . . .

Duvel gave over the dance just then, pleading breathlessness, and strolled over to lean on the spinet. Héloïse and Madeleine faced each other, mirror images almost, and arms akimbo, then shrugged and took one another as partners. Doctor Hébert, quite red in the face, ferried Emilie around in a ragged ellipse, apologizing for his clumsiness even as he committed it. The spinet made a rattling sound to Claudine's soured ear, like teeth shaken in a jar. A foolish smile spread over his face, Duvel was admiring the movement of Marguerite's plump fingers over the keyboard, but suddenly she broke off and looked up crossly.

"What *is* that gruesome noise?" And suddenly she was on her feet; Claudine had never seen her respond to anything so quickly. Indeed the crackle was much louder than before and with the spinet silent it seemed to fill the room, along with a roaring behind it. Monsieur Lambert shifted in his seat, the ghost of a frown crossing his face. One hand pressed over her pale throat, Marguerite began walking to the door. The others remained frozen as she passed onto the gallery, but Claudine rose immediately and followed.

A dry wind blew toward the house, pushing a low roller of black burned-sugary smoke ahead of it. It was the wind that roared, and mixed with that was the feverish snapping of the burning cane, and something else: a low throbbing ululation like the wind howling over a broken bottleneck. The wind shifted and the billow of smoke rolled away. The gallery was flooded with a hot orange light, though the fire was still far back in the cane field. In silhouette against the blaze Claudine saw a larger host of devils than any hallucination had figured forth for her till now.

Then she realized that Marguerite saw them too. It must be that ululation came from human throats. Marguerite screamed, staggered down the steps and began running across the compound parallel to the fire. After hesitating a bare instant, Claudine pinched up her skirts in one hand and went after her. Unused to haste, the girl ran awkwardly and was easily overtaken. Claudine snatched her hair at the nape of her neck and hurried her along a great deal faster. The compound was bordered on three sides by cane fields and Claudine rushed them into an area of cane that was not yet alight.

THE DOCTOR GAINED THE GALLERY a step behind Duvel, and by then the rebel slaves were already pouring up the steps and vaulting up over the railings. Duvel stopped with his mouth agape. A red-skinned man crouched and took a careful aim at him with a long nail spliced to a staff and drove it hard into Duvel's neck. Duvel hissed, air rushing from his trachea. The red man drew back and made another strike and when he withdrew the nail this time, a crimson jet blasted from Duvel's throat like wine spurting from a heavy, punctured skin. The bloodstream splattered a gallery post and passed beyond it into the darkness and indistinct firelight. Experimentally,

Duvel placed a forefinger over the tiny wound, and a fine spray arced out to stain several of his attackers.

Someone struck at the doctor with a cane knife and he interposed his open hand. The blade cut deeply into his palm, though for the moment he did not feel it. Duvel had fallen on his side; his eyes showed white and blood was pooling darkly round his cheek and jaw. In the cane the flames shot suddenly high and brightened all with a hellish clarity. Monsieur Lambert appeared in the door frame. His lips moved in some speech the doctor could not hear for the choral voice of the rebels throbbing in his ears. Lambert's hands were flattened before him in a mosaic gesture as though he would calm a turbulent sea. Meanwhile the blacks were tumbling through the windows at either side of the door, carrying away the mosquito nets as they burst through, and within all the women had begun screaming together. The doctor glanced through the naked window frame and saw a tall lean man with his head swathed in mosquito netting like a beekeeper's veil snatching at Héloïse and divesting her of all her clothing in a single rip. Another smashed on the spinet keys with his fists, releasing loud discordant clusters of notes, while Héloïse shrieked and jigged up and down in a parody of the dance they'd enjoyed earlier, her white buttocks fluttering.

An enormous ink-black rebel whose muscles shone with oil swung a long-bladed hoe down at Monsieur Lambert's head. Still in the midst of his temporizing discourse, Lambert sidestepped. The hoe fell on his collarbone and the doctor heard plainly the crack as it broke and Lambert pitched forward on his knees. He was surrounded, but the rebels confused themselves, all striking at once with their blades tangling in midair. Lambert's hands were upturned now; a palm filled with blood. For an instant the doctor caught his liquid eye. The hoe swept down again, the blade raking away the scalp to expose the hideous whiteness of his blood-skeined skull. Under the force of the blow Lambert's head dropped forward and remained. A rebel directly in front of the doctor drew back his *coutelas* to swing at the exposed neck, but the doctor locked an arm around his throat and dragged him away.

The main wave of attackers had passed on into the house or beyond it to the sugar mill, and no one seemed to notice the struggle the doctor was engaged in. As the rebel tried somehow to bring his knife to bear, the doctor tightened his stranglehold and overbalanced backward. His hip broke the rail as they both fell over into a patch of darkness which the house corner shaded from the fire. They wrestled there, the doctor's hands slipping on the rebel's oiled body, feeling the first pain of his slashed palm. His choke hold was broken but the other had apparently lost his knife and was content to run away once he had freed himself. A cloud of smoke blew over and the doctor gathered himself on hands and knees, coughing and spitting. When the smoke swirled away he saw Marguerite at the border of the cane field east of the compound. The white dress she wore picked her out plainly even though the fire did not much illuminate that area, and she was struggling as it looked with some darker figure. He scrambled up and ran to her.

What seemed an attacker was only Claudine in her rust-red dress, hustling the hysterical Marguerite along willy-nilly through the cane. The doctor drew abreast of them. Claudine was moving with a firm purpose though he had no idea where she thought she was going. Then some hundred yards ahead of them another fire exploded, leaped high and fanned on either side. The ululation rose again like a wall and there was a more fragmentary hooting on conch shells. The doctor swung an arm at the fire, staring at Claudine.

"Keep moving," she said, her face twisting as she splattered his face with spittle. "The ditches—"

Marguerite's feet turned under and her weight sagged. The doctor caught her other arm and went with Claudine half dragging the girl along between them. He had no notion why they should run toward the new fire and the rebels they could hear approaching them from it, except there was no good reason to remain at the compound either. Ahead, the marauders were so near that the single wall of sound they uttered began to separate into individual voices howling this or that. But before they came in sight the doctor's foot slipped out from under him and he slid down on his coccyx into a narrow irrigation trench.

Instantly he understood, and flattened himself facedown to the bottom of the ditch. With the drought there were only a few inches of water here; it was a hot sticky mud hole. Claudine was lying almost nose to nose with him, her arm across Marguerite's back. The girl said something and began to raise her head, but Claudine mashed it back into the mud and held it there, fingers digging into her scalp. Small clouds of mosquitoes moved toward them from either direction along the trench. Claudine's eye glittered in an almost reptilian way. The doctor would have liked to kiss her. Mud was sucking at his ear hole and he could see out of only one eye. Beyond the women's prostrate bodies, twenty or thirty yards along the ditch, a new band of blacks began to jump the barrier, lit now by the fire in the other *carré*. A couple of them stumbled or fell crossing the ditch but even then they hardly looked about themselves, so great their haste to reach the compound or outdistance the fresh fire racing up behind them.

When he thought they had all passed the doctor raised up on his elbows, in spite of Claudine's angry glance, and looked to where they'd come from. The fire was lacing through the standing cane stalks and, with the wind behind it, the speed of its advance beggared belief. A blast of heat parched his eyeballs; he dropped his face into the ditch. He'd thought the trench must halt the blaze, but the flames were shooting out laterally as if thrust from dragons' throats, across and into the cane on the other side. For a minute or more the three of them were overshot by long sheets of fire. A flight of mosquitoes combusted all at once with no flame touching them, only from the pure heat; they glowed like transfigured ideas of mosquitoes for an instant and were gone. The fire caught at Marguerite's loose hair and tore among Claudine's crooked fingers there. The doctor scooped a handful of sludge from under himself and doused it.

The fire had passed. A spiral of silence twisted at the doctor's ear as the roar of it receded toward the compound. He felt with his fingers around the trench. Most of the moisture had been baked away and the walls of the ditch were parched and cracking. The wind began to silt it in with flat flakes of hot ash. He could hear the shrieks of the women in the house, and horses screaming in the stable, which made him wonder if it too were afire. But now the fire was lowering at the edge of the compound, where the cleared area was too large for it to pass. At the edge of it three of the blacks did a wild dervish dance together, each holding a small keg of rum and alternately drinking from the bunghole or splattering liquor to boost the dying flames.

Inside the house the cries of the women kept ascending as if they would eviscerate themselves with screams. Marguerite lifted her fire-blackened head to peer over the rim of the trench, but there was little to see; the house was dark.

"What are they doing," she quavered. "What are they doing there?"

"They're getting married," Claudine snapped. "Didn't you want to get married too?"

The girl began to moan, her teeth chattering, and Claudine pushed her face down in the dirt. "You'd best keep silent," she muttered stiffly, "or someone will come along and *marry* you."

AT DAWN, WHEN IT HAD everywhere been silent for an hour, the three of them crawled out of the ditch and approached the house across the ashen waste of the cane field. None of the buildings had been destroyed except the sugar mill, which had been dismantled board by board and all the clay forms shattered. It seemed the horses had all been stolen or driven from the stable, though it had not burned. The bodies of Lambert and Duvel lay tumbled in the yard below the gallery, identifiable chiefly by their clothing, as neither any longer wore a head. Reluctantly, the doctor followed Claudine into the house. As they entered, Madame Lambert stirred on the floor and moved her hands to cover her blood-smeared thighs.

"It is worse than death," she said, but tonelessly.

"It is not," said Claudine. "But if you don't stir yourself you'll have a chance to make the comparison. You must get up and look to your children."

The Lambert girls were huddled in a corner, tangled with each other like a pile of terrorized puppies. Roughly Claudine hauled on their limbs to make them rise. At the opposite end of the room, the doctor looked them over, with what detachment his professional point of view could still achieve. They were bruised and torn between their legs but he thought no direct attempt had been made against their lives. Their nakedness was that of corpses; their eyes stared through and through him as though he were made of glass. Behind him, Marguerite uttered a choking sound and collapsed sobbing in the doorway.

"O tais-toi, tu m'enmerder," said Claudine. "Go find some clothes to put on these people—anything, sacks . . ."

This seemed pretext enough for the doctor to retreat into the rear of the house. In the room he'd been meant to occupy he found his spare clothing had all been taken and the pistol was gone from his saddlebags. His medicaments had been scattered but few removed; he gathered them back into their drawstring pouch. In another room he found strewn about some articles the women might wear but when he came back to the main chamber they had already managed to cover themselves with shifts and trousers the slaves had discarded during their sack of the premises.

Claudine had entered the broken storeroom and stood there clucking her tongue. "Look," she said as the doctor joined her. She peeled back a cloth covering from a silver coffeepot. "The Flaville plate—they left a fortune here."

"Strange," the doctor said. He followed Claudine out onto the gallery. It was in some ways an odd pattern of looting. They'd made off with all the wine and rum and everything resembling a weapon. The women had been stripped of their personal ornaments and yet a pair of solid gold candlesticks were abandoned in plain sight in the main room.

"Well, we may save that plate at least," Claudine said.

"Along with our lives, if luck favors us," said the doctor.

"Yes, and what are you standing there for?" she said. "Go and catch that horse."

The doctor looked along her pointing finger and recognized his own mount, Espoir, picking his way along the edge of the burned cane field, trailing the broken reins of his bridle. Someone had tried to ride off on him then, and had probably been thrown. He was unsaddled and spooky as could be. Each time the doctor was within a hand's reach of him he picked up his head and went jittering off. At last he was able to catch one of the dragging reins. He stroked the horse till he was reasonably calm, led him into the stable to search for a saddle, but there was none. On the way out he picked up a riding crop from the dirt and stuck it into his waistband. He mounted bareback and managed to overtake and noose a dun-colored mule he saw wandering near the wreck of the sugar mill.

He rode back to the house leading the mule at the end of a length of rope. Under Claudine's direction the other women were loading a flat wagon with the plate and covering it over with straw and corncobs from the outbuildings, all moving like automatons. Marguerite came dragging from the well with two slopping pails of water. The doctor hitched the mule to the wagon and they set out.

There was no conversation. Claudine drove the mule and the doctor rode alongside, his heels dangling on the horse's flank. Marguerite lay prostrate in the wagon bed and was perhaps unconscious. Claudine had forbidden her to wash herself at the well with the warning *You may yet meet a bridegroom on the road.* Soot-stained and mud-plastered as she was she was hardly an erotic spectacle.

The other women slumped silently around the wagon rails, staring blindly in different directions, but the view in all quarters was the same. When the doctor had come down this road the previous day it was like riding through a tunnel of cane, but now he could see across the wasteland as far as the warped line of the horizon. Though it was full day the sun had never really risen, as if the charnel fires had laid a permanent stain across the firmament. All around them the blasted fields still smoked dully, and fitful gusts of wind stirred up black masses of ash and blew them in their faces. Some of the cinders were still hot and the women were at pains to keep the straw in the wagon from igniting. The doctor rode along blinking often and painfully with his bare reddened eyelids. His eyebrows and lashes had been seared away when he'd raised his head from the trench to look at the fire the night before. The cut through his palm was swollen and sore. High in the soot-speckled sky a single vulture held a position directly over their heads. Every so often it spun away in an uneven loop and then returned magnetically to its pole.

They had traveled perhaps four miles in the direction of Le Cap when another party detached itself from the horizon of the road ahead. Madame Lambert turned her head wretchedly on the rail. "Is it the troops?" she said in a cracked voice.

Claudine snorted. But the doctor didn't think it was such a stupid question. The others seemed to march in a tight mass and a standard of some description was borne among them. In any case there was no possibility to turn aside with the wagon and they were already in plain view, so they simply went on at the same pace as before, Claudine snapping the reins occasionally across the mule's dun back.

After fifteen or twenty slow-moving minutes, the doctor could descry that it was a band of blacks approaching. He could not quite make out the standard raised on the pole but thought he could guess what it was and well enough he did not wish to see it any nearer. But they were coming on apace. Claudine lifted her chin to him.

"You'll outdistance them easily," she said. "They have no mounts, *comme vous voyez.*"

This possibility seemed so repugnant to him it was almost comical. He didn't bother to answer her, but she clucked her tongue and spoke again more urgently.

"Will you defend us with your riding crop? It's the men they want to kill. If you save yourself we may come through."

The doctor hesitated, shifting the reins off the slash in his palm. The band was near enough that he could begin to count its members, and he thought they were probably about twenty strong.

"Go," Claudine said, her voice dropping to a low mesmeric tone. "I'll bring us through and we'll rejoin you."

Shrugging at her, he took the riding crop from his waistband and touched up the horse, bringing it quickly to a canter, and rode down on the center of the group ahead. If they had held their ground they might have stopped the horse or dragged him from it but as he bore down on them they moved to scatter as he'd trusted they would. As he burst through the shifting line he leaned out to cut with the crop into what faces he could reach. This effort nearly cost him his seat on the horse's bare back; he dropped the crop and clung to the mane. The thing on the pole tilted toward him with its underjaw unslung as if it would bite. A hand seized at his knee and was torn away.

He had hoped to anger them with the crop and so draw them off, and a few of them did come yelling after him for a short dash before they saw the futility of the chase and gave over. The doctor pulled up the horse and swung it round to a standstill, but the band would not try for him again. They were all moving down the road toward the wagon now.

A CRAZED TATTERDEMALION CREW, uniformed in grease and bare skin or in odd assortments of the clothing they'd looted. They bore the arms of any peasant rising: sticks and staves, machetes, hoes and makeshift pikes. Some carried the whips that had been used to drive them. A few had guns and some of these Claudine could recognize from the Flaville house. One went along swinging a fowling piece by its barrel like a club and the others who had blundered into possession of firearms seemed to have little clearer idea of their use.

When they were little better than a handspan away, Claudine let the exhausted mule halt and stood straight up on the wagon seat. Her rust-colored dress clung to her stiffly and her mud-matted hair stuck out in several directions like a Medusa's snakes.

"As God sees you," she said in her raven's voice, "or whatever demon of hell you may worship, there is nothing more to be taken from us. Let us pass."

The group stopped staring. A Congo detached himself and approached the wagon. A gentleman's powdered peruke was crookedly perched on his huge shaven head and his ragged teeth had all been carefully blackened to resemble little chunks of coal and he had put on backward the sky-blue dress Emilie had worn the night before. The V of its back could not close over his chest and so he was bare almost to his navel. He carried a soldier's bayonet stuck through a rip in the cloth so it knocked against his belly and at the back of her mind Claudine wondered how he might have come by that.

He passed her, laid his hand on the wagon rail, and walked around it, humming tonelessly. Claudine felt that he was looking at the other women though she did not turn her head to see.

"Those have had the juice well wrung from them," she said. "As you may know."

The Congo grunted, circling around the wagon tail. Claudine could not help herself from glancing briefly back at him. It might have been comical, how his shoulder blades protruded from what had been meant for *décolletage*. He reached into the bed and gouged into Marguerite's leg with one finger, but the girl lay catatonic and did not stir.

"I think she's dead, that one," Claudine said. "Although perhaps that's what excites you."

The Congo spat into the mat of ashes that covered the road and continued his circuit. The lusterless gaze of the other women drilled through him on its way to the charred horizon. Claudine watched the mule's ears revolving, forcing her eyes away from the spot in the straw where the plate was hidden. There was a blue cross over the mule's dun shoulders where several flies were rising or alighting. As the Congo passed below her again she saw framed in the bodice of the dress gray cicatrice ropes of old whippings on his back.

His eye caught the wedding ring on her dangling hand and he turned back and clutched at it. Reflexively Claudine pulled back, then relaxed. Another jerk brought her down from the wagon. The wig had slipped forward over his eyes and he stopped and used both hands to adjust it, for all the world like a fop before his mirror. Claudine twisted at the ring, but her finger was so swollen to it, it would not even turn. While the Congo still fiddled with the wig, she snatched the bayonet from its cloth hanger.

A murmur ran through the band and the pole tilted, the severed head of Émile Duvel slackly smiling down on the scene with its even bloodstained teeth. The Congo surged upon her, but she indented his belly skin with the bayonet's point and made him hesitate.

"Attends," she said. *"Regardes."*

She turned and laid her hand over the wagon wheel, the one finger flattened on the iron-shod rim and the other three pressed down against the side of it. She pushed her weight against the hand to separate the finger more completely from its fellows and better expose the joint behind the ring. The blade rose to the length of her right arm and came down with a whistle and a flash. The edge of it clashed on the iron wheel rim, and ring and finger sprang from her hand in opposite directions.

The stump was mottled pink and white, too suddenly shocked to bleed at first. She tried to ball it in a fist; her other hand let the bayonet drop in the cinder-strewn roadway. "Now you will let us pass," she said woodenly, and clambered back upon the wagon seat.

The Congo stood with the ring in one hand and the finger white and wormlike in the other, gazing up at her with round vivid eyes. She crushed her left hand into the fabric of her skirt and with the other cracked the reins lightly on the mule's back. The wagon wheels began a slow turning. The Congo spoke gutturally in some African tongue and the band divided itself silently and the wagon passed through.

By the time they reached the doctor, Madame Lambert had gathered herself to climb onto the wagon seat and take the reins. She would have put an arm round Claudine's shoulders but Claudine shook her off and sat a little apart from her with her head slightly bowed. Several times the doctor sought to examine her wound but she would not allow it. They kept riding on and on speechlessly along the bald burned turning of the earth.

Chapter Twelve

WHEN NIGHT CAME DOWN TO COVER US we left the women and children hiding in the jungle on the mountain slope and we came down on the plantation of Noé, only our band going along together at first, Achille and César-Ami and Jean-Pic and Paul Lefu and Aiguy who was one of us now, also some of the others who had come out to meet us from Le Cap. We came to the edges of the Noé cane fields and we began to see others there hiding in the cane, the slaves of Noé itself and some of those who had been at Bois Cayman with Boukman. They said that Boukman was there himself somewhere though I never saw him. In the cane piece where we were waiting was a *commandeur* of Noé who had been at Bois Cayman and he had some direction to give to everyone but of course none of us maroons had to obey him and many of the Noé slaves did not obey either. They had left their families in the quarters, and we passed them going through the cane, rows of neat cabins whitewashed and well kept, but they were too quiet now, silent as death, though not empty. If I had been a whiteman in the great house I would have heard the silence and known. And maybe they did hear it, but knowing did not help them.

A moon was in the sky curved to a knifepoint at both ends of it, and the sky so clear we could see well all around. I went along between Achille and Bienvenu. Achille had found some powder and shot for his long gun and when we paused he crouched down and loaded it. Then through the stalks of cane we could see the clearing and the candles burning inside the *grand'case*.

Someone down the line from where I waited began drumming

on a little drum, a dry rasping sound, shallow, but the Noé *commandeur* came crashing through the cane leaves and stopped the noise. We waited while the quiet returned, the insects singing and nothing more. There was no sign of anything from the house or the outbuildings, only I did see a few house servants come out and go scattering into the cane at the left. It was windy, a dry wind rising and falling and knocking the cane leaves together like blades. I took my cane knife from the piece of cloth that tied it to my hip and tasted the bitter edge of it with my tongue and held it flat across my knees as I squatted. I heard Aiguy begin to hum low in the back of his throat and down the line Jean-Pic took it up and César-Ami and Paul Lefu and others too. A deep drone like a hive of bees, and the Noé *commandeur* could not stop this.

I wanted to swallow but my throat was stuck. As I might feel coming to a woman for the first time, or some special time. The drone was there inside my head and I was not quite Riau any longer and not quite yet Ogûn. My mouth was full of water and my tongue floating but I could not swallow and the water ran out at the sides of my mouth. On the far side of the compound fire broke out all at once in the cane and everyone was up and running altogether toward the buildings and Riau running too. Before this I had thought I would keep near Achille that Riau might be protected by his gun (or if he died then I might get the gun) but now Riau was not thinking about the gun or anything. He whirled his cane knife running toward the house, and felt his bare heels banging on the battered dirt of the compound. The drone of many voices pulled tighter and tighter as if it must tear and just ahead of Riau they were already splintering in the door.

Most of the whitepeople in the house had been already in their beds but for one young man in the main room, who was in shirt-sleeves and had taken off his boots. He had just the time to rise from his chair when Achille fired at him from the hip. Even so near the bullet missed him but Achille had overcharged the gun and the blast of powder blew back the whiteman's hair and burned his face. He put a hand in his breeches pocket and raised a shout, but no one answered. One of his eyes was blistered shut from the powder burn and the other was brown and swimming with fear. Riau came near enough to see this and he hacked his knife at the whiteman's head, but the whiteman dodged it partly and the stroke only caught his ear and left it dangling. He didn't seem to notice this because someone else was already stabbing him between the ribs on the other side and he folded his fingers over the blade and let them be cut to the cords inside as the other withdrew the blade very slowly, all the time looking into the whiteman's one open eye.

A glass bell that had covered a clock was swept to the floor and Riau saw the shards of it rebounding and pattering back down onto the boards as bright and slow as rain. Aiguy had seized the clock by its brass legs and danced around the room with it, shaking it and talking to it, trying to make it chime. Riau went toward the rear of the house where he heard women screaming now. A whiteman stepped into his path, dressed only in a shirt and a nightcap. His hair was gray between his legs and he was trying to charge a pistol but his fingers were shaking and he had no time to finish before Riau stabbed him in the belly, hardly breaking his step. Riau felt the blade go deep and catch between two sections of his backbone, and he twisted it loose and whipped it out the other side of the long sickle-shaped cut. Out of the hole smoked blood and a chitterling stink. Riau left the whiteman groaning, as some other blacks came up and began clubbing him with sticks. In the next room several had surrounded a whiteman who seemed to be in his sickbed and they were all flailing at him with machetes with no care to strike any vital spot, beating him as much as they cut.

Riau passed them, hurrying. In another room a whiteman hung upside down across a bed, gutted like a hog with his entrails swung from the breastbone tangling across his face, and below his stiffening open hands a naked whitewoman screamed and struggled on her all-fours. The man behind her was Paul Lefu, who kept jerking her up by the hips to meet his thrusts into her hindquarters, wanting her to support herself four-legged like an animal, but her palms would slip from under her on the blood-slickered floor and her face crash down against it.

Another whiteman, the *gérant* or the master, was pinned against the wall by the Noé *commandeur*. The whiteman was naked as if he'd been surprised in an act of love and he kept trying to talk about different acts of kindness he'd visited on the slaves of Noé, but the *commandeur* mashed the blade of his knife two-handed across his throat and held him to the wall with such a slow and steady pressure that it hardly cut at all, but only stopped his words.

The whiteman choked and his eyes bulged out, while a second whitewoman, younger than the other on the floor, flung yelping around the room until someone caught her by the hair and threw her down, catching up the hem of her loose white shift and trapping her hands and swaddling her head in the wad of cloth. Her bared body flopped on the floor like a skinned fish, crooked elbows working like fins out of water. The man who'd pinned her so was squatting on her head, unable to see quite how to improve his position, so Riau was the first to fall upon her.

Then the Noé *commandeur* had a new idea and got himself behind the master and throttled him slowly with a lace from one of the whitewomen's dresses, holding him so he was forced to watch. Each time the lace tightened the master's eyes went white, and his tongue stuck out of his blackening face while the *commandeur* cried out in a loud voice, "See! I am making a new nigger here!" Then he would loosen the lace and give him air until his eyes reopened, and begin again. Under the strangulation the master's member rose and pointed and the *commandeur* called out thunderously, "See how the whiteman is ready to take his pleasure!"

But he held the lace too long so that the whiteman died. The *commandeur* straightened, panting and sweating, and let the whiteman fall. Someone cut his penis off and crammed it into his mouth. Riau finished and got up, scrambling for the cane knife he'd dropped when he began. Another moved to take his place, but the whitewoman had suffocated in the folds of her shift and she was dead too. A mahogany-framed mirror hung over the bed and Riau looked at it and I saw myself there and Riau smashed his knife handle into the reflection. The glass shattered but held to the frame and the image splintered into dozens of Riaus and Ogûns. Riau shouted and jumped out the window and ran howling up the slope to the sugar mill.

It was a *moulin de bêtes,* powered by donkeys who circled it endlessly, each harnessed to a spoke. The mill had been running when the raid struck, and the mill hands had overcome the white refiner but had not done him much harm before Riau arrived. It seemed that Aiguy had persuaded them to feed him bodily into the mill, and under Aiguy's direction they had strapped his arms down to his sides with harness pieces and were beginning to push him in feet first. César-Ami and Jean-Pic and some others were happily poking up the donkeys to turn the mill faster. The refiner shrieked as his feet were crushed and thrashed so hard he broke most of his straps, but many hands came to hold him to the chute, Riau's among them. Riau could not even see the whiteman he was holding; he had reached across Aiguy's back to catch on, and he could see the scars the headstall had left on Aiguy's neck beginning to flush purple with his excitement.

Someone had set fire to the building and there was no need to drive the donkeys now. Crazed by the fire, they bellowed and broke into a gallop and the mill whirled the whiteman through all at once into a mass of blood and bone meal on the other side. One of the mill slaves had not let go in time and the mill sucked him up to the shoulder and he was shouting for someone to stop the mill but there was no stopping it. The high round roof of the building filled with smoke. Riau cut a couple of donkeys out of their harnesses and followed them as they ran wildly from the mill.

The *grand'case* was burning now too and when Riau saw flames shooting out the windows he saw on his eyelids as if in a dream the pistol falling from the hand of the whiteman he'd stabbed and smoothly revolving under the bed. He climbed back in through a window whose smouldering sill scorched his bare thighs. The bodies of the white people there were all so cut and torn he could not distinguish who was who, and besides the rooms were full of smoke. He went along crouching with his nose and mouth covered with one hand and entered a room past a slumped corpse whose hair was burning fitfully and felt along the floor under the trailing bedclothes, where he found the pistol or another as good. It was a handsome little weapon with a carved handle and silver chasings and an octagon barrel. Because he'd cast off his trousers during the rape he had no place to carry or conceal it. He ripped a section from a sheet and rolled the pistol in it and tied it to his waist. Still carrying the cane knife, he scuttled toward the front of the house, bent double to keep his face out of the smoke as much as possible.

Other salvagers were looting the storeroom, handing out kegs and bottles as fast as they might. Someone gave Riau a bottle of wine still corked and he carried it out onto the gallery and paused for a breath. The gallery roof was burning but the wind carried enough of the smoke away that the air was breathable. Just then the fire reached the powder in the storeroom and the explosion sent Riau pinwheeling halfway across the compound. He sat up gasping and felt for the pistol; it was still there and his knife was lying near him. The core of the house caved in on itself and burned with the luminous heat of a smelter's forge. The heat was baking Riau's face and he felt like both his ears were bleeding. Somehow he had kept hold of the wine bottle and now he broke off the neck on a stone wedged in the earth and gulped at it, not feeling how it cut his lips.

People were beginning to scatter from the compound now, and Riau got up and went down toward the quarters, sucking on the wine as he walked. A naked man tiger-striped with fresh wet blood ran with a torch from cabin to cabin setting all the roofs alight for no good reason but bloodmadness. The women and the children came pouring out looking for where they might turn for some other shelter, but as far as the jungle on the mountain slopes there was nothing at all but walls of fire. A mass of the rebels was collecting at the bottom of the quarters and Riau went there. He was losing the momentum that had carried him this far and I began to feel the scrapes and bruises he'd got in the explosion, though the wine partly numbed him.

After this we went to Galifet, where they had already attacked before, but here the whites had taken warning and were barricaded in the house with guns. I took out my pistol to shoot at them but Riau had not got any powder or lead so I could only snap it empty and put it back where I kept it again. Some of us had already been killed by bullets from the house and their bodies were lying in the open in the compound. Riau took a pair of trousers from a man who was dead there in the yard. After that we set fire to whatever was not already burning and then we went away.

Some were going back into the mountains already and many were drunk on tafia from the houses and some were lying down right in the roadways to sleep. There was no place in the fields to rest because they were all burning. I was tired enough to lie down myself but I didn't want to be alone with dreams of what Riau had done and seen although Riau wanted still to do more of the same. If Ogûn had done everything himself then Riau would not even have remembered it, but it had been part Riau and part Ogûn and I did remember but I did not know what to think or do. We went up and down the roads all night thinking we might meet some whitemen who were running away but we met no one but other bands. Of who had started with us there were just Jean-Pic and Paul Lefu and they didn't know what had happened to the others any more than I. The rest in the group were strangers and there was a big Congo wearing a whitewoman's dress that they all seemed to follow. We kept on walking that way all together until morning came.

There was only a red blaze in the smoke where the sun should have been, like it was one of the fires still burning in the cane fields all around. My eyes stung and ran from the smoke and there was a heaviness on me like I had awoken with some sickness. My mouth was swollen with cuts from the wine bottle and most of all I wanted water, but there was none. This was the hell where Jesus sends people who serve him poorly, and I saw that he had made it here for the whites as they deserved but that somehow we must be in it with them too.

After a long time walking we saw a wagon and beside it one man riding a horse. We came near but before we could see them well the horseman began riding down on us and our people scattered, thinking that what he had in his hand must be a saber or a knife, though it was only a switch when I saw it near. He swung at me with it and almost fell from the horse and I might have caught him and dragged him down but just then I saw that it was he who had killed the dog at Arnaud's place and I was so surprised that I did nothing. A few ran after him a little way but they could not keep up with the horse.

So we all went down together toward the wagon. It was pleasant to see them like they were, all stunned and blind with misery, the same expressions as our people wore when they were carted from the barracoons to the slave market at Le Cap. The Congo walked all around the wagon to admire them while the rest of us watched from where we stood. The whitewomen had all been used already till they were nothing but bloody bags, so we probably would have killed them all except for a strange thing which happened.

The one whitewoman who was driving the wagon was different from any whitewoman I had ever seen before. She stood up with an odd stiffness as though something was crowding into her body beside her, as though she was a *serviteur* though this could not be. When she spoke it sounded like the voice of a *loa*. The Congo grabbed at her as much to drive the *loa* out as to get her ring, I think, but that was not what happened. No one of us could have believed that any whitewoman would do what she did then. Of course the women of Guinée would often swallow their tongues and strangle their own children to take them home to freedom that way. But we had not thought any whitewoman could cut her own limb free of a trap and when we saw her do it, we did not know what to do about her anymore. We let them go by then, without touching them at all, not even taking the water they had with them in the wagon. They moved very slowly, and it was long before they went out of sight, long after the horseman had joined them again. An hour later I looked back and thought I could still see the wagon as a dot or a fleck of ash where the land ran into the smoking sky.

On the afternoon of that day we came upon Jeannot leading a big party back to Le Cap. So many they were they'd swollen from the road and many were walking over the fields though these were still hot enough to blister your feet. Jeannot was leading them all and carrying a white baby stuck onto a spear. The baby was newborn, or notborn even, and it was not quite dead but could still move its arms and legs a little the way a frog does when you stick it. I looked at it wondering why if it was not dead it did not cry.

It was different to see this thing than to make the words that say it—as terrible but in a different way. You cannot understand this when you only see the words I make. I knew this was a thing the whitemen had done before. They carried colored children on spears this way when they were attacking *les gens de couleur*, their cousins, in the west. But it was different to hear about it than to see it. When I looked I knew for the first time what it was we were doing and what we all wanted although I could not make the words for that either. Riau and Ogûn and I all wanted this thing together though we couldn't say what the thing was, but I knew that I would follow the spear and what was on it, where it would lead me.

Then the whitemen must have known too, carrying such a standard, they must have known where they meant to go. But it was a long time later before I thought of that.

Achille and Aiguy and César-Ami were all in Jeannot's gang then. Still there was no water I could find but César-Ami had rum so I drank some of that. From them I heard how it was that we were going to Le Cap. There should have been a rising there when the plantations were all burned on the plain, but someone had given up the secret and the whitemen had killed several of the leaders and the others were afraid, so nothing had happened—it was like in Macandal's time. Also most of them with a taste for killing had come out onto the plain with us.

But Jeannot had got word that the soldiers of Le Cap had set out for Limbé that morning, so with the city naked it seemed that we might take it after all. While we were going there another strange thing happened. A gang of young whitemen, only a few, came riding out toward us with no guns, only whips that they waved and snapped. They ordered us, in our thousands, to go back to our masters on the plantations, and told us our punishment would be light if we obeyed. This was ordinary whiteman madness, not like what that woman had done, but still I think these must have been very stupid young men. They were pulled down off their horses and Jeannot commanded them to be skinned, meaning to send their skins back where they'd come from, as a sign. But whiteman skin is so flimsy we could not get a whole pelt off any of them. At the end they lay flayed on the coals of the cane field screaming and begging for death, and we trampled over them all of us as we went on toward Le Cap, so I think they had died by the time we had all passed over.

We could not come into the city at once because of a fort with guns, so we attacked this fort and the soldiers that were there. It was not a real army that we had yet, and people ran up on the cannon carelessly and many were killed. Later I heard that Paul Lefu was killed this time, but I did not see it. It was only a low earthwork fort and if we did not fear the cannon it was easy to get into it. No one feared. I did not even have to have Ogûn in my head that time, but I could be still myself and willing to toss my body away. I was running right behind Achille when he tossed away his gun and wrapped himself around a cannon's mouth calling out to everyone behind him, "Come, brothers, I am holding it for you!" I saw the artillery sergeant's eyes swell wide and yellow while Achille grinned at him down the cannon's barrel and I almost reached him before he fired the touchhole, but not quite. Achille kept grinning and his hands held tight to the gun carriage even after the rest of him had been blown half across the field in a bloody net to catch the others' faces. I cut the artilleryman's head half off while he was trying to get his pistol unstuck from his belt and I took the pistol for myself along with the belt and his powder and lead.

The soldiers in the fort surrendered then, believing the game would be played by the rules whitemen use on each other or wanting to believe it. Jeannot lined them up and had their throats cut like cattle at the slaughter and he went from one to the next drinking their blood he caught in his cupped hands and screaming praises to the *loa*. Many of us did the same. But then the other soldiers came back from Limbé and there was a worse fight. We wanted to shoot the cannons at them but we didn't know yet how it was with cannons and when we put the balls in before the powder the cannons wouldn't fire. So after a while the soldiers drove us off.

Achille was killed and again I didn't know what had happened to the others. I didn't know what had happened to Jean-Pic or César-Ami, and I didn't know about Merbillay. We had come farther than we meant from the place in the mountains where the women and children were hidden. After the soldiers chased us away from the fort, most of us went running back to the plain, but I caught a horse I found wandering loose and rode away by myself alone.

Chapter Thirteen

In Le Cap there was no sunrise; billows of black smoke rolled in from the northern plain and blotted out the light. All through the town it was raining feathery flakes of ash, and hot cinders too sometimes, which threatened to set the roofs alight. But few attended to this danger. No blacks from the plain had breached the town's defenses, but the *petit blancs* had risen in a riot and traveled the streets in mobs, hanging whatever mulattoes they might find from the lampposts or shooting them or slashing them to death with knives, for as the first white survivors began to trickle in from the plantations the rumor spread that Ogé's colored co-conspirators had raised the insurrection of the slaves.

Captain Maillart rode about aimlessly from quarter to quarter of the town; he had been doing so for a little better than an hour. Together with the saber and dragoon's pistol he commonly carried, he had equipped himself with an infantryman's musket, carried in a makeshift sling against his saddle skirt. He had been one of the small scouting party that went out into the plain at dawn as the first refugees straggled in from the countryside, and one of a few to survive a misfortunate encounter with a huge band of brigand blacks. Badly as he'd been shaken by what he'd seen then, he'd volunteered at once for the expedition to Limbé, but Thouzard had detached him along with some few others to remain and keep order in the town—now a plainly impossible project.

Most of the other soldiers had shut themselves in the barracks to wait for the riots to wear themselves out, knowing that the *petit blancs* might attack them, in their weakened numbers, almost as readily as they'd set upon mulattoes or blacks. Maillart, however, preferred to remain on the move, though unsupported as he was he could do little of real use. The town's small body of regular police had either joined with the rioters or barred themselves behind their doors to wait it out. Some householders had banded together to do what they might to contain the present danger of fire, wetting down roofs and wooden walls and smothering hot cinders before they could ignite. The wind that brought the coals and ash in from the plain could spread a fire quickly all over the city if ever a fire was well started.

His horse at least was a steady campaigner, unafraid of smoke or sparks. But at the edge of the town even this horse grew restive, shifting its hooves and flaring its nostrils. Captain Maillart himself felt a shock to the roots of his system repeated each time he looked at the spectacle there. Beyond the ridge of Morne du Cap was something that his imagination could only compare with a storm over some brimstone lake of hell. A hundred degrees of the horizon were luridly edged with a red fire glow. Above this smoldering ring rose great black billows of smoke like thunderheads with long tongues of flame stabbing up through them to lick the belly of the sky. But there was no sky, only the sooty haze from which the ash and coals kept hailing down.

Here some few other officers of the Regiment Le Cap were ministering to the survivors still intermittently trickling out of this inferno. Most were advised to seek shelter in the houses of friends, if they had friends, since the hospital and the convent were already overcrowded. Captain Maillart looked over their soot-streaked staring faces. He would have liked to inquire about his friend Antoine Hébert, but he saw little hope in doing so. Most who survived were women and children and these could report that their men had been mostly slain on the spot, before their eyes. Maillart knew from the events of the morning that women and children would not always be spared either.

He headed his horse back into the town, where the prospect was no more encouraging. The streets were awash with a surf of *petit blancs,* scouring the neighborhoods for new victims, some now openly breaking into mulatto houses. There were no blacks or *gens de couleur* abroad, save those who hung bloody and loll-tongued from window embrasures and posts. By now the wave of murderous retaliation had mostly passed over, leaving a festival of rape and looting in its wake. Maillart was not an especially canny political analyst but he did understand that these outrages stemmed as much from resentment of mulatto wealth as from any connection *les gens de couleur* might have had to the slave rebellion. Also he recognized, exchanging glances with the pop-eyed dangling men he passed, that many in the mob would be as glad to see him swing among them.

In his unhappiness over the likely doom of the doctor, Captain Maillart began to think of Nanon and the other mulatto women who were variously attached to his regiment. Immediately he felt certain of what must have already happened to them, but just the same he nudged his horse into a trot and rode up to the area below the Place d'Armes where most of these women kept their lodgings. As he'd expected, the door to Nanon's rooms was stove in. He dismounted and stepped over the threshold, holding the horse at the length of the unslung reins. The front room was dim and quiet, there seemed to be some scurrying noise in the back. In the poor light he stepped on something and almost lost his footing: a pawn from the chess set that shot out from under the edge of his boot and twirled into a corner. The room was a ruin, all the fragile furniture overturned and dismembered, hangings slashed, the glass all hammered out of the mirror frames. At the sound of his movement a squirrel face poked out from the bedroom, a looter rolling opulent dresses into a large bundle.

"Come out of there," Maillart called brusquely, but the looter only dodged behind the door frame. The captain cursed and looked over his shoulder at the horse; he didn't dare step away from the animal, certainly not leave him tethered there. He called a warning, drew his pistol and after a moment's pause fired through the inner doorway. The looter did not stir or show himself but the ball struck loose a hinge from a bamboo jalousie and through the window thus uncovered Maillart could see some commotion in the inner courtyard. He reloaded his pistol and primed it and remounted and rode around to investigate.

Immediately he recognized the woman Fleur, with whom he'd enjoyed the occasional most exquisite dalliance; she was lying on her back near the central well with a number of men raping her in turn. There seemed no longer any need to hold her down; her arms shivered loosely in the dust like the wings of a hen under treading, and her eyes showed only white, as if she were dead. Captain Maillart wondered if she were not dead, in fact. With each lunge of the man who'd presently skewered her, the top of her head knocked against the well's bricked rim. In the shadows under a shanty lean-to against the rear wall of a house a great fat black woman in a white headcloth stood watching the scene impassively with her heavy lips set firmly together. Near her two shirtless blacks stood similarly immobile, one holding a spotted pony on a rope. They seemed less interested than the animal they held, but Maillart was no more appalled by their indifference than by his own. He could feel nothing and he thought that there was nothing he could do. With a snort one rapist withdrew and another assumed his place and despite his grunts and the mutters of those encouraging him the sound of Fleur's head bumping on the bricks seemed louder than anything else.

He would likely have done no more than ride away at this point, but just then someone burst out of the lean-to, a woman with her hands held out to him. He was distracted for a moment because the spotted pony had begun to kick and buck, jockeying the two blacks halfway across the courtyard to the well as they strove to control it. But the woman was Nanon; they must have hidden her there, beneath that heap of tattered sailcloth someone had been remaking into slave clothes. Her face was a welter of snot and tears and she called out chokingly for him to save her from the men who'd already diverted themselves from Fleur to seize her and tear at her clothing. There was Faustin the baker along with a man Maillart had never seen before, and the disreputable farrier Crozac. Maillart shouted for them to stop and took the musket from its sling without waiting to see their response.

Faustin caught Nanon by the wrist and she spun half around with both arms spread wide; she had not quite reached Maillart's horse. The captain chopped out another order and deftly fixed the bayonet to the musket. He sat the horse, balancing the unfamiliar weapon with one hand round the trigger guard. Nanon could not break Faustin's grip, but she drew her captured wrist toward her face and closed her wide mouth over his hand, crunching down on the small bones clustered like a chicken back. Faustin shouted and let go; he would have hit her with his unhurt fist but he saw the bayonet probing for his face and he fell back, along with the third man. The dozen or so other men in the yard had formed a loose line around Maillart's horse and were waiting to see what would happen.

Crozac rushed up and clutched at Nanon's hair, yanking her head back by the scalp, exposing her long pulsing neck and a taut face distorted by the sudden pain. Maillart spoke to him crisply, not too loud, trying for the tone of authority which these folk would often follow before they fully knew they would obey, but Crozac was beyond this. His eyes were furrowed shut like badly sutured scars and his face looked nothing but a mask of bad teeth. In his unconsciousness he had pressed the woman full against the saddle skirt and Maillart's booted foot. The captain touched him with the bayonet point, at the neckless join of Crozac's head and shoulders, but the man did not seem aware of him at all. Maillart returned the glance of some of the whites watching him and thought of the hanged men who'd be his blind and silent companions if his choice of action proved to be mistaken. He reversed the musket and gripped it with both hands about the barrel and brought it down with maybe half his force into the center of the farrier's forehead.

Crozac sat down sharply with a *whumpf* and a puff of dust. His eyes jumped farther open with the blow and he took a noisy breath in through his mouth. Maillart held out a hand to Nanon and she swarmed up his whole arm at once, swinging a leg over the saddle and splitting her skirt as her weight settled down. The captain lifted the reins with his left hand and with the other brandished the musket over his head like a javelin. Her arms cinched around his waist as he dug heels in the horse's side and cantered out of the yard.

Doctor Hébert and his battered and exhausted party had reached Le Cap at last, exactly when he could not say. The cinder-black sky gave no clue of the time and he felt himself to be passing within some sort of damned eternity. The Flaville family kept a house in town where the women might retreat, but after the doctor had escorted them there he excused himself and headed for the Place d'Armes, going afoot and leading his spent horse by the reins. The scenes through which he passed defeated his understanding. There was as much ruin and death about as if the slaves had overrun the town although he had been told that this had been prevented.

Whatever rage had swept the place had drifted into its doldrums and he was alone on the streets now except for the dead. He was itching to find Nanon; though there was no vestige of passion in him or even interest really, he felt a blunt obligation to see to her safety if he could.

He hitched his horse to a rail by her broken door and walked across the gutted ruin of her rooms. The floor was carpeted with splinters of furniture and chunks of broken mirror glass. The doctor stooped and picked up one of these, just large enough to show him his own eye. A heap of fresh human excrement fumed warmly near one wall. Everything that was not stolen had been carefully insulted and destroyed. The bed was stripped and marked with crisscrossing streaks of urine. The doctor stepped through the back door into the courtyard, where he saw a woman struggling feebly to get up onto her knees. She looked to have been raped to ribbons, and the doctor was becoming so inured to such sights that it took him a moment to realize that this was Nanon's sometime companion, Fleur.

He moved to lift Fleur by the shoulders, but she would not or could not stand. Her lassitude was more uncooperative than dead weight. The doctor twisted his head around until he noticed Maman-Maigre hunkered in her lean-to, and he began to back in that direction, Fleur's heels furrowing the dust as they dragged behind.

Three chickens clucked and scattered from their way. The doctor laid Fleur's shoulders down softly as he might by the dead embers of Maman-Maigre's cook fire. There was a pail of water standing near and the doctor sopped a rag of rotten sailcloth in it and uncertainly began cleaning the crust from Fleur's belly. At his first touch she moaned and convulsed onto her side. Maman-Maigre took the rag from him and continued the task herself and the doctor gratefully turned his eyes elsewhere. He did not look again until Maman-Maigre had covered Fleur's legs with the remains of her clothing. The black woman sat cross-legged, holding Fleur's head on her hammy thigh. The younger woman's eyes were closed completely now and she breathed easily as a sleeper. All over the yard the ghostly ash continued to feather down. The doctor asked Maman-Maigre several times over if she knew what had happened to Chloe or Jasmine or Nanon, but though he spoke slowly in the clearest Creole he could manage, she would not answer him at all.

At dusk he came stumbling through the northmost quarter of the town into Les Casernes, where he thought he might at least safely stable his horse. When he asked for Maillart the captain came running and almost knocked him over with the surprise of his embrace. He conducted the doctor to his quarters where he broached a bottle of brandy which the doctor was very glad to taste. With his throat so warmed he told of what had happened to him and what he had witnessed: the slaying of Lambert, and how Duvel's head had grinned down on him from its stake, and how Madame Arnaud had saved them all, as he believed, by sacrificing her finger to the Congo.

At that the captain drew in his breath and looked as if he would make some remark, but when he did speak he told another tale. How he'd gone out at dawn to reconnoiter on the plain with a small body of foot soldiers who'd unexpectedly fallen in with rebel slaves, surprised and outnumbered so completely they'd all been slaughtered save himself and a few others who'd outdistanced the marauders on horseback. Because it was only Antoine Hébert and not another military man the captain could confess the shame he felt at fleeing before blacks and the shock of knowing he had no better hope to save his life. And here he hesitated, but finally went on to say he'd seen something more dreadful than a head raised on a spear: an infant's corpse and what was worse it seemed to have been torn untimely from the womb.

The doctor set his glass aside and rubbed his eyelids with his fingertips.

"Can you imagine such bestial cruelty?" the captain said.

"Unfortunately I don't have to imagine it," the doctor said. He held his hand out before him flat and planed it back and forth across the air as if to show himself that it was steady.

"What does it mean?" the captain said. "What can it mean?"

"Ours is the age of reason," the doctor said. He took from his pocket the wedge of broken mirror he'd saved from Nanon's room and squinted into its minute reflection. "Reason must afford some answer to your question."

At that the captain only sniffed and rolled the remains of liquor in his glass.

"Hogs may eat their young," the doctor said. "They sometimes do. But not display a piglet as a trophy." He put the bit of mirror back into his pocket.

"The woman Nanon," said Maillart.

The doctor raised his head and stared at him with his bloodshot eyes. He'd been helplessly filling Nanon into Fleur's situation and now he only expected to hear some such event described more closely.

"*Oui, ta petite amie,*" the captain said. "I happened to meet her before she'd been harmed. I took her to Les Ursulines . . ."

The doctor exhaled. "You astonish me," he said. "I passed by her place—it looked as if the slaves had sacked it."

"Yes," the captain said. "She's quite all right. A little frightened. One might look out some other lodging for her. I don't suppose she's very well suited for convent life."

Then over the captain's protest the doctor went out again into the smoking evening. There was a new tumult in the streets because the main body of troops led by Thouzard had just reentered the town, having fallen back from Limbé in time to repulse a horde of blacks who'd overrun Fort Bongars. News of the garrison's massacre there . . . The roof of the house next to the Cignys had caught fire from some floating spark no doubt and a mixed part of slaves and whites were hurrying to extinguish it. But at *chez Cigny* the liveried footman was still at his post and when ushered into the drawing room, the doctor found Madame Cigny playing carelessly with her son Robert.

The boy had undone a little kit of *nécessaires* and Isabelle Cigny was laying out the instruments and prattling to him about their use. A compass, a pair of glass vials, a penknife and a small scissors . . . That dainty fop, Pascal, balanced on a spindly chair and played a country air on a violin with a disconsonant expression of seriousness. The doctor could not quite make out whether all this insouciance was courage or idiocy, but remembering Madame Arnaud he thought he would do well to reserve his judgment. Soon he found himself telling the story of his trials again under Madame Cigny's cheerful questioning, though as briefly as she would allow. While he was speaking she quietly removed the scissors from Robert's hand before he could do himself the injury he seemed to intend and raised the boy onto her lap and held him there. The doctor paused.

"Not to fatigue you with these horrors," he said. Through the cloth of his pocket he fidgeted with the bit of mirror glass. "I came for another reason . . . to ask your hospitality, your charity, I mean." He fumbled. "Not for myself but another . . ."

"A woman?" Madame Cigny said with her provocative smile.

"*C'est ça,*" the doctor said. He picked up the *nécessaire* box and examined the miniature painted on its side, a couple standing by the steps of a tiny Grecian temple all open to the air. "*Une femme de couleur* . . . hmmm . . . her home has been rendered uninhabitable. And it seems unsafe generally now."

"A woman in whom you must have some peculiar interest?" Madame Cigny lifted a fan and hid her mouth behind it; above its fluted rim her eyes looked dark, almost angry. The violin abruptly ceased and in its absence shouting voices reached them more plainly from the street. The doctor felt that he was turning purple. He knocked over the *nécessaire* box in replacing it on the table and had to reach again to set it right.

"What are her virtues, this girl?" said Madame Cigny. "Has she accomplishments?"

"Why yes . . ." The doctor bethought himself that most of Nanon's accomplishments were strictly unmentionable. "Well, she can cook. And sew."

"*Vraiment?*" Above the fan, Madame Cigny's eyes turned merry. "Then I suppose we may find some place for her here. Out of Christian charity, as you suggest. And temporarily, *bien entendu.*"

"Thank you," the doctor said. "May I bring her directly? Or no, the morning would certainly be better."

When he took his leave he was surprised to find that Pascal would accompany him out. Robert wiggled his plump hands happily, trying to reach the scissors again. And as the parlor door closed they heard Madame Cigny begin singing him a little song in Creole.

"Indeed you are a very droll fellow," Pascal said when they had reached the street.

"What do you mean?"

"To ask a Creole lady to harbor your mulatto wench?"

"I didn't see it in that light," the doctor said. "The town's in a state of emergency."

"It's of no consequence. Though I suppose the ladies must inevitably be weary of seeing their husband's bastard get in the arms of these colored women. And you must know that our Isabelle was one of the ladies who brought about the sumptuary law."

"Oh but I have only been in the country a couple of months," the doctor said.

"At the behest of our ladies an ordinance was passed which forbade the mulattresses to wear their fine clothes—out of their own doors. Nor any jewelry or ornament . . . but the women rebelled and refused to go out at all. They refused to entertain. I think you know their touch with entertainment? And so the law was hastily repealed."

"Thank you," the doctor said. "You have been most enlightening."

They parted, and the doctor went on to Les Ursulines where with some difficulty he persuaded the nuns to admit him at last. A nun was present throughout his interview with Nanon and so he remained across the room from the place where she was seated while he gave his news. After all he hardly knew how to comport himself and really it relieved him that they were not left alone. He had no wish to be touched or to touch anyone for the time being, if he could avoid it. And she seemed mute and uncomprehending; her still beauty was a mask; he had to repeat himself several times before he thought she'd understood. Then she crossed the room more quickly than the nun could stay her, sank down and wrapped her arms around his legs and laid her cheek against his knees.

Chapter Fourteen

ARNAUD RODE UP THE RIVER VALLEY from the ford, followed by his *nègre chasseur* Orion. The trail he'd been told of did exist but was hard to follow in its twistings along the mountain escarpments, going up and farther up the gorge. Below, out of his sight, he could hear the noise of some tributary stream, rushing to join the Massacre. They went slowly, their mounts picking their way, Arnaud's horse less easily than the mule ridden by his slave, though oftentimes both men had to dismount to lead them. Twice they found their way barred by obstructions they must clear: a slide of muddy rock and a fallen tree trunk half rotted over the trail. Arnaud had no choice but to put his own hand to the work and at those moments he wished he had brought more niggers along to help, although in other ways they would have hindered his journey.

A cloud brooded over the mountaintop above and ahead of them, and the jungle grew denser and damper, edging its way onto the trail. As the sun passed its zenith Arnaud began to grow uneasy. There was no sign of the men he expected to meet and he dearly wished to complete his return from the mountains before night. Across the gorge from where they made their way was the vestige of a clearing with banana suckers sprouting from what might have been terraces cut into the nearly sheer slope. As if someone had tried to carve a dwelling place and since abandoned it. It put Arnaud in mind of the maroon bands who very likely traveled these hills. He shook his head dourly and pressed on, following Orion, who had now taken the lead. The black stopped short and wrinkled his nose.

"K'eské sé?" Arnaud said.

"Fimé, lahô." Orion swept a hand widely around the area and surveyed the gorge with a slow rotation of his head. Arnaud imitated the movement, hoping to catch a glimpse of something in the corner of his eye. He saw nothing, but a ghostly odor seemed to waft his way, not smoke so much as a surreal unlikely smell of roasting meat. He and Orion exchanged a shrug and continued. Some fifty yards farther on the trail Orion stopped again and stared into the thickness of the jungle.

"Là, là," he muttered.

Still Arnaud could not see anything at first. Then at last his eye discerned another clearing within the thick bush above them and at its edge three figures waiting, posed almost as still as the trees, two blacks and what he took to be a Spaniard dressed in the kilt and boots of a *boucanier* of half a century gone, his face shaded out of view by the wide brim of his hat. There seemed nowhere on earth this party might have come from but there they were.

"De donde viene?" Arnaud called out half believingly.

"Donde va?"

The Spaniard's voice came from nowhere, or out of the whole jungle all around. Arnaud left Orion holding the horses on the trail and began to climb the slope dividing them. So high on the mountain the jungle was always very wet and his footing was so uncertain in the mud he had to haul himself up by clutching at the trunks of trees. The meat smell blew in his face again. When he reached the others he saw that they had spitted a shoulder of wild pig and were roasting it over a muddy pit. The Spaniard crouched at the fire's edge companionably with the two blacks, who were pulling off strips of the loosening meat as it cooked and eating it with their fingers.

"Ah, Michel," the Spaniard said, standing again as Arnaud came level with him. "I didn't know it would be you." He took off his hat, and with a start Arnaud recognized Xavier Tocquet, his long mass of hair tied back with a greasy bit of black ribbon, his chin obscured by a short pointed Spaniard's beard he'd grown.

"Nor I you," Arnaud said, trying to conceal his breathlessness. In climbing the grade he'd broken into a clammy sweat, though it was quite cool in the jungle shade.

"Have you yet dined?" Tocquet inquired.

Arnaud looked distastefully at shreds of meat and roasted plantains still in their skins, spread on a glossy banana leaf. It was not the plainness of the provender which displeased him so much as the casual way Tocquet partook of it alongside the blacks.

"*Merci, mais non,*" he said. "I haven't time."

"Of course." Tocquet's deep-set eyes were glittering; perhaps his beard concealed a smile. He was a head taller than Arnaud, big-boned but lean in his loose clothing. His hands were huge; he raised one and waved it farther on. "*Allez, regardez,*" he said.

Arnaud climbed a little higher. From the far side of the fire pit he could see the clearing better: another abandoned cultivation, with the plantains running wild. Here six pack mules in a train were foraging on the jungle floor. Arnaud turned back the canvas from the back of one; beneath, the blunt muskets were bundled like firewood. He went on examining load after load, roughly calculating as he went along; Maltrot had let him know that payment had already been made through some other channel, but still he thought it best to check. His habit. As he went from mule to mule he looked all around the jungle and the borders of the clearing but there was no track or any other sign to show how the pack train might have reached this place.

"Satisfactory?" Tocquet called to him, from where he hunkered over the firepit.

"*Ouais, bien sûr,*" Arnaud said. He walked back to the lead mule and slipped a finger through its halter. All the mules were harnessed in a line and the whole string came behind him docilely, stopping when he stopped and nosing again at the jungle floor.

"You're welcome to eat," Tocquet said. "Call your man up if you like." The two blacks had stopped eating; they sat back on their haunches and watched Arnaud with a quiet animal concentration. Above, invisibly, a cloud drifted over the forest ceiling and the space where they gathered grew darker.

"I want to be off the mountain before night," Arnaud said. One of the blacks relaxed himself to lift a fresh whole pepper pod from the banana leaf and begin eating it.

"You've become altogether a Spaniard, Xavier?" Arnaud said. On the plain or in the coast towns he would not have addressed Tocquet by his first name, but it was difficult to muster any formality now.

"What does it matter here?" Tocquet tossed his head back. His neck swelled against the mass of his hair. Arnaud saw the uneven curls of beard sparse on his throat.

"This place was here before our nations," Tocquet said. "I'll trade you for your horse." He jerked his head at three saddled mules which were tethered to thorny saplings at a brief distance from the fire pit. Arnaud stared at them for a moment and then burst out laughing.

"It's harder going down than up," Tocquet said.

"Vous êtes gentil," Arnaud said. He peered down toward the trail. Orion, holding the horse and mule, had pressed himself partly into the trees for shelter from the light spatter of rain that was now tapping down on the leaves overhead. "I think not, however . . ."

"As it pleases you," Tocquet said, gazing neutrally at the fat dripping onto the coals from the spitted shank, whose white bone glistened through tears in the flesh.

Arnaud tugged on the lead mule's halter, meaning to guide the pack train down the steep slope to the trail. He had not gone more than twenty paces before his feet shot from under him in the mud and leaf mold. An arm crooked over a branch stopped him from falling altogether and saved a portion of his dignity. Tocquet, expressionless, snapped his fingers, and the two blacks rose from their meal and completed the task of guiding the pack train down. Arnaud heard Orion speak to them and heard that they answered, but he could not make out if they were speaking Creole or some African tongue; it irked him not to understand what they said.

His boots were clubs of mud, and when he slipped he'd strained a muscle, his legs splaying in opposite directions. He used the branch to straighten himself and took his weight shyly on both legs.

"Go with God, Michel!" Tocquet had risen to bid him good-bye, his huge hands paddling before him like flounder. *"À la rencontre . . ."* Arnaud smiled at him speechlessly over his shoulder. With care he made his way back to the trail.

At first he took the lead on the way down, while Orion brought up the rear of the pack train. The cloud that had been raining on them detached itself from the mass that clung to the mountain peak, drifted away and dissipated. The sun began to redden, westering over the hills. Making the best haste he could, Arnaud thought of Xavier Tocquet, the times they'd ridden together after runaways in the *maréchaussée*. When the going grew too rough for horses, Tocquet would always shed his boots and go up with mulattoes and the black slave-catchers, quick as a land crab over the rocks. On those occasions Arnaud had sneered at him, along with other whites who remained with their mounts. Now he wondered, if Orion had not seen them, if Tocquet would have let them pass and climb the mountain endlessly . . . It had been more than strange to hear Tocquet mention the name of God.

More sure-footed, the lead mule kept nosing into the hindquarters of Arnaud's horse. Yet he was too stubborn to dismount, until at last the horse's footing failed it on the muddy shale and it fell spraddled across the ledge, dumping Arnaud into the bush. He picked himself up, wiped a hand at the slick of mud on his shirt sleeve. The horse lay with its neck stretched, flanks pumping air, a foreleg broken. The lead mule overlooked the disaster with a supercilious expression, as it seemed. Arnaud backhanded it across the muzzle with all his strength but the mule scarcely bothered to draw back its head.

"Well, kill it then," Arnaud told Orion, as the black made his way to the head of the train. He turned his back, and waited for the horse's final sigh of expiration before he looked again. The tendons stretched tight across Orion's back as he squatted, straining to shove the dead horse off the trail into the gorge. Arnaud watched from where he stood. He felt a revulsion against touching the animal's dead hide. Orion gave an enormous heave and the horse tumbled over the edge with limp legs flailing at the air and slid down the damp slope, crushing saplings and tearing away vines. A few yards down the carcass snagged on a cylindrical cluster of bamboo and hung there. Orion stood up, gasping from his effort. He looked over the edge and clicked his tongue.

They went on, Orion leading the pack train afoot, while Arnaud listlessly sat the uncomfortable mule saddle. Orion's mount required little guidance and Arnaud let it pick its own way without interference. Still their progress was slow. They made their way around a deep involution of the gorge, from which the trail wrapped around another outcropping. At this vantage they could again see the horse's carcass rucked up into the bamboo, but the sight of it was fading in the quickly thickening dusk.

Arnaud saw that they would spend the night on the mountain

after all. They camped, if one could call it that, across the trail itself. Out of the dark came a smell of corruption, and Arnaud thought of the horse, though it hardly could have decayed so soon. At last he realized it was the birds Orion had shot, deliquescent in the saddlebag. He scooped them out and pitched them into the ravine. They had not water enough for him to rinse his hands; he scrabbled his fingers in the damp leaves and brushed them off but a vague odor of rot still clung to them. He interrupted Orion's effort to start a fire; there was nothing to cook and he did not want to show a light. They were not provisioned for an overnight stay but there were some cooked yams in a saddlebag. Arnaud ate one of these without interest and left the rest for his slave.

The rain forest clouds sealed off the sky, raining on them fitfully. Arnaud huddled in his thin clothes. It was unpleasantly chilly, and remained so even when the rain stopped and a rent opened in the clouds so that the stars again appeared. The mules were restless on their short tethers and often Orion had to rise to quiet them. Arnaud did not think he slept at all, but when his eyes opened onto daylight he felt that he had been dreaming something which left him with a strange sense of dread. He thought his wife had somehow figured in the dream, though he could not remember it, and though he almost never dreamed of her.

His leg had stiffened in the night and was so sore he had to bite back a groan when he mounted the mule. Up the ravine, the dead horse's belly had swelled and its legs stuck out rigidly from it. Arnaud ground his teeth and started down the trail. The day was fair and clear, and the sun and the saddle's movement seemed to soften his injury. As they descended, the undergrowth above and below the trail grew dryer. Also there was a smell of smoke which Arnaud could not place, and so far there was no sign of where it came from.

Before noon they reached the ragged edge of the outmost hill where the plain and the Massacre River could be seen. Orion stopped so abruptly that the mule he was leading bumped him with its shoulder. He turned and looked back at Arnaud, aghast. Arnaud had cupped a hand over his mouth; he removed it, briefly, to speak.

"*Vasé*," he said, "Go on." But Orion remained in his frozen position.

"M'ap di ou kou l'yé a," Arnaud said. "I'm telling you now." He signaled Orion to proceed.

Orion faced forward and moved off along the trail. Arnaud felt a vague stirring of nausea, perhaps from the mule's unfamiliar motion. Beyond the Massacre the cane fields were blanketed with a heavy black smoke. Apart from that it was eerily quiet and there was nothing whatsoever to be seen.

At last they came to the river ford and crossed it. Even muleback Arnaud was wet to his knees, but his trousers had dried by the time they reached the priest's compound. Here they halted the pack train and Arnaud called out but there was no answer. He dismounted with less pain than he'd expected and looked into the *ajoupa,* then limped to the church. Both houses were unoccupied but seemed in good order; there was no sign of looting or violence, though the fires had burned up to the edge of the clearing where they stood. Seeing this, Arnaud felt somewhat reassured that things were going according to plan; fire was an unsubtle tool, but certainly the show of destruction would be all that Maltrot's cohort had intended.

He climbed back onto the mule and they continued in the direction of Ouanaminthe at a much more rapid pace than before. Still it was twilight again by the time they entered the town, coming along the Dajabón road and crossing the levee that had been raised along the riverbank. The levee was lined with men standing almost in military postures, though they did not seem to be soldiers. It was already too dark to distinguish their faces at a distance but Arnaud thought it strange that no one hailed them.

In the lead again, he rode up the street in the direction of the government house. Before he could reach it a throng of men surged across the street to bar his way. Many were armed with muskets similar to the ones his mules were bearing, and they were all mulattoes. Arnaud realized that he had not seen a white man since entering the town.

"What's the meaning of this?" he shouted at a man who had caught his mule's bridle and so held him arrested. In answer another mulatto poked a bayonet toward his belly, and for the first time he felt a twinge of fear. He looked over his shoulder, but Orion was gone.

Then someone called out a command and the bayonet was lowered from his ribs. A man was striding across from the houses with an air of authority, and the other mulattoes turned expectantly to face him. Arnaud squinted in the dusk and with a flush of relief he recognized the freckled features of Choufleur.

"You've come in good time," Choufleur informed him.

"Yes," Arnaud said. He looked over his shoulder again; some men were unloading the first two mules in the train and handing out the muskets to other, unarmed mulattoes who were coming out of the side streets in increasing numbers.

"But this must stop at once!" Arnaud called out, and looking at Choufleur, "You must stop them."

Choufleur said nothing. In the dim, the patterns of his freckles were swimming on his face, though his green eyes were steady and sharp on Arnaud as he lifted his hand. Arnaud wondered if the half-breed expected a handshake. As he was thinking this, Choufleur caught his wrist and tugged him rudely down from the saddle. Arnaud shouted incoherently, more from the insult than the pain of his wrenched leg. He would have slapped Choufleur but two other men had pinned his arms behind him.

"What do you mean by it?" he said. "Where is my servant?" He could feel that his wrists were being tied together with a prickly length of sisal cord.

"You have no servant," Choufleur said. "There is nothing that you own."

Arnaud spat at him, but Choufleur stepped aside and let the gob fall in the dust. One of the men behind him gave him a rough shove and tripped him so he fell onto his knees. Choufleur closed a hand on the back of his neck and pressed his head into the dirt, scrubbing his face across his own spittle. Then he jerked him to his feet by his hair.

The two other men hustled him forward, one leading him and the other behind. All down the pack train mulattoes were shouting with pleasure as they received the new weapons. Arnaud caught sight of Père Bonne-chance beyond this throng, standing beside the buildings in his black robes, the sole still point in the confusion swirling around him. Arnaud stared wildly and the priest seemed to look back at him, but with no reaction—as if Arnaud had been rendered invisible. A prod of a bayonet sent him hurrying on.

He was brought to the cellar of a private house which might have been used to store wine, but was empty now except for another white man who had been badly beaten about the face. The faint light that drifted in from a grating near the ceiling was scarcely enough to reveal his battered features, but he raised himself on his elbows and called Arnaud by name. Coming nearer, Arnaud recognized a Ouanaminthe planter named Robineau, some ten years his senior and a slight acquaintance.

"What's happened?" he asked. "What's happened here?"

Robineau's front teeth had been smashed out so his reply was indistinct. "The mulattoes . . ." he muttered, and did not go on.

"*Évidemment,*" Arnaud said. "Where did they get the guns?"

"Ogé," Robineau mouthed. "I heard that. The guns were hidden from the Ogé rising."

Arnaud grunted and walked toward the grating. By standing on tiptoe he could obtain an ankle-level view of the street, full of men hurrying to and fro, calling out to one another in Creole, some carrying torches now. It was awkward to keep his balance without the use of his hands. He crossed the cellar to where Robineau was propped against the wall and lowered himself into a squat.

"Would you be so kind as to get this rope off me?" He wiggled his fingers, which were beginning to swell from the pressure on his wrists, and waited, but the touch he expected did not come. He glanced over his shoulder.

"I don't think . . . I shouldn't . . ." Robineau looked uneasily toward the door. "*Mieux que vous restez comme ça.*"

Arnaud deflated, rolling off his heels to sit down on the cold flagstones, which were thinly covered with dampish straw. In Robineau's tone and fearful expression he recognized that mood of abject helplessness he'd always sought to inspire in his own slaves, and he felt it would be a matter of minutes or hours at most before he sank into this state himself. The grated window slowly glazed over into total darkness. Arnaud lowered his head. His shoulders ached and he could do nothing to ease them. The mixture of dirt and spit was drying on his cheek and he was unable to wipe it. With his boot he shuffled the straw in front of him into a little mound.

Presently the door opened and Choufleur entered, carrying a candle. "Get up," he said, pointing to Arnaud.

Arnaud squinted at him, blinking at the candle's flame. Robineau had twisted his face away from the light. Arnaud raised himself again into a squat and when he saw that Choufleur made no move to help him rise he pushed himself all the way up unassisted, scraping his shoulder along the wall for balance.

At Choufleur's gesture, he preceded him out of the room and mounted the stairs, the freckled mulatto coming behind with the candle. When they reached the street Choufleur clamped his arm above the elbow and guided him toward another building, nearer the government house. By now there was less commotion in the street, but Arnaud could hear musket shots from the edge of town, along with shouts that suggested celebration more than battle.

"I want to show you something," Choufleur said.

They entered the second house and Choufleur conducted him to a ground-floor room, furnished as an office. There were many mulattoes gathered round the desk but no one took note of their entry, and they remained standing in the shadows by the doorway. The others were all drinking wine from the necks of various bottles which they held. Arnaud's eye was reluctantly drawn to a large light-skinned man dressed in elaborate military uniform, raising a wine bottle and bubbling it with its butt thrust at the roof.

"Candi," Choufleur muttered. *"Vous n'avez pas fait sa connaissance?"*

Arnaud said nothing. The group around the desk parted and now he could see, seated behind it, a white man with graying hair who must have occupied a post of authority there, though now his arms were bound to the chair and he was so tightly gagged that the corners of his mouth were bleeding. His eyes were round and watery in the light of the oil lamp that stood on the desk. Candi set the wine bottle down and picked up the corkscrew that lay beside the lamp.

Choufleur's hand tightened on Arnaud's arm. *"Regardez,"* he said. *"Attention."*

Candi wound the old cork meticulously from the screw, and lightly tried the point of the instrument against the ball of his left thumb. He stooped, smiling, and placed the screw gently against the white man's eyeball and with a slow precision began to turn it in. The white man went rigid against the chair back, and from behind the gag came a strangulated retching sound. Arnaud's eyes squeezed shut and he bit into his lip. He heard Choufleur's voice in the dark, rapturously tonguing an English phrase.

"*Out, vile jelly,*" and in French again, "Does it not remind you of the blinding of Gloucester?" He noticed Arnaud then, and slapped him so that his eyes popped open. "Watch, or you will take his place. You must see."

Arnaud obeyed, his lids pinned back. He was having difficulty with his breathing.

"Take out the gag," Candi said, and one of the others quickly did so. What came from the white man's mouth was a kind of sigh, an *aaahhhhh.* One eyelid sagged over the bloody socket while the other eye rolled evasively. Candi sighted down the length of the corkscrew. The white man's howl was deafening when he drove it in, with a delicate gradual rotation that finally brought his knuckles flush against the other's cheek. Candi's teeth clenched, his forearm tensed: he yanked. There was a sucking *plop,* followed by a shout of appreciation all around the room. The eyeball was larger than Arnaud would have thought possible, and pudgy, like a dumpling. It depended from a number of white twisting tentacle-like cords, till someone reached with a knife to cut it completely free.

Candi held the eyeball high on the screw and grinned and laughed at it. He did a little dance step, boot heels clicking on the floor. Arnaud's bowels will-lessly released and he felt that he was soiling his trousers. Choufleur turned and inspected him with an extraordinary satisfaction.

"But probably you have not read Shakespeare at all," Choufleur said. "You see that my education is superior to yours."

Without saying anything more, Choufleur returned him to the cellar across the street, and went away closing the door silently behind him. Robineau had disappeared. The clump of straw was wetter than it had been, dripping actually, when Arnaud stirred it with his foot. It reeked of blood. Arnaud was loathe to sit down anywhere. He was aware of the stench and the clinging damp of the feces that coated the insides of his legs. The white man's scream still buzzed, distorted, in his inner ear. In his mind's eye the dead horse appeared, bloated with its necrid gasses. He stood below the grating, straining to see out; there was a column of men tramping along the street. In the aureole of their torchlight the face of Père Bonnechance appeared.

"I will hear your confession, my child, if you desire it," the priest said.

Arnaud wondered if he might not be hallucinating. "Yes," he said. "Yes." The priest vanished from beyond the grating, and a moment later the door swung open.

"But how did you get in?" Arnaud said.

"It wasn't locked," the priest said. "There's no lock on it, but you've been distracted. Hurry, you must go in front."

When they reached the street the priest pushed Arnaud's head down so it was bowed and went along half a pace behind him, chanting a paternoster in Latin. The column continued to pass in the opposite direction alongside them, most of the men now blacks dressed as field hands, but carrying the muskets Arnaud had inadvertently provided. Some glanced at them curiously as they went by, but took no further notice.

Père Bonne-chance led Arnaud down another street toward the levee and thence out onto the Dajabón road. There were bonfires lit on the levee's height and men were crying out to the stars and firing off their muskets at the sky and pouring rum from broken barrels onto the flames to make them leap. They had not got very far along the road from these festivities before they heard a party of horsemen approaching from the opposite direction.

"Quickly," the priest said, and hauled Arnaud down the steep bank into the river. The water was suddenly, surprisingly deep. Arnaud felt the priest's hand cupped under his chin, supporting him, till his flailing boot found footing on a rock. He could hear the jingle of harness as the horses passed, though he could not see them. The priest's hands worked around his wrists and as he gratefully fanned his fingers over the surface of the water he saw the length of sisal rope go drifting downriver, twisting palely in the current like a snake.

"They would have killed you," Arnaud said. "Did you not see what inhuman monsters they are?"

"It may be that they follow the old dispensation," the priest said. The skirts of his habit came floating up around him. "An eye for an eye and a tooth for a tooth."

"They might have done worse than kill you, indeed," Arnaud said, scarcely listening to his own words. With delight he felt the river purging the filth from between his legs.

"Oh, the ones who are superstitious would fear to harm me," the priest said. "Those who are educated would dislike to offend the

Church." He clambered out onto the bank and peeled out of his robes and wrung them out. Arnaud followed him, pulling off his own wet things, scrubbing his trousers on a stone as he had seen slave women do.

"But you are not really even a priest," he said.

"Because I am not chaste, you say this," Père Bonne-chance said. Arnaud could see his bullet head thrusting about in the strange light. The stars were mostly obscured by persistent smoke and they were now well away from the fires on the levee, but the sky gave off a weird red glow reflected from the burning cane fields.

"But I must believe that God approves of love," Père Bonne-chance said. He bundled his wet robe on his shoulder and began walking barefoot and naked along the roadside. Arnaud followed, naked himself but for his boots, which he was too tenderfooted to go without.

The priest looked back once over his pale and hairy shoulder. "No love is wasted," he said, with a faint smile. Arnaud nodded, though he did not understand. Boots squelching, he kept on following the priest into the dark.

Chapter Fifteen

BY MID-NOVEMBER, the Bréda plantation still stood isolate and undisturbed like an islet in the midst of the river of fire which streamed perpetually over Haut du Cap and down to the borders of the city itself. Bayon de Libertat was absent, trapped in Le Cap from the first flare of the insurrection. But there had been no burning or looting, no outrages nor much sign of any disorder at Bréda. A few slaves had slipped off to join the roving bands, no more, while the rest remained at their work, cutting and milling the harvest of cane.

This evening however there was no one at the mill, and most of the slaves had retreated within the doors of their cabins as Toussaint walked toward the *grand'case* through the cooling of dusk. Before him, a black hen bunched herself and clumsily lifted and flew to a roost on a low branch of an almond tree. Toussaint went on with his boots whispering on the dust of the path. In the garden alongside the *grand'case*, the desiccated roses hung head downward like paper bells. He climbed the steps and crossed the gallery, knocked on the door frame and waited. In a moment, Madame de Libertat called for him to enter.

The white woman took only a light repast in the evening, some biscuits and a little watered wine. Before the rising, her appetite had been hearty enough, but this abstinence was her only visible reaction to the trouble and otherwise she behaved trustingly, as if all was as usual. When Toussaint arrived, her two daughters had already dined and left the room. She looked at him directly, one finger turning a biscuit crumb in a circle on her plate. Madame de

Libertat was younger than her husband, but her eyes were pinched with wrinkles, and her skin had begun to loosen on her face, turning papery as the petals of the roses in the yard. She was solemn but not apparently unhappy. For a few minutes she questioned him on commonplaces and they talked of affairs at the plantation.

"It's quiet tonight," she said. "There's no one singing."

Without, the fronds of a coconut palm shivered together in the wind with a sound like rain. The breeze stopped and the rattle died away.

"The mill is empty," said Toussaint.

"Yes," said Madame de Libertat. "Do take some wine." At her gesture a housemaid filled a glass from the carafe and passed it to Toussaint, who turned the long stem through his gnarly fingers. The cup itself was scarcely larger than a thimble. He held it without tasting.

"Madame, you have made ready?" he asked with some reluctance. He watched the water-paled liquid revolving in the glass.

"It must be tomorrow?"

"Madame," Toussaint said. "I could not any longer answer for your safety."

Madame de Libertat passed a veiny hand across her eyes. A peculiar low drone breathed out of her; she was praying, perhaps. When she looked at him again her eyes were watery and clear.

"And will I ever see this place again?" she asked.

"I will pray and hope for an end of these troubles," Toussaint said, "as you must, Madame."

"*On doit éspèrer toujours,*" said Madame de Libertat. She nodded to him. He was free to go or to remain. He stood, placing the untasted wine glass on the table, and bowed to her and left the house.

Outside the door of his own cabin his brother Paul stood waiting. Toussaint told him that he expected him to drive Madame de Libertat down to Le Cap the next morning, as they had thought. There would be a wagon following with the household goods, as well as the coach carrying the mistress, which Paul would drive himself. Toussaint told Paul that he had already placed a loaded musket under the driver's seat of the coach; Paul nodded without asking how he had obtained the weapon.

"When you return, I will be gone," Toussaint said.

"*Ouais,*" Paul said, unsurprised.

"Stay here—if you can," Toussaint said. "While you can. Keep order. If there is trouble, you must try to cross to Santo Domingo or come to Grande Rivière. Or I will send you a message."

"Yes," Paul said. "I will be waiting." He reached to touch his brother's hand and walked away slowly down the row of cabins into the dark which was now complete.

Toussaint sat down on a plank bench just outside his door. Beyond the cabins, in a grove surrounding a watering pool, he could hear the voices of children. Isaac and Placide would be among them; they had already eaten and gone out. Suzanne came out of the house and handed him a bowl of soup. While he ate, she sat on the bench beside him, opening her dress to nurse Saint-Jean. It was a green soup, flavored with lemon grass and thickened with coconut milk. He ate it slowly, without talking at all. When he had finished he set the bowl down on the plank.

"The mistress?" Suzanne said. "I know she will be unhappy to leave this place."

"She will not show it," Toussaint said. "All month the countryside has been burning around us and she has not blinked at it once."

"It's hard," Suzanne said. The baby rolled a little forward in her arms, revealing his sleeping face. Cradling him, she closed her dress.

"It may be hard," Toussaint said. "I think I saw her praying."

"And you?" Suzanne said. "What gods have you prayed to, my husband?"

Toussaint turned his head to look into the child's smooth face. In his sleep Saint-Jean squinted and wrinkled his nose.

"What do you know of the nature of god?" Toussaint said. "We must take our gods as they come to us."

"Jesus has been kind to us," Suzanne said. "We have a good life here."

"We have no life," Toussaint said. "We are like the dead. We are yet to be resurrected."

Suzanne's face clouded over; she picked up the bowl with her free hand and carried the sleeping infant into the cabin. Toussaint waited but she did not return. From inside the cabin came a muted clattering. There was little enough for Suzanne to make ready, but he understood that no woman, black slave or Creole lady, liked to abandon a home. He leaned down and pulled his boots off and set them aside. His toes stretched in the dry dust under the bench.

Boots were not new to him, but he had only lately taken to wearing them. He sat thinking about his forty-odd years of dependence on the kindness of white people, which kindness had indeed come more freely to him than to most. Silently he said a paternoster to himself in the dark, shaping with his tongue the Latin words he'd learned from Pierre Baptiste. While doing so he thought about Jesus, the frail white man who could transmute weakness into divine power. He thought too of the god who was Jesus' father, whose son so little resembled him. Afterward his mind went blank and he sat listening to the insects and the leaves of the trees behind the cabins stroking each other with a slow susurration, enjoying the sensation of his feet freed from their boots, and hearing the voices of the children reflected from the pool within the grove.

In the morning he appeared at the *grand'case* dressed in his boots and coachman's livery, wearing the green coat with its faded bloodstains. The Libertat daughters took their seats in the carriage; Toussaint handed Madame de Libertat in to join them, solemn and mute as any slave on any such occasion. When the door was shut upon her, Madame de Libertat stretched her arm through the window, motioning as if she meant to speak, but in the end she only thanked him with a smile. He bowed and walked around the rear of the carriage, and back to the box where Paul was already seated. Toussaint ran his hand under the iron braces and felt the contour of the musket where it was strapped to the underside of the seat. Paul nodded to him, impassively, and as Toussaint stepped aside he slapped the reins across the backs of the teamed horses and the carriage moved out, squealing and jouncing toward the road.

Toussaint backed his way up the steps of the *grand'case*, watching the wagon fall into the train of the coach. Two lady's maids and the cook were perched on the bags and bundles in the wagon bed, and Toussaint had sent two men along besides the drover, arming all three as well, in case of any trouble. He knew they would not be likely to meet any of the better-organized bands on the road today, but there was more to fear from the ill-organized ones, of which he could know nothing. When the wagons had left the yard he entered the empty house, closing the door softly behind him. His boots rang notes of vacancy on the bare floors. On one wall a forgotten mirror gathered the light that leaked through the closed jalousies to itself, like a pool in a forest. Behind a chair lay one of the girls' fans half unfolded and beside it a large black beetle ticking erratically like a broken watch. Toussaint went out at the rear of the house, closing the door with as much caution as if he feared to wake sleepers within. In the garden the roses had wilted further and some were stretched to the length of their stems on the hardening ground.

Within an hour he was headed southeast, mounted on Bellisarius with Isaac riding pillion behind him, while Placide proudly bestrode his own mount, a mule. Suzanne also went muleback, carrying Saint-Jean in a sling. With them were fifteen men from the plantation, all the good saddle horses and half of the mules. The men now openly carried the muskets smuggled from the Spanish. Toussaint was quite certain they would meet no whites in this direction, but there was no way of knowing what else they might encounter. Once in the afternoon a handful of men emerged from the bush and swarmed in a bare rocky area far ahead of them, shouting and blowing on conch shells, but seeing the size and strength of Toussaint's party, they did not make any closer approach.

They camped at the foot of the mountains near the Spanish border, while there was still good light. Toussaint took off his boots and went barefoot into the jungle, gathering fresh herbs for his sack. It was dark when he returned and Suzanne was cooking over the open fire; one of the men was helping her with a big iron cauldron. They ate in near silence, and slept ringed around the coals of the fire. Placide could not sleep, it seemed; the boy was not afraid, but excited by the journey and by the sight of the two pickets Toussaint had sent out from the camp in opposite directions. Toussaint talked to him in a low voice, identifying the night sounds and what each portended, until Placide slumped against his side and slept. Toussaint covered him and went to relieve his sentries. As for himself he required little sleep; a couple of hours, near dawn, sufficed him.

By first light, they had all remounted and when the sunlight had strengthened enough to filter through the leaves and gild the way ahead of them, the ascent had grown steep. Here Toussaint parted from his wife and children, sending them on up the higher trails in the care of five of the men he'd brought. On the far side of the San Raphael mountains was a *boucanier*'s camp where they were expected; two of the men he sent with them had been to the place with him before and he was confident they would reach it before night. Isaac rode behind one of the men, clinging with his face pressed to his shirt, but Placide twisted on his mule's bare back for a look behind. Toussaint saw the baby's head joggling between Suzanne's shoulders where he was slung, but Suzanne did not look back. The trail wrapped snakelike around the mountain. He watched the smaller party out of sight around an inward turning and waited until they reappeared on the next elbow, though by then their faces were too distant to discern.

On the descent he passed the others he'd kept with him, and rode Belisarius out ahead of them all, alone. Some of the saddle horses might have kept pace with him, but not the whole string of horses and mules; they would come along a day later to Grande Rivière, which was where he was bound. He pushed hard, stopping only once to fill his gourd with water and add a few herbs to his sack: *malnommée, guérit-trop-vite, herbe à cornette*. In the late afternoon he came down into Gallifet plantation where Jean-François and Biassou were encamped.

"Happy as a nigger of Gallifet" had been a proverb of the colony, for here the slaves had been treated with much the same providence as at Bréda. But now there were no masters kind or otherwise, save Biassou and Jean-François—Boukman was raiding around Le Cap and Jeannot was camped at a little distance, near Habitation Dufailly. If happiness still obtained here, its character had changed. The Gallifet *grand'case* was still standing, alone among ruins of the mill and other outbuildings that had been burned and pulled down, and the big house now surveyed a waste of smoking ash and cinder where there had once been cane fields. On the borders of the destruction the blacks rested or wandered as it suited them. There was little shade or shelter except within the jungle green.

Toussaint came in with a stream of blacks, for there were more and more of them flooding into the camp every day, now mostly loyal slaves who would not have run away from their plantations if they had not been driven by white reprisals against any black skin within reach. If anyone gave him a second glance it was because he was one of the few with a horse and that his was better than all the others. Among the newcomers he rode the trail along the riverbank.

At a bend of the river, backed into the jungle cover, there was a tent where Toussaint dismounted. The tent was strung with curious little bones and the doorflap decorated with *ouangas*. He was looking for Biassou, but the tent was vacant except for three multicolored cats that burst out when he lifted the canvas. Also there were two large snakes coiled in a tightly woven Carib basket, curled in a torpor of black and chocolate brown. Toussaint let the flap drop.

Of the three original leaders of the rising, Toussaint now thought Jean-François the most reliable, was inclined to trust him above Boukman or Jeannot. Both of these latter (though in rather different ways) had seemed unable to recall themselves from the first delirious frenzy of revenge upon the whites. As for Biassou he had come more lately to leadership and was less of a known quantity, though the accoutrements of his tent would seem to confirm his reputation as a *hûngan*.

Somewhere up the river, in the direction of Jeannot's separate encampment, a peculiar sound was audible; it might have been the echo of a scream. Toussaint shook his head and led his horse in the direction of the Gallifet *grand'case*, where Jean-François was established. The distance was not very great; Jean-François and Biassou still acted together in close concert.

Jean-François met him coming from the house, resplendent in a gray uniform with yellow facings, a black cordon ornamented with white fleurs-de-lis. On his chest was pinned an Order of Saint Louis he'd taken from a house they'd sacked and the whole ensemble was completed with polished top boots, a plumed hat, and an enormous cavalry sword whose sheath squeaked against his belt as he walked. Someone in his retinue took Toussaint's horse away to be groomed and fed, while Toussaint retained only the herb bag that he'd carried across the saddle.

"You've come to stay?" said Jean-François.

Toussaint pushed back his bandanna to scratch at the crown of his head. There was something floating down the river toward them, an oddly thick and pale piece of wood with a short crook at one end of it.

"It will be useful," said Jean-François. "Since you are a *dokté-feuilles*." With a finger he prodded the fragrant bag of herbs.

"There's illness," Toussaint said.

"No more than usual," said Jean-François. "Some are wounded. Among the white people, a little fever."

"How many whites?" Toussaint said.

Jean-François shook his head. "I haven't counted. It's Biassou who's interested . . . "

It was the hostage white women that interested Biassou, Toussaint was well enough aware of that. He moved a little nearer to the strange object in the water. As it drifted toward the bank, an eddy turned it over and they both saw that the clubbed end of it was in fact a white man's foot, with only the great toe remaining and the others all severed individually. The leg had been cut off just above the knee. It caught itself on a snag of sticks and stones, tendrils of hair waving out from the dead flesh of the calf.

"Caymans," Jean-François said, under Toussaint's interrogative look.

"Not a toe at a time," Toussaint said. "That's not a cayman's appetite."

"No—it's from Jeannot," Jean-François said, looking away upriver. He drew out his huge sword with a grating sound and used the point to push the leg free of the snag and back into the current.

"It must not go on," Toussaint said. "It ought never to have begun."

"You know they do as much to us, and more," Jean-François said. "The white people."

"It doesn't matter," Toussaint said. "We must act differently with them."

"You say this because you are a Christian," Jean-François said.

"We will show the white people what we are," Toussaint said. "And also what we are not."

Jean-François began a question, but an upheaval a way downriver distracted him. A small party of horsemen was crossing the burned fields below the Gallifet *grand'case*, surrounded by a larger throng of men on foot, stirring up great clouds of flaky ash. All of them were shouting something but nothing could be distinguished beyond the name of Boukman. A rider broke from the main body and came cantering toward them. It was Biassou, his squat toad's body uneasy in the saddle, his hands high and loose on the reins. With some difficulty he pulled the horse up and stared at Jean-

François and Toussaint, his face running sweat and his flat nostrils flaring.

"Boukman's killed," he said, too loudly. For a moment it seemed he would lower his tone and give details, but a convulsion passed over his features and he kicked up the horse and rode off crying "*Boukman tué, Boukman tué,*" mechanically, as if an outside intelligence governed him. It was what they were all shouting, spreading dismay throughout the whole encampment.

"Boukman," Jean-François said, his face wrenched with genuine pain. "How could it happen?"

"Easily," Toussaint said. "He ran in calling on Agwé and Ogûn, waving a bull's tail around his head and thinking it would fan the bullets away from him. What's surprising is that Biassou has *not* been killed, since he tells everyone that whoever dies in these fights goes back all at once to Guinée."

Jean-François looked at him aghast.

"Yes, I know it may be true," Toussaint said. He took off his bandanna and shook it out. "It's what happens here in this world that interests me more."

"You say we must become white men, then?"

Toussaint smoothed the bandanna over his forehead and reknotted it at the base of his neck. "You look very well in your uniform," he said. "Have you become white? You may put on more than their dress and still remain what you are."

"I am the grand admiral and commander-in-chief," Jean-François said stiffly.

"Yes," Toussaint said. "And neither of us kills our horses recklessly. So the *loa* must not kill their horses without reason. Who serves the *loa* must be served in return."

Jean-François looked at him narrowly.

"It isn't Boukman," Toussaint said. "It's any life that's wasted." He smiled and shook his bag of herbs. "Come and show me to the ones who need these things."

Chapter Sixteen

THE UNIFORMED FOOTMAN laid a tray of coffee on the table before Isabelle Cigny. Her spoon jingled cheerfully against the edge of a china cup. Doctor Hébert watched the movements of her small white hand. When she beckoned him, he came forward and accepted a cup and saucer and returned to his chair. Captain Maillart, meanwhile, leaned forward from his seat on the sofa to help himself to a plate of cakes. He turned to offer one to the girl Marguerite, who sat beside him there.

Doctor Hébert inhaled steam from his coffee, without yet tasting it. The odor of the sugared brew reminded him oddly of the smell of burning that blew daily from the plain. Isabelle Cigny looked up at him teasingly, as if she had read his mind.

"Our sugar is still of a perfect whiteness here," she said at large. "We do not follow the vicious saying of that English minister."

"*Pardon?*" said Marguerite. She looked blandly about with her large blue eyes. She had declined the proffered cake, leaving her hands demurely folded on her lap.

"William Pitt has remarked on our misfortune," Captain Maillart said. " 'It seems that the French prefer their coffee *au caramel.*' "

The doctor surprised himself by blurting out a laugh (although he'd heard this bitter jest before). Madame Cigny looked at him rather sadly, three fingers pressed against her small pink lower lip. The doctor's eyes slid away from her, toward Nanon, who sat apart from the others at a small sewing table in the corner, a basket by her feet and work on her lap. By her position in the room it was unclear to what degree she might or might not belong to this social group, though of course an untrained eye would probably not have doubted her *perfect whiteness*. She had not taken coffee. Her dress was vastly simpler than before, merely a pale loose shift a little better than what a household slave might wear. Her eyes were lowered to her sewing. The doctor had had no opportunity for as much as a private word with her, nor was he certain he'd have sought her intimacy, were it more available to him. Though he came here often, twice a week, he had little idea how to comport himself with her in these half-public circumstances. She tossed a lock of hair from her face and bent again to her work; the movement was not quite enough for him to catch her eye.

"*Oui, vraiment,*" Marguerite said almost tonelessly, peering into the sugar bowl. "*C'est évident.*"

Captain Maillart looked at her, at a loss for a direction to continue. He had been trying to flirt with the girl for the past half hour, but she was most unplayful.

"And you," Madame Cigny said to the doctor. "You will be leaving us as well, I understand."

"Yes," the doctor said, and sipped his coffee.

"You tear yourself away"—Madame Cigny developed her theme with a brittle vivacity—"from our fair city, with its . . . spectacles. The gallows and gibbets. The execution wheels."

"Painfully," the doctor said. It was not an ideal choice of word. "Affairs at Habitation Thibodet have been neglected . . ."

"During your long absence," Madame Cigny said, helping him along, "and will require your most earnest attention."

"Yes, as you say."

"No word from the mistress?"

The doctor shook his head, understanding her to mean Elise. He smiled at her, in thanks for her tact. It had entered his mind that his sister might have returned to the plantation, especially if news of her husband's death had somehow reached her. But he had had no communication from anyone there and so could not know if the plantation itself was still in existence, for that matter.

"I do wish you would dissuade this child from undertaking such a foolhardy journey," Isabelle Cigny said, looking at Marguerite, who was perhaps four years her junior. No one answered her. The doctor set his cup aside, on a small table. Marguerite had been offered hospitality at the Paparel plantation, in Marmelade, and she was intending to set out for the place the next morning, escorted by Captain Maillart and a party of militia.

"You might do very well to stay here," Madame Cigny said directly to Marguerite. "I will gladly open my house to you. In any event we seem to have become a hostelry for displaced persons . . . of various sorts." Coolly she glanced at the doctor, who dropped his eyes toward the toes of his boots.

"You are kind," Marguerite said, "yet I have always preferred country living to the distractions of a town."

"It must be admitted," said Madame Cigny, "that for the moment our town is less than an ideal setting for a girl such as yourself—much as I regret to say it. Still I wonder at your journey. Is it wise?"

Marguerite smiled, sweetly or stupidly, as the disposition of an observer might interpret it, and said nothing at all. Madame Cigny got up and quickly crossed the room to her. Seating herself lightly on the arm of the sofa, she took Marguerite's face between her two hands and twisted it up toward her own. It was an abrupt movement, and to the doctor it didn't seem entirely friendly. Isabelle Cigny was examining her visage much as a horse trader might examine an animal. Captain Maillart stared at the pair of them, openmouthed.

Seeing himself unobserved, the doctor thought he might at least exchange a glance with Nanon. But when he looked her way she would not meet his eyes, or else she was insensible of his regard. She had stopped her sewing for the moment and sat with her hands folded over the work, which looked to be a garment meant for Madame Cigny's infant Héloïse. The looseness of the shift she wore gave no suggestion of her body's shape, so that the doctor, recalling what he'd been told of Isabelle Cigny's opposition to finery for colored women, wondered if she were used unkindly here.

Nanon sat with her face half turned to the wall, so that he saw her profile. Despite her pallor, there was much of Africa in her head's shape at this angle, the slant of the cheekbones, full and heavy meeting of the lips. Her face seemed fuller, rounder than before, or perhaps he was imagining this. Her eyes were open, but she seemed entranced; she might have been asleep or dreaming.

There was a sort of whisper and the doctor turned to see Marguerite's head swinging away from Madame Cigny's hands, slackly, as if its support had been abruptly severed. The girl's plump lips were parted a little, and her breath passed through them with that whispering sound he'd heard. A strand of her honey-blonde hair had come down and with her fingertip she reached absently to adjust it. Madame Cigny was looking down on her with an expression of terrible sorrow.

Captain Maillart then jumped to his feet, loudly slapping at the thighs of his breeches. "Well then, we must be going," he said. "Off to subdue the brigands." He smiled wryly. "Provided we can find them . . ."

AT MIDMORNING THE NEXT DAY their party set off from Le Cap, passing through some low earthworks hastily erected since the rising; before, the city had had few landward fortifications. Now, on one of the dirt ramparts, a pike carried the severed head of Boukman, the skin shrinking yellowly to the skull, leathery lips peeling back so that the whole head grinned deathly toward the gently smoldering plain. Briefly Doctor Hébert considered whether Marguerite would term this vision one of the "distractions" of town life; for the moment she did not seem to take notice of it at all.

Their party was some forty strong, a larger group of soldiery than the brigands (as all the black insurgents on the plain had come to be known) would commonly dare to attack. Save for Captain Maillart and a couple of other officers, these were not regular army troops, but militiamen, and an uneasy combination at that. Twelve were white Creoles, young and healthy enough, but too soft from pampering for a campaign in rough country (as Captain Maillart had somewhat bitterly explained). The rest were all mulattoes, a little older on the average, and most of them veterans of the *maréchaussée*. They were ill-trusted, for many still believed that the mulattoes were wholly responsible for the rising of the blacks, but indispensable just the same.

They carried with them two eight-pound cannons, drawn by mules, but no wagons, for the ways they'd take would be impossible for wagons to navigate. For the same reason Marguerite must go horseback; the doctor was surprised to see her riding astride like a man. Indeed, she sat the pretty gray mare she'd been given most confidently. Riding seemed to bring her out of herself. She rode alongside a lieutenant of Maillart's regiment whom the doctor knew slightly from the theater and other such occasions, and she responded to his conversational sallies with more animation than he'd ever seen in her.

The doctor himself rode behind this pair in silence, half attending to the mild flirtation going on between Marguerite and the young lieutenant. Captain Maillart, who now rode at the head of the column, had provided him with a huge dragoon's pistol, whose long scabbard scraped at his knee with every movement of his horse. But there was no enemy, no menace within view. The trail—it could not quite be called a road—went winding beside a bank that was tall with tawny lemon grass. That amiable lieutenant leaned from his horse to pluck a stalk which he presented to Marguerite, and the doctor saw the girl smile at its fresh odor of sweetness.

They were going through open country: low, gentle hills under a clear sky. Sometimes they crossed the now familiar fields of ash, but elsewhere nothing had been burned and the birds still sang. Once, at a great distance, they saw a band of the brigands who hooted and whistled at them from half a mile away, then scattered into the bush. Captain Maillart went a little more cautiously after this, despite the strength of his party and the fact that the gangs of brigands were thought to lack the skill and discipline for an organized ambush.

That night they spent at a fortified camp on the lower slopes of the mountain range. All these mountains were now strung with such camps, a cordon meant to keep the insurrection from breaking through to the Department of the West and sweeping down on Port-au-Prince. It was true as well, however, that the brigand blacks were also encamped all through the hills. Loath to risk open confrontation with armed whites in force, they skulked and raided as they could.

The trees around the palisade were ornamented with the rotting bodies of blacks who had been captured and hanged. A recent novelty of *country* life, the doctor thought, passing beneath them to enter the camp. Their stench was almost overwhelming; one of the very young Creoles masked his nose and mouth with a scented handkerchief. But Marguerite seemed to take no greater note of these carcasses than she would of crows crucified on a barn door to warn away their fellows.

They slept uneasily in that rough place, the Creole youths complaining mightily of their discomfort; apparently a couple of them had never been anywhere before without a body servant. Soon after first light, they were on the road again. Now the way went winding in and out of the gorges that raked the mountainsides, so that they must go three miles of twists and bends for one in a straight line. But in two hours they came down into the lowlands. Coconut trees were growing on a swamp flat and among them dozens of land crabs came up from their holes to watch the party passing. One of the mulattoes jumped down from his horse and ran among the trees to snatch the crabs and toss them into a bag, for they were good to eat. The men laughed to see him run, and Marguerite tittered, holding her fingers to her lips.

There were others who had used the trail ahead of them. The roadside was littered with cut coconut husks, and back in the trees were the blackened rings of small cook fires. As they continued they found peculiar cairns of stones and eviscerated birds arranged to signify some meaning. Captain Maillart sent scouts half a mile ahead of his main body, and let a couple of men trail back, pairing a white Creole with one of the mulattoes in each case.

In the midafternoon they overtook the advance riders, who'd halted just below the summit of a round hill. The doctor rode up, after Captain Maillart, half hearing their muttered conference. There was a sound of drumming from somewhere ahead. They dismounted and led the horses to the hill's crown. A long slope glided down into a grassy bowl where a hundred or more of the brigand blacks were dancing to the drums, many already transported into the queer ecstatic fits that possessed them at these *calendas*. The women were equal in number to the men, and a mambo seemed to be presiding over the whole affair.

Some of the more hot-blooded of the Creole whites wanted to mount a charge immediately, but Captain Maillart dissuaded them from this. There was no possibility of surprising them across this long savannah, and at their backs was jungle where they'd easily disappear. Outnumbered as he found himself, Maillart disliked to risk the scattering of his force. The doctor knew too that he was unwilling to endanger the girl needlessly, though he did not say so.

Captain Maillart ordered the two cannon to be brought to bear and charged. They fired the first eight-pounder down on the blacks from the hill's brow. The brigand dancers were well out of range—if the ball reached them it did so by rolling down the incline. A number of the Creoles followed up the shot with an equally futile clatter of pistol fire, disregarding for a minute or two Maillart's order to desist. A cannoneer touched off the second charge, the gun bucked in its carriage and recoiled. By this time most of the blacks had already filtered away into the forest.

On the ground where they'd been the grass was pounded flat and there were leavings of a feast, split yams and the bones of wild hogs and stolen sheep. Also in certain more orderly areas, portions of food and fruit and bowls of milk had been laid out in offering to the pagan gods. Captain Maillart passed frowning through this scene, leading his own party tightly bunched. They pressed on more speedily after that, and by nightfall had reached the Paparel plantation, at the border dividing the canton of Marmelade from that of La Soufrière.

At Paparel they grew mostly coffee, the bushy trees ranked in terraces on the slopes, red thumb-sized pods bright on their branches. Though there was plenty of water here, the land was too steep and rocky for sugar, and only a few *carrés* were in cane. Paparel did keep a small cane mill, also an indigo works, and he grew fields of provisions for sale to neighboring plantations and the towns on the coast. But the master himself was no longer present; he'd decamped at the start of the insurrection, leaving his property in charge of the *gérant*, his wife, and two grown sons and two daughters.

It was the *gérant's* family who'd tendered the invitation to Marguerite, and the daughters quickly bustled the girl away to the rear of the house to freshen herself and arrange her things. She'd brought them letters from friends at Le Cap. The doctor stayed, with Maillart and the junior officers, to dine with the family. The food was plentiful and well prepared. Maillart had requisitioned a share of the crabs caught that morning, which were served stuffed, and had a pleasant flavor.

All was in good order at Paparel, they learned. The *gérant* remained optimistic about his situation, though many neighboring plantations had been razed. Of Paparel's one hundred and fifty slaves only some thirty had defected, the others remaining loyal to the master. Mouzon's worst complaint was that the whites from the hill forts were as likely to murder a loyal black as a rebel, indeed they killed whatever blacks they found at large.

But the plantation had suffered no depredations. There were

three white men on the place, besides the family, all well armed, and Mouzon had also furnished guns to some of the most trusted slaves. Captain Maillart grumbled a little at this, but Mouzon declared that he had more faith in his best blacks than he could summon for the whites in the camps, and Maillart was bound to agree that these latter were a most uneven lot.

The doctor retired early and slept without dreaming, exhausted from the days of riding. It was pleasantly cool, a healthier climate than Le Cap; in fact the night air was almost chill. Captain Maillart awakened him next morning by kicking the soles of his feet. After a hasty breakfast they were back in the saddle once more, bound for another of the hill forts.

This next camp was tucked in a *crête* of the mountains beyond the Perigourdin gorge from Paparel plantation. Only half a day's ride distant, this was one of the strongest positions in all the Cordon de L'Ouest. The *gérant* had been willing enough to acknowledge that its proximity meant a good deal to their safety at Paparel, however much he might dislike the details of the militiamen's conduct. Maillart's party expected to reach the fort shortly before noon.

They entered the gorge and rode for half an hour along its narrow stream, then began climbing a vestigial trail that rose along one side. Here the doctor's horse picked up a stone, and he had to dismount to pick it loose from the hoof. A cool drizzle fell on the back of his neck as he stooped to the task. There was a cloud on the mountain raining down on them gently, while from another quarter the sunshine picked out a gilded aureole of mist. The doctor dislodged the stone from the frog and tossed it over the trail's bank. He set the foot down so the horse could try its weight, then straightened, stretching his stiff back. Half the column had halted behind him, because there was no room to pass. From this elevation he had an excellent view back across the fields of Habitation Paparel, even despite the haze. It was not only haze, however, there was smoke. Buildings in the main compound were burning.

The doctor pointed and uttered a great shout. Captain Maillart heard him immediately, and saw the smoke stain on the misty sky, but he was at the head of the column and it was not a simple matter to reverse direction on the narrow trail. The cannon, traveling a third of the way from the column's end, now became an obstacle. Meanwhile, six of the young Creoles who were bringing up the rear now quickly regained the floor of the gorge and began galloping pell-mell back to the plantation, with a dozen of the mulattoes following at a slightly more cautious canter.

Shouting orders and curses, Captain Maillart harassed the cannoneers until at last the gun carriage reached the bottom of the gorge. From here the remainder of the column gave chase to those who'd gone before, leaving the guns to follow as they might. The doctor rode half a length behind the captain. He had drawn the heavy pistol and its weight and awkwardness were interfering with his management of the reins.

At his left, one of the Creoles flinched and slapped a hand to his left shoulder. He rocked back in the saddle, as though his horse had stumbled, but then the doctor saw the bloom of blood across his chest. Helplessly, he passed the man by, still following Maillart at a gallop. Somehow he had heard neither shot. It was queer that the attack had begun in silence, without the usual preparatory shrieking and skirling on conchs. Behind Maillart, he reached the point where the gorge made a final twist before issuing into the outmost of Paparel's fields. Here they were immediately taken by highly organized and professional enfilading fire.

Four of the Creoles who'd been at the head of the stampede had fallen in this place; one lay half in the stream with threads of his blood flowing into the water. Several of the mulattoes had abandoned their mounts and taken cover among large boulders around the stream bed, returning fire which came not only from the mouth of the gorge but out of the dense jungle above on either side, where those of the hundreds of blacks who lacked weapons were simply hurling down huge stones. Captain Maillart wheeled his mount, crashing shoulder to shoulder into the doctor's horse. Straggling in the rear, the cannon had been overrun by swarms of blacks who now bore the guns away like ants carrying outsized clumps of sugar.

One of the young Creoles galloped past, stretched out to the length of his horse's neck like a Cossack trick rider. Behind him came another, riding erect. Doctor Hébert saw one of the mulattoes hiding in the rocks take careful aim at the second young man and fire, at such near range that the youth was carried backward out of the saddle. He looked to Captain Maillart to see if he had witnessed this treachery, but the captain had rallied those of his men still in the saddle and was ordering a charge down the gorge toward the plantation.

Maillart spurred his horse and led the charge with his saber drawn. A black popped up from directly in front of him and took a hip shot with a musket, missing in spite of the point-blank range. Maillart dealt him a crooked saber cut and rode him down. To the doctor's left another man was shot out from his horse. He saw the sudden vacancy from the corner of his eye, and then a big Ibo scrambled up in the white man's place. The doctor gasped, the Ibo grinned. Another black swung up behind him. The doctor turned his pistol to cover this pair, but numerous hands reached from the ground to drag down his arm. He struck out wildly with his other fist, and broke free, still holding the unfired pistol, cantering into the open field. He felt a small pulse of jubilation at having carried through the ambush, but just then a bullet creased his horse, and the animal bucked and ran away with him. He was carried off from the other survivors, headed into the burning cane.

A swirl of smoke from the cane field swept through a gap in the citron hedge across the road. A heavy, thick, sweet smell like a pastry afire in the oven. The doctor coughed. The heat was terrible, and flame laced through the tightly woven branches of the hedge. Parts of the hedge itself were also catching alight, consuming. The doctor had just managed to pull in his horse, but at the fire's crackling it shied under him, reared and tried to run again. Doctor Hébert held it with great difficulty, tightening the reins and twisting the horse's head down and to the left, its blubbery lips foaming on the bit, its white eye rolling. The doctor was choking and the smoke stung his eyes so he could hardly see.

But then the wind shifted and the billow of smoke swung off ahead of it and that was when the doctor saw them riding almost directly out of the fire itself. For an instant he thought it was a regular cavalry column because the leader wore an officer's shako, but it was set backward on his head and the man was naked but for that, bare skin all purple black like tar except for the whitened weals from his old whippings, everywhere across his back and arms and legs. Two human heads were slung across the shoulders of his horse, the man's queue tied to the woman's long blood-matted hair, in balance like a pair of saddle bags. Seeing the doctor he smiled in a brotherly way and whirled a long cane knife around his head. His teeth were filed to points after the occasional Congo fashion. He rode with confidence and skill. The next man behind him was dressed in a tattered blue ball gown with lace trim at the low-cut bodice and long slits ripped on either side to free his legs to straddle the horse. He had let the reins go dangling and hung on by the pommel of the saddle, grinning and looking foolishly about. A third rider waved a long crazy-looking fowling piece, the barrel bound to the splintered stock with bits of wire and string. Behind these three were more on foot, armed with knives or staves or carpenter's tools. Out of the smoke and fire reached a severed forearm, impaled on a lance, fingers still wriggling and clutching at the vapors.

So it looked to the doctor, an illusion perhaps. He had his pistol cocked and ready, but the horse kept shying and lunging, spoiling his aim. He gave the horse its head and let it run, full tilt and out of control, holding hard with his knees, his hands tangled in the reins and mane and the pistol pinched awkwardly there too. A stench of scorched blood mixed with the burning sugar; the smell could madden horses, the doctor knew. At the end of the lane he gathered the reins and guided the horse across the corner of the cane field, galloping wildly across the provision grounds. No fire here, only a mat of potato vines and worked earth, where the hooves threw up great clots of dirt as the horse went by. The slope of the provision ground was steep and bordered on two sides with the jungle winning its way back over it again. The smoke had cleared but the doctor didn't look behind him. His eyes were streaming and still it was hard to see, but he got fractured glimpses, down the hill, of hundreds of the rebel slaves bearing torches to the buildings all around the *grand'-case*. They had flushed the *gérant* out of the sugar mill and were swarming around him like ants on a spill of syrup. The *gérant* held his fists by his ears, ducking. They had hemmed him in and were prodding him with the long poles used on the ladles. Thrust and poke, then one man swung a pole far back and let it come down with an awful languor across the white man's shoulders.

The *gérant* fell, got up again, hunching his shoulders. The doctor saw another pole rise high. Then a wild ululation and blowing of conch shells seemed to rise up just at his feet, and he turned the horse frantically into the trees. A long loop of vine dropped over his chest and snatched him halfway out of the saddle, then it gave way, leaving him clinging to the side of the horse, one knee crooked where his seat should have been. Coarse hair of the mane scrubbed across his face. With a furious effort he got back astride. Something whipped at his cheek, opening a cut, and a bare rise of shale cleared out ahead. Then he was lying on his back, a crushing pain all through his ribs. The horse had rolled over him completely and lay on its side with two legs broken, screaming in a voice that was worse than human.

No sign of immediate pursuit, but the noise the horse was making could be heard for miles around, no doubt. Who would run toward such a howling? Hair lifted on the back of the doctor's neck. He was still pinned by one leg under the horse's shoulder and he couldn't free himself. For a minute or two he ceased to be a conscious human being; there was nothing left of him at all but a blur of frantic struggle. Then his bare foot popped loose from the boot and he was up and running instantly, although the pain of his exposed ankle was almost incapacitating. Impossible for him to cover any ground like this. He went slipping over the shale, biting his lips against the pain. The moans of the horse seemed a proxy for his own. He looked back once and saw beyond the horse's flailing shattered legs a single black, old and hunchbacked, his wrinkled face indented with old tribal scarification, carrying a carpenter's saw. He didn't seem to see the doctor, who rested, panting, behind a mapou tree, thinking how unusual it was to see a slave of that age in the colony, where most did not survive so long. The conch shell sounded again, very near, and there was crashing in the brush nearby. The doctor took a few more agonized staggering steps and then shot fifteen feet up a tree without knowing how he had conceived or accomplished the action.

Some kind of palm it probably was, with shiny grayish bark laid in triangular wedges, like snakeskin or scales, all pointing up. The doctor had cut his hands and his bare foot on the scales of bark while he was climbing. Still, the bark was the only thing that helped him hold his perch. There were no branches. He had thrust himself waist high into the long serrated fronds that sprang from the crown of the tree. They seemed to rattle with his breathing. There was a particolored patch on one that proved to be a giant katydid when the doctor nudged it with his thumb. Through its artifices it had turned itself the precise color of the palm leaf and mimicked veins and fibers, even a few patches of leaf rust, to make itself more completely frondlike. The doctor wished he had some similar ability.

His eyes went out of focus. He was tired, dazed. Thirsty too. It was uncomfortable to cling there in the tree and still less comfortable to speculate on what might be his chances if and when he ever came down. Supposing he escaped discovery by the blacks, he still had no way to get out of the area. The horse was still screaming in the shale. He imagined from what he had seen that the rebel slaves would be looting or destroying all the provisions on the plantation. Though one could live on the country here. There were fruit trees, other edibles too if he had known how to identify them. He licked a little blood from the heel of his hand, sliced in parallel lines as tidily as a razor could have done it, and peered down at his naked ankle. It hadn't swollen so very much, and he hoped it was only sprained, not broken, but it couldn't carry him very far or fast. The horse kept on screaming; he wished someone would shoot it. The pain in his ribs was soft, dull, not the sharp-edged sensation of a break, so maybe only bruising, though he didn't know what internal damage he might have sustained. He laid his cheek against a shiny wedge of bark and as his eyes glazed over and slid shut he saw again the severed heads swinging across that lead rider's lap. The woman's head, he now recognized, belonged to the girl Marguerite; those slack lips pulling off the teeth had been her petal mouth, that matted bloody rope her wealth and treasure of long flaxen hair.

It wouldn't do to wonder what had happened to the rest of her. The horse was still screaming, hoarsely now. It would break off for a time and then start over. Somehow it bothered the doctor more than anything else that happened all that day and he knew he would be hearing it ring in his head for a very long time afterward, supposing he survived long enough to enjoy this experience or any other. A great commotion started up around the foot of his tree. The doctor parted the palm fronds and looked down. Several rebel slaves in the tattered cotton breeches of field hands were gesticulating at him and chattering loudly among themselves in Creole. The doctor couldn't make out one word of what they said. The only arms they had were cane knives and he was a little relieved to see no guns among them. His dragoon pistol had been lost, it occurred to him now, when the horse fell or else earlier in the headlong flight.

Another man stepped into the clearing, carrying a sort of pike improvised by splinting a cane knife to a long pole from the sugar mill. The others clustered around him as if he had some special knowledge or authority. When he had spoken one ran off and the others drew a little back. The new man set the butt of his makeshift pike on the ground and stared up at the doctor. He was quite tall, emaciated, with a long face and a sorrowful expression. One of his ears had been lopped to a stump and the other was large and wrinkled like an elephant's ear. He gazed at the doctor sadly, intently; the doctor found he couldn't hold the stare. His own eyes went wandering over the treetops. There were other trees nearby he might have better chosen, taller, with branches for his seat and more leaves to hide him from the ground. The tall man said something to him in Creole, a question evidently.

"*Comprends pas,*" the doctor said. He showed an empty bleeding hand and smiled foolishly. The tall man lifted his pike over his head and probed, without especial vigor. The point of the cane knife pressed into the arch of the doctor's bare foot. Too dull to cut with such a light thrust but the pressure hurt his ankle. There was nowhere to go. He bowed out his back and worked his knees a little higher in the tree, all the long fronds clashing loudly together with the movement. The crown of the tree bent sideways with the shift of weight and the doctor found himself hanging almost upside down, while the tall man nudged the pike into his thighs and buttocks. The other bystander laughed and clapped and capered a little. The tall man's expression was gloomy and disinterested, like a bored child teasing a toad with a stick.

The doctor slipped a little way down the tree trunk, which righted itself elastically. But the tall man could now reach as high as his heart with the point of the cane knife. The doctor slapped the flat of the blade away from him, wondering if he might work it loose from its binding and get possession of it, but it seemed futile to try this project or even to succeed at it. Away out of sight the horse's screams cut off with a gurgling sigh, and then another man entered the area below the tree, riding bareback on a mule. He spoke sharply to the tall man, who lowered his pike and backed away. The mule rider craned his neck and addressed the doctor in passable French.

"You look like an ape up in that tree," the mule rider said. A red bandanna was bound tightly over his whole head, knotted at his skull's base, and he was otherwise dressed in surprisingly fresh-looking coachman's livery. He sat the mule as if he had sprouted from its hide. On his knees lay a pendulous cloth sack full of some sort of plant matter and pillowed across that a short military musket with a bayonet fixed.

"Are you an ape, or a man?" the mule rider said. "It's hard to know."

The doctor was too astounded to reply. He just stared back. The mule rider's eyes glittered darkly under the tight crimp of the bandanna. A sprig of gray hair was caught under the edge of the cloth. He too was elderly for a slave in the colony, late forties or early fifties perhaps. His jaw was long and underslung and full of long yellowish teeth separated by little spaces which his half smile revealed. The mule's long ears revolved and it dipped its head to nose at the base of the tree.

"Not a soldier," the mule rider said musingly, studying the doctor's clothes. "Not a planter. Not Creole, certainly. You'll be some sort of artisan, perhaps, or one of the adventurers that come here."

"Antoine Hébert," the doctor said. The sound of his voice pronouncing the words made him feel faint and giggly. "I was born in Lyons and trained in Paris as a doctor."

"A doctor." The mule rider pursed his lips and nodded. "*Médecin.*"

"Yes," the doctor said. He still felt like giggling, or weeping perhaps. "And yourself?"

"Toussaint," the mule rider said, disarmingly, looking at the doctor sidelong. "Just old Toussaint." A practiced obsequiousness in his tone. His eyes glinted below the bandanna and that simpering note left his voice. "Do you want to stay up in the tree and be an ape?" he said. "Why don't you come down here and be a man with me?"

"I'm afraid," the doctor admitted. It surprised him how good it felt to say it.

"Of course," Toussaint said. "So are we all. Except the pure fools."

Chapter Seventeen

Père Duguit, the priest of Limbé, visited the white women held prisoner in Jeannot's camp at Habitation Dusailly. As always when he first entered their enclosure he loudly offered a prayer for their well-being, and then solicited confessions, though none were forthcoming. A stout lady in middle age transfixed him with a stare of pure fury. The younger women simply turned their faces from him.

Père Duguit was a tall man, skinny as a thrashing stick, with long angular boney features, tunnel eyes and eyebrows tufted like the ears of a cat. The hem of his cassock was all in rags and he wore sandals so soleless he might as well have gone barefoot. His feet were painfully riddled with sores full of burrowing worms—a mortification, as he sometimes observed with a certain air of spiritual pride. A slight fever lingered with him also, though he took it as a form of intoxication.

His mind wandered, along the mazy windings of his fever. He looked about himself, dazed as if drunk. The grove of new-growth sabliers in which the white women were contained was fenced about with creeper weavings, more a symbol of a line they must not cross than any effective physical barrier. There was in any event nowhere for them to flee. The Creole ladies among them had erected some flimsy lean-to shelters, thatched with banana leaves; these were partially successful in keeping off the rains, which increased with the advance of the season.

Père Duguit squinted up toward the mountains which rose beyond the river. Another small dark squall was idling over the slate-gray peaks; it was unclear if it might blow in their direction.

Between them and the river stretched a cinder-strewn desert which had once been a cane field, and farther off there was a planting of bananas that had survived the holocaust, long flat leaves twisting like mule ears in the breeze. At the edge of the jungle proper there stood an outbuilding or small house that must have gone to ruin many years before the insurrection. A full-grown tree thrust out of the wrecked roof, with orange blossoms upturned like cups toward the uncertain sky. The priest was startled to see a brown nanny goat poke its head over a plank that barred the dark doorway of the crumbling building—surprised that no one had killed and eaten it. His stomach contracted round a vacuum. Perhaps the goat was being kept for milk.

The wail of a crying baby brought the priest's attention back to the women's enclosure. Some of the white women were attending as best they might to the infants who'd survived the first carnage of the insurrection, and a few older children ran about with a weary carelessness, their faces smudged with dirt. Père Duguit watched a lank-haired Creole wife awkwardly try to suckle a baby who until the change of circumstance would have been put to wet nurse; the mother had not enough milk and the child was crying. Another woman was watching too—milk began to move in a spreading stain on the fabric of her chemise. Murmuring, she took the crying child and loosened her garment and began to nurse it. Père Duguit regarded her; he knew this woman from Acul, and knew that she'd lost her own newborn the night the first plantations burned. That child would be in Limbo now, the priest reminded himself automatically. He studied the nursing woman, breast and thigh, and she stared back at him, her jaw set, an iron hostility burning out of her rust-red eyes. She was well formed, but would not suit Biassou—a problem of comportment.

He passed on, observing the younger girls with sidelong glances. Some of the black women had come into the enclosure and were bringing out the older women they'd taken to be servants, those who were too old to interest the black men as concubines or who'd been so used and then abandoned. These would be taken to the river to wash clothes, or to dig in the provision grounds or to grind meal and do cooking. The stout woman went out among them, and Père Duguit was pleased to see her go, misliking the uncharitable way she always looked at him.

As he paced, his gnarly hands twining together behind his back, he caught a sort of flinching movement from the corner of his eye. Something that he'd learned to value. He moved in. The girl was sitting on a stump, her head cast down. There'd been some others standing near her but they dispersed sullenly as he approached. Hélène was her name; she was eighteen or nineteen, probably. Père Duguit did not know just where she'd come from, though perhaps she was also from Acul. Her head of dark hair was neat and clean—remarkable really, as these captives were infrequently given enough water to wash. He took her chin in his hand and examined her face. Her lips trembled and her eyes were full, so he was unprepared for the quick slash of her nails across his cheek.

"A little *cat,*" he hissed, and caught her wrist as she tried a second time. He twisted her arm down toward her bosom, and leaned in closer to smell her breath, as a buyer might do with a slave on the block. Her jaws were clenched but somehow he was convinced all the same that the breath would be sweet. Her mouth worked and he saw that she would spit at him. He let go her arm and drew back out of range.

"You must cultivate humility, my child," he began. "Meekness and complaisance are most pleasing to God."

Hélène dropped her head, turning her face aside, and he admired the whiteness of her throat as it emerged from the torn neck of her dress. That burst of spirit seemed drained from her now, but still it was a becoming pose, and her figure was good. He ran a hand across his cheek. It stung where she had scratched at him, but his fingertips came away clean; she'd drawn no blood. He flushed a little, perhaps from his fever, as he went on explaining to her in a low tone the opportunities for humility which would be provided to her on that night or the next.

A few moments later he was walking across the main compound of Habitation Dusailly where Jeannot was encamped, chewing absently on half a cold yam he had picked up somewhere. Pus pumped out of his infected feet as he walked, but he was scarcely aware of the pain, or of the orange pulp of yam squeezing out the corners of his mouth. He was approaching a long brick building formerly used for the roasting of coffee, where the imprisoned men were now locked up. Within sight of the iron gate, the priest tossed away the end of his yam. From behind the grille, one of the prisoners cursed at him.

"You throw your food to the rats," he complained, "while we've had nothing these last two days but three rotten bananas and a bit of an ox's ear . . ."

The prisoner's lips were also cracked with thirst, so much so he had difficulty speaking. Père Duguit stopped at the gate, a thin smile on his lips, and breathed in the stench of human excrement. The prisoners were in irons and had no choice but to let their feces fall at their heels and remain there. There were some twenty whites. On a camp bed was stretched a half-conscious, militia officer, his back caked with blood from the two hundred lashes he'd received the previous day. There were also a few blacks who still professed loyalty to the white masters, and these too had been put in chains.

A drum began beating, off to the rear. Père Duguit recognized the approach of Jeannot's cortège. His own heart swelled and throbbed in time. *"Mes enfants,"* he said in a loud voice. *"Il faut savoir mourir, notre Seigneur Jesus Christ est mort pour nous sur la croix."* Then his heart ballooned into his throat and he was unable to say anything more.

Jeannot marched into the compound surrounded by the blacks and mulattoes who were closest to him. The drum continued to pulse slowly as the black Chacha Godard unlocked the gate and led out the white prisoners. His heart still beating powerfully, Père Duguit contemplated his instruction to them. *You must learn how to die, as our Lord Jesus Christ died for us on the cross.*

Jeannot watched the captives for a time, silently. Sometimes he would lecture the prisoners before beginning, but today he said nothing. He was a small man, muscular and coal black, with a Chinese slant to his eyes. He wore a military coat with no shirt beneath it and his chest and belly were glossy with palm oil. His eye stopped on a *grand blanc* who'd been captured with the rest.

"White man, you are too tall," Jeannot said. "Chacha, will you lower him for me?"

There followed a brief struggle which ended with the planter flattened on the ground, a black kneeling on each of his arms and a third sitting on his head. His bare ankles protruded from the leg-irons. Chacha Godard walked toward him casually, carrying a two-handed woodsman's ax. Père Duguit watched avidly, pricked his ears for the crunch of bone. Abstractedly, he picked a crust of yam from the edge of his lip with a long horny fingernail. The other whites looked down inexpressively—to close one's eyes or turn away meant joining the victim, if Jeannot noticed it, and they were to a degree inured to such sights by the events of the past few days. The drum continued grumbling throughout.

When the operation was complete, Jeannot took a step nearer to evaluate the result, chuckling in his throat as the blacks tried to balance the moaning planter on his stumps. With no feet to retain them the irons had slipped loose. Jeannot concluded that the white man was now too short, and ordered that he be hung upside down from a tree limb to see if this procedure might lengthen him to a happy medium.

Père Duguit knelt near the planter's lightly swaying head, to offer him extreme unction, but he seemed incapable of response. Footless as he'd now become, he swung from nooses at his knees, and his severed ankles drooled blood onto the ground where his loose hair was dragging . . . Père Duguit finished the ceremony and walked away to a seat behind a board laid across two kegs, a desk of sorts where he waited until his services would again be necessary. His eyes slipped out of focus for a moment; the board blurred and then reclarified. A strange metallic sort of millipede was crawling down one of the barrels, shiny as a polished bayonet. Strange how it seemed to advance without moving its multiple sections. The priest tracked it into a heap of yellowing leaves, where two mantises were engaged in their devouring act of copulation. Père Duguit thought to separate them, but knew it was impossible; they would suffer themselves to be dismembered before they would desist.

Jeannot had meanwhile caused two other whites to be bound to ladders. At his gesture, Chacha Godard went up to one of them and struck him a lazy blow with the ax. The stroke bruised as much as it cut, but there was a popping sound and a gasp from the victim that suggested it must have broken a rib. Chacha laid the ax aside, drew a small sharp knife from his belt and approached the second white man. He pushed up his chin and made a shallow cut all along the jawbone, not piercing anything vital.

Jeannot stood by, a watch in his hand. Père Duguit knew from past experience that it would be precisely fifteen minutes before he ordered the next cut. He bethought himself of writing a note to Biassou, detailing the evening's delectation. There was paper and a stub of charcoal in a cloth bag swung from his cassock's belt. He spread a bit of paper on the plank and licked the charcoal and began.

"J'ai disposé la dame une telle à vous recevoir cette nuit . . ." He thought for a moment, picturing the attitude of Hélène when he had first noticed her. *"Vous n'avez jamais eu de telle jouissance, mon cher Biassou, que celle qui vous attend ce soir . . ."**

Idly he looked about. The drummer's long flat palms caressed the skin of the drum's head, but despite the noise from the drum the priest felt that he could also hear the sound of Jeannot's watch. Of a sudden, the planter began to scream and thrash, scattering droplets of blood in a semicircle from his stumps. A barefoot black walked up and kicked him in the face; his head snapped back and his screams subsided to a gurgle. The priest was thrilled to his fingertips. He closed his eyes for a moment and pictured random scenes from the Inquisition, each sin and heresy meticulously extracted. His face stung slightly and he saw Hélène's face as she'd looked when she had struck him. He opened his eyes and wrote again.

"La petite de fait la reveche mais apportez de la pitre pour la disposer à souscrire à vos désirs . . ."†

Jeannot turned his watch over in his hand and coughed out an order. Chacha Godard took out his knife again and drew his thumb down along the blade to the point. In the woods all around, the birds were chattering, and the beat of the drum became harsher and drier. Père Duguit looked abstractedly at the two men bound to the ladders. He signed his name to the letter and folded it in three.

THE WHITE MEN HAD BEEN DYING on the ladders for four hours, sixteen cuts apiece, when Choufleur and the Sieur Maltrot strolled up to join the rear of the audience: the white prisoners who were bound to watch, and those of the blacks bloodthirsty enough to appreciate

*I have prepared such a woman to receive you tonight . . . Never have you known such joy, my dear Biassou, as that which awaits you this evening . . .
†The little thing will be obstinate, but bring along the whip with the hemp lash, to dispose her to submit to your desires . . .

this spectacle. Maltrot arranged himself in a cantilevered pose, like a Greek statue, resting the tip of his sword stick on the toe of his opposite boot. His brocaded coat was dusty with travel and his breeches were sweat-stained where they'd been in contact with the saddle, but apart from these details he appeared much as he would have on the street of any city. Choufleur stood foursquare, his arms folded, wearing a white shirt open at the neck.

Maltrot twitched, and moved his hands restively on the pommel of his cane. Jeannot had given a low grunting order and, under the direction of Chacha Godard, three blacks were untying the first white man from his ladder. They carried him, dazed and bleeding, to a *zaman* tree in whose trunk had been set an enormous butcher's hook, seven or eight feet off the ground. Standing on a stack of packing cases, the blacks raised the white man and adjusted his jaw above the hook's point. Chacha Godard yanked him down sharply by the waist to set the hook, using such force that the point broke out one of the man's lower teeth as it curled around the jawbone and emerged from his mouth.

The drumbeat turned still more shallow, dry as the whisper of dead leaves. The white man had been comatose, but under this new stimulation he enjoyed a remarkable return to life. He hugged the tree and tried to climb it, but Chacha Godard twisted his arms away and a black man tied his wrists behind him with long strips of liana. The white man hung, kicking his feet against the tree trunk. His chest and belly grumbled with a suffocated scream, but his own weight sealed his throat shut so it could not escape. Above, the rounded leaves of almond tree fanned him gently.

"You must have these monstrosities stopped immediately," said the Sieur Maltrot. His tone was customarily crisp, though he kept his voice low. His eyes cut from the hooked man to the suspended planter, who had died a couple of hours previously and was just beginning to stiffen where he hung.

"Be careful," Choufleur said. "You're not master here."

"I believe that was a friend of mine," Maltrot said, looking at the planter's blotchy face with an evident fascination. "Or an acquaintance, rather."

Jeannot was whispering something to Chacha Godard, who signaled for his assistants to reverse the ladder on which the second man was strapped, so that he hung upside down. Godard knelt at his side, his short knife drawn. The white man's eyes rolled toward the blade and then away. Jeannot was kneeling also, holding out an odd round cup or drinking bowl, which had a curious mass of tendrils dangling from it, as if it had been rooted in the ground. . . . Maltrot saw that the bowl was in fact a scooped-out cranium, with a dried scalp clinging to its underside, and the trailing hair. As he made this recognition, Godard jerked a short deep cut in the white man's neck as one might bleed a hog. Blood gushed over the edges of the skull and matted the hair where it hung beneath and spilled over to darken the gold braid on the cuffs of Jeannot's coat. Jeannot stood up ceremoniously, holding the brimming skull out from himself like a chalice. He looked at the man hooked to the tree as if he meant to propose a toast to him.

"How good it is," Jeannot pronounced, "how sweet—the blood of the white people." He raised the skull to his lips and drank, blood running from the corners of his mouth and separating into threads as it mingled with the oil on the bare skin of his chest. Maltrot hiccuped and looked away, toward the scarecrow of a priest who sat behind a sort of bench, watching the proceedings with a rapt attention. Then he looked at Choufleur's freckled profile.

"It isn't that such things occur," he said. "It's that you permit them to be shown to me."

Choufleur did not react, and Maltrot waited. Waiting, he drew out his snuffbox, took his dip and sneezed. A few of the black men gathered around looked at him curiously.

"A certain decorum ought to be maintained," Maltrot said. "But you have fractured it. I meant to say as well that instructions appear to have been exceeded quite drastically all around."

Choufleur broke from his reverie, and gave Maltrot a distant look.

"Come with me," he said. "They've finished here."

As he turned moving toward the edge of the central compound, he made a covert movement with his hand, and a group of five black men began following them at a little distance. They walked a way in silence, climbing through the terraced coffee trees.

"Who was that devil of a priest?" the Sieur Maltrot inquired. He paused, resting with one hand on his hip. His face was lightly broken out with sweat. Choufleur looked back at him noncommitally and climbed ahead.

They entered a trail that passed through the jungle and wound toward the bluff above the river. It was cool and shady under the thick-laced forest roof, and all around was the damp smell of leaf mold. A macaw flicked across the way ahead of them. Maltrot looked back, and saw that the five men were still following them, two dozen paces back.

"Who are those fellows?" he called to Choufleur. "Have they no work?"

"They work as they are ordered," Choufleur said, without turning. His back receded on the trail, a shifting patch of white on the dense green.

Maltrot shrugged and kept following him. They came out together on the bluff's edge, where the sound of the water rushing downriver reached them much more clearly. The river turned through coffee trees planted almost to its edge. It was a pleasant vista, on the whole. At the bend of the river, a party of the men who'd assisted Godard were dumping dismembered parts of bodies into the water.

"*Nous sommes arrivés,*" Choufleur said. He stood on the balls of his feet, beneath a tree lurid with red flowers whose stamens lolled from the blooms like tongues.

"*Arrivés où?*" said the Sieur Maltrot.

"*Á la fin du monde,*" Choufleur said. "*Tu comprends ça?*"

Maltrot swung at him with his stick, but Choufleur caught the end of it with an even quicker movement. Maltrot let him try his strength for a minute or more. They set themselves against each other, Choufleur straining to twist the stick out of his grip. Then Maltrot released the catch and whipped free the blade, leaving Choufleur unbalanced, holding the empty wooden sheath. He might have skewered the mulatto then, but instead he only grazed the sword's point across his cheek.

"Was that your game?" Maltrot said. "*Tu oses me tutoyer, toi?* Get down, ungrateful cur, and beg my pardon."

Choufleur stepped out of the blade's reach and touched the butt of a pistol stuck in his belt.

"Is that it?" Maltrot said. "Shoot, then. I'd welcome it—compared to what I've seen."

Choufleur winked. A black arm wrapped across Maltrot's neck; his arms were pinned by several hands. He'd forgotten the men on the trail behind, and now they'd overtaken him. The hands were peeling his grip from the sword stick, finger by finger. Choufleur moved near him, and Maltrot kicked him neatly in the groin. Choufleur gasped and dropped into a crouch, gagging from the pain. But Maltrot could not get free of the other men. The sword stick was taken from him. The black men tied him carefully into the heart of the blooming tree.

"Enough," Choufleur said. "Go now."

The black men retreated down the trail. Choufleur approached the flowering tree, with a mincing step from his injured groin. Maltrot wriggled his fingers; it was the most that he could do. They'd tied his legs below the knee so that he could not kick again.

Choufleur reached into Maltrot's vest pocket, took out the snuffbox and wrinkled his nose at the powder inside. He poured the snuff out on the ground and put the box in his own trousers pocket.

Maltrot's face had turned quite gray. "You must remember," he began, in a level, formal tone. "I've shown you every consideration, every generosity. I gave you education, sent you off to Paris, sparing no expense. I've given you land and slaves of your own."

Choufleur drew a knife from his belt and ran his tongue along the blade. Maltrot choked.

"I am your father," he said flatly.

"Do you acknowledge it?" Choufleur said.

"Yes," Maltrot said. "*Yes*—and publicly, if you like."

"If it is true," Choufleur said, "then you gave me a nigger to be my mother."

He cut a bracelet all around Maltrot's wrist, just above the thong that bound it to the branch. He made a vertical incision into the palm and turned back the flaps of skin from the whitish fatty layer underneath and began peeling it back toward the fingertips as if he were slowly taking off a glove. Maltrot ground his teeth and bit his lips till the blood ran freely, but finally he could not contain the scream and when it came it was large and loud enough to split the sky.

Doctor Hébert was coming upriver along the bluffs from Biassou's encampment, in the company or custody of a black man he'd come to know as Jean-Pic. In his pocket was a safe conduct in the name of Biassou. It was Toussaint, however, who'd signed Biassou's name to the paper—a curious instrument, the doctor thought, for none of the people who challenged him in his perigrinations could read it. And yet in every case where he was required to produce it, the document would be scrutinized (upside down or sideways like as not) and its talismanic significance acknowledged. He would pass. He was, as had been said of certain privileged slaves, *liberté de savane*—meaning that he was at liberty to go more or less where he liked, but without being truly free. The constant presence of Jean-Pic or someone like him also served as both protection and restraint.

With Jean-Pic he had been crisscrossing the bluff trail, making little ventures into the surrounding jungle to collect medicinal herbs Toussaint had taught him to recognize, and also other plants which were unknown to him and which he believed Toussaint might identify. The black man had a skill with medicinal herbs, some of which he'd used to poultice and soak the doctor's hurt ankle. Doctor Hébert was not entirely certain of their efficacy but he had recovered most of his mobility with good speed.

He was just reaching into a cluster of bamboo to pluck a section of a climbing vine with fragrant trefoil leaves and small white star-shaped flowers when the air all around him was cleaved by a scream. It was not precisely an unfamiliar sound; the doctor had grown somewhat accustomed to hearing it at some distance upriver from Biassou's camp. But now it seemed to be just at his feet. He thought that he must have strayed nearer than he should have to Jeannot's encampment, or perhaps Jean-Pic had lured him here deliberately, and this idea frightened him. But he saw that Jean-Pic was as startled as he, was parting the fronds of bamboo with great caution so that he could look down on what was happening below.

The doctor stepped up softly and looked over Jean-Pic's shoulder. At the bamboo's edge there was an abrupt drop of some fifteen feet, and below, the blooming tree. The doctor noticed the tree first, its flowers such a fresh and vegetable red that all the blood seemed flat and dull beside them. He was aware of the rank bloody smell. There was a man, two men, one operating upon the other with a concentrated and scientific precision.

The doctor had seen this sight before, or something like it, and indeed his own position on a height above reminded him all the more strongly of the operating theaters of his training, where he had learned anatomy. With the difference that here the subject was screamingly alive. The epidermis had been peeled away strategically to reveal the workings of the musculature on the hands and arms and thighs; even the cheeks were laid bare, and the lips had been cut away (so that the man must scream without a proper mouth to do it with). Two tendons had been severed, so that the large muscles of the thigh hung down below the trembling genitalia, and above these, an incision had been made into the body cavity. The operator pulled out the mass of intestines, straightened out the kinks in them and let them drop. He reached within and laid his curious hand on the liver, the spleen, the palpitating heart.

The operator was a mulatto, oddly freckled—the doctor felt he'd seen him somewhere before. The subject, on the other hand, was skinless now, deracinated, transmogrified into the internal self he possibly had always been, raw human nature laid bare to greasy viscera and a scream. The doctor had seen the assembly of these parts oftentimes before in his own chilly dissections—but this was life itself. Unconsciously he mutilated the vine he'd plucked between his fingers; new fragrance rose from the crushed leaves. He felt through his nausea and terror that he was witnessing something well beyond torture or murder. Though he could not understand or grasp it, he was seeing what it meant to be human. This was a sincere inquiry into the nature of man, not how a man is made and how his parts cooperate, but what a man *is*, in his essence, and who, in the final analysis, would be allowed to be one.

Chapter Eighteen

WHEN DAWN'S LIGHT FIRST BEGAN TO RISE, the priest was once again revealed, a pace or two ahead of the staggering Arnaud, the pale skin of his back looking speckled under its mat of bristles, his hairy buttocks jiggling with his steps. The road they were taking passed between cane fields that had been put to the torch and because of the smoke the morning light was unusually slow to penetrate. When they once could see each other plainly, the priest stopped and resumed his damp brown habit. Arnaud sat down and pulled off his riding boots. His feet were covered with watery blisters from rubbing against the wet leather, and as they walked on the blisters tore open and he saw that he was leaving dim smudges of blood on the dust with every step. He would have liked to moan or weep but before the barefoot priest he was ashamed to.

The two huts of the priest's compound were as silent and deserted looking as they'd been when Arnaud had passed that way with his pack train the afternoon before. But when Père Bonne-chance swung open the door of his *ajoupa,* Arnaud saw over his shoulder that his family had returned there, the mulattress Fontelle sitting motionless on a stool and an indeterminate number of children huddled along the wall behind her, all quiet as kittens or puppies surprised in a warm den. The children looked at Arnaud speechlessly, their eyes shining. Père Bonne-chance pushed the other stool toward him and he collapsed onto it helplessly.

Arnaud was face to face with the mulatto woman, who regarded him, as crisply still as a snake. The light coming in through the cracks in the palmiste wall laid grayish stripes along her turban and her cheek. Her nose was long and crooked and her teeth were snaggly in her lantern jaw, but with his connoisseur's eye Arnaud discerned that she was also high-breasted and slender, though full in the hips, and he recognized that the priest had a good thing in her, at least in this wise. Using his hands, he lifted one of his feet to the opposite knee, and now he finally did groan aloud, more from the revolting appearance of the blood-encrusted sores than from the pain itself, to which he'd partly become inured.

Fontelle reached out and took his ankle and raised the foot onto her lap. She looked at the sole of it critically, twisting the ankle this way and that. At her short command one of the children went out with a clay jug and returned with it full of river water. When Fontelle lifted his other foot to her knees, Arnaud was unbalanced on the stool and his head and shoulders went lolling back against the fragile wall. The woman washed his feet one after the other and packed them in a poultice of crushed aloe leaves. At her first touches a weird sensation shot through the marrow of Arnaud's bones, first an exquisite pain and then a soporific numbness. His face turned against the slats of the wall and he gave up his consciousness.

When he awoke it was night and the room was redolent with a green soup thickened and sweetened with coconut, which Fontelle was ladling into bowls. Arnaud accepted his portion and ate it wordlessly as the others; no one spoke. He lay down on the floor and slept again. Sometime during the night he woke to find that one of the little boys had rolled against him in his sleep. Arnaud let him remain there, smelling the sour-sweet odor of his breath; the child's arm shivered against his ribs in the nervousness of some dream. On the opposite side of the *ajoupa* the priest was snoring loudly. Arnaud thought of his wife by her name, Claudine, and wondered what their lives might have become if she had borne him any children. When he next came to himself it was dawn again and Fontelle was shaking him by the shoulder.

He got up with less pain than he'd expected and followed the woman out of doors. While he slept she had bundled his feet into makeshift moccasins made of rags, and his steps brought him no more than a dull discomfort through this padding. He walked behind Fontelle who walked behind the priest. The children followed them like a string of chicks or ducklings, each carrying a pack of clothes or a couple of gourds or cooking pans. Arnaud had been given a pack himself, with his riding boots tied across the top of it. When they had walked a mile or so, he asked Père Bonne-chance where they were bound, and when the priest asked if there were anywhere he wished to go, Arnaud said that he would like if possible to return to his own plantation.

Because of the children their pace was slow, and Arnaud, with his tender feet, was grateful for its languor. He watched the priest's bare toes splaying out over the gravel of the roadbed with as much amazement as if he were watching someone walk on water. The first night they stopped in the provision ground of a plantation that had been sacked. The provisions had been looted too but not completely, and Fontelle found a stalk of good bananas and sent the children to dig dasheen. They roasted bananas in their skins over an open fire and ate without conversation and slept and in the morning they rose and went on.

The way they took led through a stand of coconut trees with the ground between them razed and burned—not to destroy them this time but only to clear the undergrowth. The priest gathered coconuts and husked them where they were and gave a pair to each child to carry. In leaving the grove they came upon a starveling milk cow trailing a lead rope and the children ran after her, but the cow bellowed and bolted and would not be caught.

They were crossing open country, dry flats never yet scored with irrigation ditches. Behind them the green tufts of the coconuts receded and in the farther distance the mountains beyond the River Massacre had gone ghostly in the distance, under the purpling clouds that crowned their heights. Ahead was more jungle, then mountains again, a lower range but steep enough. They reached the tree line before night and made a camp, where they supped on coconut milk and slices of the meat. In the plump darkness Arnaud slept uneasily, waking to pinch at mosquitoes or to listen to the low liquid calling of the *siffleur montagne*. Next morning he rose with the others and they continued their way.

The land was full of small roving bands of rebel slaves, and often the priest and his companions had to leave the road to avoid them. In the heat of each afternoon they rested under cover, and when the heat had abated in the evening, they came out of the jungle to walk a couple of miles more. They changed course so many times to keep away from the brigands that soon they had departed from any way familiar to Arnaud. By the third day he had lost all sense of their position in the country.

The third night they spent in a banana grove above a small stream that ran along the edge of a burned cane field. In the early morning of the twelfth day the priest went down to the stream for water and came back hurriedly, his face leaching alarm.

"What is it?" Arnaud said.

His viscera clenched and then went watery, as if he didn't need to ask. But the priest beckoned him to the grove's ragged edge and pressed on his shoulder so that he knelt, the priest crouching beside him. A half mile distant a dull cloud of ash had been raised on the incinerated plain by the feet of a hundred or more blacks coming their way. An indistinct mass, they moved in quick rushes broken by sudden halts; when they stopped they shouted loudly to the devils they worshiped and thrust makeshift spears into the air above their heads. A large man in their forefront swung a bull's tail around his head, snapping it like a whip to urge them on.

"They saw me when I went to the stream," Père Bonne-chance muttered. Arnaud watched the blacks advancing, half mesmerized by the odd rhythm of their stops and starts.

"You must go on alone," the priest said. "If you cross this mountain you will find your own place in the plain on the far side."

"I would not leave you," Arnaud said, surprised to feel that what he said was true.

"Well, they have seen me," the priest said. "We could not outrun them in the mountains with the children. Or without them for that matter, I expect . . ."

Arnaud hesitated. The blacks were near enough now so he could pick out individual forms among them. They were singing, chanting rather.

"What do they say?" he asked the priest, as if he would know better.

"*Vodûn,*" the priest said. "Never mind—I have a better *vodûn* of my own. No doubt I've baptised some of them, besides—on more than one occasion. *Je saurai comment ménager tout ça.*"

Arnaud kept staring. His mouth hung slackly open; the inner membranes had gone dry.

"You must go quickly," the priest said, without moving or raising his voice. "As you are a *grand blanc* they will certainly murder you, and I think it will go worse with the rest of us if they find us together."

Arnaud stood up abruptly and followed the priest back to the blackened circle of last night's campfire. Fontelle had already detached his boots from the bundle he'd been carrying, and one of the children was stuffing the uppers of them with bananas and some of the tubers they'd dug the night before. Arnaud pinched the boot tops closed and swung them together over his shoulder. The priest accompanied him a few paces into the jungle.

"You have only to go up that way." Père Bonne-chance waved indiscriminately at a mass of bamboo laced together with vine. "And down the other side . . ."

Arnaud, all unsure of his intentions, dropped onto one knee. He took hold of the priest's thick spade-shaped hand and began kissing the hair-matted backs of his fingers. "Father," he said. He repeated the word. In the stiffening of his wrist he felt the priest's embarrassment. Père Bonne-chance pulled his hand free and laid it on Arnaud's head, but he said nothing. After a moment he touched Arnaud with both his hands, rubbing his ears as he might a hound's. Then he broke the contact and swung away, back to where Fontelle and the children were waiting.

Arnaud began climbing but it was impossible to make much haste. His feet were healed considerably, but the unwieldy moccasin-bundles gave him no traction on the difficult slope. He zigzagged, of necessity, there was no other way. The noise of his own poor progress alarmed him and he stopped, hearing the sound of many feet splashing through the stream below.

In the place where he had halted there was a break in the jungle cover and Arnaud overlooked the grove. The priest and his family were seated on their haunches some thirty yards below, breakfasting on dasheen and fruit as if unaware of the shouts and pounding feet approaching them. The leader flung into the clearing, his bull's tail brandished at arm's length. Père Bonne-chance looked at him in the manner of a host receiving an invited guest.

"The Lord be with you," the priest said. He picked up a banana and broke the peel and offered it. The leader's hand loosened and the bull's tail slipped slackly from it.

Arnaud began climbing again, holding his boots in one hand and clinging to bamboo and saplings to support himself with the other. He went as quietly as he could, abandoning any attempt at speed. The priest's voice carried well in the humid air, and Arnaud heard him repeating the same phrase, each time another man reached him he supposed: *Domine vobiscum*, as if he were confident of a response according to the litany.

At dusk of that day Arnaud crossed the mountain's backbone somewhere short of the peak and made it a little distance down the other side before nightfall stopped him. He groped dasheen and bananas from his boot and ate in the heavy dark. The rattle of a stream through a gorge somewhere below was a torment to him, for he had not thought to make his way to water, and now he was afraid to climb down in the dark, knowing he might fall and break a leg, if not his neck. The image of the horse he'd so wantonly destroyed on the mountain was present to his mind; in dream he saw the animal as it would look now, swollen with the death-bloat and legs stiffly projecting from its foul belly. Sometime during the night it rained a little and he could lick some moisture from the leaves. When the rain had stopped the *siffleur montagne* took up its mournful song again, but tonight it irritated Arnaud more than it soothed him.

The descent was slower and more arduous than the climb, though he began it early. Near noon he came unexpectedly into a clearing, a bare trodden area circling a single peeled tree trunk at its center. Painted on the stripped wood were images of two serpents entwined together and nearby on the ground there lay a broken gourd strung with cracked clay beads: a rattle abandoned by the dancers who'd been here. It occurred to Arnaud that this must be where his own slaves came for their *calendas*, though weeds were sprouting from the track and it seemed no one had been there for some time.

In twenty minutes more he'd cleared the jungle and could see. All the fields that had been his cane were burned to nothing. In his compound, only one hut remained standing, a row of vultures perching on the rooftree. He went down toward it. The citrus hedge had been scorched but not consumed. Arnaud plucked a shriveled orange and ate it for its juice.

His stone cane mill had been broken down by hammers, as it looked. Standing in the litter of smashed vats, Arnaud was aghast at the sheer labor this destruction must have taken. Three of the walls had been battered to rubble, and about half of the fourth was still standing, lianas working their tendrils into cracks in the mortar. His stable and the *grand'case,* which were built of wood, had both been burned to the ground. The only surviving building was the shed where he had kept his dog. Arnaud walked toward it with a dragging step.

The door was open—from it issued a vague putrid smell. This odor had drawn the vultures, undoubtedly. Arnaud stooped and picked up a stick of charcoal and whipped it side-arm at the three who sat on the roof, but the vultures only shifted their feet and looked back at him. He stopped at the threshold and peered in.

Vultures and insects had done most of the work. It was a skeleton that hung from the wall, clothed in rags and a few strips of rotten desiccated flesh, its bone wrists casually aloft in loose loops of cord. And yet it moved, or something moved about it. Arnaud squinted into the dim. A metallic sectioned thing with many legs came crawling out of one eyehole and crept into the other.

He was stumbling across the packed ground toward the black hole that had been his house. The thing in the shed was peculiarly addressed to him, he knew; it was a message, personal, as if someone had come in the night and nailed a crow to his front door. He fell on his all-fours and vomited into the ashes of his dwelling and stayed there with his head dizzily drooping, strings of spittle hanging from his lower lip. Something was gouging into his palm; he sat back on his heels and lifted the object to examine it. A silver fork, fire-blackened, melted and twisted into a new shape of deformity.

He stood up and flung the fork away. In the ashes a few yards away, a glint of something caught his attention, a surface reflecting a section of the sky like a still pool or a well brimful. Thirst drew him to it, but he found nothing but a mirror, the gilt frame burned away. Crouching over it, he saw a face, filthy and bloodshot and roughened with beard, unknowable to him. After a time he worked his fingers on the ground and began methodically to darken his cheeks with ash.

He took to wandering, in and out of the fringes of the jungle and the slopes that bordered the plain. At first he'd thought of going to Le Cap but he was afraid to expose himself on the wide waste open spaces that lay between him and the town. Eventually the logic drained away from the fear and it became a simple animal aversion. The ruined landscape was now so featureless to him that he did not know how to place himself within it.

His feet healed, toughened to a horny gloss. He would not wear his boots, but carried them strapped to his waist with a rag of his discarded shirt, as panniers for the food he was able to forage. He ate wild fruit, or raided abandoned provision grounds at dusk. Wild goats and wild hogs sometimes passed, but he was never able to run one down. Once he found a stand of mushrooms and ate them greedily, but they made him violently ill and sent him into delirious dreams. Whenever he came near other men he fled from them, because they were not of his own kind. He coated his body and face with mud, to guard him from the sun, and from others' sight. At one point he began scoring the leather of his boots with sticks or stones to mark the days, but too much time had passed for him to reckon before he began the habit and, after making some thirty such scratches, he gave it over.

A day came when he'd left a jungle trail to hide himself from something he heard coming. Horsemen, twenty or more in single file. A few regular army dragoons and the rest militia, these were the first white men he'd seen. He watched them with mere curiosity from a rock above the path, until their captain's voice broke the air.

Arnaud came scrambling down then, willy-nilly, spooking the captain's horse so that it reared. The captain struggled to bring his mount under control, and Arnaud waited meekly as the animal shivered and snorted and rolled its eyes. He'd known this officer once by name: it was M—, M—, Maillart. Who watched him with an utter lack of comprehension.

"Do you not know me?" Arnaud croaked. Getting no answer, he crumbled some of the mud from his chest, scraping the skin to bare it further to the captain's eye. "It is white, do you not see? I am like you."

Chapter Nineteen

Doctor Hébert sat on a stone high above the riverbank. Behind him was the bustle and whir of Biassou's camp; ahead, large boulders tumbled down into the water and partway across the river stream. Near the water a calabash tree was growing, oddly decorated with cords the blacks had tied around the gourds to shape them as they grew, for later use. Round the tree's foot sprouted rich red-blossoming fronds of what the doctor had heard from Toussaint was a sort of ginger.

A tickling on the back of his hand distracted him. Looking down he saw a small olive-green beetle with one yellow spot in the center of its back, walking over the hairs on his skin. Involuntarily he started and the beetle cracked its carapace and flew in a silent whirring of its transparent wings. The doctor raised his head toward the river, where five or six of the captive white women stood waist deep in the cold water, laying out clothes on boulders and scrubbing them with smaller stones. From the bank, a gaggle of black women gossiped among themselves, and occasionally called out instructions and commands. This latter group was dressed in a mélange of slave garments and finery looted from the plantations. Many of the clothes the white women were laundering might formerly have been their own.

The doctor's eye was on one of them in particular, a dark-haired girl wringing out a white chemise: Hélène. There was something about her that recalled Elise to him, though they hardly resembled one another, unless in bearing or in attitude. The doctor had not seen his sister for so long he sometimes wondered if he'd know her, if she did appear before him, changed as these women had been transformed. Hélène spread the chemise out on a boulder and scoured it with hands chapped and reddened by the cold water; her lips were pursed, and he thought that perhaps she was even humming as she worked. He studied her profile, wondering what Elise might be doing at this moment (if she were still alive) and if he'd ever see the niece he'd heard of. He had attended Hélène for a time after Biassou had discarded her, and had, a week previously, believed that she would likely die. She had been cruelly used by the black general (as he styled himself), probably by others in his retinue as well, and for her unwillingness she'd been injured in more ways than one, and cast off all the sooner. The doctor had treated the weals on her thighs and buttocks with herb poultices Toussaint had taught him to prepare, embarrassed to see the damaged flesh and touch it, doubting that his ministrations would be of great use. But the girl had surprised him by rallying suddenly, as if the ordeal had cut through to a powerful resilience at her core, and she seemed stronger now, more cheerful than she ever had before.

A mulattress, Marotte, called her to the bank. Hélène waded till she was no more than ankle deep, her thin legs storklike under the wet mass of skirt strapped up around her thighs. She shook out the chemise and displayed it to Marotte's critical eye. The doctor could see no blemish on its striking whiteness, but Marotte frowned and sent her back, with large theatrical gestures, to continue the washing. Hélène took it meekly enough, expressionless as she carried the chemise back to the boulder she'd been using as a washboard. The black women tittered among themselves at some insult Marotte called after her as she went.

Behind them there began an outcry, men's voices raised in anger in the camp. The doctor went quite rigid when he heard it; he could even feel his testicles retract. Among the rebels there was always some faction in favor of killing all the white prisoners on the spot, though as a rule they were not so badly treated in this camp, where some of them, like the doctor, were free to wander as they wished, like officers on parole. But since he had seen the white man flayed in the blossoming tree, the doctor had been wary of where his wandering might lead him. There was a fear that twisted his vitals and never really left him, tremulous below the outward aspect he struggled to keep mute. But in the camp the tumult quickly died, and he relaxed a little, watching a green-headed hummingbird flick among some vines beside him and pause to hover before a barely opened bud. The hummingbird flew. Restively the doctor shifted his buttocks on the stone. He reached into his pocket and took out the shard of mirror he'd picked up from the ruin of Nanon's rooms and somehow managed to retain all through his wanderings. Cupping the small reflection in his palm, he scanned his face section by section: eyes bloodshot and sunken darkly in the sockets, face scratched and grubby, rough beard growing down his throat.

Again Marotte ordered Hélène out of the water. The doctor pocketed his glass and raised his head to look. The white girl shook the dripping chemise out at her arm's length, revealing that the fabric had gone threadbare under too much scrubbing, holes appearing in it here and there. Marotte raised her voice and cursed Hélène for her stupidity, begging her to look more closely at the damage her carelessness had caused. The doctor remembered the mulattress from Arnaud's house, and he thought it was there she must have learned the language and the gestures she now employed. These were the caprices of Madame Arnaud which Marotte was reenacting, as was strictly natural, certainly—as chains of being bound her to do. There was, after all, something quite impersonal about it. The two woman were of a height and similarly slender, though Marotte was perhaps ten years the elder. The doctor watched her slap at Hélène's face, but weakly, meaning to shame her more than to do real physical hurt. The white girl turned her head just ahead of the blow, so the yellow hand just grazed her cheek in passing, and remained with her face averted, eyes cast down.

Toussaint was coming over the rocks, his small jockey's body erect and surely balanced, despite his slick boot soles. He snatched the chemise from between the two women and held it at eye level. Inserting his fingers in one of the larger holes, he ripped the whole thing down the middle. Cowed, the black women fell silent on the bank. Toussaint said nothing, as if the tearing were enough to rebuke Marotte's perversity. He passed between the women and came up toward the doctor, methodically tearing the cloth into long strips they'd use for bandages, once dry.

As he reached Doctor Hébert, Toussaint turned and glanced back toward the women, smiling faintly in one corner of his mouth. Marotte had turned her back to Hélène, disdaining the white girl as she gathered up the washing. The black women's voices recommenced, a little softer than before. The doctor watched Hélène raise the sodden bundle to her head; she could not balance it as a black woman would, without using a hand to steady it. He got up and followed Toussaint's beckoning. By now the ankle scarcely pained him at all, but his cracked ribs had healed more slowly, and he felt a jolt from them upon first rising from his seat.

The sick and wounded lay on pallets in a grove uphill from the main encampment, under a wall-less *ajoupa* thatched over with palm leaves against the rain. There were a few white people here, mostly fallen ill with fever, and many more blacks, some wounded in skirmishes with the white men in the hill forts all around, others from fighting among themselves, which was almost equally common. Toussaint made rounds as a white doctor might, but with less presumption, stooping to speak softly to each invalid who waked. Unlike the other blacks who held position, he had not tricked himself out in any quasi-official regalia, wearing only his coachman's livery still, the worn green coat with its old stains, bare of the decorations the other self-appointed officers liked to flaunt. Still, the odd assortment of *hûngans* and leaf-doctors over whom Toussaint had at least a nominal authority paid as much respect to the faded bandanna knotted over his head as they would to a general's bicorne cap.

It was something to be a *dokté-feuilles*, Doctor Hébert had come to recognize. He felt that his own education had begun anew from the first days he'd been held in the encampment. Despite the rustic situation, Toussaint adhered to a standard of cleaniness higher than that the doctor had known in many French hospitals, and he had for the most part dissuaded the lesser *hûngans* from practices such as packing wounds with dirt. As for Doctor Hébert himself, he'd largely been demoted to the status of surgeon, amputating injured limbs that were past saving, a point on which he and Toussaint did not always agree.

A few feet outside the *ajoupa*'s roof, an old woman called Ti-Jeanne tended a fire and a boiling cauldron. Herbs dried on a latticed rack beside the fire, and she used them to prepare the various infusions. The doctor went to help her with this work. He'd learned that the plants of the colony had virtues quite unknown in Europe, and many of these were now unlocked for him. A *tisane* of *armoire* could halt the course of dysentery. For cough, one brewed a mixture of several flowers: *gombo, giromon, herbe à cornette,* and *pectoral.* A tea of *herbe à pique* was effective against fever . . . The doctor crumbled leaves between his fingers, combined them in the bottoms of the gourds, while the old woman ladled boiling water over them. Abstracted as he was, it took him a moment to respond to the voice of Toussaint, slightly raised to call him.

Toussaint knelt at the side of a young man, who'd been quite badly hurt in a fight, no doubt over some woman or other. He'd been struck a glancing cutlass blow on the outside of his upper arm, which stripped the meat away from the bone and left the severed muscles hanging. The doctor saw him as an immediate candidate for the surgeon's saw, for such a mangling wound must certainly go to gangrene. Left to himself, he'd have taken the arm off at the shoulder.

Now Toussaint signaled him to change the dressing on the wound. The injured man turned his head and grinned at the doctor as he loosened the bandage, no mean impression in itself, since a few days earlier he'd have moaned in pain at the lightest touch on the injured arm. Inside the binding, the wound had resolved into an inch-wide gash from shoulder to elbow, crusted over and puckering at the edges. There was no proud flesh, no pus when the doctor probed the edges with his fingertips, though the other's breath came hissing hard. The wound smelt clean, and it was healing from the bottom. The doctor nodded and withdrew his hand and Toussaint began anointing the cut with a paste he'd ground in a shallow wooden bowl: aloe, *guèrit-trop-vite,* and *mal dormi*—medicinal herb used in plasters. Finished, he bandaged over the ointment and stood up, smiling sidelong at the doctor.

"White people are sometimes too free with other people's limbs . . ."

Doctor Hébert did not know if he were being accused or taken into a confidence. He simply nodded, feeling quite deracinated by Toussaint's remark, as if he no longer belonged to any category. He could recall, as well, that on the worst plantations such amputations were practiced for no medical reason, but as a punishment for runaways. They had finished here. Toussaint motioned him with a finger and they walked down the slope and through the camp until they reached the riverside again.

Moored to a stake on a muddy bank were a couple of canoes made in the ancient Carib way: the trunk of a *gommier* dug out and spread with water and hot stones, reinforced with curving struts pegged against the interior, a plank on either side to raise the gunwales. Toussaint climbed into one of these and the doctor followed, taking up the oars. Toussaint pointed and he settled to the rowing, pulling against the current of the stream. Paired pegs served as the oarlocks, the oars shuttling somewhat awkwardly between them. With his back to the prow, the doctor could not see just where they were going, but he began to break out in an anxious sweat, knowing that Jeannot's camp was this way, up the river. But before they had gone nearly so far as that, Toussaint directed him into a backwater, an abandoned paddy of sorts where rice or indigo had once been grown. A small gray heron, red-breasted, flew over the flat expanse, and far beyond it the shadows of clouds were running swiftly over the mountain slopes.

It was very hot. Toussaint undid his kerchief and trailed it in the water, then refastened the wet cloth over his forehead. The doctor was conscious of a runnel of sweat furrowing into the creases of his belly. His fear ebbed from him; it seemed to come and go sometimes, almost without reason. Toussaint pointed to a channel between two narrowly set trees. A spiderweb tore across the doctor's back as he pulled between them. Toussaint reached across and flicked the hairy bee-striped spider into the water.

The stream was only a few times wider than the boat, and tightly shelved in on either side by mangrove trees, the flat flanges of their roots coming down into the water. Here the doctor saw a great dirt nest of grubs or insects, daubed in the fork of a trunk; there a whole mangrove had been eaten out by termites, cleaved as if by a lightning strike. The current was almost imperceptible and he rowed without resistance, as he might on a lake. The water was a flat brownish green and in its surface the mangrove roots entwined with their reflections and the tree limbs joined below as well as above, so that they seemed suspended in a symmetrical barrel vault.

"*Sondé miroir . . .*" Toussaint murmured, as if to himself. He touched the ball of his finger to the water. The doctor saw it join the finger of the other Toussaint beneath the river, like a touch of life, some communion he couldn't comprehend, though he saw that it was more than mere reflection. Toussaint withdrew his hand and broke the contact. He dug into the skin of a grapefruit and broke the yellow sphere in half; the sweet acidic tang of it swelled into the still air.

The doctor shipped his oars and accepted the half he was offered. The fruit was virtually fleshless, so packed it was with juice. They ate contemplatively, discarding the peel and spitting seeds into the still water. The boat drifted sideways to the stream. Finished, they exchanged seats wordlessly and Toussaint took the oars.

His stroke was smooth and even, mesmeric, and the doctor's mind went idling, as the sweat dried on his face and chest. The farther they went up the stream, the more tightly the mangrove branches laced them in. It grew dimmer, cooler, as they went upstream. A little black crab with hairy legs circled the narrow trunk of a sapling that grew straight from the water, hiding from them shyly. Somewhere above the forest canopy it began to rain and the doctor could hear it rattling on the leaves though few drops reached through to them.

By the time Toussaint moored the canoe, the rain had stopped. The doctor climbed out on a mudbank and followed him into the jungle. The slope was steep and muddy, scattered with bright red seeds from the bead trees. The doctor went haltingly, sweating in the damp, though it was rather cool here below the mountain clouds. After a while they reached a path where the going was much easier. The trail was not only worn, but *made,* with palm-sized flints packed close together in the mud like scales. When the doctor had caught his breath, he stopped and dislodged one of the stones and held it in his hand.

"The Caribs made this road in the time before," Toussaint said. "Before the white people came." He turned and went ahead; the doctor replaced the stone in its socket of mud and followed him. The terrain was changing slightly; it was no longer so wet as it had been underfoot, and there was not much undergrowth below the tall trees. The doctor heard shifting animal movement on one side of the trail, but whenever he stopped to look he could see nothing.

The thing, or things, seemed nonsensically large, a wild boar possibly, but invisible. The doctor stopped in place when he heard a dry rattle stirring a pale patch of deadfallen bamboo leaves, still shivering.

"You're looking where he's been," Toussaint said, with his odd half smile. "You must look where he's going."

The doctor concentrated. At the next burst of ticking he raked his eyes in a circle around the troubled leaves and finally saw the lizard, blue striped and nearly a foot long, a slender beam of sunshine on the loose skin of its throat where it was breathing. Toussaint had gone on ahead. The doctor hastened to catch him up.

"Where are they now?" he said. "The Caribs."

"They are gone," Toussaint said. "All dead now, they would not be slaves . . ." He didn't look back when he spoke.

The doctor followed on. It occurred to him that for all his knowledge Toussaint was not a native of this place himself and that no one surviving here was truly native to it. As he was thinking this, they came out suddenly into a wide clear slope above another river gorge.

In this field, *lantana* grew and blossomed. Doctor Hébert automatically began gathering it, breaking off the flower tops and stowing them in his cloth bag. *Lantana* was effective against colds, pneumonia . . . Each flower top bristled with small round blooms, yellow, white, and coral rose; they had a pleasant dusty fragrance. The doctor picked his way around the edges of the clearing. The grasses were damp here, and soon his boots were sucking at his feet.

A gray fringe of low-hanging cloud drifted over; higher up the sky was purple and engorged. Then the sun cut through the swollen weight of the clouds like a cutlass slashing through a bruise, and the whole hillside was drenched in a strange green light. Doctor Hébert was exhausted and terrified. He understood he was in the presence of God. The weird euphoria lifted a little distance out of his body and above his fear. Down the slope, Toussaint continued trimming leaves from a vine, as if insensible of the ray that held him in its nimbus, and yet the doctor felt that he must be absorbing it, and that he would have the power, when he chose, to give it forth as a healing light.

They were not alone. Down toward the rapid chattering of the unseen stream appeared two men, near naked, obsidian against the jungle green. One moved restively under the doctor's observation, like a deer. Toussaint spoke without seeming to look at them, his voice low but carrying well in the damp air. "Yes, Riau, I see you. Now, come here."

. . .

I, RIAU, I CAME TO BE on that slope in the sunshine because of many things. After the fighting with the soldiers, when I had found the horse, I rode away alone to look for Merbillay. The horse was green, gun-shy and half crazy from the smell of blood all over, but Toussaint had taught me to gentle any horse.

First I rode back to the place on the mountain where the women and the children had been hiding, but they were not there anymore by the time I came. I went along the mountains looking but it was a long time before I met anyone that I had ever seen before, days and weeks. After a while it seemed good to me to be alone. Sometimes I came upon other bands but since there was not anyone I knew among them I kept away. Also I was afraid for my horse. There was fruit to find and other things Toussaint and others had shown me were good to eat, or sometimes I was hungry, but it was good to be by myself this time, only Riau.

Sometimes the soldiers came out from Le Cap and walked all over the country looking for a fight, but the bands would not stand to fight them in the open country on the plain. The soldiers could not go too far from the city either, because the bands would attack it if the soldiers were far away. There were some attacks and some came near, but our bands could not come all the way into the city like we had wanted to at first.

Later I heard this but I did not go to these fights myself. The bands were too big now and the leaders becoming too strong. Biassou and Jeannot and Jean-François were all leading big bands that were like armies though the people still did not walk in step like people in a whiteman army would do. But these leaders had all been *commandeurs* in the cane fields and often they still behaved like they were driving slaves. There were more slaves than maroons in these bands and I did not like that so much either. I think many other maroons began to go back to the mountains then, some going to Bahoruco.

While I was alone in the woods, I practiced with the pistols I had got. I learned how much powder to put into each and how to prime them so they always fired and to hit what I aimed at most times if it was not too far off. One day I tethered the horse in the woods and ambushed two soldiers who came riding over the country in a place there was no road. These were not regular French soldiers, but from the *colon* militia, brave ones surely since most of the militiamen would not go out of the towns by this time. I shot one down from his horse at once. The other got down meaning to fight me with his sword against my cane knife, but when he came near I took out the second pistol quickly and killed him with one shot. I got some more powder and lead this way, and food and the things they carried in their pockets. And I caught both the horses, warhorses both well seasoned and well trained.

Then at last I went into the big camp that Jeannot had made at Habitation Dusailly near Grand Rivière. There I found Aiguy and César-Ami and most of the women who had been in our band before the killing of the whitepeople began. Merbillay was there too which was why I had come in. Also it was hard for me to manage the three horses alone.

I gave up two horses to Jeannot when I came into the camp, the green one and a good one but the other I kept, along with the pistols and other small things Jeannot did not have to know I had got. Jeannot had made himself like a little king of Guinée in this place, but a mean spirit ruled him. Erzulie-gé-rouge was his *maît'tête,* all spite and jealousy and malice mixed together. Each morning when he woke he drank a mixture of blood and tafia from the round top part of a whiteman skull he used for a cup and he went on from there all through each day. A palisade was around a part of the camp and on each fifth post a whiteman head was stuck. Jeannot had a lot of prisoners here and every afternoon he would bring out a few and with his favorites try to think of new ways to kill them slowly. He had a whiteman priest of Jesus who had gone over to him to help him make the Hell of Jesus for these whitemen, and there were whitewomen too, a lot of them, that Jeannot used for himself or his favorites and would give to our women as slaves when they were all used up.

Merbillay had her baby in this place. He was long and thin and chocolate-colored, pale on the palms and the bottoms of his feet. His bones were a little bent at first from being folded up in there and his hands and feet were wrinkled like a turtle from the sea. He had a lot of hair in tight black curls all over his head and his eyes looked tired like he had come on a long long journey without rest.

I carried him all around the camp or sometimes I would take him out. I had a watch from one of the soldiers, and he liked to hear it ticking and watch it swing on its gold chain, or he would touch it with his fists, though he could not collect his fingers to hold onto anything yet. He would go anywhere with me gladly and almost never cried. I was the man now, since Achille was dead. Only Riau. I took him horseback up the river to a little spring that fed into it from the woods. Here there was a hollow of moss and dragonflies and butterflies would be there. The moss was soft for him to lie and sometimes I would hold him so the spring water ran over his feet. The water was cold but it did not frighten him. He would move his feet in it and make low sounds I think he meant for words.

Then we would go to the camp, through the palisade where the centipedes were crawling in and out of the eyeholes of the rotting heads and the air was torn with screams of whitemen being tortured. I had not disliked these things myself but it was a bad place for a baby, though he didn't seem to mind it. Merbillay had not given him a name.

Then Jean-Pic left the camp of Biassou and came to join us who were with Jeannot. It was he who had the idea of leaving that place and going to the maroons at Bahoruco. It was no longer good where Jean-Pic had come from, there with Biassou. The black men who were pretending to be white officers were wanting the others to be like white soldiers too. To drill and train and exercise even when there was not any fighting. It meant that they killed the whitemen more easily, with less danger, when they met them in the mountains, but still Jean-Pic did not like it. I did not like it either when I heard of it, though it was not happening then in Jeannot's camp.

Also Jean-Pic told me that Toussaint had come to Biassou. I do not know why it did not surprise me, though I think I would also have believed it if I heard that he stayed by the whitemen all along. I felt his hand in all the doing of whiteman soldier things that was beginning with Biassou, though the hand did not show. If Riau broke a horse, there at Bréda plantation, the horse would not know it was Toussaint's hand that moved Riau. I thought that I did not want to feel that hand moving me again and so I was glad when Jean-Pic said that we would go to Bahoruco.

But that was not all. Some weeks before a jolly little fat whiteman priest of Jesus had come to Jeannot's camp. His name was

Père Bonne-chance, and he prayed to a different face of Jesus than Père Duguit, the kind face instead of the cruel one. For that reason Père Duguit did not like him. Père Duguit whispered to Jeannot that he should kill the little fat father or drive him away. But the little fat father pretended not to know about this, and he went around the camp smiling kindly at Père Duguit the same as anyone else he met. The little fat father had children with a *quarteronnée* woman he had brought there to the camp, and maybe it was because of that Jeannot did not hurt him. But it was hard to know why Jeannot did any of the things that he did. Also the little fat Père Bonne-chance wanted to baptize all the children and the babies who were being born in this camp.

Merbillay did not like this, so the little fat father came to me. At first I did not want it either. After the little fat father had talked to me, I took the baby away into the jungle. I laid him in the grassy place beside the spring which ran where he could watch it bubbling. He did not know how to walk or crawl so I knew he must stay there where I left him. I went away through the jungle crying and howling and beating my hands bloody on the walls of trees. This was because I could not remember the name of my father or my mother and I didn't understand anymore the language of Guinée. I thought then that if I ever did reach *Guinée en bas de l'eau* I would be a stranger there and no one would understand me any better.

Then I thought it would be better for me to swing the baby by his heels and smash his brains out on a tree. But when I came back to the grassy place I saw how quietly he lay there trusting for me to return and bring him home again. I took him then to Père Bonne-chance, and saw him christened with the name Pierre Toussaint. I told the little fat father that I was choosing this name because Toussaint had been my *parrain* and had sponsored me when I first was brought as a *bossale* to Bréda, and that Toussaint had taught me the whiteman way of Jesus. This was a half-true thing that I said, and the little fat father smiled to hear it.

Then I did not know to go or stay. For days and weeks I did not like to see the child, a stranger with his whiteman name. Merbillay would not go to Bahoruco. She thought that Riau was not sure of the way there and she did not like the walking it would be. I did not have a horse anymore because Jeannot had taken it away. So it happened that I was going alone with Jean-Pic, carrying only the pistols I had kept hidden from Jeannot. But when Toussaint called me, I could not help but come.

At first he spoke over his shoulder without looking at us, only his voice. Then Jean-Pic stepped back into the trees, but I went toward Toussaint like I was dreaming, like there was a *loa* in my head. When he turned toward me I saw him taking a book from his coat pocket and holding it out so I could see it well. The whiteman with the short beard who killed the dog had come down to stand beside him but I did not pay him any attention then.

"I have been wanting to find you, Riau," Toussaint said. "I think that you remember how to read."

He held the book to me even nearer. It was a book I knew. Toussaint taught me to read from it along with others. Also it was the book he had been carrying when the whiteman beat him for reading in the street of Haut du Cap.

"You can read it," he said. "It doesn't matter where you begin."

When I took the book it seemed to burn my hand like *manchineel.* I let it open anywhere. The words were squirming on the pages. I saw they would burrow through my eyes like worms into my brain, to rule me. My voice was cracked and choking when I read them out.

If any person was intending to put your body in the power of any man whom you fell in with on the way, you would be vexed: but that you put your understanding in the power of any man whom you meet, so that if he should revile you it is disturbed and troubled, are you not ashamed at this?

If there was shame, it did not change anything. This was Epictetus, who had been a slave, speaking to me from the paper. But it was Toussaint, a long time before, who put the words inside my head. So it did not matter if I closed the book or burned it. Jean-Pic went on to Bahoruco, by himself, but I went following Toussaint.

AUGUST 1802

The interior of the coach was dark, sweat-smelling. Toussaint and his valet Mars Plaisir sat shoulder to shoulder and hip to hip. There was no space for them to move apart, and a sweat glue seeped through the fabric of their clothing, binding them together. Mars Plaisir's knees were uncomfortably cramped against the opposite wall of the cubicle, under the coachman's box, which was invisible to him. He stretched his long neck toward the gap between the slats nailed and blackened over the window at his right, and flared his nose for a gasp of the outside air. To his left, Toussaint was spottily illuminated by chinks of light that came through the covered window on his side, shining on the gloss of sweat that coated his cheeks. He sat erect, both alert and relaxed, as if he were mounted on a warhorse instead of nailed into this box. There was too little light for Mars Plaisir to fully see his face or make out his expression.

That none should know who was being conveyed, the windows of the coach were sealed. The guard was strong—twelve mounted artillerymen, two gendarmes and their officer—but not so numerous as to attract undue attention. A separate body of soldiers went some miles ahead to clear the roads before they'd pass. The route itself was meant to be the closest secret, but in several of the towns where they were quartered for the night, they seemed to be anticipated, and crowds of curiosity seekers pressed around the coach, vying uselessly for a glimpse of the interior.

Then would come the curses of the mounted soldiers, the warning snap of the coach whip, once the sodden crunch of a musket butt into some overeager voyeur's teeth. Next, except for the harness jingling and the beat of hooves, silence restored. It was not possible by squinting through the cracks in the window hatches to make out where they were at all in this strange land.

Holding his breath, Mars Plaisir broke wind, or let it slip as quietly as he was able. He twisted his face away from the smell of his interior corruption. He was ashamed, though Toussaint did not react. He never did, but rode in what seemed to be an easy silence, interrupting it at rare moments to tell some anecdote, often of his childhood, or the recollection of some episode he and his valet had shared. Mars Plaisir had little notion what he really might be thinking. The fetid smell lingered, and he recalled the tales he'd heard of slave ships, but those were worse. He and Toussaint were let from the coach to answer nature's call (when absolutely necessary) and at night they were taken out to bed on pallets in the jail of some small town or other. Here the local dignitaries often made a discreet visit. They came to gape, but not to mock, and usually they observed the forms of courtesy.

They were bound for the Fort de Joux, near the Swiss frontier in the Jura mountains, though neither of them yet knew it. Toussaint had had no answer to his letters to Bonaparte. He was preparing, nonetheless, to be brought to trial. But in the air around the coach, more letters of Leclerc's invisibly pursued him.

*Dans la situation actuelle des choses, sa mise en jugement et son exécution ne feraient que aigrir les esprits des noirs. . . . Ces hommes se font tuer, mais ils ne veulent pas se rendre.**

In the close interior of the coach, there was a stuttering sound, a buzz, and a leggy thing brushed across the valet's face. Startled, he gasped and clawed at himself. The fly, a huge one, bumbled across a wormhole's worth of light so that he saw it briefly. He clapped his hands around it and for an instant felt its thin legs whispering on his palm, but it worked through the lacing of his fingers and eluded him. As he moved again to seize or crush it, Toussaint caught his arm and restrained him gently.

*In this state of affairs, [Toussaint's] trial and execution would do nothing but embitter the spirits of the blacks. . . . These men will get themselves killed, but they don't want to give up.

"Quiet now," Toussaint said. "Listen."

At first, Mars Plaisir could hear nothing but the fly, whirring at cracks which were too small for it to squeeze through; he could no longer see it in the dark. Then there was something, beyond the clumping of their escort's hooves, some other party. Mars Plaisir felt his throat tightening, an odd electricity leaping in his veins. Some days previous a band of horsemen had been seen crossing the Loire and coming in their direction. They'd made no attempt, but their mere appearance brought great consternation among the guard. Toussaint had said nothing of it, but of course he would not speak of it even if there were a plan.

The two patterns of hoofbeats merged, then stopped. The coach pulled itself up shortly. Someone was arguing with the captain of the guard. In his agitation, Mars Plaisir lost his comprehension of the words, but he followed the conversation by its tones: resistance, assertion, a reluctant agreement. Someone prized open the left door of the coach. Mars Plaisir saw the fly escape, dwindling like a mote in his eye, and he blinked as the surprise of sunshine dazed him.

They were officers of the Eighty-second Regiment of the line, once garrisoned in Saint Domingue, and for time under Toussaint's command. Mars Plaisir recognized a few of their faces: Majeanti, Sigad, a couple of others. The rest were officers who'd only heard of the black general and beheld him now for the first time. It was not a rescue, but a welcome of sorts. They'd come to greet him, make obeisance, lay a finger on his sleeve. Mars Plaisir's eyes were streaming, and the light had also stunned Toussaint, who reached his hand out, like a blind man, to touch their upturned faces.

Part III

EXCHANGE OF PRISONERS

November 1791–

April 1792

Maman w ak apap w tonbe
Nan basen an, Nan basen yo tonbe
Adan avè, w tonbe wo
Nan basen an, nan basen yo tonbe
Pitit ou avè w tonbe
Nan basen an, nan basen yo tonbe
Eve tonbe
Nan basen an, nan basen yo tonbe
Eve o Eve o Eve

—BOUKMAN EKSPERYANS

Chapter Twenty

NOVEMBER WIND SWEPT A THIN ragged rain cloud over the streets of Le Cap. Most passersby scurried for shelter in the doorways, but Monsieur Cigny, determining from a glance at the sky that the shower was unlikely to last long, kept striding down the middle of the way, a few raindrops collecting on his thick black hair, glistening in the curls of his beard. He was returning from the government house to his offices on the quay, but he had it in mind that he might in passing make one of his rare appearances at his wife's salon.

The cloud passed over; it had rained scarcely enough to settle the dust. The sun shed a weak radiance through the haze. The wind had died, replaced by a damp calm settling. Monsieur Cigny crushed a mosquito against his cheek. He entered his house and mounted the steps, absently crumpling the insect's legs between his fingers.

He came into the parlor unannounced; there was a stir on the sofa cushions as his weighty steps crossed the threshold. It was Pascal, that frail and foppish youth his wife kept dangling from one of her several spider's threads, straightening hastily from where he'd been lolling on the sofa, his head in her lap perhaps? Isabelle twisted to smile at him across the sofa's back.

"An unexpected pleasure," said Madame Cigny. Her husband studied her, wondering if her flush had a source other than the humid heat. But surely it was unlikely that she would carry on her dalliance in the presence of her son, not to mention that mulatto courtesan she'd been, inexplicably, sheltering here these last few months. Nanon was sitting in the corner, amusing Robert with cat's cradles.

"*Monsieur.*" Pascal jumped to his feet and bowed.

"*Asseyez-vous.*" Monsieur Cigny circled the sofa and walked into the center of the room. Robert ran to him; he swung the boy up into his arms. Pascal shifted a silver flute from a cushion before he reseated himself. Monsieur Cigny noticed a sheaf of music on the low table there; perhaps it was this that had brought Pascal and his wife *tête-à-tête*.

"Well, I have seen our new commissioners," he announced. "*Messieurs Mirbeck, Roume, et Saint-Léger . . .*"

"Do you approve them?" Isabelle's dark eyes narrowed as she spoke. Monsieur Cigny smiled down at her, quite naturally. He recognized her good political sense, and could make use of it even when other departments of their marriage were in utter disarray.

"One must distinguish the men from their mission, I believe," he said. "Of course they are radicals, though not of the worst kind." He paused to ruminate.

The three commissioners, sent out to do what they might to resolve the disturbances in the colony, had been selected by the French National Assembly at the time of the decree of May fifteenth, which granted political rights to mulattoes, but, between their appointment and their actual departure from the metropole, there had intervened a new decree, which restored authority over all such matters to the internal governing bodies of the colony itself.

"But they are bound to support the decree of September twenty-fourth," said Isabelle, anticipating him.

"Indeed, and I believe they will not fail to do so," Monsieur Cigny said. "But they bring better news than that." Robert was tugging at his beard; wincing a little, the father disengaged the child's plump fingers and set him on the floor.

"There are troops coming," he declared. "Or so they say."

"A good number?" asked Isabelle.

"Sufficient. As many as ten thousand I have heard. Enough to put down this slave revolt once and for all." He watched Robert, who had returned to Nanon's knees.

The woman took up her loop and twirled it dexterously among her fingers. Two dancing figures made of string approached each other, suspended in the cat's cradle. Monsieur Cigny felt a returning twinge of the irritation that had pricked him when he first came into the parlor. Nanon had rebuffed him the couple of times he'd visited her room at night—this in spite of the obvious pregnancy that proved she could not be so nunnish as she affected to behave with him.

"I thought you'd want to hear the news," he muttered.

"Oh yes," said Isabelle, "I am very glad of it."

"Well then." He stared at Pascal. To be cuckolded by such a creature, whom he could have broken like a stick across his knee. And would have, if he knew for sure . . . "I must improve the hour, I suppose." He nodded, a stiff jerk of his neck, and went out.

On the street his confusion dissipated and again he felt quite cheerful. That the revolt should be suppressed at last—their property on the plain would finally be recovered. He smiled to himself a little as he walked. A freckled mulatto in fancy dress was coming toward him in the opposite direction, swinging a slim, gold pommeled cane. Cigny knew him to be some *grand blanc*'s bastard, though for the moment he did not recall just whose. The decree of September 24 not withstanding, the mulatto did not seem disposed to make way for him. But Monsieur Cigny was as emboldened by the thought of ten thousand French dragoons as if they were already at his back. Coming abreast of the mulatto he swung his shoulder forcefully into his chest, unbalancing the slighter man so that he stumbled into the gutter, with a hissing exhalation of breath. After several more paces, Cigny could not resist looking back. The mulatto was staring after him, twisting his spotted hands on the pommel of the cane in a spasm of impotent fury. Monsieur Cigny smiled at him ironically and continued his way, well pleased.

In the parlor, Pascal had taken up his flute again. He held it crosswise to his lips and blew across the sounding hole, with a noise like the wind in a bottleneck, short of a true note. Isabelle crossed the room to the window and stood pensively looking down at the street below, then she turned to face the room again. Pascal lowered his instrument.

"The news is good," he said hesitantly. "The troops?"

"Oh the *troops*," Isabelle said, in her jingling tone. "I will believe in them when they debark—if then."

"What do you mean, 'if then'?"

"An English general sailed later with eighteen thousand men to conquer Cuba," said Madame Cigny. "Two months later, he had eighteen *hundred* left to him."

"I've heard that story."

"Yes, it's well known." Madame Cigny wrapped her arms about herself and shuddered. "I'm chilled," she said, though in fact there was a light sheen of perspiration overlying the pallor of her face. She clapped her hands and sent the footman for wine.

In the corner, Nanon was showing Robert how to arrange the cat's cradle string on his own fingers, but the boy soon lost patience and began shrieking and yanking furiously at the loop. Isabelle, who'd been pouring the wine, replaced the decanter on the tray and went to pick him up. Robert kicked and twisted in her arms, his face empurpling. Disgusted, she set him down and he slid belly-down to the carpet, crying and writhing. Nanon watched him with her large liquid eyes. In her hands another cat's cradle spun itself, as if unconsciously.

The footman entered and announced the name "Maltrot." Isabelle, wineglass in hand, beckoned for the caller to be admitted. Choufleur walked into the room holding the slender cane with two hands across his groin, smiling into the corners of the room, a strangely fixed expression on his face, like a petrified cat.

"Ah," he said. "Good afternoon."

He looked around, his eyes passing over Nanon with no particular sign of interest. Robert's tantrum had wound down. He still lay on the floor, with his feet cocked up and crossed behind him, raised on his elbows to watch her cat's cradles through his drying tears.

No one answered Choufleur's greeting. Pascal's hands were trembling slightly, rustling the sheets of music he'd picked up. Madame Cigny's skin stretched over the sharp bones of her face as if it were tacked to season on a tannery wall.

Choufleur propped the cane on the arm of the sofa. He stooped over the tray for the decanter, poured himself a glass of wine. The glass was egg-sized, leafed with gold, supported by a garnet-colored stem. Choufleur raised it as if in a toast.

"*Santé,*" he said, and drank half the glass. "And thank you."

"I regret that I can*not* make you welcome," Madame Cigny said brittlely.

"Is it so?" Choufleur said. "As it happens, I've come to call not on you but on this lady." He looked at Nanon, who averted her eyes. Robert had climbed up from the floor and stood beside her knees; one of her hands went carelessly combing through his curls.

Choufleur looked at Pascal and Madame Cigny as if he expected them to clear the room to afford him greater privacy for his interview with Nanon. He drained his wineglass and replaced it on the tray, then picked up his cane. The silence that followed the tap of the glass on the tray was so heavy that they could all hear one another breathing.

Nanon stood up. She wore a long loose shift of white cotton, and when she rose it hung to the floor uninterrupted from her breasts, so that her pregnancy disappeared behind the straight, clean fall of it. She left the room at the measured pace of a sleepwalker, looking neither left nor right. Choufleur favored the others again with his catlike smile and followed her.

"The audacity—" Pascal began, but Isabelle signaled him to be silent. Robert, looking at the knotted loop of string abandoned on the cushion of Nanon's seat, looked as if he might weep again. Madame Cigny sent him out with the footman, off to find his nurse.

"The effrontery of that creature, to come here!" Pascal said. "To impose himself upon you—with that name."

"Oh don't be tiresome." Madame Cigny looked across at him with unmasked contempt. She picked up the glass Choufleur had used and rolled the bowl of it across the palm of her left hand.

"If my husband had still been here . . ." she mused.

"Ah, madame, your *husband* . . ." Pascal said.

With a quick spasmodic clench she crushed the glass in her left hand; it made a muffled sound like a wet stick breaking. She let the stem fall to the floor and opened her hands to dust the bloodstained shards down onto the carpet. Pascal gasped.

"You've hurt yourself."

"It's nothing." Madame Cigny covered her palm with a handkerchief. "Now leave me, please."

When he had gone, she stood at the window again, alone, squeezing the ball of her handkerchief in her left hand. After a few minutes, she inspected her palm: the pale crisscross of fine cuts there—mere scratches, really.

. . .

Nanon's room was a whitewashed cubbyhole underneath the eaves. There was a single small window, circular like a porthole on a ship, overlooking an alley beside the house. Its light passed through the fabric of her dress and outlined the rondure of her pregnancy again.

"This room is better made for lying than standing," said Choufleur, who had to stoop under the slanting eaves.

"Do you think so?" Nanon motioned him toward the single straight-backed chair. There was a white-sheeted pallet and a small table near it, but no other furniture. Choufleur sat down, balancing the cane across his knees.

"It makes a change for you," he said. "I would not have looked for you in such a spartan setting."

"I am well enough here," said Nanon, who remained standing near the window. "Or I was, until today."

"Yes, I see that." Choufleur pointed the cane's tip at her midsection. "Is it his?"

"Whose?"

"You know very well what I mean." Choufleur's lips twisted unpleasantly around the words. "Am I to expect a bastard brother?"

"You have nothing to expect from me," Nanon said.

Choufleur did not speak for a moment. He sat, rolling the cane on his knees. A mosquito dropped from the ceiling and whined elliptically to settle on the back of Nanon's neck. Inattentively, she pinched it away.

"You've taken on his manner," she said. "Along with his name . . . and his stick. It doesn't suit you."

"The cane, you mean?" Choufleur released the catch and exposed two inches of the sword stick blade, then shot it back into its wooden sheath. Nanon smiled, in spite of herself.

"No, the sword stick agrees with you very well," she said. "I meant the manner. And what would he say to hear you use his name?"

"The name is mine," said Choufleur. "I'll be his heir. In name, in property, and all the rest."

"Impossible."

"I claim it," Choufleur said. "It is my *birthright*. Besides, he'll have no other. I will make this be." He stood up, round-shouldered under the eaves, and reached to touch her face. She broke from him, turning to the window.

"You prefer white men," Choufleur said. "To live in a white household . . . as a *ménagère* or what you will. To bear white bastard children."

"When have you offered me *your* protection?" Nanon said. "You were away—you didn't see what it's been like. If they had not taken me in here, I'd have been killed in the streets, or worse."

"There is no worse," Choufleur said.

"You don't believe that."

"No, I don't," he said, with a half smile. "You understand me very well."

Nanon didn't respond to him. She stared down at an angle through the porthole. A bare-chested slave was walking down the alley, some loaves of bread bundled under one arm and a basket of fruit balanced on his head. A green parrot perched on his left shoulder, and this somehow reminded her of the afternoon she'd encountered Doctor Hébert in the Place de Clugny.

"I brought you something," Choufleur said softly.

Nanon looked around. In the palm of his hand was the silver snuffbox embossed with the fleur-de-lis. She laughed at it.

"Do you take me for Maman Maig'?" she said. "It's pretty, but I don't use snuff."

"Open it," Choufleur said.

Cupped in his palm, the heavy silver caught the light and seemed to glow. When she reached for the box, it was warm to her touch. With her thumb she flipped back the lid and looked. Inside the box was a shriveled brownish thing with a head like a mushroom; at first she thought it was a mushroom but its texture was parchment dry, like a mummy's skin.

"It was his once," Choufleur said. "Oh, it was most intimately rooted to him. I think he would have wanted you to have it. But I wonder, did it give you pleasure?"

Nanon blanched. "Never," she said. "Never in my life, not once."

Choufleur smiled. "I hope that it will please you better now."

Nanon snapped the box shut and pushed it toward him.

"You must keep it," Choufleur said. "Or do what you will with it, *n'importe quoi*. A token of my intentions, let us call it. You see that they are very serious indeed." He picked up his cane and went out without waiting for any reply.

Nanon put the snuffbox on the rickety table, beside her clay candlestick there. She backed away from it, then moved forward to pick it up again. She opened it and looked at the petrified member curled inside. It was close in the little room, quite airless, and very hot below the lowering roof. A pulse was beating in her throat like a door slamming in the wind. She closed the box and put it on the table.

The door latch clicked and Isabelle Cigny came into the room, her face drawn with anger. She saw the snuffbox first of all, there being no other ornament or bibelot in the whole room, and crossed to take it up.

"Did he bring this?"

"Yes," Nanon said, indifferently.

"A lover's gift, *je vois bien.*" She made as if to open it but the handkerchief wadded in her left hand hampered her and she set the box down on the table, still shut.

"You are not to receive your half-breed lovers here." Madame Cigny slapped Nanon's face with her right hand. The blow was limp-wristed, without heat, meant to insult rather than to sting. Nanon dropped into the chair Choufleur had occupied and sat with her head lowered meekly over her folded hands.

"I will not have them come here," Madame Cigny said. "Your . . . whatever you may call them. My house is not a bordello, do you understand?"

"I understand," Nanon said tonelessly. Madame Cigny put her hands on her hips and glared at her.

"Yes, and I know that my husband has come scratching at your door at night," she snapped. "Tell me, why did you turn him away?"

"I have a respect for you," Nanon murmured, still looking down at the floor.

"I could turn you out at once," Isabelle said. "I don't know why I haven't done it."

"You are of a stronger character than the people who surround you," Nanon said.

Isabelle snorted. "Do you think you can flatter me?"

"No," Nanon said. "I don't think that."

Chapter Twenty-One

"WRITE WHAT I SAY," Toussaint told to me, Riau, who had become an *I* again from listening to him make me make his words. I sat on a stone above the river with a paper on my knees, waiting to be mounted by the voice of Toussaint the way I would wait sometimes for Ogûn. Beside me, also on the rock, was sitting the little whiteman doctor with the beard, and he also held a pen.

The wind was blowing, so the leaves turned back and tossed. Below the rocks by the river shore a red rag clung to a stick where the women had been washing. The rag went streaming along the wind in tatters. Toussaint did not say anything, it seemed like a long time. I thought that when he went away I would climb down the rocks to where the red rag was sticking there.

"Monsieur," Toussaint said. "Yes—write that."

I moved my pen, so did the doctor.

"Monsieur," Toussaint said. *"We have never . . . sought to . . .* to depart. No—don't write depart. To wander. No. To *deviate. Monsieur, we have never sought to deviate from the duty and from the respect we owe to the King's representative, nor indeed, to His Majesty."*

The doctor had stopped moving his pen a long time before I could finish these words. Then Toussaint moved around to stand behind us, looking at what we each had written.

"You have not done it well, Riau," he said. "Look, see the hand of the doctor. You must make the same letters that he uses in each word."

But just then someone came calling him from the camp, so he could not go on with his speaking and our writing. I watched him go walking back toward Biassou's tent. A little bowlegged, swinging his arms. The wind was teasing at the ends of his kerchief, below the knot. He looked back over his shoulder once.

"You must teach him," he called to the doctor. "The way I taught you herbs."

I looked at the little doctor sideways, and he looked back at me with half a smile. So I put my paper down and climbed over the rocks until I reached the stick where the rag was hanging. Toussaint had set the doctor over me, to guide my writing. But I was set over the doctor too, to guard him and to keep him safe. This pleased Toussaint, it made him smile. Always he liked to arrange his people so.

Toussaint was not yet what he would become, or if he was he did not show it. They still called him *Médecin Général*. He went around the camps doctoring and showing the whiteman doctor the ways to use the leaves. It was Biassou, Jean-François, Jeannot, who were called generals then. But they were not fighting many battles any longer. No one wanted to fight the whitemen in open country by that time. We had learned that we could not hold the mouths of cannons shut with our hands. A *hûngan*'s word would not often stop a musket ball, and even Ogûn could not always catch a bullet in his teeth. In the mountains to the west the whitemen were strong in their forts and we could not break through the line to the rich land of the western department.

Being a *hûngan* himself Jeannot held *petro* dances in his camp, and being there I danced at these; there I was Ogûn's horse. Biassou was a *hûngan* also but in this camp I could not dance or lose my head. My head was full of Toussaint's words and letters and the words were thinking Toussaint's thoughts. That the rebellion might not last the winter. The Spanish whitemen were sending guns and powder but they could not send food. We had burned so much of the northern plain by then that it was hard to forage for so many. So many all together, stripping the land of food and firewood. Among the Creole slaves were many who did not know how to make an *ajoupa* well enough to keep off the rains. I met men from Bréda, or other places where the slaves were treated well, who would have returned if they had been able. For three days *congé* and abolition of the whip, like the King In France had promised us. Or even without those things which had been promised.

The Spanish whitemen spoke to us of kings, the King In France and the king in their own country. But from the French whitemen we often heard that the King In France was a prisoner in his land. Yes, and we had kings of our own who were made slaves and not one of them ever returned to rule in Guinée unless he passed *en bas de l'eau*. What was coming from France instead of the king's promises was an army of ten thousand soldiers who would sweep the camps of Grand Rivière and hunt and kill us through the mountains.

Jeannot and Biassou and Jean-François were living like kings of Guinée then, but their only wealth was in the women they could take and the men who would follow them. They did not have many yams or cattle. The words were thinking in my head that they were like the corrupted kings of Guinée who sent the raiders to my village and sold me and my people to the whitemen on the coast. And it was true that Jean-François and Biassou were thinking of selling us then, although I did not understand this until later.

Toussaint helped, or he seemed to help. So did the whiteman doctor, and so did Riau, making words on paper for the *colon* whitemen to read. But Toussaint was learning the way to make the words in knots instead of lines, so that they twisted like mating snakes upon each other and would say more than one thing.

The words were struggling in my head as I went climbing down the rocks. I wished that I had run away to Bahoruco with Jean-Pic. At the same time the words thought of Merbillay and of the name of the baby, Pierre Toussaint. I came to where the rag was and held it in my hand and felt it trembling across my fingers, wind pulling it against the piece of stick that held it where it was. Then I saw them coming down the river, him and the woman and all the children, I knew who they were before they were near enough for me to see their faces.

DOCTOR HÉBERT'S HAIR had grown very long and the damp wind was whipping the grease-stiffened ends of it across his parted lips and teeth. A cloud had passed across the sun and a thin line of rain was marching up the river, stippling the surface of the water, rain and not-rain divided by a clear frontier. The wind teased at the papers on his lap; he lifted a sheet and puzzled over Riau's strange orthography, similar to Toussaint's, in fact. The words were French, not *patois,* though one could not tell by looking. One must sound out the syllables to know.

He looked to where Riau had climbed on the rocks below, apparently to retrieve a bright scrap of rag down there—a childish project, though Riau was not a child, nor was he stupid. Far from that. The doctor saw from a change in his posture that he had noticed something, and he looked upriver, where Riau was watching.

There were seven or eight of them coming along the riverbank, making their way among the rocks: the woman and the children and the white man in a priest's brown cassock. The apparition of a priest was bizarre in this place; the doctor would scarcely have been more surprised to see a robed cleric descending from a cloud. Then he remembered hearing of a priest in the camp upriver who helped Jeannot select who would be tortured—that and worse.

The priest was sweating, Doctor Hébert saw as he came near. Exhausted too, and stumbling as he moved among the rocks, coming toward Riau, who'd pulled the rag loose from the stick and was twisting it around his hand. He carried a child, some five years old, across his chest, so no doubt it was the burden that so tired him.

"Ah, Riau," he said, approaching. "Your son is well. And of course the mother."

Riau said something in reply, but his voice was so low that the doctor could not well hear it. Still holding the red rag in one hand, Riau clambered backward up the rocks, holding out a hand to assist the priest in mounting with the child he carried. The other children stood perched on the points of various stones nearby, raindrops stinging them through their ragged clothes.

"She has an awful fever, our Paulette," the priest said. "And a cough—we had heard that there was someone here, a *dokté-feuilles*."

Doctor Hébert looked over the priest's shoulder into the child's face. Her hair was sweat-matted and her eyes were slits. She breathed hissingly through bubbles of mucus in her nostrils. The doctor touched her forehead and drew his fingers back from the heat.

"I can help her," he said. The priest turned to him, his round red face flushed from his effort, his expression open. The doctor felt a thrust of revulsion—this face had arranged for the rape of Hélène by Biassou. Riau had caught the sick girl's attention with the red rag. He'd bundled it doll-like around a finger and was making it nod what seemed to be its head.

"Follow me," the doctor said curtly. He turned his back and went stalking toward the camp.

He and Riau had made themselves a snug *ajoupa* on the slope below the makeshift hospital, with walls of sticks laced horizontally and the roof well thatched with palm. Riau's design—they'd shared the labor. Coals from the morning's fire still smoked under an adjacent lean-to. Riau blew them into flame and boiled water. The priest and his children, meanwhile, filed one by one into the *ajoupa*. It was raining harder now, and generally, drops patting softly down on the palm thatch, but under the roof the dirt floor was cool and dry.

The doctor reached into one of his several collecting bags and began crumbling dried *lantana* flowers into a gourd, then added some crushed leaves of *giromon* and *herbe à cornette*. He pointed to the priest where he might lay the sick girl on the pallet where he slept himself. Riau came in with the kettle and poured hot water over the herbs to steep. Doctor Hébert wet a rag from the kettle and carefully began cleaning the girl's snot-sticky face. When the tea had brewed sufficiently, he motioned to the mother to raise the child's head. As he moved the gourd toward the girl's cracked lips, she coughed rheumily, and Fontelle, murmuring something, took the gourd out of his hands.

The doctor straightened and took a step back. The children scattered from him, like mice along the wall. They all smelled damp and woolly, rather like wet sheep. In the small space it was impossible not to be near the priest.

"I had not known that Riau was father to a son," the doctor said, stiffly, unable to quite resist his curiosity on that point.

"I believe so—one cannot be certain," the priest said. "But the boy exists. I baptized him."

"I would have assumed that the last rites were more your specialty," the doctor said.

The priest chuckled uncomfortably. "Perhaps you've confused me with Père Duguit," he said. "Jeannot's . . . confessor, as you might say."

"Is it not yourself?" The doctor glanced around the walls of the *ajoupa*, seeing the priest's jovial beaverlike features repeated darkly in the faces of the children.

"As you see, I am guilty of many venalities, which I would not wish to deny," said Père Bonne-chance. "Père Duguit, however, has unfortunately gone insane and lost all control over his own actions. God no longer hears the cries of his unreason."

"I misapprehended you," the doctor said. "I must apologize."

"It's nothing," said Père Bonne-chance. "I notice that you yourself are not entirely what you seem."

The doctor bowed and stepped out of the shelter. Rain collected on his beard and seeped into the corners of his mouth. Then it began to slacken. Riau appeared a step behind him and plucked at his ragged sleeve.

"*Nou alé*," he said. "Let's go."

"*Ki koté?*" the doctor said.

"*Viân*," Riau said. "Meat." The doctor had already turned, automatically, to follow him up the slope and into the denser trees.

They climbed above the whole encampment and passed through jungle that was thick with the black boles of wet *gommier* slick-slimy from the rain, overrun with creepers and the vivid wild flowering orchids. The way was very steep and the doctor was in such difficulties he could not much observe the flora, but had to go scrabbling along on his hands and knees sometimes, as the wet leaf-mold was too uncertain a footing for him to walk upright with security. He was sweating very much despite the rainy chill. Meanwhile Riau proceeded ahead of him, always erect and with gazelle-like poise, turning now and then to wait. The black man carried a small cloth-wrapped bundle under his arm and sometimes he would lift a flap and peek at whatever was inside of it.

The rain stopped, but it did not lighten where they were; all remained a cool subaqueous green. They climbed, cutting crossways on the slope. The sounds of the encampment were no longer audible. They had walked perhaps an hour and a half before they came to a gorge where jagged triangles of rock stretched out above a stream some thirty feet below. Here Riau stretched out on his stomach. The doctor, after a moment's hesitation, joined him. The sun was shining on this place and the surface of the stone was warm and dry.

"We came for this?" the doctor said. "To sunbathe like a pair of snakes?"

Riau hushed him with a gesture and unwrapped the ragged bundle. Inside were the two pistols which the doctor knew the black man to possess; one an unornamented, long-barreled dragoon's pistol, the other a lighter, fancier gun with a damasked barrel and silver chasings on the grip. Riau passed the larger one toward the doctor, butt first, then turned again to look over the gorge.

Doctor Hébert closed his hand over the dragoon's pistol unbelievingly; it was much the same as the one he had lost at the time of his capture. He checked the priming. The gun was properly loaded and the powder was dry, so that, if he wished, he could blow the back of the black man's head off and . . . then what? The truth was that he had no great wish to injure Riau even if he had believed himself capable of making his way back to the coast alone.

The doctor stretched out and propped himself up on his elbows, holding the pistol grip in his two hands. The pitted surface of the stone was warm and gratifying on his belly through his rags. Following Riau's glance, he looked down the gorge. A heavy-billed toucan came flying over the gap and lit in a leafy swag of a creeper and remained there lightly swinging and turning its thick horny bill to and fro. Below, in a clear patch lowly overgrown with wide flat ferns, two spotted goats had quietly appeared.

Riau nudged him, mimed picking up the pistol, and pointed down at the big billy goat, crowned with long gray twists of horn. The doctor turned and mimicked the gesture, inviting Riau to take the first shot. But Riau rolled his eyes till they showed only white and exhaled hissingly through his nose; he was insisting.

The doctor lifted the heavy pistol and adjusted it in his double grip, scraping the rounded butt on the stone. It was a long shot at a queer angle—down to the patch of clearing where the stream ran out of the gorge and the goats were drinking. Sour juices squelched into his stomach, for he was at least as hungry as Riau. The doctor closed one eye and stared down the pistol barrel. He was very confident that he would miss.

"No," Riau whispered to him. "Not like that." He made a hideously strained grimace of squinting concentration. "Like this . . ." He made a pistol of his hand and lowered it quickly to the angle of fire and immediately snapped the hammer of his thumb. "Like when you shot the dog."

"Dog?"

"At Habitation Arnaud."

Again Riau demonstrated the movements he evidently believed he had once seen the doctor make.

The doctor shrugged. As good a way to miss as any . . . He sat up and raised the pistol two-handed till it pointed to the sky. For about a minute he stared at the billy goat, just at a place behind the muscle of the shoulder, until his eyes began to blur. He dragged the pistol down and when the muzzle covered the place he had been staring at he pulled the trigger. Riau had slightly overcharged the pistol and the flare from the flashpan blinded the doctor for an instant. When he could look again he saw that the nanny goat had bolted and the billy had been knocked over dead; it lay on its side with the foreleg reflexively kicking and pawing the air.

Riau had jumped up and was doing a capering dance on his toes. Of a sudden he skidded onto his knees and seized the doctor by the shoulders.

"Listen, *blanc*," he said. "You will teach me this new way of shooting."

"I don't know what there is to teach," the doctor said. "I don't understand at all. Habitation Arnaud? How did you see me shoot the dog?"

"Moin caché." Preparatory to goat-skinning, Riau had pulled out his knife and he was grinning across its edge. "I was hiding."

WITHIN THE WEEK, Père Bonne-chance had erected a church of leaves and sticks, comparable to one he'd used on the outskirts of Ouanaminthe, and was celebrating Mass there daily. His oldest son, a skinny boy of fifteen whom everyone seemed to call Moustique, served him as an acolyte. Doctor Hébert, though he'd rarely entered a church before his capture, took considerable comfort in these services. Toussaint was also faithful in his attendance, and fluent in the Latin responses. A few others came, Toussaint's familiars. Riau stood in the back, his face dark and clouded. Jean-François and Biassou stayed away from these occasions, but the priest, like the doctor and Riau, was admitted to their councils, where Toussaint made the best use of their literacy that he might.

So after one Sunday's Mass they adjourned to the tent of Biassou, ornamented with skulls on its four corners, with strings of snake bones swinging in the wind. Biassou sat in a low carved chair, stroking a small striped cat that stretched across his military tunic.

"We must make him *some* answer," Toussaint was saying, referring to Governor Blanchelande's demand for the immediate, unconditional submission of the slaves. His pale pointed fingernail tapped on the paper which the doctor had drafted to the group's dictation.

"This answer will bring the soldiers down on on us," said Jean-François from his corner of the table.

Toussaint pinched his fingernail between his teeth. "Yes, the ten thousand soldiers . . ."

"A letter like this will madden the whites," Jean-François said. "You know it."

"Would you crawl to them?" Biassou said. "Let the soldiers come."

"You have a *ouanga* to stop them," Jean-François said. "Is it so?"

"Perhaps the soldiers will *not* come," said Toussaint.

Jean-François cleared his throat. "You must know the whites will never accept what the letter says."

"No," said Toussaint. "But we must not give ourselves up for nothing. And it is possible to send more than one message at one time."

"*Comment ça?*" said Jean-François.

"Jeannot," Toussaint said, as if nothing more were needed than the name. For some reason everyone in the tent looked at Père Bonne-chance.

"Do you mean to assassinate Jeannot?" the priest said.

"Bring him to justice," Toussaint said, "I had rather say. Put an end to murders for amusement. An end to rape." He looked at Biassou, who glanced down at the cat purring on his belly.

"*And* send this letter," Jean-François said.

"*And* let them see we can be treated with," Toussaint said. "That we keep order in our camps. We are not a mob but an Army."

He looked around at the others' faces. No one gainsaid him. He folded the letter over twice and began softening a stick of sealing wax in a candle flame.

"Whose army?" asked Biassou, and the cat raised its head inquisitively at his grunt.

"Of course," Toussaint said smoothly. "We are the army of the King of France."

THE WAX FELL ON THE LETTER'S SEAM and spread like a brilliant globe of blood. By the time it crossed the wasted northern plain to reach the hands of Governor Blanchelande in Le Cap, the seal had dried and hardened to the color of a scab. Blanchelande, whose gray hair had paled toward white in the last months, turned the letter over and over without opening it. He was in the presence of several members of the Colonial Assembly, all immoderate *Pompons Rouges,* who thought his hesitation rather strange.

"Shall we get on with it?" one of them said. Blanchelande sighed and broke the seal, turned up the top fold of the letter.

"Allow me," he said wearily, and began to read.

" '*Galliflet Camp*

" '*Sir,*

" '*We have never sought to deviate from the duty and from the respect we owe to the King's representative, nor indeed, to His Majesty. But you, General, who are a just man, come among us and see this land which we have sprinkled with our sweat or, rather, with our blood; these buildings which we have raised, and that in hope of a just reward. Have we obtained it, General? The King, the universe, have bemoaned our fate and have broken the chains we bear. And we, humble victims, we were ready for anything, not wishing at all to abandon our masters. What am I saying? I am wrong! Those who should have been as fathers to us, after God, they were tyrants, monsters unworthy of the fruits of our labors, and you wish, brave General, that we should be like sheep and go and throw ourselves into the wolf's mouth? No, it is too late. God, who fights for the innocent, is our guide. He will never abandon us. This is our motto—Conquer or Die.*' "

"No nigger could have written that," one of the assemblymen said.

"Possibly not," Blanchelande remarked. "I'm told they have a few bush priests in league with them."

"If it is not all the work of royalists and the *émigrés,*" said the assemblyman.

"Yes, Governor," said another among the *Pompons Rouges.* "Why do they campaign under the white flag and fleur-de-lis? Why do they talk so much of kings?"

The paper shivered in Blanchelande's hand. "May I continue?" he said, and raised an eyebrow.

" 'To prove to you, worthy General, that we are not as cruel as you may believe, we wish, with all our hearts, to make peace. BUT on condition that all the whites, whether from the plains or the hills retreat in your presence and return to their homes and so leave Le Cap, without any exception, and take with them their gold and jewels. We only seek after that so precious thing, beloved liberty.

" 'There, General, our profession of faith which we will uphold until the last drop of our blood. Then will all our vows have been fulfilled and believe me, it costs our hearts dear that we have taken this course.

" 'But, alas! I finish by assuring you that the entire contents of this is as sincere as if we were before you. The respect which we have for you, and which we swear to maintain, will not disappoint you, think that it is weakness, as we shall never have another motto: Conquer or Die for Liberty.

" 'Your humble and obedient servants,

" 'The Generals and Chiefs who make up our Army.' "

"There's only one answer possible to *that,*" said the first assemblyman. The second snatched the paper from the desk, threw it on the floor and stamped on it.

TWO HOURS BEFORE DAWN THEY WOKE US, those who would go to Jeannot's camp. There was a way worn through the jungle between the one place and the other. That priest of Jesus might have used it, if he had known where it led, instead of finding his own way down the river. It was wide and easy, like a road. Biassou and Jean-François went horseback in their uniforms with the braid and sashes and ornaments taken from the whitemen, and Toussaint was mounted too, though he wore only his old green coat, but I, Riau, I was going on my feet, with the musket they had given me on my shoulder. There were fifty men, the trusted ones, and each with a good musket from the Spanish whitemen. They had all been training to walk in rows like whiteman soldiers, and our line went into the jungle two by two, although we did not make the noise that a whiteman column would have made. Everyone stepped softly on bare feet and Toussaint had even wrapped the horses' feet in rags and tied up the rings of the bits so they would not jingle.

But before we had gone very far from our own camp, we at the end of the line heard a noise behind, a gasp and the sound of stumbling. Quietly a pair of us went back, I, Riau, and another. It was that little priest of Jesus who had been following us and although I tried to send him back he would not go and finally we agreed to let him come, walking beside me in the column.

It was raining when we first began to travel, and very dark under the big *gommier* trees the trail passed among. We could see nothing, and went along by touch, nose to the neck of the man ahead. Some rain leaked down through the leaves above and I doubled my hands over the flashpan of my musket, to keep the powder dry. We did not know if there would be any real fighting, though we hoped that there would not. After a while the rain stopped and we could hear the voices of birds speaking in the high branches as if they could see light somewhere. When we came out into the clearing of Jeannot's camp the sky had cleared and the stars were there, and a little crescent of moon like a fingernail.

All of the camp was sleeping, no one had yet stirred. Dogs began to bark as we came across on our soft feet, but no one raised his head before we reached Jeannot's *ajoupa*. We went around in a circle, the first man facing in and the second out—to protect the place from the people of the camp. Jean-François opened the *ajoupa* by kicking down a wall, which made me think again of how the raiders first came to our village in Guinée, bursting through the walls of all the huts . . . A woman jumped up from beside Jeannot and broke out of the circle screaming. Her voice mixed with the barking of the dogs and then the camp began to wake.

By then the light was turning silver and the piece of moon began to fade. There were a couple of men in the *ajoupa* with Jeannot but right away some of us knocked them down with musket butts. Looking at all the gun barrels pointed at his head, Jeannot had already begun to cry like a woman and beg.

Toussaint said something to Jean-François, who opened our line to a half-circle, so that we faced the camp, and the people there could see and hear what we were doing. People were coming up quickly, women and children and men. Some of the men had weapons, but no one raised them against us. I watched Toussaint, whispering again to Jean-François.

"This is a military tribunal," Jean-François said in a loud voice. "You, Jeannot, have offended against the King In France. You have broken the law of our Army. How? You have done unspeakable things to women. You have killed helpless prisoners with torture, you have drunk their blood . . ."

And Jean-François went on speaking this way for a long time, but I stopped listening to him. In the crowd that was silently watching I saw Merbillay, with Pierre Toussaint on her hip. Her face was sober, and the baby hid his face against the cloth under her breasts. Jeannot was kissing Jean-François's boots and crying that he would serve him in chains for the rest of his life, if he were only let to live, and I remembered how he had been in the first fights against the whitemen, facing their guns with his chest bare, and calling insults at them. But this bravery was not his own, it belonged to *Maît'Carrefour,* who was hungry for death. Jeannot had fed him well, in the fights and with the prisoners in the camp. But the Baron's hunger is bottomless. Time now for Jeannot to feed the grave with his own flesh.

Jean-François kicked Jeannot's face away from his boots and took a few steps back. The priest came forward then, the little fat man who had walked with us, for Jeannot's bad father had run away in the jungle when he first heard that we had come, and no one ever saw him again in that place. The priest was holding out his cross with God nailed to it and he was talking in a low voice about the kindness of Jesus. But Jeannot clutched him and held him with his arms and legs like the priest was a woman and Jeannot wanted to do the thing with him.

It needed five men to pull him loose. They tied Jeannot to a tree. The priest came to him again and spoke to him and showed him the cross, but it seemed that Jeannot would not hear him. He pulled against the sisal ropes so that they tore his skin, and his face was so twisted with screaming that we could not see his eyes. They picked ten men to shoot him with their muskets. I was glad that they did not choose me.

After this, Jean-François ordered Jeannot's body to be hung by the jawbone from a hook in a tree, the way he'd once hung living men. Jean-François collected together all the whiteman prisoners who were still alive, and then we went away. I was thinking, if Jeannot was going home to Guinée, he had not looked happy to go there.

Jeannot's camp was breaking up, with the people going off in all directions, many of them following us. We went raggedly through the jungle going back, not so much like a column of whiteman soldiers now. The sun had come out clearly and it grew hotter as it climbed the sky. I doubled back and found Merbillay walking with the baby among the other women and children who were following. Partway I carried the baby on my shoulder. I had kept the piece of red rag and I did tricks with it to make him smile.

When we came to our camp again, I took Merbillay to the *ajoupa* that I and the doctor had built. The *sang-mêlé* girl Paulette was in there resting. Her fever had broken but she was still weak. I saw her smile to see the baby. She stood up and raised him with his hands in hers and moved him so he seemed to walk, though he could not walk, not really.

After this, Toussaint did not make me go into Biassou's tent any more to listen to the talk, although the doctor still went there, and the priest too. Toussaint knew I would not have liked what they were talking about then, and I did not learn just what it was until a while later. Toussaint kept me away. But he still gave me things to copy out, so that I would put the same letters in each word that the priest and the doctor used.

6 December 1791

Great misfortunes have beset this rich and important colony—we were involved in it and there is nothing more for us to say to justify ourselves. One day you will give us back all the justice that our position merits. The mother country demands a completely separate form of government from the colonies; but the feelings of clemency and goodness, which are not laws, but affections of the heart, should cross the seas and we should be understood in the general pardon which the king granted to everyone indiscriminately.

We see from the law of the 28th September that the National Assembly and the king grant you leave to pronounce finally on the status of nonfree persons and the political status of colored men. We defend the decrees of the National Assembly and your own, invested with all the necessary formalities, to the last drop of our blood. A large population which submits with confidence to the orders of the monarch and the legislative body which it invests with its power definitely merits some consideration. It would, in fact, be interesting if you declared, by a decree sanctioned by the general Assembly, that your intention is to take an interest in the fate of the slaves. Knowing that they are the object of your concern and knowing through their leaders, to whom you would send this work, they would be satisfied and that would help restore the broken equilibrium, without loss and in a short time.

Jean-François, General. Biassou, Field Marshal.

Desprez, Manzeau, Toussaint, and Aubert, ad hoc Commissioners.

Now I copied out each word of this letter very carefully with the words lined up like soldiers on the paper. But when I had done, I saw that Toussaint had learned a way to make his words march in more than one direction. They looked at first as straight as tiny whiteman soldiers, but if I took my eye from them, they would begin to twist and turn. And if a word on a paper could do this, I was thinking, why not I?

AFTER THEY HAD SHOT JEANNOT and hung his body from the hook, all the people went away from that camp near Habitation Dufailly. The whitemen who were prisoners came into the camp of Jean-François, and no one kept them penned up any longer. No one thought that they would run away. It would be too far for them to go before they found any of their whiteman friends. Also Biassou told them that any one of them who ran away and was caught again would have the leg cut off he used to run with, and I am sure that they believed this because they had done this thing to us so many times before.

Of Jeannot's people, some of them ran away altogether after he was dead and others of them came with us, like Merbillay. Of the ones who ran away at first, some came later to the camp of Jean-François, but others never did. They had gone away to be with the maroons, or were just gone. The priest of the cruel Jesus who had followed Jeannot was not seen again anymore by any of us. Anything could have happened to him, he could have gone anywhere, but I believed that he died alone in the jungle then, where no one ever found his body, because he had been sick for a long time with fever, and the cruel Jesus rode him all the time and never let him rest. He ate only to feed the cruel Jesus, and he could not get any food for himself. So I think that he must have died for that reason, though no one ever found his bones.

Then Jeannot's camp was empty, and no one would go there anymore, except that I, Riau, I went there sometimes. I didn't know what I meant to find. For weeks the vultures hung over that place, because Jeannot did not bury the dead, and he did not always throw them in the river. The birds would ride on their black wings in a circle around the tree where Jeannot was still hanging, like a wheel rim goes around and around the axle pin. I went there sometimes and I saw how they flew this way.

I don't why I would go there, but sometimes it would happen, when I was tired of reading and writing with the little whiteman doctor, tiring of learning to walk and think the whiteman way. Then I would become a *petit marron* for a day, creeping away from the camp of Jean-François, sometimes carrying a musket or my pistols. Sometimes it would really be that I went hunting and would come back with an *agouti* or at least a *manicou*. Or I would go with the doctor and watch the way he had of shooting, which I could not learn. It must be that it came from some *ouanga* that he had, because he did not seem to know himself how he did it. But other times I went alone and only went to Jeannot's camp, as if I were looking for something there, but I did not know what it was.

A place was there where Jeannot had left the bodies he did not cut up and throw into the river, north of the camp and a long way from the river shore. The dead people were lying in a grove of young thorn trees, wherever they had fallen or been dropped, and later scattered. Wild pigs tumbled them all around, for a wild pig will eat any kind of flesh. Sometimes I could have shot a wild pig in this place, but I did not like to think of eating what had eaten the meat from those bones. But soon enough all this dead meat had disappeared, and the bones lay there quietly, yellow-white, with long grasses sprouting up through ribs and eye holes, vines wrapping over them to bind them to the earth. You would not have known then that these were mostly whiteman bones. I thought that it would be a long work for Jesus to put them all together, the way they had been mixed and jumbled, so that each whiteman could have his *corps-cadavre* again. What a long work it must be to raise them . . .

The cross of Baron Samedi was in this place. Someone had carved it onto a little barrel and strung it up high in one of the thorn trees. But I thought that Ghede did not want these bones. Maybe Jesus didn't want them either. They were alone like sticks or rocks, sinking into the jungle floor, with leaves falling down to cover them. The vultures and pigs didn't come anymore, but the butterflies flew over the bones, through the patches of sun that came down through the leaves of the thorn trees.

Then, after I had looked at them for a little time, I went back to the camp of Jean-François.

Now there were many people staying in that *ajoupa* I had showed the whiteman doctor how to help me build. The little *sang-melée* girl Paulette would lie there all the day with her fever. Then the fever passed and she sat up, and she could eat a little, eating solid food for the first time. But for some days she was too weak to move very far from the *ajoupa*. When her brothers and sisters ran away playing, she could not go, but she would lie quietly, or sit up with her back against a pole. Her breath still whistled a little from her sickness.

We kept a wall of the *ajoupa* open in the day, and at night too if no rain came, and the priest's children would sleep outside unless it rained. I and Merbillay and the priest and his woman and the doctor all slept in the *ajoupa*, close together. When Merbillay and I were lying together, I did not think at all about who was near, because I was glad to be with her again after the long time she had stayed in the camp of Jeannot after I had come away with Toussaint. Other times I could hear the priest lying with Fontelle, both of them trying to do the thing quietly. I heard the doctor trying to make his breath sound more like sleep, and then I wondered, what voice might be speaking in his head while he lay there making himself be still in the dark. I wondered if he, a whiteman, could have a *ti-bon-ange*, and where his *ti-bon-ange* might travel while he was dreaming.

By daylight the *ajoupa* would be empty except for Paulette lying on her pallet, and for Pierre Toussaint, who Merbillay began to call Caco. She called him this because of sounds he made that Merbillay thought were like the squabbling of the parrots. When Paulette grew stronger, Merbillay would leave the baby there with her, if she went out to dig in the provision grounds or looking for fruit trees in the jungle. The women had to go farther and farther to find food now, because there were so many of us living in this one place.

On one afternoon I came in from a day of my *petit marronage* and I found them there, under the roof. Caco was crawling to Paulette, his mouth open making a toothless wet shape of joy because he had learned how to crawl. When he reached her she took his hands and raised him to his feet and held him swaying there at his arms' length. She turned him so he faced me and he smiled and laughed to see me, there where I had come very quietly up to the open wall of the *ajoupa*, swinging a *manicou* I had killed by its scaly tail. I felt a happiness then to look at him and see this smile he had for me, although most of those days my mind was uneasy with strange whisperings.

Toussaint did not make me go anymore to the meetings in Biassou's tent. He wanted me to think it was because he did not mean to punish me any longer with words and the work of writing. But I know he did not really mean it so, because he still had me write and copy with the doctor, but only after the doctor had come out of Biassou's tent again. It meant that Toussaint was still making Riau ready for another time, so maybe he did believe that time would come. Even then, he might already have believed it. He must have thought of it. He did not have me copy their letters to the whitemen anymore. The doctor would read to me from the book of Epictetus, and I would write down what he said, and he would read it over. But I knew that in the tent they were still making letters to send to the whitemen on the coast. Toussaint didn't want Riau to know what these letters meant to say. They did not want anyone to know, but they were too many whitemen in the tent with them, the doctor and the priest and some others who were prisoners there and knew of writing. Among all us who were outside the tent there were others who heard uneasy whispering in their heads, and some were already beginning to whisper to each other.

I, Riau, I hated all of this. Riau wanted Ogûn in his head again instead of all the shadowy thinking words. I wanted my *maît'tête* to come again. Each week all us would dance and feed the *loa* with Biassou serving, or some smaller *hûngan*. Riau would be there dancing with the rest, hearing the drums the others heard, but Ogûn did not want to come into my head because it was too crowded with the words Toussaint was putting there, and there were new words growing too that Riau was trying to learn to make in answer.

Toussaint was scheming in the tent and he sent me, Riau, to see to the horses. He knew I liked to do it. There were many of the good horses of Bréda there, even the stallion Bellisarius, that Toussaint used to ride more than the master did, when the master had grown too old to handle him. Also the big sorrel I had brought into Jeannot's camp was there. I don't know what had happened to the other horses—the green one and the other that Jeannot took from me—maybe they had been lost when the camp at Dufailly broke up.

Bellisarius had thrown a shoe. I went to the blacksmith box Toussaint had brought from Bréda. So many things he'd taken from that place, like he himself was a thieving maroon . . . There was a tool for trimming the stallion's hoof and when I had finished this I found one of the shoes that had been forged for Bellisarius and I nailed it on.

I thought that I might ride him then, but I did not. I groomed the other horses that came from Bréda and rubbed their noses and felt them whicker into my hands. There was not any sugar to give them, not even green cane since it all was burned, and they were hungry because fodder was short. I put a bridle on the sorrel gelding and led him out to ride him bareback.

The river went twisting, south of the camp. On the other side, the mountains rose up hard and high, and a wind blowing down from the mountains cooled my face and moved the hair of the sorrel's mane across his neck. I turned the horse from the river and rode across some cane fields that were burned, him picking through the scorched stubble, over the ash. In the next *carré* the cane was still standing and we rode along the side of this cane piece, outside of the hedge.

After a while we came up across the lower slope of another mountain, where it had been cleared and planted with coffee trees. When we had passed around the curve of the hill, the river was in sight again. The sun was going down behind the mountain we rode on. I watched the trees shifting in the wind on the mountains behind the river, and I thought how Riau might ride away alone, not coming back. I thought of Bahoruco, where Jean-Pic had gone. But even though I had never been to the Bahoruco mountains I knew I could never ride my horse so high.

I pulled the sorrel up again and sat him quietly, leaning a little to stroke his neck. It was foolish to think that he was mine. He was not owned by Jeannot either, or Toussaint, or even the officer I had killed to get him. He was just a sorrel horse, like I was just Riau. Bayon de Libertat had fooled himself to think that he had owned Riau, one time . . . I felt these things were true that evening, but I soon forgot it all, and it was a long time before I thought of it again.

The sun had gone by the time we came riding back to the camp.

I looked for chickens going to roost, but all the chickens were already eaten. Some dogs came out of the camp to bark at me. They were hungry too, but they ran off when I got down from the sorrel horse. I led him to his place again and tethered him, and I stayed there until the stars came out, listening to the horses shift and breathe.

In going back toward our *ajoupa* I went by the place where the whitewoman prisoners were sleeping. While I was going along I saw a man come out of the trees on the other side and walk among the sleepers, all crouched down. He passed between me and the stars and I saw it was Chacha Godard, from Jeannot's camp. But Chacha did not see me at all. He went crouching among the whitewomen, and I knew that not all of them were sleeping. They were watching Chacha, not moving anything but their eyes, like hens will watch a cat that walks below the branch where they are perched.

Then Chacha jumped onto one of the whitewomen and stuffed her mouth with a rag or leaves, something, I could not see what. She did not fight him very much, only a little struggle, like wings beating in a bag. Chacha dragged her away into the trees, and I went after him, a few steps back. Under cover of the trees I could not see much. But Chacha was doing the thing to her, of course. They did not make much noise. It was like in our *ajoupa*, except that sometimes if I heard the priest with Fontelle I would want to do the thing myself. But when I heard Chacha it made me think that maybe I would never want to do the thing again.

There was someone else there watching Chacha too. I could not see who it was, but I heard a sound of metal touching metal. Chacha didn't hear the sound. He finished on the whitewoman and went away, leaving her lying against a tree. I didn't see what way he went. The whitewoman sat up with her back against the tree, crying in the pale way whitepeople do. Then she got up and limped back to where the other whitewomen were lying. When she came into the starlight I saw that Chacha must have filled her mouth with dirt, because there were mud streaks now running from the corners of her mouth.

The whitewoman went to lie down among the others, where she had been. I heard the metal sound again and I saw the other man step out of the trees not far from where I was still hidden. It was Biassou, and this surprised me, to see him walking alone at night, because Biassou had already the fears of a big chief. The metal sound was coming from the coins taken from the whitemen he had pinned across his chest, to look like a whiteman general. They clicked together when he stepped or changed his weight. Biassou looked toward me, like he could see me even in the dark under the trees. Then he turned and walked away with the coins all clicking and the spurs ringing softly on the heels of his boots.

I followed Biassou until he came to his tent. When he had lifted up his tent flap he looked back at me, still like he saw me, but he went without saying any word. I came nearer the tent flap because he had left it open. The light of a candle began shining inside.

"Come in," Biassou said. "Riau."

I was inside when he said my name to me. Biassou waved that I should drop the tent flap. He was sitting with one of the cats curled on his shoulder and the *asson* on his knee. I looked at the baskets where the snakes lived, I could not see them in the baskets but I felt that they were there. Among the *ouangas* strung from the ridgepole were hanging some puffer fish. He must have brought these from some other place because it was far from the sea, where we were at Grande Rivière. The fish had dried blown up with their spines prickling out like soursops. When Biassou began to shake the *asson,* I saw the fish begin to move, like they were again in water, their spiny shadows moving on the tent roof like shadows of a *loup-garou.*

Biassou's *asson* was a special one, carved and blackened to look like a fish, with eyes and a diamond pattern on its back. There were seeds of the gourd that sounded inside it, along with the beads strung outside the shell. Biassou had a way of moving it that was less like one little gourd of an *asson* than a whole *rada batterie.* But he stopping shaking it for a moment and spoke to me.

"You saw Chacha, the thing he did."

I said that I had seen Chacha. Biassou began shaking the *asson* again in his special way. I looked at the fish face, the fire-blacked nose. I could feel the sound balanced between my ears.

"Chacha disobeyed the order," Biassou said. His eyes were in shadow, I saw only a glint. He had grown very fat in this camp. His cheeks were glossy and fat and the buttons of his whiteman soldier tunic had pulled away to show his stomach rolls. I saw that watching Chacha do the thing made Biassou want to do it too, but Biassou had not brought any whitewoman to his tent since Jeannot was killed. No one did the thing to the whitewomen after that. Jean-François and Biassou ordered it so, but it was Toussaint moving them. I looked at Biassou but I could not tell if he felt who it was that moved him.

"If Jean-François knows what Chacha did, then Chacha will be shot," I said. "Or Biassou can order Chacha shot himself." It was hard for me to say these things because of the way Biassou was moving the *asson*. My mouth was only half my own. And I felt that Biassou stood between me and Ogûn, like Legba sitting on the gate. If I don't feed Legba, he will not open the gate to let the great *loa* come through.

"Chacha will die," Biassou said. "But Chacha will not die of shooting. You will see his *corps-cadavre* walk again, Riau."

My mouth hung open, but I did not speak. In my head I saw the bones where they lay in Jeannot's camp, not meaning anything to anyone. Spittle pooled inside the corner of my mouth.

"It's true, Riau," Biassou said. "What I say will be."

"*Ouais,*" I said. "It's true." My voice came back to me from a long distance, but Biassou stopped the *asson* and put it aside so suddenly that the silence struck me like a blow.

OUTSIDE, WALKING AWAY FROM BIASSOU'S TENT, I felt a tearing in my whole body, like I had been torn away too soon from lying with a woman. I spat on the ground, all the water that had gathered in my mouth, but the tearing stayed. At our *ajoupa* they were all sleeping, only Caco woke as I came near. He began crying, so I lifted him from Merbillay's side and carried him a little away until he would quiet. He kicked at the pouch that hung on my waist, because he had learned that there I kept the watch I had taken from that soldier.

I took it out and let him hold the chain while I wound it for him to hear. Usually I never wound the watch, though I always carried it with me. I did not like to hear it chopping up the time with no one looking at it, the way a book will measure words even when no one reads it. Let the whitemen chop up time.

Then Riau did not think of any time but the one he was living. Now, Riau must say *then*. But to Caco the watch sound was like the crickets in the jungle or water running from the spring into a pool. He did not make much difference between these things, only he liked the watch because it shone. While I sat holding him on my knees, the torn feeling passed away from me, and I began to feel better than I had felt when I first left Biassou's tent.

Chapter Twenty-Two

DAMP, NAKED, SWADDLED IN TOWELING, Arnaud twitched nervously in the wooden chair that had been shifted to the center of the *salle de bains*. The long shears of the barber-surgeon snicked along the back of his hair.

"Be still," the barber-surgeon said. Arnaud's breath snagged. Unintentionally, he went rigid. The barber-surgeon was a white man, a piratical-looking fellow, some sawbones absconded from a ship, undoubtedly. Le Cap had always been awash with scurf like that . . . The inner voice responsible for these observations seemed to reach Arnaud as from the bottom of a well. Exhaling, he twitched again. A scissor point pricked his neck.

Some hours before, just a short time before sundown, he had entered the town riding pillion behind Captain Maillart, in the midst of the excursionary party. Their aspect drew attention, finally a small crowd, children calling up and down the alleys that the soldiers had captured a weird ape in the jungle, hirsute, fanged, strangely pale and fully as big as a man. Arnaud clung to Maillart's back, turning his face away from the voyeurs. He'd whispered into the captain's ear that he might find shelter at the house of the *négociant*, Bernard Grandmont, but it was a long journey through the catcallers, across town to the neighborhood near the quay.

This was Grandmont's house, his *salle de bains*; the *négociant* had summoned the barber. His slaves had drawn a bath for Arnaud, hot water in a copper tub. It had taken three waters and much assiduous scrubbing for the slaves to bring the mud plasters and grime off his hide. Scoured to a sore flush, Arnaud's skin revealed its intricate patterning of insect bites and superficial scratches. His hair was hopeless, a carpet of burrs and twigs and thorns. Cut it off and wash and comb whatever might remain.

The barber tipped him backward and plunged his head into a basin. Arnaud stiffened; his arms flailed like the legs of an overset beetle. He concentrated and made his muscles still. Soap was stinging one of his eyes, and his feet jerked spasmodically through pools of water on the flagstone floor. From the doorway, Bernard Grandmont covered him with a grave regard.

Something more than a mere acquaintance, Grandmont often had joined Arnaud's carouses when the planter came to town. Arnaud was fondest of the ladies, while Grandmont, fearful of the pox, preferred cards or dice. But there was sufficient intersection of their tastes. Grandmont, who served as factor for Arnaud's sugar and other export goods, had always been ready with a loan if his friend's *amours* put him out of pocket (though indeed, he charged a usurious rate on such accommodations). When Maillart had brought Arnaud to the house, Grandmont had at first tried to chaff him over his tatterdemalion appearance, but soon could see that Arnaud, so far from resenting those japes, did not even appear to understand them.

Behind the chair, the barber stropped his razor. He laid one hand on Arnaud's shoulder; Arnaud trembled in response. Grandmont shifted his weight against the door frame, crossed one buckled shoe above the other.

"*Doucement,*" he said soberly. "*Doucement, Michel.*"

His tone was that you'd use to calm a restive horse. The razor was chill on Arnaud's cheekbone. His breath pulled into a bulbous *cul de sac* at the rear of his throat. He could draw it no deeper, it would not reach his lungs. The blade stroked down, sheared off the hair. It was sharp enough it hardly pulled, but Arnaud's skin still crawled behind its path. With a rough movement, the barber twisted his head back, exposing the stubble on his neck. An odor of tainted meat breathed across Arnaud's face, and the barber snickered as he spoke.

"Be *very* still," the barber said. "*Sinon,* I'll cut your throat."

ARNAUD HAD ALWAYS KEPT A CHANGE or two of clothing at Grandmont's house, since he often stayed here when visiting Le Cap. In an earlier period, Claudine had sometimes accompanied him here. Was that a faint trace of her scent when Grandmont drew open his closet door?—No, it was impossible.

During his errors through the jungle, Arnaud had lost his plumpness, and the old clothes fit him poorly now, the trousers hanging slackly from his hipbones. By the light of a candle flickering in Grandmont's bedchamber, he faced the mirror, startling at the sight of his own eyes. His cheeks had lost their convex curve and in the hollows below the bones the barber had missed twin patches of shallow stubble that glistened now in the candlelight.

"Yes, you are quite yourself again," Grandmont said. "Or if not quite, at least recognizably so. You must have an appetite—for something better than bananas or salt beef. Shall we go out? Or—

"*Mais non.*" Arnaud turned sharply from the mirror. His hands were shaking; he looked down at them in confusion.

Grandmont reached into a corner and presented him with a walking stick. Automatically Arnaud grasped it with both hands. It was dark in color, surprisingly lightweight, and formed in a curious double spiral that ran its full length. He looked up uncertainly at Grandmont as his fingers slipped naturally into the grooves.

"A bull's pizzle," Grandmont said. "You must have seen them made so in France."

Arnaud kept staring.

"Haven't you always carried a cane?" Grandmont said. "I give it to you—a present. Come, we'll eat in the kitchen."

Grandmont's kitchen was brightly lit, scarcely a shadow in it anywhere, and in fact Arnaud did feel more comfortable there, especially after Grandmont had dismissed his cook. The odor of well-cooked, well-seasoned food excited him, and the first bite brought a painful burst of saliva at the rear of his jaws, but he could not eat as much as he desired; his stomach had shriveled. He pushed aside his plate and sat, sipping the wine that Grandmont had served him, and rolling the spiral cane across his knees. The movement seemed to stop the trembling of his hands.

Grandmont completed his own meal and raised his head to look across the table. He had clear eyes and a straight nose, but his chin was weak and he had more teeth than his small mouth could accommodate; they jostled together and pushed outward to deform his lips, giving his whole face a ratlike aspect. Because he presented his face confidently, with no apparent idea of its ugliness, it had small effect on the people he knew.

"Coffee? Or rum?" Grandmont asked. "There is no brandy to offer you at the moment, I am sorry . . ."

"Yes, rum," Arnaud said. Grandmont got up, clearing the plates with his own hands, and brought a bottle and two glasses to the table. He reached into an inner pocket and took out two cheroots and passed one to his guest. Arnaud leaned forward to light his at the candle. He felt an unaccustomed giddiness; it was long since he had smoked.

"Well, you doubtless have your tale to tell." Grandmont said, exhaling toward the ceiling. "Whenever you are ready."

Arnaud began to unfold his story. He rolled the cane back and forth over his thighs, kneading them—his old mannerism. As he did so he felt his voice better integrated with himself, and he was surprised and grateful for Grandmont's subtlety in offering him the cane. The taste of rum and tobacco were sweet familiarities. He reminded himself not to drink too much, and this thought too was proper to Michel Arnaud, *grand blanc,* proprietor, and manager of men. In the telling he was careful to falsify the purpose that had brought him to Ouanaminthe, for Grandmont, so far as he knew, had not not been privy to the Sieur Maltrot's plot. This caution too belonged to his ancient character. When he told what he had seen of Candi, he was scrupulous to omit the role of Choufleur.

"Ah, Candi, yes . . ." Grandmont leaned back and blew smoke rings at the ceiling, neatly targeting the second through the dissipating circle of the first. "Perhaps you don't know that he has become our ally now . . ."

"*Comment!*" Arnaud lurched forward in his chair.

"Yes, he has been accepted into our militia," Grandmont said. "As a junior officer. I know it must seem strange to you, but he brought many men, and you know that the situation is desperate now, you know it better than I, I think."

"Yes, but it's unthinkable—that monster." Arnaud snapped, feeling a thrust of his old seigneurial rage.

"Who can say any longer what is possible?" Grandmont said. "But never mind. When things are settled, there'll be another reckoning. For Candi . . . among others. I think you understand."

Arnaud caught his breath, then went on with his tale. He told of the priest and of his rescue, how they had set out together to regain his plantation, the manner in which they'd been forced to part.

"Et après?" Grandmont asked.

"I blundered onto the place in the end," Arnaud said. "Home. There was nothing left of it, nothing at all, all burned to the ground. Ashes and charcoal." His mind's eye slipped over the single shed left standing, with its contents. "The slaves all run away—or murdered. And God only knows what happened to my wife—"

"Ah, Claudine!" Grandmont said suddenly. "Of course, forgive me, you could not have known."

Arnaud grew attentive, bending his ear for notes of artificiality. Grandmont knew something of the estrangement between Claudine and himself.

"She is here in this town, and she is well—she is safely here, at least."

"How did she come here?" Arnaud said.

"Well may you ask," said Grandmont. "It is a most extraordinary story."

BIDDEN TO DINE *CHEZ CIGNY*, Claudine Arnaud found herself seated at a table that included her hostess and her husband, the *philosophe* Maillart, the *négociant* Bourgois with his wife, and some others whose names Claudine had not registered. Of late she had often been summoned to *fêtes* of this kind, and often at the home of perfect strangers. Emilie Lambert, seated directly across the table from her, was the only person here Claudine had known previously, and neither her mother nor her sisters were present. Claudine had not seen the family all together since she had left the Flaville townhouse to seek her retreat at the convent of Les Ursulines.

She ate mechanically, timing her forkfuls by those of the other ladies at the table. The food went down, dry and tasteless. Wine evaporated in the glass that had been set at her left hand. She had not moved to touch it. Her fork was pinched in the fingers of her right glove, for she always wore gloves now, even to eat. Her left hand was cuddled on her lap, the empty ring finger of the glove pinned to the palm.

There was conversation, in which Madame Arnaud took the smallest possible part. Monsieur Bourgois and a youth whom Isabelle Cigny addressed as Pascal would pay her occasional compliments. These she deflected, often without so much as a word, only a deprecating flip of her gloved right hand. She scarcely listened to anything that was said, but her eyes took in the state of things beneath the surface of their chatter.

In Monsieur Cigny she recognized an irritable cuckold who most certainly would have preferred to spend his evening elsewhere. It was the reverse of the situation that had obtained between herself and Arnaud; Isabelle Cigny threw it in her husband's face. Both of the two young men seated right and left of her, Pascal and the junior officer called Henri, had clearly been her lovers at one time, but Claudine sensed that she was bored with them now, that in general she must suffer from *ennui.* Madame Bourgois, some twenty-five years younger than her husband, had only recently come out from France, and was clearly unfamiliar with Creole ways, and altogether too admiring of her friend Isabelle. Monsieur Bourgois for his part seemed oblivious to the dangers inherent in this acquaintance. Emilie Lambert, meanwhile, had her own recent experience of male nature to try to reconcile with all this worldliness.

The plates were cleared, the wine refilled. Madame Cigny got to her feet; her husband, grumbling, followed suit. A little murmur ran round the table. Isabelle Cigny lifted her glass with two hands like a priest raising a chalice.

"Let us do honor to our guest," she said. "To her great determination—to her beautiful courage. Madame Arnaud!"

The toast was taken—a muted cheer erupted from the gentlemen. As the dinner party resettled itself, Claudine deliberately raised her left hand and laid it next to the right, in the space on the table where her plate had been. She felt how all eyes rolled to the maimed glove.

"You must tell us," Monsieur Cigny began, in tones of someone whose toe has just been crushed by his wife's heel, "tell us how you found such resolution."

"But perhaps the recollection is too painful," said Isabelle Cigny, with a polished insincerity.

"Oh tell, do tell." It was a chorus. Claudine was well enough prepared for it. She cleared her throat, but her voice was still croaking when she spoke.

"*C'etait rien.* Any one of you would certainly have done the same." She pressed her fingertips to the table and raised her palms like a pianist. Several people talking at once denied what she had said. Pascal turned to Emilie Lambert.

"Don't let her hide behind this modesty," he said to her. "*You* must tell us how it was."

Emilie's eyes were moist in the candlelight. *Ah, child,* Claudine thought, but with little bitterness, *we have both to sing for our supper now.* That was always the way of it; some member of the Lambert survivors would be coerced into attendance, to draw Claudine out, fill in details that she omitted. And tonight the story was unfolded in like manner, a series of coy hesitations; only Claudine understood the deeper reluctance that was masked. Tonight, she let Emilie bear the brunt of it. She felt for the girl, but could not move herself to help her. When obliged to, she put in a word or a correction. The shadow of her crippled hand wavered on the table's polished wood. She raised her palm a little higher, to see how the empty finger was clipped to the cloth. Formerly Arnaud had been in the custom of chaining up the ankle of a recaptured runaway to an iron collar round his neck, so that the slave must skip about with one leg drawn up behind; this was the punishment that preceded amputation. Emilie had come to the point where the Congo's band intercepted the wagon.

"And then Madame Arnaud stood up," she said. "Like a statue, or a figurehead . . ."

"Like a goddess." Madame Bourgois supplied the simile.

Like a witch, Emilie thought privately. "She denounced them," she went on. "She shamed them from our path."

"'In the name of God,'" said Madame Cigny in a ringing tone. "'Let us pass.'"

There was a moment's silence. Claudine turned her palm up so that her stigmatum could be witnessed. As customary, the description of her actual sacrifice was elided.

"She saved you," Madame Bourgois, pinkening with excitement, said to Emilie, "from a terrible violation."

Claudine watched the pulse beating in the hollow of the young wife's throat. *Dear lady,* she whispered to herself, *you would not have enjoyed the fact so much as you seem to enjoy the thought.*

"Yes," Emilie murmured, with a lopsided smile. Her eyes looked as if they would well over. "Yes, of course." Many had turned to admire the purity of her virginal emotion. In the interest of her daughters' futures, Madame Lambert had concealed what actually had happened to them. Thus the stage was inadvertently set for the exquisite cruelty of these recitals to be visited upon them all.

"Others have been less fortunate," Claudine said, releasing Emilie from the skewer of attention.

"*Vraiment,*" said Isabelle Cigny. "Even some of those who owed you their salvation." She turned to Maillart. "We have heard from your gallant cousin that Doctor Hébert and the girl Marguerite were lost on that unlucky expedition."

"Yes," Maillart said gravely. "Thus far there has been no word of them."

Isabelle Cigny clicked her tongue. "So reckless of them. To expose themselves a second time. Can one look for *two* miraculous interventions?"

"We must pray for their safety," Maillart said sonorously. "There may still be hope."

A silence fell. After a moment, Madame Bourgois punctured it. "The horrors one hears of," she said, bending again toward Emilie. "From those less fortunate than yourself."

"Madame Dessouville, for example," Claudine said. All attention at once swung back to her, that she would raise this subject in mixed company.

"I have not heard of Madame Dessouville," Madame Bourgois said expectantly.

"She was waylaid with her husband in attempting to escape from Dondon," Claudine said. "They raped her across her husband's dead body, though she was pregnant and near her time. When they had done, they cut the infant from the womb and slaughtered it before her dying eyes."

"*Tout á fait comme d'habitude,*" Isabelle Cigny said quickly. What she said was true enough, though the routine character of such atrocities was seldom alluded to. She smiled thinly around the table, then stood up. The ladies would withdraw for coffee, leaving the gentlemen to their wine. Claudine had the right of precedence, but she hung back, and Madame Cigny caught her sleeve and held her in the doorway.

"Should I apologize?" she asked.

"*Comment?*"

"For making you a spectacle," said Isabelle Cigny, and Claudine thought fleetingly of strangling her or clawing her eyes out there on the spot.

"I did so want to meet you," Isabelle continued.

"Yes," Claudine said. She looked into the other woman's face and found her stare met firmly. After all, she could not quite dislike her. Isabelle Cigny clutched at both her hands.

"Tell me, how did you do it *really*? *La verité.*"

"The truth?" Claudine said. "I wanted to know if I could feel something." She smiled politely, let it fade, and turned to follow the other ladies toward the drawing room.

IN THE MORNING ARNAUD left Grandmont's house rather early to set out for Les Ursulines. It was a considerable distance, but he walked the whole way, scarcely noticing his surroundings. He carried the cane Grandmont had given him, though he found he could not swing it so freely as he'd been wont to do with the one he'd formerly possessed, but had to make actual use of it sometimes, to support him through the dizzy spells that occasionally overtook him.

Midway he crossed the path of a pair of Negroes bound together in a cart, en route to their place of execution. A crowd was milling all around, screaming insults and throwing stones. Arnaud took only the slightest notice. The cart rolled by, the crowd went with it, the noise and shouts receding. He went on until he'd reached the convent, where he made his business known. A nun escorted him to a small stone room, undecorated but for a brass crucifix screwed into the masonry. He waited. The room was cooler than he would have expected, almost dank. Vines laced over the iron grille that covered the single small window, so that it was quite dim inside.

Presently Claudine came in and sat in a chair beneath the crucifix, at the opposite end of the room from him. Arnaud inspected her from his own seat, not knowing what to say. She wore a loose pale shift and her hair was pulled back very tight, drawing the skin sharply against the bone of her face. In her temples, blue veins forked like lightning.

"My husband," Claudine said tonelessly. "You've fallen off."

Arnaud glanced down at his bagging breeches. "I was taken prisoner," he said. "After my escape I was a long time wandering." He gave no more detail and she requested none. His eye roved to the crucifix, then to the window, where a hummingbird hovered before a blossom on the vine. Claudine sat with her gloved hands decorously folded, right over left in her lap. Arnaud used his stick to help him to his feet.

"They tell me you are become a sort of heroine," he said.

"They are greatly deluded." Claudine turned her face to the wall. He crossed the room more quickly than she could react, raised her maimed hand and turned it over. For an instant it appeared to him that the pin passed not only through the glove's palm but also the skin beneath.

"Everything is destroyed," Arnaud blurted. "All our plantation. It's all gone as if it never was—all but the dog shed. There's something in there—did you know of it?"

Claudine mutely shook her head. Her lips sucked in across her teeth; she would not look at him. Arnaud dropped to one knee. He clawed the glove from her left hand and frantically began kissing the stump. In a moment she had snatched her hand away from him. Arnaud fell back and groveled at her feet.

"I'm sorry," he said. "I know I've done you many injuries."

"No—it's nothing," Claudine said. She had placed both hands across her stomach, as if to quell a pain. "It's only—I am with child."

Arnaud got to his feet and took a backward step, staring at her in amazement, wonder even.

"Don't mistake yourself," Claudine said. "It's no cause for rejoicing. If ever you see it, you will know."

"Do you mean—?"

"I don't mean that," Claudine said. "The child is yours." She rose silently from her seat; wraithlike, she left the room.

ARNAUD REACHED THE STREET in a welter of unfamiliar feelings. He stumbled along for quite some distance without paying any attention to his direction. As he began to regain a sense of his surroundings, he noticed a young mulatto in a brocaded coat coming along the way toward him.

"*Bonjour*," Choufleur said, smiling ironically. "So pleased to see that you are well."

Arnaud's eyes bulged. He looked at the cane which Choufleur was negligently dangling. "That cane belongs to the Sieur Maltrot," he said.

"Formerly," Choufleur said. "It *belonged*. I have inherited it."

"You yellow bastard," Arnaud said, and swung Grandmont's bull pizzle back behind his shoulder for a blow. "When I denounce you, you'll be hung from the nearest lamppost—I'll see you broken on the wheel."

Before he could bring down the stick, Choufleur darted inside his striking range and grabbed him by the neck. There was strength enough in his one free hand to shut down Arnaud's air supply.

"And if I denounce *you*?" Choufleur hissed. "The *Pompons Rouges* have a recipe for royalist conspirators. Don't you remember *le chevalier de Mauduit?* They'll cut your balls off and make you swallow them, just as they did with him."

Choufleur shoved Arnaud against the wall. "Do you see the strength of our mutual interest?" he grinned. "Good day."

For a moment, Arnaud floundered dizzily, small black dots spinning behind his eyes. He coughed and regained his breath. Rage swelled all through him as he pushed himself upright with both hands on the stick, but Choufleur was right; he could do nothing now. He kept on walking, there was nothing else to do. But with the flood of anger in him, he felt much more himself than he had done for a long time.

Chapter Twenty-Three

A LITTLE BREEZE TURNED OVER THE LEAVES of the thorn trees that grew alongside the hospital *ajoupa,* and ran through the open sides of the *ajoupa* itself, stirring the yellowing palm leaves of its thatch. It cooled the sweat that was running off the freckled bald slope of Doctor Hébert's head, gathering in droplets on his eyebrows. He looked up from his task for a moment, turned his face into the wind. His patient relaxed his gritted teeth and sighed. Behind him, a few places down the row, the doctor could hear the click of the priest's rosary and the murmur of a prayer.

"Sa ou fi mâl?" The doctor looked down at the injured man, who smiled back at him thinly. He was cheerful enough, under the circumstances. Foraging far from the camp, he'd stumbled into a deadfall trap dug out by some other hunter, and skewered both his feet and calves on the bamboo stakes at the pit's bottom. The wood had broken off in the wounds and the doctor had been engaged for more than an hour in fishing out the fragments with a pair of long-nosed pliers.

The priest's daughter Paulette was looking on; she'd recovered herself enough to help around the hospital now, and the doctor found her quick and willing. *"M'ap kòmâsé,"* he told her now, and Paulette, sucking in her yellowish cheeks, tightened her grip on the hurt man's right ankle. The doctor probed at the ball of the foot. A stake's point had broken off well inside the wound, and so far he'd been unable to extract it. It splintered further whenever he tried to grip it with the pliers. The iron edges of the instrument grated on the edge of the tough callus at the borders of the cut. The leg stiffened, kicked reflexively. Paulette, ever determined, swung her leg over the shin and rode it like a bucking horse. The doctor loosened his grip on the pliers and straightened. The breeze had died, and he blinked back the salt of the sweat than ran into his eyes. He called down the slope for Marotte, who was tending the fire, to come and help.

"Be still, man," the doctor said, as the wounded man grunted and flexed his bloody toes. "It's not so bad. You won't lose the leg." The doctor was cheerful saying this, confident that the promise would come true. He had learned enough of herbal medicine to be sure enough that he could keep off gangrene.

"All the time I tell him to be still," the hurt man said, sighting down the bare length of his leg. "But he keep moving."

Marotte slapped him on the muscle of his thigh, and hunkered down to fasten her hands on the shin just below the knee, giving Paulette a wink as she took her position. The doctor stooped and dug again, spreading the pliers' jaws slightly within the wound. The broken butt of the bamboo shifted from him, and the injured man gasped and twisted his head, but Marotte and Paulette held him fast between them. The stub slipped within the pliers' mouth and the doctor felt that he had caught it. He groped a little farther toward the point, grasped and pulled back with a smooth, steady pressure. The sliver resisted, gave a little, and plopped free in his hand. The patient's breath hissed out and, as if with the same exhalation, a quantity of blood flowed from his foot, spilling onto the doctor's fingers. With his free hand he flexed the corners of the foot. The blood looked clean. A centipede was walking off the edge of the straw *paillasse,* jointed and metallic; the doctor couldn't see its feet. He straightened up, waving the two-inch bamboo splinter over his patient's head.

"You see?—No barb." He waggled the splinter between the teeth of the pliers. "You are lucky. And not poisoned either, I don't think."

The hurt man's eyes had slid half closed, but they suddenly started open again, as Marotte thrust his foot into a kettle of disinfectant brew that had just come off the fire. He twisted to one side and tried to raise his knee.

"Leave it," the doctor said. "Let it work, it will draw the corruption." The hurt man breathed out whistlingly through his teeth, and relaxed enough to let Marotte bring his foot back into the hot water. The doctor turned and flicked the splinter away, spinning it past a live thorn-studded sapling that Riau had incorporated into the roof's support. He wiped the pliers on his pants leg and walked down to the fire to wash his hands. In a moment, Père Bonne-chance had joined him.

"Success?" the priest said. The rosary was still looped over his hands and he inattentively continued to shift the beads under his thumb.

"Je pense que oui . . ." the doctor said. "She's a very useful person, your daughter." He had come to the point that he could allude to the priest's children without any particular self-consciousness.

"She might owe you a lifetime of usefulness," the priest said, inclining his head. Doctor Hébert reddened slightly and looked away.

"It's nothing," he said. "And yours?"

"That one has died," said Père Bonne-chance. Drying his hands on a shock of grass, the doctor turned to face him.

"Are you certain? Come then, let's go look at her."

They reentered the hospital *ajoupa*, and the priest led the doctor to the pallet where the dead girl lay. The doctor knelt, felt for a pulse, held a finger underneath her nostrils, but a glance would have sufficed to confirm the priest's diagnosis. The girl was ten or twelve years old, or had been. She lay on her back with her mouth slightly open, the white of her teeth and her eye whites exposed. The velvety black of her skin was turning gray. Her arms and legs were so emaciated that the knobs of her joints looked painfully swollen, and the gaseous balloon of her belly puffed out between the sharp blades of her rib cage.

"Starvation," the priest muttered.

"Yes, or worms, possibly." A fly circled the dead child's head and the doctor fanned it away before it could light. He stood up. Downhill, a plunking of sour-sweet notes began; it was Riau, playing an instrument he had lately made for himself, which he called a *banza*. Another fly swooped toward the dead girl, but this one was a dragonfly, and it whirred past without stopping. The doctor followed it out, stooping a little to pass under the fringed eave of the *ajoupa*. Beyond it, several dragonflies were circling each other in a green and sunstreaked glade.

From here he could look down to see Riau, who sat just outside the *ajoupa* where they slept at night, cradling the *banza* in his crossed legs. The instrument was made of a planed length of mahogany attached to half of a large round calabash over which had been stretched a drumhead of sheepskin parchment. There were three strings, twirled out of the guts of an *agouti* Riau had killed. The doctor admired the ingenuity of the whole production, though the music the thing could make grated on his nerves, tending to produce melancholy. He raised his eyes toward the horizon, where the lush green of mountains blued in the distance, the plain a scorched gap passing in between them.

"They've been a long time gone," the priest said, as he came out, echoing the doctor's thought. He was referring to the pair of mulattoes, Raynal and Deprés, who had gone to present the peace proposal so carefully drafted and signed by Toussaint and the others to the Colonial Assembly in Le Cap some days before.

"I wonder . . ." the doctor said, trailing off. The child Merbillay and Riau called Caco came out of the *ajoupa* and began turning bowlegged circles to the notes of the *banza*. Riau beat out a rhythm with the heel of his hand on the skin head as he plucked.

"If it goes well?" the priest said.

"How could it not?" the doctor said. "We—*they* ask so little. Four hundred manumissions, to bring all the rest of them back to the fields?"

"If they *can* bring them," the priest said softly.

"They're starving," the doctor said. "I'd think many of them would gladly come in." He moved toward a twig where a dragonfly had lit, its opalescent wings shimmering in the uneven light. The insect flew, and he turned back toward the priest, who'd seemed to shrivel in his brown robes over the weeks. The doctor felt the boniness of his own face and hands. They'd all become familiar with short commons. These great encampments laid waste to the land like a plague of grasshoppers or locusts.

"It would be madness for the assembly to refuse," the doctor said.

"Yes . . . there is madness enough to go round, I think." From the hollows of his sinking eyes, the priest held his gaze. "Well, but it is an unpleasant thing."

The doctor looked down through the trees, toward where Riau played the *banza* and his son danced around him in slow circles. "What do you mean?" he said.

"Betrayal," said the priest. "These hundred thousand given up to buy the freedom of their leaders."

"Do you see it so?" The doctor stooped and picked up a bright seed of a bead tree and began scraping the mud from it with his thumbnail.

"What's your opinion?" asked the priest.

"I don't know," the doctor said truthfully. "It isn't at all clear to me."

"Now that's a feeling I have shared," the priest said, and gave his unaffected smile. He let the rosary drop to his waist and began making his way down the slope, holding to the thorny saplings to preserve his balance.

The doctor watched him out of sight. He'd felt no guilt, in fact, in helping to work up the compromise, for after all he'd made no promise that could be betrayed, and yet he was uneasy in his mind. Here in this place, he came and went much as he would—seemed free without truly being so. The prospect of real freedom had unbalanced him. His bones seemed to ache for it, but he was also more afraid than he had been in quite some time.

IN THE MIDDLE OF THAT AFTERNOON, the doctor retreated into the shade of the sleeping *ajoupa*, and dozed off there without quite meaning to. Strangely, he dreamed of being cold, of wandering in a featureless, snow-covered landscape like nothing he'd ever known in his waking life. From behind the icy crest of a ridge, a huge howling rose to the violet sky. Wolves. He woke then, sweating and confused. He could still hear that howling—it was still going on.

Nine or ten blacks, all strangers to him, came bursting into the *ajoupa*. The doctor got up onto one knee and was jerked forward, out of the shelter. He saw that the priest was similarly chivvied out, his harriers pricking at him with swords' points. They were sweeping through the hospital as well and flushing out such whites as lay there ill or injured. Fontelle had collected all of her children that were at hand and was shepherding them uphill into the bush. She looked back at the priest but he could not see her. Someone had hit him in the face and blood was running into his eyes.

A couple of musket shots sounded, random, people firing at the sky. Conchs were whistling here and there, their shrills punctuating the deep, throbbing ululation that seemed to blend into a single voice, like a low chord on an organ. The doctor was running willy-nilly down the slope, branches lashing across his face. They menaced him with cutlasses from right and left, and someone directly behind him kept slamming him across the shoulders and the lower back with something that felt like either a tree limb or a plank, blows so powerful he could scarce keep his feet. The whites were being herded in from all directions, toward the clearing within the grove where the white women slept; they were all screaming and weeping now. The blacks pressed on them from every side, cursing them and howling. Among the white men there was a half-organized effort to link arms to shelter the women in the center but there were not enough of them to close a circle.

Doctor Hébert locked elbows with the priest and stood breathing shallowly against the bruises on his back. Behind, a woman's voice kept plaintively calling something indistinct. In the moil of shrieking black faces turned against them the doctor could make out no single individual he knew.

Then an avenue opened in the mob and at its farther end Biassou appeared. The blacks nearest him quieted a little, so that the doctor hoped for some return to order, some revelation of the logic of the situation, if any there was. But Biassou raised both his hands above his head, one holding a short knife whetted to a silver gleam, and cut shallowly across his other palm and waved the hand to show the blood around. A froth was sizzling at the corners of his mouth; he was transfigured. "Kill the white men!" he was shouting. "Kill the women. Kill them all."

Behind them, within the circle of linked arms, some of the women renewed their screaming. Among the blacks, there seemed a total willingness to carry out Biassou's suggestion on the spot, but before the butchery could begin, Toussaint appeared at the head of a troop of the best-disciplined men, all of them carrying new Spanish muskets. They cut between the prisoners and the mob and quickly formed into a line.

Toussaint was standing directly in front of the doctor, his gray pigtail twisted over the greasy collar of his old livery coat, green fabric stretched taut across his shoulders with the browned old bloodstains scattering over it like the map of some undiscovered archipelago. Toussaint spread his hands high, palm-down over the crowd that faced him. He made a number of smoothing motions, like a woman smoothing dough across a bread board. The people nearest him lowered their knives and began to listen with a sulky attention. Even Biassou was silent. The doctor had not heard what he had said.

Toussaint turned around to face the white people. "Kneel down," he shouted. "All of you down on your knees." The doctor wanted very badly to connect with Toussaint's eyes, but they shot over his shoulder, even as Toussaint switched his leg and hooked the doctor's feet from under him so that he dropped deadweight onto the ground. Then all the white men began loosing their arms and kneeling. The doctor bowed his head and looked at the scuffed dirt; he felt as if he were waiting for the fall of an executioner's ax.

"Put them in irons," Toussaint shouted out. The doctor squinted up at him sidelong. The kerchief that covered his head was dark with sweat, his face was twisted, his eyes were shriveled away in their sockets. He was still shouting, something unintelligible, as if his rage was one with Biassou's. A cart pulled up, drawn by a donkey; Riau and another man walked alongside it. The bed of it was piled high with rusting old slave shackles. Toussaint dropped his fisted hand, or let it fall. The whole crowd sagged accordingly. In the quiet that followed they could hear the birdcalls and the chink of the chains as Riau began tossing them down out of the wagon onto the ground.

The blood mood was broken, and the mob had begun to dissolve and drift away. There was the ringing sound of Riau pounding rivets into the irons with a blacksmith's hammer as he made his way around the circle of white men. The doctor sat on his heels, waiting his turn. He was watching Biassou, who stood in slack confusion, the sacrificial moment snatched from under him. Toussaint approached him, braced his arms on Biassou's shoulders. They spoke for a moment, too low to be overheard, then Biassou broke away and stalked off through the trees.

It grew calm enough for Doctor Hébert to turn to the priest and briefly examine the cut above his eye, more superficial than he would have supposed from the amount that it had bled. "You're a free bleeder," the doctor began to say, with an attempt at half a smile, but one of Toussaint's guards chopped a musket barrel down on his wrists, knocking his hands away from the priest's face and, grunting in a low harsh voice, warned him not to speak.

How automatically one thought of them as *Toussaint's* guards . . . The doctor knelt rigidly like a man at prayer, numbly obedient, looking at nothing but the trampled ground between his knees, until Riau came to him. He was a long time selecting a set of irons, which he fit loosely over the cracked rotting uppers of the doctor's boots. After he had driven in the rivets, he ran his finger around inside the shackles and gave the doctor a look of some significance which the doctor could not fathom. Riau reached out and squeezed the muscle of his shoulder, giving him a little shake, then his eyes went blank and he passed to the next man.

Still the doctor was facing forward, his feet sticking straight out before him now. Toussaint had remained at the edge of the trees, after Biassou's departure, and now the doctor saw him take his headcloth off and wring it out slowly, hand over hand to the sweat-dripping corners. He shook the kerchief out into a square and let it billow in the breeze, then tied it carefully around his head again before he left the clearing.

Twilight came down, cool, gray and cloudy. Two big green parrots flew from tree to tree. Toussaint's guards still loosely enclosed the prisoners, less to keep them in than to protect them from a fresh assault, the doctor surmised. They were free to move about within the circle if they chose. Only the men had been put in chains, the women and children left as they were.

The doctor got up and shuffled to the edge of the ring. When a guard noticed him, he gestured at his breeches; the guard nodded and waved him toward the tree line. There he unbuttoned and relieved himself with a painful difficulty. His urine was bloody from the blows his kidneys had received.

He closed his trousers and shuffled back, crossing the center of the circle. The chain on his shackles shortened his step, but he was more discommoded by the simple weight of the iron. He came upon the erstwhile procurator of Vallière crouched among some of the other men and a few of the older women. His teeth were almost chattering from agitation as he spoke in a low urgent whisper. The doctor squatted down among them. "What has happened, do you know?"

"The lunatics at the Assembly rejected the proposal." The procurator sprayed his face with a nervous spittle as he spoke. "Would not even have it read or hear it. Would not treat with them at all till every man surrendered, in advance."

The doctor's heart bulged and contracted. He must have known this, he felt now, from the moment that he woke that afternoon, but it was still a shock to hear it.

"*O mon Christ,*" the doctor said. "It *is* madness, truly."

"And the commissioners?" someone said.

"What about them?" the procurator said in a breaking voice. "What can they do? *C'est foutu et c'est tout.* Do you understand that? We are already dead."

A woman moaned and mashed her face into her tattered sleeve. The doctor stood up in his shackles, his sudden movement dizzying him. The inner walls of his mouth had gone as dry and rough as sandpaper. He closed his eyes and tried to breathe, but instead of a blanket of comforting darkness he seemed to see that tree so redly flowering, tonguelike stamens lolling from the blooms as if they'd lick the raw flesh of the white man who'd been skinned alive there. What difference was there, under the skin? He'd believed Toussaint had saved them, but probably it would have been better if they'd all been shot at once. He took a step and then another, the bare pressure of his shinbones against the bands of iron. He kept on going among the others with that same shuffling gait of any other member of the walking dead.

I, RIAU, WHEN I CHAINED THOSE WHITEMEN, I nailed the chains as tightly as they would have done on me. But with the doctor, I put the irons outside his boots, and loosely too. In the dark, if he had taken off the boots, he might have twisted his heels out of the irons, I set them loose enough for that. But he did not understand it, though I shook him by his shoulder to try to make him see. I did the same for the little fat father also (he was not so fat anymore by that time) and I saw by his eyes that he knew what I was doing, but I saw too he would not run away.

I did so because I didn't want those two to have to die then, even if I would have been happy to have killed the others all myself—all the whitemen and whitewomen who were there. It was not that they were kind, the doctor and the priest, because the kindness of whitemen is so shallow it does not even go so deep as their thin skins. But because I had helped them as much as they helped me, building them a shelter and hunting food for us to eat, and we had eaten and slept all together like brothers, and with our women and the children in the one *ajoupa*. I wanted to save them because they were mine. But neither one of them knew how to live in the bush alone, and if they had run away they would have been caught and shot, surely, that night or the next day. So it was useless, what I had done. That was a word Toussaint put into my head, *useless*. But it happened that they did live longer, at least for a little while.

When I heard that the *colons* in Le Cap had turned away the messengers and spat on the paper where the two-faced words of Jean-François and Biassou were written without even letting the words begin to speak, I was ready to start killing the whitepeople again. I chased down to where they were holding them, with all the rest of us, and I would have torn them into pieces and scattered their arms and legs across the ground. I was ready to kill like Biassou, though that was *useless* also, because the two-faced words of that paper would have freed Biassou but not Riau. Then Toussaint came and stopped the killing before it could begin.

It is not true that Toussaint loved whitemen, not so much as people sometimes said he did, at least not always. But he would never kill without a use in it. Almost never.

It happened that Biassou had run out calling for the death of the whitemen before Deprés and Raynal had finished all they had to say. Toussaint stayed back and heard them through. He heard that the two-faced paper had grinned and whispered to the commissioners who had come from oversea and now these commissioners wanted to make a meeting with our leaders.

So it was done. Toussaint calmed Biassou by telling him this thing, so he did not talk anymore of killing the prisoners for that time. Still Biassou would not go to the meeting, but Toussaint went, and Jean-François, and I, Riau, went riding with them. There were not so many of us going, even though we were expecting soldiers to be there.

The meeting was to happen at Saint Michel plantation, and this is where we were riding to. Some of the fields around this place were burned but as we rode nearer to the *grand'case* there was still some cane standing in the fields. The cane looked like maybe they had been working it, even, though I didn't see anyone working then.

We came along the road that went between the whole cane field and one that had been burned, and so we came to the other road that led to the *grand'case*. This was a long straight *allée* with tall palm trees planted on either side, many times the height of a man, with coconuts growing at their tall bushy tops. Looking down to the end of this road, we saw the *grand'case* was still standing too.

We pulled up our horses there, and Toussaint spoke to Jean-François, a little apart from the rest of us. Then Toussaint spoke to me and told me to go riding around the fields to see whatever I could see of the main compound, while they stayed there to let the horses rest in the shade of the palm *allée*. I kept riding around the cane field path. I had my good sorrel horse to ride on.

The cane was so high that I could see no more than the rooftops but when I had come around behind the buildings on the side where the little slave *cases* stood, the road climbed up on top of a bank above the cane. From this place I could look over the tops of the cane leaves and see into the main compound.

There were soldiers there like we had thought, but not so many, not so many more than we. Most of them were the walking soldiers, I saw only a few horses tethered in the yard behind the *grand'case*, where the soldiers were standing. They had not as many horse soldiers as we, I thought. I rode back then, to meet the others in the palm *allée*. The soldiers must have seen me too, because it was all open country. But they did not stir or shoot a gun, or give any other sign.

I told Toussaint what I had seen, that these whitemen were not strong enough to frighten us. Then all of us who had come rode down to the end of the palm *allée* until we had come to the place where there was a garden in front of the *grand'case*. It was a garden of flowers arranged in a design with paths in between and in the center there was a fountain, though the fountain was not running anymore, and the flowers were dying and grown over with weeds. There where the *allée* opened onto the garden, all us waited with our horses, and only Toussaint and Jean-François and two others went ahead. But we were near enough to see everything that happened.

Some whitemen, *colons* and the ones who came from oversea, were sitting on the gallery of the house. Toussaint and Jean-François got down from their horses and began walking toward them through the path of the garden, but before they could get there, another whiteman came riding out from behind the house where the soldiers were waiting. He was not a soldier, but a *colon*, and he was shouting before he had come near them, and he had a whip in his hand. He rode the horse across the flowers that were still living there, and when he came near enough he began cursing Jean-François and beating him with the whip.

I don't think this whiteman knew who he meant to beat. He picked Jean-François because he wore his fine uniform with the ribbons and coins pinned to it, while Toussaint still wore only his old green coachman's coat. The whiteman never called the name of Jean-François while he was beating him, but we knew his name. This whiteman was Bullet, who had been Jeannot's master. Those were famous names for cruelty, Bullet, Le Jeune, Arnaud. Bullet made Jeannot from nothing. Without Bullet, Jeannot could never have been all that he was, and he learned many of his torture tricks from Bullet, though also he had ideas of his own.

Jean-François did not draw his sword to defend himself from the whip, or take his pistol and shoot Bullet down from his horse. He only covered up his face against the whip and came staggering back to his own horse and climbed into the saddle. Then he and Toussaint and the other two came riding back to us. We would have all of us gone away then, except for a strange thing that happened.

Some soldiers came out and caught the bridle of Bullet's horse, and began leading him away. Bullet swore at them and for a moment he looked like he would strike them with his whip, but these were not militiamen, they were soldiers coming from France, and I think these soldiers would have shot him if he used the whip. Bullet must have thought so too, because he let them lead the horse around behind the *grand'case*, him still sitting on it with his whip hand hanging down.

When Bullet had gone, we saw that a little man had come down from the gallery and was coming toward us, on foot and all alone. We could see from the clothes he wore that he was not a *colon*, but that he must have come from oversea. Also he was not carrying any weapon when he came into the palm *allée*. Two of our men pointed their pistols at him, but he did not stop or even slow his step until he had come near enough to speak to us without raising his voice. So then we saw that he was not afraid to trust us.

He told us that his name was Saint-Léger and that the King In France had sent him on Commission. He said that he was sorry for what Bullet had done, that no one had known that he was going to do it, and that Bullet had been taken away and would not be let to come near us anymore. He said that he wanted peace and that if the generals Jean-François and Biassou would talk with him, he would make a peace between them and the *colons* of the Assembly.

Jean-François had had his fine uniform coat torn across the shoulders by Bullet's whip. Some of the coins pinned on his chest had been whipped away, and one of the ribbons hung loose at one end. He got off his horse and knelt down at the feet of Saint-Léger.

When I saw him do this I thought of something strange. I thought how Jean-François would sometimes sell slaves himself from out of the camps over to the Spanish. He claimed that those were criminals, troublemakers, *mauvais sujets*, but it was not true of all of them. Sometimes women and children were sold, and how could a child be a *mauvais sujet*? He sold them for the money he could get, the same way a whiteman would do. Biassou had done the same, along with making *zombis*.

Saint-Léger raised Jean-François to his feet and took him with Toussaint and some others back to the gallery with the whitemen there. They were there a long time talking in the *grand'case* while we waited with the horses in the palm *allée*. It was near night before they returned and we started riding back to the camps at Grande Rivière. I was riding near to Toussaint in the dark, and I knew that he was happy, and Jean-François too, because there would be a peace and a stop to all the killing and burning. But the blood was dark running in my heart, because I thought that Jean-François had sold some of us before, and now he would sell all of us.

Then we were going to give up the whitemen prisoners, but many of us did not want to give them back alive, because we thought we were going to be sold back into the cane fields. Many were whispering for the deaths of all the prisoners again, but Biassou did not call for them to be killed now, because Biassou would be free. And I, Riau, when it came time to move them, I struck the irons off the legs of the whitemen so they could walk. The whitewomen and the children were all loaded into carts.

No one raised a hand against the prisoners then, but I knew that they would be attacked somewhere along the road and I would have been there too, Riau, with my pistols and my knife. Only Toussaint called me apart and he told me to go with the guards and with him protecting the white prisoners along the way. I am not sure why he called me to do this or why I chose to go. Toussaint often could see through my head to look at what was in my heart and know it, so it may be that he knew I would be in ambush at La Tannerie if he did not bring me along with the guards. Maybe I was thinking that if I went with Toussaint and the men he had chosen, then I would be free myself, with them and him and Biassou and Jean-François. Even though I had not been in the tent when the two-faced letters were written, I had heard that there would be four hundred men made free. It happened, though, there were no freedoms given.

The carts with the prisoners started off then, with the whitemen walking behind them and the guards on either side, all of us with the new Spanish muskets and carrying boxes with many cartridges on a sling. At La Tannerie the people came out to kill the whitemen. They were in hundreds and they could have run over us all, even though our guns were better, but they did not really want to fight with us. We did not really want to shoot them either. There I, Riau, came face to face with César-Ami who had been with us in the band of Achille and helped to kill many whitemen and who had come at last to the camp of Biassou. César-Ami raised his cane knife to strike past me to the whitemen who were prisoners but I showed him my musket with its bayonet and he backed away. So we brought the whiteman prisoners through unhurt, nothing worse happening than shouts and a few stones thrown. Then we brought them down to Saint Michel again and gave them to their friends, who were waiting there.

After this was done, we went on to Le Cap to make the peace with the *colons*, like Saint-Léger had fixed it. Jean-François and Biassou did not go, this time Toussaint was going as the messenger. But the *colons* of the Assembly would not keep the promises that Saint-Léger had made. There would not be any freedoms, and no peace either then. I saw Toussaint coming away from that meeting with his eyes shining with sadness. I knew that he was sick with the blood and the killing, and I knew he was angry too because the prisoners had been given up for nothing, and because the *colons* of the Assembly were all fools.

Then we went riding to Bréda plantation. I was not so sorry that the lives of the white prisoners had been saved. I thought maybe I would kill some of them later on in a fight but it was not the same as killing them like cattle in a pen. I was not so sorry that the peace had failed either.

We spent a night at Bréda, because Toussaint wanted to see how things were there, the same as he had managed things for Bayon de Libertat. Most of the slaves were still at work there, and there had not been any burning. Toussaint's brother Paul was there, still serving as a *commandeur*. It was a good night to spend for me talking to people I had not seen for a long time. Most were happy enough with the way it was at Bréda then. The work was easier because the whitemen had all run away, but still they stayed and worked.

In the morning we rode out from Bréda, and while we were passing through Haut du Cap some men from the *colon* militia attacked us. They were not so many as we, but they must have still believed that we would not know how to stand to an attack of whitemen in the open, when we had no jungle to run into. So I think they were surprised when we had killed them all.

One of these whitemen was the one who had beaten Toussaint that time so long ago when he was walking back to Bréda from the church, reading the book of Epictetus. Toussaint rode him down with his horse. He had the good horse that day, the stallion Bellisarius. The whiteman took shelter in a doorway and Toussaint got off the horse to go after him. He was so angry I could see his shoulders shaking from behind when he slapped at the seams of his green coat.

Do you know who I am? he said. The whiteman did not answer him. The bayonet was fixed on my musket and Toussaint grabbed it from me and killed the whiteman with the bayonet, I think he must have killed him a hundred times.

I wondered then, was there a *use* of killing this whiteman? I think there must have been. This was not the only time I saw Toussaint kill a man in anger, but it was rare. There were tears in his eyes after he had done. When he finished and the whiteman was lying dead half in and half out of the doorway, he took off his green livery coat, and he dropped it over the whiteman's face. He took off his shirt too and dropped it somewhere on the body.

All the way back to Grande Rivière he rode with no shirt. Toussaint was an old man, for this place. In Guinée I had known old men, but here most men had died before they had the years Toussaint had then. When we were riding back to Grand Rivière I could see the strength in his body he didn't often show, how the muscles were hard under his tight skin and gritty white along the ridges like worn stone. He was thin still, but no one would anymore think to call him *Fatras-Baton*. There were no whip scars on his back, because Toussaint had never been under the whip.

That was the last day he wore the green coat. Later on, he began to wear the uniform of a whiteman officer.

RIAU POUNDED THE RIVET OUT OF THE DOCTOR'S remaining shackle, and the iron opened and fell away from his boot, splitting like two halves of a nut. Reflexively he took off his boots and rubbed along the ridge of his shins, though the boot uppers had protected from any hurt. Père Bonne-chance, who was bare-legged, had his ankles blistered and rubbed raw. The doctor might have made a salve for them, but his herbs and medicines were at the hospital *ajoupa*, and it soon appeared that he would have no chance to return for them before all the prisoners were taken away.

The heavy wood wagon wheels grated and began to turn, and the men fell into line behind them. They marched in a double column with guards flanking them on either side. The camp at Grande Rivière was oddly silent as they left and none of the blacks came out to see them depart from that place. Père Bonne-chance was a long time looking back over his shoulder, and the doctor knew that he must be thinking of Fontelle and the children, but he had nothing to say to him because he had no better idea than the priest where they might have gone. For other reasons than that, his mind was uneven. One rumor ran back through the captives that they were to be released but there were other voices urging that they were merely being taken to some other place to be killed there.

They marched along by a low swampy place where egrets were standing spindle-legged in the dark water and hairy little black crabs had climbed the trees. Mosquitoes boiled out in swarms to bite them there. They climbed over a mountain pass where the women and children had to get down from the wagons and the guards must work in harness with the mules to draw them over the summit. As they came down the other side, a wild goat dashed across the head of the column and two of the guards gave chase and shot it. Toussaint rode back and rebuked them for breaking ranks and firing a shot without an order, but he halted the march long enough for the goat to be bled and gutted, and they went on with two men carrying it with its legs lashed to a pole.

By the time they came to La Tannerie, the march had degenerated into a stagger. A crowd of blacks was waiting for them there, all in a sweat and a fury, flailing sabers and cane knives. They knew that the prisoners were going to the coast to be released, but they said that they would kill them and send only their heads to Le Cap. There was a flurry as the mob pressed up against the guards. A stone or a stick clipped the corner of the doctor's mouth, and he tasted his own blood another time. Toussaint was shouting something from the back of the big stallion he rode, but the clamor from the others drowned him out almost completely. Riau was holding his musket braced like a crossbar to shield them against further blows, and Doctor Hébert saw a saber descend on the barrel and ring aside. He saw too that the swordsman did not really mean to hurt Riau, for if he had he easily could have stabbed him in the body.

So they came through. A couple of men among the prisoners were bruised or lightly cut and the women had all flattened themselves across their children in the wagons. The goat was lost, tumbled in the dust behind the column. As the doctor looked, he saw a group of scavengers quarreling for possession of the meat. They went on. The doctor noticed he had been slashed deeply across the meat of his forearm. It must happened during the scuffle at La Tannerie, but he had not felt it then and now it gave no more than a dull ache, which rather troubled him. He walked cradling the arm; the blood flow slowed and stopped and the blood dried to a black crust and blowflies whined around the edges of the wound. He had no resource for his own cure for he had left his herb bag at Grand Rivière and in any case he could not stop to treat the injury.

At evening's end they came to the edges of the Saint Michel cane fields. The doctor wondered to see cane still standing—it had been so long since he'd seen anything but ruin or wild jungle. By the time they reached the palm *allée*, a deep blue darkness had lowered over them. No one spoke as they rode down the *allée* toward the *grand'case*. It was very quiet except for the creaking of the wagon wheels and the hooves of the horses sounding on the packed earth. In the gap of sky above the palms there hung a sliver of new moon and the long leaves of the palms shivered together with a sound that reminded the doctor of rain.

In the garden before the *grand'case* they had lit many torches, so that the arrangement of the plots could be well seen. A simple affair: a cross and concentric circles producing a pattern of crescent-shaped beds expanding from the stilled fountain at the center. Some of the beds had been trampled over and the flowers and shrubs battered down, and all were suffering from neglect, but still the doctor's eye was taken by the firm regularity of the design. It was mostly jungle foliage, but all strictly ranged by human hands.

He stood a little apart from the others. The fringes of hair at the sides of his head had grown long during his captivity, and now they were lifted up to tease at his bald crown by the same wind that shivered the palm leaves. His hurt arm had gone numb, and the thought of the wound had ceased to trouble him. The column of guards had fallen away, and Toussaint was holding his horse well back. There were white men on the gallery, and some infantrymen standing in loose order on the far side of the garden. The distance was too great and the light too poor for them to make out one another's faces.

No one moved, on either side. As if they each awaited an order from the other, a signal or a sign. Then one of the women cried out and swung her skirted legs over the rail of a wagon. She called a word, a name, something indistinguishable, and began running toward the people gathered near the *grand'case*. The doctor thought it was Hélène, but he might have been mistaken, for whoever it was carried a child in her arms. Then all the women and children were scrambling down from the carts and dashing toward the *grand'case* with their arms outstretched, calling out the names of the people they knew, and trampling more of the flowers in their haste.

A group of three or four women had fallen in immediately with the soldiers. They had not come from the camp at Grand Rivière, but had joined the column along the march from La Tannerie, so the doctor did not know them. But they all seemed to be pointing at him, and calling, *That's the one, there, c'etait lui . . .*

Three or four of the infantrymen came thumping across the flower beds. Brushing past the doctor, they laid hold of the priest.

Someone drove a gun stock into his side, and as he moved away from the blow he stepped on the hem of his cassock and fell. On the ground, he rolled about rather nimbly, to avoid the kicks that were coming his way. Two soldiers snatched him up by the elbows and hustled him away.

It all happened too quickly for the doctor to react; besides, his capacity for astonishment was greatly attenuated. He advanced a little way and stopped again, within the first precincts of the garden's scheduled pathways. Others of the released prisoners were still rushing past him, calling out greetings to friends that they knew, but the ranks of white faces around the steps to the gallery were still foggy to the doctor, no more than a blur. He was quite alone where he was standing there. Someone was calling *Antoine, Antoine!* and a man threw his hat into the air, and caught it. A man in uniform, Captain Maillart. The doctor remained as if rooted on the garden path, swaying slightly from his knees. It seemed to him that he had completed the errand on which he had come and that he was now free to return to the camp with the others and take up his duties at the field hospital there. He looked over his shoulder to where Toussaint sat his horse, his face sealed away in the shadows; he looked for Riau but could not find him. He was free, alone, his freedom was equal to his isolation. After a long time, as it felt to him, he broke from his place and began walking along the curved garden pathway to join the other white people.

Chapter Twenty-Four

THE WHITE MULE PICKED A WAY down to the cove, finding its best footing with a natural agility, needing no guidance on the reins. The trail was twisting and seamed with rock; quick brown lizards skittered through the shale on either side, away from the mule's carefully placed hooves. The trees on the hillside were sparsely set and there was little undergrowth. So unlike the thick jungle of the interior was this place, it might almost have been some European wood.

The trail opened into a wide spread of tall lemon grass that sloped over the curve of the headland into the cove. From this vantage the doctor could see the sail of a little sloop making for the Le Cap harbor, around the point to the east. The day was still, and the water below was fantastically clear. Beneath its translucent turquoise, a shelf of white sand fanned out and dropped off into deeper, colder blues.

The cove was empty, as he always found it. He unslung the reins from the white mule's neck and tied them to an overhanging branch of a *zaman* tree. The beach was lined with sea grape, a few coconuts, more *zaman*. Nanon had told him of this place, where mulattoes had often come to bathe, before the trouble. Her pregnancy was too far advanced for her to come herself, or rather Doctor Hébert would not allow her to accompany him, although she gladly would have done. With the bands of wild blacks roaming the plains and the hills, no one came here latterly, but if the doctor was afraid, the fear affected him as it would the lizards scattering from the path; it did not prevent his going.

He undressed, folding his clothing meticulously and laying the garments atop each other in the *zaman*'s shade. The sand was mostly white, streaked with a laval black underlayer that his feet disturbed as he walked toward the water. There was no surf, only the lightest lapping on the shore. He waded into the water waist deep, then threw himself forward. The water was just cool enough to refresh him. He swam froglike, parallel to the beach. The salt of the water stung his hurt arm but it no longer put any hitch in his stroke.

He rolled over in the water and floated on his back for a moment, then stood up. The water was just deep enough that the gentle swell of it shifted him on and off his feet. The ship had passed out of sight around the headland, and the horizon was completely empty to the seaward side. On shore, the mule's pinkish ears revolved lazily in the shade of the *zaman* tree. The doctor had tied it loosely enough that it could lower its head to nuzzle the clear freshwater stream that wound out of the sea grape to join the great blue water.

He rolled onto his stomach and swam out over the reef. His cut had adjusted to the brine now, so that he no longer felt the sting. He dropped his face into the water and looked down for as long as he could hold his breath. On a peak of the coral a few feet below, anemones waved their fronds to him; there were the black brittle glassine spikes of the sea urchins. He raised his head gasping and dropped it again, propelling himself farther with a flutter of his feet. His eyes were burning from the salt. In a deep cleft of the reef was a Z-shaped basketwork fish trap of the kind some blacks had learned to make from the extinguished Caribs. A long gray predatory something hovered over the trap, tail flicking in the current; the doctor couldn't make out what it was. A trio of opaque pink squids appeared at his left side, each no bigger than his hand. They wriggled their tentacles in a gay, engaging manner, but when he moved to look more closely, they jetted nervously away.

He swam back into shallower water where he could stand on the soft sand. A swarm of minnows clustered curiously around his knees and nipples. He raised the hurt arm from the water and inspected it. The wound was scarring over pinkly; the swim had softened the scab that still lined the center, and dissolved the itchy scales around the edges of the cut. There was no proud flesh at all.

It was healing nicely with no more treatment than the ocean soaks and the herb poultices he'd learned while prisoner of the blacks; without these, he considered, he might well have elected to amputate, for such wounds were quick to go gangrenous in such a tropical clime. He laid the arm back on the surface and let it sink of its own weight, watching the minnows scatter from the movement. The water was so clear that he could see his feet, toes digging into the sand as he walked up onto the beach.

He had brought no food, only a bottle of fresh water. Naked, he gathered a few pods fallen from the *zaman* trees along the shore. He sat on the pad of his folded trousers and shelled the nuts from their thick spongy husks and ate them slowly. His left hand stirred layers of the sand together, unconsciously mixing them to an even shade of brown. When the sun had dried him, he dressed and got back on the mule and rode up the trail again. Among the grasses on the headland a white-haired man was gathering *lantana* and other herbs. The doctor thought he recognized him as the *affranchi* who lived in a hut by the town cemetery, a *dokté-feuilles* also supposed to be a sorceror. He called out a greeting as he rode by on the mule, but the old *affranchi* only looked at him as if he were some apparition and though the doctor hailed him again he could not get an answer.

It was midafternoon when he had reached the city and most people had fled indoors from the heat. He rode into Crozac's stable yard; when he had dismounted, a groom came out wordlessly and led the mule to its stall. The doctor repaired to his rooms, took off his boots and rested in the close warm motionless air of the interior.

In the evening Doctor Hébert made his way to the jail where Père Bonne-chance was being held, and negotiated his entrance to the priest's cell, paying the guards a customary compliment of money, that they be left in private. There was a single barred window high in the heavy stone wall, and the priest was standing on a stool beneath it, his face upturned and smiling in a glow of sunset light. In his outstretched right hand was a long thin *baguette* split lengthwise. The doctor saw within the frame of the window a tiny red-throated hummingbird hovering before the end of the loaf. But the sound of the door closing behind him startled the bird and it flew off.

"How do you do it?" the doctor said.

Père Bonne-chance turned and grinned at him, lowering his arm. "Sometimes he comes all the way inside," he said. "I soak the bread in honey. We used to do it that way—at Ouanaminthe." His face clouded slightly as he stepped down from the stool. He motioned for the doctor to take a seat. There was a second stool, by a small round table laid with a chipped plate and an earthenware cup.

The doctor sat. He took a flask of rum from his inner pocket and poured a measure into the cup. The priest sat opposite him and raised the cup and sipped it. Even in jail he had regained much of his plumpness. Fontelle had mysteriously reappeared with her children in the city; she cooked and carried meals to him. The priest set down the empty cup.

"Drink with me," he said, "be of good cheer." Obediently, the doctor poured two fingers into the cup and drank it off. The warmth spreading through his chest inspired him with a strange desire to weep. A bar of sunset red cleaved the table between them and formed a crisp bright slash on the inner wall. The priest stretched out his hand and dabbled his fingers in the light.

"I'm very fond of this time of day," he said. "When I was a child, it frightened me. I would be frightened and very sad and lonely. Blood-red stains across the lawn and shadows reaching toward me from the trees . . . well, that feeling is the natural one, I suppose. That's why one drinks at sunset. And now I've come to love the hour—thanks to you, of course. And to your bottle." He poured himself a fresh measure and drank it a little more quickly.

"They say the trial begins in four days," the doctor blurted out.

"Yes, I expect so," the priest said indifferently. "Come, drink with me."

"But it was not you who did those things," the doctor said. "It was Père Duguit."

"Ah well, you know this because I told you so," said the priest. "And as Père Duguit is not to be found, someone must bear the burden of his sins, you see."

The bar of sunlight was shifting on the wall; it glared into the doctor's face and he moved his stool to avoid it.

"Those women who accuse you are deranged by their suffering," he said. "You must have witnesses of your own. Can you remember no one's name?"

"*Après tout,* this matter is not quite so important as you imagine," the priest said, smiling pleasantly. He poured more rum and lifted the cup.

"I was never really suited for the priesthood," he said. "Spirits and women—my tastes are more those of a soldier. Perhaps I would have done better with some army. But being a younger son, I had no choice. I became a Jesuit because they seemed martial but it seems I was not so well suited to that either." He laughed softly. The sun dropped below the sill and the light died as suddenly as a lamp snuffed out.

The doctor had brought along two new candles. He took one out and lit it, dripping a little hot wax to affix it to the tabletop. The priest poured rum into the cup and pushed it toward him. The doctor sipped. He was not uncomfortable remaining there, but he could think of nothing more to say. He fidgeted in his pockets for a moment, then cleared his throat.

"Fontelle will be here," the doctor said, and stood up. "She will be waiting. Is there anything at all you would like for me to do?"

"Pray for me," the priest said.

"I shall endeavor to do better than that," said Doctor Hébert. He pressed the other's arm, and with his head bowed, left the cell.

Fontelle in fact was waiting in the corridor, flanked by Paulette, who held a covered dish, and one of the older boys, that skinny one who was called Moustique. Her face was hard with anger and despair, but this was an expression the doctor could meet almost anywhere he turned these days. He exchanged a wordless nod with her. As he passed, he kissed his fingertips and touched them lightly to Paulette's cheek.

In going down the steps of the building he encountered a figure familiar enough to make him reverse himself once he'd gone by.

"*Pardon?*" he called. "*Mais . . .*"

The other man turned in the light of the doorway. "Indeed," he said. "I thought I knew you, yes, but I don't recall your name."

It was Michel Arnaud, the doctor saw, but greatly changed. He had lost weight, his face was gaunt, and that odd trace of effeminacy had altogether vanished.

"Antoine Hébert," he said. "I was your guest, this summer past, before the rising."

Arnaud's eyes narrowed. "Yes, of course," he said. "I believe you are the one who killed my dog."

"I believe you may have been the one who set the dog upon me," the doctor said.

"I believe my wife had been a visitor to your room, that night before . . ."

The doctor colored. "Yes, but all in innocence," he said. "She was ill and sought advice of my profession."

"Is it so?" Arnaud said. "Well, let it be." On his lips appeared the sneering smile of his seigneurial amusement. "It was most extraordinary shooting, I must say, especially for a man of *science*. I compliment your marksmanship."

"I regret the loss my markmanship occasioned you."

"Think nothing of it," Arnaud said. "What brings you to this place?"

"I came to visit Père Bonne-chance, the priest who has been wrongly accused."

"Strange," Arnaud said. He twitched his cane; the doctor noticed it was a different one, twisted and black. "I am come on the same errand."

"You know him? Then you must know he cannot have done the things they claim. He is a kind-hearted man and a true Christian, as I believe, and have seen."

"Of course the whole affair will be cleared up soon enough," Arnaud said.

"Do you believe so?"

"I will vouch for him myself," Arnaud said firmly. His smile was thinner than the doctor remembered, though his arrogance seemed only slightly diluted.

"Well, then," the doctor said. "And madame your wife? I hope she is well? Is she still in the city?" Of a sudden he felt himself remiss, not to have called on Madame Arnaud, but then the woman rather unnerved him.

Arnaud twitched his cane. "Yes, she is here, and well enough."

"Please convey my greetings to her," the doctor said, and went his way.

That night he took an early supper with Captain Maillart and some other young officers, but excused himself directly the meal was over. *Chez Cigny*, he found a typical company assembled over coffee in the drawing room, but since his visit was meant to have a professional character, he remained on his feet and kept the exchange of compliments as brief as he might. He already knew the way to Nanon's little room under the eaves.

She was sitting up in bed, working on some piece of sewing by the light of the small lamp. The small round window was dark, uncurtained; it reflected the doctor's lower body as he walked across the room. She looked up and smiled at him, not speaking. He took the work from her hands and looked at it: a little linen cap, trimmed in lace with lace strings to tie it under the chin; he had bought the material for her himself at the market in the Place d'Armes.

The stitches were exceedingly fine and regular. He pinned the needle through the cloth and laid the cap on the table, between the lamp and a slender vase that held several pale yellow blossoms of an orchid, closed now for the evening and depending like raindrops from a single green stem. There was nothing else on the table but an expensive-looking snuffbox—strange appurtenance for a woman in advanced pregnancy, the doctor thought, but no doubt it contained flower petals, or candy, perhaps. He drew a chair up to the bedside and asked her a number of medical questions, to which she responded carelessly. He lifted her arm to take her pulse.

"What have you done all the day?" she said.

The doctor was looking at his watch and counting. "I went to the cove," he said.

"What did you do there?" Her eyes were closed, long black lashes shadowing her cheek.

"I swam, and sat upon the beach . . ." Her image sharply appeared to him, naked and slender, graceful and erect, walking slowly out into the still water as if all unaware that it was not her natural element. He cast about for something else to tell her.

"I sat so quietly there the crabs came out to look at me. A little gray crab with his eyes on stalks came as near to me as I am to you. I winked at him and he put his eye down on one side . . ."

He was still holding her by the wrist; of a sudden she reversed the grip and drew his arm up to her face. She kissed the point of the wound, then traced the length of the healing scar with her tongue's catlike tip. The doctor trembled. She was smiling, her eyes still closed. He was alive with desire for her, but with her condition so advanced—it was impossible. Gently he disengaged his arm.

A flicker of disturbance crossed her face and her eyes opened. She caught his hand again and moved it to the high rise of her belly.

"No," she said, as he stiffened to withdraw. "Only feel him."

She dragged up the skirt of her nightgown under the sheet, tucking it up beneath her swollen breasts, and shifted his hand against her drum-tight skin. Something bulged into his palm and rolled away: a foot, an elbow maybe.

"Does he hurt you?"

"No."

The doctor lowered his head and flattened his ear against her belly. The skin was very smooth and warm. Listening for a second heartbeat, he closed his eyes. The susurrus of her inner currents recalled for him the sound of the ocean licking on the shore. When he opened his eyes again he saw Isabelle Cigny standing in the doorway, looking down on them with an ironical smile. He sat up sharply, jostling against the table. The orchid shivered in the vase.

Madame Cigny remained where she was, one hand on the door frame, her expression fixed. She seemed disposed neither to speak nor to leave them in privacy. The doctor cleared his throat.

"Best that you sleep now," he said, in a quasi-professional tone. He stroked his fingers briefly across Nanon's forehead, then reached to lower the wick of the lamp.

When he stood up, Madame Cigny moved out of the doorway. He followed her down the turning of a stair, into a room he'd never seen before. It was small and close, the windows curtained, fabric hangings covering the walls. He noticed a low daybed of the sort Nanon had kept in the rooms she occupied before the riots, this one covered with a fringed silken shawl. As Madame Cigny did not sit down, he also remained standing.

"The patient is well, I trust?" she said.

"To the best of my estimation."

"You are a most attentive physician. I would hope to secure your services to myself," she smiled, "should I be so misfortunate as to lose my health."

"Why madame, your health is radiant," the doctor said perfunctorily.

"You are kind." Madame Cigny relaxed her manner slightly. She caught her lower lip in her top teeth and released it to a little blush.

"My friend," she said, "believe me, I know everything you must be suffering at such a time as this—"

"I don't think I understand you," said the doctor. Before he could quite complete the sentence, she had slipped within his boundary. He overbalanced, dropping backward onto the daybed. This was sheer surprise, for her weight was nothing, she was not half the size of Nanon. Her mouth had opened his, her cool tongue darted and fluttered like the hummingbird. He felt her nails on the back of his neck. Her other hand had opened his trousers all unaided; the doctor was astonished at this dexterity. She cupped his testicles as though she'd weigh them, then milked his member upward with a languid, confident stroke. The doctor tore his mouth from hers, so as to moan. With that she sat up and away from him. He opened his eyes and moved to reach for her, but she was prim, unruffled, the cunning hands neatly folded in her lap.

"There is something you must know," she said. "Who marries a black woman becomes black. Do you understand it?"

The doctor stared. She stretched out her hand and flicked the head of his penis with her middle nail. It rebounded, ticking back and forth like the wand of a metronome.

"Be careful how far you are led by *ce monsieur-la,*" she said. "He is not always a wise instructor." She smiled at him, crisply, distantly, stood up and smoothed her skirts and left the room.

The doctor sagged back on his elbows. His breathing echoed off the masked walls of the room like the sound of a saw on a barrel. He waited for his erection to subside but it would not. After all, it was a stupid thing; thus far Madame Cigny was absolutely right. When a couple of minutes had gone by with no change in his condition, he crammed it back into his breeches and returned to the more public areas of the house.

Chapter Twenty-Five

Claudine Arnaud waited in Madame Cigny's parlor; she accepted coffee, suffered a biscuit to be laid on her plate. There was conversation in which she joined without attending to what was asked of her or what she said in answer. She nibbled the edges of a piece of fruit . . . At length the little doctor crept down from the upper story where he had been attending his pregnant mulatto *demimondaine*. He seemed to be in some confusion, lit uneasily on the edge of the chair where Isabelle Cigny bade him sit, declined all refreshment offered him, and excused himself in rather a shorter time than politeness should have dictated. Madame Arnaud fixed her blank eyes on his nervous display. Something untoward had evidently passed between the doctor and their hostess, but she could not guess the nature of the transaction, nor was she much interested, in fact. When the doctor rose to go, she craved the favor of his escort on her own way.

He attempted no pleasantries, on the stairs or on the street, and Madame Arnaud appreciated that, though his bald head had flushed under its tan, and she saw he was uncomfortable in her company. She knew he was a little afraid of her, though she was beyond taking any satisfaction from that state of things.

"You must take me to Père Bonne-chance," she said.

"*Comment?*"

"You must take me to Père Bonne-chance," said Madame Arnaud, in the same flat and grating tone. The doctor's hand flapped madly at a black fly that was buzzing near his eyeball.

"The priest who is supposed to have committed those crimes in the camps of Grande Rivière," she reminded him.

"He never did them," the doctor said automatically.

"So says my husband also. Not that it matters . . . not to me."

"Why yes, *monsieur* your husband visits there. He might well introduce you."

"I prefer it should be you."

Doctor Hébert glanced across at her as they walked. She had not looked at him once so far, but faced resolutely forward, so that he saw her profile. She was much changed since their first meeting. Her color had improved, on the whole—she had more of a look of health than previously. The doctor had had some opportunity of observing her and it was his impression that she no longer drank spirits, or even wine. She had lost her alcoholic palsy, but her eyes were sunken and dark around the sockets as though she were exhausted by some long travail.

"Tell me why it is that you would go?" he said.

"I wish him to hear my confession."

The doctor stopped in the middle of the street and stared at her. "But surely, *madame*, there are other priests. At Les Ursulines, for instance . . ."

"This one. *C'est lui qui je veux.*" She put her maimed hand on his arm. He glanced down at the gloved finger on his sleeve, the one which was folded under, resisting his first impulse to jerk away.

"Of course," he said, "I could refuse you nothing." The fingers on his arm were bird-bone light. "I will oblige you. Tomorrow if you wish."

SHE MOVED INTO THE PRIEST'S ROOM in a cloud of muslin, footless, drifting like a wisp of fog. It was evening, and the sunset stripe was measuring out its minutes over the stones of the wall beyond the table. She sat down on the stool without awaiting invitation. He saw that she had been pretty once, to say the least, but her face was eroded by some torment. There was the strange, disanimated way she moved, as though she ran on wires or clockwork instead of possessing an inner life. Momentarily, Père Bonne-chance felt puzzled as to what might be her derangement. As for Claudine, she smelled the rum that he had just been drinking with the doctor, and was a little nauseated by the lingering fumes. She covered her mouth with her gloved hand.

The priest looked at her curiously, a ghost of a smile on his broad cheeks. His skin was rather oily. Claudine arranged her hands at the table's edge. There was an unlit candle, two rum-smelling cups, and an end of bread sticky with honey.

"Bless me, father, for I have sinned," she said.

But nothing more. The priest was waiting. "Tell me your trouble," he finally said. At his back, he felt the failing light.

"This awful country," she said finally. "This dreadful place."

"Some find it beautiful," said the priest. "I among them. God intended it to inspire awe, if that is what you mean."

"God never meant for us to come here."

"Perhaps you're right." The priest leaned back, considering. "They say the Indians who lived here were a gentle race—before the Spanish came."

"I would that I had never come here," she said. "It is evil."

"It's ourselves," the priest said.

Claudine was taking off her gloves. "I knew you'd understand me. Only you."

"Ah well," the priest said. "So far you've told me little." He waited. Certainly her hands were very pretty, pleasantly shaped, the fingers long, graceful and expressive. The stump on her left hand was a rough shock. Of course, he'd heard the story many times; it was inescapable.

"This is a place which debases men," she said. "It makes them brutal. My husband has a love of torturing his slaves. He also fornicated with them. They bore his children. All of this happened many times."

She stopped. The priest shifted his legs under his cassock, watching the red seam of cicatrix that sealed the stump of her left ring finger. "Was it your husband's sin you came to confess, or your own?"

She didn't answer him at once. The light had shifted so her face was in shadow, and he could not well make out her expression. While they were silent, the hummingbird appeared outside the window, hovering, then darted in. It hung apparently motionless in the space above the table. From a distance it seemed black, but as it lowered one began to see the iridescent green of the feathers that lay on its neck and breast like scales.

The priest rubbed a finger on the tacky surface of the bread, smeared it in the center of his opposite palm and raised it. Within the curve of his blunt fingers the hummingbird was suspended, long beak needling the skin of his palm.

"It's a miracle," Claudine breathed.

The priest laughed. "Oh, I don't think so." He dropped his hand and the bird snapped out the window, instantaneously as a shot.

"It's only a bit of sugar," the priest said.

"Yes . . ." She was looking at the wall, where shadows of the vine leaves flickered between shadows of the window bars. "Once I detested my husband's cruelty," she said. "The place worked its change on me as well. There was a maid he'd bought me, as a 'gift,' he called it. I knew that he had taken her to his bed—I never told myself but *oh,* I knew . . . I used her cruelly as I was able—as my imagination would allow. He got her with child, of course, and then one day when she was near her time and he was absent from the place, I had her bound up in a shed . . ."

She stopped, still staring at the wall. The priest's back pained him. He leaned forward on the stool and propped his elbows on the table.

"Oh, the power I had over her," Claudine said. "It was absolute. How could I make you understand it? No one can know."

The priest lowered his face into his hands. Suddenly he felt very tired, and rather drunk as well. His forehead was humid with a rummy sweat.

"And so you murdered her," he said.

"And worse." Making its way around the table, the sunlight smashed her full in the face. It looked as if it might have blinded her. Perhaps it had.

"I cut the child from her womb alive," she said. "I cut it out and left it there. To die. No one would go near. Not me. Not anyone. But still it lives. It comes to me. I cannot bear it. I cannot nurture it. I am barren, you see. I will never have a child."

"I believe I understand you," said the priest.

"And then . . ." said Claudine. "Of course you know what happened next. It was I who caused the insurrection. I delivered it to this world on my blade's edge. Do you see? Because I *could not bear it!"*

"Yes," the priest said. He rubbed the sore red rims of his eyes. "Yes, my child, I see your difficulty. You must sacrifice your pride."

"My *pride?"* Claudine seemed to look upon a lunatic. The priest smiled back at her pleasantly enough.

"Do you know why pride is the deadliest sin? Because it enables us to root out all the others." He chuckled a little, under his breath. "I myself am not so terribly afflicted with it. Others I have in generous supply. Gluttony, lust and sloth . . . At least those three, and in sufficient quantity to earn me a warm place in hell. But now, you see, I will be spared this. The Lord has laid my table before me. He will catch me at the brink.

"So I must tell you, offer up your pride, my daughter, stop thinking of the greatness of your crime. One sin is not so much greater than another in God's eye. Be humble and be kind to others, as you have opportunity, and especially be kind to children, as Christ suffered them. When you do so, your heart will be softened, and you may yet awaken to the language of love." He laid his hands palm up on the table. "Pray for me also (I will not have much time to pray for you). Have faith that the Lord will provide for you, even as He has provided for me."

Her face was stricken in the blast of sunset. The priest hardly knew if she heard him or not, but he was exhausted himself by all he'd had to utter. Without knowing he'd do it, he yawned in her face.

"Forgive me, I am very weary," he said. "*Ego te absolvo.* Go in peace."

But Madame Arnaud remained rooted in her chair, gazing through and through him with her unseeing eyes.

"What was her name?" the priest said. "The maid, I mean to say."

Madame Arnaud seized him by the ribs and clung. She drew herself partway across the table. No sound escaped her, but she was weeping now, as though she'd fill his open palms. With the strange light still full in her face, it looked as if she was weeping tears of blood.

NEXT DAY WHEN HE RETURNED to the Cigny house, the doctor found no one in the parlor—no one about at all in the lower floors save a brown-skinned maid and the footman who'd admitted him. Between these two there seemed to be a strange charged atmosphere. He waited dutifully for his presence to be officially recognized, thinking that Madame Cigny would certainly appear in time. When he first heard the shout from above he went racing up the stairs in triplets and burst into Nanon's room without a knock.

She lay on her back with her knees drawn up, one hand tearing weakly at the hem of her pillowcase; the pillow seemed to discommode her, and Madame Cigny pulled it away. Nanon's head dropped back on the flat, sheeted mattress. Her eyes closed, then were shocked open by a long writhing spasm that seemed to the doctor to begin at the base of her spine and shudder all through her till it sent her head lashing back and forth against the linen.

As the contraction passed, he walked to the head of the bed and took her hand. Her face was glossy with a sheen of sweat, and her eyes looked glazedly past him, into the queer angles of the ceiling under the eaves. Then she went rigid from head to toe, and twisted snakily against the mattress, a groan pressing out of her clenched jaws. She crushed down on his hand as if she'd break it, then relaxed with a fainter gasp.

Across the bed from him, Madame Cigny moved with quick concentration, arranging strips of cotton at the bedside. The brown-skinned maid came in carrying a basin of water which Madame Cigny took from her and placed in a corner. She pulled down the sheet and drew up the hem of Nanon's gown. Automatically Nanon pushed up her hips so that the fabric could roll under. She moaned and jerked and crushed the doctor's hand. Madame Cigny glared across the heaving swell of her stomach, seeming to see him for the first time.

"You'd better go," she told him, her tone neutral. "You'll find there's nothing you can do."

"No, no, I must stay by," the doctor said, unconfidently. He made an effort to look wise and imperturbable. In truth he had attended few scenes of birth and knew next to nothing at all about it. Madame Cigny flicked her fingers at him, but said nothing more.

A new spasm ran through Nanon, sharper and stronger than the others it must have been. She raised up on her elbows and began cursing the doctor in close detail, with a thorough attention to every part of his anatomy, alternating between good French and wild obscure Creole epithets that tried the doctor's recent knowledge of *patois*. As she fell back exhausted, Isabelle Cigny smiled and twinkled at him across the bed.

"Well, stay then. *Comme vous voulez*. Allow her to relieve her feelings."

Nanon lay with her wide lips slightly parted, so that her teeth and tongue's tip showed; the whites of her eyes were also showing through a gap in her slack lids. Her breathing was loud and laborious but except for that it looked like death, and the doctor realized how frightened he was.

"How long . . ." he said, uncertainly.

"She's tired already," said Isabelle Cigny, who seemed not to have heard him quite exactly. "A first child . . ." She shook her head, then dipped a cotton rag in the water basin and began bathing Nanon's temples, but Nanon had jerked up again with another spasm and was cursing the doctor as before. As she subsided this time she spoke in a loud biting tone.

"Go get Maman-Maigre . . . Ma'maig' . . . *go get Maman-Maig'!*"

Doctor Hébert looked wildly across the bed. Madame Cigny pursed her lips and nodded . . . Some moments later he was flying out the door, pounding his way toward the Place d'Armes through the midafternoon heat. By the time he found the right courtyard he was all in a lather. The huge old black woman was sitting in the shade of a lean-to by the wall, talking to another slave and playing with an old polished chicken bone, which made a fluting sound when she blew on it. Doctor Hébert exhorted her to come, to hurry, using his most fluent Creole. For a long time Maman-Maigre's face was blank, and when finally she'd grasped the message, or shown herself willing to receive it, she prepared herself with torturous lethargy. She packed a basket with herb preparations, cold biscuit, a change of clothes. At last he saw her put into the basket a little tortoiseshell kitten before she closed the lid. He was dancing around her like an overwrought lapdog, as she marched grimly back toward the Cigny house. But what in God's name could she need a kitten for?

In Nanon's room not much had changed. Maman-Maig' set down her basket. She spread her fingers on Nanon's head for a moment as if to weigh her down; in fact the touch did seem to calm her slightly. Then she gripped Nanon's legs and spread them and peered between; she groped, then grunted something. As she withdrew, Nanon pulled away and screamed. Maman-Maig' drew a root from her basket and cut a strip of it with a clasp knife and gave it to Nanon to hold between her teeth.

It went on. The doctor stayed stubbornly in the room, though from time to time the women tried to throw him out. He would come forward to hear her curse him, curse all men; when the spasm passed, she would sometimes apologize. Sometimes he sat down to rest, drawing a chair beside the porthole window. New chairs had been brought into the room; there was an extra table now. Across the alley, colors of sundown swirled and faded on the opposite wall. It was dark, then late. The tortoiseshell kitten came out of the basket and chased a ball of lint through shadows of candlelight and under the bed. Doctor Hébert caught it up and brought it to Nanon to look at, touch—for a moment it seemed to distract her from her pain but that was very temporary.

Madame Cigny forced him to go down and sit behind a plate of supper, across the table from her sour, close-lipped husband. Monsieur Cigny was content to eat speechlessly, which was well. The doctor chewed and chewed but could not swallow. Upstairs again, he took a little of the broth that Nanon had been given to keep up her strength—so Maman-Maig' said. She seemed to choke on it; she pushed the bowl sloppingly away.

There was a lull. Sitting by the dark round of the window, the doctor took out his watch and dangled the chain. The kitten raised up on its hind legs and batted at the links so that they jingled and sparked in the lamplight.

It was past midnight. He went down and out into the street—for air, a few black gulps of the thick humidity. When he returned, the room was once again a box of screams. He was given to understand that the child was trying to be born sideways or backward, that the cord was looped around its neck and that Maman-Maigre's desperate manipulations were meant to rectify all this. The chicken bone was in her mouth, whistling with her exhalations as she rubbed and worked. Isabelle Cigny drew him aside, and held him by the window. At last Maman-Maig' looked up with a grin and nodded. She herself had sweated through her head-cloth.

"*Now* you must go," Madame Cigny snapped at the doctor.

The doctor stared and mutely shook his head. Madame Cigny had moved back to the bedside.

"Damn you, then," she said. "Be useful, if you refuse to leave. Well, come here and hold this leg." She beckoned him and showed him how to do it.

Their positions were symmetrical, either side of the bed. One of the doctor's hands was locked somewhere on Nanon's thigh and the other supported her foot like a stirrup. At every new contraction both he and Isabelle pulled back as if on a pair of oars. Maman-Maig' knelt between Nanon's legs like a worshiper, one hand spread across her belly and the other doing something down below.

"Li prèt," said Maman-Maig' in her low flat tone. "He's ready." Nanon raised up, face starkly white, lips closed on a tight, silent line as she was pushing, while the doctor and Isabelle Cigny hauled back on her legs.

"Come on," said Madame Cigny. *"Allons*—you must concentrate. *Plus fort."*

Nanon's head rolled back, and she subsided, whimpering. There was a pause before the coming stroke.

"Li prèt," Maman-Maig' said again. It went on. Isabelle was leaning into Nanon's face. *"Allons,"* she called. *"Pousses—plus fort que ça."* Her face was shining, a blaze of power and light pouring down on Nanon; the doctor was in awe of both. And Nanon slipped back, a thin wail sighing from her as her jaws relaxed.

"Li prèt," said Maman-Maig'.

The contractions came in patterns like sets of waves running in on the beach. Somewhere there was hot water steaming, filling the room with a hot mist. Blood ran out from Nanon's legs, filling a barber's basin the brown-skinned maid held underneath her. Everyone was screaming, shouting exhortations. The doctor was probably screaming himself, but mostly he only heard Isabelle, saw her glowing transfigured face as her head leaned near to Nanon's.

Maintenant pousses plus fort que ça tu peux tu dois plus fort que ça si tu m'aimes pousses maintenant!

"Têt li désân," said Maman-Maig' with reverence. "The head is coming."

The doctor turned his own, but could not see. Nanon sobbed out, with relief this time, and Isabelle's voice was gentler now as she stooped again to stroke back the sweat matted hair from Nanon's brow.

Allons, pousses, encore une fois. . .

What shot out into Maman-Maigre's hands was at first so alien that the doctor could not even read it. It was purple, slimed with blood, connected by a ropy pulsing vein; it looked like some internal organ, a liver or a spleen.

"Regardes-moi cette tête," said Madame Cigny softly.

Then, upside down, he recognized the face, as Maman-Maig' scooped off the mucus with her fingers. At once there was a small harsh cry that strengthened as it went. He saw the molded limbs drawn up in that odd rabbity way; the whole body was scarcely the size of the head, it looked, and the head was doubled, enormous. There was a mass of material above the face that made it seem as though the baby were wearing a gigantic conical hat.

Nanon's hands fluttered weakly over the infant's back. They had laid it on her breast, and Maman-Maig' was tying up the cord to cut it. The doctor understood that all was well. Nanon was slipping into sleep. He drew his watch out of his pocket and was amazed to see that more than two hours had passed since Maman-Maig' first raised her grinning face and announced that it was time.

Now he was hungry, ravenous. He went to the kitchen alone and ate whatever he could find. Madame Cigny had gone to bed, he thought, and Maman-Maig' was also sleeping somewhere in the house.

He returned upstairs, inattentively brushing crumbs from the corners of his mouth. It could not have been much later, for the brown-skinned maid was still there, tidying the room. Quiet now, with the mother and child asleep, and the signs of the struggle being gradually effaced. Some damp rags hung unnoticed over a chair back. Maman-Maigre's chicken bone had been set aside on a table where it lay with a mute authority, and there was a basin of blood on the floor.

Blue had begun to show at the porthole window. The maid unlatched the casement and swung it out, to admit a breath of cool predawn air. The doctor felt drifty, cloudlike, though he was not really so very tired. The maid moved through her tasks with the same measured composure that he felt within himself. An hour previous, she must have been screaming with the rest of them. A wave of affection for her passed over him. He asked her name: *Jacqueline*. The syllables were melodious in his ear, and even the blood in the basin had beauty.

She left a lamp burning for him when at last she went out. By its light the doctor saw that the infant had quietly awakened and was looking toward him with its round dark eyes from the basket they'd arranged near Nanon's bed. He took it up carefully, afraid of a cry that would wake the mother, but the baby stayed quiet. They'd put a conical cotton cap like a sailor's on its head, but the doctor slipped it off, noticing at once that the skull itself was relaxing to a more ordinary shape. A quantity of rust-colored hair covered the scalp; the doctor stroked its furry softness with the thumb of the hand supporting the head. A warmth and texture like new-risen bread dough. It was a boy. His hands and feet were covered with an ancient wrinkly skin; one hand wrapped around the doctor's finger. All the while the baby looked at him from great owl eyes as if he'd truly see and know him.

A thin gray rain came up with the dawn, drops beading on the open porthole casement. Before Isabelle Cigny snuffed out the candle, the doctor had not noticed her come in. She crossed the room, her long nightgown trailing on the floor, and peered over his shoulder into the child's face. The warmth and softness of her breast pressed unconsciously against his arm, but for once he was unembarrassed, as she was unaware.

"What woke you?" he said. "You must be very tired."

"Ah, there's nothing like it, is there?" She did not look at him when she said this, but kept her wistful smile turned on the baby. The doctor understood that she meant not children, but the birth itself, in which they were bound together as witnesses. One of her fingers reached out to touch the newborn cheek.

"He's very white," the doctor said.

"On the first day it's always so," she said. "After that, one sees the color." She lifted one of the fingers from its tiny grip. "You can see it now, in the base of the nail."

There was no rancor in her tone, and the doctor did not resent it. On the contrary, he loved her as well as he loved the maid, Jacqueline. Some little while later she must have left the room, but he was no better aware of her going than of her arrival. The rain was tapping on the window and hissing on the street below. Still the child regarded him intently. Already his small face was changing. When the doctor had first seen it emerge, the face had been without a doubt his own grandfather's. There were still the odd dog-shaped, crumpled ears, a Hébert family trait, but the other features were settling into something that belonged to this one child alone. Not himself, not Nanon, but a mingling—something new. This, the doctor realized, was what all the trouble was about.

. . .

AT THE TRIAL OF PÈRE BONNE-CHANCE, these charges were upheld: That he had aided the rebellious slave called *Jeannot* in the torture and murder of many white prisoners. That he had deliberately pandered and prostituted helpless white women to many of the rebel black slaves. That from the very beginning he had helped to instigate the insurrection and had inspired the slaves to destroy so much property and take so many lives and overthrow the rule of order in the colony.

None of those who had accused the priest appeared against him in person. The charges were general in their form. A letter which had been found and preserved by someone who'd survived the camp of Jeannot was read out in the court.

*J'ai disposé la dame une telle à vous recevoir cette nuit . . . Vous n'avez jamais eu de telle jouissance, mon cher Biassou, que celle qui vous attend ce soir . . . La petite de fait la reveche mais apportez de la pitre pour la disposer à souscrire à vos désirs . . .**

The signature had been been partly torn away, and what remained of it was scarcely legible. Père Bonne-chance denied that he had written the letter, but without much force. He had little else to say. On the whole he did not appear to take much interest in any of the proceedings.

Doctor Hébert testified haltingly on behalf of Père Bonne-chance, describing his assistance at the field hospital in Jean-François's camp. The spiritual comfort he'd brought to white prisoners and black rebels alike. The evident sincerity of his religion . . .

Michel Arnaud followed the doctor's testimony, disparaging every accusation made against the priest as if it were unworthy to be heard, especially the charge of prior conspiracy. He'd mustered up all his old swagger for the occasion, and for the time it took him to tell his story he succeeded in making the charges seem absurd. His performance had more authority than the doctor's, though unfortunately he had also been more remote from the scene.

Still, the judgment was never in doubt. Père Bonne-chance had no defenders who'd actually been present in Jeannot's camp to say that he had *not* done those things he was accused of. In any case, it was plain that he was not what he appeared to be. His numerous

*I have prepared such a woman to receive you tonight . . . Never have you known such joy, my dear Biassou, as that which awaits you this evening . . . The little thing will be obstinate, but bring along the whip with the hemp lash, to dispose her to submit to your desires . . .

progeny proved that he did not keep the priestly vow of chastity. Then too, he was a Jesuit disguised in robes of another order. Had not the Jesuits been expelled because of their too great sympathy for the slaves?—which in itself suggested most strongly that Père Bonne-chance must have conspired with the rebels. Besides, even the doctor could not deny that he'd helped with the composition of their latest, most outrageous demands.

Two days after the sentence was passed, they brought the priest to the Place de Clugny. A large crowd was present for the execution. His children had been kept away, but Fontelle was there, and the priest was permitted a last embrace with her. There was a frank lustfulness in his touch of her, and the crowd mocked them both for it, and threw stones and dead things they had saved for the occasion.

Père Bonne-chance was bound spread-eagled to the wheel and broken. The executioner used a great iron hammer to smash his arms and legs, his ribs and clavicle. *Domine, non sum dignus,* the priest shouted out at the first few strokes. The mob was unnerved by this, and virtually silenced. But after the fifth blow his cries became unintelligible and the mob was released again to jeer and catcall. When all of his bones had been appropriately shattered, they called for him to be left in that state, for slow death over hours or days as it might be. But the executioner, a kindhearted fellow who was known to carry a pet mouse in his vest pocket even as he did his duty, took out the knife and slit his throat.

Michel Arnaud and Doctor Hébert were both present for the execution. Arnaud was aghast, in a state of shock; it seemed that the repudiation of his testimony had shaken him more deeply than anything else that had yet befallen him. The doctor was obviously, catastrophically drunk, swinging a brandy bottle from his slack fingers and weeping openly without shame. Between them stood Claudine Arnaud, watching closely and missing no detail; her eyes were parched and hot as burning stones.

SEPTEMBER 1802

M. PLACIDE LOUVERTURE, *Belle-Isle-en-Mer,*

M. Placide, mon ami fils de mon maître I am write to tell you of what am arrive to M. v. père mon maître. I have been four week one month since we are coming at the end of this one journey across the France. This place is a crête in the mountains as it would be in Sainte Domingue but so much far inside the France and so much high. The name it is Fort de Joux. Going we aren't to see nothings of where we go there, not I and not M. v. père mon maître. We are in a close carriage with no way of regard outside. we are go up and up through some very tight turning like the lace of a boot and the coach do twist and rock on every side. Worse like the ship but for less long.

When they have open the coach to take us out we are come again inside the walls so we don't see nothings of where we are. Only to see the sky one time and feel the cold which is much colder than our mountains even in the summer here of France.

I am not to see how this fort is there until I am three weeks they take me out bring me away. They take me out though I would not go I would stay near to M. v. père mon maître even if they would make me free but they did not. I am now in this prison of Nantes. I have trapped to myself a sickness of cold from the fort de Joux where it is cold even in summer and wet. No one to me tells what have done what crime

Each day M. v. père mon maître have speak to me of you you mother you brother Isaac & St. jean. Between us we remember much of you and we are talk only of you between us when we together come. If my heart will fall too low he does upraise it, and I so to him when it is able to me. This fashion I serve him and can not any other because we have no things in this two cachot where we are place. May Be that you will have words of M. v père also to you because the commandant of Fort dejoux have allow him things of write.

Now I will tell you how it is this place of M. v. père mon maître at this Fort de joux that you when you know of it your hearts will be together. One must pass three keyholes to come to this cachot all like an underground. One place wet like a bad hole of crab. Then after that one comes one corridor with two cachots one for M. v. père and one for MARS PLAISIR. *That is all.*

I would they lock us in one same cachot but not. We are together each day some hour or two only. Some hour each day they will bring me out to walk inside the walls, under the guard as you will see. For M. v. père mon maître, they make this never to him. Only in cachot all day and enduring the night. There is one small fire but not enough of wood.

Our happiness it is talk of you you mother and you brother and remember between us manything of you. Now we are each alone and in far places. I was nothing when my master raised me up to stand beside him. Now I am in this prison of Nantes, how will I raise him up?

I am pray to n. seigneur jsuschrist, there is no other gods in France. May Be, not even that one.

I have trapped to myself this one bad sickness. In the chest and in the head. Also in this prison of Nantes I have not the money for food or fire. I would even be at fort dejoux if I am able. So I am not alone like here in Nantes prison. They allow me things of write but I do not well say. I know M. v. père mon maître is each day write to government in French. They will not tell me any crime because I did not do any one.

When they are take me down the mountain they do not the coach closing. This way I am to see how how much a cold a highplace is this Fort de Joux. Going down these lacets I would not see the fort above the cliffs and turns. After when we were in a low place and there is the Fortdejoux ten thousand lieux above me of the mountaintop. It was not to be brought there and put down but dug there in the mountaintop like the crab digs his hole in mud. It was like a grave of stone. A man will rise from a grave of dirt, but how will he come out of stone?

A day when I am make my walkings by the walls, the guard am bring me back some different way to the cachot from like before. We are stop inside this different voûte, for him me show this well. One well set in the stone going down so long away in the dark I am to think myself it must be slaves of France who are make this one. This one well narrow like one man head but a body would not pass it.

The guard have give me a pebble to throw in, this one sharp little stone. I have drop it, how he sign for me to do. I have hear this one stone hitting on the sides of this stone well but never have I hear it strike into the bottom. Still I do listen this long time but I don't hear it strike.

M. Placide mon ami fils de mon maître, I am pray to n. seigneur jschrist that one day we will all be free. I have trapped a sickness so I don't know long to live. I do not know how to have a letter or any words of you. I am write you mother you brother also but this another day I am

v. serviteur

MARS PLAISIR

BAILLE, THE COMMANDANT OF THE FORT DE JOUX, was afraid of something, as Toussaint could sense at once. He was an aging man, heavy, white and lumbering, as though he were unused to daylight or disliked it. Toussaint could feel Baille's lack of ease, and knew that Baille was not afraid of him but of his being there. This cheered him, though he showed nothing of his cheer.

An officer of the guard stood by the wall. Baille asked Toussaint to empty out his pockets. He did so. With a fearful gingery touch, Baille stirred the articles on the tabletop: a broken quill pen, some coins of small denomination, a couple of letters and a watch and chain. Toussaint had kept back two letters and some gold pieces in an inner pocket; he was concerned about a body search, but it did not come.

Baille opened the watch case front and back, looked first at the face and then into the works. He studied the inaudible contractions of the fine silvery spring that moved the second hand. Toussaint leaned a little forward. He knew what troubled Baille so much: the escape of two imprisoned officers of the Vendée from this very place only a few weeks before. The thing Baille feared must certainly be possible. The fear itself might make it possible . . . But Toussaint did not show his smile.

Baille returned the watch to him. The other items were put into a bag and taken from the room. Toussaint stood up then, as if it were his prerogative to terminate the interview. Baille did not seem startled or surprised.

They passed along the vaulted corridors in this order: first a guard with keys, then Toussaint, then the officer of the guard, and Baille bringing up the rear. It heartened Toussaint that the commandant was so reluctant to be near him. He kept his face a neutral blank. The cold of the tunnels troubled him but he suppressed any visible shiver. The vaulted ceilings were so low that the taller men must stoop to pass, but Toussaint, with his jockey's build, could still walk erect.

Baille carried his own ring of keys, and paused to lock each door once they'd passed through it. The door before them was never opened until Baille had locked the door behind. Each door had a small cross-barred hatch set in it, no larger than palm-size, each a head higher than Toussaint's eye level. The double thickness of the wood of every door was bound with bolts and bands of iron.

The third corridor they traversed was damper than the others; a sheen of water seeped on the raw rock wall to their left side, and water had collected on the floor so that the splashing echoed as they went through. In the next vault, the floor was dry again, or only damp. At its end, the guard unlocked the final door, and stood aside that Toussaint might enter.

When he had gone into the cell and walked as far as the middle of it, he turned to look back. The other three had all remained without, watching him through the doorway. Baille bowed to him, without apparent irony. Toussaint returned the bow. When he raised his head again, the door was already quietly closing. He heard the crunching of the iron teeth of the lock.

He walked first to the end of the *cachot*, where the window was. It had been bricked up over the lower two-thirds of its height, and above this barrier he could just see a section of a slate-blue sky, beyond the outer end of the deep-set embrasure. He turned and walked back, passing the bedstead, a square table with two chairs pushed up under it. To his left was a small fireplace, but no wood.

He had reached the door. His eyes were just flush with the lower edge of the barred peephole. From beyond, he heard the doors locking down along the line of vaults. On the way in, the guard had opened each almost with stealth. Going out, he seemed to prefer to slam them.

Toussaint turned again. The wall opposite the fireplace was quarried out of living stone. There was a glisten of damp on it as well, though it did not run with water so freely as had the wall in the third corridor.

On the table stood a pitcher; when Toussaint lifted it he found it mostly full. He poured some water into his palm and washed his face and hands. There was a cup on the table too, and he poured an inch of the water into the cup and drank it. The water had a faintly brassy taste.

He took out his watch and looked at it, let it depend and swing gently at the length of its chain, then snapped it up into his hand and put it in his pocket. It was just past four, in the afternoon. Certainly it was an illusion that he could *feel* the tick of the watch against his fifth rib.

He walked to the window and again to the door. It was almost automatic to count the steps required for the circuit, but he repressed the number. Standing before the cold fireplace, he became aware that he had wet his boot leather, crossing the third vault.

He picked up one of the chairs and positioned it before the window. Standing on it, he could look over the top of the brickwork. The view was somewhat altered by this change of angle. Now he saw the top of a wall, the corner of a guardpost, and a sentry walking along the rampart.

The iron bars at the end of the embrasure were old and rusting, but the mesh screen beyond the brickwork was much newer. Those officers of the Vendée had filed the bars of their cell, and bribed a guard. Toussaint reached to his arm's length to touch the screen. The mesh was too fine to admit his fingertips, too fine for even a rolled paper to be pushed through.

He drew his hand partway back, turning it this way and that at the top of the brickwork. An ambiguous current of air stroked across his fingers. A scrap of gray cloud was hastening across the strip of sky he saw above the wall but disoriented as he was, he could not guess which way the wind was blowing.

Part IV

ILLUMINATION

August 1792–June 1793

Don't try to hold me up
On this bridge now
I got to reach Mount Zion . . .

—Bob Marley

Chapter Twenty-Six

Léger Félicité Sonthonax stood on the afterdeck of the ship *America*, tight curls of his black hair whipping around his long, pale and anxious face. His co-commissioner Polverel was with him; Ailhaud was somewhere belowdecks, ill or indisposed. They were watching the light ship sent out in advance of the commissioners' small fleet to assay conditions and attitudes in Saint Domingue—which ship had just lately returned and was standing a way off from them, tacking against the stiff wind that carried them all westward toward the colony.

They were lowering a boat from the smaller ship into the chop. Sonthonax guessed by his uniform that the officer scrambling awkwardly down the rope ladder was Lieutenant-Colonel Etienne Laveaux, though the distance was too far for his features to be legible. The sound of the boat knocking against the ship's hull came to them hollowly across the rough water. The boat plunged and as Laveaux (it must have been he) stepped backward off the ladder he lost his balance and fell hard upon the seat of his trousers. They threw a despatch bag down to him from the ship; in leaning out to catch it, Laveaux almost fell out of the boat. Sonthonax's stomach rolled. He glanced sidelong at the gray and balding Polverel, who did not seem so much perturbed.

Two sailors were laying into the oars. As the boat drew near, Sonthonax threw down the ladder with his own hands, shouldering aside the sailors of the *America* who'd have managed the affair. A burst of salt spray filmed over his face; he blinked away the sting and scarcely noticed it. It was Laveaux, indeed, coming up, swinging the despatch case by a strap. Sonthonax was squeezing his upper arm and slapping him on the shoulder with his left hand while clawing into the despatch bag with his right. A roll of paper uncurled and blew; Polverel, suddenly alert, moved to intercept it.

"*De la patience,*" he said to Sonthonax. "Come, we'll go below. For shelter." He gave a speaking look. "And for *privacy* . . ."

Sonthonax bit his lip and went after Polverel, despatch case gathered under one arm, drawing Laveaux along by the cuff of his uniform coat. They followed the older man toward the hatches.

In his cabin, Sonthonax pushed back from the small round table where the documents were spread, wedging his back against the bulkhead that straightened the curve of the ship's outer hull. A lantern rocked with the ship's motion, swinging a scythelike shadow over the papers and the three men's faces, while a glass prism set in the deck above let in a little greenish daylight. Sonthonax was reading and simultaneously asking questions of Laveaux, then interrupting before the other could answer him.

It was all enthusiasm, Polverel understood. Each day of their two-month-long voyage, Sonthonax would array himself in the formal dress of his office—the tricolor sash and engraved gold medal (*Civil Commissaires* on one face, *Nation, Law and the King* on the reverse)—though in truth there was hardly anyone, in the middle of the Atlantic, for so much grandeur to impress. But Sonthonax had been, would have always been, a small provincial lawyer. The Revolution had dizzied him by shooting him so rapidly to his present height. He was just twenty-nine years old. Laveaux was even some few years his junior.

"Yes, I believe it is all sincere," Laveaux was saying. "No, not sincere, but genuine. I mean—it is politic, it is only practical. Of course there is race prejudice. But they do accept the law of *quatre Avril!* At least, in practicality . . . after all it is their common cause against the rebel blacks . . ."

"Yes, of course," Sonthonax said, half attending as he shuffled papers. "So far as it is in their interest . . . but when the elections must be held?"

Still, he was broadly smiling, thoroughly elated. Polverel knew him to be quick and canny, never mind his youth, or his occasional excesses. He shifted in his seat so as to be able to read over Sonthonax's shoulder, a longish letter from Governor Blanchelande.

"In July, the white men even gave a dinner for *les gens de couleur,*" Laveaux was saying. "And shortly afterward the colored men returned the compliment . . . Of course they would not ordinarily mingle, but . . ."

"They do accept the law," Sonthonax said. "In time, will they accept the spirit of the law?" He chewed his fingernail.

Polverel leaned toward Blanchelande's despatch. He could not greatly trust the author, long suspected of royalist dispositions, but still the news seemed good. Of the four thousand French troops already in the colony, nearly half were in hospital or otherwise incapacitated, but that might be a blessing in disguise, for the commissioners could better depend on the loyalty of the six thousand soldiers they'd brought with their own fleet. By Blanchelande's account, this force would be warmly welcomed, and he urged that they be put into the field against the insurgent blacks as soon as possible. If the civil war between the whites and mulattoes had truly been resolved, there might be real hope of suppressing the slave insurrection once for all . . .

Polverel covered a belch with his hand and stretched out his legs beneath the table. He too had been troubled by doubts and anxieties which he took more care than his younger colleague to conceal. On April 4, the king had made law a decree of the French National Assembly that henceforth *all* free mulattoes of Saint Domingue regardless of birth should enjoy equal rights with the whites of the colony. The mission of the second Civil Commission was to enforce this law and to hold new elections in which the newly enfranchised *gens de couleur* could participate. It was a worthy work, certainly, but they had all misdoubted whether or not they might be received with cannon fire, discover themselves at open war with the colonists when they arrived.

So Polverel was also warm with relief. He watched Sonthonax, who had calmed himself now, and was reading more slowly, silently, ignoring the continuing stream of Laveaux's speculations. It might be that the news was too good to be entirely true. Sonthonax would be trying to read between the lines . . .

. . . and leave the colonists, perhaps, to do the same. On September 18, the commissioners debarked at Cap Français, following a mild controversy with the expedition's military commander, the elderly General Desparbés, about the proper movement of the troops.

But there was no resistance, no immediate sign that resistance would come. The attitude of the colonists seemed uneasy but submissive, as Daugy, president of the Colonial Assembly, described it:

"Gentlemen, we are in your hands as a jar of clay, which you may break at will. This is, then, perhaps the last moment vouchsafed us to warn you of a vital truth ill understood by your predecessors. This truth, already recognized by the Constituent Assembly in its closing moments, is that there can be no agriculture in Saint Domingue without slavery, that five hundred thousand savages cannot be brought from the coast of Africa to enter this country as French citizens; lastly, that their existence here as free citizens would be physically incompatible with the coexistence of our European brethren."

Sonthonax, resplendent in his sash and its gold medal, was immediately on his feet. His words were persuasive, perhaps even to himself; Polverel (who'd had previous opportunity to study his oratorical performances) suspected that the momentum of his discourse might sometimes carry him where he had not meant to go . . .

"We declare, in the presence of the Supreme Being, in the name of the mother country, before the people and amid its present representatives, that from this time forth we recognize but two classes of men in Sainte Domingue—the free, without distinction of color, and the slaves." He paused, significantly; the medallion winked in the area of his navel. "We declare that to the Colonial Assemblies alone belongs the right to pronounce upon the fate of the slaves. We declare that slavery is necessary to the cultivation and prosperity of the colonies; that it is neither in the principles nor the will of the National Assembly of France to touch these prerogatives of the colonists; and that if the Assembly should ever be so far misled as to provoke their abolition, we swear to oppose such action with all our power." He drew in a large breath and stretched out his arms. "Such are our principles. Such are those given us by the National Assembly and the king. We will die, if need be, that they may triumph!"

A flutter of applause ran round the chamber when he had thus concluded; it grew stronger as the import of his remarks began to sink in. There was even an isolated cheer. Michel Arnaud, however, was sitting on his hands. He turned partway toward Doctor Hébert, who'd also come along as a spectator, and muttered out of the side of his mouth.

"See how winningly he lies," Arnaud said, "this godless Jacobin—one shade of a nigger is as good as another to him, I'll wager." He caught himself short and inspected the doctor for reaction, but the other's face was studiously blank.

When the installation of the new commissioners had been perfected, Doctor Hébert returned—home, as he might come to think of it at last. Nanon's two rooms near the Place d'Armes had been restored and refurnished, the doctor drawing on the Thibodet accounts at the house of Bourgois to cover the expense. It was better so. Since the declaration of the law of *quatre Avril*, Nanon's situation had become more strained than ever *chez Cigny*. Curious how the law had changed things. Such casual friendliness as might sometimes (rarely) have obtained between whites and *les gens de couleur* was fairly stifled by it. All became a matter of rule—open hostilities were repressed, but so was any genuine goodwill. In this climate, the charity of Isabelle Cigny had withered, shriveled in the dry heat of other aspects of her character. No doubt there had been additional pressure from her husband too. Doctor Hébert understood as well that the presence of the infant did nothing to ease matters, although of course he had never gone so far as to acknowledge that the child was his.

It was twilight, and the air was cool and damp when he turned into the last street. The forked shadow of a bird flashed over him; he looked up, but it was gone. A pitch apple tree bloomed in the dooryard, a ring of dusty red circling the round white petals of the flower. Nanon had scratched the child's name—Paul—and his birthdate on one of the waxy green leaves; the impression had remained legible these last six months. The doctor blinked at the token. He took the key from his watch chain, unlocked the door and went in.

A gray cat rose from the rug over the boards, arched his back and rubbed against his leg. The doctor had acquired it to replace the dead monkey; he'd suggested another monkey, but Nanon said it would not do. He bent and ran his fingers over the cat's fur, then walked to the cabinet and poured himself a glass of red wine from the counter. On the cabinet's highest shelf were two loaded pistols in a case; he took them down and checked their priming and replaced them, then did the same with the long octagon-barreled rifle that hung over the door. There had been no more insurgencies from the *petit blancs* of the town since the riots of winter and spring, for Colonel Cambefort and the Regiment Le Cap were keeping them under virtual martial law, but still the doctor had thought well to arm himself, and had even bullied Nanon into learning the use of the weapons.

The girl Paulette was playing with the baby in a corner; she would raise him up, his plump hands wrapped around her fingers, but each time she did it he'd let go and thump back solidly onto his bottom. Each time it happened, the baby gave a sort of soundless laugh, his mouth working itself into a perfect round O of pleasure.

"*Paul et Paulette*," the doctor grinned, and the priest's daughter looked up with a smile. He tilted his glass, rolling the red fluid around the transparent bell, then moved to a table and lit a lamp, for the dark had now shut down outside the closing door.

"*Et maman*?" he said.

Paulette pointed to the back room, and the doctor carried his wineglass through the curtain. Nanon was stretched on the bed, propped up on cushions, a rug spread over her bare feet. The doctor smiled at her and sat on the edge of the bed. She accepted the glass of wine from his hand, took a sip and returned his smile. Doctor Hébert scraped off his shoes and swung his legs up onto the bed beside her.

They lay in the darkening room and talked for a time, sharing the one glass between them. She told him of all the child had done that day, while he rehearsed for her the events he'd witnessed in the town. Presently Paulette brought in the baby, and Nanon took him to her breast. As she went, Paulette paused to light a candle.

The child nursed with a snuffling sound, and soon enough had fallen asleep. The doctor picked him up and held him to his shirt; the baby molded there like warm, soft, living clay. His lashes were long, and his loose cheek mashed against the doctor's buttons, taking their imprint, while his mouth pulled partly open. The doctor held him for a few rapt minutes, automatically rocking from foot to foot. Nanon got up, closing her bodice, put on slippers and went out to see to the meal. The doctor laid the child in his cradle and came to table when she called for him.

They dined on the legs of the big *grenouille*—mountain chicken as they called it here. There was rice cooked with peppers and a dish of greens, afterward a bowl of chopped fruit and some flat sweet cakes. Fontelle had helped in the preparation. She and her children had found lodging in a building across the courtyard and the doctor gave them work and money as he could manage it.

He and Nanon took no coffee and went early to bed. For the look of the thing the doctor had taken rooms for himself in a building nearby, but he spent so little time there he had scarcely troubled himself to furnish them. One chamber was set up as a crude medical laboratory; he received his mail there, and that was all.

In the middle of the night he came alive to the sound of hoarse screaming and the grip of hands restraining him. He shook himself upright gasping and, on discovering where he was, he recognized the hands were Nanon's, her voice softly calling him, *stop, wake up, you are dreaming* . . . He let his breath out in a whistling sigh.

"What was it?" Nanon said. "Was it the camps?"

"Nothing." The doctor got out of bed, wiping a slick of sweat from his forehead. "I have forgotten." In the dark, he padded toward the baby's cradle and crouched beside it, his head cocked till he heard the light sound of his breathing, a series of the clicks and gurgles the child would make in sleep . . .

His knees cracked as he stood back up. Nanon was still sitting up in the bed; her face turned in his direction; he felt this though it was too dark to see.

"What was it?" she asked again as he rejoined her.

"C'etait rien," he said. Superstition prevented him from telling a dream before daylight, lest it come true. He fumbled on the night table among his keys and watch until he found the shard of broken mirror he'd kept all through the time of his captivity among the risen blacks and carried daily in his pocket still. His *ouanga*, it might be. In the darkness he could not see a trace of its reflective glint but the pressure of the broken edge against his palm helped relocate him. He put the mirror piece back on the table.

Nanon snorted and rolled onto her stomach; the doctor stroked his fingers over the small of her back. The nightmare image printed and reprinted itself on his inner eyelids. A golden infant thrust aloft into the clouds, skewered through its rib cage on a spear. He forced his mind away from the image, thought of anything else at all. As usual, he was only able to calm himself by imagining the look of his weapons and the weight they'd have in his hands. It was something under an hour before he could return to sleep.

The lengthening of the fall brought cooler weather, and so the fever season was somewhat abated. Doctor Hébert had been casually impressed into the makeshift medical corps that treated both the new troops and the old. As always among soldiers so freshly out from Europe, disease was rife: dysentery, dengue, malaria, a few fatalities from *mal de Siam*. The doctor grew popular among the troops for his success in easing the symptoms of several of these afflictions, though some would also mock him for the herbal concoctions he employed, calling him an old woman and a witch.

But many of his preparations worked. At least they'd seem to palliate most fevers. For *mal de Siam* he understood no cure, although some few patients did survive it. He knew the symptoms well by now; the yellowed eyes, chills and fever and the deeper bone ache, then days of black treacly vomiting which usually presaged death. As for himself, he was immune and knew it now. Perhaps some time before he'd suffered a mild case—a spell of fever with mild nausea, in his first days at Habitation Thibodet, or even at Arnaud's, or in the camps. Sometimes, inexplicably, an attack was fairly mild, and left the survivor inoculated against another. The doctor was acclimated now, as much as any seasoned slave or soldier. Death was ever at his shoulder, it was everywhere among the military hospitals, but now he knew he would not die of fever.

Of an evening he inattentively played *chemin de fer* against the house bank of the Regiment Le Cap. Arnaud, Captain Maillart, and the *négociant* Grandmont were playing too, while the roly-poly young Lieutenant Baudin served as banker. Only Arnaud was on a winning streak, the others were all losing—Grandmont quite heavily. The doctor played more cautiously than the others, though he was slightly drunk, folding his poor cards early, letting his small stakes leave him as the price of an hour of male company and a share of brandy and water from the regiment's store.

"Well, and what of your patients today?" said Captain Maillart.

The doctor shrugged. "Much the same as yesterday," he said. "Some recover and others fall ill. I'd give you a third or quarter of them *hors de combat*."

"Among the new troops?" Arnaud said.

The doctor nodded, and folded his hand. Grandmont grinned with his bad teeth as he flipped over his losing cards and shoved his stake across to Baudin. The seriousness of his losses did not seem to trouble him much. Laughing, he rose and walked to a shelf where he took up a pen and wrote out another note to borrow yet more money from the bank. Already he had gambled away perhaps three hundred pounds of sugar . . . Mentally, the doctor tried to translate the loss into *main-d'oeuvre,* the labor and lost lives of slaves, but could not do it. He sipped his brandy. Arnaud was still looking at him with an odd fixity.

"And are more affected among the troops of the line?" he said. "Or among those National Guards?"

The doctor noticed that Maillart had shut his cards up in his fingers and was awaiting his reply with a close attention.

"I couldn't say." The doctor forced an unnatural chuckle. "Diseases don't commonly make such nice political distinctions." He looked back and forth from Arnaud to Maillart, thinking it odd how thickly they'd thrown in together these last weeks, when their characters were so poorly matched, or so he thought. Of course Arnaud had lately been very energetic in raising companies of militia . . . and yet the regular troops of the line would ordinarily despise such reinforcements.

"*En tout cas,*" the doctor said, seeking to turn the conversation, "it would be for the better if all these fresh troops were moved out of the city. Away from the coast and the bad air of the *marais* . . ."

"Yes, and where they might accomplish something," Arnaud said, returning his attention to the fresh hand he'd been dealt. "So long they've been here, and not the first move against the brigands. No, they leave the troops to rot in Le Cap until they are decimated by disease. This Desparbés is a weak old man . . ."

"Desparbés is a good soldier," Captain Maillart said rather sharply. "But he's hamstrung by the commissioners. They will not give him rein enough to act . . . he has no course but to hold his hand."

"And a plague on the Commission too," Arnaud snapped. "What have they done since they arrived but stir up the white *canaille* against us?" He drew to nineteen—a jack turned up —and disgustedly shoved his coins toward Baudin.

"Perhaps Roume will accomplish something with them," Grandmont said reflectively. Roume, the only member of the first commission still in the colony, had come up from the west to confer with his successors; previously no one had much trusted him, but now, by contrast to these new Jacobin commissioners, he was much better liked among these circles than before.

"Ridiculous," said Arnaud. "He'll succeed as well as Blanchelande did."

"There's a man I pity," Grandmont said, turning up the corner of his hole card.

"*Comment ça?*" Arnaud said. "A waste of your emotion."

"He has a date with Madame Guillotine," Grandmont said.

Captain Maillart sniffed. "But he requested his own recall."

"That was before," Grandmont said. "Sonthonax deported him—in disgrace, as you'll remember. They'll put him on trial when he reaches France—well, a trial is what they call it."

The worn pasteboards whisked through Baudin's hands as he shuffled, redistributed. The sound put the doctor briefly in mind of the whisper and rush of a dropping blade. The silence persisted a moment before Arnaud spoke.

"That's his desert for trying to serve two masters. If not more. One must be bold enough to take a stand and hold it."

Captain Maillart frowned at him; Grandmont looked away. The silence lingered. Captain Maillart cleared his throat.

"Have you been riding out today?" he said to the doctor. "Gone for your sea bathing?"

"Yesterday," the doctor said. He pushed his top card to one side—a queen.

"What do you mean, sea bathing?" asked Baudin.

"Why, this one rides over the hills every day to swim at the beach beyond the point," Maillart said.

"What, *alone?*" Baudin said.

"Not every day," the doctor said mildly. Unconsciously, he scratched his scar through his sleeves. "Not since my arm has healed—I only go to find the herbs I need."

Baudin stared at him. "*T'es fou,*" he said. "It's utter madness."

The doctor shrugged. "I never see anyone in the hills—almost never." He turned over the ace beneath the queen.

"Yes, you are a witch," Baudin grunted. He pushed over a small scattering of coins. Arnaud also had won again, a larger bet; he gathered in the money and stacked it up in rows. It was quiet again except for the suck of Grandmont's breath as he leaned to light a cigar in the candle flame. Then they heard the clatter of hooves, iron shoes clashing on the stones of the court. Immediately there followed a hammering on the door. Maillart got up and jerked open the door so suddenly that the knocker almost tumbled inside.

Major O'Farrel of the "Dillon" regiment—the Irishman was a stranger to the doctor. "Where's Colonel Cambefort?" he said, in his weirdly accented French. "There's news—it's urgent."

"A raid?"

Arnaud and Baudin were also on their feet, while Grandmont leaned back, smoking. Not long since, a party of insurgent blacks had breached the defenses of Le Cap and penetrated as far as the civil hospital before they were turned back.

"No, the king," said the Dillon officer. "Word just came in at the harbor . . ."

"What, dead?" said Arnaud.

"Deposed," the Dillon officer said. "Quickly, we must find Colonel Cambefort."

There must have been others come with him from the harbor, for the square courtyard of Les Casernes was milling with troops by the time they went outside. Men were shouting confused tidings; the doctor thought he could make out that a mob had stormed Les Tuileries, that the king was divested of all his powers, and some sort of new government had been installed in Paris.

In the midst of the tumult and tossing torchlight, Colonel Cambefort appeared on a high step. He held out his flattened palms and waited for silence; when it came, he snapped a crisp order for all to return to their quarters. Beckoning Major O'Farrel and a couple of others to follow, he turned smartly on his heel and walked inside. Captain Maillart and Baudin surged forward, along with other officers, but the door slapped shut in all their faces.

They reconvened around the card table, but no one had heart to continue the game. Grandmont still sat in the same chair, contemplatively chewing the wet end of his cigar while the other smoldered. Had he risen to follow them out at all? The doctor was not sure of that.

"C'est foutu," Arnaud said, and cracked his cane against a chair

leg. "You see, this decline won't stop before the Jacobins are dictators over us all."

"Sit down," Grandmont said, pulling the cigar from his mouth, as Arnaud whirled in the corners of the room. "It may be that something may yet be done here." He glanced at Captain Maillart, who nodded.

"We must look to Cambefort," the captain said slowly.

"Yes, and to Desparbés." Grandmont blew a smoke ring toward the ceiling.

Among them all there seemed no one who'd willingly meet the doctor's eyes. He scraped back in his chair. "I believe I must be going."

Baudin winked at him then. "*Mais oui,* you've got such a sweet morsel to return to . . ." Lasciviously he kissed his fingers.

The doctor stared, not precisely at him, but directly through a point on the bridge of his nose to a chip on a brick in the wall behind his head, like lining up the two sights of a gun. It was a trick he had learned in the camps. He touched the shard of mirror in his pocket. In a moment, Baudin had dropped his eyes and turned away in some confusion. The doctor drained his glass with an air of carelessness, stood up, bowed, and took his leave.

The streets were full of criers and couriers, and all the *petit blancs* were in a state of high excitement. Another day, the troops would have turned out to drive them back inside their doors, but since the arrival of Sonthonax, the soldiers were kept in barracks and the popular demonstrations continued unrestrained. No sign of a uniform anywhere tonight. The doctor passed by a tavern which had become a meeting place for one of the Jacobin clubs Sonthonax had encouraged among the *petit blancs*. The place was jammed, a mass of jerking heads. Through the orange-lit window he thought he saw some hero raised aloft on a chair. Moved by curiosity, he turned back and went in.

Another night he might have been challenged at the door. As best as he might make mystery of his political sentiments, whatever they were, he could have been denounced as an associate of officers, aristocrats, the *grand blancs* in general. But tonight the mood of elation was too high for him to be noticed at all, and besides he saw no one he knew even by sight, except for the baker, Faustin.

He did not know the man they'd swung aloft in the chair to cheer him. He was a lean black-bearded fellow, hatless, with the red cockade stuck behind one ear. Almost everyone in the common room was also sporting the *pompon rouge;* the doctor rather felt naked without one of his own. But no one seemed to have remarked him or his lack. A barrel of rum turned longways on a high counter flowed from its bunghole while cups or cupped hands were thrust under the stream. The doctor saw one half-shaven enthusiast twisting his face sideways to lap at the overflow like a dog . . .

Liberté! Egalité! Fraternité! There was a massive outcry of these slogans, while from other quarters of the room began a garbled anarchic rendering of *La Marseillaise.* Someone jostled the doctor into the door frame. In an opposite corner he saw the farrier Crozac, grinning and shouting with the others . . . There was a crack as the chair leg snapped, and the black-bearded fellow fell down laughing into the crowd. But not all were so amused. The doctor saw the splintered chair leg rise again, come clubbing down. A fist swung in a semicircle, blood, a grunt and the click of a splintered tooth against the wall. A surge of men rippling out from the focus of the fight pressed the doctor back out the street door.

He thought it better to remain without. He'd broken a sweat while pressed in the crowd; now, in the humid cool of the night, it turned clammy on his cheeks and forehead. He straightened his lapels, and felt under his coat for one of his pair of pistols that he'd concealed in an inner pocket. All seemed in order there. The roar and outcries from the tavern faded behind him as he went on his way toward the Place d'Armes.

GRANDMONT CHEWED AN UNLIT CIGAR, sitting across a bare table from Colonel Cambefort. Captain Maillart was looking absently through the window into the courtyard of Les Casernes, where a couple of cavalrymen were brushing down their horses.

"We can turn out a well-organized militia," Grandmont was saying. "Small numbers, but they'll be properly armed and should acquit themselves well against the disorder of a mob."

Colonel Cambefort pulled at his mustache. "We may count absolutely on the Regiment Le Cap." He glanced at Major O'Farrel. "Dillon and Walsh as well, I should think."

"A gang of Englishmen," Arnaud said distastefully.

"Irishmen, mostly," said O'Farrel. "They'll be true to us—they're good king's men."

"I think we may also rely on the troops of the line who came out with the commissioners," Cambefort said. "Although we must be very cautious in speaking to Monsieur Desparbés."

"Do you doubt his loyalty?" said Grandmont, his mouth turning down toward the weak chin.

"To the king? No," Cambefort said. "So far as his personal sentiments go. But he is aging, and he certainly does not mean to settle here among us. He must consider that one day, and not long hence, he will answer for his actions here in France. As you all know, it has always been *convenient* for the home government to set the military and civil authorities here in competition with each other. According to their documents, the commissioners do have plenipotentiary powers. For Desparbés to defy them openly would be a serious matter."

"Well, he has defied them tacitly," Arnaud said. "He refuses to order the troops out against the brigands . . ."

"To take him beyond that point would require a sudden shock," said Cambefort. "I've sounded him and that's my estimation."

"The shock must come," Grandmont said quietly. "In a military situation, the military commander stands supreme. When it does come, Desparbés will choose the lesser evil and declare for us."

Colonel Cambefort looked out the window. "I think you may be right. Well. Let us consider our strength. With Dillon, and Walsh, and the Regiment Le Cap, we may field fifteen hundred men. As for the new troops . . ."

Captain Maillart returned his attention to the room. "Disease has discriminated neither for nor against us," he said. "So we may use the ordinary numbers. Two thousand troops of the line will certainly follow us—with Desparbés or even perhaps without him. Then there are four thousand National Guards to reckon with."

"Can they be swayed in our favor?" said Cambefort.

Grandmont took the cigar from his mouth and inspected the frayed spittle-soaked end of it. "I'm doubtful of that," he said. "They are all *political* recruits. One can't say for certain which way they'll jump, but we'd be wiser to assume they'll stand by the commissioners."

"Yes, I agree," said Cambefort.

"But they've none of them been long in the field," Arnaud said. "They're ill-disciplined—your regular troops will chew them up."

"We may hope so," said Cambefort. "*Bon ça*, what have we then?"

"Thirty-five hundred regular troops," Grandmont said. "I could promise no more than five hundred militiamen."

"To set against your four thousand National Guards," Arnaud said. "The numbers being equal, superior discipline will carry the day in our favor. Drive the commissioners onto their ships and let *them* account for their conduct in France."

"It's a pleasant notion," Cambefort said. "We have also to consider the entire mass of the *Pompons Rouges*. Not to mention *les citoyens de quatre Avril*—who, whatever else you may say of them, are not to be underestimated in battle."

There was brief silence in the room. In the courtyard, a horse snorted, and a trooper clucked to it and led it away across the cobbles.

"The unity of *those* two factions might not withstand much pressure . . ." Grandmont said, stroking his underslung jaw.

"That's an imponderable, is it not?" Cambefort said. "We have rather too many imponderables. I would we were more certain of Monsier Desparbés."

"How does it stand, then?" asked Arnaud.

"A clear opportunity may present itself but I would say it has not yet done so," said Cambefort. "When it does come, we must not lose it."

THE MORNING OF OCTOBER 17 was cool and foggy. Doctor Hébert walked toward the hospital in a pleasant humor; he was in no hurry, so he stopped to take a second cup of coffee at a tavern that had set out a few wooden tables along the edge of the Place d'Armes. The chairs had been dampened by the mist, and he wiped one down with his handkerchief before he sat down. As he sipped the coffee, his eye was caught by some odd white placards that had been pasted up overnight on the walls of the buildings surrounding the square.

He set down his cup and strolled idly across for a closer look. Each card bore a rough sketch of one or another officer of the royalist regiments, Le Cap, Dillon and Walsh—and all were depicted as hanging in chains. Cambefort and Desparbés had been gleefully included and some of the civilian *grand blancs* were represented as well. For some time, the doctor had been aware that *La Société des Amis de la Convention*, as the Jacobin Club was formally known, had been circulating a list of "traitors to the Republic" whom they hoped the commissioner would deport to France. But this new tactic seemed more violent. The sketches were awkwardly done, but not without a certain verve, and each was plainly recognizable. The doctor was truly brought up short when he saw the caricature of Captain Maillart.

Others had come out to admire this artwork, which they mostly seemed to appreciate and enjoy, pointing and chuckling among themselves. Then there appeared a black-mustachioed officer of the Walsh regiment, who whirled when he noticed the posters, and with an outraged shout began tearing them down from the walls. The brawl broke out so suddenly that the doctor didn't see it start. The Irishman was clubbed to his knees by the mob of *petit blancs*, though he swung his hairy fists at them and swore at them in English. Someone was running up with a noose and there was a call for the officer to be hanged on the spot, but before they could fix the rope to his neck, more soldiers came double-time into the square and seized him back. The two parties broke up in a jumble of individual fistfights or grapples, and someone fired a gun into the air.

Doctor Hébert touched his own pistol grip through his coat, then went back to Nanon's rooms at his best pace short of a run. He collected Fontelle and her children and brought them all in with Nanon. For the rest of the day and on into the night they sat behind closed doors and blinds. The smaller children played dress-up with Nanon's finery, while the doctor engaged Nanon and the older son Moustique in alternate games of chess. Sometimes he'd hush them all, to listen to the shouting that approached or receded in the surrounding streets, and sometimes he'd pace and fidget with his guns. On two occasions there came loud knocking at the door, but he'd allow no one to answer.

In the late afternoon of that day, Arnaud and Grandmont came riding hell for leather into Les Casernes with the news that the *Pompons Rouges* had broken into the arsenal and were arming themselves apace. There was no answer at Cambefort's quarters, but Arnaud soon found Captain Maillart.

"Here's your opportunity," Arnaud spluttered.

"*Where is Colonel Cambefort!*" Grandmont said, sprinting back across the cobbles.

"Gone with Desparbés to the commissioners," Maillart said. "To demand the Jacobin Club be disbanded immediately."

"They'll have to be disbanded with grapeshot now," said Grandmont. "Who's in authority here? We can lose no more time."

Before the captain could answer them, they heard hooves beating over the stones of the court and Colonel Cambefort rode in astride a splendid gray stallion. All three of them clustered at his stirrup.

"What news?" said Captain Maillart.

"The Jacobins were there before us." Cambefort's face was drawn and weary, but his eyes had an excited gleam. "They've asked for my deportation and that of Desparbés."

"And the answer?" said Grandmont.

"None given," said Cambefort.

"But where is Desparbés?" Arnaud said.

"He has broken with the commissioners and is ordering out the troops even now."

"Well, God be thanked," Arnaud cried out.

The Dillon and Walsh regiments were already falling out into the courtyard with their weapons in hand. General Desparbés appeared on the high step of the general officers' quarters. He was stooped with the seventy-three years of his age and seemed to need to hold the door frame for support. Cambefort rode across toward him, the others following on foot.

"The National Guards do not obey the order . . ." Desparbés voice was shaking slightly. His eyes were rheumy. Captain Maillart veered away before he could catch Cambefort's response, rushing toward the barracks where the National Guards were quartered. Someone called after him but he paid no mind. Grandmont was striding along a pace or two behind him.

As they clattered up the steps, Lieutenant-Colonel Etienne Laveaux appeared in the doorway. He smiled down at Maillart (for these two liked each other well enough despite the difference of their politics) but at the same time pressed his palm against the opposite door jamb and stiffened his arm to bar the captain's passage. Maillart stopped on the top step and peered into the dim interior hall, where another officer was lecturing the republican troops.

"Why, will you shoot your brothers only to satisfy the barbarous humor of a handful of aristocrats who only wish to destroy the human race . . . ?"

Grandmont twisted his face aside and spat on the cobbles through his crooked teeth. Laveaux's eyes were grave and sad above the fixed contortion of his smile. Captain Maillart backed down the steps and walked away. Cambefort had dismounted and now stood alongside Desparbés, gesticulating as he argued with his superior, while Arnaud, standing by, was unconsciously mangling his hat in his hands. But before the captain had reached them, Desparbés thrust Cambefort aside and drew himself erect. In a loud, clear, and almost perfectly steady voice, he gave the order for the troops of the line to disassemble and return to their quarters.

On the following day, Sonthonax went with Polverel to address the public in the Place d'Armes; this public included a sizable civilian mass, *Pompons Rouges*, a few *grand blancs*, some *citoyens de quatre Avril*. Both the royalist troops and the National Guards were out in force, ranked at opposite ends of the square. Sonthonax's face was waxen and stippled with little beads of sweat. The speech was very brief for him, and strikingly unornamental. He told the assembly that Desparbés and Cambefort had been placed under arrest and would soon be deported. He pleaded for calm and asked the people to disperse.

After perhaps two minutes of frosty silence, the two bodies of troops began to file out of opposite corners of the square. The commissioners then disappeared from the scene with a noteworthy precipitousness. Captain Maillart, numb and exhausted, walked in his place behind Lieutenant Baudin, scarcely attending the gangs of *petit blancs* who ran alongside catcalling at them. A man in a soiled bricklayer's apron was paying peculiar attentions to Baudin, who suddenly wheeled and spat in his face.

"Scum of the earth," Baudin began, and was just drawing breath to continue when the bricklayer took out a pistol and shot him in the mouth.

His cavalry sword was in the captain's hand, and he stabbed the bricklayer through the belly without a thought, not even knowing he had done it until he saw the dark blood welling over the hilt onto his hand. As the bricklayer fell sideways, his twisting weight broke the sword from the captain's hand. The skirmishing was general all around them now, but most of the troops had already left the square. Then Laveaux came riding through, controlling his horse with his knees alone. He was calling out for peace and calling the names of the men he knew and reaching out with both hands to touch them gently as a priest. Both soldiers and civilians allowed themselves to be so manipulated and the fight was over before it had well begun.

Laveaux's warm palm settled on the captain's brow. When he removed it, Maillart began unconsciously to weep. Half blinded, he went staggering away from the square.

IT HAD BEEN JUST OVER TWENTY-FOUR HOURS since the disturbances had begun. Doctor Hébert answered the door with a pistol in his fist. Through the crack he could just see a bloodstreaked hand and a uniform cuff. He grabbed the wrist and twisted it and jerked the man inside, pressing his face against the door and jamming the pistol into the hollow at the back of his neck.

"Christ, man, don't you know me?" Captain Maillart said. The doctor relaxed his grip. Nanon had come up to pull him away, while the children all watched round-eyed from the corners of the room.

"I'm sorry," the doctor muttered. He laid the pistol carelessly on the chessboard. "We've been . . . a trifle anxious."

"So it would seem."

"What's happened?" said the doctor.

Maillart wiped at his bloodshot eyes. "We're done for in this country. Cambefort and Desparbés will be deported—with *all* the senior officers loyal to the king."

"But not you," the doctor said.

"Not yet," the captain said. "Perhaps I'll find a passage to Martinique, or else . . . They've murdered Lieutenant Baudin, you know. And I was very fond of that fellow."

The doctor picked up the pistol and returned it to the box on the high shelf. In the back room, the children had resumed their game; there was a rustle as a stiff silk dress slipped down from a hanger.

"It's true, there was no harm in him," the doctor said. "I'm sorry."

He circled a chair and sat down in it. After a moment, the captain followed suit. Nanon came out from the back with a basin of water and clean cloth. She knelt down at the captain's side and began to sponge the blood marks from his hand.

Chapter Twenty-Seven

After what happened at Saint Michel, and later at Le Cap, when we took the prisoners there, and when we passed Bréda on our way back to Grande Rivière, there was not much I wanted to do anymore except to kill whitemen. It was not Ogûn wanting to kill them as it had been before, but it was I, Riau, who wanted this thing for myself. With all our people there was anger and a hunger for blood, because we had let the white prisoners go for nothing and because the *colons* had tricked us again.

In this time we did kill many more of them. In this time, the way of our killing whitemen changed. Toussaint did not call himself a general yet, but he did not anymore call himself *médecin*. His old green coat was gone, but he had not then put on the coat of a whiteman officer. He would only whisper into the ear of Biassou, and other men, the younger ones he was teaching now, Moise and Dessalines and Riau and Charles Belair. Riau would be in the tent for talking and writing with these black men, because there were no whitemen anymore among us, no prisoners to be used for writing or planning. When writing was to be done, Riau would do it, or Charles Belair. But most of this time we did not write anything but only talked about the ways that were good for killing whitemen.

Jean-François did not like to hear the voice of Toussaint anymore in these days. He mistrusted him and was afraid, because he saw that Toussaint was sly, like a tricky spider of Guinée—the fly will not know he has touched his web until he is rolled up in it. And the spider only comes when he is ready. Jean-François had even moved his camp away from our camp. But when it was time for fighting,

Jean-François and his men went with us. They were all ready to kill whitemen, and our new way for that worked well.

In the first beginning time after Boukman danced and the fire was struck and the blood was running, we used to fight like we were dancing *petro*. It would be a big crowd screaming and beating drums and blowing conchs, most ridden by the *loa*, or else half in our heads half out. We were many, and with *les Invisibles* at our backs, and maybe we would kill all the whitemen, or if they killed us instead we would only be going to join *les Morts et les Mystères* in the Island Below Sea, where is our home, Guinée. But now Toussaint was teaching this new way, because he did not want us to go to be with the dead any longer.

The whitemen had made strong places in the mountains of the east which were between us and the plain of Fort Dauphin. Many of these whitemen were old Creole *colons* who knew the hills, and there were too the soldiers of France with them, and also *gens de couleur*, Candi's men who had changed their side, and all good fighters. But now the rains were heavy, and in the mountains it was cold at night. These whitemen were wet in their wool clothes, and they were beginning to sicken there. They had been holding these mountain places a long time.

When we moved into the mountains of the east, we did it slowly and not many at one time. I, Riau, and a few others went in front along with some of Toussaint's band while the crowds of men belonging to Jean-François and Biassou came after us, in cover of the jungle. If we saw a few whitemen scouting or hunting away from their camps, then we would kill them all, but if they were many, we did not show ourselves at all. All this time when we were moving and watching, you would not know anyone was there at all except for the silence of the birds.

We had a game we liked to play, I and Chacha Godard and Jean-Jacques Dessalines. I did not like Chacha any more than Toussaint trusted him. He was not with us in the tent. And I knew what Biasssou meant for Chacha in the end. Still I saw that he would be a tricky spider in the dark. At night we went to a whiteman camp that was backed into some rocks. One side of it was fenced around with logs of wood that we could not come over, and there were sentries there. But we climbed around over the rocks and came down the cliff face on the strangler vines that hung down over it, slipping very quietly down the vines, with our knives held in our teeth. These were little knives and very sharp, much sharper and smaller than the big *coutelas* they use in the cane fields. We did not bring any guns at all for this game.

It was raining a little as we came down these vines, but very thinly, and sometimes the cloud would blow away from the moon, to make a little light. I saw the moon shine on Chacha Godard's wet shoulders as he came down. We were naked all three of us except for our testicles bound up, and oiled like the warriors of Guinée.

The moon rode behind the cloud and it was dark again. I did not hear Dessalines come down behind me, but I felt that he was there. At one end of the camp was a small smudgy fire under a canvas, but it did not give much light. I could only see Chacha going over the rocks low like a crab toward a place where there was snoring to be heard. A minute later, the snoring stopped. By then I had crawled under an *ajoupa* where two whitemen were sleeping, and there I cut the throats of both. All this time there was no sound from anywhere except for sizzling when water ran off that canvas piece to drip into the fire.

When we came to the place where our camp was, we looked to see how many ears we had brought away each. Chacha had more, I had the same as Dessalines. But Dessalines traded us his share of *tafia* for our ears that we had taken. With a thread he sewed them altogether as a white *pompon* which he wore on his hat to show that he was for the King In France.

Toussaint did not like it though. Toussaint did not say a word when he saw this cockade of ears by daylight. He swung his sword and cut the ears loose from Dessalines's hat and kicked them into the fire with his toe. It was a heavy sword and that surprised me, how he could cut the ears clean away without even knocking the hat crooked on the head of Dessalines. That whole time Dessalines stood straight and still like a soldier with a whiteman officer cursing him and his face did not change. No one said a word about it then or later. After this, we still took ears when we went out at night, but we did not show them.

There were others who played this game, besides us three. Sometimes the men from our old band of Achille, César-Ami and Paul Lefu, or sometimes others that I had not known before. So we made the whitemen fear, and we learned to know how all their camps were laid and how nearly we could come to them. The men of Jean-François and Biassou had all come up through the jungle by that time. By night we took our places all around the camps. I was so near the whiteman I had chosen I could hear him breathing through the night, but he knew nothing about me. We waited till first light came up, to have light for the killing. When I could see the slick black trunks of *gommier* and *bois bander*, and water beading on the elephant ears all around, then I saw the hairs of the mustache of my whiteman, and so I shot him with my gun.

Once the shooting started there was not a reason to be quiet and tricky any longer, so we blew conchs and screamed and beat the drums, and then we heard the voices of the *loa*. It was all right to frighten the whitemen then. Most of them were killed then at this camp and many of the others there were killed or chased away. Then the *cordon de l'est* was broken and we came into the eastern plain and burned the plantations there and killed all of the whitemen we could find. We could not come into the town of Fort Dauphin, though, because of many soldiers who were there, and if we had fought them in the open, too many ones of us would have gone to be with the dead.

After this fight was finished up, Biassou took some people to fight the whitemen at Le Cap. Toussaint did not go that time, but some of his men slipped away, and so did I, Riau, because I was still hot for the death of more whitemen. Along the way we gathered some men of Pierrot and Macaya who were camped on the northern plain or in the hills outside the city, but still there were not so many as we had been on that plain by Fort Dauphin.

But the walls on the landcoming side were not so strong at Le Cap, because these *colons* who first built the town only expected war to come from oversea. We came over the low dirt walls fighting well and we ran all over the hospital of the *Pères de la Charité*, which was there at the edge of the town. That was the place where Biassou had been a slave and there was his mother still a slave, and he had come to take her from this place. It was the only thing he wanted, so when he had taken her he did not want to fight the whitemen anymore.

Then we all stopped the fight and went away. If not for Biassou, maybe we would have killed all the whitemen of Le Cap that time. But then I understood why it was that Toussaint did not go.

Toussaint had made two whitemen prisoners in the fighting around Fort Dauphin, an old whiteman who had been an officer, and one other of the militia too. When I came back from the fighting by Le Cap, I saw how these whitemen were drilling Toussaint's people. The one old whiteman with his gray hairs, and the younger *colon* with his beard growing rough, were marching our people up and down. Moise and Dessalines and Charles Belair were with these whitemen, calling out commands like *halt* and *about face* and *quick march*. There was Moise, whose skin was black and shiny like a wet tree trunk, dressed in nothing but a dirty pair of cotton trousers hanging in rags around his knees. He had not even any shoes, but he was wearing two horns of a hat and shouting orders like a general.

These things all seemed foolish to me, because it was not our way to fight. It was for whitemen to row out in lines or box themselves in squares for shooting. Ours was another way. Also I did not like to see our people moving to these orders that came from the thin cold lips of these whitemen.

I wanted to stay away from Toussaint then, because when I saw what Moise and the others were doing, I knew that Toussaint would tell me to do the same, doing the words of the whiteman officers. I went to the *ajoupa* I had made and played with Caco and that night I lay with Merbillay. It was next day Toussaint came. We had already eaten in the morning and I was playing on the *banza*, sitting outside the *ajoupa* while Caco walked around smiling and shaking a long pod from a tic-tic tree I had picked for him to have for a rattle.

Toussaint was standing over me so that he was between me and the sun. He told me that I must go and learn the whiteman way of soldier with the others, as I had been knowing he would say. I could hear them already this morning, below in the clearing, the officers all barking like some *casques* outside a cowpen and the drum of men's feet moving on the ground. There were seven or eight hundred men to fight with our band then—that was before Laveaux attacked us.

I could not tell Toussaint no or yes. I made the guts of the *agouti* cry under my fingers and I hit the drum of the *banza* with my hand. I was thinking how it might feel, if I did what he asked. I had not followed the say of any whiteman since I had fourteen years and ran away from Bréda. I thought of how Toussaint had taken the doctor and the priest and other whitemen into the tent at Grande Rivière and left us out, and how they would have sold us again to the *colons*, and I thought too of how he had taken my bayonet to kill this one whiteman at Haut du Cap who had once beaten him long ago. There was one thing I wanted to know of him but I did not know what I would ask before I heard my mouth start speaking.

"Tell me about Béager."

Toussaint laughed. He must have been surprised. He did not often show his teeth in laughter, though he did smile behind his hand, and sometimes he would grin at you.

"What do you want to know, about Béager?"

"The story that they tell of him and you," I said.

Toussaint squatted down beside me and the sun struck on my face again. Caco had broken the pod open and was spilling beans out of it onto the mud. Toussaint blinked at him. He hunkered with arms wrapped around his knees, all wrinkled up and knotted like old Legba. I knew that if he wanted he could squat so for one hundred years.

Béager was *gérant* of Bréda before Bayon de Libertat. I did not know him because he was gone before they sold me there, but not long gone. Bayon de Libertat was a kinder master, and the slaves of Bréda talked of that sometimes. But Béager had not been cruel like Lejeune or Arnaud, only hot-tempered, hasty and quick to strike in his anger.

"I was young then," Toussaint said, looking at Caco smiling with his pink mouth open over the beans he was pushing in the mud. "I had no wife, but there was more than one woman that I knew." He smiled his usual way, behind his hand, and above the hand the eyes looked at me craftily. "Then I worked mostly with the horses. It was summer, very hot. There was a fine horse, a black gelding with white socks and a white star on his forehead. They named him Treize. Béager took him out riding in the heat of the day. When I saw him come in I thought they must have gone at a gallop all the way to Le Cap and back. It was still hot when he brought him in all foamed up and slobbery. Béager took him to the water trough."

"That's how you kill a horse," I said. "He must have known—what was he thinking?"

"I don't know," Toussaint said. "Sometimes I still wonder. Maybe he thought he had killed the horse already. And you know, Riau, that sometimes a Creole will destroy a thing only to show that he is master of it."

"*Ouais,*" I said. "I know it well."

"I called him to stop," Toussaint said, "to think what he was doing." His eyes were far away, over my shoulder. "He did not listen. I caught the bridle out of his hand. He pushed me out of the way and led the horse nearer the trough. I hit him with my fist before I knew that I would do it—never knew I'd done it till I saw him sitting on the ground."

I laid the *banza* on the ground and breathed out through my teeth. I heard this story times before but never from Toussaint.

"It was all in the open," Toussaint said. "You know where we water the horses at Bréda. There must have been twenty slaves that saw it. No white men, though. Béager got up. He touched his mouth and showed me blood on his fingers. He took a step toward me where I was holding Treize still. The horse was tossing his head because he wanted to go drink the water and die. Then Béager turned around and went into the *grand'case* by himself."

I, Riau, I had not believed this story before. It was like stories that you hear of jesus. In that time, before we rose, no slave could strike a whiteman and live afterward, it was unknown.

"What did you do," I said.

Toussaint shrugged and rocked back on his heels with a slow rhythm. "I walked the horse," he said. "Circles and circles, on into the night, till he was cool again. All that time I knew I was a dead man. I was walking like a *zombi*, Riau, do you know how it feels?"

"*Ouais,*" I said. "I know it."

"Béager never came out of the house," Toussaint said. "The horse was saved though. It was five days before I saw Béager again. He never spoke of it or of the horse. We went on as before. Maybe he thought that a good horse was worth more than a nigger after all. I won't ever know what he was thinking. I was walking like a dead man for five days."

Toussaint stood up then, and his shadow fell across me.

"Who knows, Riau," he said, "do you? Maybe I have been dead all the years since then, only I don't know it." He grinned at me then, and went away without saying anything more.

So I did not go to train with the soldiers that day or the next. But in some days that followed I saw that of all those I had fought with around Fort Dauphin, the only other one who did not go was Chacha Godard.

After I began training with the others, Toussaint made me a lieutenant, like he did Moise and Dessalines and Charles Belair. Lieutenant Riau. Now when I met Paul Lefu or César-Ami while they must stand very straight and throw me a salute, though it was hard for them to do it without laughing. And sometimes I must laugh myself at this Lieutenant Riau. But not where anyone could hear my laughing.

There were good things about this way of training, I soon saw, beyond the foolishness of lines and squares. It made that each man would know to keep his musket clean and ready to fire. Each man would always have his musket and his bayonet, good weapons that had come from the Spanish whitemen, and each man would wear two leather belts across his shoulders with two cartridge boxes always full. Every man would always know to have these things all of the time, even if he had no shirt or shoes, and most did not.

Also we could make many men move as quickly as one man and all together. And any one man or any few would do what they were told to do, that moment they were told it and no question—as slaves do. But it was good to know these things when fighting came. And it was good that we had learned it, because it was not long after that Laveaux came out from Le Cap to fight us with new soldiers.

These were new soldiers who had come oversea from France, they had not long been in the country so they were not yet sick. They were not like the old soldiers of Blanchelande or the militiamen, we could not scare them so easily, and when we spread away in the jungle, they would still come after us very fast. There were thousands of them too. It was not long before they had broken up most of the men of Jean-François and Biassou and made them run away.

All we who were with Toussaint were left to hold the hill called Morne Pélé, which was keeping the whitemen out of our camps at Dondon and Grande Rivière. Toussaint knew we could not win this fight, I think. We were hundreds, but there were four thousand soldiers coming. Toussaint was meaning to make time for Biassou and Jean-François to get their men away into the mountains. This was a new thinking which came from him talking to the whiteman officers. But he did not tell us that we could not win the fight at Morne Pélé.

At Morne Pélé we began on the high ground and we killed very many whitemen with our guns while they were coming up the hill. But they were many and they did not stop charging and at the last we could not keep them from coming among us with their swords and bayonets. I saw Toussant fighting a whiteman officer face to face with a sword. It was the Chevalier d'Assas, we found out later, and he gave Toussaint a big cut on his arm, but neither one of them died from this fight.

We were chased back to the fort that Toussaint had made us build at La Tannerie. But next day we attacked them again on the top of Morne Pélé. Toussaint wore his arm in a sling, all bandaged with the herbs he knew to use. All the other men he had tended through the night went to this fight behind him, all the wounded who could walk and use a hand. We surprised the whitemen just at dawn on the top of Morne Pélé, and drove them down the hill again to the place that they had started from, but still they would not give it up.

They were very tough then, these soldiers of d'Assas and Laveaux. All this second day they kept on charging up the hill. In the afternoon, they broke us once, but Dessalines caught the horse of some whiteman officer who was killed and rode it down on them, alone at first, calling the others to follow which they did, even I, Riau, charging with the bayonet, and only I not Ogûn in my head to lead me. Dessalines was young then, a tall man, red-skinned like a coal in a fire, and he wore no shirt or coat that day. We could see the tangle of white scars of old whippings all across his back, because he had a bad master when he was a slave.

That day Dessalines was hurt in the foot, but not so that he could not fight. We held the whitemen one time more, but we had many killed, and when they charged again we could not hold and so they chased us back and we had again to run to our fort of La Tannerie.

Toussaint thought then we could not hold La Tannerie either. I know he was sorry to leave this place, and I too, for all the work of building. I saw men crying to give up this fight, still they had not known they could not win it. But we had many dead, almost two hundred, and Toussaint said that we must go. In the night he sent out men ahead to drag the cannons we had there at La Tannerie, and all through the hours before dawn we began to slip out of the fort to the place in the Cibao mountains to the east where Toussaint had sent our women and children a few days before.

By morning, we were all gone out of La Tannerie. Only I, Riau, and Chacha Godard stayed there, hiding in the tops of trees outside the fort, so we could see these soldiers and know what was their strength. When the sun was well up, columns of soldiers began to come out of the jungle, very carefully at first, with their guns ready, but soon there was shouting all back down the line when they found the place was empty.

Then the officers came up, Laveaux and the Chevalier d'Assas. They walked up and down under the tree that I had climbed to hide, and I could hear all that they said. Laveaux was carrying a little riding crop and he pointed this at all the things Toussaint had made us build—the deep ditch full of water we had run in from a stream, the palisade of logs with their sharp points sticking out behind this ditch, the gates all covered with copper plates to keep out the cannon balls.

On the far side of the ditch, where my tree was, there was clear ground, and not far from the trees, Toussaint had told us to drive some stakes, so that the musket men would know their range. When whitemen came as far as the stakes, that would be the time to shoot them, but we never got to try it at La Tannerie. Laveaux flicked his crop against one of the stakes and frowned and then he pointed the crop at one of the places in the palisade we made for the cannons to look out.

"*Vous voyez ça,*" he said to d'Assas.

"What of it?"

"Gun embrasures," said Laveaux.

"But these niggers have no cannon," d'Assas said.

"I think they do," Laveaux said. "I think they have them still, wherever they have gone. What manner of men are these?"

"There must have been thousands of them here," d'Assas said. In my tree, I could have laughed to hear that, but they would have caught me.

"Whatever they are, they are not savages," said Laveaux. D'Assas pulled his mustache and did not answer him.

All that day Chacha and I hung in those trees, watching the soldiers make camp at La Tannerie. I had not known they were so many. I could not believe we had been fighting so many for two days. When night had come, Chacha wanted to cut throats and take ears before we went away, but I wanted to get off from that place alive, and I brought Chacha with me. A few ears taken would not have frightened these soldiers out of our place anyway.

So we came into the Cibao mountains, near the Spanish border, or across it maybe—who could know in that place. In the mountains it was cold and raining almost all the time because the heads of the mountains stuck up into the clouds. We had our women and our children though, more than Biassou and Jean-François had theirs. Their men were in big camps not far from us, but they had run so fast away they left their women and children behind, and many of them who were left so gave themselves up to the whitemen and were slaves again.

There were then six hundred men of Toussaint's band who were not killed. We did not know what we would do. It was all hunting and looking for food, and taking care of the ones who were hurt in all the fighting.

I made a tight *ajoupa* to keep the rain off Riau and Merbillay and Caco. I had brought my *banza* with me from the other camps, with my pistols and my musket and my cartridges. I sat under the roof watching the rain while I played the *banza*.

One day I was sitting in the *ajoupa* and Toussaint came and asked for me to play something for him. I was surprised, but I picked up the *banza* and did what he asked. I had not thought he cared anything about a *banza*. At Bréda, he would never go to any kind of dancing, or if he did go he would not dance. But I played a slow sad song for him because I was thinking of the ones who had been killed while we were fighting all the time. Paul Lefu had been killed there at Morne Pélé and I had been the friend of Paul Lefu.

When I stopped playing, there was no sound but the rain coming down on the leaves of the *ajoupa*. Toussaint was looking out into the rain. Then he looked at me with a queer smile.

"Have you heard the violin, Riau?" he said. I did not answer him but still he said, "When we are in the government house at Le Cap, then we will hear violins and golden horns."

He sat by me for some while more before he got up and walked away into all the rain that kept leaking down from the high trees that shut out the sky. It seemed strange to me then, what he had said, but later I thought he must have always known that we would go there one day, where he said that we would go.

Chapter Twenty-Eight

DOCTOR HÉBERT WAS IN SOME ANCIENT MOUNTAIN FORT, alone and unattended except for his wife and child. The place was under attack, it seemed, with men wearing chain mail and curious antique helmets charging the gate with a battering ram, the shock sounding a throaty bass note, repeated at a slow interval. The baby was crying, somewhere out of view, and the doctor looked about himself for help or some means of defense. There was only a rusty medieval pike, leaning against the huge rough-cut stones of the wall. As he reached for it, he overbalanced and was falling—then came to himself sprawled over the floor beside the bed, tangled in a snarl of mosquito netting. Insects thirsty for his blood had clustered on the netting and he had evidently crushed a good number of them in falling out of bed; there were a good many small bloody smudges on the pale planks of the floor. The knock at the door repeated itself, but with no more than ordinary force.

It was still daylight, though dim from rain, and he had dropped asleep without intending to. He sat up on the floor and pried the piece of mirror from his pocket. In the cupped palm of his hand his one eye hung suspended as within a pool. He closed his fingers over it, put it into his pocket again. Sweat was running in the hollow of his throat. The knocking, which had ceased, commenced again.

He cleared the net from his legs, bunched it and tossed it on the bed, then walked to the door and opened it a crack. Since the deportation of Desparbés and Cambefort there had been fewer open disturbances in the town, and the *petit blancs* were again kept mostly in check by the troops the commissioners had brought, along with two thousand other soldiers under the command of Rochambeau, who'd lately been denied a landing at royalist Martinique. These things being so, the doctor no longer felt compelled to answer the door with a weapon actually in hand.

A blurry identification of the uniform of the Regiment Le Cap moved him to pull the door open wide. But it was not Maillart who entered. The face above the uniform collar was pale, but swirled with chocolate freckles. The doctor stepped aside to let him pass, remaining near enough to the door that he might easily have reached the rifled long gun down from its pegs above the lintel. He had come to know Choufleur by sight and by his sobriquet, though he had never spoken with him. Choufleur was not a usual caller here, and the doctor thought that Nanon seemed ill at ease when speaking of him, that she avoided the topic when she could and even tried to keep the two of them apart.

But Choufleur was not attending to him now. No more than if the doctor had been Nanon's footman at the door. He walked over the rugs in the center of the room, silver spurs jingling at the heels of his military boots, looking superciliously at the pieces scattered over the chessboard, then at some bibelots arranged upon a cabinet shelf. With a suppressed chuckle he picked up a small silver snuffbox and turned toward the doctor.

"Do you take snuff?"

The doctor shook his head blearily. "Nor would I recommend its use to anyone," he said. "It fouls the nasal passages and conduces to catarrh."

Choufleur snorted and set the snuffbox down, unopened, on the high shelf beside the pistol case. He resumed his idle circuit of the room, twirling a slender gold-pommeled cane, its tip describing loops an inch or two above the carpets. The doctor hid a yawn behind his hand. In the heat of the day he had broken off his medical rounds and returned here to rest for an hour, but he had not intended to sleep so heavily as he seemed to have done. It was later than he'd thought. He was enough confused to imagine that he might still be dreaming.

"Was it me you wished to see?" he asked.

Choufleur turned and glanced at him dismissively. "I came for the lady," he said in an easy tone.

"I believe she has stepped out," the doctor said. He stooped slightly to peer out the window.

Outside, a mass of purple cloud was beginning to be pierced by a few shafts of evening sun. The rain had momentarily stopped, but it was very close and humid in the room, and he was still sweating from his nightmare. Barefoot, he padded to a stand and poured some water from a pitcher into his hand, then dabbed it at his temples. He had mostly undressed before lying down, and now wore only a pair of loose trousers and a blousy white shirt, untucked.

"You are much at home here," Choufleur observed.

"You caught me asleep," the doctor said simply.

Choufleur kept looking at him, but he did not elaborate. The mulatto turned and moved past the pallet where the girl Paulette lay sleeping, toward the cradle. Doctor Hébert took note again of the uniform he wore and wondered what it might portend. Of recent weeks, Sonthonax had been raising more and more mulattoes to posts of importance in the military and the civil government. The commissioner's speeches inveighed more and more heatedly against race prejudice; in turning against the local Jacobins, he had denounced them all as *"aristocrates de la peau."* The doctor knew from Captain Maillart that these developments, especially the military promotions, were causing a rise of tension in the Regiment Le Cap.

Choufleur shifted the mosquito net from the crib on the point of his cane. The doctor moved up on him quickly and quietly, standing just behind his shoulder. The child was sleeping quietly enough.

"What pains she takes," Choufleur murmured, his tone half mocking, half wistful.

The baby clicked his tongue in sleep, and made a nursing movement with his loose lips. His hair was dark and straight and fine; his skin indistinguishable from white. Of course there were the fingernails, as Madame Cigny had explained. A mosquito lowered whining from the ceiling, toward where the netting gapped above the child's head. The doctor crushed it with a one-handed clench; his fingers made a smacking sound against his damp palm. He stooped to detach the net from Choufleur's cane tip and replaced it over the crib. When he straightened, Choufleur was looking at him with a sardonic twist to his lips.

"Yes, I think he does resemble you," he said, as though he had been considering the point for some time and only now had come to his conclusion. "What do you say?"

The doctor stroked his spade-shaped beard. "On the day he was born he most resembled his great-grandfather," he said. "Since then I believe he has come to take after the mother's side a little more." He waited for Choufleur to sort through the implications of this remark.

"You are a strange man," Choufleur said.

"People are always telling me so," said the doctor. "I confess that I do not find myself so remarkable."

"One insults you, but you are not insulted," said Choufleur. "A *grand blanc* would have called me out, perhaps."

"A *grand blanc* would not have lowered himself to duel with a mulatto," the doctor said, raising his chin slightly so that his beard's point seemed to jut, "but would more likely have arranged for you to be hung from some lamppost, I imagine."

Choufleur's lips tightened for a moment under the cloud of his freckles. The doctor saw that the colors had not mixed in him, but remained particulate, at odds with each other all across his face. The mouth opened and Choufleur laughed.

"I will not be insulted either," he said. "I will be equal with you. But it is strange—that you should keep the company of a man like Michel Arnaud, or officers of the *ancien régime* like your Captain Maillart, and all the while live openly with a *femme de couleur*."

"Consider that I am a friend of the world," the doctor said. "I see by your uniform that you and Captain Maillart are become comrades in arms."

"Oh, but you are mistaken there," Choufleur said. "The Regiment Le Cap refuses to receive me or acknowledge my commission. Their suggestion is that I be posted to the Sixth—with the other mulattoes, you understand." With quick clicking steps, he walked to the door. "But I will have my place there in the end . . . if the Regiment Le Cap continues to exist."

The doctor looked at him where he stood framed in the open door, rain-gray daylight behind him. "Shall I tell Nanon that you called for her?"

"You needn't trouble," Choufleur said. "No doubt I'll find her at home some other day."

He went out, slapping the door behind him. The doctor opened his hand, brushed away a mosquito leg. The blood was browning in the creases of his palm—he wondered what mixture it might be, and smiled to think it hardly mattered.

He turned back toward the crib. No doubt the baby had not cried at all; that part had been only dream. He yawned. The visit had unsettled him, and yet he would have liked to detain Choufleur, and ask him a few more questions. Nanon was always uncomfortable in speaking of their acquaintance, would only say that they had been born on the same plantation, near Acul, and had known each other as children, before she came to Le Cap and he was sent to Europe to commence another sort of education. The doctor knew that women in Nanon's position would often keep a lover of their own color—quite unbeknownst to their *grand blanc* whoremasters, as a rule. But if there were rivalry, he still might be counted the winner, thus far—after all, the child was his.

CAPTAIN MAILLART WAS HAVING SOME DIFFICULTY concentrating his mind, for the meeting room of the Regiment Le Cap officers' quarters was a welter of confusion, with all the young men talking at once. There was chaos too in the court of Les Casernes. Through the windows he could see enlisted men milling about in a state of excitement. Some members of the suppressed Jacobin club had arrived with a handcart and were distributing copies of what purported to a proclamation of the French National Assembly, making it illegal for colored officers to command white troops in the colonies. Within the room, the arguments carried on unmoderated.

"Look at that rabble—and the troops are listening to them! When they ought to be clubbing them down with their musket butts—"

"But what if the proclamation is true?"

"Of course it is an arrant fabrication!"

"Don't be so sure, and if it is not true, it ought to be."

"Gentlemen," said Captain Maillart, "let us have at least some semblance of order." But the hubbub did not abate. So many senior officers had been deported with Cambefort and Desparbés that there was no one clearly in authority in this group.

"Let them listen to it," someone was saying. "Let them believe it. It would be the very thing we need to rid us of the Jacobin dictatorship of this Sonthonax . . ."

"And throw in our lot with that *petit blanc canaille?* It's scarce two months since they were all arming *themselves* to murder us . . ."

"But if they are the enemies of our enemy, after all—"

"This Sonthonax is a slippery fish," said Captain Maillart. "Who knows whose enemy he really is? He raised those *petit blancs* up to be his Jacobin brothers, and now he reviles them as *aristocrates de la peau* . . ."

"Well and it may be that white skin will be our last aristocracy in this place," someone said sarcastically.

"Can't you see through him then?" said another officer. "I'll tell you what he is at bottom—a bloody abolitionist."

There was a brief, surprising silence at that. In the courtyard, disbanded members of the Jacobin Club were still crying the "news" of the National Assembly.

"If Desparbés had not lost his nerve," someone said in a lower tone, "we might have done it in September. And if *we* do not lose our nerve, we may yet do it now."

It continued quiet in the small square room, with the men all looking at each other tensely. There were fifteen or sixteen of them there, and scarce a one over twenty-five years of age.

"We have again the National Guards to reckon with," said Captain Maillart. "The mulattoes of the Sixth . . ."

Someone leaned over and spat conspicuously on the floor. Captain Maillart raised his voice just slightly.

"These *petit blancs* are not to be relied on, even if our interests have momentarily coincided. Then there are the two thousand troops who arrived with Rochambeau, which I predict will remain loyal to the Commission . . ."

"What are you saying, Maillart?" someone said. "Whose side are you on?"

Captain Maillart turned his hands palm out, an unconscious mimicry of Cambefort's signal for calm.

"Well, and if we'd only denied the commissioners a landing as they denied Rochambeau at Martinique, we'd be in a better situation now . . ." someone said.

"Here's to that," said Captain Maillart. "I am for the king, as I always was."

Quiet again. "*Vive le roi,*" someone said, but the phrase fell flat in the still room, less like a cheer than a prayer of unbelief.

Some change transpired in the quality of the disturbances in the court, and Maillart looked out the window to see that Laveaux had dismounted from a horse, tossing his reins to a trooper to hold, and was striding across toward the building where they were gathered. Soon he'd passed within the portal, in a moment he'd be in the room.

"Oho," someone said. "So they did call him back."

Laveaux had entered, or almost; he stood handsomely within the door frame. His air was almost diffident, for although he had been promoted to full colonel following the September riot, he did not like to presume on his rank in any less than formal situations. Once again the room had fallen silent.

"May I come in?" Laveaux said.

There was a murmur, and someone pulled out a chair for him. Laveaux sat down. He looked from face to face, but most eyes turned away from him, though he was well liked by almost all of them, partly because he shared their youth.

"Let us come quickly to the point then," Laveaux said. "There are rumors of insubordination, mutiny even. I hope to discover them all false."

No answer.

"Monsieur Sonthonax has been greatly concerned—" Laveaux began.

"Monsieur Sonthonax has set himself up as a despot here, since Ailhaud ran away to France and Polverel went to Port-au-Prince. There is no Commission here, it is government by caprice. The faintest whisper of dissent and you are deported to France on the instant. Or even if you do not whisper, it is enough that your name appear on the black list of that infamous Jacobin Club to find yourself sailing for the guillotine—"

"But Sonthonax has suppressed the Jacobin Club—" Laveaux said.

"Oh, be sure that your Sonthonax is a straw to twist in whatever wind blows strongest—"

"Enough," Laveaux said. "It is not his conduct we are to discuss, but your own. You will not acknowledge the commission of *le citoyen Maltrot*—"

"—who not ten weeks gone was calling himself *le Sieur Maltrot*—"

"—jumped-up nigger, that Choufleur—"

"*Je vous en prie!*" Laveaux said. "Whatever he may have been, he is now a citizen of the French Republic for better or worse—as are we all. And he is only one man. All the other regiments have accepted a single colored officer—"

"Will you say it is only a token? That's what they claimed about the law of May 15—a mere four hundred votes for the mulattoes. Now they are all enfranchised and set over us to boot, Sonthonax takes them into the government, they supersede the Colonial Assembly—"

"Peace," Laveaux said. "Let us keep to the point. Would you throw everything over for this one man? Can you doubt the capabilities of *les gens de couleur?* They have proved themselves in the field time and again."

"They have proved a facility for drawing out eyeballs with corkscrews, you mean —"

"The mulattoes are very well in the Sixth. And the Regiment Le Cap is very well without them."

Laveaux sighed and looked at the tabletop. Maillart studied him—his face was drawn with weariness, and his laced fingers strained against each other slightly.

"Consider this," Laveaux said in a low voice. "Our first mission is to suppress the slave insurrection, as I think you'll all agree—and even with Commissioner Sonthonax, on this one point. Our campaign against the rebels was going famously well—until I was recalled to deal with disturbances here. The threat of these disturbances means we cannot field the troops we need to put down the insurrection once for all, and this has been true for a long time, as I think you understand. And soon enough we will be at war with Spain, most likely England as well. If these troubles find us quarreling among ourselves, we may very probably be destroyed altogether."

"Colonel," Maillart said, "so far as you are concerned, yourself, we all of us would follow wherever you might lead."

Around the room there ran a murmur of assent, but someone spoke more bitterly.

"After all, are you not *le comte de Laveaux?*"

"It's true that I originate from the *noblesse de l'epée,*" Laveaux said. "Exactly as you have it. But my first loyalty is to the nation." He looked at Maillart. "If you truly mean what you just said, then I believe that all of you will find your duty clear."

With that, Laveaux stood up and left the room. When he had gone, one of the junior officers cleared his throat as if to speak but found no words. Maillart remained in his seat, staring out the window, while the others scraped back their chairs and gradually dissipated from the room. His head hummed with unconcluded arguments, and he had small doubt that the others were in much the same condition.

NEXT MORNING, the morning of December 2, the command came down the line for the Regiment Le Cap to assemble on the Champ de Mars. At first no one misdoubted the order. The men fell out, carrying their weapons but all unloaded—it was only a dress parade. Captain Maillart was startled at first by the numbers of civilians who lined their way as they marched out the barrack gate and onto the big parade ground. He'd seen many of the same faces screaming abuse at him and his fellows when the riots broke out in September, but now the men who wore the *pompon rouge* were presenting themselves as allies of a kind . . . not that he much trusted them.

The morning was gray, misty and cool, though the rain had stopped. A mist gathered on the captain's forehead, and he felt the cold sweat start from under his arms as he moved through the cool humid air. Tramping into the Champ de Mars, they found the mulattoes of the Sixth already waiting for them, standing at attention, muskets dressed crossways across the breast. Maillart was relieved to see that these men too had fallen out without their ammunition boxes. And yet a little thrill coursed up his spine.

"Curse his arrogance," someone said behind him, in a voice loud enough to carry across the field. "He has no right to wear that uniform."

Captain Maillart looked over and saw Choufleur, a little apart from the lines of the Sixth, still arrayed in the uniform of the Regiment Le Cap. Sonthonax, his commissioner's medallion shining over his navel, stood near to him, along with Laveaux. From the crowd of civilians that lined all four sides of the field, a high thin voice called out, *"Massacre!"*

The captain could not make out who had raised the call. The Regiment Le Cap halted, faced right, and dressed its ranks, facing the Sixth at some fifty yards distance. The men stood down, musket butts resting lightly on the packed earth of the field, a hand curled around each barrel. Laveaux was crying out in a loud voice that the Sixth Regiment was without ammunition also, and that a peaceful assembly was all that anyone intended. Then Sonthonax took a step forward and began to speak. His hands described strange arabesques in the air, and he was all atremble like an excited hunting dog. Captain Maillart could not at first understand what he was saying, distracted and disturbed as he was by his groundless premonition that something much more serious than talk was likely to occur.

A deeper voice called from the mass of *Pompons Rouges*. "The truth, Sonthonax. You mean to abolish slavery! Set the niggers to rule over us all—and all of us know what's in your black heart!"

Sonthonax, his face reddening in his agitation, screamed that the maintainance of the institution of slavery in this colony was his most sacred principle—one he'd die, if need be, to defend. The question of the day was not slavery at all but the rights of *les citoyens du quatre Avril* . . . Captain Maillart's attention drifted once again. His eye rose from Sonthonax's gesticulating figure to the mass of blue-veined cloud that swirled above Morne du Cap. The cloud parted, and a shaft or two of sunlight chiseled through.

"*Massacre!*" the same high voice cried. "Fly—fight! *Sauve qui peut*—Look there, they are bringing cartridges to the Sixth!"

"It's bread, you idiots," Laveaux shouted. "It's only bread."

Maillart turned to the center of the confusion. An aged mulatto was making a way through the civilian crowd toward the lines of the Sixth, bent double under the weight of a man-sized duffel sack. If this was bread, Maillart was thinking, it must be the heaviest bread ever baked.

But some of the *Pompons Rouges* had overpowered the old man and jerked the pack away from him, ignoring Sonthonax's hoarse admonitions. Men of the mulatto Sixth stepped up to protect him. The men around Maillart broke ranks and rushed up into the center of the confusion. The captain could not think how to restrain them or if they ought to be restrained. He let himself be carried forward by the movement, and when the rotten canvas of the duffel ripped from the many hands tugging at it, he saw that there were loaves, indeed, on top, but underneath were many ammunition boxes.

Men of all parties were fumbling over the torn sack and scrabbling for the spilled and scattered ammunition on the ground. By instinct the captain dove for a cartridge box himself and caught it by its strap. The troops of the Regiment Le Cap had spontaneously charged the Sixth and were fighting them with gun butts and fists before they could load, if they had meant to load. Captain Maillart could not tell who had got control of the contraband ammunition. When the first shots began snapping he did not know who had fired. Unconsciously he was passing out cartridges from the small supply he'd recovered to the men nearest him. Then he saw Choufleur, who'd somehow got astride a horse. The freckled mulatto rode low on his horse like a Cossack and he had got the half-full ammunition sack slung across its withers and he was distributing cartridges to the rear ranks of the Sixth, who would have more leisure to employ them. Choufleur straightened in his saddle and called out an order to the front lines to draw back, passing through the ranks of those who stood behind. Captain Maillart saw what would happen and he could not but admit that Laveaux had not overestimated the competence of this one colored officer at least.

He snatched the man nearest him by the back of his collar and threw him headlong on the ground, calling out an order for all to follow suit as he plunged into the dirt himself. The first volley from the Sixth passed clean over their heads and behind them the captain heard a wounded man cry out in outrage and somewhere a horse was screaming. He raised himself on his elbows and saw the first rank of the Sixth kneeling to reload while powder flared from the barrels of the men who stood behind; an instant later came the noise of the volley like a cloth raggedly tearing. Maillart kissed the earth with his teeth. When he heard an answering volley from behind him he could have wept for joy. They must after all have brought up some ammunition from the arsenal at the barracks.

A charge of the Regiment Le Cap passed over him; when it had gone by he got up and reformed his own unit and supervised the distribution of cartridges from an ammunition cart that had been wheeled up. The mulattoes of the Sixth had held off the charge; they were still keeping up a disciplined fire, standing to shoot and kneeling to reload. Still the captain thought that they could not hold long. They would not have much ammunition, and they were now cut off from resupply.

He thought. Some of the *petit blancs* were contributing fire from small arms or hunting guns to the melee, but apart from their participation it was a well-drawn, clear-cut battle, so utterly different from those anarchic encounters in the jungle with the blacks. In this respect, the captain was much reassured. He massed his men and moved them up, stepping over bodies of the fallen. They came to a halt to fire, moved up again. This time it was corpses of the Sixth they walked among. The mulattoes counterattacked, charging the front line of the Regiment Le Cap—a brave ploy, but probably a desperate one; with ammunition low they must elect hand-to-hand fighting if they could.

The Regiment Le Cap stood off the charge. The mulattoes were in retreat again, but keeping good order. Gradually they were being driven from the Champ de Mars and into the broken ground beyond the field, then withdrawing into the cemetery proper, the marshy ground of La Fossette.

The low ground of the cemetery was virtually a swamp at this time of year, and the men slipped and slithered and fell as they tried to charge across it. Captain Maillart was staggering over the bones of those many comrades of his who'd died of fever in this place . . . Every movement brought clouds of stinging mosquitoes out of the stagnant pools to persecute them. Surely they ought to have annihilated the mulattoes by now, the captain thought, and would have too, had it not been for the calm and courage of their officers, for the colored men were now outnumbered and outgunned. But the momentum of the white troops had bogged down in the cemetery swamp. The mulattoes had gained higher ground on the other side, and were holding it well. Captain Maillart saw Choufleur, still on horseback, directing fire, and thought how useful it would be to bring him down. He recharged his big dragoon's pistol and carefully sighted on the freckled face, but when he fired there was no effect. He reloaded and took aim again, holding the heavy gun with two hands, but held his fire.

The range was possibly too great. And Choufleur himself was pulling back, suddenly—with about half the remaining men of the Sixth as well. The pistol swung down in Captain Maillart's numbing hands, bounced off his thigh and bruised it. A trapdoor slammed in the back of his throat; for a second he thought he'd actually vomit. There was nothing he or anyone could do but watch, while Choufleur's part swept over the thinly manned earthworks that defended the town from landward attack.

Now the men of the Regiment Le Cap had fought their way off the marshy ground and were breaking the skirmish line of the Sixth that had been left to hold them off—but it was too late. The mulattoes controlled the earthworks now—and there'd be ammunition aplenty there. The Regiment Le Cap was charging once again but now it was mere folly. The mulattoes were cutting them down from the cover of the breastworks, and Maillart could still see Choufleur's uniform moving, distinct among the yellow uniforms of the Sixth—he was ordering the cannon to be turned around to bear on the town and its defenders.

One man made it up the earthwork almost to the top, but someone shot him full in the face and he tumbled over backward. Cannon fire cut three separate swaths through the advance of the Regiment Le Cap, halting the charge. As the men were wavering, Laveaux came riding across the front lines, calling them to fall back, withdraw out of range. Now, at last, they heard him and obeyed.

The retreat went staggering over tangled bodies, white and colored laced together. A drummer boy was beating a loud tattoo, which Captain Maillart seemed to hear now for the first time, and all at once the firing had stopped. Not far from him, Laveaux pulled up his horse and faced the earthworks. He had lost his hat in the confusion, and his chest heaved with his breathing; above, his fine features looked completely stricken. The drumming stopped, and from the hills they heard the calls of crows. It seemed to the captain they had been fighting only a few minutes, but it must have been nearer to four hours, for the sun was plumb vertical overhead, a pale disk searing through the haze. Out of range of the cannon, the men of the Regiment Le Cap stood down.

BY NIGHTFALL THE SKY HAD CLEARED COMPLETELY and now the stars and a hangnail's worth of moon appeared to mark the slopes of Morne du Cap on the horizon. When the darkness was complete the movement of many torches could be seen on the dark face of the mountain. Sonthonax and Laveaux were advancing cautiously toward the earthworks, under the cover of a few guards. As a sort of mental fidget, Sonthonax tried to count the lights by multiplying their rows, but they kept shifting, kept increasing, and soon he saw he could not number them.

"Would it be more *gens de couleur* coming in from the countryside?" he muttered to Laveaux.

"The blacks moving up from the plain, more like."

"*Eh, mon Dieu . . .*"

"*Justement,*" Laveaux said grimly. "*On verra . . .*"

There were torches aplenty among their own party, as they had no wish at all to come upon the mulatto position unobserved. They were thirty yards out from the earthworks when someone fired a warning shot and a voice called out to know their business. Laveaux drew his breath deep into his belly and shouted back his name and that of Sonthonax and said that they were come to remedy the *misunderstanding* that had taken place that afternoon (Sonthonax having prompted him to this phrasing). After a couple of minutes a different voice hailed them from the earthworks and gave permission for them to approach.

Sonthonax and Laveaux clambered over the dirt ramparts, leaving their attendants to hold their horses. The damp curve of the wall was overgrown with vine and grasses, going back to jungle. Sonthonax slipped on the wet growth and fell to one knee; Laveaux reached a hand back to pull him up.

There were three soldiers of the Sixth who escorted them along the twisting declivity between the earth walls to a place where a small fire was burning. Choufleur and another colored officer named Villatte were just within the aureole of its light, seated on the carriages of the cannons that had been turned to cover the town. With them were two black men whom Sonthonax and Laveaux had never seen before, one dressed in a mismatched assemblage of military clothing, the other bare-chested and breech-clouted and ornamented like some chief fresh out of Africa.

"Please be seated," Choufleur said, "*Bienvenu . . .*" Laveaux and Sonthonax took places on gun carriages of their own. Beside the fire an orderly was brewing coffee in a fired-clay pot. Choufleur snapped his fingers at him and he offered Sonthonax and Laveaux each a cup.

"There has been reckless impetuosity on both sides—" Sonthonax began.

"You mean," said Choufleur, "that through this so-called *impetuosity* the royalist troops betrayed that conspiracy they had long been hatching to exterminate all *les citoyens du quatre Avril*."

Sonthonax sniffed his coffee and turned to set it down, untasted, near the touchhole of the cannon he was sitting on. All his intelligencing during that evening had failed to discover just whose conspiracy was whose, nor could he even learn just who had sent that pack of ammunition into the ranks of the Sixth, or why.

"Perhaps there are some few officers of the *ancien régime* who have difficulty in accepting the changes with which the times present them," Sonthonax said. "But I assure you that these matters will be expeditiously resolved and that you and your fellow officers will be accepted with no further difficulty."

"Oh, that is without importance now," Choufleur said. "I and my fellow officers, as you put it, have no longer the slightest interest in serving with the Regiment Le Cap. *Au contraire*, I believe that *all* of our men would absolutely decline to serve in any force into which the Regiment Le Cap was incorporated."

Sonthonax swallowed dryly and looked toward Laveaux, who seemed to be enjoying his coffee; he frowned and shook his head just slightly, but Laveaux did not notice him. Sonthonax's head had been filled with stories of poisoning since he arrived; he rather delectated on these tales, but though a republican he feared poison as much as any king.

"I see," said Sonthonax. "You know of course that our Commission's most important duty here is to maintain *le loi du quatre Avril* and so to protect the rights of all new citizens."

"I have heard much lip service paid to that notion," said Choufleur. "It strikes me that if it were sincere, then any factions who continue to resist the law would have been disposed of with less delay."

"Don't presume that you can dictate terms," Sonthonax said. "You must remember that the Commission is the highest authority in this land."

"Forgive my discourtesy," Choufleur said. "I've failed to introduce my two compatriots. Pierrot" —he indicated the black man in the uniform, who was staring broodily into the coals of the fire without apparently following the conversation— "and Macaya. No doubt you will have heard their names."

Pierrot did not acknowledge the introduction at all, but Macaya, when he heard his name pronounced, raised his head and grinned fixedly at the two Frenchmen. He was of a coppery color, compared to Pierrot's glossy black, and had high cheekbones that seemed to pinch his eyes in slits. His hair had grown very long during the time of the rebellion, and it was propped up with little bones and stiffened with clay in a shape that resembled a peacock's fan.

"Yes," Sonthonax said. "I know these reputations." Immediately he covered his mouth with his hand, out of fear his chin might tremble. He knew that Pierrot and Macaya were the chieftains of the mob of rebel slaves who swarmed in the nearest vicinity to Le Cap; these were far less organized than the men collected under Jean-François and Biassou, but their sheer numbers presented an almost overwhelming threat.

Villatte raised his head and also smiled, but neither he nor Choufleur seemed disposed to make any further remark. Sonthonax studied the neutral faces of Pierrot and Macaya for a moment more and decided to risk the assumption that they understood only Creole, not proper French.

"I had not known," he said to Choufleur, "that men such as these were precisely your *compatriots*."

"Ah, but we live in a time of rapidly shifting alliances," Choufleur said. "Do we not? You will have observed this truth since you arrived here on our island . . ."

"*Vraiment.*" Sonthonax stood up. "Allow me a moment with my colonel." He plucked at Laveaux's sleeve and drew him away into the dark.

On the hill above them the lines of torches continued to snake and circle down. A drumming had begun just at the edge of earshot, thin and parched like a rustle in dry leaves or the first irritating tickle of a cough. Sonthonax turned in the direction of the town and rested his elbows on the breast-high barricade. The lights of Le Cap were interrupted by the mute curve of the barrel of a sixteen-pound cannon.

"How many are they, do you suppose?"

"Fifty thousand? A hundred thousand?" said Laveaux. "No one has had the opportunity to count."

"And Pierrot and Macaya control them all."

"*Control* is perhaps not the most exact term," Laveaux said. "I expect that they can deliver them."

"What is your estimation, then?"

"*Bon,*" said Laveaux. "They are *already* inside our defenses—assuming the mulattoes act in concert with them. With disciplined troops of the Sixth to stiffen the spine of this African horde, I have no doubt they could sweep us all into the sea in a matter of hours. Thus an end of French rule in the north and possibly in all of the colony."

"Ah," said Sonthonax. "It is fortunate, then, that *les gens de couleur* have no good cause to side with these insurgent blacks."

Laveaux took off his hat and scratched the back of his head unconsciously. The tone of his civilian superior suggested that he was practicing his words for some other audience.

"No," Sonthonax continued. "It is well that the fortunes of *les gens de couleur* are so closely allied with our own. For *we,* after all, have been pledged from the beginning to defend their rights as citizens; we recognize only two classes of men in Saint Domingue: the free and the slaves. Equality is irresistible! Whoever stands against it must be swept away."

"Let us hope that they will yield to such persuasions," said Laveaux.

"But it is not at all a matter of persuasion." Sonthonax began leading Laveaux back toward the fire; he noticed now that the two rebel chieftains had withdrawn, or been dismissed, from the circle of light.

"*Courage,*" Sonthonax said. "We have only to *recall* for them the mutuality of our interests."

ON THE MORNING OF DECEMBER 3, Sonthonax returned to Le Cap with the regiment of mulattoes at his back. The rebel blacks from the northern plain had fallen away beyond Morne du Cap, and no one spoke of the threat they had presented, but there was no further resistance to the integration of *les gens de couleur* into the French troops. Or if resistance did appear, it was sharply and suddenly put down.

Within days, Sonthonax had deported the Regiment Le Cap *en masse*. He set up a tribunal to purge *"les aristocrates de la peau"* from the civilian townspeople as well, and these also soon began to fill the holds of ships in the harbor bound for France. "It is hard for Frenchmen to rule by terror," Sonthonax wrote to his new minister of marine, Mongé, "but one must so rule here at Sainte Domingue, where there are neither morals nor patriotism, neither love of France nor respect for her laws; where the ruling passions are egoism and pride; where the chain of despotism has weighed for a century on all classes of men from governor to slave. I have chastised; I have struck down: all the factions are in fear before me. And I shall continue to punish with the same severity whosoever shall trouble the public peace, whosoever shall dare deny the national will—especially the holy law of equality!"

During these same days, Laveaux was scurrying among the various military departments, taking such steps as he might to retain those officers whose services he was loath to lose. It was not long before he came to Captain Maillart, who sulked in his quarters in a fog of gloom, expecting his own deportation hourly.

"Now hear me out before you answer—" Laveaux took a bundle of paper from his coat and strummed it against his opposite palm. "I have here a commission transferring you to a regiment under Rochambeau . . ."

Maillart sat up in his chair with a start. He saw at once that this could be the salvaging of his career, for he did not doubt that in France all the officers of the Regiment Le Cap were likely to be ignominiously dismissed from service.

"Will I serve *under* colored officers?" Maillart said.

"Eventually, perhaps . . ." Laveaux said, then changed his mind. "Yes, undoubtedly you will. And you will do it honorably."

Maillart lowered his eyes and chewed on a fingernail.

"Should you accept this new commission," Laveaux said, "I have also papers for a six-week furlough—long overdue in your case. It will allow you time for reflection. Now I can scarce give you more than a day. You know the situation. But I trust you, Maillart. Never once have I doubted your loyalty. You are a good officer and I refuse to let all my good officers be swallowed up by these political disturbances. Tomorrow I must return for your decision."

He turned and made to leave the room. Maillart stood up.

"I accept," he blurted. "I accept the commission."

Laveaux turned back and nodded. "Good," he said. "I hoped you would."

"With thanks," Maillart said.

Laveaux smiled slightly, his hand upon the doorknob. He opened the door and put a foot through it.

"Colonel," Maillart said. Laveaux turned back, raising an eyebrow.

"Have you not trusted me too easily?" Maillart said. "Is not your confidence too great?"

"I cannot say," Laveaux said. "I don't think so. I do not believe so. I think you will be moved to justify whatever confidence is reposed in you." And he went out into the stony barracks yard before Maillart could think of another word to hold him back.

Chapter Twenty-Nine

"Will I teach you to turn your coat?" Isabelle Cigny's voice was low, light, a little husky; her small white teeth were near enough the captain's ear to bite. He felt her breath against the lobe. It was not the first time she had brought him to the secret room, but it was still a novelty; his throat was yet so swollen with excitement that he could not answer her.

On a small table in the corner, an oil lamp glowed like a ruby within its red glass shade. In the swimming red light she shucked him out of his uniform tunic as easily as peeling a banana, and slid his trousers down the lean poles of his legs. Her deft fingers worked in the crisp black hair of his belly. In a moment she had laid him stiff and bare on a soft mound of carpets in the middle of the floor. Her skirts swung up and over him like a bell and then she settled, nestling, almost like a hen. He smiled at the thought. Then they were joined.

Her long skirts shrouded their point of union; her bare heels locked under his knees and drew them up. From the waist up, she was tidily arranged as for reception in her parlor, only for the mottled flush spreading across her deep décolletage and rising on her throat. Her eyes were half-lidded, there was a hint of hurry in her breathing. Captain Maillart felt a deep desire to work some change in her composure. With certain more assertive movements he was able to move her face into a pinch, a sort of frown, shadowed by the clouds of troubling thoughts, as it appeared. Her mouth twisted; her hand clawed through the fringes of a shawl spread where they lay, long nails driving back into her palm. The captain thought he was shouting at her, perhaps, he could not well hear. Waves of red light from the lamp washed over them like blood. She rode him to a gentler, rocking stroke, and her face gentled, mouth softening as her lips were parted in a sighing ring.

At the end, she slumped over him, holding herself up by her elbows. A strand of pinkish coral beads swung down toward his nose. He raised his head to kiss the cleft between her breasts, but smilingly she turned his chin away. From some distant recess of the house came the muted sound of a small child crying. Abruptly she swung her leg clear of him and sat upon a divan, pinning up a loose tendril at the back of her hair. Her skirts had fallen into perfect order around her when she stood. The captain sat up, a little dizzied by his movement. He was sticky and hollow as an empty, unwashed bowl. On either side of him lay one of a pair of beaded white satin slippers, improbably delicate and frail. He picked them up and, naked still, knelt down to slip them onto her feet. She smiled at him absently. Without, the street door opened and closed.

"You must hurry," she said carelessly, and left him in the secret room.

It was the first word to pass her lips, after their congress. The door closed softly on her back. Maillart picked up his uniform coat—true enough it was of a different design, since he'd accepted the commission Laveaux had arranged for him. He dressed, and extinguished the lamp before leaving.

DOCTOR HÉBERT HAD NOT BEEN WAITING long in the parlor when Madame Cigny came in, carrying Héloïse on her hip, with Robert at her heels, trailed by his black nurse. She offered him her free hand and he bowed and murmured over it. Robert picked up a gilt-stamped leather book from the sofa and flung it on the floor. With a crafty look around the room, he picked it up and made to throw it farther. The nurse, his slave, looked pained, but would not interfere with him before his mother. Pascal, slouching in an armchair, had preceded the doctor on this call, and had evidently been waiting for some time; he regarded the scene with a faintly ironic air of detachment.

"Well, stop him, someone." Isabelle set down the smaller child. "Must I do everything myself?" she trilled, flashing her inconsequent smile. With a pretty movement, a flirt of her hem, she bent to pry the book from her son's chubby fingers. Héloïse, meanwhile, pulled herself up by the edge of a low table, oversetting a glass of wine which splashed purply all over the front of her white dress.

"Well, take them out then," Madame Cigny cooed at the nurse. "Change that dress—and see that it's cleaned *immediately.*" Her face impassive, the black woman led the children out. As they left the room, Captain Maillart came in.

"Well, you are going then," said Madame Cigny to the doctor. "Again you are going." She looked at the captain. "So I am told."

"Oh, I shall not be long from your side." Maillart regarded her with something close to open astonishment. How could she have come to this room ahead of him? Fresh as she seemed, she must still be fragrant from their late encounter . . . He glanced at her slim hand—yes, the palm was still indented with faint nail marks. The captain noticed that Pascal had fixed on him a hostile stare. He grinned at him pleasantly, twirled his mustache, and sat down on the sofa.

"One may venture to hope that this sally will be more successful than your last," said Isabelle, balancing herself winningly on the edge of a chair.

"After all," the captain said serenely, "we did return to tell the tale."

"But of course," cried Madame Cigny. "A pity that the girl you were protecting could not share in that good fortune."

The captain colored and emitted a cough.

"*Eh bien,* she was too good for this world, your Marguerite," said Madame Cigny. "Or perhaps she was simply too stupid." She turned smilingly upon the doctor. "And your mission will be the same as before?"

The doctor laughed. "To learn if on a third essay I may at last discover Ennery. I have hopes that my sister may have returned to Habitation Thibodet."

"Your hopes are grounded?"

"*Chère Madame,* they are without a clear foundation," said the doctor. "Like so many human hopes."

THEY LEFT THE TOWN ON AN EARLY MORNING, eight men well mounted and heavily armed: the doctor, Maillart, a lieutenant named

Vaublanc who'd also survived the purge of the Regiment Le Cap, Arnaud, Grandmont, and three other Creole militiamen. The Creoles, since they were white, whiled away the first hours of the journey with bitter and sarcastic commentary on the rise to power of the mulattoes in the town, and the general ascendancy that *les gens de couleur* seemed to have obtained over Sonthonax and the Commission. The captain held himself aloof from this discussion, and the doctor too kept silence.

On the far slopes of Morne du Cap they dismounted to take their noon repast. They sat cross-legged on stones or stumps, under the cover of the jungle leaves, chewing on chicken legs and cold sweet potatoes, drinking a little red wine from the skins they carried with them. All during the morning it had been raining fitfully, but it was clearing now, though a few drops still pattered on the leaf canopy. A fringe of cottony gray cloud trailed away over the peaks of the southwestern range of mountains, and as the cloud mass parted some shafts of sun leaked through to gild the green of the trees.

Doctor Hébert wore the long duster in which he almost always rode; he'd also acquired a broad-brimmed hat, against the constant rain. Together the two outsized garments seemed to dwarf him. While the others were preparing to remount, he meticulously checked the priming of the two pistols he carried in his belt and of the rifled long gun which was fitted into a scabbard on his saddle skirt. Captain Maillart chuckled audibly to see his concentration. The doctor looked up, alert and inquisitive.

"What is it?"

"Nothing. Only—you seem so piratical, in that garb, with all your weaponry."

The doctor shrugged, and looked at his shoes. "It's only practical."

"Hah," said the captain. "What could you hit with it?"

"Whatever you like," Arnaud said, from the far side of his horse, whose girth he'd been tightening. He spoke before the doctor could respond. "And that I'll wager."

"Oh, let it pass," said Captain Maillart, a little irritably.

"But I am serious," Arnaud said, coming around his horse's head. "Throw up your hat."

"*My* hat?" Captain Maillart said. "Throw up your own."

"I will if *you* will fire at it," Arnaud said. "I should be safe enough." He grinned, and held up a gold piece between his thumb and forefinger. "This says our man of science will be the better marksman."

Maillart reddened and dug into his pocket.

"Excellent," said Arnaud. "I knew you for a sportsman. Bernard will hold the stakes." He passed the coins to Grandmont, who rattled them in his loosely curled fingers, showing his brown snaggle teeth in a sort of smile. Two of the other militiamen came up to him to negotiate a side bet. Arnaud took off his hat and turned the brim through his thumb and forefinger.

"How, with a pistol?" the captain said irritably. "But it is absurd."

"*Mais bien sûr,*" Arnaud said. "Hold your pistol down, just so. When I have thrown it, take your aim and shoot." Arnaud stepped out of cover onto the trail, swinging his hat at knee level. Rain had begun lowering again, fine as mist, stippling the captain's cheeks as he followed Arnaud into the open, holding his dragoon's pistol barrel-down across his hip.

"*Vous êtes prêtes?*" Arnaud said.

The captain nodded. Arnaud flung his hat straight up above him and took a quick step back. The hat rotated smoothly, etched black against the dull overhanging mass of cloud. The captain tracked it, like a fowl, right hand braced over his left wrist. It did not fall so quickly as all that, and yet he knew that he would miss before he pulled the trigger.

Arnaud stepped briskly down the trail and retrieved the unharmed hat. "And now for the good doctor," he said, returning.

Doctor Hébert stepped onto the trail, fidgeting with the flashpan of his pistol, his lips pursed. Sighing, the captain took off his cap and fingered the bill. He was facing the doctor, twenty paces up the slope of the trail, as if they were preparing for a duel.

"All right, Antoine?" the captain said.

The doctor stood with his pistol hanging down; the overlong sleeve of his dustcoat covered his fingers on the grip. He looked up anxiously.

"*Oui, commences.*"

The captain flung his cap aloft. It turned unevenly, because of the bill, with a sort of fluttering movement. But Maillart's eye was on the doctor. He saw the other's thickish wrist thrust out of the dustcoat sleeve, hand rock-steady on the pistol grip. The clouds parted overhead and a sudden flood of sunshine made the captain blink. He had just time to draw a breath while the powder burned in the flashpan, before the ball discharged. A gasp came from the men around him, then a shout of approbation. The captain's hat dropped in a stunned curve through the mist-glittering sunshine and caught on a bush twenty-five yards down the gorge from the trail, above a twittering run-off stream.

The captain tapped his boot toe restively. "All this useless shooting may well attract the brigands."

"Come, don't be churlish," Arnaud said, collecting his winnings from Grandmont. "It was a fair contest, was it not?"

"Of course," the captain said. "Well shot." He approached the doctor and shook his hand, squinting disbelievingly into his face as he tightened his grip. Then he stepped to the edge of the trail and stared glumly down to where his hat hung on the bush.

"I'll get it for you," the doctor said, embarrassed.

"No, no . . ." Maillart scrambled down.

The damp foliage wet him to the hip as he waded through it. The hat had been shot clean through, front to back. The char-rimmed hole at the front would just accommodate his forefinger; at the back, the felt had been blown out in a tripartite tear. The captain put his hat on and adjusted it. On the trail the other men were laughing at him, but in spite of this he grinned as he looked up. The doctor had not joined in the laughter, but stood recharging his pistol with an uncertain fastidiousness as if he'd seldom done that task before.

They mounted and rode on until dark and passed that night in an old provision ground a hundred yards above the trail. The planting was untended and had all been dug over by looters so they found no provender there excepting a half-rotted stalk of bananas sprung up from a runner shoot. They ate some dried meat they carried with them along with bananas roasted in their skins and afterward slept propped up on their saddles, always keeping two men on watch. In the morning they saddled their horses and went on.

The day was luminously clear, the sun bright and warm upon their backs once the mist had parted, so that they sweated in their rain gear. Ahead of them the involutions of the mountains, carpeted smoothly over with green jungle, went on and on like folds of a crumpled fabric. In the forenoon, as they passed in single file along an exposed and rocky outward bend of the trail, they came in view of an enormous throng of brigand blacks on the plain below—the rebels noticed them soon enough, and set up a great shout and stir, seeing their numbers were so few. A shiver ran over the doctor then, though the blacks were more than a mile distant down the mountain, and could not possibly overtake them on that difficult terrain.

In the afternoon they came upon flocks of birds and shot a great many and strung them up on their saddlebows. The fresh fowl assured them a warm welcome at the fort of the *cordon de l'ouest* which they attained before dark. That night they passed around the garrison's fire, talking to the soldiers. The latest news from Ennery was that all continued peacefully there, though the news was not so recent. In the morning they rose and went on at first light.

In the midafternoon of that day Grandmont spotted carrion birds circling over a rocky defile of the mountains about a mile ahead. He pulled his horse abreast of the captain's and requested a halt. Maillart resisted at first—vultures were no uncommon sight in these parts, these days—but something about Grandmont's odd conviction finally swayed him.

They drew their horses up above the trail and took positions behind a ragged line of boulders overgrown with fern. There they waited, fifteen minutes, twenty. The captain's watch ticked in his pocket. There was no talk, but the exchange of fretful glances. The doctor had laid his rifle across a stone, and crouched behind it, aiming at leaves on the trail. The blacks, being barefoot, made no sound when they came up, but seemed to have materialized from nothing beyond the forward bead of his gunsight. There were four of them, dressed in breechclouts or ragged field trousers and all with muskets of the same make. Their leader was a big Congo with broad flat nostrils, and pockmarks all over his face that the doctor thought must have come from a bout with *la petite vérole*. He stopped the others and sniffed slowly, a luxurious inhalation, turning his head in a slow contemplative curve, eyelids lowered so that only the whites showed. Feeling the force of his attention, the white men all held their breath.

Arnaud wanted to gun them down at once, but Grandmont and the captain held him back; it was well that they did so, because ten minutes after the advance scouts had passed along the trail, the main body came up. The leader, who was also marked with smallpox scars, rode horseback, and from his saddle horn hung by their hair a number of bloody desiccated severed human heads, flies buzzing eagerly around them. The doctor wondered how the horse could tolerate the stench of rot. The men who marched in a regular column behind their mounted chieftain all carried muskets and their bare chests were crossed with bandoliers; there looked to be more than a hundred of them.

It took them some little while to pass, and the white men waited a half hour more when they had gone, before they led their horses cautiously down to the trail. While they were waiting, the captain watched the doctor sighting down his rifle barrel and felt strangely reassured by his proximity. Within the hour they had come to the place where the vultures were turning but down the defile there was only the carcass of a long-horned cow who must have strayed there, already mostly devoured or decayed, the bones showing whitely through the rotten hide.

They passed. Next day they crossed a corner of the plain as speedily as they were able, disliking the exposure when their strength was so slight, and swiftly began ascending the pass that led to Ennery. Toward sundown of that day they came down out of the jungle through the terraces of coffee trees that were the outlying cultivation of Habitation Thibodet. They crossed the irrigation trenches and rode alongside the bristly green *carrés* of cane. As they filed through the quarters, the *gérant* Delsart came out the door of a cabin, buttoning up his pants. When he looked up and saw the doctor at the head of the troop he staggered back as though it were a ghost, just catching himself on the cabin's wattled wall.

They rode down to the stables where the doctor dismounted and scared up a couple of grooms to see to their horses. It did seem after all that many of the Thibodet slaves *had* remained on the plantation. But the windows of the *grand'case* were shuttered and silent.

The doctor swung his saddlebags up over his shoulder and started toward the house. The porch bowed and groaned under his feet . . . long in need of a shoring up. He stepped into the dusky outer room, blinking. The musty interior space was all striped by bars of reddish sunset light admitted through the palmiste strips of the jalousies. The doctor blinked and turned about. A calico cat startled him by appearing out of the shadows to curve and purr against his shins. Atop a tall chest, a fancy clock ticked mutedly, the disk of its pendulum sweeping between four twisted brass columns that supported the works, like a canopy covering a cathedral altar.

Through the rear door there came a scurrying sound. The cat pulled away from the doctor's boots and loped after it. The doctor proceeded in the same direction, his footfalls dampened by a runner of carpet. Thibodet's house was scarcely a mansion but its appointments had a greater air of permanence than those of many Creole residences. Elise had brought some of the carpets and furniture out from France with her trousseau; the carpet which the doctor stalked along had once lined a hallway of their house in Lyons.

He stood within the door frame of the master's chamber. The great carved bed where Thibodet had died was undisturbed, its rich coverings silted over with a skein of dust. Atop the near pillow a glossy black beetle as large as a teacup clicked and shifted its mandibles. The doctor leaned over and brushed it to the floor; it shifted itself under the bed, without haste.

He walked down the narrow passage and into the smaller room beyond the next partition. It was not so different from the room he'd slept in at Arnaud's, or from a spare room at any other *grand'-case* in the colony. As the single window was quite small and faced away from the sunset glow, it was rather dark inside. The bed was a low wooden frame strung with rope to support the mattress. The doctor dropped his saddlebags in a corner, divested himself of all but one of his pistols, and turned to hang his duster on the accustomed peg. Here he'd lain night after night, pondering the disappearance of his sister and listening to Thibodet's delirious ravings as they floated over the top of the partition, wondering if he'd desire to cure this man of his disease, supposing it had lain in his power to do so.

He went back out onto the gallery where Maillart, Vaublanc, Arnaud and Grandmont had seated themselves in chairs. As the doctor approached them, Maillart looked up.

"No sign of your sister, then?" Maillart said.

Before the doctor could reply, Delsart came up hurriedly and swept off his hat to make a low bow. As he straightened, the doctor observed that his handsome, rather swarthy features were marred by several venereal sores.

"There will be eight to dine and pass the night," the doctor said. "Have we hands enough to manage that?"

"Without a doubt," Delsart said. "I shall give the orders now." He struck out briskly for the outbuilding housing the kitchen, only staggering slightly from his visible drunkenness.

"If that's your manager," said Maillart, "I'd say you haven't by any means returned too soon."

THE MOON WAS FAT AND SLEEK THAT NIGHT, only one day short of the full. It rose early, large and yellow, and whitened and shrank as it climbed the sky. During the moonrise the white men dined inside the house, drank a decent amount of brandy, and went early to bed, as all were fatigued from their days of hard riding.

Propped up on his low bed with his back against the wall, Doctor Hébert flipped through a botanical book he had left in this house at his last departure, but his attention failed him. Damp had worked its way into the paper and a gray-green mold was forming a filigree over the print. The doctor could not force his mind beyond this pattern.

The doctor let the book fall shut, and closed his eyes, but his mind was still too active for repose. After a little time, he got up and carried the candle into the master's room. A maid had come to clean at his instruction; the floor was swept and the bed freshly changed. The doctor pulled open the big mahogany wardrobe and fanned his hands across Elise's dresses which hung there. Many of them were expensive, but they had not been aired for a long time and the damp had somewhat damaged them; a few were stained with mildew. Some he recognized from France, but most were new. Unlike Elise to abandon it all here. The wardrobe door drifted from his hand; he clicked it shut.

In the main room, some brandy still remained in the bottle. Delsart had run very heavily into Thibodet's stock, but the supply had been large to begin with, so there was still a reasonable amount in store. The doctor took the bottle by the neck, then changed his mind. The moon shone so brightly at the windows that the light of his candle was inconsequential. He snuffed it out and went onto the gallery.

The chairs stood empty along the board floor. It was quite pleasantly cool, and there were no mosquitoes just at the moment. Under the brilliant moonlight, the doctor walked down through the quarters and beyond. The wind drifted caressingly through the cane, the long leaves whispering together. This rustle receded as he began to climb the terraces of coffee trees. The stiffness of the ride was loosening from him, and he felt cheerful and alert.

Where the coffee trees ended and the jungle climbed uninterrupted over the mountain, he stopped also. Habitation Thibodet was spread before him like a pale shawl in the moonlight, which silvered the irrigation ditches that marked out the *carrés* of green cane. No human light shone from any building, but in the quarters a woman's low voice rose to sing a mournful tune in some African tongue. The doctor wondered passingly if it was an infant she was soothing, or if she sang to please herself, for her own comfort. At his back the jungle insects had composed a wall of sound. If he had chosen, the doctor thought, he might have gone farther into that warm wet darkness, with small fear. So much at his ease he was, he had not even troubled to bring along a pistol—though it was strange, for this wild place had seemed pregnant with menace when he'd first come here months before, and certainly it was no safer now.

Chapter Thirty

NOW WHEN WE HAD BEEN IN THOSE Spanish mountains for some weeks, the people all were very hungry, because there was not much fruit to find, and no meat at all to eat. Also Toussaint said we must not hunt with guns because we had not so many bullets or powder then, or any way to get more of those things. All we could do was dig for roots and take birds by glue or by smoking them in their trees, but soon the birds were eaten and new ones did not come. It was always raining there. The clouds sat so low on those big mountains that it rained there even in the summer heat.

Then that one who had run from Habitation Arnaud, who we called Aiguy, was fighting with another man. The fight was about a woman whose name was Achuba. They fought in the old way, using round-headed clubs with nails, and Aiguy was very quick and clever with his club. He broke the head of the other man and left him bleeding, leaning against a tree with the white of his bone showing through the blood and black hairs. The man was hurt almost to his death, and Aiguy was afraid then, because Toussaint was against this kind of fighting, and would sometimes shoot the ones who fought so, especially if there came a death. And I, Riau, I too believed that it was foolish we should fight each other in this way.

Then Aiguy wanted to go away, and also we were very hungry. Aiguy had a story that on the plains of the Spanish whitemen beyond the mountains there were hundreds of cows who ran wild so that we could take them. Merbillay and Achuba were hungry for meat, and that is how we came to go. We took the boy Epi with us, who had been a small boy in Achille's band but had grown bigger now, to help us cure and carry meat if we did find it.

I left my musket there at the camp and one of my pistols too, also my *banza* and some other things I did not want to carry, and my horse I left with the horses of Toussaint. A horse could not go where we were going anyway. Maybe Riau always meant to go back, leaving these things behind the way he did, but when we left I was not much thinking of return. Before we went I made two good spears, using scrap iron I could shape in the heat of the blacksmith's forge, and binding the iron blades to the shafts with lianas in the old Carib way. I had one of my pistols also to take with me but I meant to save its bullets for killing whitemen later on.

We could not go so quickly in these mountains, which were steep and sudden and all cut through with crevices dug by streams. No trails were here or any Carib road that we could find. Merbillay was carrying Caco in a sling across her back. By that time he could walk a little, but he could not have followed in this country. On the third day we found two brown and white goats and killed them with our spears. So far away in the bush away from men, the goats were not even very shy. We were happy then, that night, eating goat meat around the fire till our bellies were tight and hard like melons and our faces shone with fat. The she-goat had milk in the udder for Caco to drink, and I cut small pieces of meat with my knife and Merbillay chewed them for him. So we were happy, only Aiguy wanted *tafia* to drink, but I, Riau, I did not care.

Next day we built a frame across the fire for drying the meat we could not finish fresh, and Achuba and Merbillay were scraping the two goat hides with stones to clean and soften them. Next day we went hunting again, Riau and Aiguy, and came onto a boar-hog before we knew we'd find him. I put the blade of my spear between the boar-hog's shoulders but this did not stop him charging me. Thinking how it would be before, I had lashed a crossbar on my spear a foot below the blade when I first made it, but the boar came so hard and fast that the crossbar broke and the shaft went through him like a drink of water. I slipped on the mud and wet leaves, and he knocked me down and maybe he had killed me, but Aiguy came then and killed him with the other spear.

Then we had hog meat to eat beside the goat. The boar was big and very fat. He had cut my legs with his yellow tusks, but not so badly I could not walk. We stayed in that place where we had camped for three or four more days, eating and drying the extra meat. My legs were hurting where the boar had gashed them, but I had learned some herbs from Toussaint, at Bréda and later on when he was teaching herbs to the whiteman doctor. I sent Merbillay into the jungle to look for *guérit-trop-vite* and when I used this for a few days, my wounds were closed and dry.

After this, we all went back to Toussaint's camp. Aiguy wanted to go on into the Spanish country. I, Riau, would have liked to see those hundred cows he spoke about, but I had heard another story how the Spanish whitemen used killing dogs to hunt maroons, dogs bigger than Arnaud's, big as the cows themselves or nearly. I thought Aiguy feared to go back because of the man that he had hurt, but I told him it would all be forgotten by the time that we came to the camp again. We had big packs of dried meat to carry, so we went even more slowly returning.

But when we came to the camp again, they caught us by the skin and the neck all at once, Riau and Aiguy, and dragged us to Toussaint's tent. Right away Aiguy was taken off somewhere to be beaten, only a little, not enough to break his skin, because the man he had clubbed had not died after all. But when they brought me into the tent, Toussaint shouted out an order, and Chacha Godard jumped up and screwed the barrel of his pistol into my left ear.

I stood at attention then, exactly like a whiteman soldier. Chacha had drawn back the hammer of his pistol, so eager he was to taste my death—he loved death so much he did not care it was Riau. I did not know if even Toussaint's word could hold his hand. If it had been Riau only, or Ogûn in my head, he would have fought and snatched at Chacha's arm. Then Chacha maybe would have killed me. But all the time I stood stock still and stared straight ahead. *Lieutenant Riau,* I spit to hear those words, like Toussaint spat the words he said to me.

Toussaint was angrier than I had ever seen, his face was swollen and all the rest of him was shaking, he jumped up and down before me like an angry dog, but his words were sharp and pointed like cat's teeth. It was all because I was *lieutenant* he was angry. Because I was *officer* in his army and so I had *desert,* and the desert of an officer was a thousand times worse than when another man desert because if the officer desert, a thousand men could follow him. So when a desert officer was captured, the punishment was to be shot.

White bubbles were at the corners of Toussaint's mouth when he said this, and Chacha's finger trembled on the trigger, and I felt Chacha's breath against my neck. Charles Belair was in the tent with us this time, and he jumped up to ask for mercy, but Toussaint ordered him to go out. Toussaint asked me if I understood what he had said.

"*Oui, mon general,*" I said. "*Je comprends bien.*" I don't know why I said it, because I did not understand. Then Toussaint sent Chacha away too. At first Chacha would not hear the order, and Toussaint had to pull the pistol down with his own hand.

Toussaint told me to sit down. There was a shiver in my belly when I did it, and my legs pained me where the boar had hurt them, and my ears were ringing like Chacha had really fired his gun so I was already on my way to the Island Below Sea. But Toussaint was smiling to himself and looking into a sack where he kept all the books he always carried with him. He looked inside the bag and handed me one book I had not seen before.

"Read this," he said, and opened the book on my knees. "Read this page to me."

I looked down at the paper and through my mouth the words began to speak.

If self-interest alone prevails with nations and their masters, there is another power. Nature speaks in louder tones than philosophy or self-interest. Already are there established two colonies of fugitive negroes, whom treaties and power protect from assault. Those lightnings announce the thunder. A courageous chief only is wanted. Where is he, that great man whom Nature owes to her vexed, oppressed and tormented children? Where is he? He will appear, doubt it not; he will come forth and raise the sacred standard of liberty. This venerable signal will gather around him the companions of his misfortune. More impetuous than the torrents, they will everywhere leave the indelible traces of their just resentment. Everywhere people will bless the name of the hero who shall have reestablished the rights of the human race; everywhere will they raise trophies in his honor.

When I had done, Toussaint was smiling on me.

"What do you think of that?" he said.

I was thinking about the maroons of Bahoruco where Jean-Pic

had gone, how the whitemen gave them a paper to say that they were free. I thought that these maroons were free with a paper or without one, but I did not think Toussaint would like to hear this thought. So I told him that I believed what I had read in the book must have been written by a black man, but that I had not known any black man would write a book.

"No," Toussaint said. "It was a white man who wrote that, a priest. His name is Abbé Raynal and he is the friend of the King In France."

So I asked Toussaint how long he had known this book and when he said it was even while I was still a slave at Bréda, I asked him why he did not show it to me there.

"The time was not then, Riau," he said. "But now, now is the time." He was walking up and down the tent again with his excitement, a small man in his tall soldier boots. Then he stopped to look at me.

"Your little son, Pierre Toussaint," he said. "He was not born in slavery, *he* was born free. Always remember this, Riau."

"Oui, mon général," said Lieutenant Riau. But I did not need him to tell it me, there was no chance I would forget. It was Toussaint who forgot that Riau was born free in Guinée, while only he, Toussaint, was born to slavery.

Then Toussaint sat down and began to ask me many questions about Laveaux, the whiteman soldier who had finally whipped us at Morne Pélé and driven us into the mountains. He had me tell him many times over how Laveaux had looked at the fort of La Tannerie when I and Chacha spied on him from trees, and say to him the things that he had said. Times over he made me say the sentence of Laveaux—*Whatever they are, they are not savages.* Then he smiled and let me go.

After all this I was not beaten, not even a little. The dried meat we had carried back with us did not feed our six hundred for even as long as one day. But we did keep the goatskins, one for Caco and one for the baby Aiguy had put into Achuba that time while we were hunting.

In the next days, we all came together in Toussaint's tent, Riau and Dessalines and Moise and Charles Belair, writing a letter to this whiteman soldier Laveaux. Each of us wrote the letter many ways, and Toussaint listened to all the ways and changed from one way to the other until every word of the letter was perfect to his ear. At last, when the letter was sent, it told Laveaux that Toussaint would bring our men to fight with the French against the Spanish, because there was war now between these whitemen overseas. It promised to bring the men of Jean-François and Biassou also, though Toussaint did not know for certain if he could bring those men or not, but the letter did not tell that part to Laveaux. The letter said that we would do these things only if the French whitemen would admit that all we black men and women were free, not only the soldiers but all the people of Guinée who were in the island then.

So the letter went to speak to Laveaux, and we were a long time waiting for an answer. While we were waiting, we made another letter to speak to the Marquis d'Hermona who was a soldier of the Spanish whitemen. This letter said the same as the other, but in different words that we and Toussaint were a long time in choosing. This letter told that Toussaint would bring our men to fight with the Spanish whitemen against the French if the Spanish whitemen would admit the freedom of all the people of Guinée on the island also.

All this time Riau was thinking with two heads. One way I thought that I was glad of this Abbé Raynal and the King In France and how whitemen were in the world that could believe black men were free. But the mind of Ogûn in me thought that all whitemen meant evil to us and that all their words were lies and that Ogûn must kill them all or drive them back into the ocean. Then I thought Toussaint was very wrong. Then I would go down to the camp of Biassou and feed the *loa* with the others who were dancing and feel *l'ésprit* of Ogûn in my head. Alone with Biassou in his tent, I helped him make the *ouangas* against Chacha Godard, and I was happy to make *ouangas*, thinking that now Chacha had come so near to the taste of my blood he could not rest before he drank it all.

But even then Biassou was going to go over to the Spanish, to be given ribbons and coins to wear on his uniform and to have new officer names of power. Jean-François was gone already to the Spanish whitemen. So I went back, always, into the camp of Toussaint.

When Laveaux's answer came at last, he only said his heart was with us, but he could promise nothing. And because even the promises of whitemen seemed not to be worth much, Toussaint was not pleased with this. Marquis d'Hermona did not send a letter. Instead the gunrunner Tocquet came one day. He did not bring any guns this time, but powder and shot, also some salt and flour. With him came the Père Sulpice. I did not know this priest so well even though he had sometimes come to the camp of Jeannot, but I thought he must pray to the cruel Jesus because of the beads he wore on the string of his black robe. The beads were wood and each not bigger than a fingertip and on one side the face of Jesus was but on each other side it was a skull. He used the beads to count his prayers, though I think he did not love blood so much as that other, Père Duguit.

It was this Père Sulpice who had brought Jean-François and Biassou away to the army of the Spanish whitemen, so Riau knew what he meant to do when he came to us, and so did we all know. I was happy that Toussaint did not send us out of the tent this time when Père Sulpice and Tocquet came in. We all stayed there, Riau and Moise and Charles Belair and Dessalines, to hear what words the whitemen said.

The whiteman priest Sulpice told to us then that the Marquis d'Hermona promised these things only, that we who would fight for the Spanish whitemen against the French would be free forever after. They would give ribbons and coins and new uniforms to wear and bigger louder names for our officers to call themselves. Also some money they would give. But Père Sulpice did not say anything about freeing *all* the children of Guinée. He did not even say anything about our women, or the children we had with us in that place. I did not like the way he played with the skulls on his bead-chain while he talked. But I did think Toussaint would do the thing he said.

All this time Tocquet the whiteman gunrunner sat with his wide hat still on his head, so his eyes were in shadow, but I saw his eyes missed nothing. They were quick and bright and black as the eyes of a crow. Sometimes Toussaint would stop the Père Sulpice from talking and look very hard into the black eyes of Tocquet and ask him if what that *père* said was true and if he, Tocquet, had heard it with his ears from the Marquis d'Hermona. Tocquet would hold his eyes steady when Toussaint asked him a question, while the eyes of the priest went sliding all the ways around the tent walls when he spoke. But Tocquet said it was all true, what the priest told. He never took his hat off and except when Toussaint asked a question he did not want to say anything at all.

All this time at the cook fires outside the tent they were making flat breads from the flour Tocquet brought. I smelled the bread frying on the iron and the juices started in my stomach, and in my mouth the juices came hard and sharp enough to sting. I knew we would not be staying in those wet mountains for much longer.

So we came down then, to the Spanish town of San Raphael, all we six hundred men and the women and children too. It was not Marquis d'Hermona at that place, but one called General Cabrera of the Spanish army. Here Toussaint was made a general and a *maréchal du camp* and a knight of the order of Isabella who was the queen of the King In Spain. He had a fine new uniform to wear, the uniform of a general, with a general's hat. They gave to me, Riau, this louder name of *capitain*. They gave me a uniform and also boots, only I would not wear the boots because they pinched my feet. Also they gave money to the pocket of my uniform, because these whitemen pay to kill each other, instead of doing it from their desire.

All at once when we had come to San Raphael, Toussaint wanted to hear prayers to jesus, which he had not heard for a long time, since the little fat whiteman priest had gone away from our camp. The Spanish whitemen were all very happy that Toussaint wanted to have their god in his head and so many of them went inside this church with Toussaint. Then Père Sulpice was a long time talking to jesus and all in a language no one could understand, all the time counting his words on his string of skulls. When he was finished talking, he put a piece of jesus meat into Toussaint's mouth and gave some blood of jesus to Toussaint to drink. All these things were done before the uniforms and the new names were given.

Now *Capitain Riau* had an army tent for himself, instead of building an *ajoupa* like before. I saw the Spanish soldiermen did not like to see me keeping Merbillay and Caco in my tent. They did not like to see me sit outside the tent to play on the *banza*. But while Toussaint was General, it did not matter much what those whitemen liked.

In those days Madame Suzanne and Toussaint's children came back to the camp. I think they had been hiding on the Spanish side all this time since we first began burning and killing whitemen. Of his sons, only Placide remembered Riau from Bréda. But sometimes I would take Placide and Isaac riding out onto the Spanish plain, bringing Aiguy along with me. The Spanish whitemen did not much like us to go away from camp, but these were General Toussaint's sons, and Riau, who was Toussaint's *aide de camp*, I was more free.

After the first hundred cows were a hundred more and then more hundreds. They all did run wild on the plains, the way Aiguy had told it. We did not see very many cane fields. These Spanish whitemen were not like the French. No matter how many cows they had, they did not seem to know that they were rich. They would not grow anything out of the ground, only provisions, and these they grew poorly. When they were hungry, they would kill a cow and make a *boucan*. If they were not too lazy, they might cure the skin.

Now we all of us had plenty meat to eat. These whitemen on the plain did not know how many cows they had, I thought. But they were selling cows to the army, and if a cow was stolen, they would somehow know it, and sometimes I saw bad trouble over this.

These Spanish *colons* lived in cabins not much better than *ajoupas*, except they used planks of wood instead of sticks to make them. They had not many slaves, and the slaves they had slept in the cabins by the whitemen, and how a slave lived was not so different from a whiteman. They were not very like the French *colons*. But if a slave would run away, they hunted him with dogs and when they caught him they might give him alive to the dogs to eat. I saw that the whitemen who were on the plains were not happy to see us in the Spanish soldier uniform. But because I was near to Toussaint, our general, no one ever troubled me.

So I brought the children back, to Toussaint's tent again. Soon it was going to be time to go and fight and kill more of the French whitemen. Toussaint was not anymore speaking to me of Abbé Raynal, or showing the book that came from that man's head. I did not much know what was in his mind. He was glad to have his wife with him again, and his sons I know, so maybe he was not thinking of much else all through those days.

But on a day he called me into his tent alone. From a little wooden writing desk he was keeping there, he took out a paper. The General Cabrera gave him this little desk for a present, and it had much work of carving in it like the priest's beads, but it was made here, by a slave. When I looked at the paper I saw Toussaint had written it himself. I could not understand it well at first. His letters all had a bad shape and he did not put the right letters in the words. It was hard for me to make this paper speak.

Then I saw that the Toussaint he had put into my head had learned more about writing down words than the Toussaint who sat across the tent from me. I felt strange inside myself to think this. But Toussaint took the paper from my hand and read to me in his own voice.

"*I am Toussaint. . .*" He stopped here, holding out one empty hand while he held the paper high before his face, in his other hand. *"Upon a day, you will hear my name. I am coming to fight for you and your people . . ."*

He stopped again. These were the only words that were on the paper. I saw these words had not satisfied him.

"I am Toussaint . . ." he said again. He held out the empty hand like he was feeling for a weight to balance the word that he was speaking. But I did not know what to say to him. Of course I knew he was Toussaint.

"It wants something," Toussaint said. "More—another name."

"Toussaint Bréda," I said then.

"*No,*" he said. "Not that." He was even angry I had said this. But he had been called Bréda forty years. I was not sorry though, if this name was finished for him then.

"Who is the letter going to?" I said. "Who is it for?"

"Of course it is for you," Toussaint said, smiling on the far side of his mouth. "For you and for all the world also."

"I don't understand," I said. And I did not. We had never before written a letter to *everyone*. I would not know how to start doing that. Always we knew who would read the letter and so we shaped the words to fit into the ear of this one man.

Toussaint put the paper back into the desk and shut the wooden lid and tapped it with his fingernail. The nail was thick and cracked and yellow like old cowhorn.

"Maybe I don't understand it either," he said then. "The letter is not finished yet. But you will help me finish it, Riau. When it is done, not long from now, then we will both know all that there is to know about it."

Chapter Thirty-One

A CURTAIN OF RAIN PARTED BEFORE Captain Maillart as he walked across the Le Cap quay in the direction of the fountain, and continued withdrawing a pace or two ahead of him, shimmering like a waterfall, stippling the stone pavement with pinpoints of damp. As the cloud tore and lifted off completely, that last faint misty sheet of rain was all at once spangled through with sunlight. The captain had not bothered to cover his head, but walked gaily swinging his hat at his side. The fitful shower had scarcely dampened the stiff newish cloth of his uniform.

He strolled up to the fountain's rim. A pace away from the lip of the basin, an old white-haired *affranchi* sat cross-legged on the ground. Perched on his shoulder was an enormous green parrot, head as large as a small dog's. The old man was feeding the bird with fibrous pinches of soursop from a fruit that lay divided in his lap. The parrot looked askance at each, turning its head sideways, and harshly croaked, *cela m'emmerde, c'la m'emmerde,* but still accepted every proffer from the crooked black fingers.

Maillart smiled, turning to face the opposite direction down the quay. From a knot of cloud above the southern mountains there arced three bands of brilliant rainbow color driving down into the water of the harbor. It was very still. A French merchantman had negotiated the channel and was drifting silently toward a mooring. The hour was still very early and though a couple of men had come out to catch the lines tossed down from the ship's upper deck to be made fast, the quay was not very busy as yet.

The parrot clicked, repeated its phrase, turned its head for a sidewise inspection of another fingerful of soursop. Its beak was curved and black, irregularly marked with paler cracks and chips, strong and sharp enough to sever a man's finger, Maillart knew. There was a short slapping sound of a small-bore cannon firing over the flat water, and he quickly turned his head in that direction. The ship at the mooring had fired a gun from a starboard port; a wreath of blue-gray smoke lazed away from the square trapdoor high in the hull. Now the noise of confused shouting came to Maillart down the quay, as more and more men came out of the buildings to see what was the issue. He could not make out what anyone was saying, but the smoke seemed to darken as it dissipated over the still water, and the brilliance of the day turned chill. Maillart jammed his hat on his head and hurried over the pavement toward the strange ship.

Several men had emerged from the warehouses nearer him and were hastening along in the same direction. Maillart was not acquainted with any. He saw his brother officer Vaublanc speeding up toward him and toward them all, raking unhappily at his hair with one hand and clutching a Paris newspaper in the other. His spurs made a harsh rattling sound with each jolt of his boot heels against the stone *pavés*. As he came farther within earshot Maillart heard him calling out in a hoarse voice that the king was dead, that Louis and Marie Antoinette had both been slain on the guillotine, and that the French monarchy was now altogether fallen.

"What does it mean," Maillart said, hardly conscious of his words. He snatched the paper from Vaublanc's hands and scanned the columns blindly; the words tangled on the page and he could make no sense of them. Two other men stood by looking curiously on while a third had run deeper into the town to cry this news.

"It means that we are finished." Vaublanc seemed unaware that he was weeping, though his pale face was all in sheets of tears. "Done for in this country, done for in France. There *is* no France. Well, I shall sell my sword to the Spanish, I suppose, and that straight away—will you come too?"

"Yes," Maillart said, mechanically. "What are you saying? Do you really mean to go?"

"I do," said Vaublanc. "Only imagine the demonic joy the monster Sonthonax will have of this intelligence. I would not serve that man another hour. No, but if the Spanish win this island, there may be some refuge here—some order and some decency. Only tell me, will you come?"

"Yes," Maillart said. He knew, of course, that he'd find friends among the Spanish forces now, for many officers had deserted in the aftermath of that unlucky skirmish between the mulatto Sixth and the Regiment Le Cap. All this he knew, but when he spoke his tongue felt numb between his lips.

He arranged to meet Vaublanc by noon, on the road out of the city that passed by La Fossette. Vaublanc had an affair or two of business to terminate in the town; he believed he might be able to raise some small amount of money. For Maillart there were no such considerations. He went back to Les Casernes in the wake of the riot that ran through the city ahead of him. In the barracks all was equally in turmoil. Laveaux was organizing patrols to quell the confusion in the city, but only the National Guards seemed much disposed to obey his orders.

The captain moved through the courtyard unnoticed, as he thought, and went into the room to pack his gear. The task would not occupy him long, as he had only his linen, a change of uniform, a book or two and a slack purse containing the few coins left of his last pay. When he came into the courtyard again carrying his light saddlebags across his shoulders, Laveaux caught his eye and called out a quick command for him to go with a detachment of ten men to settle a disturbance that had arisen near the Place de Clugny. But Laveaux turned quickly away once he had spoken, allowing no time to observe the captain's response. So Captain Maillart would not need to openly display his insubordination. All the same, the ten men followed him once he had mounted and ridden through the barracks gate. He looked blankly at them, over his shoulder, touched up his horse and rode away, leaving them there.

Now he might have wept himself, but he would not give way to the impulse. He controlled himself, forcefully emptying his mind. It being unseasonably warm, he was sweating a little under his tunic. Some blocks ahead he heard shouting and the snap of small arms fire; he took his way into a different street.

It was early yet, still short of eleven, and the captain did not want to wait long for Vaublanc under the broiling sun in the open country round La Fossette. The mosquitoes were very bad in that place.

It was this distaste, more than the thought he owed her some farewell, that prompted him to call on Madame Cigny. She had been demonstrably cool to him since his return from Ennery, and there'd been no renewal of their trysts.

The parlor was empty when the footman escorted him into it. Shortly afterward, Major O'Farrel of the Dillon regiment came in—from some inner recess of the house, the captain was convinced, because his clothes were definitely rumpled and he was blinking as if he'd come from darkness into light. They had time to pass a word or too before their hostess interrupted them. Today her *déshabillé* was such as to leave few secrets of her trim light body unsuggested. The captain was inclined to take this as a personal affront. He rose from his seat and moved very near her; yes, he could smell it on her—she was hot and wild as a little cat. A loud throat-clearing from the major helped him suppress his impulse to slap her insolent face. Then Isabelle took his hand in both of hers and when she spoke her voice was kind, atypically sincere.

"Grim news today, my friend."

"Yes," the captain said. "It is grim indeed."

She held his hand a moment longer, neither squeezing nor caressing but only sheltering it in the cage of her own fingers. Then she let it go and walked to the window.

"What will you do?" she said, staring into the street. "I have heard the intentions of Major O'Farrel."

"I'm going over to the Spanish, I believe," the captain said, "and so it is I'm come to take my leave of you."

Isabelle turned from the window, her pretty fingers still on her bare throat. "I would away to the mountains myself, had I the power."

"You have more power than many suspect," the captain said, but with no rancor. He had not even meant to say it. And he had no reply of her, except her somewhat wistful smile.

After all it was no hour for embraces. He and the major left the house together, O'Farrel preceding Maillart out the door. Looking at the other man's broad back, the captain felt his resentment flare again. He toyed with a pair of gloves in his pocket and with the notion of snapping them across the major's russet beard.

O'Farrel turned smartly as if he'd read the captain's mind. "No," he said. "We shan't quarrel over her."

The captain started back a pace, as the street door clicked shut behind him. "No?" he said.

"I think it unlikely." O'Farrel smiled, yellowish teeth foxy in his beard, as he glanced up at the windows above them. "Of course she is an extraordinary woman, but you cannot believe she takes us very seriously. If we were to be so foolish as to fight a duel, say, why she would be laughing in her sleeve at both of us all the while."

"*Bien*, I never offered you any quarrel, did I?" Maillart said somewhat irritably.

"Of course not," the major said. "You are a sensible fellow. You might come in with me to the Dillon regiment—I will be going to La Môle in six days time."

"Thank you, I am resolved to forswear any further service to these Jacobins," the captain said.

Major O'Farrel cut his eyes quickly along the street and stepped a little nearer to the captain. "No more than I," he said. "And no more than many of us with Dillon. There may be something to be hoped of the English, before long . . ."

"The *English*." Maillart twisted his lips in the form to spit.

"Well, if you are so much fonder of the *Spanish*," O'Farrel remarked. "Do you recall how half Le Cap put on the black cockade when the Englishman Bryan Edwards sailed into the port?"

The captain shook his head—though he did remember well enough. "At any rate, we shall not quarrel over that," he said. "I wish you joy of whatever course you take."

"Yes, and the same to you," Major O'Farrel said. He slapped the captain on the shoulder, just below the fringe of his epaulette. "*Bon voyage et bonne chance*."

He had delayed long enough that Vaublanc was already awaiting him in the barren field by La Fossette. Their horses fell automatically into step with each other, going along the hard-packed road, which had only a surface layer of damp this day, had not yet gone to mud and ruts. Captain Maillart was gloomy and dour, thinking of acquaintances who had been killed in this place the last September, during the skirmish with the Sixth. At a distance of a hundred yards they passed the hut of the *hûngan* who was established at the cemetery's end. Drums were beating there and there were white-clothed celebrants dancing in the *hûnfor*.

"Vodûn," Vaublanc said, contemplatively.

"Are they so overjoyed to learn the murder of the king?" said Maillart.

"I don't think it probable," Vaublanc said. "After all most of our black brigands appear to be of a royalist bent."

Maillart snorted.

"You were there at Habitation Saint Michel, recovering the prisoners," Vaublanc said. "Do you not remember that green silk flag the brigands round Jean-François were displaying? *Ancien régime* it said on one side—I forget what it said on the other."

"Vive l'ancien régime," Maillart said, surprised to hear the bitterness of his own voice.

They passed through the earthwork defenses, riding out beyond them in the direction of Morne du Cap. As they went through, a mulatto officer hailed them with some ironic salutation and fired a musket into the air. The shot's echo faded behind them in the empty land and they rode on.

They went from fort to fort of the *cordon de l'ouest* spreading their ill tidings on their way. At some of these white encampments the garrison was Jacobin and their news was greeted with scarce-suppressed pleasure, but elsewhere the despair it engendered was black as their own, and some of these latter forts emptied out behind them, the defenders scattering for the Spanish border or south to Les Cayes and Jérémie, which were reputed still to be *émigré* strongholds.

As they came nearer to the River Massacre there were no more forts at all and they sought shelter for the night at the house of a free mulatto coffee planter on the lower slopes of the mountains there. He received them gladly enough notwithstanding their color, and told them that despite the burning and looting on the plain, he was carrying on his work without molestation, still harvesting and roasting coffee beans. He was helped by his wife and two young sons and there were a dozen workers in that place, both black and colored; if these were slaves or *affranchis* it was not clear.

Next day they came down to the bank of the river itself, where in the midst of the razed cane fields the little church and *ajoupa* were still standing. Someone had planted two *carrés* with provisions, so that now the ash-blackened land was beginning to brighten with the green of banana shoots and potato vines. There were children working those provision grounds with sticks, but it was not until the tall angular woman in the turban came out to join their labor that Captain Maillart recognized the place from the tales which Arnaud and the doctor had told him.

He left his horse for Vaublanc to hold and walked into the field afoot to speak with Fontelle, whom he remembered seeing once or twice around Le Cap, and at the last in the Place de Clugny, when they had executed the little priest. She did not know him, but seemed pleased when he explained himself. He was curious to learn how she had made her way back to this place with all her children, but she would make no definite answer to his questions. She did tell him how to find a ford without going too riskily near the town of Ouanaminthe, and gave him a sack of yams to carry on their way. She seemed reluctant to accept the coins he offered in exchange, but he pressed the money on her, though his purse was light.

The ford was passable as she had said, and they crossed it with no difficulty and doubled back on the opposite shore, riding back toward the Spanish town of Dajabón, which they reached just at dusk. The place was without much to recommend it, but both officers were unsure of their next direction. Vaublanc was rather wary of going deeper into Spanish lands while wearing their French uniforms. He thought they might change to civilian dress here in Dajabón, which was a smugglers' town, but Captain Maillart was loath to go in disguise, if only because he pictured a fine scene when he would dramatically cast off his French coat in the presence of grateful Spanish officers.

They debated this matter for a few moments with no result, then Vaublanc suggested they refresh themselves at the tavern. Better in funds than the captain, Vaublanc ordered drinks for them, and returned to their rickety table with two cups of *tafia*.

"They have no wine at present," Vaublanc said. "Nor ever have had any, I suspect."

"I'm glad enough of whatever I can get," Maillart said, losing no time in warming his inwards with a good gulp from the brim.

He had taken care to seat himself against the wall, and now Vaublanc also hitched his chair around, so that they sat side by side, surveying the room together. Two men were lying on the floor, asleep or drunk or dead perhaps, and three mulatto women were draped against the rough-hewn counter, turbaned heads tilted like flamingos'. A drunken white man kept trying to insert his fingers into the bodice of one of these ladies who as often slapped his hand away. In the corner opposite their own, some black men and a couple of whites were playing dice around a larger table.

"Our troubles are over," Vaublanc said.

"What do you say?"

Following the other's gesture, Captain Maillart took note of a white man leaning back into the corner, arms folded across his chest, frowning over the game as it seemed, though it didn't appear he'd placed a bet. His long greasy black hair was pulled tightly back to the nape of his neck, and his throat was roughened with a week's dark growth of beard. He wore a white shirt of coarse cloth, loose in the belly and the sleeves and stained with many days of sweat and dirt.

"It's Xavier Tocquet, look there—" Then Vaublanc was on his feet and speaking louder. "Xavier, well met—" He halted suddenly. Tocquet had jerked upright, away from the wall, and was just slipping a hand into his bloused shirt belly . . . Captain Maillart laid a hand on his own pistol grip, concealing his movement beneath the table.

"Wait, man," Vaublanc said. "You know me."

"Of course," Tocquet said. "Only you took me by surprise." He revealed his hands again on the tabletop, each empty. "Come on, then, and bring your drinks."

The men made space for them to draw up their stools, and Tocquet with a gesture invited them to join in the dice game.

"I fear I've played my stake already," the captain said, demurring.

Vaublanc put up a coin, and watched the play sidelong as he explained their situation to Tocquet.

"Well, your moment is propitious," Tocquet said when he had done. "Though I'd counsel you to keep clear of San Domingo City for the moment . . . go instead to San Raphael. They are fitting out new regiments there—to invade you," he smiled, showing the tips of his teeth, "or for you to invade them, would it be? *Comme vous voulez*. In any case they will be glad to find white officers."

"*Parfait,*" Vaublanc said, smiling fixedly as one of the black men gathered in the coin he had staked. Tocquet reached into his shirt again, took out three slim black cheroots and offered them to the French officers.

"Merci bien," said Captain Maillart, leaning toward the candle flame. Inhaling, he coughed on the strong smoke. *"Mais . . . un moment.* You're suggesting I command nigger troops?"

Across the table, two of the black men grew quiet and watchful—Maillart wondered if they'd reacted to the sudden stiffness of his tone or if they understood his French.

"I am suggesting that you serve under a nigger general," Tocquet said with a slightly contemptuous bite. He turned to Vaublanc. "You might have known the man—Toussaint Bréda. He had been coachman and *commandeur* at Haut du Cap, on the lands of the Comte de Noé."

"I might know him by sight, perhaps," Vaublanc said. "I certainly did not know he was so elevated . . . but didn't he sign one of those absurd letters that were sent in from the plain?"

"That I can't say. But he is a general officer now," Tocquet said, "in the Spanish army. Supposing I had a taste for the military life, which I do *not,* I had sooner serve under him than any of your Spanish boobies. I tell you this because you asked." His dark eyes snapped toward Captain Maillart. "Of course, you may do as you like, and be damned to you."

The captain swallowed. He felt too foolishly disoriented to follow up the challenge. "I meant you no offense," he said haltingly. "You see I am a stranger in this place . . . and to these times."

"As are we all." Tocquet reached out his hand; the captain grasped it. "I do not take offense so easily," Tocquet said. "Good luck to you, whatever you choose."

"I think I have not ever been to San Raphael," Vaublanc said.

Tocquet toyed with the frayed brim of the large hat that lay on the table near his drinking cup. "I will be going there myself before long, though not directly," he said, showing his thin smile. "I have business with the quartermaster there—I and my companions . . ." he glanced at the two black men who had grown wary when the captain first spoke. "I might offer you an escort if you wish it—if you are not in too great haste."

Vaublanc looked toward Captain Maillart, who hitched his shoulders uncertainly.

"Where have you left your horses?" Tocquet said.

Vaublanc flipped his hand over casually. "Just there, outside the door."

Tocquet clicked his tongue. "You are carefree . . . there is a stable on the next street which would be much more trustworthy."

OUTSIDE THE INN IT WAS COMPLETELY DARK and beneath a sickle moon a small wind gently combed the palm crowns. On the opposite side of the street two dirty white men were fighting empty-handed, but they were so incapacitated by drink they could scarce find each other with their fists. Captain Maillart was much relieved to find the horses still where they had left them. He and Vaublanc unhitched the animals and walked toward the stable which Tocquet had recommended to them.

"Will we go and offer our services to this black general then?" the captain said.

"I think we will," Vaublanc said. "I'm a stranger to these times as much as you, but Tocquet always falls on his feet, wherever the moment may drop him."

"I can well believe that," said Captain Maillart. "What was the name of this black fellow, Toussaint? Toussaint what?"

"I don't recall," Vaublanc said, cheerfully enough. "What does it matter?"

Chapter Thirty-Two

THE NIGHT WAS THICKENED BY THE CLOUDS circling the ring of hills that shelved in Habitation Thibodet, and toward dawn it rained but only a little. Lying in the sag of his roped bed, Doctor Hébert was vaguely aware of the thickening of raindrops on the roof, as he drowsed between consciousness and dream. The light sound lulled him and he slept more deeply. When he woke again it was good daylight and the housemaid Zabeth was setting a tray with coffee on the floor beside the bed, turning her shy smile from him as she did so.

The doctor dressed, taking sips of coffee from the demitasse. On the gallery, Zabeth served him another cup, some bread and a jam made from mango. The doctor peeled a banana and ate half of it. Presently Delsart joined him and without speaking helped himself to coffee.

A mass of rain cloud crawled easterly over the hills like a great gray caterpillar, toward the peaks of the Cibao mountains, which were sheathed in a pale fog. To the west, the sun had shot the dissipating vapors with white light. The doctor finished his banana and folded the peel on his plate.

"*Comment allez-vous aujour d'hui?*" he inquired of Delsart.

"*Pas mal, pas mal . . .*"

In fact it did appear that the *gérant*'s health had taken a turn for the better. The sores on his face had healed to pinkish patches of new skin. The doctor had him under a mercury treatment for the pox, and had frightened him away from the quarters by telling him that if he did not altogether abstain from venery, an amputation would certainly be necessary to save his life. He had also contrived to limit Delsart to a pint of tafia a day. If altogether deprived of rum, the *gérant* began to hallucinate and turned completely useless.

"You'll go to the coffee again today?"

"*Ouais, bien sûr,*" Delsart said. He brushed a crumb from his cheek and stood up, reaching for his tattered hat. The doctor got up also, nodding to Delsart, and walked down the path to the infirmary.

This building he had caused to be erected as soon as Maillart's party had left the plantation, overriding Delsart's complaints about the loss of *main-d'oeuvre*. Delsart had maintained that the institution of a hospital would only lead to more malingering, but in fact, the opposite seemed to hold: after a few days of treatment and recuperation, the ill or injured performed much better than before, and the morale of the whole *atelier* seemed boosted. Besides, the infirmary was far from luxurious, nothing more than a rectangular shelter built on the model of the slave cabins, but about three times their size. One wall had been left open to the air, with palmiste blinds that could be lowered in case of a blowing rain.

Today, the blinds were rolled up to the eaves. The doctor had ordered the making of six rope beds similar to the one he used in the *grand'case*, but only two of them were occupied at present. At least two other women, erstwhile inamorata of Delsart, were sick with the pox, but the doctor could spare no mercury for them. Delsart was essential; he'd have been helpless in the management of the plantation without the *gérant*'s aid. Unfortunately, Toussaint's repertory as a *dokté-feuilles* had included no specifics for venereal diseases.

He first approached the bed of a twenty-year-old Senegalese with a pair of nasty puncture wounds, one in the forearm and the other in his calf. This one had a tale of being knocked over and slashed by a boar in the jungle, but the doctor did not much credit it. He had learned the difference between knife wounds and tusk wounds, and he thought the injuries more likely came from a fight, though he saw no use in prosecuting the matter.

He changed the Senegalese's leg bandage and applied a fresh poultice of herbs. While he was so engaged, Zabeth came from the kitchen shed and served the *tisane* he had ordered for the other patient, an elderly slave who was sick with the grippe. When the old woman had received her bowl, the doctor beckoned Zabeth over and watched as she redressed the Senegalese's arm wound, nodding approvingly as he stroked his short beard to its point. He was pleased with Zabeth; the girl was quick and clean and gentle, and she had talent as a nurse.

A wind was blowing pleasantly from the west and by the time the doctor left the infirmary, the sky had cleared all around the horizon so that the jungled peaks of the eastern mountains were sharply etched against the bluing sky. Already it was beginning to be hot, but the breeze cooled the sweat that sprang on him as he proceeded. He walked through the *carrés* of cane, untended for the moment, and climbed the terraces of coffee trees toward the edge of the jungle.

The *atelier* had started on the highest terrace and the slaves were picking their way down. It was much easier work than cane, so today the singing was spontaneous. Delsart had not even bothered to carry a whip up the hill. The doctor exchanged a word or two with him. He selected a red pod from the basket of the slave Politte, cut the husk with his thumbnail and peeled it back. The coffee taste was fresh and lively in the opaque jelly stuff surrounding the seed, when he popped the bean into his mouth. There was something he heard, though, a beat behind the singing. The doctor made a cutting motion and Delsart called out for the singers to cease.

In the decline of the *gérant*'s voice, the doctor slowly turned his head from side to side, straining his ears, but there was nothing, only the sigh of the western breeze. Delsart looked at him curiously. The small oval leaves of the coffee trees fanned back, then righted themselves as the wind relaxed them.

"C'etait rien," the doctor said, blinking his reply to Delsart's shrug. The slaves took up their song again as the doctor walked back down the hill.

He crossed the main compound and entered the cane mill. The slave Barthelmy was in charge of two others who were cleaning and repairing the refinery gear, which had been left in sticky disarray since the last pressing. They were also supposed to go over the equipment necessary for the refinement of white sugar. Doctor Hébert had insisted that Delsart teach him this process, though in truth they were now too short-handed to work both cane and coffee simultaneously. Habitation Thibodet had fared much better than most plantations of the north, but many of the slaves had run away, if not murdered or abducted, so that they now commanded only two-thirds of the original workforce.

The poles of the disused *moulin de bêtes* swung down from the central turn-peg. Barthelmy was scrubbing the interlocked grooves of the cane press cylinders with a stiff brush. He stepped back as the doctor approached, and swung a pole to turn the press, exposing new-brightened metal. Doctor Hébert smiled at him and left the mill.

He went to the stable, saddled his horse, and rode out on the cattle trail behind the main compound. In a scabbard by his knee he carried a big *coutelas* which he used to chop the overgrowth from the path—weekly the jungle tried to take it back. Every so often he stopped to gather useful herbs. Allowing for these pauses, it took him nearly two hours to reach the area where the sheep were foraging.

Again in despite of Delsart's protest, the doctor had diverted two slaves in their prime, Coffy and Jean-Simon, to serve as shepherds—that because he was quite distressed over the drastic diminution of the flock over the months that he'd been absent, since Thibodet had died. But today, no more of the sheep had been lost, and three new lambs were safely born.

Coffy and Jean-Simon seemed very glad to see him. He had brought them food, manioc flour and some dried peas that they could boil. But Coffy, especially, seemed distinctly ill at ease. He asked the doctor if he had brought his pistol. The doctor said that he had not.

He thought no more of this matter until, partway down the trail, he heard the drumming start again. It was faint and very distant, but unmistakable—no longer to be dismissed as an illusion, as he had done among the coffee trees. He thought for a moment, then doubled back on the trail and returned to his pair of herdsmen.

"Why didn't you tell me?" His tone was sharp. Coffy rested his stave on the ground and looked down at the dirt between his bare toes.

"How long since it began?" the doctor said.

"Only since this morning," Jean-Simon muttered.

The doctor cocked his head again. He did not understand much about the drums, but this sound seemed fuller-throated, deeper, more like the drums of Biassou's followers than the harsh dry rattling beat he had heard coming out of Jeannot's camp once upon a time. Ought that to be a reassurance?

"We had better bring the sheep back into the corral," he decided.

Jean-Simon and Coffy both looked visibly relieved. The doctor stayed to see them organize the movement, but Jean-Simon had been training a little dog to drive the sheep, so they didn't seem to require his help. Only each must carry one of the newborn lambs in his arms, because they were too small to make the pace. The doctor took the third lamb over his saddlebow and preceded the others down the trail.

As he rode, the drumming became less distinct behind him and, by the time he reached the main compound, he could no longer hear it at all. Going at a faster pace, he had arrived well in advance of the herdsmen and the few remaining sheep. It seemed useless to raise any alarm, but he could not quite think what to do. All was quiet in the compound now, with the work party resting in the quarters, waiting out the midday heat. This term of the old Code Noir was one the doctor scrupulously observed, which was one reason he was infinitely more popular with the *atelier* than Thibodet had been.

He stabled his horse, and since he did not know what else to do with the new lamb, he carried it with him into the office behind the cane mill. The lamb nudged bluntly into the doctor's armpit, hunting the teat. He set it down on the floor, where it balanced on its bunched legs, heavy head swaying. The doctor took one of the heavy mold-spotted ledgers from a shelf and opened it across the desk. Of late he had taken over all account-keeping, which Delsart had reduced to a sad confusion. The doctor had rearranged affairs into three books: one for coffee, one for cane, a third for provisions and the livestock. Now he dipped a pen and recorded the new births, two ewe lambs and the little ram who had now drifted into a corner and stood bleating at the join of the walls.

It was very hot in the close brick room, although the large shutter had been thrown completely clear of the window. The doctor finished his entry and fanned the pages back. Delsart's uncertain watery handwriting lay in webs across the sheets, translucent from his weak, diluted ink. The doctor raised his head, almost before he heard the sound, and then a woman's voice broke into a crazy ululation somewhere in the quarters.

The doctor dropped his pen and rushed into the yard. Coffy and Jean-Simon were just coming in, the little dog yapping at the tails of the hot and dusty sheep. At the doctor's sign, the two slaves hushed the barking. At the same time the woman's wailing stopped and in that crisp passage of silence the doctor heard drumming again in the distant hills. Then the woman's voice again took up the cry, her thread of terrorized notes interrupted now by lower hoarser voices which perhaps were trying to calm her. But all was confusion: looking down the trail the doctor saw the whole *atelier* swarming out of the cabins.

Delsart was coming around from the rear of the *grand'case,* rubbing his eyes wearily. Jean-Simon and Coffy stared at the doctor to see what he might do. Doctor Hébert waved them on to the corral—they turned from him and began herding the sheep through the gateposts.

"They're coming!" It was that woman's cracking voice, crying somewhere among the agitated slaves.

"Quiet, then," the doctor said loudly, but no one seemed to notice him. Delsart had just come up. "It may be nothing," the doctor said to the *gérant.* "They may well pass us by."

Delsart frowned and spat to the side. The petals of a bloodshot flower had unfolded on the white of his left eye. "Whether they come or not, we had better do something or our blacks will all bolt."

"To join them?" the doctor said.

"Not this crew," said Delsart. "These are afraid . . ."

"All right," the doctor said. "Get them together and bring them all up to the yard. Women and children, everyone. Break out the cane knives for the men as well." The doctor started for the *grand'case,* then called back over his shoulder. "Bring beanpoles too. Beanpoles and twine."

By the time Delsart had marshaled all the slaves into the compound, the doctor had opened the storeroom and taken out the powder and shot and what firearms there were: five rusting pistols (apart from his own), two old smooth-bore muskets, four bird guns and his own rifled piece. He rowed the weapons out on the gallery floor, while the crowd in the yard shuffled and breathed. The doctor straightened, laid a hand on the gallery rail as he drew breath into his tightening chest.

"There is nothing to fear," he said loudly. "I don't think we will be attacked. If we are," he picked up a musket, "we will be ready."

He tossed the musket to Delsart, who caught it one-handed, leaning forward to snatch it before it hit the ground. The doctor picked up the second musket and passed it butt-first to Jean-Simon.

"Only remember," he said, raising his voice another notch. "There is nowhere to run. Here is the safest place for all of you." He lifted his own rifle and thumped the stock on the gallery floorboards. "If we stand fast, they cannot overwhelm us—they will not even dare to try."

He turned aside. The slaves were quiet at first, then came the muttering of whispered conversations. Delsart came creaking up the gallery steps. "Do you believe that?"

"No," the doctor said. "I had to tell them something. You'd better start them making cartridges. Jean-Simon and Coffy, they are quick. Have the other men make pikes from the cane knives and the beanpoles."

"Much use those will be," Delsart said. "All the brigands have guns from the Spanish now."

"Yes," the doctor said. "But it will calm them to have this occupation."

"They won't stand to fight, you know," Delsart said. "They'll break and run at the first shot."

The doctor shrugged. "We have guns and powder enough, we may defend the *grand'case* with only a few."

"Until they burn us out," Delsart said.

"Of course," said the doctor. "Perhaps it will not come to that."

The clock ticked in the shadowed interior of the blinded front room, pendulum winking as it swung between the stripes of daylight. Going along the dim rear corridor, the doctor collided with Zabeth, who plumply recoiled, gasped and rushed into another room. In his own small chamber, he loaded both his pistols. He laid one of them back into the case where it was kept and stuck the other into his belt. As he came out onto the gallery again, he pulled his shirttail out of his waistband, letting it hang loose to cover the pistol grip.

A circle of blacks in the yard was engaged in splinting cane knives to beanpoles, as he had instructed. The doctor smiled thinly to himself to recall where he had come by this notion. His old ankle injury was paining him a little. He felt the eyes of Delsart on him as he went walking out of the yard.

He climbed the hill at such a good speed that he was soon sweating freely, but once he had passed the last coffee terraces and entered the jungle shade, the moisture turned cold on him, though he remained damp and humid. It was quiet beneath the forest canopy, only for the crying of the birds. He heard no drumming. The sounds of his breathing and his heartbeat seemed loud to him.

Unsure of his purpose, he went along slowly, climbing the steep slope, still soft and slippery underfoot. The mud was spotted here and there with the bright vermilion seeds from the bead trees. The doctor came to vine-covered rocks that edged a shallow ravine; in the bed of it a slender stream went singing down the hill. He continued, climbing alongside it. At a distance above he heard the drums again but then they faded, perhaps around some sudden turning of the slopes.

Toward the top of the ridge was a slash in the jungle where some big *gommier* trees had been logged out by Thibodet. Skirting the edge of it, the doctor saw that it was later than he had thought, for the light of the sun was sharply slanting. Somewhere nearby was a larger stream and he could hear the rush of the water, though he did not see it. All the air was dazed with moisture. He kept going, circling the cut. Never before had he climbed so high; plantation work had allowed him no time for such explorations.

When he crested the ridge, he found one of the flint-paved Carib roads that ran along the backbone of the mountain. Because he had not expected it to be there the discovery quite unnerved him and he left the road immediately, although it would have been easier going, of course, if he had kept to it. It was then that he noticed that all birdsong had ceased. Only, down below him now, a big dark-winged macaw went gliding across the cut as silently as a hunting owl.

The doctor moved toward a rock face which had been hollowed out a little by the rush of water and was overhung with vines that hung as straight and evenly as rain. There was just enough space behind the vines for him to stand erect. He waited, the damp of the rock face chill against his back. From this vantage he could admire a pale orchid which sprouted near a rotting log, white drooping blossoms strung in a row like harness bells.

He took the shard of mirror from his pocket and cupped it in his hand. Amid the wrinkles of his palm his single eye gazed back at him. He turned his wrist and the mirror swam plaid with the muted jungle colors. Why this movement gave him comfort he could not have said.

The first two men appeared in the slanting shafts of reddened light, below and to the doctor's right; he had not heard or seen them come. Each wore breeches of army issue, and one had a shirt, while the other was bare-chested, black skin gone coppery in the crepuscular glow. Both their chests were crossed with straps of cartridge boxes and they both carried muskets at the ready and they went quietly, carefully on their splayed bare feet over the slippery grade. He saw five more men filtering around the edges of the cut, then ten, fifteen. All was silence still, until from above him he heard the tramp of many marching feet. He surmised they would still be following the Carib road, which had led them out of the secret heart of the mountains.

A black man in the uniform of a captain in the Spanish army appeared quite near the deadfall log and the white orchid. He was empty-handed, though he wore two pistols in his belt. He turned and explored the fringe of vines with his attentive eyes before he made his way farther down cautiously over the difficult footing. The doctor noticed that he had a pair of high-topped boots slung over his shoulder, though he went barefoot like the other men. Of course, that was altogether like him. It was the uniform and the unfamiliar captain's hat that had delayed his recognition.

The doctor parted the vines and stepped into the clear. First he whistled, then called out.

"Riau."

The barefoot captain pivoted on the ball of his forward foot, reversing his direction as he threw himself down; he'd drawn a pistol as he spun and now he lay propped on his elbows, training the barrel precisely on the center of the doctor's chest. The doctor spread his hands and waggled the fingers slowly, the mirror shard still caught in his left palm. Quite suddenly, Riau broke into a smile and sat back on his heels. His hat had fallen off when he threw himself down, so that he looked more like himself as the doctor had known him.

Doctor Hébert relaxed and took a couple of rapid steps forward, so much too quickly that his feet shot out from under him and he went sliding down the grade, plowing twin tracks through the mud with his blunt heels. He rolled half over and stopped himself by catching hold of a sapling's base, fetching up beside Riau, who was now laughing heartily and pounding the flat of his thigh with his free fist.

"Mwê môtré sa," Riau said, prying at the doctor's left hand.

"What?" Unconsciously the doctor had closed his fingers over the mirror shard when he fell. He let Riau unfold them, so the mirror's wink appeared.

"Oh," said Riau. "There is your *ouanga*."

"My *ouanga*?"

"It is the eye you see to shoot with."

Riau smiled, but the doctor saw he was not joking. He shrugged, and put the mirror in his pocket.

"How did you come here?" he said, wringing some wet mud from his fingers.

"Following my General Toussaint."

"Your general?"

Riau pointed, back toward the rock face where the doctor had cached himself. At the height of the bluff a number of other foot soldiers had materialized. The Carib road must have continued just behind them, for there was Toussaint indeed, astride a gigantic black stallion and wearing a Spanish general's hat resplendent with a curling ostrich feather plume. The doctor scraped some mud from the back of his neck, then waved tentatively. Toussaint swept the hat from his head and bowed to him from the saddle.

It was agreed that the doctor would go ahead with Riau and some few men of the advance guard to prepare the *atelier*, so that the slaves would not panic when the main force arrived. Fifteen minutes later, the men began filing into the yard. Descending the jungle slope, they had fanned out, but once they reached the coffee terraces they reformed into a column and came lockstep and two by two, through the coffee trees and then the fields of cane. In the yard they regrouped into squares, each division with its officer stiffly standing at attention: Riau, Dessalines, Moise, and Charles Belair. Toussaint dismounted and stood beside the doctor, relaxed but perfectly erect. His military bearing seemed as natural to him as his good horsemanship.

They were reviewing the troops, the doctor perceived. His own spine stiffened. The Thibodet slaves stood in a loose group, round-eyed and silent.

"You'll camp here?" the doctor said.

Toussaint inclined his head.

"Above the provision grounds is a likely spot." The doctor waved his arm. "We had been clearing land for a new planting."

"*Bon ça,*" said Toussaint.

He called an order in a louder voice. His officers saluted him and the men spun the thread of their column once more and began marching out the opposite end of the yard. In the corral, a single ewe kept bleating piteously. As Toussaint's soldiers marched out, the Thibodet slaves began to laugh and gesticulate and chatter among themselves.

"So the work has been going forward here?" Toussaint said.

"Yes, we have enjoyed enough tranquillity so far . . ." Was it guilt the doctor felt? After all, it was forced labor.

Toussaint nodded, noncommittally, stroking his clean-shaven jaw. "Show me, then."

The sun had fallen behind the mountain and the light was blue. The doctor paused to ask Delsart to contribute some yams and a barrel of *tafia* to the cookfires of Toussaint's encampment. The men were carrying supplies of their own, so Habitation Thibodet would not immediately be picked clean. Delsart went off to execute the order.

"You know," the doctor said, "I hoped it would be you."

"You hoped?" said Toussaint.

"When we first heard the drumming . . . "

"You heard no drumming from us, I think," Toussaint said. "That would be Biassou—but he is still a long way off, behind that mountain."

The doctor raised his head and looked toward the eastern peaks, though now it was perfectly silent there. Above, the first and brightest stars pricked pinholes in the violet sky.

The doctor escorted Toussaint around the compound, showed him the hospital, the other projects under way. In response to his occasional questions, he explained his plan to resume the manufacture of white sugar. He told how gravely affairs had failed during Thibodet's illness, when both the slaves and crops had been neglected and ill used, and too many decisions left to the drunken and debauched *gérant*. He explained how he had sought to rectify these abuses, by building the infirmary and allowing for adequate food and rest, by denying Delsart use of the whip in all but the most desperate cases—and since these policies were instituted there'd been no desperate cases.

It was dark when they came to the cane mill again. The doctor lit a candle stub and held it high, while Toussaint explored the cane press. Then they went together into the office behind the mill. The little ram had been forgotten there; when they came in it jumped up and began bleating. Toussaint picked it up and it soon quieted. The doctor reached outside the window to draw the shutter to. In the corral, the ewe was still bleating but the shutter muffled the sound when it was closed.

"Yes," Toussaint said, returning to the tale the doctor had told him of Delsart. His hands were folded over the lamb, which nuzzled at his finger. "It's often so. And from that, many wrongs will come. And when the *gérant* drives the slaves to make a secret profit for himself as well as for the master . . . "

"I don't suspect Delsart of embezzlement," the doctor said. "It's not his vice. He is interested in wine and women but not money."

Toussaint leaned back and stared abstractedly into a cobwebbed corner of the ceiling.

"You know," he said, "if all the white men did as you, these troubles would have long since ended."

"And now?"

Toussaint looked directly at the doctor. The whites of his eyes had yellowed with his age. "You've seen my men. What do you think?"

"What do you mean?"

"The Spanish king has said that they are free if they will fight for him. Do you believe that they are free?"

The doctor looked at Toussaint's hands, long fingers lightly folded over the lamb's thin wool; beneath the wool the fragile skin showed pinkly. The candle cast a shadow over the black man's face. He thought that he might ask Toussaint if he were himself a prisoner of the Spanish authorities at this point, for Toussaint's arrival did represent the invasion of a foreign power . . . He recalled Monsieur Panon, whose lecture had sought to locate blacks somewhere in the chain of being between mules and men. There was Michel Arnaud, that night the doctor had first met him, releasing his cane and catching it just before it escaped his grasp. He remembered holding Nanon's baby soon after it was born and how hungrily the infant had searched him with its eyes, and he thought that it would be absurd to say that all men were born to freedom. In his peregrinations around this place, he had often felt as helpless as a newborn.

"I believe they are as free as I am," the doctor said.

"Ah," said Toussaint. "That will do."

The doctor exhaled and stretched out his legs. If it had been a test, he must have passed it.

"There is a woman in Le Cap," he said. "Also a child. I had thought to go for them, and bring them here. What do you think?"

"Yes." Again Toussaint lowered his head, perhaps to hide his smile. "I think you might be free enough for that."

They returned the lamb to the ewe in the corral, then strolled to the encampment where they ate with the other men around the fires. When they had done, the doctor offered Toussaint the hospitality of the *grand'case*, but the other declared that he would stay with his men. The doctor bade him good night and returned to the house alone through the gathered darkness.

As he lay in his low bed he could hear singing from the camp. Some of the Thibodet slaves had brought up instruments they had made, and there *was* drumming now. Although Toussaint suppressed *vodûn* among his troops, there would be an impromptu *calenda* danced tonight. The doctor thought that on the morrow, he must give the slaves a day's *congé*.

His candle sputtered low on the stick, but he did not extinguish it; there was not enough of the stub to bother saving. He was very weary, but the thought of Nanon had quite electrified him, so that his legs were tingling under the thin sheet. He closed his eyes and pictured a black fig, slightly wrinkled, pendulous and ripe to bursting. The fig would be cool in his palm's hollow, and he would hesitate, considering how to enter it.

When he opened his eyes, Zabeth was standing in the doorway.

She smiled and at once hid her face against her shoulder, while with both hands she raised the hem of her white shift to her neck, so that she showed herself to him entire. Her nipples and the soft brush of her nether hair were like dark chocolate layered onto light.

Presently the doctor said, "No, no, my dear—you must go to the dancing."

When he opened his eyes again, Zabeth had gone. He smiled weakly, touching his lips with his tongue. She offered herself so to him because she was a well-meaning person, and she wanted to show him a kindness. So far he had always declined the gift. Sometimes he thought that it would be wrong to hold Delsart to a higher standard than he himself could attain. Sometimes he gave himself another reason.

When the candle drowned in its molten pool of wax, the fig was firmly in his hand. He required neither knife nor nail, only stroked the glossy darkness of the skin with the balls of his thumbs; gladly it opened itself to him. The black skin parted to disclose the creamy whiteness of the flesh within, but still he would go deeper, deeper still, to reach in the teardrop heart of the fruit the wet red viscera it held. How strange it was that a fig tree should also bear red flowers with those thrusting tongues! His dissection needed no instruments; he would pursue it further. When he had passed entirely through the body of the fruit, his being would be washed in the colorless light of another soul.

Chapter Thirty-Three

East of the town of San Raphael were the traces of a large encampment recently departed: tent-peg holes, *ajoupas* abandoned, the grasses beaten down and the earth churned by horses' hooves and the feet of many men. Tocquet rode through, his head inclined, eyes bent hawklike on the ground, reading sign. Maillart and Vaublanc followed him in single file, the two blacks, Gros-jean and Bazau, bringing up their rear. The captain aimed his own glance wherever Tocquet seemed to look. Here and there was the impression of a booted foot but it seemed that most of the legible tracks had been left by barefoot men.

"De la merde, encore," Tocquet clicked his tongue. "I believe we have missed him."

"Where have they gone?" said Vaublanc.

"I suppose they must be invading you," Tocquet said, without looking back at his interlocutor. "Invading *us* rather . . . would it be?" He chuckled, perhaps—a growling sound low in his throat. "We shall see who is left in the town, if anyone. *Ouais, on verra, on verra . . ."*

The principal street of San Raphael looked no great matter. It was unpaved, so that the hoofbeats of their horses were still muted as they rode. A flock of speckled hens scattered in advance of them, cackling, and a little black boy dressed in only a shirt ran into a doorway and turned to peer back out. They halted before one of the more considerable dwellings, built in the Spanish fashion around a central court. Tocquet dismounted and knocked on the door. When some minutes had passed without response, he took a pistol from his belt and hammered much more loudly with the butt of it.

Presently, a young man in the uniform of a Spanish lieutenant opened the door; he raised his eyebrows superciliously but said no word. Tocquet winked at him.

"Is the general here?"

The lieutenant remained mute.

"Yes, he will receive us," Tocquet said decisively.

He put some pressure on the door, and the lieutenant gave way and let it swing completely open. Tocquet entered, the two French officers following. As the white men walked into the house, Bazau and Gros-jean led the horses around the outer corner of the building. Maillart blinked his way through the dim, stale-smelling interior. They emerged into the center court, which was unevenly paved with flagstones. In one corner a huge iron kettle rested crookedly on the dead embers of an extinguished fire. Some few straight chairs were grouped around the wicker table where they all took seats.

"He will be with you shortly," the lieutenant said, and went back into the house.

Captain Maillart slumped in his chair. He was stiff and sore from their hard and rapid ride from Dajabón, and would best have liked to recline, to sleep. Neither of his companions spoke. Maillart rolled his head back on the top rail of the chair and looked dreamily up at the fat cottony clouds suspended in the blue well of the sky. Beyond the house wall, a hummingbird shot up vertically from the bowl-shaped orange blooms of a tree.

A woman's voice roused him, and he pulled himself erect. She was a white woman, but oddly dressed in a short jacket and a man's white shirt. Also her thick straight hair was cut very short, just below the lobes of her small ears. Maillart thought that Tocquet had not embraced her; he only dallied his fingertips on the edge of her small hand.

"Je vous présente Madame Tocquet."

Cutting off his yawn, Captain Maillart jumped to his feet and bowed; Vaublanc was a little in advance of him with this courtesy. The woman nodded, smiling. Her chin was a little weak, but it was an agreeable smile, and her large brown eyes looked merry.

"Please sit down," she said. "You must be weary . . ."

Maillart resumed his seat. The woman took a step back from the table, hands on her hips, and as she moved her black skirt separated and he saw that it was not a skirt at all, but rather a pair of loose-cut trousers that stopped just short of her ankles.

Madame Tocquet had caught him staring at the division of her legs. She smiled more brightly still. "My husband has lately presented me with a mule," she announced. She spun around, presenting herself to Tocquet; her trouser legs flowed together and joined again as one. "Will this win your approval as a riding habit?"

"Yes, I believe so." Tocquet grinned, half concealing his mouth behind one hand as he turned to the French officers. "One cannot ride sidesaddle, where we are going."

Vaublanc started. "You cannot mean to take your wife into those mountains."

"Oh yes," the woman said. "I am going to Ennery."

Tocquet nodded. "She has an inheritance to claim."

She faced them, still smiling confidently, while the captain stared and reappraised her. It was the same, the eyes, the lips, the ears quite small but curiously shaped like cup handles. Even the weak chin, which the doctor's short beard sought to conceal, was much the same. Of course he had seen her in Lyons a time or two but that was long ago when she was a child.

"But you must be Elise Thibodet," the captain blurted. "I mean to say, Elise Hébert."

"Elise Tocquet—as I now find myself." She glanced at the man. "It's as he told you." Now she seemed more careful to choose her words. "We were married after the death of my first husband."

"*Pardonnez-moi,*" the captain said. "I am the friend of your brother Antoine—I have been in your house in Lyons, even. I think you would not remember. But your brother will be overjoyed to recover you—he is at Ennery now, if you are going there, I left him at Habitation Thibodet."

"I did not know he was in the colony." Elise had colored, placing her fingers to her throat.

"Why, he has been here for several months, and searching for you everywhere."

A door hinge whined and boots came clattering over the irregular paving stones: General Cabrera was approaching, flanked by the lieutenant and another orderly. Elise dropped them a curtsy, fanning the loose cloth of her trousers as though it were a skirt after all, and went hurriedly toward a door at the opposite side of the court.

"You are behind the time," the general said to Tocquet, and looked askance at the two officers in their French uniforms.

"These gentlemen are seeking to enter the Spanish service," Tocquet said. "Out of loyalty to their murdered king—and the other usual motives."

"Interesting." Cabrera continued to eye them coldly. Maillart felt the stiffening of the muscle along his spine.

"Perhaps you will find them suitable uniforms, at least," Tocquet said. "I will bring them to Toussaint myself—if you have cargo for me."

"Yes, I think so." The general turned and directed one of the orderlies to go in quest of uniforms, then looked again at Tocquet. "Certainly they will have need of powder and more lead. We may also find some victuals for you to carry . . . Though Biassou may be in greater need—his is the larger force."

"Toussaint is the wiser quartermaster," Tocquet said. "When one furnishes him powder, one may at least believe it will not be set afire to please the *vodûn*."

"You overestimate the man," Cabrera said. "He is too old, he was too long a slave. He has the slave's servility, which has shaped his mind."

"Do you think so?" Tocquet said.

The general sniffed. "Reading Epictetus—what sort of military man would be guided by the philosophizing of a slave?"

Tocquet laughed aloud and slapped the palm of his hand upon his thigh. "Meanwhile I doubt that Biassou can read as much as his own name."

"Well, we do not employ these fellows for their scholarship," the general said, glaring at the Frenchmen. "If your companions have determined to join Toussaint, I shall not quarrel with them—let him make of them what he can."

"Well enough," Tocquet said.

Captain Maillart felt a discomfiting desire to wriggle, though he held himself perfectly still. He'd been brought closer than he'd ever thought to be to the sentiments of a slave displayed on the market block.

"What news have you," Tocquet asked.

"What is there?" The general seemed to muse. "Oh yes, it appears that Galbaud has managed to pass the English blockade and is safely arrived at Le Cap."

Tocquet snorted. "Exchanging the devil for the witch."

"Galbaud?" Vaublanc inquired.

"Sent out from France as the new governor-general," Cabrera said.

"A curious choice," said Tocquet. "I think there will be trouble there. Galbaud is married to a Creole lady and I have heard he has considerable property here."

"I have heard the same," said the general. "It has long been the French policy to set the governor-general at odds with the intendant."

"But there is no longer any intendant to reckon with," Vaublanc said.

"There's Sonthonax," Maillart said.

"My thought precisely," Tocquet said. "It's much the same thing."

"If the military and civil authorities owe fealty to different factions," Cabrera said, "they are less likely to conspire together."

"Small chance of conspiration, these days," Tocquet said, stroking the stubble along his jaws. "Paris is far distant for the management of marionette strings as long as that. I wonder if this policy has perhaps outlived its usefulness."

"I suppose," said Maillart said, with more bitterness than he'd thought, "that if Galbaud ventures to dispute the Jacobinism of Sonthonax, he will only go the way of Desparbés."

"I take your point," Tocquet said, "but Galbaud is not so elderly a man as Desparbés, nor yet so frail. *Attendez, on verra . . .*"

As he spoke, the orderly came back into the court, carrying two uniform coats across his arm; he had brought no trousers at all. Expressionless, he displayed the goods. Both were faded and riddled with moth holes; one was missing all but one button and the other had most of the frogging ripped away. Captain Maillart felt the blood draining from his head, though he couldn't know for certain that the insult was deliberate.

"Control yourself." Tocquet watched him intently; his voice was sharp. "I tell you, Toussaint is the better quartermaster. Leave it to him to fit you out. Till then, I'll find you clothes of my own to wear."

NEXT MORNING THEY RODE OUT AT THE HEAD of an eight-mule train and by midday were well into the mountains, despite delays caused by the uneasiness of Vaublanc's and Maillart's horses on the abrupt and tangled slopes. Tocquet's horse, meanwhile, seemed preternaturally adapted to the difficult ascent, quite as nimble as a mule. And for the first hours of the journey he carried the little girl before him in his saddle, while Elise bestrode her white mule all alone, and ably as any old campaigner.

The child, whom they called Sophie, was Elise's, and it appeared that Tocquet claimed paternity; the girl let herself go to him with a familiar ease. Vaublanc had been shocked all over again by her appearance among their party, for the little girl looked altogether too delicate for such a trek, with her pale stick-thin limbs, her large dark eyes, and general air of frailty. She could have been no more than two. Captain Maillart, however, had grown numb to new astonishments. At first the little girl was sufficiently cheerful in her place, prattling and pointing and staring round-eyed at everything they passed. Tocquet kept one arm close around her waist, managing the reins with his other hand, and she seemed secure and comfortable. But later on Sophie grew restive and began to cry.

"This won't do," Tocquet said, after trying a few minutes to calm her, without success. "They can hear her howling for twenty miles at least." There was no asperity in his tone; he was simply stating the neutral fact. He dismounted, then lifted the child down and carried her to Elise, who took her up into the mule saddle. But Sophie was not reassured; she cried even louder.

"I don't want to ride anymore," she said. "I want Anna, where is Anna?"

"Anna could not come with us," Elise said softly.

"Why *couldn't* she?"

"Because she cannot ride a mule."

"*Mais pourquoi pas!?*"

There was a thunderhead on the mountain; in its shadow, Elise's face looked worn and fatigued. She caressed the little girl's shoulders, gathering the loose folds of her brown-figured calico dress.

When this failed to soothe her, Elise opened her shirt and gave suck to the child, who instantly closed her eyes and quieted. To manage this, the woman dropped her reins on the mule's neck, and the mule found its own way forward without guidance, following Tocquet, who had not once looked back. Captain Maillart would have liked to render her some assistance, but he was in difficulties of his own; he must needs get down and lead his reluctant horse across an especially problematic passage of their climb.

He could tell from the other man's sharp inhalations that Vaublanc had been dismayed once more at these fresh improprieties, but Captain Maillart, for his own part, was simply interested. The only thing he dreaded was the rain, but it did not begin; instead the cloud dragged its cold tendrils over them and shifted to a farther slope. In the fresh sunny radiance, Maillart regarded Elise and the nursing child as frankly as he might have gazed upon a painting, and indeed, she seemed as tranquil as any madonna, all unaware of her surroundings. Sophie was sleeping now, black lashes long upon her cheek, her face tucked against a milk-wet spot on her mother's thin chemise. Both seemed entranced, and Maillart also moved as in a dream, thinking of Isabelle Cigny again but without even wistfulness, only curiosity. It would have seemed impossible to imagine her in such a situation, but now he was not, after all, so sure . . .

So they went on, the two French officers afoot more often than not, leading their eye-rolling, head-tossing horses unwillingly along behind. It grew chill as they climbed higher, but still Maillart sweat-soaked the clothes Tocquet had lent him. The trousers were enough too long that their cuffs kept slipping under his bootheels; slickered with mud, they sometimes made him fall. Both he and Vaublanc were tired and irritable, but in the presence of the woman and the child they did their best to refrain from cursing. Presently Sophie awakened, but now she made no complaint; she contented herself in her mother's lap and looked around her owlishly.

By late afternoon they had completed numerous ascents and descents of the crags and sharp defiles of the mountains, and had come to the height of another peak whence they could see the sun streaking the western hills with an orange light. Tocquet had brought them faultlessly to a strange unlikely pathway made of rocks wedged in the mud; it ran ribbonlike down the mountain's spine, not quite wide enough for two men to walk abreast on it.

Tocquet got down from his horse and walked a little way ahead with his eyes lowered, examining the surface of this trail.

"*Incroyable,*" said Maillart. "How did this come here?" Vaublanc had come up breathlessly beside him.

"An Indian road," Tocquet said. "From the time of the *caciques.*" He stooped and shuffled through leaves at the trail's edge, then raised a horseshoe in his muddy hand; the iron was bright along a cut where a sharp stone must have gashed it.

"He'll make someone answer for the loss of this." Tocquet laughed shortly as he brandished the shoe. "If I know him."

"Who?" Vaublanc said.

"Toussaint." Tocquet hung his hat on a pack saddle and lifted the sweaty mass of hair from the nape of his neck. Following his eye, the captain saw that indeed there were prints of hooves and human feet to either side of the rocky road, which was so firmly laid that there was no mark directly on its surface.

"He will be going to Dondon, I think," Tocquet said. "That will be convenient for us."

He called out crisply to the two blacks. Bazau began loosening the girths of the pack saddles, while Gros-jean took a *coutelas* and began chopping undergrowth above the trail to clear a space where they might camp. Tocquet held up his hands to Elise and took the child onto his hip, then helped the woman down from the mule. They were still hand-in-hand as they left the trail and walked toward the sound of rushing water. Tocquet looked back and beckoned to the Frenchmen.

"Come."

So they followed him across the slope, among flat glossy elephant ears that grew against the larger trees, across a carpet of strange ferns. The rush of water became almost a roar. It was dim in the shade where they were going, but of a sudden they came into an open space where evening sunlight poured into a pool carved out of rock. A waterfall dropped sparkling from a stone lip fifteen feet above the pool, and Maillard wondered at how it steamed when the column met the smoother liquid surface.

"Hot springs," Tocquet said, as if he'd asked the question. He kissed Elise's cheek, then handed her down toward the water. "Just as I promised you."

The woman smiled at him and took the child from his hip, then made her way surefooted down to the gravel shoal beside the pool. Tocquet crooked his finger at the other men and they began climbing around to the lip of the falls, clinging to saplings to make their way. The captain staggered and panted out a laugh; Tocquet looked back at him curiously.

"You know, the Normans claimed that a horse must go anywhere a man can go without using his hands," the captain said. "I believe you have even exceeded that standard . . ."

Tocquet stepped out onto the rim above the falls, the two others in his train. From below came the delighted giggle of the child, Elise's musical laughter chiming in. Sophie was naked, waist-deep in the steaming pool, and Elise had rolled up her trouser legs to wade after her. She looked up at the men and waved; Tocquet smiled back.

"Come, let us give them privacy," he said. "I promised her this, at the day's end."

They went upstream, some hundred yards, clambering over boulders, then Maillart threw back his head and gasped. Above was a much higher fall; a sheer drop of sixty feet or more. Tocquet was already climbing toward it. The way grew steeper, vertical in spots, and the captain found himself climbing by notches in an ancient log. This rather unnerved him; he paused and called ahead.

"Will they be safe? Down there alone?"

"They're not alone." Tocquet was just reaching the foot of the larger fall. "Bazau and Gros-jean will look out for them. Besides, there's no one here. Those steps were cut a hundred years ago."

Maillart scrambled up beside Tocquet. The fall drove into a wider, shallower stone basin than the one below, and here too it was steaming. Tocquet shucked off his boots and stripped himself and stood directly beneath the tumbling stream with his legs set wide, gasping, his neck arched back so that the water blasted on his face and throat. In a moment he had moved away and was floating idly in the shallow water of the basin.

In his turn, Maillart undressed, then walked over, carefully on the slick underwater stone, and stood breathless under the weight of the warm falls. He dropped his head like a weary ox and let the stream pound the soreness out of his shoulders. Vaublanc joined him, laughing crazily. Water sluiced through the captain's ears. He withdrew from the waterfall and lowered himself gingerly onto his back so he was floating on his elbows not far from Tocquet.

"It's wonderful here," the captain said. "Nature . . . never have I seen nature so powerful."

"I agree with you." Tocquet lay back with his eyes half-lidded, black hair snaking around his head in the water. "Nature is very strong here indeed. A man could come up with nothing but a *coutelas* and a fire-drill and live out the rest of his natural life in happiness."

The captain stretched his toe in the warm water, thinking that Tocquet might already have put this notion to the test.

"The *caciques* might have held out forever here," Tocquet said. "The Spanish would not have reached them with an army, in these mountains."

"Why didn't they?" Maillart said.

Tocquet sat up and tossed his hair back over his head. He propped his back against a boulder. "I think they died of grief," he said. "Some say they were a gentle people. I believe it. Anyway, they would not be slaves. They threw themselves from the cliffs in droves—five hundred thousand of them." He scratched his stomach idly and let his fingers trail off in the water. "You see, it's not the first time this island has been washed in blood."

The captain drifted, the warmth of the water rather stupefying him. Vaublanc was floating alongside them. "How did you ever find this place?" he said.

Tocquet twirled a finger in the air. "I belong here," he said. "It may be that I have a touch of the brush, you know. Carib blood, not black."

"Blood will out?" the captain said.

Tocquet stirred his legs in the water. "Then there were no other women here, but Indians," he said. "My great-grandfather was a pirate. One of the faction that won Saint Domingue for France. But neither France nor Spain can hold it. It is mine and it is no one's. Or yours too, as you find it." Tocquet raised his dripping hand and spread it on a stone. Near his fingers, a small striped frog sat unalarmed, eyes protuberant and its loose gullet pulsing.

"I don't follow," Maillart said.

Tocquet gave his caiman smile. "I will tell you my great secret, then. I am the only one to know it. No man can own land *or* people, though a man may have their use. Those two down there, Gros-jean and Bazau—I paid a sum of money for them, but all three of us know that each belongs to himself alone. Do you understand me?"

"No," the captain said, feeling himself strangely incapable of lying.

"My friend, you had better think a little harder," Tocquet said. "Consider, who owns you? A week ago you were a Frenchman. What are you today?"

AT FIRST THEY FOUND THE GOING MUCH EASIER when they set out on the following day. But the Carib road did not run uninterrupted all the way to Dondon. It petered out, or was washed out altogether, and again they found themselves struggling through the untracked jungle, a day, a night, another day, and so until at last they struck the road again, near Ennery. They followed the road for four miles more and camped above it as they had done on other nights. On the afternoon of the next day they left the road again according to Tocquet's estimation of their position and soon broke out of the jungle into the coffee plantings above Habitation Thibodet.

From the hilltop they could see at once that the crops were well tended and they could see the slaves at work in the cane, a white man in a tattered straw hat directing them. As yet the new arrivals had not been observed and the work went forward with no interruption. The slaves were singing as they swung their hoes and the sound came thin but clearly to Tocquet's party on the crest of the hill.

"Look there," Tocquet said, drawing his horse up beside Elise's mule. "All in good order, just as I told you . . ." He reached across to ruffle Sophie's hair. "What are you thinking, little one?"

The child rocked between her mother's knees as the mule's feet shifted. She looked down dazedly over the plantation.

"Of course she doesn't remember," Elise said. "When we left here she was a babe in arms."

A shout went up from the *atelier*. They had been seen. There was a stir among the workers, but their foreman soon reorganized them—all save one, who was dispatched to run quickly back across the main compound and over to the provision grounds south of the *grand'case*. Another slave came out of the cane mill, paused to stare up the hill, and went for the *grand'case* at a trot.

Now the single runner had reached the new-cleared area above the provision grounds, which had been pitched with military tents. Some hundreds of black soldiers were there involved in a parade-ground exercise.

"So," Tocquet said. "It isn't Dondon." He reached into his saddle-bag and raised a small brass spyglass to his eye. In response to whatever message the runner had brought, a detachment of twenty men fell out and began marching back down toward the *grand'case*, guided by one officer.

Tocquet sniffed. "Well, we are to be received with military honors."

"If we are not to be repulsed," said Captain Maillart.

"No, it's all right." Tocquet passed the glass to the captain. In its ground glass circlet, Maillart saw that the officer commanding the twenty, a coal-black man with heavy, shelving brows and lips, wore the insignia of a Spanish major.

"Moise," Tocquet said. "He's Toussaint's nephew—so they say. A capable fellow, I think you'll find."

He squeezed his horse with his heels and moved to the head of their small column. In a few minutes they were on the flat and leading the mules through the cane. As they came abreast of Delsart he recognized Elise, tore off his hat and burst out laughing in amazement. Elise gave him a weary smile; Tocquet saluted him half-mockingly as he turned toward her from the saddle.

"That scoundrel looks in better health than when I last laid eyes on him . . ."

Elise's eyes, ringed by fatigue as if with kohl, were riveted on the house; she did not answer. The twenty black soldiers were drawn up in a double row at the yard's edge. Tocquet greeted Moise with a sharp upward jerk of his fist, then turned to point at the pack train.

"Munitions for your general, major," Tocquet said. "With your permission, we'll go straight along. Only, I think we'll leave the mistress to settle herself here."

Maillart looked over the black soldiers, barefoot men. Irregularly dressed, they still stood stiffly to attention, each with a musket held at the present-arms position. He searched their inexpressive faces; their eyes stared through and through him blindly as the eyes of statues. Tocquet, meanwhile, dismounted and lifted the girl down from the mule saddle. Sophie kicked up her leg and ran in a merry half-circle, holding her skirt out in both hands and flouncing it about. Elise took both of Tocquet's hands and swung lightly down to stand beside him.

"Come, Sophie." She caught the little girl by the hand and led her toward the steps of the *grand'case* gallery. Tocquet touched her on the shoulder as she passed, then swung back up into his saddle. The pack train moved along; Moise's soldiers faced left at his command and marched alongside of the mules. As they went by, Bazau reached out and caught the dangling reins of Elise's white mule and led it on behind the others.

At the top of the gallery steps, Elise hesitated, looking toward the darkness of the door, and then went on.

Formerly, in those last months, she had endured a lowering of her spirits whenever she passed this doorsill. Now she felt nothing of the kind. The main room was much as she remembered it, warm and humid, dominated by the ticking of the clock. At once, Sophie let go her hand and went to stand below the chest where the clock was placed, rapt in the swinging movement of the pendulum.

"Yes, you may touch it," Elise said, thinking how much Thibodet would have disliked her to do it. Tentatively, the child reached up her hand and arrested the swinging disk. The clock stopped. Elise began to laugh as Sophie turned to her, moonfaced with surprise. In the silence left where the tick had been, an insect whirred and thrummed behind a jalousie. Apart from that the house felt empty; there was no sign of Antoine.

"Come." Elise led the girl into the bedroom of her husband.

It was brighter here, for the blind was rolled up, and the room's window faced the sun. Thibodet's effects had been removed, but otherwise all was much as it had been before. The sight of her marriage bed did not particularly affect her, except that she was glad to see that it looked freshly made. She pulled open the door of her wardrobe and saw that her dresses seemed mostly intact. Impulsively she gathered clusters of the fabrics to her cheek and closed her eyes. The odor of the cloth was only slightly musty. She had been able to take scarcely anything with her when she made off with Tocquet, and she detested what fashions were available in Spanish San Domingo. She sat on the bed and spread a striped silk skirt across her knees. The calico cat came into the room and jumped into her lap. Smiling, Elise lifted it from the silk and sniffed its fur.

Sophie had picked up a tiny porcelain vase and was closely examining the enameled pattern of flowers and vines. Just then Zabeth came into the room.

"*Maîtresse?* Oh!" She sank to the floor and gazed at Sophie. "Look at the child." Zabeth winked, then wrinkled her nose like a rabbit, while Sophie put her finger in her mouth and smiled around it.

Elise sat down on the edge of the bed and began dragging at the heels of her riding boots. Immmediately Zabeth moved to help her. As the the second boot sucked off, Elise gasped with the pleasure of relief. "Oh, Zabeth," she said. "I'm glad to see you."

Zabeth smiled up at her with real good cheer, her fine teeth bright in her full, pleasant face. Elise saw that her own feeling was genuinely reciprocated.

"And my brother?" Elise said. "I had heard that he was here . . ."

"*Maîtresse,* he would be desolated to have missed you—he has gone on an errand of business to Le Cap."

"And will return?" Elise drew her legs up onto the bed, too weary to attend to Zabeth's answer.

"Yes, of course, he will return, within the fortnight," Zabeth said. "A bath, *maîtresse?*"

"Oh yes, a bath." Elise stretched her back against the coverlet, half closing her eyes as she flexed her cramped toes. "A bath, with plenty of hot water."

Above the provision ground, Toussaint's camp was flawlessly neat, free of debris, the ground hard-packed by movements of the men and horses. Tocquet and the two French officers dismounted outside the general's tent. As they did so, a hand pulled back the tent flap, and Toussaint stepped out and straightened in their presence. Maillart was somewhat surprised to recognize the man—he remembered seeing him, inconspicuous among the other blacks who'd delivered Doctor Hébert and the other prisoners to Habitation Saint Michel—but he looked different now. In the uniform of a *maréchal de camp* he seemed much more imposing, though the cavalry sword suspended from his sash looked almost absurd against his short jockey's legs. His posture was very straight, and he looked at Maillart and Vaublanc unblinkingly for a long time while Tocquet explained to him their reason for being there. The whites of his eyes were in fact somewhat yellow, with an amber, tobacco tint, like the eyes of many aging Negroes. Still, something in his look seemed to hold the captain in thrall, so that when Toussaint spoke he saw his lips move but did not hear a word of what he said.

Another black, in a captain's uniform, held up the tent flap, and Toussaint and Tocquet went in. Automatically, Maillart made to follow, but the black captain barred his way.

Tocquet looked back from the gloom of the tent's interior. "No, no, he'll see you later," he said. "After he's done with me."

Vaublanc smirked, then turned three-quarters away from Maillart and stared at the ground. Across the beaten earth from them, a mule hitched to a gun caisson lifted its tail and defecated. Immediately a man ran out from behind the general's tent and spaded up the steaming dung and carried it down to scatter on the potato vines in the provision ground.

There was a drumbeat, not the drums of *vodûn*, but a regular French military snare. A division of men was drilling to the beat, the officer called Moise commanding them. Some few of these black infantrymen wore complete Spanish outfits, while most were as irregularly garbed as militia. An effort had been made to give them a more uniform appearance with a standard issue of belts, slings and cartridge boxes. Certainly their weapons, short smoothbore muskets each fixed with a bayonet, were standard, and most of them seemed quite familiar with their handling. Maillart saw that the commanding officer had dispersed the green recruits in among the veterans, so that the inexperienced men could be supported, wherever they looked, by someone else who knew the drill. As it looked, there were many more green men than seasoned, but all in all there was much better order and discipline among them than Maillart could conceivably have anticipated.

The familiarity of the drumbeat lulled him into a sort of daze. He was much wearier from their traveling than he'd known, he was swaying, whirling on his rubber legs . . . When Tocquet tapped him on the shoulder, he started fully awake.

"He's ready for you now." All traces of the intimacy that had grown among them in the mountains was now gone from Tocquet's smooth and neutral tone.

Maillart lowered his head to pass under the tent flap. Within, no lamp was lit, only daylight straining through the canvas, so that Maillart, as he took the place indicated for him on a camp stool, thought that he could be seen much more clearly than he could see. Toussaint sat on a similar camp stool, a wooden lap desk balanced on his knees. The black man in the captain's uniform stood behind his chair.

"Your name, sir? Your rank in the French army? Which is your regiment?"

Maillart related these statistics. He had expected Toussaint's searching look so he was surprised that it was withheld. Toussaint had turned his face sideways, seemed not to look at Maillart at all, seemed only to be listening. Above his seat, the face of the black captain was hawk-like, cruel; there was anger there but Maillart could not know if he was the object of it.

"Tell me, sir, why you are out of uniform."

Maillart told of their circumstances. He had launched an account of their discomfiting meeting with General Cabrera before it occurred to him that it was not strictly necessary for him to do so. What was there in the black general's disposition that invited such extraneous confidences? Toussaint had taken off his hat, but his whole head was bound up in a madras cloth, triple knotted at the base of his skull, after the fashion affected by many slaves and by some wealthy planters. Against his crisp field uniform it made a strange impression. Toussaint asked him another question; Maillart replied. Each time, he told more than he must, and found himself, surprisingly, giving a full account of his relations with Laveaux, the expulsion of Desparbés, and the battle that had erupted between the mulattoes of the Sixth and the Regiment Le Cap.

The black captain had taken the desk from his general's legs and begun making notes. Maillart kept talking, adding details—a strange fit of glossolalia. Toussaint gave no sign whether he had any prior knowledge of the events of which Maillart was informing him. When he did turn his full gaze on the captain, Maillart was startled by the full force of it. Emerging from the shadows of the tent, Toussaints eyes were more penetrating. They probed his face through to the bone, searching his features inch by inch, as if the black general thought to sculpt his portrait.

"Well, I am satisfied with you, captain," Toussaint said at length. He stood up, and Maillart followed suit, clicking his heels.

"You will retain your former rank," said Toussaint. "You will report directly to Major Moise." He made a quarter-turn toward the black captain at his left. "Captain Riau will find you the suitable uniform—without mothholes, but with buttons."

Maillart saluted. "Thank you, sir," he said. He thought of permitting himself a smile, but Toussaint had remained wonderfully inexpressive.

"Since the troubles began," said Toussaint, "We have learned much of European warfare."

"I can well see that," Maillart replied, somewhat impulsively.

"We have still much to learn." Toussaint remained correct, unbending. "You will remain with Captain Riau. Captain Riau will make you familiar with your men. You will instruct Captain Riau in the arts of European war. Each of you will be a guide and teacher of the other. Do you understand?"

"*Oui, mon général.*"

This time, Toussaint returned Maillart's salute. The captain was warm with a blush as he stepped out of the tent into the full daylight, so that Vaublanc looked at him oddly when they passed. Maillart had resolved, days before their arrival here, to treat Toussaint with complete military courtesies, but what confused him was that he had done so without thinking.

Twenty minutes later Captain Maillart, now arrayed in a good, newish uniform from Toussaint's supply store, stood to stiff attention on the impromptu parade ground while Captain Riau, in a loud harsh voice, announced him to the troops. Now he could see them clearly, much more clearly. Perhaps three-quarters of them must have come straight out of Africa: Congos, Mandingues, Ibos and Senegalese . . . a year or five years since they would all have been fighting each other with bows and lances and clubs. Now, but for the masks of tribal scarification, the filed teeth, dyed locks and feathers braided in the hair, there was not so much in their bearing to distinguish them from the Creole blacks and the scattering of colored men.

He began to command them. They obeyed him readily, smartly enough, marching, wheeling, forming into squares, then columns—though it occurred to him that many probably could not comprehend his French. When they reversed direction from him, at his order, he saw on the backs of many the cicatrix lacings of ancient whippings. For all of that, their spines were stiff enough.

Beside him, Captain Riau stood in a posture of attention that somehow, weirdly, also seemed relaxed. Captain Maillart found him most inscrutable, though he also felt certain that his own least gestures were being very minutely observed. Maillart stared into the faces of the men arranged before him in a single line, their arms at rest. He seemed again to feel the doctor's lips at his ear: *If a white man and a black man come together, what will you call their offspring?* The captain looked into the black and yellow faces with a curiosity he'd never felt before. *Is it something else or is it human?* Maillart was very weary; for a moment, the faces before him blurred and swam together. One face, one façade—this façade was Toussaint's. His vision cleared. The face of this seedling army was Toussaint's face, the one he chose to show—impossible that it could be so simply what it seemed.

Chapter Thirty-Four

Why is it that whitemen believe that only jesus could come back from the dead? All men could do it. All black men do. More paths than one lead back from the Island Below Sea. There is the *zombi astrale* and the *zombi cadavre*. Les Morts et les Mystères are also there. This thing that jesus did, to come back in the body, I, Riau, could do it too.

When the whitemen brought Riau from Guinée, that was the same as death. The ship was a big wooden graveyard for men and women of Guinée, and each with a space to lie no larger than those wooden boxes whitemen use for burying. That was the first time Riau must pass through death.

Now it was Captain Riau in the hills by Habitation Thibodet, drilling and marching and learning how to be a whiteman officer. There was this other whiteman captain Toussaint gave to me, wanting us each to be a *parrain* to the other, so that Riau would turn into a whiteman officer, and this other would learn the ways of the men of Guinée. Captain Maillart. He was not so bad a whiteman, and he taught to Captain Riau many new things about drilling and marching and all the special ways that whitemen know for fighting and killing each other. But at the end of the day when Captain Riau took off his uniform, I had to look at myself all over very carefully to be sure that my skin was not fading into white.

Now we were free black men, free soldiers, as Toussaint said, and also those Spanish generals had said so. But slaves were still there at Thibodet. Every day they went into the fields to work the cane and coffee. They went singing like slaves of a good master, like the slaves at Bréda used to sing. But when I watched them in the cane, I thought I saw *zombi cadavre*. Where was the *ti-bon-ange*? Where was the *gros-bon-ange*? No one is there in the head of a slave, only *cadavre*.

Then the little whiteman doctor went away. After all, he was not the master of this habitation, only something like a *gérant*, but the Thibodet slaves told to us that the master had died. Then, a few days after the doctor had gone, the Thibodet mistress came back from before, only she had then a new whiteman who was the gunrunner Tocquet, and had taken his name as whitepeople do. Now Tocquet was master of this *habitation*. The slaves of the fields were afraid of him at first. The little doctor was good to them, but Thibodet had whipped them all, so they waited, afraid Tocquet would whip.

Captain Riau knew this whiteman from another time, when he carried guns to us at our camps of Grande Rivière. Two black men were always with him then, Gros-jean and Bazau, and all three of them could live in the mountains like maroons. Tocquet was the strangest whiteman Riau had ever seen, and sometimes I thought he might not be a whiteman at all, but some strange pale kind of *homme de couleur*, only other whitemen treated him like one of them always. At this Habitation Thibodet, Tocquet lived in the *grand'case* with the white madame, but Gros-jean and Bazau built themselves new cabins in the quarters. Toussaint sent a detail of our free black soldiers to help them build it.

Tocquet and his white madame were very friendly with Toussaint, and often they asked him to eat at their table in the *grand'-case*. Sometimes Captain Riau, or Moise or Dessalines would go with him to eat from this table, always dressed in a fresh washed uniform with the buttons newly polished and bright. Sometimes Captain Maillart went too, or the other whiteman officer Vaublanc. Around this whiteman's table would be what they called conversation, and we ate the same as they. But sometimes Riau began to think that this friendship of Tocquet for Toussaint was like the friendship Bayon de Libertat had for his good *commandeur*.

Then also Toussant began to send details of soldiers into the fields for Tocquet. Not every day, but when the work was big—digging to plant new cane, or helping to repair the cane mill. I, Riau, went to direct them like a *commandeur* myself, still wearing my uniform of captain, but the men took off their uniforms if they had them, so when I saw them working I could not know them from the slaves of Thibodet. This seemed very bad to me. None of the Thibodet slaves wanted to run away then, because here was food enough and no whippings, and we soldiers kept them safer than any place they knew to run. No, all of them were singing there, that time. But if any had tried to run away, I thought Toussaint would send us after them to bring them back, the same like we were with the *maréchaussée*.

We did not have any drums in our camp except for drilling or any dances for the *loa*. Only prayers to jesus, even though we had no whiteman priest this time. Toussaint would make the prayers himself. The Père Sulpice was so happy with what he said to jesus in San Raphael that he had given Toussaint a rosary, without any skulls or jesus faces, only plain wood beads, and Toussaint knew how to count his prayers with this. Still in the night I did hear drumming from the mountains, where was the camp of Biassou.

In the night I was sleeping in my tent but my dream was in the fields of Thibodet. My *ti-bon-ange* went walking in my dream to see for me how things were there. The slaves were in the fields to work at night as well as day, and all of them were dressed in white, and my *ti-bon-ange* saw how all of them were *zombi*. When I woke, I heard the drum and so I went to it.

There at Biassou's *calenda* Riau was a long time dancing but Ogûn would not come into my head. The drum tried very hard to move me but I could not be moved, I was yet I, Captain Riau. So I gave it up, and put on my coat of officer again, which I had taken off to dance. I sat down with my back against a thorn tree. Ghede came walking to me then, all stiff-legged and turning his head like a snake. He had snaky eyes that looked at me, though he was mounted on the body of Jean-Pic. I had not known Jean-Pic had come again to the camp of Biassou.

"Give me bread," Ghede said, but Riau had no bread to give to him. Ghede took hold of the uniform coat and rubbed the cloth with his stiff fingers.

"Give me BREAD," said Ghede. "I am hungry—you must give me something."

I put my hand into my pocket and brought out some coins that were there and offered them, but Ghede only laughed to see them.

"I cannot eat these metal pieces," Ghede said. "I ask you *bread.*" With his stiff arm he struck my hand from underneath so that the coins went all scattering. Ghede laughed at me, and then I felt afraid of him.

"Would Ogûn come to a whiteman's head?" Ghede was sneering at the uniform of Captain Riau. "No better will Ogûn come to you. Besides, you are a bad *serviteur*. It is too long since you have fed the *loa*."

Ghede pushed me in my chest and I fell down against the tree. I watched Ghede go walking away to do his feasting in some other place. The coins were spilled all around me but I had no heart to pick them up, I did not want them anymore.

It went on long, this feeding of the *loa*. I sat by the tree, thinking I would be very tired on the next morning, when it was my time to do my work of officer, dancing with the Captain Maillart. But I did not go away. After a while, when Ghede had left the head of Jean-Pic, Jean-Pic noticed me and came to talk.

I asked him if he had gone to find the maroons of Bahoruco, as he had said he would do. Jean-Pic told me that he had done this, and it was very good there, better than even he had thought. He told me how they did things there, and how he was meaning to go back there, and he asked me if I would come with him. I pointed to my uniform and said I could not go. I told him how it was to be Captain Riau, what was the meaning of *désert*, and what would happen to an officer if he would desert. All the time Jean-Pic squatted by the tree, smiling and shaking his head slowly like he could not believe what I was telling. When I had done, he told me that no soldiers would ever reach those caves in Bahoruco.

Then Jean-Pic asked me about Merbillay, if she and Caco were with me in the camp of Toussaint. I told him that she was not there, because all the women and the children had been left behind in the mountains above San Raphael, we could not bring them with us to fight the whitemen in the whiteman way of fighting. Jean-Pic smiled and shook his head, like he did not believe that either.

Then Biassou passed by, walking slowly and making a small sound with his special *asson*. He looked at me, so I got up and followed him. Jean-Pic came too.

"*C'est l'heure,*" Biassou said, when we came in his tent. "Chacha has not gone to his *ajoupa*, but soon he will go."

In Biassou's tent there were all the things we had been making ready for the *coup poudré*. Long before we had put a toad into a box with a snake to make it angry, then we had killed the toad and dried it and ground it to a powder. We had cut out the insides of a puffer fish and dried them in the sun. We had taken graveyard dirt, and dust ground from the skulls saved from that place in Grande Rivière where Jeannot had liked to throw his bones. Now Biassou was mixing all these things together, while the strings of snakebones shivered from the ridgepole of the tent, and his cats watched from the corners with their strange-colored eyes. Biassou mixed everything together, and he also put in some *pois-gratter* and some pieces of broken glass.

When it was finished, Biassou put everything into a bag and gave it to me. He shook the *asson* lightly and stared into my face, his eyes as strange to me as those cats' eyes. I felt a feeling then, even if Ogûn had not come. I did not feel my uniform so much.

Then Riau and Jean-Pic left the tent, Riau carrying the bag. It was true, Chacha had not come to his *ajoupa* yet. Jean-Pic waited outside while Riau went in. In the place where Chacha would lie down, Riau poured the powder to make the *vévé* of Baron Cimitière. As he was going out, Riau poured the powder in the shape of a cross on the place inside the door where Chacha must step.

Then we went a little way into the jungle to wait for Chacha to come back. It was not so long before he came. When he first stepped on the burrs inside the doorway, he said a whiteman's curse and dropped down on the floor of the *ajoupa*. I thought he must be holding up his foot to feel what it was that had bitten him, and maybe he even rolled over onto his sleeping place then, so that the *vévé* touched him with its broken glass. Then Chacha stopped his cursing and gave an awful moan of fear, because I think he must have known then what had happened to him.

In a little while it was silent there, and so we went away. I felt strange to myself all the time going back to Toussaint's camp, and strange all the next day while I was doing my soldier work. It was not the same as cutting someone with a knife, or shooting someone with a gun. It was not even the same as the things Riau had done in those first days when we were burning the plantations.

In the afternoon, Jean-Pic came to tell me that Chacha had died in the night, and that they had already buried him this day.

. . .

FOR THREE MORE DAYS I DID MY WORK OF CAPTAIN, being *parrain* to Captain Maillart and he *parrain* to me, but I did not feel so much like a whiteman anymore then. Chacha was in the earth three days, the same as jesus. On the third night, Jean-Pic came for me, and I went back along with him to the camp of Biassou. I wore my uniform of captain and I took my two pistols with me, and the watch, but I did not take anything else with me, not even the *banza*.

Chacha was not buried very deep, about three feet. Then it did not take so long to dig him up. Riau dug while Jean-Pic held the torch, or I would hold it while Jean-Pic was digging. The torch was made from *gommier* wood and it burned very bright, with a sizzling sound. People from Biassou's camp could see the light of it through the trees, but I think they were afraid to come there to see what we were doing.

Chacha's eyes were open, under the ground, as the eyes of the dead must open if you do not weight the lids. His jaws were closed tight but the lips had pulled away from them, so that he gave a dead grin of a skull. Dirt was lying on the white part of his eyes, and the earth had stained his teeth. I saw that he was truly dead enough he could not blink the dirt out of his eyes.

But then Biassou came crouching over him, like Chacha used to crouch over the bodies of his women when he still lived. Biassou pried his jaw open with a spatula of bone, and pushed in a paste of dark shiny leaves that he had mashed together, and poured in a *tisane* the leaves had been boiled in. There was nothing, because Chacha was gone, there was only *corps-cadavre*, and the *tisane* ran back out of his jaws like a cup that is overflowing. As dead as that. But Biassou's eyes were shining in the torchlight. He put his lips to Chacha's lips and blew his breath in him. He pushed the paste in deeper with his piece of bone, and rubbed on Chacha's throat and pushed his jaw so that it made the chewing movement.

Then Biassou sat back. How his eyes were shining—Riau cannot forget. If the jaw of the *corps-cadavre* was still moving it was only that Biassou had pushed it, Riau thought. Or it still moved itself like a machine. The thing was choking, spluttering out the leaf paste. Then the thing was sitting up, spitting out dirt and leaves across its knees. It put its hands on the edges of the grave and rose.

It was not Chacha, it did not even look like Chacha anymore.

There was no shining there around the body, and it could not cast a shadow anymore. The *gros-bon-ange* was gone away. The *ti-bon-ange* was gone. Maybe someone could catch the *ti-bon-ange* for the making of a *zombi astrale*, but it was the *corps-cadavre* that Biassou had come to take.

Biassou made the *zombi* eat more of the leaf paste. He took it under the shoulders and raised it up to stand beside the grave hole. He picked up a rod the thickness of three fingers bunched together, and he beat the *zombi* across the back and shoulders until it fell down to its knees. The *zombi* moaned and cried out like the wind across a rum bottle, like the dead thing which it was. Biassou kept on beating it until it put its face into the ground and covered the back of its head with its dead hands. Biassou was sweating and breathing like a runner and a lover. He kept on beating the *zombi* until the rod broke in his hand.

Riau thought he must have killed it, that it could not move again. But when Biassou commanded it to get up, the *zombi* rose once more. It stood with its head swinging and its two arms hanging down.

Biassou led the *zombi* to the edge of the trees, where some other men were waiting. They would take the *zombi* away somewhere. Maybe it must go to the farm which we had heard of, where Biassou had fields of *zombis* who must work for him. Or maybe he would sell it for a slave. He was still selling slaves over the Spanish side, we knew.

Jean-Pic and Riau did not wait for Biassou to come back from where he had taken the *zombi* into the trees. We stuck the torch in the loose dirt by the grave, still burning, then we left that place.

His *ti-bon-ange* and his *gros-bon-ange* were still with the body of jesus when jesus came out of the grave where they had laid him. That is the story Toussaint tells, and all the priests. I remembered the beads of the Père Sulpice, all those jesuses and skulls. It was not that way with Chacha. I wanted to raise the dead to life! Instead, we made a dead thing walk.

So I took off my uniform of captain, and hung the coat and trousers in a tree. I took off the soldier boots that crushed my feet. I was not going back to Toussaint now, but I was going to Bahoruco, with Jean-Pic. I had only a cloth to bind around my sex part, and a pouch hanging over my shoulder to hold my knife and pistols and the watch. I was only sorry to leave the *banza*, but if they did come after I would not want to carry it. All this time I was pretending to be a whiteman soldier, I did not have much time to play it anyway.

In Guinée I was alive, but they brought me out a dead thing. I was not three days but three months in my tomb. Each day they brought us on the deck and made us eat and made us dance, still nothing moved but the *corps-cadavre*. As a dead thing I was sold to Bréda. There Toussaint was my *parrain*, and there could be none better. Toussaint taught me how to be a slave, how to bear my death. It was the *hûngan* Achille, when he came down from the mountain with his band, who touched my lips and eyes and made me live again.

So I was running behind Jean-Pic, quick and sure-footed in the dark below the trees. No one was chasing us, but we ran because we liked to. The air of the night was sweet on my whole skin, and they were both the good black color. I could not see Jean-Pic or see myself in all this dark, but I knew I was Riau again, only Riau, and I was glad to be running away to Bahoruco.

Chapter Thirty-Five

"YOU ARE FORTUNATE," Monsieur Bourgois informed the doctor, "or they are fortunate on whose behalf you manage these affairs . . . That Thibodet brown sugar was certainly one of the last cargoes to be safely embarked; were you to arrive with it today, we scarce could contrive a secure passage. But as it is . . ."

Monsieur Bourgois reversed the ledger on his desk, so that the doctor might examine it. His face was even ruddier than Doctor Hébert remembered it, the cobweb of burst capillaries spreading farther from his nostrils across his cheeks. The *négociant* gave his amiable smile and stood up as the doctor leaned forward to peruse the latest figures. A tidy balance in the favor of Habitation Thibodet was there recorded. At his usual somnolent, drifting pace, Monsieur Bourgois had reached his drinking cabinet.

". . . let us toast your most excellent profit." The *négociant* stepped from the cabinet, holding a brandy bottle in his right hand, two tumblers pinched together in his left.

"Vous êtes gentil," said the doctor, as Bourgois poured the first measure. "I think I must accept."

"Santé," said Monsieur Bourgois. They clicked their glasses.

The doctor sipped and lowered his glass to rest beside the open ledger. Noticing the heavy book, Monsieur Bourgois folded it shut and slipped it into a desk drawer. Hitching halfway around in his chair, he turned his hazy regard to the window. The doctor followed the direction of his glance, enjoying the threads of alcoholic warmth that spread through his belly from the drink. The middle of the afternoon was just passing, with some slight abatement of the heat. Beyond the casements, the air was brilliant, clear, and still.

"No word of Madame Thibodet?" said Monsieur Bourgois.

"I have had none whatever," the doctor said. "I suppose I need not ask if there has been any result to your inquiries."

"Not the slightest." Monsieur Bourgois tilted the bottleneck to pour them each another glass. "I'm told that you have been most assiduous in your searching."

"One may say that I have fairly quartered the country." The doctor delivered himself of a wintry smile. "Whether by accident or design."

"I fear for her, and the child most of all." Monsieur Bourgois's eyes were welling, the doctor was surprised to see. Perhaps only from the sudden vigor with which he took his brandy. "There have been so many atrocities since the time they chose to vanish . . ."

"Oh, I have hope still she may have escaped all that," said the doctor. "It may be they were out of the country before the troubles came."

"But it's I who ought to be reassuring you," said Monsieur Bourgois. "I ask your pardon."

"Well, never mind it," the doctor began. But just then came the sound of heavy feet upon the stairs, and an urgent rapping on the office door. Monsieur Bourgois called to the knocker that the door was open. His black beard bristling, Monsieur Cigny strode into the room.

"You're in a state," said Monsieur Bourgois. "What is it, man? You'd better have some brandy."

"You'd better lock up your bottle and come along to the quay," Cigny said. "Something's happening—in the harbor."

Monsieur Bourgois stood up with unusual alacrity. "Galbaud."

"What of Galbaud?" said the doctor. "I thought he had been deported."

"He took ship, but has not left the harbor," said Cigny. "There were boats going back and forth from ship to ship for half the night, and on into the morning."

"More deportations, doubtless," Bourgois said. "It no longer requires even a word against these Jacobins—if only a thought should cross one's mind, then Sonthonax descends."

"Yes, but I think he has overstepped himself this time," said Cigny. "You know how his mulatto troops have been harassing the sailors on the quay . . . I think it is more than their pride will bear. But you would do well to come see for yourself."

Through the open casements of Bourgois's window, the doctor could see only an irregularly shaped section of the harbor, bounded by roofs of the intervening buildings. A pair of warships anchored in the area of his view were lowering longboats full of men—one, two, three . . . It was difficult to tell from this angle (and now Monsieur Bourgois had thrust his head through the window frame, interrupting more of the doctor's view), but the boats seemed to be making in the direction of Fort Bizoton.

"Come down," said Monsieur Cigny impatiently. "You can't see anything here."

There were a good many other onlookers already hurrying out of the warehouses all along the waterfront, though not enough to constitute a crowd. Some were already raising shouts of excitement, or dismay. It seemed that every ship was lowering its boats and all the boats were full of armed men. Some few of them were rowing toward the harbor forts and the rest were coming straight for the quay, toward a point near the fountain some way to the left of where the doctor and his companions stood to watch.

"How many sailors with the fleet?" the doctor asked.

"Two thousand, three thousand." Cigny's teeth flashed in his beard. "You may count them for yourself."

"Then there are the deportees, who knows how many hundreds?" said Bourgois. "All the ships of the harbor are cram full of those."

"I believe they have decided to undeport themselves," said Cigny. "Look there—they have reached the fort."

"The soldiers are not firing on them," Bourgois said wonderingly.

"No, and I don't think they will," Monsieur Cigny said. "Those are troops of the line in those forts—the last shreds of the old regiments. Sonthonax stuck them there to be out of the way, you see? So they would not interfere with the oppressions of his colored army in the town . . ."

"Let him reap the fruit of that wisdom now." Monsieur Bourgois was grinning too.

"Indeed. Galbaud is still governor-general to those soldiers," said Monsieur Cigny. "No matter what fault that slithering weasel of a law-parsing Sonthonax may have found with his Commission—and be damned to every trick clause hidden in the disgusting *loi de quatre Avril.*"

The doctor stared. The men in the boats so rapidly approaching appeared to him as on the opposite side of a thick glass wall; doubtless the humidity promoted this odd sensation. He took off his hat and wiped a film of sweat from his balding dome. The beginnings of an unpleasant headache were focusing behind his eyes. The men laid on their oars so smartly that the boats almost seemed to leap from the water, and now the doctor could hear the goading shouts of a coxswain as the boats drew near. Monsieur Cigny had laid a brotherly arm around each of their shoulders.

"*Mes amis,*" he said, "I think we shall see a great righting of wrongs this day."

Smoothly, Monsieur Bourgois disengaged himself. "I hope you are right," he said. "Still, each must look to his own good now. I know for a fact those navy men have not had one pay in six these last nine months . . ."

"*Évidemment,*" said Cigny. "There will be looting, certainly."

"Therefore I beg you to excuse me." Monsieur Bourgois set out for his offices, at a high bounding step. The doctor remained in Monsieur Cigny's peculiar embrace.

"He's right about the looting," said Cigny. "We'll see a lot of that. You had better round up your colored harlot and her brat and bring them back to our house, for the moment. Oh, they have been comfortable enough there before, have they not? No, don't say a word—we should be glad of another arm." Still holding the doctor in the crook of his elbow, Cigny winked at him. "Arnaud has told us of your prodigies of marksmanship. You would be doing us a favor."

"Is it so?" The doctor freed himself, ducking under Cigny's arm. "You have a curious way of asking it."

THE TROOPS OF THE LINE IN THE HARBOR forts went over to Galbaud's party without the slightest hesitation, and soon had joined the assault on the town. With his brother Cézar leading part of his force, Galbaud struck first at the arsenal, which was easily taken, none of the whites of the town being of a mind to defend it from them.

Most of the *petit blancs* went over to Galbaud's faction immediately, acting in concert with the *grand blancs* on this one rare occasion.

Sonthonax himself, however, was not to be so easily overcome. The National Guards, under Laveaux's command, remained loyal to the commissioners, and the mulatto brigades were fighting well enough—so well that Cézar Galbaud, who'd overextended himself in their vicinity, was made prisoner before the end of that first day. To further boost the commissioners' morale, all the black slaves of Le Cap spontaneously volunteered to fight in support of the *affranchi* and mulatto troops.

"Slave master! Whoremaster! Traitor to France!" Sonthonax was in such an apoplectic state that he sprayed Cézar Galbaud with spittle when the prisoner was paraded before him in the old Jesuit House where the commissioners were in residence. "Chain him! Let him taste iron for himself, and feel the shackle. But best of all, get him out of my sight."

Cézar, speechless, was taken out. From a corner, Choufleur observed the scene, chewing on a cinnamon stick and half concealing his sardonic smile behind his fingers. Laveaux and Polverel sat soberly, though both were electrified by the general tension.

"Those ingrates who called themselves Jacobins—their treason is most bitter." Sonthonax was traversing the room in a series of short lunges from his desk, like a wild dog roped to a tree. "I brought them the rights of French republicans, but they are all repulsive traitors, all *aristocrates de la peau . . .*"

"Yes, of course," Polverel said, a trifle wearily. The older commissioner saw no use in observing that Sonthonax had disbanded the local Jacobin Club months before and since then had used his mulatto troops to hold its former members under martial law.

Sonthonax spun toward them, his pale face shining under the usual slick of sweat. "The *slaves* have joined us—good," he said. "Now, we must lay open the *prisons.*" He aimed a vibrating finger at Laveaux. "Go at once and—no, you are worse needed here." Sonthonax rushed over to Choufleur and hauled him up by his elbow. "You will go and liberate the prisons . . ." Together, they left the room; Laveaux and Polverel could hear Sonthonax's voice still raving on the landing beyond the door.

"It's not my place to say it," said Laveaux, "but this decision strikes me as intemperate."

"He is in a transport, as you can easily see," said Polverel. "It may be that he believes this will be a reprise of the storming of the Bastille—I think he regrets missing it the first time . . ."

GALBAUD WAS UNABLE TO REDUCE the Jesuit House that day; at nightfall, he withdrew most of his force to the safety of the ships. The town was not left precisely quiet, however, for there were parties of sailors still roaming the streets in search of pillage, skirmishing with bands of the local slaves who were abroad on similar missions of their own.

The night was busy with scattered shots, isolated cries. At the Cigny house, no one even tried to sleep. Arnaud and Grandmont had joined in the defense of the place, along with the doctor; Arnaud had tried to bring his wife to this shelter, but she insisted on remaining at Les Ursulines. Pascal, Madame Cigny's disfavored young dandy, had also sought refuge *chez Cigny*. The men would periodically climb onto the roof to stare toward the harbor, and to soak the shakes with water; no fires had broken out near them as yet, but fire was their great fear, in this disorder. There were no slaves to perform this labor now, since all the household slaves but the children's nurse had absconded to loot, or join the commissioners.

Monsieur Cigny, for his part, seemed less irascible than usual at passing the entire evening in his own salon. He and the doctor whiled away the time by teaching Isabelle and Nanon to load and prime the firearms. The doctor was feeling too unwell to join the bucket brigade on the roof. His strange sensations of the afternoon seemed to be flowering into fever, and now he very much regretted that he had not taken time, in going for Nanon and the child, to collect his herb stores from his makeshift laboratory.

Sometime short of midnight, there was a commotion on the street, and someone lobbed a stone through one of the Cignys' ground-floor windows. Pascal, who'd been increasingly agitated for most of the night, returned fire with a pistol shot taken targetless from the middle of the room before the doctor could move, somewhat woozily, to prevent him.

"Sit down, you stupid whelp," said Monsieur Cigny, seizing the hot gun from Pascal's powder-blown fingers. "Go whimper in the corner if you must, but keep out of the way."

From the street came a shout in Creole to the effect that if they did not open and surrender their valuables, the marauders would set the house on fire.

"Well, it doesn't sound like he hit anyone," said the doctor.

"No," said Monsieur Cigny. "But I don't like those torches."

They had blown out the lamps within at the first disturbance so they could be less easily seen from the street, and now the torchlight threw a gay, red glow through the windows and onto the litter of broken glass in the middle of the carpet. The doctor picked up his rifle and went to the second-floor salon, where the women were waiting. Isabelle had crept to the window and was covertly observing the situation outside. As they came in, she turned toward them with pinched lips and her hands cocked on her hips.

"My own footman, if you please. Come back to sack the house . . ."

"And in his livery too," said the doctor.

He settled himself beside the other window, kneeling down and bracing his heavy rifle barrel on the sill. There was a gang of twenty-some blacks on the street below him; he didn't know if they'd seen his movement, but they brandished their torches and cried out new threats.

"He will certainly know where the plate is hidden," said Isabelle.

"*Sans doute,*" said Monsieur Cigny. "But come away from the window, please."

The doctor leaned over his long gun and sighted on the footman, who was the largest man among the group, and, in his bright and fancy livery, far and away the most inviting target. Then he sat back on his heels, to take a more general view. The thought came to him that some among the mob might know his reputation as an herb doctor . . . which was the next best thing to *hûngan*.

"Listen to me!" the doctor called. "You have no business with us—we don't intend you any harm, but we are well armed and ready to defend the place. It's I, Doctor Hébert. Leave us be, I say. Pass on."

There was a stir among the blacks, some of them expostulating. Doctor Hébert could make out only the phrase *dokté-feuilles,* frequently repeated. He changed his angle (keeping his head well within the window frame) so he could peep down to the ground floor. Musket barrels belonging to Arnaud and Grandmont were lipped over the sills below.

"Bring that villain down for me." Monsieur Cigny pointed at the footman.

"But what if it only enrages them," said the doctor. "Perhaps a warning shot?"

Among the gang, a fissure of disagreement seemed to have opened, with some apparently willing to withdraw, while others influenced by the footman were urgent to press the attack. The doctor laid his cheek against the cool curve of his rifle stock. A triangle of silver brocade at the peak of the footman's tricorne hat seemed to make an appealing mark. When he closed one eye, the brocade seemed to leap to the very end of his gun barrel. He squeezed the trigger smoothly and the hat flew backward. The footman slapped at his head and howled.

"*Grand Seigneur!*" said Cigny. "Arnaud did not exaggerate."

The mob broke up and scattered either way along the street. The punctured hat had fallen on a doorstep, near a dropped torch that slowly died, smothered by the dust of the unpaved thoroughfare.

Hébert stood up, passing the rifle to Nanon to reload. The report of the shot had awakened the child, and the doctor took him from Nanon's arms, seeing she was very weary. He walked up and down the hall outside the salon, murmuring and singing snatches of song that he remembered from his own childhood in Lyons—odd how they returned at such a time. The baby's mouth was damp against his shirt and his collarbone, lips slackening as the child relaxed again toward sleep. The doctor's ears were ringing, and not only from the shot. He hoped his indisposition might be one of the more survivable malarias, not *mal de Siam*, but the headache worried him considerably.

A couple of hours before dawn, a party of marauding sailors from the fleet approached the house. They did not threaten it with fire, but seemed willing to beat in the doors with the axes that they carried. Inside, the men took up their firing positions as before.

"Gentlemen," Monsieur Cigny called from the second-story window. "We are in total sympathy with your aims—you are our liberators! Here's to the governor-general, Galbaud! Understand just the same that we are determined to protect our property. Trouble us and we won't hesitate to shoot you."

"Open to us," said one of the sailors, "if you are friends, open and let us drink the health of the governor-general in your wine."

"I don't think so," said Monsieur Cigny, who might have laughed, if not for the strain. "But I *can* say you'll find the houses of the richest niggers near the Place d'Armes or the Place de Clugny."

When the sailors had gone by, there was no more unrest in their immediate vicinity. As the light began to blue into the day, the town slipped into its first full silence of the night. Nanon led the doctor upstairs to the room she'd formerly occupied, and forced him to lie down, for she saw that he was sickening. For a couple of hours he slept fitfully, twisting through the weirdness of his dreams. But by midmorning he was awakened by the sound of a cannonade.

That morning Galbaud renewed the attack and, fighting steadily from street to street, soon overcame the remaining resistance except for the defenders of the Jesuit House. Infuriated by their stubbornness, Galbaud brought up cannons from the fleet and began to bombard the building. Sonthonax, whose passions had plagued him so violently he had not slept a moment of the night, emerged onto a balcony to harangue the opposing troops—being as ever a convinced believer in the powers of his own rhetoric. Galbaud had his gunners aim at him directly, and a cannonball must infallibly have carried him away, if Laveaux and Polverel had not dragged him back.

The building was not defensible against artillery. Villatte, Laveaux, and Choufleur marshaled their troops and managed to conduct an orderly retreat. The commissioners reached the fortified lines inland of the city with their small force intact, which under the circumstances was no mean achievement. Galbaud, meanwhile, was technically master of the town, though by no means in complete control of it. Apart from the troops of the line who'd deserted from the harbor forts, the discipline of his motley army was very poor, and once the real fighting had lulled, the general looting was redoubled. Looking in the direction of the harbor from the roof of the Cigny house, Arnaud and Grandmont could see isolated columns of smoke betokening houses set afire—but it seemed that there was still enough organization among the citizenry that these, if not completely extinguished, at least did not spread generally.

The commissioners still held Cézar Galbaud—this hostage was their best negotiating pawn. At noon, they dispatched an envoy, Polverel's son, across the sweltering flats between their lines and the town. The proposition was that Cézar be given up in exchange for Galbaud's complete withdrawal, and even Sonthonax had not laid much hope upon it. He was playing for time, though he did not yet know what use he would make of whatever time he could recover.

Before they had word back from this sally, the commissioners removed their seat to Haut du Cap, and had taken over the *grand'case* of Bréda as their temporary headquarters. It was there that the envoy's escort reached them with the lugubrious intelligence that Galbaud, flouting the flag of truce, had made the junior Polverel his prisoner and now proposed to trade *him* for Cézar.

Sonthonax had an unfailing instinct for the dramatic moment, even when his passions were only those of impotence. Twirling his coattails in the middle of the Bréda drawing room, he banged his right hand across his heart, stabbed his left hand toward the chandelier, and declared that the decision must pass to his colleague. "*Tu es père,*" he declaimed. "You are a father. Do what you must; I agree to anything."*

Polverel was not ordinarily given to such demonstrations, but now he was weeping openly, though he remained seated, stolidly as ever, in an armchair which had molded somewhat since Bayon de Libertat and his family had decamped.

"I adore my son . . . He might perish . . . I will make that sacrifice to the Republic . . . My son was a parliamentarian treacherously arrested by rebels . . . Cézar Galbaud was taken with arms in his hand against the delegates of France . . . No, my son cannot be exchanged for a guilty party."

Hearing this, Sonthonax passed to an even greater height of exaltation. He looked as though he'd weep himself—perhaps he did, a little.

"My friend, your words do you great honor," he said. "They will not profit by this treachery. We will defeat them, against all odds." But this speech seemed to deflate him as he uttered it, and he crashed down into a chair opposite Polverel, who reached to press his hands.

"I fear we have no hope of defeating them against the odds which we now face," said Polverel.

Then Choufleur turned from the window—for the last hour he'd been staring out, in what seemed a sort of rapture of ennui.

"There is a way," he said.

Sonthonax looked up at him, uncomprehending, his eyes sunken and dark from the sleepless night. Choufleur had not troubled to remove the cinnamon stick from his mouth; it continued to ride his lips as he spoke.

"Pierrot and Macaya," he said laconically. "They are encamped not two miles distant—with ten thousand men."

Sonthonax stared at him, agape. He had not a word to say.

"You will remember them, I think? Pierrot? Macaya?"

"Absolutely." Sonthonax's teeth clicked as he set his jaw. "So," he said. "If we promise them liberty?"

"I think so," said Choufleur. "I think you must also promise them the town."

Sonthonax paled, even he, at that. "What do you mean?" Although of course, by then he knew.

"They would never try to hold it," Choufleur said. "Only . . . a matter of a day, a few . . . " He took the cinnamon stick from his mouth and inspected it with an air of surprise, then looked at Sonthonax more sharply. "The choice is yours. I will arrange it, if you wish."

BY THE CLOSE OF THAT DAY, Le Cap seemed on the verge of calm, at least from the windows of the Cigny house. The doctor was feeling better, able to drink some broth, and pace the floor. He was thinking it might soon be safe enough for him to go and recover his medicine bags, which he would have liked to accomplish before dark. When night fell, he expected his fever to worsen.

Above the harbor, the sun had slipped away through a slit in the cloud cover. A great trunk of cloud sprouted up from the horizon line, expanding at the top into a bloom or an explosion. Diffuse sunset radiance tinted this whole mass of vapor with rose and a sulfurous yellow. In a fever just high enough to make him slightly giddy, the doctor gazed upon this spectacle.

It was very still, until a heart-stricken cry went up from the roof, where Grandmont and Arnaud had gone for their hourly reconnaissance. Without thinking, the doctor snatched up a pistol and ran to the top floor, where he scrambled out a dormer to see whatever it was they saw. He joined the other two men astride the rooftree.

Both Arnaud and Grandmont were staring, aghast, in the direction of Morne du Cap; they both seemed petrified, but at first the doctor could not make out what it was that had so transfixed them. From the fever, his vision was rather blurry, but he squinted and rubbed his eyes. There was a movement on the face of the mountain, as if all Morne du Cap were a vast anthill, with marching columns of army ants all swarming out of its core.

"What is it?" the doctor said, for if he saw, he did not quite believe it.

"The brigands." Grandmont's voice was strangled to a whisper. He cleared his throat but it didn't seem to help. "Do you see? No one is defending the line—they have already passed it."

The air stirred now, a draft opening in the thick wet suck of the humidity. A land breeze was starting up, combing back their hair and cooling the sweat on their faces. It was true what Grandmont said. The first wave of the huge black mass had already passed the landward earthworks and was coming to the fringes of the town, across the lowlands around La Fossette.

Arnaud pointed his pistol in the air and pulled the trigger. "The brigands!" he shrieked. "The brigands are coming!"

No one heard him. The hot wet air closed over his words. Arnaud kept holding the pistol high, as if despair immobilized his arm. The wisp of smoke from the warm barrel broke up into particles and slowly sailed away down to the water.

The men of Macaya and Pierrot had no vestige of military organization, nor were they especially well armed, but these disadvantages didn't matter much, because Galbaud's troops were dispersed and mostly drunk by the time the first wave of the attack struck into the town. Besides, the numbers of the blacks were completely overwhelming; it was one of those mad, berserker charges, like the suicidal charges against cannon in the revolt's first days. But now the few cannons available were not in position to do them any harm.

The blacks had seen it all before, among the plantations on the plain, though never on such a grand scale as this. Never till now had they breached one of the cities of the coast. Still, the order of operations was much the same as elsewhere: kill, rape, loot and burn.

Some of Galbaud's men held out better than others. There were pockets of stubborn fighting, house to house and street to street, up until nightfall. But in the end the white men could not hold. The attackers were innumerable and they seemed to come directly out of the fire, like salamanders, or like legendary demons. Fire was general now in the town, driven ahead of the strengthening land breeze, down toward the harbor. Now it was night, but there was no darkness.

From the Cigny roof, Doctor Hébert and Grandmont could see very well how the fires proceeded, lashed by the strengthening wind from roof to roof, and constantly joining with each other to form one larger, more colossal fire. Fish crows flew screaming, ragged-winged, through the black cinders that rose up to blot the sky. The fire was not two houses from Cigny's—it was not even one. The roof next to theirs was already blazing, with a heat so great the doctor felt his eyebrows singeing, his lips begin to parch and flake. He wet his shirttail in one of the buckets they'd brought up to dampen the roof and pulled the wet cloth across his nose and mouth. Smashed horizontal by the wind, the flames on the next roof sped across the gap between the houses to flutter over the Cigny shingles. On the lower floors, the window glass began exploding from the heat.

Grandmont stood tall and heaved his bucket hopelessly into the fire on the next house. Then he ducked inside through the dormer window. Breaking his horrid fascination with some difficulty, the doctor followed him.

On the second floor, Isabelle Cigny was folding garments into a trunk, aided by the children's nurse; Robert and Héloïse were watching her, frightened but quiet, clinging to the nurse's skirt. Monsieur Cigny also looked on; the doctor paused beside him. Stooping over the trunk, Isabelle felt a stray lock of hair tumbling in her face. She straightened and turned to the mirror to adjust it, without either haste or lingering, then went back to her work.

"Look at her," said Monsieur Cigny, laying his hammy hand on the doctor's forearm. "Say what you will about Creole women—what should I care for the horns she gives me?"

Even under these extraordinary circumstances, the doctor thought it unwise to respond to that question. A spatter of gunfire from outside distracted them all. The doctor stepped to the shattered window to see. A squad of sailors was retreating down the street toward the harbor, hotly pursued by seventy or eighty blacks who could just barely be held at a distance by small-arms fire—there were enough of them to choke the street.

Isabelle had closed the trunk, Monsieur Cigny swung it up onto his shoulder and carried it toward the stairs. He seemed to handle its weight and awkwardness with ease, though he could not be much used to physical work, the doctor thought; no white man could be, in this country.

It was chokingly hot going down the stairs, from fire already pressing against the near wall. Monsieur Cigny descended first, balancing the trunk. The nurse led the two children after him. Her eyes were closed, and through her tight jaws came a keening sound, with now and then a word of Creole, song or maybe a vodoun supplication. The doctor followed them down. On the ground floor, Arnaud, Grandmont and Pascal had hoisted bundles and bags of the Cigny belongings. The horses of the household had bolted or been stolen earlier in the day, so they must make their way to the harbor on foot.

The doctor took the child from Nanon, and arranged his loads, two pistols in his belt, the rifle in his right hand, child in his left arm, forked across his hip. Balancing a bundle on her head with her unique grace, Nanon glided through the door onto the street. In the approach of his evening delirium, the doctor thought he saw her as he'd seen her first, striding ahead of him through the throngs at the market in the Place de Clugny, wearing the basket of fruit like a tiara. But the men who pressed around her now had less benign intentions.

The rifle discharged as he dropped it—the range was too short for him to use it now, even if he could have managed it one-handed. The doctor shot the nearest one point-blank in the face and handed the pistol to Isabelle Cigny to reload and drew the other to shoot the next man in the chest, twisting sideways to shelter the child on his hip the best he could. Isabelle handed him the first pistol reprimed and he dropped another man with a shot to the temple and the others ran away. There had been six of them, stragglers from the larger mob that had just passed through.

The doctor sank down onto one knee, heavily; his head hurt horribly and his fever was suddenly very much worse. The child clung to him, pressing his face against his chest. It had all taken hardly an instant, was over faster than any of the other men had even been able to train their arms, but this time no one paid the doctor any compliments on his marksmanship. He could not make out which were the men he had just killed because there were so many other corpses littering the street. Blood and scorched flesh covered them with its stench. The doctor saw that Robert, clinging to his nurse's arm, was looking at the bodies too.

"Come quickly," said Monsieur Cigny.

The doctor stood up. Nanon had reloaded his second pistol; he took it from her and tucked it in his waistband. In the house next to the Cignys' a beam gave way and the entire roof collapsed in a cascade of sparks.

"We are not going to the ships," the doctor said. "We have concluded to go instead to Ennery."

Isabelle Cigny dropped what she was carrying and took a step nearer him. "You're delirious," she said. She looked at Nanon. "This man's insane."

Nanon gazed at her steadily; she could not gesture with her head, or the bundle would have fallen. "We have spoken of it earlier," she said calmly. "It's as he told you."

Isabelle walked closer to the doctor. The fire illumined her face with a strange red glow; he thought that she might scratch him with her nails. "Is it your romance?" she said. "Is it *love?* Don't be a fool. In another country she could pass for white."

The doctor looked from her face to the others. In the hellfire light cast all about them, there was no longer any skin tone; Isabelle was exactly the same hue as her black servant. The doctor could not speak at all. Stupid, brutal as a beast, he only shook his head.

Isabelle Cigny turned again to Nanon. "The man's insane," she said again. "But save yourself. You must come with us."

When Nanon had murmured her refusal, Madame Cigny's shoulders clenched as with a sob. It was the first time, the doctor thought cloudily, that he'd seen her show the faintest sign of weakness. Her husband's admiration might have been well placed. He watched as she leaned forward to kiss Nanon on the lips.

"God help you then," she said. "I will not see you again upon this earth."

. . .

ARNAUD SAID NOTHING TO THE DOCTOR as they parted; he could not think of anything to say. Armed with a pistol and a musket, he was bringing up the rear of the Cigny group. At the first corner, he looked back and saw the doctor and Nanon still standing near the burning houses; when he looked again, thirty paces farther along, they had gone. In the next block, the Cignys fell in with a platoon of regular army soldiers who were still making forays into the town to evacuate what citizens they could. There were several other families already in their charge, and in this strength they made their way to the harbor in greater safety than they could have hoped.

The ink-black surface of the water threw back eerie reflections of the flames that blanketed the town. Still, the fire would not pass across the wide stone esplanade dividing the harbor from the burning warehouses. Some hundreds of white refugees were clustered on the paving stones, babbling, weeping, or cursing their enemies—all those not struck completely dumb by what was passing. Eastward along the waterfront, a double line of soldiers fired alternating volleys in a regular one-two rhythm, holding off some two thousand of the blacks.

There were not enough boats, and too many people were trying to get into those there were. Someone was crying out in loud disgust that Galbaud himself had been seen to fling himself into the water in his urgency to secure a place in one of those few boats. Arnaud listened without attending. He had not thought of his wife all day, but now her image ballooned to fill his mind.

WITHIN THE WALLS OF LES URSULINES, the nuns were at vespers, singing and praying for deliverance, but Claudine Arnaud had remained in the small cell she paid them for, embroidering a little dress for the layette of the infant she expected, in whose existence only she believed. When the fires overarched the convent roof, one of the sisters, Félicité, came in and urged Madame Arnaud to flee the place with them. Claudine ignored her. She had lately come to dislike the nuns, because they stole her baby clothes while she was sleeping, hoping thus to distract her from her mania.

"Maybe you have the right of it." Sister Félicité was weeping, tears scalding on her round pale cheeks as the ovenlike heat from the stone walls blasted them. "It won't go much better for us outside than in."

But Sister Félicité was not long gone before the furnace heat drove Claudine out also. The nuns were descending the steps of the convent in orderly single file, demure in their black robes and white wimples, hands folded before them in prayer. As they reached the foot of the stair, the blacks laid hold of them and yanked their skirts above their heads to rape them, or sometimes simply slit their throats.

At the head of the stairs, Claudine Arnaud drew up her skirts and pushed her hands against the bare skin of her shrunken belly. All around her burning embers were crashing down from the roof.

"Now hell has finally come to us, little one," she cried to the thing she addressed inside her. "Now at last you can be born."

One of the blacks mounted the stairs to snatch at her. Claudine picked up a burning stake and stabbed it at his face, her skirts dropping around her legs again when she released them. The first attacker fell away, but another came from the other side; it seemed to her that he was that same Congo, from the other time, though he was no longer dressed in women's clothes. She swiped the burning stake at him, but he grinned and swayed back from his hips, mocking her with his dancer's grace, letting the fire pass over him, then springing back to his place. She thought to show him the stump of her finger then, but he only laughed at that.

She saw that she must show him something more. It was only a light shift that she had on; with one hand she could rip it to the hem. When she'd shrugged out of it entirely, she stooped and picked up a second brand, holding it by its hot coal, for its whole length was afire. She rubbed the flames over her bared skin, smiling to show her indifference to the pain and harm of it. Then she began to dance and shriek in much the same manner as the blacks all around her. Seeing her to be possessed by some spirit too powerful for him to master, the Congo ran off, and was followed by the others.

When Arnaud reached the convent, she had just had the inspiration of setting her hair aflame. He saw her in that fiery halo, raising a blazing sword above her head in her two joined hands. She stood on tiptoe, her head thrown back and to one side, resting on her collarbone, bare scorched breasts lifting and her muscles strained as if she were depending from a hook somewhere above her. Arnaud recognized her posture but without knowing why. When he called to her she did not seem to hear him. But when he was near enough, she brought her flaming sword down on him with all her force.

The brand cracked across his shoulders. Arnaud ducked, came up again, once more he called her name. Her hair had burned down almost to the scalp. She hissed and thrust the burning stake at him; he caught it firmly between his two bare palms and closed his grip. The shock of the pain slammed all the way into his shoulders, but he did not let go. Now he felt the very thing that she was feeling, and he saw, when he looked in her eyes, that she acknowledged this.

Together they rolled down the steps, and as they did so, much of the fire about her was extinguished. With his blistered palms, Arnaud beat the flames down in the blackened stubble of her hair. When he was done, he saw that she had fainted. He picked her up and carried her back to the harbor, where a few boats were still plying, picking up the last survivors. The town was all in flames around them as they went, and by some freak, no one troubled or hindered them all of their way.

THE DOCTOR TRIED TO SECURE a dampened cloth across the nose and mouth of the child, to protect him from the smoke and ash, but the contact troubled him and made him cry. Without it he was quiet, so the doctor gave it up. He and Nanon began walking, generally in the direction of the Place d'Armes, although many detours were required because of the fires. A great number of bodies were scattered about—soldiers and sailors and civilians, women and children mixed with them indiscriminately, some mauled and mutilated, others just dead. Many of the black invaders had also been killed. In one block they traversed, the corpses had been dragged out of the middle of the street and neatly arranged along the house walls, so that the doctor was moved to wonder what agent had accomplished this work and with what purpose.

How exotic was this impulse to bring order into hell's worst chaos! As the doctor was contemplating this phenomenon, two gangs of hostile blacks appeared at opposite ends of the street they were traveling. As it happened, they were just by an alleyway that would have let them directly into Crozac's stable yard, but unfortunately this passage was sealed by walls of flame.

The doctor returned the child to Nanon and produced one of his pistols. Two men were rushing up in advance of the first group and one had painted designs on his face and chest with gouts of human blood. The doctor fired and brought him down and felled another with the second pistol, but Nanon was not yet ready with the first; he had passed them both to her too quickly, and she was busy with the child. The blacks did not seem greatly dismayed in any case. There were so many corpses strewn over these streets that a couple more did not much matter.

He aimed the rifle and pulled the trigger, but there was not even so much as a click; he had forgotten to reload it after it had accidentally gone off in front of the Cigny house. The blacks on either side no longer seemed to hesitate. The doctor thought that maybe there was nothing for him to hope for at Crozac's—the whole place might already be destroyed. Certainly the tavern where he'd once resided was already rising in a crackling cone of flame. But as they were without alternatives, he gathered Nanon in the crook of his arm and rushed her into the burning alley.

Through the fire's roaring came a hoarse scream that might have been either hers or his own; he could not tell. The carpet of coals they walked across was searing through his boot soles—he could well imagine what it must be doing to the fragile shoes she wore. He felt himself coughing but could not hear the sound of it. The flames leaping in their faces refined themselves yellow to blue, next to a crystalline, piercing white, finally a single colorless blade of heat.

Then they were through, stumbling into the stable yard. One of Crozac's grooms was running from stall to stall opening all the doors; the fire had already caught the stable roof though it had not yet burned through. The horses and mules all came out in a screaming terror. The groom swung himself up to the bare back of one and rode out the opposite corner of the yard, where there seemed to be no live fire but only smoldering, another unnumbered horseman of this apocalypse.

When the doctor pried the child's head away from Nanon's bosom, he straightaway began to howl, an excellent sign he had not been seriously injured. Relieved, the doctor sat down on the ground and began reloading all the guns. At Nanon's desperate shriek he jumped up with a pistol in either hand. One of the blacks had been frenzied enough to follow them through the fire after all, but before he had quite emerged from the alley, the doctor shot him through the forehead and he toppled over backward into the bed of multicolored flames.

The child was sobbing quietly now, exhausted from his screaming. Nanon opened the bodice of her gown and gave him suck to comfort him. Her head was bare now, hair all scorched and singed; she'd lost her bundle in their passage through the fire.

The doctor reloaded his pistol and walked over to peer in the open door of Crozac's living quarters. It appeared that the fleeing groom, or someone else, had paused to slit the farrier's throat. The dead man lay in a scorching pool of his own blood; all around him, fire was gnawing through the floorboards.

"Don't look," the doctor said to Nanon, and all at once was racked with laughter. The idea she should be disturbed by the sight of a dead body . . . Tears spurted from his eyes; his sobs were like vomiting. She remained ice-white, ice-calm before him, as if she were walking in her sleep. Or was it really vomiting? Really *mal de Siam*, in the end? He was on his hands and knees, her hands on his shoulders, pressing to soothe him. At length he composed himself enough to stand.

He had brought them there in hope of finding a horse, but they had all stampeded off when the groom had let them go. The doctor walked along the row of empty stalls. In the last but one, there was a mule; the stall was open like the others but for some reason the mule had been tied to the feedbox, and stood there snorting and lashing against the restraint. The doctor slipped to its head and undid the lead and brought it out. Seeing the flames, the mule began to jerk its ax-shaped head and scream. It took all the doctor's remaining strength to keep control of it.

The animal was too panicky for Nanon to mount, and because the tack room was fully on fire there was no question of bridle or saddle. They left the stable yard still on foot, following in the direction the groom had taken. The northern quarters of the town were already burned almost to rubble, and the marauders who still frolicked among these ruins were too engaged in their own ecstasies to notice the pilgrims who crept by with their half-mad mule.

From La Fossette a pestilent fog was boiling, cool and full of mosquitoes and of *mauvaisces humeurs*. The doctor was glad of this thickening of the darkness. Now the mule had calmed enough for Nanon to ride, first slashing a vertical rip in her long skirt so she could straddle the animal. The doctor handed the child up to her, noticing then that her light satin shoe was burned to a rag around her ankle. The sole of her foot was horribly blistered; he lowered his head and kissed the air above it.

He led the mule around the lower curve of Morne du Cap and on into the jungle. Maybe he had at last become familiar with the ways and byways, or maybe it was the gruesome pain in his head that led him onward like a beacon, but whatever the cause he seemed able to choose their direction without hesitating. They went on.

IT SEEMED TO HIM THAT IT WAS day again and that he was slumped over the mule's back, Nanon leading it and also carrying the child, and while he tried to protest she insisted he must ride and rest. Again, some other time, another night, Nanon was feeding him a paste of mashed bananas she must have foraged somewhere, but he could not swallow it and he signaled her that she must give it all to the child instead. His fever no longer abated with daylight; instead it seemed to worsen. Now he could not even keep down water. He crawled away from the trail on hands and knees, puking a black stinking bile he knew was his own rotten blood. Another time, lying on his back, he saw some sprigs of herbs he thought might help him, and he motioned Nanon to pluck them and put them in his mouth to chew. The leaves could not be brewed, for out of all that fire and destruction they'd brought away no means to strike a light of their own.

They went on, through dark to light to dark again. The doctor chewed his bitter herbs, which won him no remission. How greatly he had deluded himself with his belief he would not die of fever. The pain was extraordinary, like a nail through his skull, and he heard himself repeating the phrase aloud: *Comme cloué, comme cloué*. Then, *No*, another voice answered, *you are not nailed*. Nanon's hand upon his forehead was now Toussaint's, but he had to tell this darker man that he was surely dying. Then Toussaint said that he would not die yet, that there was still a use for him upon the earth. At this the doctor choked on a cry and protested that he had lately killed more men than he'd had the leisure to count and that he was not a healer but a murderer. Toussaint smiled and stroked his burning brow and said that out of all this death and ruin it would still be possible for them to work a healing.

On his fire-blistered feet the doctor staggered through mountain passes always leading the mule where Toussaint, dressed in his green coat and knotted headcloth and carrying his bag of herbs across his knees, seemed to have replaced Nanon and the child. As he had sometimes done before, Toussaint quizzed him about European politics and science and asked him his interpretation of all he recently had witnessed.

Tell me, Toussaint said. Tell me all you think of what you've seen. Let me know the reasons that you'd give for it.

Well I don't know, the doctor said. But there must be some reason.

Why must there? Toussaint said. Give me the reason of it. What does it mean?

The doctor's back was to Toussaint on the mule but still he heard him well enough and felt the old man's foxy smile.

I can't tell you. But it does mean something. It must mean something. It can't mean nothing. It cannot.

That night he slept beside the trail full of a confidence that the world was as sensible as he'd declared it was, even if he'd never grasp the sense of it. When he woke, an hour before dawn, his fever had completely broken. At first light they continued their way. He was visited by no more hallucinations and whenever he looked back he recognized it was Nanon astride the mule with the child on her lap looking about with calm alert interest at everything they passed. The distance still to go was less than he'd supposed and the sunrise was just clearing the mountains when they came into the groves of coffee above Habitation Thibodet.

If his head still hurt the pain was comfort, now an aspect of the clarity he had regained—he contained it, rather than it surrounding him. There was order in the world spread out below him. In the camp of Toussaint's six hundred, they were just extinguishing their breakfast fires. From the quarters, the slaves came marching in a double column toward the cane, Delsart directing them and their *commandeur* counting cadence while the rest of them all sang cheerfully enough. The doctor looked up at Nanon, who returned his smile, gazing at him dreamily. He snapped the lead rope and led the mule down past the coffee trees and through the cane fields into the yard.

There was someone on the *grand'case* gallery, a total stranger, though he did not seem unfriendly. He had on a loose white shirt and long dark hair gathered loosely at the back and he was cleaning his nails with an enormous knife. He looked up at them with some considerable surprise, then turned to shout a word into the house, perhaps a name.

What a sight they must present, indeed. The doctor felt like laughing. He took the child from Nanon and set him down. A semicircular area of grass had been maintained just in front of the gallery, and now the doctor noticed that some flowers had been freshly planted round the border. He offered his hand to help Nanon get down. When she had dismounted, he noticed for the first time that the mule was a dark whiskey color and that there was a blue cross over its shoulders and down its spine.

Up the hill among the coffee trees there was still a late cock crowing, though now the sun's round was fully in the sky. The child sat cross-legged in the grass, chuckling and fingering the blades; some of them were still damp with the dew. He was too young yet to stand unsupported, though he might pull himself up on the edge of a table or a chair.

A door clapped inside the house, and in his inner ear the doctor heard the name that the man had called. *Elise*. It was not his sister though, who first appeared, but a little girl in a blue-printed dress, running barefoot down the steps toward them. Her eyes were only for the baby, the doctor saw. She ran toward where he sat in the damp grass, waving her arms in winglike sweeps and shaking dark ringlets back from her face. But when she had come almost within reach of them she stopped and stood abashed.

The doctor looked toward the *grand'case*. Now Elise had appeared on the gallery; she froze for an instant, then drew in her breath and came forward again, walking down the steps toward him. Her robe was somewhat overlong so that he couldn't see her feet, so that she seemed to float. After all, he could not absolutely meet her eyes. He looked down. The baby had scooted on his bottom, nearer to the little girl, and he was reaching both arms up to her, wanting to touch the pattern of her dress, or possibly to raise himself on her. The little girl looked up at the doctor uncertainly.

"Yes," the doctor said. "He is your cousin. You may take his hands."

Envoi

THE FIRE IN LE CAP BURNED FOR THREE DAYS. *Throughout that time no darkness fell, the night was brighter than the day, sufficient for men on the decks of the ships in the harbor to read their letters and despatches without the aid of other light, while ash and cinder rained all over them, and during that first darkless night the same fiery glow was cast on Polverel and Sonthonax in the salon of the great house of Bréda where the older man paced along the windows in rapidly exchanging states of exaltation and despair, as the younger one would more commonly do, but now Sonthonax had entered that state of grim fixity he would reach whenever the world itself outran his tongue and so with the blades of firelight redly flicking at his page he wrote:*

WE DECLARE THAT THE WILL OF THE FRENCH REPUBLIC AND OF ITS DELEGATES IS TO GIVE FREEDOM TO ALL THE NEGRO WARRIORS WHO WILL FIGHT FOR THE REPUBLIC UNDER THE ORDERS OF THE CIVIL COMMISSAIRES, AGAINST SPAIN OR OTHER ENEMIES, WHETHER INTERNAL OR EXTERNAL—

. . . and he licked the tip of his pen and wrote:

THE REPUBLIC AND THE CIVIL COMMISSAIRES ALSO WISH TO IMPROVE THE LOT OF THE OTHER SLAVES—

. . . and upon the conclusion of this sentence he thought for a moment more and then he wrote:

ALL THE SLAVES DECLARED FREE BY THE DELEGATES OF THE REPUBLIC WILL BE EQUAL TO ALL FREE MEN . . . THEY WILL ENJOY ALL THE RIGHTS BELONGING TO FRENCH CITIZENS—

. . . all these words being necessary (at least to him) because Sonthonax, ever the avocat, *forever sought to clothe the event in words to give it a more advantageous meaning, or perhaps he even believed what he was saying, and had always intended it, as his admirers and accusers would later main-*

tain (later, when the fire flashed in their eyes) and some would claim that Sonthonax intended these words only to frighten Galbaud away, but that would have been superfluous: Galbaud and his whole faction being already so thoroughly disposed of that on the morrow morn the entire fleet set sail, away from the unceasing precipitate of ash and coal (dawn being darker than the night in truth, so long as that great fire still burned) toward Baltimore, where some of those several thousands of refugees would forget Saint Domingue in their urgency to begin new lives, and others would gnaw their bitterness until they died, and others still would plot to recover all they'd lost and some of these latter would indeed be determined or mad enough to return—still none of them tarried to impress themselves with Sonthonax's latest proclamation; they were gone, and with their going came if not the absolute end of white power in Haiti, at least the beginning of that end, a thought which those mostly African illuminati must certainly have cherished as they reveled in the roast and ruin of Le Cap throughout the three days Sonthonax had promised them and would faithfully deliver (although General Lasalle had come up with fresh troops from the south and begged to be allowed to restore order in the city), for Sonthonax was after all a man of his word—while Polverel fretted and chewed his nails to the bloody quick and Choufleur sucked his cinnamon stick and smiled behind his hand—all of them foregathered in the house at Bréda where the first agents provocateurs had made Toussaint the initial payment for organizing this all-too-successful provocation, and by day or night the firelight bathed them; it would be with them all their lives, as it pursued Galbaud's fleet on its voyage to North America, shining so winningly on the billows that bore up the ships, for this was a most assiduous fire, determined to throw its light upon the future; it would not burn low, and it still burned in Sonthonax, tingling to his fingertips when, before the end of summer (still astonished at the fact that the bands of Pierrot and Macaya, once Le Cap had been utterly despoiled, abandoned the white French republicans to return to their roving on the northern plain, indifferent to any enticements in or out of his power to offer them), he wrote another proclamation which emancipated ALL THE SLAVES, *not freeing them any more than Lincoln did in the next century but simply admitting that they were free (and it may be that Sonthonax believed so all along but he was so devious, so studied in his cunning, that none could ever fathom his beliefs) and so the fire passed over Sonthonax as well, razing him to a scorched stump at last in spite of his remarkable resilience, for this wise fire was all-consuming as history itself, as Toussaint might have put it, there in his camp at Ennery or later in the Fort de Joux, Toussaint having been as best he could manage a student of history all his life, learning that what had once been could be again, so coming to believe that he could be in truth the black Spartacus Abbé Raynal had predicted to come forth and achieve the freedom of his people; therefore the fire was his intimate friend, and he knew how to use it (certainly Toussaint used all his friends, being far more cunning than even Sonthonax) as a weapon or simply as a light, a light he'd live with longer than he wished to, for it shone on him (however faintly) through the layered bars and gratings of his cell at the Fort de Joux, so that he stretched his hand and probed his fingers through the grate, turning and turning them in hope of reaching some shadow of the warmth of that old fire, but it was useless; he had passed too far into the future, and those coals were dead for a decade, were they not? or perhaps indeed they were not, so that if Toussaint had been able to lure the First Consul to his cell, he could have produced a live coal from the pocket of his waistcoat, holding it between his finger calluses in the manner of a countryman lighting his pipe—but Bonaparte would not come, so that Toussaint must turn backward toward that time when the fire originally was bright, when by the light which disseminated itself from the pyre of Le Cap to Ennery he first began to scrutinize the intentions of Sonthonax, wondering if they were more or less consonant with his own design than those of the Spanish, or the English, or even the Americans toward whom he also turned this illumination; meanwhile he began to pass over the country in his own extraordinary fashion (those first six hundred men increasing to tens of thousands) and the fire followed him but did not consume him or his works; under his command nothing was burned nor any man killed without reason—not all or everything was saved but everything was used for a purpose—and General Laveaux, seeing these things, threw down his hat and declared "this man makes an opening everywhere" (but he was already Toussaint-Louverture; he had already finished the letter) and he would still use the fire as need presented, knowing the old coals could always be blown again to life, as he would rekindle them a few years later to burn rebuilt Le Cap to the ground a second time—yes, if he had to he'd use this instrument more broadly still, denying the land to white invaders, he would burn the island so close to its bedrock that a crow could not fly over it without risk of starvation—let the fire take it before the enemy enjoyed it—and it was ever a hungry fire, rapacious to consume time as well as distance, reaching with its lava-dripping salamander digits to grasp and devour Galbaud, Sonthonax, Leclerc, Napoleon himself, whoever sought to leave it in the past it would pursue them, still burning across oceans, across centuries, a wind out of time's vortex driving it on to level cities of the new lands of the future for whenever it burned down to coals a breath would bring them back to the flame-flower (this fire would return from the least spark even, being so tenacious); and out of that long smoldering the fire that started in Le Cap is burning still, still rendering and dividing, so that everyone must be compelled to admire how whitely the flames rise in their pallor above the black charcoal, though the firelight has such a terrible time to travel through, like the light of a long-dead star, emerging from a history so remote and distant it seems almost quaint: the far-off screaming deaths of all those people whose fat came sputtering down into the coals of the ruined city's white-hot foundation, whose stories were written on their skins as if their skins became the parchment of the pages you turn and examine by the light of a lamp whose oil was rendered off their bones—such a fire as that may fade but never grow entirely dark, never to be extinguished altogether, it is burning still, still striving to find its way into the future, wanting to burn through to you who believe yourself inured to atrocity, to murder in the streets, to throw some illumination on your life be it faint and slight as the pinprick of green luminescence on your watch dial—it is coming still, it is still here. But no one sees the light.*

Chronology of Historical Events

Before the revolution, the colony of Saint Domingue was divided into three sections: The North, the West, and the South. Cap Français, commonly called Le Cap, was the principal commercial city of the entire colony. In the West, Port-au-Prince was the principal town. Towns in the South were smaller; among these, Jacmel and Les Cayes were significant. The eastern half of the island, separated by mountain ranges from the French colony, was a Spanish possession, with a much smaller population, few slaves, and no significant plantation economy.

1757

A plot to poison all the whites in Saint Domingue is discovered and aborted at Le Cap. The plot was organized by Macandal, a runaway slave who became a leader among the large communities of runaways, or maroons, inhabiting the mountains of the colony.

1758

Macandal is captured at a dance at Dufresne plantation near Le Cap. In March of this year, Macandal is publicly burned.

1787

In France, Louis XVI promises to call the Estates-General.

1788

February: In France, the society of *Les Amis des Noirs* is founded, complementary to an abolitionist organization founded in London in 1787.

April–May: News of the activities of *Les Amis des Noirs* reaches Saint Domingue via articles in *Mercure de France*, causing much consternation.

July: The Colonial Committee, composed of absentee planters, is founded in France. There also exists in France another profoundly conservative alliance of absentee planters called the *Club Massiac*, divided from the Colonial Committee on some issues but united in opposition to *Les Amis des Noirs.*

1789

January: *Les gens de couleur*, the mulatto people of the colony, petition for full rights in Saint Domingue.

May 5: In France, the Estates-General opens.

June 20: The Tennis Court Oath is taken in France. The Colonial Committee joins the Third Estate.

July 7: The French National Assembly votes admission of six deputies from Saint Domingue. The colonial deputies begin to sense that it will no longer be possible to keep Saint Domingue out of the revolution, as the conservatives had always designed.

July 14: Bastille Day. When news of the storming of the Bastille reaches Saint Domingue, the *petit blancs* flock to the French revolutionary tricolor and lynch those who oppose them. Wearing the *pompon rouge* as a badge of Revolutionary allegiance, they march from Le Cap to Port-au-Prince.

August 26: The Declaration of the Rights of Man and Citizen causes utter panic among all colonists in France. The Colonial Committtee and *Club Massiac* now band together.

September 27: The French National Assembly grants a Colonial Assembly to Saint Domingue, in response to petitions from the Colonial Committee and the *Club Massiac*. This Colonial Assembly, assured of *grand blanc* planter control by property qualifications, has power over internal affairs and reports directly to the king, rather than to the French National Assembly.

October 5: The Paris mob brings king and National Assembly to Paris from Versailles. The power of the radical minority becomes more apparent.

October 14: A royal officer at Fort Dauphin in Saint Domingue reports unrest among the slaves in his district, who are responding to news of the Revolution leaking in. There follows an increase in nocturnal slave gatherings and in the activity of the slave-policing *maréchaussée.*

October 22: *Les Amis des Noirs* collaborate with the wealthy mulatto community of Paris, organized as the society of *Colons Americains*. Mulattoes claim Rights of Man before the National Assembly. Abbé Grégoire and others support them. Deputies from French commercial towns trading with the colony oppose them.

November 1: A new Provincial Assembly of the northern section of Saint Domingue, dominated by a revolutionary group of *petit blancs* called Patriots, meets in Le Cap. The *petit blancs* seize control of the administration from the royalist governor.

Persecution of mulattoes in Saint Domingue intensifies. Some mulattoes begin to make public addresses demanding political rights. The response is lynching of the speakers. More atrocities follow (including, in the western section, pogroms by whites against mulattoes where colored infants are impaled and displayed on spears). Class hatred breaks out, stimulated by fear and by *petit blanc* jealousy of the wealthy mulattoes. In the absence of royal authority, these resentments are more freely acted out.

December 3: The French National Assembly rejects the demands of mulattoes presented on October 22.

1790

March 8: A decree of the French National Assembly declares the colonies to have control over their own internal affairs, and that the constitution of the mother country will not govern the colonies in all respects. Among other things, the decree turns the mulatto-rights issue over to the Colonial Assembly.

In Saint Domingue, a mulatto rising in the Artibonite fails to attract any support and is suppressed by the militia and the *maréchaussée*. In the aftermath, new configurations emerge. The mulattoes, traditionally protected by the royal government, become increasingly royalist. Conservatives move to abate persecution of the mulattoes. But the possibility of stabilization is sunk by the arrival of the March decrees from France.

March 25: In Saint Marc, three Patriot-controlled assemblies convene to form a new Colonial Assembly, responding to modified instructions from France which arrived in January.

June: The Chevalier de Mauduit, a royalist officer, arrives in Port-au-Prince to become colonel of the Royal Infantry Regiment there, and begins to win leadership of the conservative faction. By August, Mauduit and his royalist supporters control the western department from Port-au-Prince, but Mauduit's repressive measures against the *petit blancs* increase tension there.

October 12: The French government dissolves the Colonial Assembly officially. By the decree of October 12, the National Assembly reaffirms the concept "that no laws concerning the status of persons should be decreed for the colonies except upon the precise and formal demand of their Assemblies."

October 28: The mulatto leader Ogé, who has reached Saint Domingue from Paris by way of England, aided by the British abolitionist society, raises a rebellion in the northern mountains near the border, with a force of three hundred men, assisted by another mulatto, Chavannes. Several days later an expedition from Le Cap defeats him and he is taken prisoner along with other leaders inside Spanish territory. This rising is answered by parallel insurgencies in the west, which are quickly put down by Mauduit. The ease of putting down the rebellion convinces the colonists that it is safe to pursue their internal dissensions . . . Ogé and Chavannes are tortured to death in a public square at Le Cap.

November: News of the National Assembly's dissolution of the Colonial Assembly reaches Saint Domingue. The Patriots refuse to submit.

During the winter of 1790–91, the Vicomte de Blanchelande is appointed governor of the entire colony.

1791

March 2: Military reinforcements from France sail into Port-au-Prince, mutiny, and join the Patriots.

March 4: The royalist forces of the Regiment Port-au-Prince change sides and Blanchelande flees the town. Mauduit is killed, castrated by a woman among the *Pompons Rouges,* his mutilated body paraded through the streets. In the following days, the royalists are overthrown all over the west, and the *Pompons Blancs* are disarmed. Blanchelande and the remnants of the government establish new headquarters in Le Cap and a new standoff begins on this basis. The Maltese ruffian Praloto controls a new democratic goverment at Port-au-Prince. The remains of the local royalist opposition, mostly country planters unable to flee their habitations, establish a center at Croix Les Bouquets, the main town of the Cul de Sac plain in the western section.

April: News of Ogé's execution turns French national sentiments against the colonists. Ogé is made a hero in the theater, a martyr to liberty. Planters living in Paris are endangered, often attacked on the streets.

May 11: A passionate debate begins on the colonial question in the French National Assembly.

May 15: The French National Assembly grants full political rights to mulattoes born of free parents, in an amendment accepted as a compromise by the exhausted legislators.

May 16: Outraged over the May 15 decree, colonial deputies withdraw from the National Assembly.

June 30: News of the May 15 decree reaches Le Cap. Although only four hundred mulattoes meet the description set forth in this legislation, the symbolism of the decree is inflammatory. Furthermore, the documentation of the decree causes the colonists to fear that the mother country may not maintain slavery. *Re* Article 4 of the March 28 decree, the French National Assembly says that it originally meant to declare the political equality of free-born mulattoes, because the "rights of citizens are anterior to society, of which they form the necessary base. The Assembly has, therefore, been able merely to discover and define them; it finds itself in happy impotence to infringe them."

The colonists rise against this news. Governor Blanchelande is alarmed by rumors of colonial receptivity to an English intervention.

July 3: Blanchelande writes to warn the minister of marine that he has no power to enforce the May 15 decree. His letter tells of the presence of an English fleet and hints that factions of the colony may seek English intervention. The general colonial mood has swung completely toward secession at this point.

Throughout the north and the west, unrest among the slaves is observed. News of the French Revolution in some form or other is being circulated through the vodoun congregations. Small armed rebellions pop up in the west and are put down by the *maréchaussée*.

August 9: A new Colonial Assembly forms at Leogane to oppose the May 15 decree, and sets a meeting for August 25.

August 11: A slave rising at Limbé is put down by the *maréchaussée*.

August 14: A large meeting of slaves occurs at the Lenormand Plantation (where Macandal had been a slave) at Morne Rouge on the edge of the Bois Caiman forest. A plan for a colonywide insurrection is laid. The *hûngan* Boukman emerges as the major slave leader at this point. The meeting at Bois Caiman is attended by slaves from each plantation at Limbé, Port-Margot, Acul, Petite Anse, Limonade, Plaine du Nord, Quartier Morin, Morne Rouge, and others. The presence of Toussaint Bréda is asserted by some accounts and denied by others.

In the following days, black prisoners taken after the Limbé uprising give news of the meeting at Bois Caiman, but will not reveal the name of any delegate even under torture.

August 21: Blancheland arrests slave suspects in a conspiracy against Le Cap and takes precautions to secure the city against rebellion.

August 22: The great slave rising in the north begins, led by Boukman and Jeannot. Whites are killed with all sorts of rape and atrocity; the standard of an infant impaled on a bayonet is raised. The entire Plaine du Nord is set on fire. By the account of the Englishman Edwards, the ruins were still smoking by September 26. The mulattoes of the plain also rise, under the leadership of Candi.

August 23: Fugitives from the Plaine du Nord begin to reach Le Cap. That morning an expeditionary force of regulars and militia sets out under command of Thouzard and is turned back by the rebel slaves. For the next while no further expeditions are attempted by the whites.

Blancheland goes to work fortifying the heights against a land attack. Elsewhere the mountainous borders of the Plaine du Nord are fortified to prevent the rebels from reaching the Department of the West—these lines will not be broken until 1793.

There follows a war of extermination with unconscionable cruelties on both sides. Le Cap is covered with scaffolds on which captured blacks are tortured. There are many executions on the wheel. During the first two months of the revolt, two thousand whites are killed, one hundred eighty sugar plantations and nine hundred smaller operations (coffee, indigo, cotton) are burned, with twelve hundred families dispossessed. Ten thousand rebel slaves are supposed to have been killed.

During the initial six weeks of the slave revolt, Toussaint remains at Bréda, keeping order among the slaves there and showing no sign of any connection to the slave revolt.

In mid-August, news of the general rebellion in Saint Domingue reaches France. Atrocities against whites produce a backlash of sympathy for the colonial conservatives, and the colonial faction begns to lobby for the repeal of the May 15 decree.

September 24: The National Assembly in France reverses itself again and passes the decree of September 24, which revokes mulatto rights and once again hands the question of the "status of persons" over to colonial assemblies. This decree is declared "an unalterable article of the French Constitution."

Late in the month, the Englishman Edwards arrives in Le Cap with emergency supplies from Jamaica, and is received as a savior with cries of "*Vivent les Anglais.*" Edwards hears much of the colonists' hopes that England will take over the government of the colony.

October: By this time, expeditions are beginning to set out from Le Cap against the blacks, but illness kills as many as the enemy, so the rebel slaves gain ground. The hill country is dotted with both white and black camps, surrounded by hanged men, or skulls on palings. The countryside is constantly under dispute with the rebels increasingly in the ascendancy.

In France this month, a more radical Legislative Assembly convenes, alarming conservative colonists further. One hundred thirty-six new Jacobin members are seated in the *Legislatif* that meets on October 1. This body will set itself against the appeals for arms and aid made by both the Civil Commission and Blanchelande. Radicals in the Legislative Assembly suggest that the slave insurrection is a trick organized by *émigrés* to create a royalist haven in Saint Domingue. The arrival of refugees from Saint Domingue in France over the next few months does little to change this position.

October 24: A party of whites in the hill camps, including the procurator Gros, are captured by Jeannot's forces and brought to Grande Rivière, where many are killed by slow tortures, day by day.

November: Early in the month, news of the decree of September 24 (repealing mulatto rights) arrives in San Domingue, confirming the suspicions of the mulattoes.

Toussaint arranges the departure of the family of Bayon de Libertat from Bréda, then rides to join the rebels at Biassou's camp on Grande Rivière. For the next few months he functions as the "general doctor" to the rebel slaves, carrying no other military rank, although he does organize special fortifications at Grand Boucan and La Tannerie. Jeannot, Jean-François and Biassou emerge as the principal leaders of the rebel slaves on the northern plain—all established in adjacent camps in the same area.

November 14: News of the death of Boukman in skirmishing around Le Cap arrives at the black camps around Grande Rivière.

A short time later, Jeannot is executed for his atrocities by the other black leaders and the white prisoners are brought to the camp of Biassou, where they receive somewhat better treatment.

November 21: A massacre of mulattoes by *petit blancs* in Port-au-Prince begins over a referendum about the September 4 decree. Polling ends in a riot, followed by a battle. The mulatto troops are driven out, and part of the city is burned.

For the remainder of the fall, the mulattoes range around the western countryside, outdoing the slaves of the north in atrocity. They make white cockades from the ears of the slain, rip open pregnant women and force the husbands to eat the embryos, and throw infants to the hogs. Port-au-Prince remains under siege by the mulatto forces through December. As at Le Cap, the occupants answer the atrocities of the besiegers with their own, with the mob frequently breaking into the jails to murder mulatto prisoners.

In the south, a mulatto rising drives the whites into Les Cayes, but the whites of the Grand Anse are able to hold the peninsula, expel the mulattoes, arm their slaves and lead them against the mulattoes.

November 29: The first Civil Commission, consisting of Mirbeck, Roume, and Saint-Léger, arrives at Le Cap to represent the French revolutionary government. Immediately on their arrival, the commissioners announce the swift arrival of military reinforcements from France.

December 10: Negotiations are opened with Jean-François and Biassou, principal slave leaders in the north, who write a letter to the Commission expressing hopes for peace. The rebel leaders' proposal asks liberty only for themselves and a couple of hundred followers, in exchange for which they promise to return the other rebels to slavery. As these negotiations proceed, plans develop to surrender the white prisoners. But when news of the leaders' planned betrayal leaks to the black masses, they move to kill the prisoners instead. The whites are saved by Toussaint's intercession and brought safely to Saint Michel plantation.

December 21: An interview between the commissioners and Jean-François takes place at Saint Michel Plantation, on the plain a short distance from Le Cap.

Toussaint appears as an adviser of Jean-François during these negotiations, and represents the black leaders in subsequent unsuccessful meetings at Le Cap, following the release of white prisoners. But although the commissioners are delighted with the peace proposition, the colonists want to hold out for total submission. Invoking the September 14 decree, the colonists undercut the authority of the Commission with the rebels and negotiations are broken off.

In the aftermath of this failure, the black insurgents strike against Le Cap. They break through the Eastern Cordon and sack and burn the Plain of Fort Dauphin. Negroes and mulattoes of La Môle revolt and take the Cordon of the West from the rear, massacring a large camp of refugees.

Also during this time occurs a widening breach between the Commission and the Colonial Assembly. The commissioners wish to claim dictatorial authority, while the radicals in the Colonial Assembly begin trying to get rid of them altogether. The Le Cap radicals begin to seek support outside the Assembly, among the *petit blancs* of the town.

1792

January 11: The September decree is reaffirmed by the Legislative Assembly in France.

January 25: Governor Blancheland writes that the recalcitrance of the Legislative Assembly in sending military aid "is reducing the people to absolute despair." In France, the Jacobins maintain their policy even though it is practically self-destructive—with people at home discontent over sugar and coffee shortages. In England, William Pitt jests that the French prefer their coffee *"au caramel."*

February: Jacobins in France renew their attempts to repeal the September decree. Even conservatives in France begin to become impatient with the white colonial refusal to accept the mulattoes as political equals, given that the mulattoes themselves are unalterably opposed to black emancipation. A rejoinder from the colonists suggests that for the mulattoes political equality is meant as a step on the way to social equality, intermarriage, etc.

March 30: Mirbeck, despairing of the situation in Le Cap and fearing assassination, embarks for France, his fellow commissioner Roume agreeing to follow three days later. But Roume gets news of a royalist counterrevolution brewing in Le Cap and decides to remain, hoping he can keep Blanchelande loyal to the Republic.

April 4: In France there occurs the signing of a new decree by the Legislative Assembly, which gives full rights of citizenship to mulattoes and free blacks, calls for new elections on that basis, and establishes a new three-man Commission with dictatorial powers to enforce the decree and an army to back them.

April 9: With the Department of the West reduced to anarchy again, Saint-Léger escapes on a warship sailing to France.

May: War is declared between French and Spanish Saint Domingue.

May 11: News of the April 4 decree arrives in Saint Domingue. Given the nastiness of the race war and the atrocities committed against whites by mulatto leaders like Candi in the north and others in the south and west, this decree is considered an outrage by the whites. By this time, the whites (except on the Grand Anse) have all been crammed into the ports and have given up the interior of the country for all practical purposes. The Colonial Assembly accepts the decree, having little choice for the moment, and no ability to resist the promised army. The mulattoes are delighted, and so is Roume.

August 10: Storming of the Tuileries by Jacobin-led mob, virtual deposition of the king, call for a Convention in France.

September 18: Three new commissioners arrive at Le Cap to enforce the April 4 decree. Sonthonax, Polverel, and Ailhaud are all Jacobins. Colonists immediately suspect a plan to emancipate the slaves (which may or may not have been a part of Sonthonax's original program). The commissioners are accompanied by two thousand troops of the line and four thousand National Guards, under the command of General Desparbés. But the commissioners distrust the general and get on poorly with him because of their tendency to trespass on his authority.

Unsure of his welcome, Sonthonax sends a fast ship ahead and gets news from Blanchelande before his arrival. Blanchelande reports fewer than fifteen hundred troops fit for duty against an estimated sixty thousand rebel slaves on the northern plain.

The Commission organizes a Jacobin Club for the *petit blancs* of Le Cap, who are chafing under virtual martial law imposed by royalist Colonel Cambefort. Soon the commissioners deport Blanchelande to France.

October 12: The commissioners dissolve the Colonial Assembly, and set up a *Commission Intermédiaire* composed of six whites, five mulattoes and one free black. Around this time, news of the August 10 capture of the king reaches Saint Domingue and freshens colonial fears of the commissioners and the Jacobin movement generally. The royalists of Le Cap, with strong support from Cambefort's Regiment Le Cap and from two battalions of Irish mercenaries, begin to plot against the Commission, profiting from General Desparbés' disaffection.

October 17: Fighting breaks out between the royalist troops and the Le Cap Jacobins. The Jacobins seize the arsenal, and Desparbés orders troops out against them. A face-off ensues between the mercenaries and the Le Cap regiment against the National Guard, the latter standing by the commissioners. Desparbés backs down and is sent along with Cambefort and other royalist officers to France as a prisoner. This defeat practically destroys the northern royalist faction.

October 24: General Rochambeau, expelled from Martinique which is now royalist-controlled, lands in Le Cap with two thousand men and is appointed to replace Desparbés as governor-general.

The Commission led by Sonthonax begins to fill official posts with mulattoes, now commonly called "citizens of April 4." During this period, Rochambeau's efforts against the rebels on the plain are frustrated by the need to keep troops in Le Cap to hold down dissension stimulated by Sonthonax. Sonthonax is alienating the *petit blancs* by creating a bureaucracy of mulattoes at their expense. In the end, Sonthonax closes the Jacobin Club and deports its leaders.

The Regiment Le Cap's remaining officers refuse to accept the mulattoes Sonthonax has appointed to fill vacancies left by royalists who have either been arrested or had resigned.

December 1: Young Colonel Etienne Laveaux is sent to try to recall the disaffected Le Cap officers to the fold, but his efforts are ineffective.

December 2: The Regiment Le Cap, without cartridges, meets the new mulatto companies on parade in the Champ de Mars. When it's discovered that cartridges (hidden under bread) are being supplied to the mulattoes, fighting breaks out between the two halves of the regiment and the white mob. The mulattoes leave the town and capture the fortifications at the entrance to the plain, and the threat of an assault from the black rebels forces the whites of the town to capitulate.

In the aftermath, Sonthonax deports the Regiment Le Cap en masse and rules the town with mulatto troops. He sets up a revolutionary tribunal and redoubles his deportations.

Laveaux and the Chevalier D'Assas mount an attack on the rebel slaves at Grande Rivière. By this time, Toussaint has his own body of troops under his direct command, and has been using the skills of white prisoners and deserters to train them. He also has gathered some of the black officers who will be significant later in the slave revolution, including Dessalines, Moise, and Charles Belair.

Toussaint fights battles with Laveaux's forces at Morne Pélé and La Tannerie, covering the retreat of the larger black force under Biassou and Jean-François, then retreats into the Cibao mountains himself.

December 8: Sonthonax writes to the French Convention of the necessity of ameliorating the lot of the slaves in some way—as a logical consequence of the law of April 4.

1793

January 21: Louis XVI is executed in France.

February: France goes to war against England and Spain.

Toussaint, Biassou and Jean-François formally join the Spanish forces at San Raphael. At this point Toussaint has six hundred men under his own control and reports directly to the Spanish general. He embarks on an invasion of French territory.

March 8: News of the king's execution reaches Le Cap. In the absence of Sonthonax, who's traveling to the western department, Laveaux must hold the city under martial law.

March 18: News of the war with England reaches Le Cap, further destabilizing the situation there.

April: Blanchelande is executed in France by guillotine.

May: Early in the month, minor skirmishes begin along the Spanish border, as Toussaint, Jean-François and Biassou begin advancing into French territory.

May 7: Galbaud arrives at Le Cap as the new governor-general, dispatched by the French National Convention which sees that war with England and Spain endangers the colony, and wants a strong military commander in place. Galbaud is supposed to obey the Commission in all political matters but to have absolute authority over the troops (the same intructions given Desparbés). Because Galbaud's wife is a Creole, and he owns property in Saint Domingue, many colonists hope for support from him.

May 29: Sonthonax and Polverel, after unsatisfactory correspondence with Galbaud, write to announce their return to Le Cap.

June 10: The commissioners reach Le Cap with the remains of the mulatto army used in operations around Port-au-Prince. Sonthonax declares Galbaud's credentials invalid and puts him on shipboard for return to France.

Sonthonax begins to pack the harbor for another deportation, more massive than ever before. Conflicts develop between Sonthonax's mulatto troops and the white civilians and three thousand-odd sailors in Le Cap.

June 19: The sailors, drafting Galbaud to lead them, organize for an assault on the town.

June 20: Galbaud lands with two thousand sailors. The regular troops of the garrison go over to him immediately, but the National Gúards and the mulatto troops fight for Sonthonax and the Commission. A general riot breaks out, with the *petit blancs* of the town fighting for Galbaud and the mulattoes and the town blacks fighting for the Commission.

June 21: By dawn, the Galbaud faction has driven the commissioners to the fortified lines at the entrance to the plain. But during the night, Sonthonax deals with the rebels on the plain, led by the blacks Pierrot and Macaya, offering them liberty and pillage in exchange for their support. During the next day the rebels sack the town and drive Galbaud's forces back to the harbor forts by nightfall. The rebels burn the city.

Sonthonax's proclamation for the day states that "all slaves declared free by the Republic shall be the equals of all men, white or any other color. They shall enjoy all the rights of French citizens."

June 22: Fifteen thousand more rebel slaves enter Le Cap from the plain. Galbaud empties the harbor and sails for the United States (Chesapeake Bay) with ten thousand refugees in his fleet.

That night, General Lasalle arrives from the west with a force of mulatto dragoons, but Sonthonax, keeping his promise to let the rebels from the plain plunder the town, refuses his request to intervene. Not until the evening of June 24 is Lasalle allowed to enter with a small force.

In the aftermath of the burning of Le Cap, a great many French regular army officers desert to the Spanish. Toussaint recruits from these, and uses them as officers to train his bands.

August 29: Sonthonax proclaims emancipation of all the slaves of the north.

This same day, Toussaint issues a proclamation of his own, assuming for the first time the name "Louverture."

September 19: The British invasion begins. The English land nine hundred soldiers at Jérémie.

December: Toussaint, still fighting for the Spanish, occupies central Haiti after a series of victories.

1794

February 4: The French National Convention abolishes slavery.

In Saint Domingue, news of these events causes more and more mulattoes to fall off from the Republic, so that Sonthonax and the commissioners, in Port-au-Prince, are forced into increasing reliance on black support.

By the spring of 1794, Toussaint has about four thousand troops under his command, the best-armed and disciplined black corps of the Spanish army.

May 6: Toussaint changes sides to join the French Republican force with his four thousand black soldiers, first massacring the white Spanish troops under his command. The disorganized Spanish soon withdraw from the territory in the north they'd occupied. Toussaint routs the other black leaders.

May 30: The English strike against Port-au-Prince. After their victory, the English ranks are decimated by an outbreak of yellow fever.

June 12: Sonthonax and Polverel are arrested by order of the French National Convention and shipped back to France.

By the end of the year, Toussaint has swept the Spanish out of the north and has driven the English back from the Cordon of the West, and a mulatto army under the command of the mulatto leader Rigaud has captured Leogane. Toussaint's army is still growing.

1795

This year, Toussaint completely expels the Spanish from the French part of the island. The Spanish are already negotiating a peace with the French Republic.

September: News of the Peace of Basel reaches Saint Domingue. By this treaty, Spain cedes its part of Saint Domingue to the French, but deferring transfer "till the Republic should be in a position to defend its new territory from attack."

After the conclusion of this treaty, Jean-François retires to Spain. Most of his troops go over to Toussaint.

As the foreign threats are reduced, the possibilities of race war increase among different factions: free and slave mulattoes, free blacks of the ancien régime, and (sometimes, unreliably) the maroons—all allied against the slaves freed since Sonthonax's proclamation, who are now led by Toussaint.

1796

March 20: The Le Cap mulattoes imprison Laveaux. Toussaint comes to Laveaux's rescue with ten thousand troops.

April 1: Laveaux proclaims Toussaint lieutenant-governor of Saint Domingue. Toussaint makes his own pronouncement: "After God, Laveaux."

May 11: The Third Commission arrives as emissaries of the Directory government in France. The chairman of the Commission is again Sonthonax, who has beaten the charges he'd been served with previously, purged himself of his Jacobinism and reincarnated himself as a Thermidorean. The Commission is backed by three thousand white troops commanded by Rochambeau.

During this year, Sonthonax's policies increasingly show favor to Toussaint and the blacks and work to the disadvantage of the mulatto factions led by Antoine Rigaud and others. Toward the end of the year, Sonthonax and Toussaint collaborate in getting Laveaux out of the country by arranging his election as a deputy for Saint Domingue in the French legislature.

1797

May: Toussaint officially becomes commander in chief of all French armies in Saint Domingue.

August 20: Toussaint disposes of Sonthonax by electing him as a deputy to the French legislature, and brings in troops to speed his departure. Sonthonax struggles to intrigue his way out of this predicament, but can't find any black generals willing to back him.

Toussaint sends a special envoy to the Directory to make the claim that Sonthonax suggested that they declare independence in Saint Domingue and set themselves up as kings. Toussaint then makes further assaults on the English, driving them back to Môle, a small bit of the west coast, and two forts on the Grande Anse.

1798

May 2: A treaty is concluded between Toussaint and British general Maitland, stipulating a complete British withdrawal from Saint Domingue. The treaty has a secret rider giving Britain trade rights in the colony, but Toussaint turns down a suggestion that Britain would recognize him as king of Haiti.

An effort by French emissary General Hédouville to negotiate a peace between Rigaud and Toussaint does not succeed.

October 20: Toussaint expels Hédouville by raising the cultivators of the north with a rumor that the general has come to restore slavery. When the ex-slaves reach Le Cap with Toussaint among them, Hédouville embarks for France, leaving behind an order for Rigaud to disregard Toussaint's authority. This parting shot makes it increasingly difficult for Toussaint to continue displaying loyalty to the French Republic.

1799

As preparations for a war against Rigaud develop, Toussaint disposes of Raymond (the next to last member of the French Commission still on the island) by arranging his election as deputy to the French legislature. To have some sanction from French officialdom, he recalls Roume from the Spanish side.

April: War breaks out between Toussaint and Rigaud—"The war of knives." Roume and Toussaint proclaim Rigaud a traitor to France. Toussaint assembles an army of ten thousand at Port-au-Prince.

June: Toussaint puts down the mulatto revolt in the Artibonite, then goes to Le Cap, sending Dessalines to Môle. This campaign is attended with much torture and massacre.

In the ensuing three months, Toussaint slowly pushes Rigaud back into the Grand Anse.

1800

March 11: Pursuing the war against the mulattoes, Toussaint invades the south. In this campaign, the men give up their guns for knives and teeth, so great is the race hatred.

July 5: Rigaud is defeated at Acquin. Roume and Vincent persuade him to give up the struggle.

July 31: Rigaud sails for Saint Thomas, while his corps of seven hundred mulattoes goes to Cuba.

August 1: Toussaint enters Les Cayes and pronounces a general amnesty. But he leaves Dessalines in charge of the south. Throughout the fall Dessalines, perhaps without Toussaint's knowledge ("I told him to prune the tree, not uproot it"), systematically exterminates about ten thousand mulattoes—men, women and children.

October: Toussaint proclaims a system of forced labor on the plantations. Under this system, productivity and prosperity return to the colony. At this time, Toussaint begins to invite the white colonists back to manage their property, recognizing that their technical and management skills would speed the return of prosperity.

1801

January 28: Toussaint enters San Domingo City with his army and takes over the Spanish half of the island in the name of France.

July: Toussaint proclaims a new constitution for Saint Domingue, which makes him governor for life and gives him the right to name his successor. His acknowledgment of French sovereignty is merely nominal at this point.

In the fall, Toussaint sends the reluctant white Colonel Vincent to present the new constitution to Bonaparte in France.

October 1: The Peace of Amiens ends the war between England and France. Bonaparte begins to prepare an expedition, led by his brother-in-law General Leclerc, to restore white power in Saint Domingue.

November 25: Toussaint proclaims a military dictatorship.

1802

February: Leclerc's invasion begins with a strength of approximately seventeen thousand troops. Toussaint, with approximately twenty thousand men under his command, orders the black generals to raze the coast towns and retreat into the interior, but because of either disloyalty or poor communications the order is not universally followed. Black general Christophe burns Le Cap to ashes for the second time in ten years, but the French occupy Port-au-Prince before Dessalines can destroy it.

In late February and March, the French forces pursuing Toussaint fight a number of drawn battles in the interior of the island, with heavy casualties on both sides.

April 1: Leclerc writes to Bonaparte that he has seven thousand active men and five thousand in hospital—meaning that another five thousand are dead. Leclerc also has seven thousand "colonial troops" of variable reliability, mulattoes but also a lot of black soldiery brought over by turncoat leaders.

April 2: Leclerc subdues the Northern Plain and enters Le Cap.

Early this month, the black general Christophe goes over to the French with twelve hundred troops, on a promise of retaining his rank in French service. But Toussaint still holds the northern mountains with four thousand regular troops and a great number of irregulars. Leclerc writes to the minister of marine that he needs twenty-five thousand European troops to secure the island—i.e., reinforcements of fourteen thousand.

May 1: Toussaint and Dessalines surrender on similar terms as Christophe. Leclerc's position is still too weak for him to obey Bonaparte's order to deport the black leaders immediately.

While Toussaint retires to Gonaives, with his two thousand life guards converting themselves to cultivators there, Dessalines remains on active duty. Leclerc frets that their submission may be feigned.

May: A severe yellow fever outbreak begins in Port-au-Prince and Le Cap at the middle of the month, causing many deaths among the French troops.

June: By the first week of this month, Leclerc has lost three thousand men to fever. Both Le Cap and Port-au-Prince are plague zones, with corpses laid out in the barracks yards to be carried to lime pits outside the town.

June 6: Leclerc notifies Bonaparte that he has ordered Toussaint's arrest. Lured away from Gonaives to a meeting with General Brunet, Toussaint is made prisoner.

June 15: Toussaint, with his family, is deported for France aboard the ship Le *Héros.*

June 11: Leclerc writes to the minister of marine that he suspects his army will die out from under him—citing his own illness (he had overcome a bout of malaria soon after his arrival), he asks for recall.

This letter also contains the recommendation that Toussaint be imprisoned in the heart of inland France.

In the third week of June, Leclerc begins the tricky project of disarming the cultivators—under authority of the black generals who have submitted to his authority.

June 22: Toussaint writes a letter of protest to Bonaparte from his ship, which is now docked in Brest.

July 6: Leclerc writes to the minister of marine that he is losing one hundred sixty men per day. However, this same report states that he is effectively destroying the influence of the black generals.

News of the restoration of slavery in Guadeloupe arrives in Saint Domingue in the last days of the month. The north rises instantly, the west shortly afterward, and black soldiers begin to desert their generals.

August 6: Leclerc reports the continued prevalence of yellow fever, the failure to complete the disarmament, and the growth of rebellion. The major black generals have stayed in his camp, but the petty officers are deserting in droves and taking their troops with them.

August 22: En route to the Fort de Joux, Toussaint reaches Besançon.

August 24: Toussaint is imprisoned at the Fort de Joux in France, near the Swiss border.

August 25: Leclerc writes: "To have been rid of Toussaint is not enough; there are two thousand more leaders to get rid of as well."

September 13: The expected abatement of the yellow fever at the approach of the autumnal equinox fails to occur. The reinforcements arriving die as fast as they are put into the country, and Leclerc has to deploy them as soon as they get off the boat. Leclerc asks for ten thousand men to be immediately sent. He is losing territory in the interior and his black generals are beginning to waver, though he still is confident of his ability to manipulate them.

As of this date, a total of twenty-eight thousand men have been sent from France, and Leclerc estimates that ten thousand five hundred are still alive, but only forty-five hundred are fit for duty. Five thousand sailors have also died, bringing the total loss to twenty-nine thousand.

October 7: Leclerc: "We must destroy all the mountain Negroes, men and women, sparing only children under twelve years of age. We must destroy half the Negroes of the plains, and not allow in the colony a single man who has ever worn an epaulette. Without these measures the colony will never be at peace . . . "

October 10: Mulatto general Clervaux revolts, with all his troops, upon the news of Bonaparte's restoration of the mulatto discriminations of the ancien régime. Le Cap had been mostly garrisoned by mulattoes.

October 13: Christophe and the other black generals in the north join Clervaux's rebellion. On this news, Dessalines raises revolt in the west.

November 2: Leclerc dies of yellow fever. Command is assumed by Rochambeau.

By the end of the month the fever finally begins to abate, and acclimated survivors, now immune, begin to return to service. In France, Bonaparte has outfitted ten thousand reinforcements.

1803

March: At the beginning of the month, Rochambeau has eleven thousand troops and only four thousand in hospital, indicating that the worst of the disease threat has passed. He is ready to conduct a war of extermination against the blacks, and brings man-eating dogs from Cuba to replace his lost soldiery. He makes slow headway against Dessalines in March and April, while Napoleon plans to send thirty thousand reinforcements in two instalments in the coming year.

April 7: Toussaint-Louverture dies a prisoner in the Fort de Joux.

May 12: New declaration of war between England and France.

June: By month's end, Saint Domingue is completely blockaded by the English. With English aid, Dessalines smashes into the coast towns.

October: Early in the month, Les Cayes falls to the blacks. At month's end, so does Port-au-Prince.

November 10: Rochambeau flees Le Cap and surrenders to the English fleet.

November 28: The French are forced to evacuate their last garrison at Môle. Dessalines promises protection to all whites who choose to remain, following Toussaint's earlier policy. During the first year of his rule he will continue encouraging white planters to return and manage their property and many who trusted Toussaint will do so.

December 31: Declaration of Haitian independence.

1804

May: In France Bonaparte becomes emperor on May 18, 1804.

October: Dessalines, having overcome all rivals, crowns himself emperor.

1805

January: Dessalines begins the massacre of all the whites in Haiti.

Another Devil's Dictionary

abolition du fouet: abolition of the use of whips on field slaves; a negotiating point before and during the rebellion

acajou: mahogany

affranchi: A person of color whose freedom was officially recognized; most *affranchis* were of mixed blood but some were full-blood Africans

agouti: groundhog-sized animal, edible

ajoupa: a temporary hut made of sticks and leaves

à la chinois: in the Chinese manner

allée: a lane or drive lined with trees

Les Amis des Noirs: an abolitionist society in France, interested in improving the conditions and ultimately in liberating the slaves of the French colonies

ancien régime: old order of pre-revolutionary France

aristocrates de la peau: aristocrats of the skin. Many of Sonthonax's policies and proclamations were founded on the argument that white supremacy in Saint Domingue was analogous to the tyranny of the hereditary French nobility and must therefore be overthrown in its turn by revolution.

armoire: medicinal herb for fever

asson: a rattle made from a gourd, an instrument in vodoun ceremonies, and the *hûngan's* badge of authority

atelier: idiomatically used to mean work gangs or the whole body of slaves on a given plantation

au grand seigneur: in a proprietary manner

bagasse: remnants of sugarcane whose juice has been extracted in the mill—a dry, fast-burning fuel

baguette: bread loaf

banza: African instrument with strings stretched over a skin head; forerunner of the banjo

Baron Samedi: vodoun deity closely associated with Ghede and the dead, sometimes considered an aspect of Ghede

bête de cornes: domestic animal with horns

bienfaisance: philosophical proposition that all things work together for good

bois bander: tree whose bark was thought to be an aphrodisiac

bossale: a newly imported slave, fresh off the boat, ignorant of the plantation ways and of the Creole dialect

boucaniers: piratical drifters who settled Tortuga and parts of Haiti as Spanish rule there weakened. They derived their name from the word *boucan*—their manner of barbecuing hog meat.

cachot: dungeon cell

caciques: Amerindian chieftains of precolonial Haiti

calenda: a slave celebration distinguished by dancing. *Calendas* frequently had covert vodoun significance, but white masters who permitted them managed to regard them as secular.

canaille: mob, rabble

carré: square, unit of measurement for cane fields and city blocks

casques: feral dogs

les citoyens de quatre Avril: Denoting persons of color awarded full political rights by the April 4 decree, this phrase was either a legal formalism or a sneering euphemism, depending on the speaker.

clairin: cane rum

colon: colonist

commandeur: overseer or work-gang leader on a plantation, usually himself a slave

congé: time off work

Congo: African tribal designation. Thought to adapt well to many functions of slavery and more common than others in Saint Domingue.

cordon de l'est: eastern cordon, a fortified line in the mountains organized by whites to prevent the northern insurrection from breaking through to other departments of the colony

cordon de l'ouest: western cordon, as above

corps-cadavre: in vodoun, the physical body, the flesh

coup poudré: a vodoun attack requiring a material drug, as opposed to the *coup á l'air*, which needs only spiritual force

coutelas: broad-bladed cane knife or machete

Creole: Any person born in the colony whether white, black, or colored, whether slave or free. A dialect combining a primarily French vocabulary with primarily African syntax is also called Creole; this patois was not only the means of communication between whites and blacks but was often the sole common language among Africans of different tribal origins. Creole is still spoken in Haiti today.

crête: ridge or peak

Damballah: vodoun deity associated with snakes, one of the great *loa*

déshabillé: a housedress, in colonial Saint Domingue apt to be very revealing. White Creole women were famous for their daring in this regard.

dokté-feuilles: leaf-doctor, expert in herbal medicine

Erzulie: one of the great *loa,* a vodoun goddess roughly parallel to Aphrodite. As Erzulie-gé-Rouge she is maddened by suffering and grief.

enceinte: pregnant

esprit: spirit; in vodoun it is, so to speak, fungible

faience: crockery

fatras-baton: thrashing stick. Toussaint bore this stable name in youth because of his skinniness.

femme de confiance: a lady's quasi-professional female companion

femme de couleur: woman of mixed blood

fleur-de-lis: stylized rendition of a flower and a royalist emblem in France

gens de couleur: people of color, a reasonably polite designation for persons of mixed blood in Saint Domingue

gérant: plantation manager or overseer

Ghede: one of the great *loa,* the principal vodoun god of the underworld and of the dead

gilet: waistcoat

giromon: medicinal herb for cough

gombo: medicinal herb for cough

gommier: gum-tree

grand blanc: member of Saint Domingue's white landed gentry, who were owners of large plantations and large numbers of slaves. The *grand blancs* were politically conservative and apt to align with royalist counterrevolutionary movements.

Grand Bois: vodoun deity, aspect of Legba more closely associated with the world of the dead

grand'case: the "big house," residence of white owners or overseers on a plantation. These houses were often rather primitive despite the grandiose title.

grand chemin: the big road or main road. In vodoun the term refers to the pathway opened between the human world and the world of the *loa.*

grenouille: frog

griffe: term for a particular combination of African and European blood. A *griffe* would result from the congress of a full-blood black with a mulatto or a *marabou.*

griffone: female *griffe*

gros-bon-ange: literally, the "big good angel," an aspect of the vodoun soul. The gros-bon-ange is "the life force that all sentient beings share; it enters the individual at conception and functions only to keep the body alive. At clinical death, it returns immediately to God and becomes part of the great reservoir of energy that supports all life."*

guérit-trop-vite: medicinal herb used in plasters to speed healing of wounds

habitation: plantation

herbe à cornette: medicinal herb used in mixtures for coughing

herbe à pique: medicinal herb against fever

homme de couleur: man of mixed blood; see *gens de couleur*

hounsi: female vodoun acolytes

hûnfor: vodoun temple, often arranged in open air

hûngan: vodoun priest

Ibo: African tribal designation. Ibo slaves were thought to be especially prone to suicide, believing that through death they would return to Africa. Some masters discouraged this practice by lopping the ears and noses of slaves who had killed themselves, since presumably the suicides would not wish to be resurrected with these signs of dishonor.

intendant: the highest civil authority in colonial Saint Domingue, as opposed to the governor, who was the highest military authority. These conflicting and competing posts were deliberately arranged by the home government to make rebellion against the authority of the metropole less likely.

Island Below Sea: vodoun belief construes that the souls of the dead inhabit a world beneath the ocean that reflects the living world above. Passage through this realm is the slave's route of return to Africa.

journal: newspaper

la-place: vodoun celebrant with specific ritual functions second to those of the *hûngan*.

lantana: medicinal herb against colds

Legba: vodoun god of crossroads and of change, vaguely analogous to Hermes of the Greek pantheon. Because Legba controls the crossroads between the material and spiritual worlds, he must be invoked at the beginning of all ceremonies.

les Invisibles: members of the world of the dead, roughly synonymous with *les Morts et les Mystères*.

liberté de savane: freedom, for a slave, to come and go at will within the borders of a plantation or some other defined area, sometimes the privilege of senior *commandeurs*.

loa: general term for a vodoun deity

loi du quatre Avril: decree of April 4, 1792, from the French Legislative Assembly, granting full political rights to people of color in Saint Domingue.

* Wade Davis, *The Serpent and the Rainbow* (New York: Simon and Schuster, 1985), p. 181.

loup-garou: in vodoun, a sinister supernatural entity, something like a werewolf

macandal: a charm, usually worn round the neck

macoutte: a straw sack used to carry food or goods

main-d'oeuvre: workforce

Maît'Carrefour: vodoun deity closely associated with Ghede and the dead, sometimes considered an aspect of Ghede

maît'tête: literally, "master of the head," the particular *loa* to whom the vodoun observer is devoted, by whom he is usually possessed (though the worshiper may sometimes be possessed by other gods as well)

mal de Siam: yellow fever

malnommée: medicinal herb used in tea against diarrhea

mambo: vodoun priestess

manchineel: jungle tree with an extremely toxic sap

Mandingue: African tribal designation. Mandingue slaves had a reputation for cruelty and for a strong character difficult to subject to servitude.

manicou: Caribbean possum

marais: swamp

maréchal de camp: field marshal

maréchaussée: paramilitary groups organized to recapture runaway slaves

maroon: a runaway slave. There were numerous communities of maroons in the mountains of Saint Domingue, and in some cases they won battles with whites and negotiated treaties that recognized their freedom and their territory.

mauvais sujet: bad guy, criminal

ménagère: housekeeper

les Morts et les Mystères: the aggregate of dead souls in vodoun, running the spectrum from personal ancestors to the great *loa*

moulin de bêtes: mill powered by animals, as opposed to a water mill

mulatto: person of mixed European and African blood, whether slave or free. Tables existed to define sixty-four different possible such admixtures, with a specific name and social standing assigned to each.

négociant: businessman or broker involved in the export of plantation goods to France

nègre chasseur: slave trained as a huntsman

noblesse de l'epée: French aristocracy deriving its status from the feudal military system, as opposed to newer bureaucratic orders of rank

Ogûn: one of the great *loa,* the Haitian god of war. Ogûn-Feraille is his most aggressive aspect.

ouanga: a charm, often worn round the neck

paillasse: a sleeping pallet, straw mattress

pariade: the wholesale rape of slave women by sailors on slave ships. The *pariade* had something of the status of a ritual. Any pregnancies that resulted were assumed to increase the value of the slave women to their eventual purchasers.

parrain: godfather. In slave communities, the *parrain* was responsible for teaching a newly imported slave the appropriate ways of the new situation.

patois: dialect

Patriots: name assumed by Jacobin factions in Saint Domingue; see also *Pompons Rouges.*

pavé: paving stone

petit blanc: member of Saint Domingue's white artisan class, a group which lived mostly in the coastal cities and which was not necessarily French in origin. The *petit blancs* sometimes owned small numbers of slaves but seldom owned land; most of them were aligned with French revolutionary politics.

petit marron: a runaway slave or maroon who intended to remain absent for only a short period—these escapees often returned to their owners of their own accord

la petite vérole: smallpox

petro: a particular set of vodoun rituals with some different deities—angry and more violent than *rada*

pois-gratter: itching pea, an abrasive plant

Pompons Blancs: members of the royalist faction in post-1789 Saint Domingue; their name derives from the white cockade they wore to declare their political sentiments. The majority of *grand blancs* inclined in this direction.

Pompons Rouges: members of the revolutionary faction in post-1789 Saint Domingue, so called for the red cockades they wore to identify themselves. Most of the colony's *petit blancs* inclined in this direction.

poteau mitan: central post in a vodoun *hûnfor*, the metaphysical route of passage for the entrance of the *loa* into the human world

***pwasô* (Creole):** fish

quarteronné: a particular combination of African and European blood: the result, for instance, of combining a full-blood white with a *mamelouque*

rada: the more pacific rite of vodoun, as opposed to *petro*

rada batterie: ensemble of drums for vodoun ceremony

ramier: wood pigeon

ratoons: second-growth cane from plants already cut

redingote: a fashionable frock coat

sacatra: a particular combination of African and European blood: the result, for instance, of combining a full-blood black with a *griffe* or *griffonne*

salle de bains: washroom

sang-mêlé: a particular combination of African and European blood: the result, for instance, of combining a full-blood white with a *quarteronné*

serviteur: vodoun observer, one who serves the *loa*

siffleur montagne: literally, "mountain whistler," a night-singing bird

tafia: rum

ti-bon-ange: literally, the "little good angel," an aspect of the vodoun soul. "The ti-bon-ange is that part of the soul directly associated with the individual. . . . It is one's aura, and the source of all personality, character and willpower."*

tisane: infusion of herbs

vévé: diagram symbolizing and invoking a particular *loa*

***vodûn* or vodoun:** generic term for a god, also denotes the whole Haitian religion

yo di: they say

zaman: almond

z'étoile: aspect of the vodoun soul. "The *z'étoile* is the one spiritual component that resides not in the body but in the sky. It is the individual's star of destiny, and is viewed as a calabash that carries one's hope and all the many ordered events for the next life of the soul."†

zombi: either the soul (*zombi astrale*) or the body (*zombi cadavre*) of a dead person enslaved to a vodoun magician

* Wade Davis, *The Serpent and the Rainbow,* p.181.

† Wade Davis, *The Serpent and the Rainbow,* p. 181.